BULFIN
MYTHO

THE AGE OF
CHIVALRY
and LEGENDS OF
CHARLEMAGNE

OR ROMANCE IN THE MIDDLE AGES

Tales of kings and knights reprinted from the original edition
by Thomas Bulfinch, with a section on Knights of
English History from the 1884 Halley edition

With a New Foreword and Notes by
NORMA LORRE GOODRICH

LOVE, HONOR,
AND THE CHIVALRIC CODE

Epics, sagas, and folklore of the fabulous Middle Ages, tales of great Christian kings, legends of King Arthur and the Round Table, the love story of Tristram and Isolde, the ancient Welsh myths and Frankish epics that are buried in Europe's history—all come to life in Thomas Bulfinch's enduring classic. Bulfinch captures the myth and romance of medieval times with these two volumes of mythology, combined into a single edition.

Bulfinch's versions of these tales, so popular when originally published that his name quickly became a household word, will be read today for entertainment and treasured for reference as they provide the themes that have shaped much of Western art, music, and literature. This celebrated work contains Thomas Bulfinch's complete, original text of the legends of King Arthur and the story of Emperor Charlemagne's reign, as well as the section on "The Knights of English History," from the famous 1884 revision by Edward Everett Hale.

THOMAS BULFINCH (1796–1867) was educated at Boston Latin School and Harvard College. He lived most of his life in Boston.
NORMA LORRE GOODRICH is Emeritus Professor of French and Comparative Literature and former Dean of the Faculty at Scripps College. She is the author of thirty-one books, including *Medieval Myths* and *Ancient Myths* (both Meridian).

THOMAS BULFINCH

Bulfinch's Mythology
The Age of Chivalry
AND
Legends of Charlemagne
or
Romance in the Middle Ages

With a New Foreword and Introductions
by Norma Lorre Goodrich

A MERIDIAN BOOK

MERIDIAN
Published by the Penguin Group
Penguin Books USA Inc., 375 Hudson Street,
New York, New York 10014, U.S.A.
Penguin Books Ltd, 27 Wrights Lane,
London W8 5TZ, England
Penguin Books Australia Ltd, Ringwood,
Victoria, Australia
Penguin Books Canada Ltd, 10 Alcorn Avenue,
Toronto, Ontario, Canada M4V 3B2
Penguin Books (N.Z.) Ltd, 182–190 Wairau Road,
Auckland 10, New Zealand

Penguin Books Ltd, Registered Offices:
Harmondsworth, Middlesex, England

Published by Meridian, an imprint of Dutton Signet,
a division of Penguin Books USA Inc.
Previously published in somewhat different form in a Mentor edition.

First Meridian Printing, August, 1995
10 9 8 7 6 5 4 3 2 1

REGISTERED TRADEMARK—MARCA REGISTRADA

Library of Congress Cataloging-in-Publication Data:
Bulfinch, Thomas, 1796–1867.
    [Mythology]
    Bulfinch's mythology / Thomas Bulfinch ; with a new foreword and
introductions by Norma Goodrich.
        p.   cm.
    Contents: The age of chivalry — Legends of Charlemagne, or,
Romance in the middle ages.
    ISBN 0-452-01153-1
    1. Arthurian romances. 2. Charlemagne, Emperor, 742-814—
Romances. 3. Mythology. 4. Folklore—Europe. I. Title.
PN685.B82 1995
398.2'094'02—dc20   95-11107
                                                                   CIP

Printed in the United States of America

CONTENTS

THE AGE OF CHIVALRY

PART I

KING ARTHUR AND HIS KNIGHTS

v

PART II

THE MABINOGEON

PART III

THE KNIGHTS OF ENGLISH HISTORY

LEGENDS OF CHARLEMAGNE

FOREWORD

In this sequel to *The Age of Fable* Thomas Bulfinch chooses subjects very close to his heart, both "The Age of Chivalry" and "The Legend of Charlemagne." What he most enjoys is not history, neither that of chivalry, nor that of the Emperor Charlemagne, but the "romance of history." That phrase bears pondering, for it seems a contradiction in terms. The word *romance* has come to mean love, and a literary text called a romance is a love story written in a romance language: here, French and Italian. (*Romance* comes from the Latin word *Romanus,* meaning "of Rome" and implies a derivation from the Latin language of Rome.)

Thus, Bulfinch cuts us off from his *Age of Fable,* whose stories were written in the classical languages of ancient mythology, Greek and Latin. Now we are referred to works written for popular consumption in the new vernaculars of western Europe, languages derived from Latin but read popularly by people of all classes. Latin was elevated above the crowd (*vulgus*), reserved henceforth for the educated, university-bred upper classes and professional scholars.

In his *Age of Chivalry* and *Legends of Charlemagne* we turn now to romances. These are works of literature that deal with the High Middle Ages, the twelfth through the fifteenth centuries in France, Spain, and Italy. There, and also in Britain, resided speakers of romance languages. Such romances dealt with the loves of noble knights and ladies in medieval courts—ergo, with "courtly love." The ladies were "courted." And frequently, if unreasonably, several such died for love.

How can Bulfinch speak, then, of the "romance of history"? It would seem he has fallen into a trap. Love is romantic. Romances are romantic. Knights court cruel ladies. Some die for love. Some die in games or tournaments. History will bring Bulfinch to account for all this by asking

ix

the old questions historians must ask: When? Who? Where? Why? But "when" alone catches him out. "The Age of Chivalry" goes back, he says, to five centuries after the death of Christ. We begin (Chapter IV) with King Arthur who died in the year 542 at the battle of Camlan. He was "buried at Glastonbury" (not settled before 800); and his grave was opened by King Henry II "about 1150." The leap from 542 to 1150 can be forgiven because Bulfinch thought Arthur was mythological anyway, as did such a source as John Milton; so easily does history vanish before romance.

Thomas Bulfinch had every right to prefer romance and scorn history. The discrepancy between an Arthur who lived in the fifth and sixth centuries (*c.*475–542), who witnessed, as Bulfinch attested, the Roman withdrawal from their western provinces, Gaul and Britain, and who became the romantic Arthur of knighthood in the twelfth century, should not trouble anyone. Romance is not history! Therefore Bulfinch chose John Milton to cite and not the great historian of that age, Edward Gibbon (1737–1794).

In Volume 4 of his *Decline and Fall of the Roman Empire,* Gibbon smiles at the "fond credulity" (p. 95) of the Norman conquerors of Britain in 1066 as they heard how Arthur conquered the Saxon invaders and other such tales that "adorned the popular romance of Arthur and Knights of the Round Table.... The voluminous tales of Sir Lancelot and Sir Tristram were devoutly studied by the princes and nobles who disregarded the genuine heroes and historians of antiquity." Gibbon concludes (pp. 95–96):

> At length the light of science and reason was rekindled; the talisman was broken; the visionary fabric melted into air; and by a natural, though unjust, reverse of public opinion, the severity of the present age is inclined to question the existence of Arthur.

After Arthur's death in 542, the whole of Britain "had returned to its primitive state of a savage and solitary forest" (p. 98).[1]

Bulfinch situates the King Arthur who lived and died in the Dark Ages indiscriminately in the High Middle Ages, either 1150, he offers, or 1257, or even 1300. He adds that

Arthur came from Rome into Britain. His authorities are Geoffrey of Monmouth's *History of the Kings of Britain* (1134), certain ballads or popular poetry, and John Milton's *History.* Milton had been urged, but declined to write an epic of King Arthur. Unlike Bulfinch, Milton feared the smack of some pagan mythology. The Christian Church of France and Rome found fourth-century Britain highly suspect in dogma and ritual. The prelates questioned the teachings and practices of both Pelagius and Saint Patrik, and ignored Merlin.

The Age of Chivalry originated inside France about 1150 and spread to England through her French kings and queens. Romances are in every sense aristocratic literature based upon love, beauty, and the charm of lovely ladies. This literature emphasized refinements in living standards, manners, customs, clothing, and language. Gallantry in the hero became all the rage. The hero was first of all an ideal lover of a Valentine Lady whose favors he sought to win. He offered her his devotion, his service, and his total obedience. He wrote lyric poetry for her. Together they listened while professional entertainers, *troubadours* and *trouvères,* recited romances to them. The Lady remained aloof, distant, unattainable, and beloved above all else. To a lady poet like Marie de France (fl. 1160–70), love was the tender passion on the lover's part. He swore eternal fidelity and devotion to her, and to her alone. Often he fell into a state of sadness, even melancholy, as his beloved retreated farther and farther away from him. His sacrifice, which he was then called upon to make, was the supreme offering of his life to her.

This way of court life was endorsed and promoted by the leaders of the aristocracy in the twelfth century, notably by Queen Eleanor of Aquitaine. She was a great heiress who became, by her marriage to King Louis VII of France, queen of that kingdom. In her court city of Poitiers, Queen Eleanor maintained two celebrated troubadours from her native *langue d'oc* (the language of southern France), Marcabrun and Cercamon, and other poet-musicians who were also composers. When his French queen produced only two female children, she was divorced by King Louis. A map of France in the twelfth century shows clearly that the English kings owned all of France except Champagne, Burgundy, and Toulouse.[2] Louis needed sons to win back France from them.

The Capetian King of France acted too late to stop his former queen from eloping to England with Henry Plantagenet. The latter became King of England in 1154, adding to his estates Queen Eleanor's vast realms, Anjou and Aquitaine. Her new husband reigned as Henry II, successfully at first. The queen promoted him via the legends of King Arthur as *ruler of all Britain* (which Henry certainly never had been, but which he yearned to become, in war or in peace). She hired the best poets and translators available, Bernard de Ventadour and Wace, to translate Geoffrey of Monmouth's life of Arthur from Latin into Old French.

These thrilling romances of King Arthur and his Queen Guinevere were also promoted inside France by two lovely noblewomen, both daughters of Eleanor by Louis. The stories which Thomas Bulfinch tells us in his *Age of Chivalry* hail from these writers and from these three ladies. Countess Marie married Count Henri I of Champagne. Her younger sister Aélis married Count Thibaut V of Blois Castle on the Loire River. She in turn employed three other most distinguished poets. They were soon supported by Count Geoffrey II of Brittany, a son of Henry and Eleanor. His patronage explains the Breton belief that King Arthur lived in Brittany (now a part of France, but then a separate realm). From this greater Plantagenet family of royalty and wealth the spirit of fashionable, courtly love spread across western Europe, thence into Italy (as Bulfinch will show us in Part IV), and into Spain where royalty itself translated Geoffrey of Monmouth.

This reverence for the royal and noble Lady extended to, or also stemmed from, an exalted worship of the Queen of Heaven, Star of the Sea, Rose of Sharon: the Virgin Mary. The towering Gothic churches of France were dedicated to her as their rose, as western windows bear witness. Nobody enters Nôtre-Dame de Paris, Our Lady of Paris, or Nôtre-Dame de Chartres without a leap of wonder that the minds and hands of persons by the hundreds of thousands could work together over centuries to create such awesome, lovely, wonderful monuments in sculpted and towering stone:[3] Chartres, Paris, Laon, Noyon, Rheims,

Amiens, Rouen, Bayeux, and Coutances, as examples. The pious queens of France hastened to build cathedrals there and in the Holy Land, just as King Arthur's ancestors from Wales had after the year 326 done for Christ. The British Empress Helena had built the first Church of the Holy Sepulcher in Jerusalem.

The greatest saints composed Latin hymns to the Virgin Mary during the High Middle Ages. They said she represented Wisdom itself and that the seven sculpted columns of her cathedrals represented the Seven Liberal Arts studied for advanced degrees; Bachelor of Arts or Sciences (B.A. or B.S.) and Doctor of Philosophy (Ph.D.).

> Oh Maria! Stella Maris!
> Dignitate singularis,
> Super omnes ordinaris
> Ordines coelestium!

Henry Adams quotes and translates (p. 103):

> Oh Maria! Constellation!
> Inspiration! Elevation!
> Rule and Law and Ordination
> Of the angels' host![4]

This love of the Virgin dominated both literature and art for centuries while for their parts great queens ruled France. The Empress of Germany Matilda (Maud) restored by her second marriage the rule of England to her son Henry II. The Empress earned the title "Lady of England" (1141). Queen Blanche became Regent of France twice and successfully defeated the claims of the English to the French land Henry II acquired through marriage. The son of Queen Blanche became King Louis IX (1214–1270), whose Queen Marguerite rebuilt the Holy Sepulcher in Jerusalem. These queens personally negotiated the release of the crusading Louis IX, who later became Saint Louis. Queen Eleanor of England personally negotiated payment in silver and gold for the release of her son (by Henry), King Richard I (Coeur de Lion). She had earlier travelled to Jerusalem to deliver Richard's bride to him in the hope that he would consummate his marriage. Queen Eleanor was finally exiled to France when Henry II saw that his vicious sons, Richard I and John (Lackland), were causing him to lose all the territories he had won, stolen, or inherited, and which were about to cause his death.

As for noblemen, the era of chivalry obliged them because of their claims to nobility to train for combat at least from the age of seven. During the Hundred Years War between France and England, a war which was to decide if English rulers could continue to rule both nations, the French nobles allowed no commoners to combat on the battlefield; and they lost every battle until Joan of Arc stepped forth to command them. A small noble boy in France became a page at age seven in an uncle's castle, where he learned his first lessons in *noblesse oblige*: service and humility. He practiced in castles, abbeys, churches, festivals, tournaments, jousts, and travels. From kitchen boy, waiter, errand boy, valet, and groom he rose to become squire to a knight. Then he cared for armor, weapons, horses, livery, pennants, and caparisons. He also then accompanied his lordly master into battle.

After long hours of vigil, on his knees nights and days without food or drink, before the altar, the young candidate was dubbed knight in a magnificent ceremony of state. While he still remained kneeling, the young aspirant's spurs were fastened to his boots by his noble sponsor. Solemn vows of courage, honor, sacrifice, courtesy, and duty were imposed upon him. He was dubbed with the flat of a golden sword on each shoulder and then on his head. He was asked to swear mighty oaths. Finally he was allowed to rise and was addressed for the first time as "Sir Knight." These chivalric orders of the High Middle Ages survive in holiness today: Knights of Saint Lazarus, Knights of Malta, Knights of Saint George, Knights Templar.

The candidate was also taught how to compose lyric poetry, as we see from the fifth stanza of a poem composed by that prisoner, King Richard I, who here employs the set form entitled "complaint":

> Ce sevent bien Angevin et Torain,
> cil bacheler qui or sont riche et sain,
> qu' enconbrez sui loing d'aus en autrui main.
> Forment m'amoient, mes or ne m'ainment grain.

De beles armes sont ores vuit li plain.
Por tant que je sui pris.[5]

(Bachelor knights from Anjou and Touraine
Gay today stay happy and sane
While I am sole, closed, loaded with chain.
They all loved me then. So now I complain:
Gone are the tourneys adorned my domain.
Prisoner. I.)

What the aristocrats of those Middle Ages wanted, consumed, and commissioned endlessly were lyrics and the longer court romances written in lofty verse. An entire body of literature, often called the most extensive body of poetry and prose in the world, dealt primarily with the heroic figure of King Arthur. Since the collection of mythology which enfolds this particular hero is so large, it has seemed appropriate from one generation to another and still seems so now, some 1500 years after his death, to ask why.

The figure of the once historical hero encloses in its accounts "racial memory," first of all. A recital of his deeds sinks deep into the hearts of readers and listeners, triggering things almost forgotten. Thus, Arthur appeals to what C. G. Jung termed our shared "collective unconscious." The hero was the only man who benefitted all mankind. The hero is adored, worshipped even, because of these benefits:

1. Hercules brought man the golden apples (food)
2. Ulysses pioneered the sea routes (emigration)
3. Hector fought sea-borne invaders (defense of his country)
4. Theseus drew the sword from under the stone (leadership)

King Arthur performed all the above functions:

1. He brought the pig from the underworld god (food)
2. He crossed the seas to conquer Norway (Isle of Man) and Wales (emigration)

3. He defended his land successfully (obviously not England)
4. He drew the sword from the stone (became commander)

The more Arthur is shrouded in mystery, "wrapped in a gray cloak of fog as he gazes over the sea," the more he is studied and adored. Everyone seeks Arthur or repudiates him at will, and for deep, underlying personal reasons. Studies have shown that political passions weigh heavily toward declaring King Arthur legendary only. Thus, questions of genealogy arise in the *History of the Kings of Britain* concerning him and his descent from the Empress Helena and her son, the Emperor Constantine.

Heroes are frequently born unusually—both the epic Hercules and King Arthur were sired by two fathers, but born to one mother only. Heroes often spend their childhoods in seclusion—both Theseus of Athens and Arthur of Britain hidden until manhood, around age fifteen. Heroes usually make a long journey toward their first appearance and recognition rites.

In Arthur's case, Merlin had given the ascertainment of right to the throne, or command, or crown. Oedipus from Thebes had to guess the riddle of the Sphinx. Gawain from Galloway had to learn whose severed head lay on the Grail platter. Navigating heroes of Polynesia had to steer by ocean currents and stars. Arthur's constellation was Arctos and the Great Bear (our Big Dipper), the circumpolar stars.

All heroes are called upon to vanquish some otherworldly creature—dragon or giant—as Odysseus defeated the one-eyed Polyphemus. Each must find an especially holy site on earth—an island, a cave, a mountain, perhaps. Arthur "went west" when he died, or to Avalon, the western isle where all heroes go in death.

Each must therefore understand mythology's quadrangle, which held that the earth had four sides: North (savagery), West (death), South (civilization), and East (religion). Each must learn lucky numbers and some pentenary system. Most of all, the hero must know his dictionary of symbols so well that he discerns intuitively his cryptic instructions: languages, dreams, grammar (glamor), art, religion. He understands that he is to volunteer, to advance fearlessly, to fight against great odds and in hostile environments, that he is never to flinch, never to show fear. In one sense every great hero is free. He accepted in childhood from his professional handlers one simple truth: that he is at all moments, times, places, and in all perilous situations *completely expendable.*

There is no hero greater than King Arthur, whether we look at him according to this vastest literature, which has accumulated in his wake over fifteen centuries now (and is growing). Surely this fanatical absorption with him and over his (missing) dead body stems from that insoluble mystery: Is Arthur historical or legendary?

This editor has concluded that he is less an epic-style hero, like his contemporary Beowulf, than an historical personage, like his contemporary Emperor Justinian at Constantinople. We must praise those Welsh Chroniclers who, from the earliest copy of their Annals we have (*c.* A.D. 800), gave us:

> The names of Arthur's twelve victories (located, and situated for the most part along the seventy-five-mile-long Roman, or Hadrian's Wall that separates Scotland from England)

> The date of his final, twelfth, or greatest victory at a "mons badonis," which we take to be Dumbarton Rock—Dum (mountain) Breaton (of the Britons)—in the Clyde River estuary adjacent to the modern metropolis of Glasgow

> The date of his death (A.D. 542) and place of his death at the battle of Camlan (from the Roman fort Camboglanna) on Hadrian's Wall close to Arthur's fortress Camelot (the chief Roman legionary fort at Carlisle)

The Welsh chroniclers give additional scores of allusions to Arthur and his Welsh enemies and/or relatives in the Annals, and also in quasi-fictional works, such *romances,* if you like, as the *Mabinogion.*

Outstanding historians and editors of the twentieth century, like O. G. S. Crawford, Lewis Thorpe, Geoffrey Ashe, and John Morris have pronounced Arthur historical, even "the last Roman Emperor" in the west. For truly, the last Roman Emperor in Rome, Romulus Augustulus, had been deposed before the year 500. Wales claims King Arthur, and Merlin also—or two great men named Myrddin—as native sons. The subject of Merlin is approached today just as virulently in Wales as it was broached in the twelfth century when the Welsh cleric Geoffrey of Monmouth trod ever so neatly back and forth, up and down, and around it.[6]

King Arthur's biography lent itself easily to medieval romancers. His fathers were doubled. His mother was born into Celtic royalty and finally married to a Roman imperial line. The lad became Commander by trial, as Theseus had done so many centuries before him, both drawing a sword from a stone. The boy appeared out of nowhere at his majority, his age the pentenary number fifteen. That day he stood like all army generals, a sacrificial victim if and when he lost a major pitched battle. He fought twelve battles, names of places identifiable, however, just as Hercules before him and the medieval French hero Aymeri de Narbonne had done. Arthur chose three first lieutenants, all justly celebrated: Gawain, Lancelot, and Perceval.

What is most magical about Arthur are, first of all, the animal totems of a primitive world: the Arctic grizzly bear of the ancient Finnish epic (*Kalevala*), and the red dragon of the Roman praetor and the North-Welsh kings. Then we have his magical sword, Excalibur, which, being of Gaelic origin, puts Arthur back again in the far north of Great Britain. The word *Excalibur* is not Latin; it derives from *Calad-bolg,* Sword of Lightning. But the star of first magnitude which rises over north Britain is named Arcturus—a name very similar to Arthur's Latin name: *Arturus* and *Ille Arturus* (*the* Arthur). Arthur is related also to thunder rolling across the sky. His Wain or Great Wain (Wagon) is the British name for our constellation the Big Dipper. These are again the truly Northern stars which circle the North Star every night. Together they form the umbrella or circumpolar constellations, or dome of heaven. Arthur's biography is complete in seven episodes:

1. Birth
2. Accession to command at age 15

3. Wedding to the heiress Guinevere (whom Bulfinch calls Guenever)
4. Twelve Battles, victory of Mount Badon
5. Defeat at Camlan
6. Departure on a ship for the Isle of Avalon
7. Grave—or "no grave for Arthur," as Welsh writers claim

Citizens of Cumbria, on and around Hadrian's Wall, today point to the Arthuret Church, to the landing stage down the cliff, below it, and to the waters of the Esk River. Downstream from there, they say, he went into the Solway Firth, out into the Irish Sea, thence to the Isle of Avalon. The site is not so much remarkable as unforgettable: river, high bank, three conical hills, graveyard, and behind all of it that Arthuret Church—old, moldering, ancient, ancient.

King Arthur died, said historians of Scotland, on Hadrian's Wall because he tried to cross this Roman line of fortifications, and seventeen "forts of the line," that separates the Lowlands of England from the Highlands of Scotland—and still does separate them. He was leading a troop carrying the body of Lancelot into Edinburgh for burial. The illustrious dead of Scotland are interred, still today, on Calton (Royal Caledonian) Hill opposite the extinct volcano Arthur's Seat. The escarpment along the volcano's base are still called Salisbury Crags, "Salisbury" being one of King Arthur's most illustrious victories.[7]

Gawain, King of Galloway, say English historians, was King Arthur's first deputy commander, he who then also carried the Roman *imperium* (power of command), or was said "to be in command" (*esse cum imperio*). In the romantic tradition Gawain is portrayed as very amorous, as a sort of curly, black-haired seducer like Aries the Ram in astrology. He is the oldest son of King Arthur's oldest half-sister and, as such, the first royal nephew to rally to Arthur's side. Modred (or Mordred) is the youngest son of this half-sister. Legend will have it that Arthur and Modred "slew each other," but local historians of Scotland deny this vigorously. The original Latin text is no assistance here, translated either as (1) they rushed together, or (2) they rushed at each other. Fortunately so, for mystery only adds its spice to this sad event.

Gawain remains a very great hero, and he died along with Lancelot, apparently at a sea landing, and was buried on a beach. His most appealing romance is told so graphically that it forms pictures constantly before the eyes. The Lady he courted required Gawain to jump his horse across a chasm—or a swift river—or perhaps across the Arthurian "Perilous Passage." He was required by the Proud Lady to bring her a certain branch she desired. Was it holly? or mistletoe? Both were ancient, Druidical symbols—the latter, medicinal. Then too, warriors both male and female in Arthur's wars were recognizable in battle by the "branch" they wore on their headgear. The Plantagenet Kings of England were still known by the Spanish (yellow) broom flowers they wore: *plante genêt*. King Arthur was called an "alder tree" king by the branch he wore, from the alder trees that surrounded each Celtic necropolis. You will remember the Lady Elaine, Lily Maid of Astolat, being floated downstream to her burial in the riverine necropolis, in Tennyson's *Idylls of the King*.

The "Perilous Passage" occurs frequently as one of several landmarks that Arthurian personages cross, or where they meet crowds of persons at some great, exciting public spectacle. (There Queen Isolde from Ireland successfully attested to her purity. People came from far and near to watch her do it. That day King Arthur sat as supreme court judge.)

In the English romances, however, the chief geographical site is their little country village of Glastonbury in southern England. This dairy farming community lies west, quite some distance, from places connected to Arthur: Stonehenge on the Salisbury Plain, and again quite some distance by one-lane roads from Bath. Residents, and local historians, and all the champions of romance and the legendary Arthur, claim Glastonbury. It was Arthur's royal seat, they believe, and also the Christian bishopric to which Arthur's Queen Guinevere was kidnapped and held prisoner for a year—while Arthur dallied. Furthermore, both Arthur and Guinevere lie buried there, they say, under the ruins of the Benedictine Abbey King Henry VIII had torn down.

King Henry II had Arthur and Guinevere exhumed to prove that they had reigned over England, and preferably over all of Great Britain, as he hoped to do. He sent down to Glastonbury several of his most illustrious secretaries. Unfortunately, the bodies were exhumed in the dark of night. Furthermore, the exhumation was done behind curtains. Even more unfortunately, no account submitted to King Henry by his employees tallied with any other. Glastonbury's right to great holiness still draws the respect and devotion of the whole world, however.

They claim that Joseph of Arimathea, who buried Christ, came to Glastonbury and died there. They believe that Glastonbury, from Celtic, means sacred "city of glass" or "isle of glass" (*Isle de Voirre*), and not "a colony settled [around 800] by Anglo-Saxons named Glasting." They say that Glastonbury was once an island to which Arthur's body was floated by ship from Cornwall, north down the stream called Brue. Perhaps the little brooklet really was, once, a rushing river that flowed a hundred or so miles north from Cornwall. Annual pilgrimages there, and thousand upon thousands of American tourists, now make the yearly ritual journey to venerate King Arthur's burial in Glastonbury, just as Benedictine monks did during the High Middle Ages. They believe Glastonbury is the British Jerusalem, as in the hymn by the visionary poet William Blake (1757–1827). Thousands also believe it the fabled Isle of Avalon where the dead heroes went by ocean-going funeral barges.

King Arthur's body was escorted by several queens whose names were not listed, but Queen Morgan le Fay and Queen Guinevere must have been chief among them. In any case, Queen Guinevere's tomb today stands inside a small glass room constructed by and at the expense of women in the Scottish village of Meigle (in the Vale of Strathmore, northeastern Scotland, near to the large town of Coupar Angus). Visitors are very welcome, and there is no admission charge. One may look suspiciously at Cairn Ryan near Stranraer (port of the king) on Scotland's west coast; but there are as yet no graves found for Gawain or Lancelot. And Perceval, last King of the Grail Castle, left Britain so he could die in the Holy Land. The Holy Grail left Britain then also—presumably for Montségur in the French department Pyrénées-Orientales.

In Alfred Lord Tennyson's *Idylls of the King,* and in Sir Thomas Malory's *Le Morte d'Arthur,* one's most beloved hero has been from childhood Lancelot, called "of the Lake." Young Lancelot is a girl's dream come true, and it is not difficult even now to, say why. Lancelot enters a girl's dream standing, walking, striding forward. He is as handsome in manhood now as he was fifteen centuries ago when throngs crowded both river banks of the Perilous Passage to see the Prince ride past. All the medieval chronicles could think of to convey to readers this epitome of youthful, princely manhood is that when Lancelot rode into the lists, he gave every man present the measure of masculine excellence. Lancelot was Queen Guinevere's champion to the death. When she stood stark naked in a crowd of people who watched her undergo her test for holiness, only Lancelot took off his cloak, strode through the crowd, and covered the trembling queen. Only he ripped off his tartan and swore to defend her in combat then ... immediately ... and to the death. And he killed her attackers except when Queen Guinevere descended into the arena and requested him to spare them.

After the unforgettable hero story of Arthur the King, the hero stories of Lancelot, Gawain, and Perceval came in close seconds. But then, to compound delight, we have two love stories. Men in love, young ladies in love, send shivers down the spine; for these romantic persons rise beyond themselves in ecstasy. The most beautiful romance in the world unites Lancelot and Guinevere, both at an emotional height that sweeps them to an apogee of human transcendence.

Guinevere and Lancelot had been raised together, say other non-English texts, two little children educated by the Lady of the Lake in her hidden castle in the Irish Sea. The older girl sweetly helped her little brother, as it were, to walk and to speak. As they grew older, he began to protect her. While the future queen learned reading, writing, manners, dress, courtesy, and the behavior of a princess, the younger prince practiced weaponry, combat, athletics, oratory, and stoicism. An undying love united the pair during the fifteen years of his preparation for war under King Arthur. Lancelot swore fealty first to Guinevere, second to the King.

The romance was not satisfying. That was not love to such experts! The love story they penned—not true for the

British historian Geoffrey of Monmouth but for the French troubadours commissioned by Queen Eleanor, long spurned by her philandering husband Henry—turned upon the key interpretation: adultery. In romances, Lancelot and Guinevere were adulterers! The contrary seems to have been true in history. Guinevere bore no children—neither to Arthur nor to Lancelot. Whenever the pair, Lancelot and Guinevere, meet in the story, the scene reads not like passionate and/or adulterous love, but as if the queen were in some ceremony one strains to understand, investing him, as in holy orders.

For her sake, in other words, as we struggle to comprehend what is going on—and the reader is urged to puzzle it out all over again—Lancelot undertakes horrible ordeals. Fighting to reach her, he goes through underground passages and fights foreign, nightmarish monsters in order to arrive at her "altar." It could well be that under this overcoating of "courtly love" Queen Guinevere was and remains a white-clad, virginal priestess. And also that she is doubled—that she is the first-born of twin girls. We know that Lancelot was the younger of twins, for which reason he was at birth cast to die in a "lake." (In the Middle Ages it was thought that the second-born of twins was not the father's child but the child of a devil; the mother of twins was routinely executed.)

The writers of romances, under the spell of Queen Eleanor's thirst for "courtly love," plotted two triangular, ergo adulterous, love relationships:

Guinevere

King Arthur   Lancelot

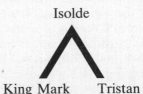

Isolde

King Mark   Tristan

The first triangle has become popular again by way of Bulfinch's *Age of Chivalry,* as in the musical *Camelot,* and the movie version of it, in which Vanessa Redgrave played Guinevere (1967). The second trio has become illustrious all over again through Bulfinch and T. H. White, but also in the German opera by Richard Wagner: *Tristan und Isolde*

(1865). Despite the erotic treatment, again we fall really into mystery concerning Isolde. Who is she? Why does she have to undergo this strange fire-walking ordeal at the Perilous Passage? Answer: She also may be a white-clad, copper-belted, long-haired Druid Priestess.[8] These two triangular romances have raised the wrath of clergymen, and one understands why.[9]

In contradistinction to these abstruse romances and so-called stories of adulterous love between the Arthurian royal persons, we have at the opposite end of the spectrum the long, complicated material on "The Holy Grail." The Grail stories are separated into those involving a Quest for the Grail and the Grail Castle, and the Grail's manifestations on an altar at a ceremony in the castle itself. When the various candidates, Gawain, Lancelot, and Perceval principally, actually see the Grail, they are blinded. Afterward (usually the following morning) they awaken to an empty, deserted castle. They dress, saddle their horses, and cross the drawbridge. Sometimes it falls, all by itself, heavily enough to cut a horse in two. Then Perceval usually meets his priestess/sister, who berates him: "Why did you not ask a question when you saw the Grail?" Poor Perceval does not know why. Nor can he remember how to find his way to the Grail Castle once again. This castle can only be stumbled upon, as it were.

A concordance of viewings by these heroes chosen to become initiates into the highest mysteries has informed us finally that the Grail object manifests itself as a hook, a platter, a chalice, and a vessel (ciborium). On the platter is a head—a severed, human head. A Grail today may be seen in La Seo Cathedral in Valencia, Spain. Another Grail was revered, if not worshipped, at Montségur, France, in the French Pyrénées-Orientales. Or on the Spanish side, according to Renaissance writers of romance, at the Spanish national shrine of San Juan de la Peña. Or the descending dove of the Holy Grail may be seen and revered today on the east window of the Arthuret Church in Longtown, Cumbria (near the city and in the diocese of Carlisle, England).

The Holy Grail remains one of the world's most tantalizing puzzles, and a true mystery. The word *mystery* derives from the Latin word *mysterium,* which means religious service, a ritual performed in church—like communion, mass, wedding, baptism, funeral. The Grail services resemble such ceremonies, and particularly one of the initiation of a young person by a greatly respected elder, the Grail King, and young princesses acting as priestesses. The ceremony always commences with a procession of beautifully clad royal maidens. We know therefore, reading the various accounts, that we are still in the so-called "Dark Ages" because women officiate at a religious ceremony. There is present, for another instance, a royal Grail Queen. Now, women were not expelled from the priesthood by the Christian Church until after the death of Queen Guinevere, which was, say, about 542. Women today (1995) are still slowly regaining positions of respect and honor.

Accounts of the Holy Grail, its processants, its necropolis, its castle, from its greatest Grail King, Arthur, to its last Grail King, Perceval, also reveal astonishing history. One is amazed to read a touching scene like this: Perceval as a little lad is taken by his father to pay respects at the tomb of a holy martyr. Perceval's young father is destined, like most warriors of his day, to die in battle while still hardly more than an adolescent himself. The father counts the generations since the death of Christ. Perceval learns that his ancestors left Jerusalem for Britain about five hundred years ago! At present Perceval grows up during the reigns and lives of the Emperor Justinian at Constantinople (483–565) and King Arthur in Britain (*c.*475–542). Thus, some medieval romances are often uncannily accurate in chronology.

If the Holy Grail is a mystery worth pondering, the personage of Merlin really staggers the mind. In his case there remains a "Prophecy" allegedly written by Merlin himself. This weird body of writing was first edited and restored by Geoffrey of Monmouth prior to his *History of the Kings of Britain* in 1134. It is reproduced in another original translation by myself in *Merlin* (1987), where it is argued that in Arthur's day Merlin could only have been another person, the real Saint Dubricius, a Celtic Archbishop (not recognized by the Catholic Church). Both Merlin and Dubricius died in the same year: 536. Here are the last lines of Merlin writing his pseudo-Biblical "Prophecy":

The chariot of the moon shall disturb the Zodiac and the Pleiades shall burst into tears. None shall return to his appointed course. But Ariadne behind a closed door shall seek refuge in her causeways. At a stroke of the wand the winds shall rush forth and the dust of our forefathers shall blow on us again.[10]

All this fervor from the Dark Ages to the High Middle Ages six or seven hundred years later dissolves into a last great courtly romance by Sir Thomas Malory. His book, largely translations from such medieval French poets as Marie de France, Chrétien de Troyes, and Robert de Boron, he called *Le Morte d'Arthur* (1468–69). It was magnificently edited and introduced by the Welsh scholar Sir John Rhys in two volumes, published by J. M. Dent and E. P. Dutton (London and New York, respectively, 1906; 1961).

Most of Bulfinch's romances of King Arthur *et al.* come directly from this late medieval telling by Sir Thomas Malory. His book is a last jewel in the crown of the Middle Ages, which were drawing to an end as he wrote. The year 1453 saw the victory of Islam over the Crusaders with the fall of Constantinople, the last of the Eastern Roman Empire. Rome had fallen by 1495. The Treaty of Cadillac, also in 1453, settled, in the favor of the Capetian Dynasty of French kings, the Hundred Years War with England. The death of King Richard II in 1499, as Shakespeare said, "in a triangular castle by the sea" (Flint Castle on the North Welsh coast), saw the end of the "French" Kings of England. The year 1492 saw the expulsion of Jews and Moors from Spain and, as we all know, the discovery of the Americas by Christopher Columbus.

Whoever he was, nobody wrote romances better than this unknown English-speaking person, Sir Thomas Malory. For wit, beauty, glamor, and gorgeous English prose, this *Morte d'Arthur* is a treasure and a treasury of the lost Middle Ages, recoverable in all their chivalry and idealized or "courtly" love through his immortal pages. Wielding mighty pen, writing not for money, fame, or glory, Sir Thomas Malory composed a dream world of starry eyes, tender lovers, Valentines, and the moon-June-tune of true love. Ah, Romances!

NOTES

1. Edition Dent (London) and Dutton (New York), 1910; 1976; introduced by Christopher Dawson, vol. IV.

2. See *Medieval Europe: A Short History* by Warren Hollister. Wiley (New York, 1978), p. 208.

3. See Chapter IV, "The Virgin of Chartres," from *Mont-Saint-Michel and Chartres* by Henry Adams, Doubleday Anchor (Garden City, 1905, 1933), pp. 95–113.

4. Literally, the Latin says, "Oh, Mary! Star of the sea! / [Woman] unique in dignity, / Ranked above all [the] / Heavenly hosts!"

5. From *Lyrics of the Troubadours and Trouvères,* ed. and Introduction by Frederick Goldin, Anchor (Garden City, 1973).

6. Various editions of Geoffrey of Monmouth are available, such as Penguin Classics, tr. and Introduction by Lewis Thorpe (Middlesex, 1966).

7. See *King Arthur* by Norma Lorre Goodrich, HarperCollins (New York, 1989).

8. See works by Reverend Denis de Rougemont (Paris, 1939, 1961); the first is translated as *Love in the Western World.*

9. See *Heroines* by Norma Lorre Goodrich, Chapter II ("The Love Story of Tristan and Isolde"), HarperCollins (New York, 1993).

10. See *Merlin* by Norma Lorre Goodrich, Franklin Watts (New York, 1987), HarperCollins (New York, 1989), p. 157.

BULFINCH'S MYTHOLOGY

THE AGE OF CHIVALRY

TO MRS. JOSEPH COOLIDGE

DEAR MADAM:

To you, who have sympathized in my tastes, and encouraged my researches, I dedicate this attempt to depict the age of chivalry, and to revive the legends of the land of our fathers.

Your friend and cousin,

T. B.

Here may we read of Spenser's fairy themes,
    And those that Milton loved in youthful years,
The sage enchanter Merlin's subtle schemes;
    The feats of Arthur, and his knightly peers.

                                        Wordsworth

PREFACE

In a former work the compiler of this volume endeavored to impart the pleasures of classical learning to the English reader, by presenting the stories of pagan mythology in a form adapted to modern taste. In the present volume the attempt has been made to treat in the same way the stories of the second "age of fable," the age which witnessed the dawn of the several states of modern Europe.

It is believed that this presentation of a literature which held unrivalled sway over the imaginations of our ancestors, for many centuries, will not be without benefit to the reader, in addition to the amusement it may afford. The tales, though not to be trusted for their facts, are worthy of all credit as pictures of manners; and it is beginning to be held that the manners and modes of thinking of an age are a more important part of its history than the conflicts of its peoples, generally leading to no result. Besides this, the literature of romance is a treasure-house of poetical material, to which modern poets frequently resort. The Italian poets, Dante and Ariosto, the English, Spenser, Scott, and Tennyson, and our own Longfellow and Lowell are examples of this.

These legends are so connected with each other, so consistently adapted to a group of characters strongly individualized in Arthur, Lancelot, and their compeers, and so lighted up by the fires of imagination and invention, that they seem as well adapted to the poet's purpose as the legends of the Greek and Roman mythology. And if every well-educated young person is expected to know the story of the Golden Fleece, why is the quest of the Sangreal less worthy of his acquaintance? Or if an allusion to the shield of Achilles ought not to pass unapprehended, why should one to Escalibur, the famous sword of Arthur:

> Of Arthur, who, to upper light restored,
> With that terrific sword,
> Which yet he brandishes for future war,
> Shall lift his country's fame above the polar star?*

It is an additional recommendation of our subject, that it tends to cherish in our minds the idea of the source from which we sprung. We are entitled to our full share in the glories and recollections of the land of our forefathers, down to the time of colonization thence. The associations which spring from this source must be fruitful of good influences; among which not the least valuable is the increased enjoyment which such associations afford to the American traveller when he visits England, and sets his foot upon any of her renowned localities.

The legends of Charlemagne and his peers are necessary to complete the subject, but they must be given, if at all, in a future volume.

*Wordsworth.

PART ONE

KING ARTHUR AND HIS KNIGHTS

CHAPTER I

The Age of Chivalry depended on masculine courage, and manly behavior centered about knighthood. Today also the word *knight* conveys this same meaning to every warrior and veteran although the Age of Chivalry was set in the twelfth through the fifteenth centuries.

In the Middle Ages, the most famous knights, from Iceland east to Germany, were certainly four of the many Arthurian heroes: King Arthur, Lancelot, Gawain, and Perceval. Then the knight was a combatant, but he also was a nobleman since commoners were not allowed in France to fight alongside him.

This rule obtained generally until the battle of Agincourt in 1415, say the French chroniclers, who were eyewitnesses, when the English King Henry V used commoners as archers. They were concealed in the woods on either side of the downslope along which the mounted French knights would plunge in serried ranks. The knights were equestrians, mounted upon horses as large as Percherons or Clydesdales. They were dressed in tons of armor, with helmets that entirely covered the faces. Their visors were movable, up and down. When the French Constable commanding gave the signal to advance, the French lowered their visors, leveled their pikes, and spurred downhill, gaining speed fast. After only a hundred feet, their horses became tragically mired. This was Flanders, where rainfall is heavy even in late summer. The heavily loaded horses sank knee-deep in mud. It had been raining steadily for days.

The first rank fell, face down, over their horses' heads. The second rank plowed into them and fell face first as well. And so on, rank after rank. To compound this tragedy, English archers armed with longbows fired at the knights from either side of the hill, having no trouble at all finding and reaching targets. Chroniclers from both sides reported the numbers of casualties, but no two ever came close to any agreement. But the French reported that of all the noblemen then alive in France, and of an age to bear arms, only six knights survived.

The rules of knighthood in such a total victory as this by the English require the victors to spare any defeated warriors who have surrendered. Despite this law of chivalry, King Henry V ordered axmen, who were commoners, to behead many French knights still alive—even the wounded, claimed the French. The beheading went on all the rest of that day. The English king took only a few prisoners. One French prince was found unconscious, but he regained consciousness near nightfall. The English king had a personal hatred of this prince, Charles of Orléans, the future poet and future father of a king of France. Charles had married the princess whom Henry V had hoped to marry. Charles was taken prisoner and held in solitary confinement for twenty-five years. His unusual survival only points up the fact that the majority of French knights who fell on that hill drowned or suffocated. Because of their heavy armor most were unable to open their visors.

This terrible loss of French knights sounded a heavy knell for the end of both armor and chivalry. Another portent was the use of commoners on a field of honor heretofore reserved for hereditary lords. The slaughter of prisoners who had surrendered is always a deterrent to total war, as charged in the recent Gulf War. But Saint Joan of Arc and the artillery expert Count Dunois, the brother of Charles of Orléans, turned the tables in the fifteenth century, coming as they said, to release

Duke Charles of Orléans from his English prison. And the Maid of Orléans died as much for her "chivalry" as for enlisting armies led by the Duke of Albany, from Scotland, who fought beside her. The first charge against Joan of Arc was that she was an unwomanly woman because she wore trousers, or long pants, under her armor. She claimed she often had to wear armor for as long as three days without disrobing, and that the undergarments protected her skin from chafing. Her English Court condemned her to be burned at the stake.

Thus, by the early fifteenth century knighthood in war was almost dead. The use of cannons and explosives also in the fifteenth century and the arrival of artillery specialists like Count Dunois sounded not only the end of the Middle Ages, but the end of this Age of Chivalry. The English, or Lancastrian, dramatist we call "Shakespeare" continued to celebrate, in his Henry V plays, this English king as brave, gallant, and knightly, but his vanquished opponents judge him unknightly.

In the twelfth century a knight was first of all a member of the hereditary and landed nobility. He was a mounted combatant, therefore a cavalier, or in French, a *chevalier.* Hence, the word *chivalry.* He was a hero, and defender of helpless persons: priests, women, and children. Because theoretically he defended, and only attacked other knights in defense of the weak, he was esteemed as supremely humanitarian; his knightly service pledged him to his liege lord to whom he had sworn obedience, and to the lady to whom he paid homage. He was a heroic military man, skilled in war, but often courteous in battle, benevolent toward the knight he vanquished, and magnanimous in victory. These are the very qualities and very conduct of the great Arthurian knights. In literature of the Middle Ages they became ideals for the world to admire and follow. King Arthur and his knights, then, set a standard of manhood that some fighting men today still follow, and a pattern for behavior that other men still follow, also.

All western Europe adopted the rules of knighthood. The German *Ritter,* the French *chevalier,* the English knight or knight-errant wandering in search of adventures, and the knight questing for the Holy Grail follow laws and strive for perfection according to the code of chivalry. The knight serves a lady as her *cavalier servant.* The virtues of knighthood establish forever a noble hero's education: piety, bravery, loyalty, honor, and humility. The Church warned French knights especially to beware of the sin of pride. The French hero Roland, who was knight under the Emperor Charlemagne, died because he was too proud to blow his war horn to summon aid and reinforcements.

During the Crusades the great Orders of Chivalry were established by such leaders as Saint Bernard of Clairvaux (*c.*1090–1153), who so eloquently preached the Second Crusade in 1146. This holy man also urged the founding of the chivalric Order of Knights Templar, whose primary charge was to defend the routes from western Europe to the Holy Land. They were called "Templar" from their residence in the Temple of Solomon in Jerusalem. The Teutonic Knights from the Germanies were also founded during the Crusades. An even larger Christian Order were the Knights Hospitalers, or Knights of Saint John, who maintained a church and a hospital in Jerusalem and thus cared for wounded or stranded pilgrims to that city. There orders were responsible for the establishment and maintenance briefly of the Latin Kingdom of Jerusalem.

The French Church, which has always claimed to sit at the right-hand side of the Holy Father in Rome, had attempted from King Arthur's days in the Dark Ages to supervise religion in Britain. When the Norman French conquered England in 1066 and crowned King William in London, Christmas Day of that year, they once more brought the French Church and French ideas of chivalry across the Channel. By 1190 their systems attendant upon both courtly love and knight-errantry obtained even into Scotland. The complicated and ever-popular system of heraldry spun off from ancient chivalry with its earlier arms and devices.

In heraldic terms a *device* is an emblematic design used as a heraldic bearing, like a motto, for example. One such is the key to chivalry: *noblesse oblige,* which means that noble birth obliges a knight to follow a chivalric code of behavior. The closed helmet of the later Middle Ages encouraged the use of devices so that persons could recognize each other and rally to the defense of a friend on a field of honor (i.e., a battle field). Heraldry offered the knight a distinguishing badge or mark, which indicated his nationality, clan, or military unit. Examples would be the Plantagenet flower, or yellow broom, the red dragon of the Welsh kings, the grizzly bear of King Arthur, the tartans and badges of the Scottish clans (the purple thistle as national badge of Scotland). Heraldic insignia grew in importance during the Third Crusade (1189) because one had suddenly to distinguish at a glance each of the three nations who went to the defense of Jerusalem: Germany, France, and England.

In addition to his sword, spear, and shield, the knight required a badge and other heraldic bearings. The King of France and his princes were recognized by his colors, blue and silver, while the King and princes of England wore red and gold. Lancaster wore a red rose; York, a white rose. Tudor chose a white lion as emblem. The Prince of Wales wore as badge three ostrich feathers. Ireland chose the shamrock. The Clan Campbell, largest of Scotland, bore the wild myrtle or the fir club moss. The most ancient peoples of Scotland, the Picts from whom Queen Guinevere was born, wore the *rugh* or rue as tribal badge; it is now joined to the thistle. Crests were worn atop the helmet of knights. The only lady known to have worn helmet and crest in battle or elsewhere was Joan of Arc. She bore the banner of Prince Charles of Orléans—whom she came to save, she said, and saved.

Knighthood, or chivalry, also employed animals and monsters as charges. These were figures borne on the field of battle, or a heraldic bearing: griffin, dragon, salamander, chimera, bear, sphinx, centaur, harpy, phoenix, or mermaid. The mermaid could well have been Queen Guinevere's charge, for she was represented in a famous text of Lancelot as holding a mirror and combing her long tresses. Knights chose familiar charges: the red lion (of royal England), the silver fleur-de-lis of French royalty, the black bear, the mastiff (of Lancelot), the boar's head of Christmas, the green armor of Merlin.[1]

Lancelot seems also to have worn as animate charge a leopard. He is often compared to a leopard for ferocity in battle, for grace, and for speed. Tristan (when in Scotland) is often referred to as a mastiff, and described as a gigantic dog (of an ancient breed), very good at tracking from scent alone, extremely loyal, easy to retrain, and absolutely dependable. Although chained for a long period of time, his dog still followed the track of Tristan and Isolde a long distance across a dense forest and rallied to them (wrote the earliest *Tristan* author, Beroul). It is well known that Britain raised dogs for Rome and used them in war just as the ancient Africans, as reported by Lucan, had used enormous snakes in battle.[2]

King Arthur's arms, say Breton Heralds, were azure blue with three (or thirteen) golden crowns. The French scholar of heraldry Michel Pastoureau describes Gawain as oldest son of King Loth and "principal hero of Arthurian legend" with arms in purple with a golden, bicephalous eagle adorned with gold, or two golden eagles with azure beaks. Gawain wore his father's shield and weapons. Lancelot's shield is silver with three wide, red bands. His charge was a golden falcon. Supporters on his arms were two naked savages. These heraldic bearings of Lancelot remained generally accepted throughout the Middle Ages, ergo the easiest for us to recognize today. Furthermore, they strike the reader as the most appropriate. Lancelot always enters into battle frenzy like the Irish champions of old who frothed at the mouth in combat, bit and kicked whenever possible, and literally could not be calmed. In the literature he always fights in the heat of day. His red rages always draw blood. Lancelot usually goes for the kill, and always when Guinevere gives him the thumbs-down signal. July is his month and his weather, a hot sun. Arthur's motto was: "All for Arthur!"

Perceval's arms are the royal purple (our fuschia color), for he is the Elect at the Grail Castle. His purple is sewn with tiny golden crosses, and his bearing is the

Gold Cross. (He is the Gold Cross Knight.) His supporters are two griffons, which are ancient Greek mythological monsters, half lion and half eagle. Two griffons
always stood as defenders guarding either a precious
treasure or an especially holy place like the Grail Castle.

Tristan's arms are green like Merlin's person when
garbed as the Green Knight attacking Gawain. Tristan
bears a golden lion on a green shield and owns a lion's
head as charge. His supporters on either side are two
golden lions—the lion as symbol of royalty being probably the most common of all charges, and represented in
heraldry in all postures and colors. The less common
wolves' heads are, on the contrary, usually silver. Leop-
ards' heads are traditionally red, like Lancelot. Animals,
birds, and horses notably, were then preferred gifts.[3] Tristan was represented by a *lion* not only in France, England, and Scandinavia, but thus through the Middle
Ages; in Germany alone he was represented with a *boar*
as his cognizance. His motto was: *"C'est pour Isolde!"*
("It's for Isolde!"). Then perhaps the green (*"sinople"*)
of his arms paid homage to her birth in Dublin, Ireland.

Chivalry with its mass of symbolism went, as it still
does, hand in hand with romance and with the romances
which first depicted this medieval courtly world. Scholars
suppose that this reverence for women must have hailed
from Persia (Iran) and its heroic literature, thence via
the Moors in Spain because it assuredly did not come
from either Rome or Greece. In ancient Rome a girl,
daughter, or wife was totally in the power—that of life
or death without question or law to the contrary—of the
male householder/father/husband. Chivalry, hand in hand
with romance, inaugurated and upheld a new literature,
an upheaval in manners, and a presentation of noble
women as respected persons, able even to govern France.

One of the greatest medieval scholars, D. D. R. Owen
of Scotland, concludes for us: "There is probably no area
in medieval studies that merits, or indeed currently receives, more attention than Arthurian romance." He
urged a deeper emphasis on history, even in such romances as those narrated by Thomas Bulfinch, which
glow like jewels. Owen asserted that any interpretation

that flies in the face of what is historically verifiable may be anachronistic, whatever merits it may have.[4]

The main subject of the romance is love, as we see from the special section in our bookstores today: hundreds of romances in inexpensive paperback volumes, most written by women, and all always purchased, say the salespersons, by women. In the Middle Ages the lovers were emphasized in the face of history, which preferred Guinevere as a battle queen, Isolde as a virginal priestess, and Morgan le Fay as a scholar competent in Arabic and astronomy. It is the accusation of adultery which has made Guinevere so titillating to male readers of medieval romances. It is the puzzle of Tristan and Isolde sleeping with the drawn sword between them which has sold books. But much more seriously, the great remainder of the Middle Ages pondered the doctrine of *fin amor*.

What is the real meaning of *fin* (faith, truth) and *amor* (love): how strong are the bonds which unite young lovers? How deep is true love? How true is it? The Provençal poets, troubadours all, were so skilled and so intellectual that no one can for sure decode their various styles of composition in order to pare off the skin and reach their thought. They wrote in *trobar ric* (rich style), *trobar clus* (closed style), or *trobar clar* (non-hermetic style). Theirs was "la belle dame sans merci":

> Dame, en vostre baillie
> Ai mis cuer et cors et vie.
> Por Diew, ne m'oubliez mie.
> La ou fins cuers s'umelie,
> Doit on trouver
> Merci, aïe
> Por conforter.[5]

> Lady, in your bailiwick I've
> Sat heart and my body alive.
> For God's sake, forget not me, nigh.
> Where true hearts kneel. Thereby
> ought ever discover
> Grace, whereby
> Solace.

There lies a case for the Royal Princess Marie, Countess of Champagne, to hear in her Courts of Love. She hands down judgment upon the Lady who, the poet complains, has failed to show her lover mercy commensurate with his pains and the offer of his heart, body, and life itself. This Countess is that same daughter born to Eleanor of Aquitaine when she was Queen of France. Marie's husband returned from Scotland bringing their Annals. These he commissioned Chrétien de Troyes to rewrite in Old French, as Arthurian romances.[6]

Those great French ladies who sat in judgment in cases of love had at their disposal, it is said, the thirty-one Laws of Love as drawn up by Andreas Capellanus (André le Chapelain) for ladies at the court of Henry II: Queen Eleanor, Countess Ermengarde de Narbonne, Countess of Bologne, and the Countess Marie. These "laws" derive in large measure from the Roman poet Ovid. Many are shocking, such as that a man may only rape any low-class woman whom he would never dream of marrying; that love made public never lasts; that only jealous persons really love; that good character makes all men worthy of love; and so on.[7]

As the Middle Ages drew to a close, with the Hundred Years War concluded (1452), with the Crusades understood as a series of disasters, with France finally pleased to recover her Continental kingdom, and with her Capetian dynasty still standing as the English Plantagenet kings faded away, there burst upon the literary scene the greatest of all romancers: Sir Thomas Malory. He collected and organized the most romantic of the Arthurian legends and presented them in an English prose which for charm, feeling, and wit can only be compared with one often named by English scholars as the greatest writer of English romances: Jane Austen.[8]

Malory reasons that Queen Guinevere made a good end because she was a true lover. Now, true love resembles a summer, he explained several times and at considerable length. People fall in love in the month of May, a lusty month that gives courage to lovers.

But, Malory adds (Book XVIII, Chapter XXV), love must be virtuous. In the old days "men and women could love together seven years . . . and then was love, truth, and faithfulness . . . love in King Arthur's days.

But nowadays men can not love seven night but they must have all their desires: that love may not endure by reason; for where they be soon accorded, and hasty heat, soon it cooleth. Right so fareth love nowadays, soon hot soon cold: this is no stability.[9]

NOTES

1. *Scottish Heraldry Made Easy* by G. Harvey Johnston, Heraldic (New York, 1972).

2. Lucan, *Civil War,* World's Classics, tr. Professor Susan H. Braund, Oxford University Press (1992), pp. 193–6, 199, 201.

3. See Michel Pastoureau's long study, "Armoiries et devises des chevaliers de la Table Ronde," in *Finistère d'Autrefois,* Vol. III (Quimper, 1980), pp. 29–127.

4. *Arthurian Romance, Seven Essays,* ed. by D. D. R. Owen, Scottish Academic Press (Edinburgh, 1973), Foreword.

5. Maurice Valency, *In Praise of Love,* Macmillan Paperback (New York, 1961). See "True Love," p. 142 ff., and his translation of these verses on page 299.

6. *King Arthur*; *Merlin*; *Guinevere*; *The Holy Grail* by Norma Lorre Goodrich, HarperCollins (New York, 1989; 1989; 1991; 1992).

7. *The Art of Courtly Love,* Andreas Capellanus, tr. by John Jay Parry, ed. by Frederick W. Locke. Frederick Ungar (New York, 1964).

8. See Eugene Vinaver's *The Rise of Romance,* Oxford University Press (1971) and also his magisterial, three-volume edition of Malory's *Le Morte d'Arthur.*

9. *Le Morte d'Arthur* (vol. II), Preface by Sir John Rhys, J. M. Dent, E. P. Dutton (London and New York, respectively, 1906; 1961), pp. 314–35.

CHAPTER II

THE MYTHICAL HISTORY OF ENGLAND

The illustrious poet, Milton, in his History of England, is the author whom we chiefly follow in this chapter.

According to the earliest accounts, Albion, a giant and son of Neptune, a contemporary of Hercules, ruled over the island, to which he gave his name. Presuming to oppose the progress of Hercules in his western march, he was slain by him.

Another story is that Histion, the son of Japhet, the son of Noah, had four sons—Francus, Romanus, Alemannus, and Britto, from whom descended the French, Roman, German, and British people.

Rejecting these and other like stories, Milton gives more regard to the story of Brutus, the Trojan, which, he says, is supported by "descents of ancestry long continued, laws and exploits not plainly seeming to be borrowed or devised, which on the common belief have wrought no small impression; defended by many, denied utterly by few." The principal authority is Geoffrey of Monmouth, whose history, written in the twelfth century, purports to be a translation of a history of Britain brought over from the opposite shore of France which, under the name of Brittany, was chiefly peopled by natives of Britain, who from time to time emigrated thither, driven from their own country by the inroads of the Picts and Scots. According to this authority, Brutus was the son of Silvius, and he of Ascanius, the son of Æneas, whose flight from Troy and settlement in Italy will be found narrated in *The Age of Fable*.

Brutus, at the age of fifteen, attending his father to the chase, unfortunately killed him with an arrow. Banished therefor by his kindred, he sought refuge in that part of Greece where Helenus, with a band of Trojan exiles, had become established. But Helenus was now dead, and the descendants of the Trojans were oppressed by Pandrasus, the king of the country. Brutus, being kindly received among them, so throve in virtue and in arms as to win the regard of all the eminent of the land above all others of his age. In consequence of this, the Trojans not only began to hope, but secretly to persuade him to lead them the way to liberty. To encourage them, they had the promise of help from Assaracus, a noble Greek youth, whose mother was a Trojan. He had suffered wrong at the hands of the king, and for that reason the more willingly cast in his lot with the Trojan exiles.

Choosing a fit opportunity, Brutus with his country-men withdrew to the woods and hills, as the safest place from which to expostulate, and sent this message to Pandrasus: "That the Trojans, holding it unworthy of their ancestors to serve in a foreign land, had retreated to the woods, choosing rather a savage life than a slavish one. If that displeased him, then, with his leave, they would depart to some other country." Pandrasus, not ex-pecting so bold a message from the sons of captives, went in pursuit of them, with such forces as he could gather, and met them on the banks of the Achelous, where Bru-tus got the advantage and took the king captive. The re-sult was that the terms demanded by the Trojans were granted; the king gave his daughter Imogen in marriage to Brutus and furnished shipping, money, and fit provision for them all to depart from the land.

The marriage being solemnized, and shipping from all parts got together, the Trojans, in a fleet of no less than three hundred and twenty sail, betook themselves to the sea. On the third day, they arrived at a certain island, which they found destitute of inhabitants, though there were appearances of former habitation, and among the ruins a temple of Diana. Brutus, here performing sac-rifice at the shrine of the goddess, invoked an oracle for his guidance, in these lines:

> Goddess of shades, and huntress, who at will
> Walk'st on the rolling sphere, and through the deep;
> On thy third realm, the earth, look now, and tell
> What land, what seat of rest, thou bidd'st me seek;
> What certain seat where I may worship thee
> For aye, with temples vowed and virgin choirs.

To whom, sleeping before the altar, Diana in a vision thus answered:

> Brutus! far to the west, in the ocean wide,
> Beyond the realm of Gaul, a land there lies,
> Seagirt it lies, where giants dwelt of old;
> Now, void, it fits thy people: thither bend
> Thy course; there shalt thou find a lasting seat;
> There to thy sons another Troy shall rise,
> And kings be born of thee, whose dreaded might
> Shall awe the world, and conquer nations bold.

Brutus, guided now, as he thought, by divine direction, sped his course towards the west, and, arriving at a place on the Tyrrhene sea, found there the descendants of certain Trojans who, with Antenor, came into Italy, of whom Corineus was the chief. These joined company, and the ships pursed their way till they arrived at the mouth of the River Loire, in France, where the expedition landed, with a view to a settlement, but were so rudely assaulted by the inhabitants that they put to sea again and arrived at a part of the coast of Britain, now called Devonshire, where Brutus felt convinced that he had found the promised end of his voyage, landed his colony, and took possession.

The island, not yet Britain, but Albion, was in a manner desert and inhospitable, occupied only by a remnant of the giant race whose excessive force and tyranny had destroyed the others. The Trojans encountered these and extirpated them, Corineus in particular signalizing himself by his exploits against them; from whom Cornwall takes its name, for that region fell to his lot, and there the hugest giants dwelt, lurking in rocks and caves, till Corineus rid the land of them.

Brutus built his capital city and called it Trojanova (New Troy), changed in time to Trinovantum, now London*; and, having governed the isle twenty-four years, died, leaving three sons, Locrine, Albanact, and Camber. Locrine had the middle part, Camber the west, called Cambria from him, and Albanact Albania, now Scotland.

---

* "For noble Britons sprong from Trojans bold,
  And Troynovant was built of old Troy's ashes cold."
  SPENSER, Book III, Canto IX, 38

Locrine was married to Guendolen, the daughter of Corineus; but, having seen a fair maid named Estrildis, who had been brought captive from Germany, he became enamored of her and had by her a daughter, whose name was Sabra. This matter was kept secret while Corineus lived, but after his death, Locrine divorced Guendolen and made Estrildis his queen. Guendolen, all in rage, departed to Cornwall, where Madan, her son, lived, who had been brought up by Corineus, his grandfather. Gathering an army of her father's friends and subjects, she gave battle to her husband's forces, and Locrine was slain. Guendolen caused her rival, Estrildis, with her daughter Sabra, to be thrown into the river, from which cause the river thenceforth bore the maiden's name, which by length of time is now changed into Sabrina or Severn. Milton alludes to this in his address to the rivers—

Severn swift, guilty of maiden's death;—

and in his Comus tells the story with a slight variation, thus:

There is a gentle nymph not far from hence,
That with moist curb sways the smooth Severn stream;
Sabrina is her name, a virgin pure:
Whilom she was the daughter of Locrine,
That had the sceptre from his father, Brute.
She, guiltless damsel, flying the mad pursuit
Of her enragéd step-dame, Guendolen,
Commended her fair innocence to the flood,
That stayed her flight with his cross-flowing course.
The water-nymphs that in the bottom played,
Held up their pearléd wrists and took her in,
Bearing her straight to aged Nereus' hall,
Who, piteous of her woes, reared her lank head,
And gave her to his daughters to imbathe
In nectared lavers stewed with asphodel,
And through the porch and inlet of each sense
Dropped in ambrosial oils till she revived,
And underwent a quick, immortal change,
Made goddess of the river,
&c.

If our readers ask when all this took place, we must answer, in the first place, that mythology is not careful of dates; and next, that, as Brutus was the great-grandson of Æneas, it must have been not far from a century subsequent to the Trojan War, or about 1,100 years before the invasion of the island by Julius Cæsar. This long interval is filled with the names of princes whose chief occupation was in warring with one another. Some few, whose names remain connected with places or embalmed in literature, we will mention.

BLADUD

Bladud built the city of Bath and dedicated the medicinal waters to Minerva. He was a man of great invention, and practised the arts of magic, till, having made him wings to fly, he fell down upon the temple of Apollo, in Trinovant, and so died, after twenty years' reign.

LEIR

Leir, who next reigned, built Leicester and called it after his name. He had no male issue, but only three daughters. When grown old, he determined to divide his kingdom among his daughters and bestow them in marriage. But first, to try which of them loved him best, he determined to ask them solemnly in order, and judge of the warmth of their affection by their answers. Goneril, the eldest, knowing well her father's weakness, made answer that she loved him "above her soul." "Since thou so honorest my declining age," said the old man, "to thee and to thy husband I give the third part of my realm." Such good success for a few words soon uttered was ample instruction to Regan, the second daughter, what to say. She therefore to the same question replied that "she loved him more than all the world beside," and so received an equal reward with her sister. But Cordelia, the youngest, and hitherto the best beloved, though having before her eyes the reward of a little easy soothing and the loss likely to attend plain-dealing, yet was not moved from the solid purpose of a sincere and virtuous answer and replied: "Father, my love towards you is as my duty bids.

They who pretend beyond this flatter." When the old man, sorry to hear this and wishing her to recall these words, persisted in asking, she still restrained her expressions so as to say rather less than more than the truth. Then Leir, all in a passion, burst forth: "Since thou hast not revereneed thy aged father like thy sisters, think not to have any part in my kingdom or what else I have" —and without delay, giving in marriage his other daughters, Goneril to the Duke of Albany and Regan to the Duke of Cornwall, he divides his kingdom between them and goes to reside with his eldest daughter, attended only by a hundred knights. But in a short time his attendants, being complained of as too numerous and disorderly, are reduced to thirty. Resenting that affront, the old king betakes him to his second daughter; but she, instead of soothing his wounded pride, takes part with her sister and refuses to admit a retinue of more than five. Then back he returns to the other, who now will not receive him with more than one attendant. Then the remembrance of Cordelia comes to his thoughts and he takes his journey into France to seek her, with little hope of kind consideration from one whom he had so injured, but to pay her the last recompense he can render— confession of his injustice. When Cordelia is informed of his approach and of his sad condition, she pours forth true filial tears. And, not willing that her own or others' eyes should see him in that forlorn condition, she sends one of her trusted servants to meet him, and convey him privately to some comfortable abode, and to furnish him with such state as befitted his dignity. After which Cordelia, with the king her husband, went in state to meet him, and, after an honorable reception, the king permitted his wife Cordelia to go with an army and set her father again upon his throne. They prospered, subdued the wicked sisters and their consorts, and Leir obtained the crown and held it three years. Cordelia succeeded him and reigned five years; but the sons of her sisters, after that, rebelled against her, and she lost both her crown and life.

Shakespeare has chosen this story as the subject of his tragedy of King Lear, varying its details in some respects. The madness of Lear and the ill success of Cordelia's attempt to reinstate her father are the principal variations, and those in the names will also be noticed. Our narrative is drawn from Milton's History; and thus the reader will perceive that the story of Leir has had the distinguished honor of being told by the two acknowledged chiefs of British literature.

FERREX AND PORREX

Ferrex and Porrex were brothers who held the kingdom after Leir. They quarrelled about the supremacy, and Porrex expelled his brother, who, obtaining aid from Suard, King of the Franks, returned and made war upon Porrex. Ferrex was slain in battle, and his forces dispersed. When their mother came to hear of her son's death, who was her favorite, she fell into a great rage and conceived a mortal hatred against the survivor. She took, therefore, her opportunity when he was asleep, fell upon him, and, with the assistance of her women, tore him in pieces. This horrid story would not be worth relating were it not for the fact that it has furnished the plot for the first tragedy which was written in the English language. It was entitled Gorboduc, but in the second edition Ferrex and Porrex, and was the production of Thomas Sackville, afterwards Earl of Dorset, and Thomas Norton, a barrister. Its date was 1561.

DUNWALLO MOLMUTIUS

This is the next name of note. Molmutius established the Molmutine laws, which bestowed the privilege of sanctuary on temples, cities, and the roads leading to them, and gave the same protection to ploughs, extending a religious sanction to the labors of the field. Shakespeare alludes to him in Cymbeline, Act III, Sc. I:

> Molmutius made our laws;
> Who was the first of Britain which did put
> His brows within a golden crown, and called
> Himself a king.

BRENNUS AND BELINUS,

the sons of Molmutius, succeeded him. They quarrelled, and Brennus was driven out of the island, and took refuge in Gaul, where he met with such favor from the king of the Allobroges that he gave him his daughter in marriage, and made him his partner on the throne. Brennus is the name which the Roman historians give to the famous leader of the Gauls who took Rome in the time of Camillus. Geoffrey of Monmouth claims the glory of the conquest for the British prince, after he had become King of the Allobroges.

ELIDURE

After Belinus and Brennus, there reigned several kings of little note, and then came Elidure. Arthgallo, his brother, being king, gave great offence to his powerful nobles, who rose against him, deposed him, and advanced Elidure to the throne. Arthgallo fled and endeavored to find assistance in the neighboring kingdoms to reinstate him, but found none. Elidure reigned prosperously and wisely. After five years' possession of the kingdom, one day, when hunting, he met in the forest his brother, Arthgallo, who had been deposed. After long wandering, unable longer to bear the poverty to which he was reduced, he had returned to Britain with only ten followers, designing to repair to those who had formerly been his friends. Elidure, at the sight of his brother in distress, forgetting all animosities, ran to him and embraced him. He took Arthgallo home with him and concealed him in the palace. After this, he feigned himself sick and, calling his nobles about him, induced them, partly by persuasion, partly by force, to consent to his abdicating the kingdom, and reinstating his brother on the throne. The agreement being ratified, Elidure took the crown from his own head and put it on his brother's head. Arthgallo, after this, reigned ten years, well and wisely, exercising strict justice towards all men.

He died and left the kingdom to his sons, who reigned with various fortunes, but were not long-lived, and left no offspring, so that Elidure was again advanced to the throne and finished the course of his life in just and virtuous actions, receiving the name of *the pious,* from the love and admiration of his subjects.

Wordsworth has taken the story of Artegal and Elidure for the subject of a poem, which is No. 2 of "Poems founded on the Affections."

LUD

After Elidure, the Chronicle names many kings, but none of special note, till we come to Lud, who greatly enlarged Trinovant, his capital, and surrounded it with a wall. He changed its name, bestowing upon it his own, so that thenceforth it was called Lud's town, afterwards London. Lud was buried by the gate of the city called after him Ludgate. He had two sons, but they were not old enough at the time of their father's death to sustain the cares of government, and therefore their uncle Caswallaun, or Cassibellaunus, succeeded to the kingdom. He was a brave and magnificent prince, so that his fame reached to distant countries.

CASSIBELLAUNUS

About this time it happened (as is found in the Roman histories) that Julius Cæsar, having subdued Gaul, came to the shore opposite Britain. And having resolved to add this island also to his conquests, he prepared ships and transported his army across the sea, to the mouth of the river Thames. Here he was met by Cassibellaun, with all his forces, and a battle ensued, in which Nennius, the brother of Cassibellaun, engaged in single combat with Cæsar. After several furious blows given and received, the sword of Cæsar stuck so fast in the shield of Nennius that it could not be pulled out, and, the combatants being separated by the intervention of the troops, Nennius remained possessed of this trophy. At last, after the greater part of the day was spent, the Britons poured in so fast that Cæsar was forced to retire to his camp and fleet. And finding it useless to continue the war any longer at that time, he returned to Gaul.

Shakespeare alludes to Cassibellaunus, in Cymbeline:

> The famed Cassibelan, who was once at point
> (O giglot fortune!) to master Cæsar's sword,
> Made Lud's town with rejoicing fires bright,
> And Britons strut with courage.

KYMBELINUS, OR CYMBELINE

Cæsar, on a second invasion of the island, was more fortunate, and compelled the Britons to pay tribute. Cymbeline, the nephew of the king, was delivered to the Romans as a hostage for the faithful fulfilment of the treaty, and, being carried to Rome by Cæsar, he was there brought up in the Roman arts and accomplishments. Being afterwards restored to his country and placed on the throne, he was attached to the Romans, and continued through all his reign at peace with them. His sons, Guiderius and Arviragus, who make their appearance in Shakespeare's play of Cymbeline, succeeded their father and, refusing to pay tribute to the Romans, brought on another invasion. Guiderius was slain, but Arviragus afterwards made terms with the Romans and reigned prosperously many years.

ARMORICA

The next event of note is the conquest and colonization of Armorica by Maximus, a Roman general, and Conan, lord of Miniadoc, or Denbigh-land, in Wales. The name of the country was changed to Brittany, or Lesser Britain; and so completely was it possessed by the British colonists that the language became assimilated to that spoken in Wales, and it is said that to this day the peasantry of the two countries can understand each other when speaking their native language.

The Romans eventually succeeded in establishing themselves in the island, and after the lapse of several generations they became blended with the natives so that no distinction existed between the two races. When at length the Roman armies were withdrawn from Britain, their departure was a matter of regret to the inhabitants, as it left them without protection against the barbarous tribes, Scots, Picts, and Norwegians, who harassed the country incessantly. This was the state of things when the era of King Arthur began.

The adventure of Albion, the giant, with Hercules is alluded to by Spenser, Faery Queene, Book IV, Canto xi:

> For Albion the son of Neptune was;
> Who for the proof of his great puissance,
> Out of his Albion did on dry foot pass
> Into old Gaul that now is cleped France,
> To fight with Hercules, that did advance
> To vanquish all the world with matchless might;
> And there his mortal part by great mischance
> Was slain.

CHAPTER III

MERLIN

Merlin was the son of no mortal father, but of an Incubus, one of a class of beings not absolutely wicked, but far from good, who inhabit the regions of the air. Merlin's mother was a virtuous young woman, who, on the birth of her son, intrusted him to a priest, who hurried him to the baptismal fount and so saved him from sharing the lot of his father, though he retained many marks of his unearthly origin.

At this time, Vortigern reigned in Britain. He was a usurper who had caused the death of his sovereign, Moines, and driven the two brothers of the late king,

whose names were Uther and Pendragon, into banish-
ment. Vortigern, who lived in constant fear of the return
of the rightful heirs of the kingdom, began to erect a
strong tower for defence. The edifice, when brought by
the workmen to a certain height, three times fell to the
ground, without any apparent cause. The king consulted
his astrologers on this wonderful event and learned from
them that it would be necessary to bathe the corner-
stone of the foundation with the blood of a child born
without a mortal father.

In search of such an infant, Vortigern sent his messengers all over the kingdom, and they by accident discovered Merlin, whose lineage seemed to point him out
as the individual wanted. They took him to the king; but
Merlin, young as he was, explained to the king the ab-
surdity of attempting to rescue the fabric by such means,
for he told him the true cause of the instability of the
tower was its being placed over the den of two immense
dragons, whose combats shook the earth above them. The
king ordered his workmen to dig beneath the tower, and
when they had done so they discovered two enormous
serpents, the one white as milk, the other red as fire.
The multitude looked on with amazement till the
serpents, slowly rising from their den and expanding their
enormous folds, began the combat, when every one fled
in terror, except Merlin, who stood by clapping his hands
and cheering on the conflict. The red dragon was slain,
and the white one, gliding through a cleft in the rock, disappeared.

These animals typified, as Merlin afterwards explained,
the invasion of Uther and Pendragon, the rightful princes,
who soon after landed with a great army. Vortigern was
defeated and afterwards burned alive in the castle he
had taken such pains to construct. On the death of
Vortigern, Pendragon ascended the throne. Merlin became his chief adviser and often assisted the king by his
magical arts. Among other endowments, he had the power
of transforming himself into any shape he pleased. At
one time he appeared as a dwarf, at others as a damsel,
a page, or even a greyhound or a stag. This faculty he
often employed for the service of the king and sometimes
also for the diversion of the court and the sovereign.

Merlin continued to be a favorite counsellor through the reigns of Pendragon, Uther, and Arthur, and at last disappeared from view, and was no more found among men, through the treachery of his mistress, Viviane the fairy, which happened in this wise.

Merlin, having become enamored of the fair Viviane, the Lady of the Lake, was weak enough to impart to her various important secrets of his art, being impelled by a fatal destiny, of which he was at the same time fully aware. The lady, however, was not content with his devotion, unbounded as it seems to have been, but "cast about," the romance tells us, how she might "detain him for evermore," and one day addressed him in these terms: "Sir, I would that we should make a fair place and a suitable, so contrived by art and by cunning that it might never be undone, and that you and I should be there in joy and solace." "My lady," said Merlin, "I will do all this." "Sir," said she, "I would not have you do it, but you shall teach me, and I will do it, and then it will be more to my mind." "I grant you this," said Merlin. Then he began to devise, and the damsel put it all in writing. And when he had devised the whole, then had the damsel full great joy, and showed him greater semblance of love than she had ever before made, and they sojourned together a long while. At length it fell out that, as they were going one day hand in hand through the forest of Brécéliande, they found a bush of white-thorn, which was laden with flowers; and they seated themselves, under the shade of this white-thorn, upon the green grass, and Merlin laid his head upon the damsel's lap and fell asleep. Then the damsel rose, and made a ring with her wimple round the bush and round Merlin, and began her enchantments, such as he himself had taught her; and nine times she made the ring, and nine times she made the enchantment, and then she went and sat down by him and placed his head again upon her lap. And when he awoke and looked round him, it seemed to him that he was enclosed in the strongest tower in the world and laid upon a fair bed. Then said he to the dame: "My lady, you have deceived me, unless you abide with me, for no one hath power to unmake this tower but you alone."

She then promised she would be often there, and in this she held her covenant with him. And Merlin never went out of that tower where his Mistress Viviane had enclosed him; but she entered and went out again when she listed.

After this event, Merlin was never more known to hold converse with any mortal but Viviane, except on one occasion. Arthur, having for some time missed him from his court, sent several of his knights in search of him, and, among the number, Sir Gawain, who met with a very unpleasant adventure while engaged in this quest. Happening to pass a damsel on his road and neglecting to salute her, she revenged herself for his incivility by transforming him into a hideous dwarf. He was bewailing aloud his evil fortune as he went through the forest of Brécéliande, when suddenly he heard the voice of one groaning on his right hand; and, looking that way, he could see nothing save a kind of smoke, which seemed like air, and through which he could not pass. Merlin then addressed him from out the smoke and told him by what misadventure he was imprisoned there. "Ah, sir!" he added, "you will never see me more, and that grieves me, but I cannot remedy it; I shall never more speak to you, nor to any other person, save only my mistress. But do thou hasten to King Arthur and charge him from me to undertake, without delay, the quest of the Sacred Graal. The knight is already born, and has received knighthood at his hands, who is destined to accomplish this quest." And, after this, he comforted Gawain under his transformation, assuring him that he should speedily be disenchanted; and he predicted to him that he should find the king at Carduel, in Wales, on his return, and that all the other knights who had been on like quest would arrive there the same day as himself. And all this came to pass as Merlin had said.

Merlin is frequently introduced in the tales of chivalry, but it is chiefly on great occasions, and at a period subsequent to his death, or magical disappearance. In the romantic poems of Italy and in Spenser, Merlin is chiefly represented as a magical artist. Spenser represents him as the artificer of the impenetrable shield and other armor of Prince Arthur (Faery Queene, Book I, Canto vii), and

of a mirror, in which a damsel viewed her lover's shade.
The Fountain of Love, in the Orlando Innamorato, is
described as his work; and in the poem of Ariosto we are
told of a hall adorned with prophetic paintings, which
demons had executed in a single night under the direction
of Merlin.

The following legend is from Spenser's Faery Queene
(Book III, Canto iii):

CAER-MERDIN, OR CAERMARTHEN (IN WALES), MERLIN'S TOWER, AND THE IMPRISONED FIENDS

Forthwith themselves disguising both, in straunge
And base attire, that none might them bewray,
To Maridunum, that is now by chaunge
Of name Caer-Merdin called, they took their way:
There the wise Merlin whylome wont (they say)
To make his wonne, low underneath the ground
In a deep delve, far from the view of day,
That of no living wight he mote be found,
Whenso he counselled with his sprights encompassed round.

And if thou ever happen that same way
To travel, go to see that dreadful place;
It is a hideous hollow cave (they say)
Under a rock that lies a little space
From the swift Barry, tombling down apace
Amongst the woody hills of Dynevor;
But dare not thou, I charge, in any case,
To enter into that same baleful bower,
For fear the cruel fiends should thee unwares devour.

But standing high aloft, low lay thine ear,
And there such ghastly noise of iron chains
And brazen cauldrons thou shalt rumbling hear,
Which thousand sprites with long enduring pains
Do toss, that it will stun thy feeble brains;
And oftentimes great groans, and grievous stounds,
When too huge toil and labor them constrains;
And oftentimes loud strokes and ringing sounds
From under that deep rock most horribly rebounds.

The cause some say is this. A little while
Before that Merlin died, he did intend
A brazen wall in compas to compile
About Caermerdin, and did it commend

Unto these sprites to bring to perfect end;
During which work the Lady of the Lake,
Whom long he loved, for him in haste did send;
Who, thereby forced his workmen to forsake,
Them bound till his return their labor not to slack.

In the mean time, through that false lady's train,
He was surprised, and buried under beare,*
Ne ever to his work returned again;
Nathless those fiends may not their work forbear,
So greatly his commandëment they fear;
But there do toil and travail day and night,
Until that brazen wall they up do rear.
For Merlin had in magic more insight
Than ever him before or after living wight.

CHAPTER IV

ARTHUR

We shall begin our history of King Arthur by giving
those particulars of his life which appear to rest on historical evidence, and then proceed to record those legends
concerning him which form the earliest portion of British
literature.

Arthur was a prince of the tribe of Britons called
Silures, whose country was South Wales—the son of
Uther, named Pendragon, a title given to an elective
sovereign, paramount over the many kings of Britain.
He appears to have commenced his martial career about
the year 500, and was raised to the Pendragonship about
ten years later. He is said to have gained twelve victories
over the Saxons. The most important of them was that of
Badon, by some supposed to be Bath, by others Berk-
shire. This was the last of his battles with the Saxons,
and checked their progress so effectually that Arthur
experienced no more annoyance from them, and reigned
in peace, until the revolt of his nephew Modred, twenty
years later, which led to the fatal battle of Camlan, in

* *Buried under beare.* Buried under something which enclosed him
like a coffin or bier.

Cornwall, in 542. Modred was slain, and Arthur, mortally wounded, was conveyed by sea to Glastonbury, where he died, and was buried. Tradition preserved the memory of the place of his interment within the abbey, as we are told by Giraldus Cambrensis, who was present when the grave was opened, by command of Henry II about 1150, and saw the bones and sword of the monarch, and a leaden cross let into his tombstone, with the inscription in rude Roman letters, "Here lies buried the famous King Arthur, in the island Avalonia." This story has been elegantly versified by Warton. A popular traditional belief was long entertained among the Britons that Arthur was not dead, but had been carried off to be healed of his wounds in Fairy-land, and that he would re-appear to avenge his countrymen and reinstate them in the sovereignty of Britain. In Warton's Ode, a bard relates to King Henry the traditional story of Arthur's death, and closes with these lines:

> Yet in vain a paynim foe
> Armed with fate the mighty blow;
> For when he fell, the Elfin queen,
> All in secret and unseen,
> O'er the fainting hero threw
> Her mantle of ambrosial blue,
> And bade her spirits bear him far,
> In Merlin's agate-axled car,
> To her green isle's enamelled steep,
> Far in the navel of the deep.
> O'er his wounds she sprinkled dew
> From flowers that in Arabia grew.
>
> There he reigns a mighty king,
> Thence to Britain shall return,
> If right prophetic rolls I learn,
> Borne on victory's spreading plume,
> His ancient sceptre to resume,
> His knightly table to restore,
> And brave the tournaments of yore.

After this narration another bard came forward who recited a different story:

> When Arthur bowed his haughty crest,

No princess veiled in azure vest
Snatched him, by Merlin's powerful spell,
In groves of golden bliss to dwell;
But when he fell, with winged speed,
His champions, on a milk-white steed,
From the battle's hurricane,
Bore him to Joseph's towered fane,*
In the fair vale of Avalon;
There, with chanted orison
And the long blaze of tapers clear,
The stoled fathers met the bier;
Through the dim aisles, in order dread
Of martial woe, the chief they led,
And deep entombed in holy ground,
Before the altar's solemn bound.

It must not be concealed that the very existence of
Arthur has been denied by some. Milton says of him:
"As to Arthur, more renowned in songs and romances
than in true stories, who he was, and whether ever any
such reigned in Britain, hath been doubted heretofore,
and may again, with good reason." Modern critics, however, admit that there was a prince of this name, and
find proof of it in the frequent mention of him in the
writings of the Welsh bards. But the Arthur of romance,
according to Mr. Owen, a Welsh scholar and antiquarian,
is a mythological person. "Arthur," he says, "is the Great
Bear, as the name literally implies (Arctos, Arcturus),
and perhaps this constellation, being so near the pole,
and visibly describing a circle in a small space, is the
origin of the famous Round Table."

---

* Glastonbury Abbey, said to be founded by Joseph of Arimathea,
in a spot anciently called the island or valley of Avalonia.
Tennyson, in his Palace of Art, alludes to the legend of Arthur's
rescue by the Fairy queen, thus:

"Or mythic Uther's deeply wounded son,
    In some fair space of sloping greens,
Lay dozing in the vale of Avalon,
    And watched by weeping queens."

KING ARTHUR

Constans, King of Britain, had three sons, Moines, Ambrosius, otherwise called Uther, and Pendragon. Moines, soon after his accession to the crown, was vanquished by the Saxons, in consequence of the treachery of his seneschal, Vortigern, and growing unpopular, through misfortune, he was killed by his subjects, and the traitor Vortigern chosen in his place.

Vortigern was soon after defeated in a great battle by Uther and Pendragon, the surviving brothers of Moines, and Pendragon ascended the throne.

This prince had great confidence in the wisdom of Merlin and made him his chief adviser. About this time, a dreadful war arose between the Saxons and Britons. Merlin obliged the royal brothers to swear fidelity to each other, but predicted that one of them must fall in the first battle. The Saxons were routed, and Pendragon, being slain, was succeeded by Uther, who now assumed in addition to his own name the appellation of Pendragon.

Merlin still continued a favorite counsellor. At the request of Uther, he transported by magic art enormous stones from Ireland, to form the sepulchre of Pendragon. These stones constitute the monument now called Stonehenge, on Salisbury Plain.

Merlin next proceeded to Carlisle to prepare the Round Table, at which he seated an assemblage of the great nobles of the country. The companions admitted to this high order were bound by oath to assist each other at the hazard of their own lives, to attempt singly the most perilous adventures, to lead, when necessary, a life of monastic solitude, to fly to arms at the first summons, and never to retire from battle till they had defeated the enemy, unless night intervened and separated the combatants.

Soon after this institution, the king invited all his barons to the celebration of a great festival, which he proposed holding annually at Carlisle.

As the knights had obtained the sovereign's permission to bring their ladies along with them, the beautiful Igerne accompanied her husband, Gorlois, Duke of Tintadiel, to one of these anniversaries. The king became deeply enamored of the duchess, and disclosed his passion; but Igerne repelled his advances and revealed his solicitations to her husband. On hearing this, the duke instantly removed from court with Igerne, and without taking leave of Uther. The king complained to his council of this want of duty, and they decided that the duke should be summoned to court, and, if refractory, should be treated as a rebel. As he refused to obey the citation, the king carried war into the estates of his vassal and beseiged him in the strong castle of Tintadiel. Merlin transformed the king into the likeness of Gorlois and enabled him to have many stolen interviews with Igerne. At length the duke was killed in battle, and the king espoused Igerne.

From this union sprang Arthur, who succeeded his father, Uther, upon the throne.

ARTHUR CHOSEN KING

Arthur, though only fifteen years old at his father's death, was elected king at a general meeting of the nobles. It was not done without opposition, for there were many ambitious competitors; but Bishop Brice, a person of great sanctity, on Christmas eve addressed the assembly and represented that it would well become them, at that solemn season, to put up their prayers for some token which should manifest the intentions of Providence respecting their future sovereign. This was done, and with such success, that the service was scarcely ended when a miraculous stone was discovered, before the church door, and in the stone was firmly fixed a sword, with the following words engraven on its hilt:

> I am hight Escalibore,
> Unto a king fair tresore.

Bishop Brice, after exhorting the assembly to offer up their thanksgivings for this signal miracle, proposed a

law that, whoever should be able to draw out the sword
from the stone, should be acknowledged as sovereign of
the Britons; and his proposal was decreed by general acclamation. The tributary kings of Uther and the most
famous knights successively put their strength to the
proof, but the miraculous sword resisted all their efforts.
It stood till Candlemas; it stood till Easter, and till Pentecost, when the best knights in the kingdom usually assembled for the annual tournament. Arthur, who was at
that time serving in the capacity of squire to his foster-
brother, Sir Kay, attended his master to the lists. Sir
Kay fought with great valor and success, but had the
misfortune to break his sword, and sent Arthur to his
mother for a new one. Arthur hastened home, but did
not find the lady; but having observed near the church a
sword, sticking in a stone, he galloped to the place, drew
out the sword with great ease, and delivered it to his
master. Sir Kay would willingly have assumed to himself
the distinction conferred by the possession of the sword;
but when, to confirm the doubters, the sword was replaced in the stone, he was utterly unable to withdraw
it, and it would yield a second time to no hand but
Arthur's. Thus decisively pointed out by Heaven as their
king, Arthur was by general consent proclaimed as such,
and an early day appointed for his solemn coronation.

Immediately after his election to the crown, Arthur
found himself opposed by eleven kings and one duke who,
with a vast army, were actually encamped in the forest of
Rockingham. By Merlin's advice Arthur sent an embassy
to Brittany, to solicit the aid of King Ban and King Bohort, two of the best knights in the world. They accepted
the call and, with a powerful army, crossed the sea,
landing at Portsmouth, where they were received with
great rejoicing. The rebel kings were still superior in
numbers; but Merlin, by a powerful enchantment, caused
all their tents to fall down at once, and in the confusion
Arthur with his allies fell upon them and totally routed
them.

After defeating the rebels, Arthur took the field against
the Saxons. As they were too strong for him unaided,
he sent an embassy to Armorica, beseeching the assistance of Hoel, who soon after brought over an army

to his aid. The two kings joined their forces and sought the enemy, whom they met, and both sides prepared for a decisive engagement. "Arthur himself," as Goeffrey of Monmouth relates, "dressed in a breastplate worthy of so great a king, places on his head a golden helmet engraved with the semblance of a dragon. Over his shoulders he throws his shield called Priwen, on which a picture of the Holy Virgin constantly recalled her to his memory. Girt with Caliburn, a most excellent sword, and fabricated in the isle of Avalon, he graces his right hand with the lance named Ron. This was a long and broad spear, well contrived for slaughter." After a severe conflict, Arthur, calling on the name of the Virgin, rushes into the midst of his enemies, and destroys multitudes of them with the formidable Caliburn, and puts the rest to flight. Hoel, being detained by sickness, took no part in this battle.

This is called the victory of Mount Badon, and, however disguised by fable, it is regarded by historians as a real event.

The feats performed by Arthur at the battle of Badon Mount are thus celebrated in Drayton's verse:

They sung how he himself at Badon bore, that day,
When at the glorious goal his British scepter lay;
Two daies together how the battel stronglie stood;
Pendragon's worthie son, who waded there in blood,
Three hundred Saxons slew with his owne valiant hand.
Song IV

GUENEVER

Merlin had planned for Arthur a marriage with the daughter of King Laodegan of Carmalide. By his advice Arthur paid a visit to the court of that sovereign, attended only by Merlin and by thirty-nine knights whom the magician had selected for that service. On their arrival, they found Laodegan and his peers sitting in council, endeavoring, but with small prospect of success, to devise means of resisting the impending attack of Ryence, King of Ireland, who, with fifteen tributary kings and an almost innumerable army, had nearly surrounded the city. Merlin, who acted as leader of the band of British knights, announced them as strangers, who came to offer the king their services in his wars, but under the express condition that they should be at liberty to conceal their names and quality until they should think proper to divulge them. These terms were thought very strange, but were thankfully accepted, and the strangers, after taking the usual oath to the king, retired to the lodging which Merlin had prepared for them.

A few days after this, the enemy, regardless of a truce into which they had entered with King Laodegan, suddenly issued from their camp and made an attempt to surprise the city. Cleodalis, the king's general, assembled the royal forces with all possible despatch. Arthur and his companions also flew to arms, and Merlin appeared at their head, bearing a standard on which was emblazoned a terrific dragon. Merlin advanced to the gate and commanded the porter to open it, which the porter refused to do without the king's order. Merlin thereupon took up the gate, with all its appurtenances of locks, bars, bolts, &c., and directed his troop to pass through, after which he replaced it in perfect order. He then set spurs to his horse and dashed, at the head of his little troop, into a body of two thousand pagans. The disparity of numbers being so enormous, Merlin cast a spell upon the enemy, so as to prevent their seeing the small number of their assailants; notwithstanding which the British knights were hard pressed. But the people of the city, who saw from the walls this unequal contest, were ashamed of leaving the small body of strangers to their fate, so they opened the gate and sallied forth. The numbers were now more nearly equal, and Merlin revoked his spell, so that the two armies encountered on fair terms. Where Arthur, Ban, Bohort, and the rest fought, the king's army had the advantage; but in another part of the field, the king himself was surrounded and carried off by the enemy. This sad sight was seen by Guenever, the fair daughter of the king, who stood on the city wall and looked at the battle. She was in dreadful distress, tore her hair, and swooned away.

But Merlin, aware of what passed in every part of

the field, suddenly collected his knights, led them out of the battle, intercepted the passage of the party who were carrying away the king, charged them with irresistible impetuosity, cut in pieces or dispersed the whole escort, and rescued the king. In the fight Arthur encountered Caulang, a giant fifteen feet high, and the fair Guenever, who already began to feel a strong interest in the handsome young stranger, trembled for the issue of the contest. But Arthur, dealing a dreadful blow on the shoulder of the monster, cut through his neck so that his head hung over on one side, and in this condition his horse carried him about the field, to the great horror and dismay of the pagans. Guenever could not refrain from expressing aloud her wish that the gentle knight, who dealt with giants so dexterously, were destined to become her husband, and the wish was echoed by her attendants. The enemy soon turned their backs and fled with precipitation, closely pursued by Laodegan and his allies.

After the battle Arthur was disarmed and conducted to the bath by the Princess Guenever, while his friends were attended by the other ladies of the court. After the bath, the knights were conducted to a magnificent entertainment, at which they were diligently served by the same fair attendants. Laodegan, more and more anxious to know the name and quality of his generous deliverers, and occasionally forming a secret wish that the chief of his guests might be captivated by the charms of his daughter, appeared silent and pensive, and was scarcely roused from his reverie by the banters of his courtiers. Arthur, having had an opportunity of explaining to Guenever his great esteem for her merit, was in the joy of his heart, and was still further delighted by hearing from Merlin the late exploits of Gawain at London, by means of which his immediate return to his dominions was rendered unnecessary, and he was left at liberty to protract his stay at the court of Laodegan. Every day contributed to increase the admiration of the whole court for the gallant strangers and the passion of Guenever for their chief; and when at last Merlin announced to the king that the object of the visit of the party was to procure a bride for their leader, Laodegan at once presented

Guenever to Arthur, telling him that, whatever might be his rank, his merit was sufficient to entitle him to the possession of the heiress of Carmalide. Arthur accepted the lady with the utmost gratitude, and Merlin then proceeded to satisfy the king of the rank of his son-in-law; upon which Laodegan, with all his barons, hastened to do homage to their lawful sovereign, the successor of Uther Pendragon. The fair Guenever was then solemnly betrothed to Arthur, and a magnificent festival was proclaimed, which lasted seven days. At the end of that time, the enemy appearing again with renewed force, it became necessary to resume military operations.*

We must now relate what took place at and near London while Arthur was absent from his capital. At this very time, a band of young heroes were on their way to Arthur's court for the purpose of receiving knighthood from him. They were Gawain and his three brothers, nephews of Arthur, sons of King Lot, and Galachin, another nephew, son of King Nanters. King Lot had been one of the rebel chiefs whom Arthur had defeated, but he now hoped by means of the young men to be reconciled to his brother-in-law. He equipped his sons and his nephew with the utmost magnificence, giving them a splendid retinue of young men, sons of earls and barons, all mounted on the best horses, with complete suits of choice armor. They numbered in all seven hundred, but only nine had yet received the order of knighthood; the rest were candidates for that honor, and anxious to earn it by an early encounter with the enemy. Gawain, the leader, was a knight of wonderful strength; but what was most remarkable about him was that his strength was greater at certain hours of the day than at others. From nine o'clock till noon his strength was doubled, and so it was from three to even-song; for the rest of the time it was less remarkable, through at all times surpassing that of ordinary men.

After a march of three days, they arrived in the vicinity

---

* Guenever, the name of Arthur's queen, also written Genievre and Geneura, is familiar to all who are conversant with chivalric lore. It is to her adventures, and those of her true knight, Sir Launcelot, that Dante alludes in the beautiful episode of Francesca da Rimini.

of London, where they expected to find Arthur and his court; and very unexpectedly fell in with a large convoy belonging to the enemy, consisting of numerous carts and wagons, all loaded with provisions, and escorted by three thousand men, who had been collecting spoil from all the country round. A single charge from Gawain's impetuous cavalry was sufficient to disperse the escort and recover the convoy, which was instantly despatched to London. But before long a body of seven thousand fresh soldiers advanced to the attack of the five princes and their little army. Gawain, singling out a chief named Choas, of gigantic size, began the battle by splitting him from the crown of the head to the breast. Galachin encountered King Sanagran, who was also very huge, and cut off his head. Agrivain and Gahariet also performed prodigies of valor. Thus they kept the great army of assailants at bay, though hard pressed, till of a sudden they perceived a strong body of the citizens advancing from London, where the convoy which had been recovered by Gawain had arrived, and informed the mayor and citizens of the danger of their deliverer. The arrival of the Londoners soon decided the contest. The enemy fled in all directions, and Gawain and his friends, escorted by the grateful citizens, entered London, and were received with acclamations.

CHAPTER V

ARTHUR

After the great victory of Mount Badon, by which the Saxons were for the time effectually put down, Arthur turned his arms against the Scots and Picts, whom he routed at Lake Lomond and compelled to sue for mercy. He then went to York to keep his Christmas, and employed himself in restoring the Christian churches which the pagans had rifled and overthrown. The following summer he conquered Ireland, and then made a voyage with his fleet to Iceland, which he also subdued. The kings of Gothland and of the Orkneys came voluntarily and made their submission, promising to pay tribute. Then he returned to Britain, where, having established the kingdom, he dwelt twelve years in peace.

During this time, he invited over to him all persons whatsoever that were famous for valor in foreign nations, and augmented the number of his domestics, and introduced such politeness into his court as people of the remotest countries thought worthy of their imitation. So that there was not a nobleman who thought himself of any consideration unless his clothes and arms were made in the same fashion as those of Arthur's knights.

Finding himself so powerful at home, Arthur began to form designs for extending his power abroad. So, having prepared his fleet, he first attempted Norway, that he might procure the crown of it for Lot, his sister's husband. Arthur landed in Norway, fought a great battle with the king of that country, defeated him, and pursued the victory till he had reduced the whole country under his dominion, and established Lot upon the throne. Then Arthur made a voyage to Gaul and laid siege to the city of Paris. Gaul was at that time a Roman province, and governed by Flollo, the tribune. When the siege of Paris had continued a month, and the people began to suffer from famine, Flollo challenged Arthur to single combat, proposing to decide the conquest of the province in that way. Arthur gladly accepted the challenge and slew his adversary in the contest, upon which the citizens surrendered the city to him. After the victory Arthur divided his army into two parts, one of which he committed to the conduct of Hoel, whom he ordered to march into Aquitaine, while he, with the other part, should endeavor to subdue the other provinces. At the end of nine years, in which time all the parts of Gaul were entirely reduced, Arthur returned to Paris, where he kept his court, and, calling an assembly of the clergy and people, established peace and the just administration of the laws in that kingdom. Then he bestowed Normandy upon Bedver, his butler, and the province of

Andegavia upon Kay, his steward,* and several other provinces upon his great men that attended him. And, having settled the peace of the cities and countries, he returned back in the beginning of spring to Britain.

Upon the approach of the feast of Pentecost, Arthur, the better to demonstrate his joy after such triumphant successes, and for the more solemn observation of that festival, and reconciling the minds of the princes that were now subject to him, resolved during that season to hold a magnificent court, to place the crown upon his head, and to invite all the kings and dukes under his subjection to the solemnity. And he pitched upon Caerleon, the City of Legions, as the proper place for his purpose. For, besides its great wealth above the other cities,† its situation upon the River Usk, near the Severn Sea, was most pleasant and fit for so great a solemnity. For on one side it was washed by that noble river, so that the kings and princes from the countries beyond the seas might have the convenience of sailing up to it.

* This name, in the French romances, is spelled Queux, which means *head cook*. This would seem to imply that it was a title and not a name; yet the personage who bore it is never mentioned by any other. He is the chief, if not the only, comic character among the heroes of Arthur's court. He is the seneschal, or steward, his duties also embracing those of chief of the cooks. In the romances, his general character is a compound of valor and buffoonery, always ready to fight and generally getting the worst of the battle. He is also sarcastic and abusive in his remarks, by which he often gets into trouble. Yet Arthur seems to have an attachment to him, and often takes his advice, which is generally wrong.

† Several cities are allotted to King Arthur by the romance-writers. The principal are Caerleon, Camelot, and Carlisle.

Caerleon derives its name from its having been the station of one of the legions, during the dominion of the Romans. It is called by Latin writers Urbs Legionum, the City of Legions. The former word being rendered into Welsh by *Caer*, meaning city, and the latter contracted into *lleon*. The river Usk retains its name in modern geography, and there is a town or city of Caerleon upon it, though the city of Cardiff is thought to be the scene of Arthur's court. Chester also bears in Welsh the name of Caerleon; for Chester, derived from *castra*, Latin for *camp*, is the designation of military headquarters.

Camelot is thought to be Winchester.

Shalott is Guildford.

Hamo's Port is Southampton.

Carlisle is the city still retaining that name, near the Scottish border. But this name is also sometimes applied to other places, which were, like itself, military stations.

On the other side, the beauty of the meadows and groves and magnificence of the royal palaces, with lofty gilded roofs that adorned it, made it even rival the grandeur of Rome. It was also famous for two churches, whereof one was adorned with a choir of virgins who devoted themselves wholly to the service of God, and the other maintained a convent of priests. Besides, there was a college of two hundred philosophers, who, being learned in astronomy and the other arts, were diligent in observing the courses of the stars, and gave Arthur true predictions of the events that would happen. In this place, therefore, which afforded such delights, were preparations made for the ensuing festival.

Ambassadors were then sent into several kingdoms, to invite to court the princes both of Gaul and of the adjacent islands. Accordingly there came Augusel, King of Albania, now Scotland; Cadwallo, King of Venedotia, now North Wales; Sater, King of Demetia, now South Wales; also the archbishops of the metropolitan sees, London and York, and Dubricius, Bishop of Caerleon, the City of Legions. This prelate, who was primate of Britain, was so eminent for his piety that he could cure any sick person by his prayers. There were also the counts of the principal cities and many other worthies of no less dignity.

From the adjacent islands came Guillamurius, King of Ireland; Gunfasius, King of the Orkneys; Malvasius, King of Iceland; Lot, King of Norway; Bedver the butler, Duke of Normandy; Kay the sewer, Duke of Andegavia; also the twelve peers of Gaul; and Hoel, Duke of the Armorican Britons, with his nobility, who came with such a train of mules, horses, and rich furniture as it is difficult to describe. Besides these, there remained no prince of any consideration on this side of Spain who came not upon this invitation. And no wonder, when Arthur's munificence, which was celebrated over the whole world, made him beloved by all people.

When all were assembled, upon the day of the solemnity, the archbishops were conducted to the palace, in order to place the crown upon the king's head. Then Dubricius, inasmuch as the court was held in his diocese, made himself ready to celebrate the office. As soon as the king was invested with his royal habiliments, he was conducted in great pomp to the metropolitan church, having four kings, viz. of Albania, Cornwall, Demetia, and Venedotia, bearing four golden swords before him. On another part was the queen, dressed out in her richest ornaments, conducted by the archbishops and bishops to the Church of Virgins; the four queens, also, of the kings last mentioned, bearing before her four white doves, according to ancient custom. When the whole procession was ended, so transporting was the harmony of the musical instruments and voices, whereof there was a vast variety in both churches, that the knights who attended were in doubt which to prefer, and therefore crowded from the one to the other by turns, and were far from being tired of the solemnity, though the whole day had been spent in it. At last, when divine service was over at both churches, the king and queen put off their crowns and, putting on their lighter ornaments, went to the banquet. When they had all taken their seats according to precedence, Kay the sewer, in rich robes of ermine, with a thousand young noblemen all in like manner clothed in rich attire, served up the dishes. From another part, Bedver the butler was followed by the same number of attendants, who waited with all kinds of cups and drinking-vessels. And there was food and drink in abundance, and everything was of the best kind and served in the best manner. For, at that time, Britain had arrived at such a pitch of grandeur that, in riches, luxury, and politeness, it far surpassed all other kingdoms.

As soon as the banquets were over, they went into the fields without the city, to divert themselves with various sports, such as shooting with bows and arrows, tossing the pike, casting of heavy stones and rocks, playing at dice, and the like, and all these inoffensively and without quarrelling. In this manner were three days spent, and after that they separated, and the kings and noblemen departed to their several homes.

After this, Arthur reigned five years in peace. Then came ambassadors from Lucius Tiberius, Procurator under Leo, Emperor of Rome, demanding tribute. But Arthur refused to pay tribute and prepared for war. As soon as the necessary dispositions were made, he com-

mitted the government of his kingdom to his nephew
Modred and to Queen Guenever, and marched with his
army to Hamo's Port, where the wind stood fair for him.
The army crossed over in safety and landed at the mouth
of the River Barba. And there they pitched their tents
to wait the arrival of the kings of the islands.

As soon as all the forces were arrived, Arthur marched
forward to Augustodunum and encamped on the banks
of the river Alba. Here, repeated battles were fought, in
all which the Britons, under their valiant leaders, Hoel,
Duke of Armorica, and Gawain, nephew to Arthur, had
the advantage. At length, Lucius Tiberius determined to
retreat and wait for the Emperor Leo to join him with
fresh troops. But Arthur, anticipating this event, took
possession of a certain valley and closed up the way of
retreat to Lucius, compelling him to fight a decisive battle, in which Arthur lost some of the bravest of his
knights and most faithful followers. But on the other
hand Lucius Tiberius was slain and his army totally defeated. The fugitives dispersed over the country, some
to the by-ways and woods, some to the cities and towns,
and all other places where they could hope for safety.

Arthur stayed in those parts till the next winter was
over and employed his time in restoring order and set-
tling the government. He then returned into England and
celebrated his victories with great splendor.

Then the king stablished all his knights, and to them
that were not rich he gave lands, and charged them all
never to do outrage nor murder and always to flee
treason; also, by no means to be cruel, but to give
mercy unto him that asked mercy, upon pain of forfeiture
of their worship and lordship; and always to do ladies,
damosels, and gentlewomen service, upon pain of death.
Also, that no man take battle in a wrongful quarrel, for
no law, nor for any world's goods. Unto this were all the
knights sworn of the Table Round, both old and young.
And at every year were they sworn at the high feast of
Pentecost.

KING ARTHUR SLAYS THE GIANT OF ST. MICHAEL'S MOUNT

While the army was encamped in Brittany awaiting the arrival of the kings, there came a countryman to Arthur and told him that a giant, whose cave was on a neighboring mountain, called St. Michael's Mount, had for a long time been accustomed to carry off the children of the peasants, to devour them. "And now he hath taken the Duchess of Brittany, as she rode with her attendants, and hath carried her away in spite of all they could do." "Now, fellow," said King Arthur, "canst thou bring me there where this giant haunteth?" "Yea, sure," said the good man; "lo, yonder where thou seest two great fires, there shalt thou find him, and more treasure than I suppose is in all France beside." Then the king called to him Sir Bedver and Sir Kay and commanded them to make ready horse and harness for himself and them, for after evening he would ride on pilgrimage to St. Michael's Mount.

So they three departed and rode forth till they came to the foot of the mount. And there the king commanded them to tarry, for he would himself go up into that mount. So he ascended the hill till he came to a great fire, and there he found an aged woman sitting by a new-made grave, making great sorrow. Then King Arthur saluted her and demanded of her wherefore she made such lamentation; to whom she answered: "Sir Knight, speak low, for yonder is a devil, and if he hear thee speak, he will come and destroy thee. For ye cannot make resistance to him, he is so fierce and so strong. He hath murdered the duchess, which here lieth, who was the fairest of all the world, wife to Sir Hoel, Duke of Brittany." "Dame," said the king, "I come from the noble conqueror, King Arthur, to treat with that tyrant." "Fie on such treaties," said she; "he setteth not by the king, nor by no man else." "Well," said Arthur, "I will accomplish my message for all your fearful words." So he went forth by the crest of the hill and saw where the giant sat at supper, gnawing on the limb of a man, and baking his

broad limbs at the fire, and three fair damsels lying
bound, whose lot it was to be devoured in their turn.
When King Arthur beheld that, he had great compassion on them, so that his heart bled for sorrow. Then he
hailed the giant, saying, "He that all the world ruleth give
thee short life and shameful death. Why hast thou murdered this duchess? Therefore come forth, thou caitiff,
for this day thou shalt die by my hand." Then the giant
started up, and took a great club, and smote at the king,
and smote off his coronal; and then the king struck him
in the belly with his sword and made a fearful wound.
Then the giant threw away his club and caught the king
in his arms, so that he crushed his ribs. Then the three
maidens kneeled down and prayed for help and comfort
for Arthur. And Arthur weltered and wrenched, so that
he was one while under, and another time above. And
so weltering and wallowing they rolled down the hill, and
ever as they weltered Arthur smote him with his dagger;
and it fortuned they came to the place where the two
knights were. And when they saw the king fast in the
giant's arms, they came and loosed him. Then the king
commanded Sir Kay to smite off the giant's head, and to
set it on the truncheon of a spear, and fix it on the
barbican, that all the people might see and behold it.
This was done, and anon it was known through all the
country, wherefor the people came and thanked the
king. And he said, "Give your thanks to God; and take
ye the giant's spoil and divide it among you." And King
Arthur caused a church to be builded on that hill, in
honor of St. Michael.

KING ARTHUR GETS A SWORD FROM THE LADY OF THE LAKE

One day, King Arthur rode forth, and on a sudden he
was ware of three churls chasing Merlin, to have slain
him. And the king rode unto them and bade them, "Flee,
churls!" Then were they afraid when they saw a knight,
and fled. "Oh, Merlin," said Arthur, "here hadst thou
been slain, for all thy crafts, had I not been by."
"Nay," said Merlin, "not so, for I could save myself if I

would; but thou art more near thy death than I am." So, as they went thus talking, King Arthur perceived where sat a knight on horseback, as if to guard the pass. "Sir Knight," said Arthur, "for what cause abidest thou here?" Then the knight said, "There may no knight ride this way unless he just with me, for such is the custom of the pass." "I will amend that custom," said the king. Then they ran together, and they met so hard that their spears were shivered. Then they drew their swords and fought a strong battle, with many great strokes. But at length the sword of the knight smote King Arthur's sword in two pieces. Then said the knight unto Arthur, "Thou art in my power, whether to save thee or slay thee, and unless thou yield thee as overcome and recreant, thou shalt die." "As for death," said King Arthur, "welcome be it when it cometh; but to yield me unto thee as recreant, I will not." Then he leapt upon the knight, and took him by the middle and threw him down; but the knight was a passing strong man, and anon he brought Arthur under him, and would have razed off his helm to slay him. Then said Merlin, "Knight, hold thy hand, for this knight is a man of more worship than thou art aware of." "Why, who is he?" said the knight. "It is King Arthur." Then would he have slain him for dread of his wrath, and lifted up his sword to slay him; and therewith Merlin cast an enchantment on the knight, so that he fell to the earth in a great sleep. Then Merlin took up King Arthur and set him on his horse. "Alas!" said Arthur, "what hast thou done, Merlin? Hast thou slain this good knight by thy crafts?" "Care ye not," said Merlin; "he is wholer than ye be. He is only asleep, and will wake in three hours."

Then the king and he departed and went till they came to a hermit, that was a good man and a great leech. So the hermit searched all his wounds and applied good salves; and the king was there three days, and then were his wounds well amended, that he might ride and go. So they departed, and as they rode Arthur said, "I have no sword." "No matter," said Merlin; "hereby is a sword that shall be yours." So they rode till they came to a lake, which was a fair water and broad. And in the midst of the lake Arthur was aware of an arm clothed in white samite,* that held a fair sword in the hand. "Lo!" said Merlin, "yonder is that sword that I spake of. It belongeth to the Lady of the Lake, and, if she will, thou mayest take it; but if she will not, it will not be in thy power to take it."

So Sir Arthur and Merlin alighted from their horses and went into a boat. And when they came to the sword that the hand held, Sir Arthur took it by the handle and took it to him, and the arm and the hand went under the water.

Then they returned unto the land and rode forth. And Sir Arthur looked on the sword and liked it right well.

So they rode unto Caerleon, whereof his knights were passing glad. And when they heard of his adventures, they marvelled that he would jeopard his person so alone. But all men of worship said it was a fine thing to be under such a chieftain as would put his person in adventure as other poor knights did.

CHAPTER VI

SIR GAWAIN

Sir Gawain was nephew to King Arthur, by his sister Morgana, married to Lot, King of Orkney, who was by Arthur made King of Norway. Sir Gawain was one of the most famous knights of the Round Table, and is characterized by the romancers as the *sage* and *courteous* Gawain. To this Chaucer alludes in his "Squiere's Tale," where the strange knight "salueth" all the court

> With so high reverence and observance,
> As well in speeche as in contenance,
> That Gawain, with his olde curtesie,
> Though he were come agen out of faërie,
> Ne coude him not amenden with a word.

* *Samite,* a sort of silk stuff.

Gawain's brothers were Agravain, Gaharet, and Gareth.

SIR GAWAIN'S MARRIAGE

Once upon a time, King Arthur held his court in merry Carlisle, when a damsel came before him and craved a boon. It was for vengeance upon a caitiff knight, who had made her lover captive and despoiled her of her lands. King Arthur commanded to bring him his sword, Excalibar, and to saddle his steed, and rode forth without delay to right the lady's wrong. Ere long he reached the castle of the grim baron and challenged him to the conflict. But the castle stood on magic ground, and the spell was such that no knight could tread thereon but straight his courage fell and his strength decayed. King Arthur felt the charm, and before a blow was struck, his sturdy limbs lost their strength, and his head grew faint. He was fain to yield himself prisoner to the churlish knight, who refused to release him except upon condition that he should return at the end of a year, and bring a true answer to the question, "What thing is it which women most desire?" or in default thereof surrender himself and his lands. King Arthur accepted the terms and gave his oath to return at the time appointed. During the year, the king rode east, and he rode west and inquired of all whom he met what thing it is which all women most desire. Some told him riches; some, pomp and state; some, mirth; some, flattery; and some, a gallant knight. But in the diversity of answers, he could find no sure dependence. The year was well nigh spent when, one day as he rode thoughtfully through a forest, he saw sitting beneath a tree a lady of such hideous aspect that he turned away his eyes, and when she greeted him in seemly sort, made no answer. "What wight art thou," the lady said, "that will not speak to me? It may chance that I may resolve thy doubts, though I be not fair of aspect." "If thou wilt do so," said King Arthur, "choose what reward thou wilt, thou grim lady, and it shall be given thee." "Swear me this upon thy faith," she said, and Arthur swore it. Then the lady told him the secret, and demanded her reward, which was that the king should find some fair and courtly knight to be her husband.

King Arthur hastened to the grim baron's castle and told him one by one all the answers which he had received from his various advisers, except the last, and not one was admitted as the true one. "Now yield thee, Arthur," the giant said, "for thou hast not paid thy ransom, and thou and thy lands are forfeited to me." Then King Arthur said:

> Yet hold thy hand, thou proud baron,
>   I pray thee hold thy hand,
> And give me leave to speak once more,
>   In rescue of my land.
> This morn, as I came over a moor,
>   I saw a lady set,
> Between an oak and a green holly,
>   All clad in red scarlett.
> She says *all women would have their will*,
>   This is their chief desire;
> Now yield, as thou art a baron true,
>   That I have paid my hire.

"It was my sister that told thee this," the churlish baron exclaimed. "Vengeance light on her! I will some time or other do her as ill a turn."

King Arthur rode homeward, but not light of heart, for he remembered the promise he was under to the loathly lady to give her one of his young and gallant knights for a husband. He told his grief to Sir Gawain, his nephew, and he replied, "Be not sad, my lord, for I will marry the loathly lady." King Arthur replied:

> Now nay, now nay, good Sir Gawaine,
>   My sister's son ye be;
> The loathly lady's all too grim,
>   And all too foule for thee.

But Gawain persisted, and the king at last, with sorrow of heart, consented that Gawain should be his ransom. So, one day, the king and his knights rode to the forest, met the loathly lady, and brought her to the court. Sir Gawain stood the scoffs and jeers of his companions as he best might, and the marriage was solemnized, but not with the usual festivities. Chaucer tells us:

> There was no joye ne feste at alle;
> There n'as but hevinesse and mochel sorwe,
> For prively he wed her on the morwe,
> And all day after hid him as an owle,
> So wo was him his wife loked so foule! *

When night came, and they were alone together, Sir Gawain could not conceal his aversion; and the lady asked him why he sighed so heavily and turned away his face. He candidly confessed it was on account of three things, her age, her ugliness, and her low degree. The lady, not at all offended, replied with excellent arguments to all his objections. She showed him that with age is discretion, with ugliness security from rivals, and that all true gentility depends, not upon the accident of birth, but upon the character of the individual.

Sir Gawain made no reply; but, turning his eyes on his bride, what was his amazement to perceive that she wore no longer the unseemly aspect that had so distressed him. She then told him that the form she had worn was not her true form, but a disguise imposed upon her by a wicked enchanter, and that she was condemned to wear it until two things should happen; one, that she should obtain some young and gallant knight to be her husband. This having been done, one half of the charm was removed. She was now at liberty to wear her true form for half the time, and she bade him choose whether he would have her fair by day, and ugly by night, or the reverse. Sir Gawain would fain have had her look her best by night, when he alone should see her, and show her repulsive visage, if at all, to others. But she reminded him how much more pleasant it would be to her to wear her best looks in the throng of knights and ladies by day. Sir Gawain yielded and gave up his will to hers. This alone was wanting to dissolve the charm. The lovely lady now with joy assured him that she should change no more; but as she now was, so would she remain by night as well as by day.

* N'as is *not was*, contracted; in modern phrase, *there was not*. *Mochel sorwe* is *much sorrow*; *morwe* is *morrow*.

Sweet blushes stayned her rud-red cheek,
  Her eyen were black as sloe,
The ripening cherrye swelled her lippe,
  And all her neck was snow.
Sir Gawain kist that ladye faire
  Lying upon the sheete,
And swore, as he was a true knight,
  The spice was never so swete.

The dissolution of the charm which had held the lady
also released her brother, the "grim baron," for he too
had been implicated in it. He ceased to be a churlish op-
pressor and became a gallant and generous knight as any
at Arthur's court.

CHAPTER VII

CARADOC BRIEFBRAS; OR, CARADOC WITH THE SHRUNKEN ARM

Caradoc was the son of Ysenne, the beautiful niece of
Arthur. He was ignorant who his father was, till it was
discovered in the following manner. When the youth was
of proper years to receive the honors of knighthood,
King Arthur held a grand court for the purpose of knight-
ing him. On this occasion, a strange knight presented
himself and challenged the knights of Arthur's court to
exchange blow for blow with him. His proposal was this
—to lay his neck on a block for any knight to strike, on
condition that, if he survived the blow, the knight should
submit in turn to the same experiment. Sir Kay, who
was usually ready to accept all challenges, pronounced
this wholly unreasonable and declared that he would
not accept it for all the wealth in the world. And when
the knight offered his sword, with which the operation
was to be performed, no person ventured to accept it,
till Caradoc, growing angry at the disgrace which was
thus incurred by the Round Table, threw aside his mantle and took it. "Do you do this as one of the best

knights?" said the stranger. "No," he replied, "but as one of the most foolish." The stranger lays his head upon the block, receives a blow which sends it rolling from his shoulders, walks after it, picks it up, replaces it with great success, and says he will return when the court shall be assembled next year and claim his turn. When the anniversary arrived, both parties were punctual to their engagement. Great entreaties were used by the king and queen, and the whole court, in behalf of Caradoc, but the stranger was inflexible. The young knight laid his head upon the block, and more than once desired him to make an end of the business, and not keep him longer in so disagreeable a state of expectation. At last the stranger strikes him gently with the side of the sword, bids him rise, and reveals to him the fact that he is his father, the enchanter Eliaures, and that he gladly owns him for a son, having proved his courage and fidelity to his word.

But the favor of enchanters is short-lived and uncertain. Eliaures fell under the influence of a wicked woman, who, to satisfy her pique against Caradoc, persuaded the enchanter to fasten on his arm a serpent, which remained there sucking at his flesh and blood, no human skill sufficing either to remove the reptile, or alleviate the torments which Caradoc endured.

Caradoc was betrothed to Guimier, sister to his bosom friend, Cador, and daughter to the king of Cornwall. As soon as they were informed of his deplorable condition, they set out for Nantes, where Caradoc's castle was, that Guimier might attend upon him. When Caradoc heard of their coming, his first emotion was that of joy and love. But soon he began to fear that the sight of his emaciated form and of his sufferings would disgust Guimier; and this apprehension became so strong that he departed secretly from Nantes and hid himself in a hermitage. He was sought far and near by the knights of Arthur's court, and Cador made a vow never to desist from the quest till he should have found him. After long wandering, Cador discovered his friend in the hermitage, reduced almost to a skeleton and apparently near his death. All other means of relief having already been tried in vain, Cador at last prevailed on the enchanter Eliaures to disclose the only method which could avail for his rescue.

A maiden must be found, his equal in birth and beauty, and loving him better than herself, so that she would expose herself to the same torment to deliver him. Two vessels were then to be provided, the one filled with sour wine and the other with milk. Caradoc must enter the first, so that the wine should reach his neck, and the maiden must get into the other, and, exposing her bosom upon the edge of the vessel, invite the serpent to forsake the withered flesh of his victim for this fresh and inviting food. The vessels were to be placed three feet apart, and as the serpent crossed from one to the other, a knight was to cut him in two. If he failed in his blow, Caradoc would indeed be delivered, but it would be only to see his fair champion suffering the same cruel and hopeless torment. The sequel may be easily foreseen. Guimier willingly exposed herself to the perilous adventure, and Cador, with a lucky blow, killed the serpent. The arm, in which Caradoc had suffered so long, recovered its strength but not its shape, in consequence of which he was called Caradoc Briefbras, Caradoc of the Shrunken Arm.

Caradoc and Guimier are the hero and heroine of the ballad of the Boy and the Mantle, which follows:

THE BOY AND THE MANTLE

In Carlisle dwelt King Arthur,
   A prince of passing might,
And there maintained his Table Round,
   Beset with many a knight.

And there he kept his Christmas,
   With mirth and princely cheer,
When lo! a strange and cunning boy
   Before him did appear.

A kirtle and a mantle
   This boy had him upon,
With brooches, rings, and ouches,
   Full daintily bedone.

He had a sash of silk
   About his middle meet;
And thus with seemly curtesie
   He did King Arthur greet:

"God speed thee, brave King Arthur,
  Thus feasting in thy bower,
And Guenever, thy goodly queen,
  That fair and peerless flower.

"Ye gallant lords and lordlings,
  I wish you all take heed,
Lest what ye deem a blooming rose
  Should prove a cankered weed."

Then straightway from his bosom
  A little wand he drew;
And with it eke a mantle,
  Of wondrous shape and hue.

"Now have thou here, King Arthur,
  Have this here of me,
And give unto thy comely queen,
  All shapen as you see.

"No wife it shall become,
  That once hath been to blame."
Then every knight in Arthur's court
  Sly glanced at his dame.

And first came Lady Guenever,
  The mantle she must try.
This dame she was new-fangled,*
  And of a roving eye.

When she had taken the mantle,
  And all with it was clad,
From top to toe it shivered down,
  As though with shears beshred.

One while it was too long,
  Another while too short,
And wrinkled on her shoulders,
  In most unseemly sort.

Now green, now red it seemed,
  Then all of sable hue;
"Beshrew me," quoth King Arthur,
  I think thou be'st not true!"

                * New-fangled—fond of novelty.

Down she threw the mantle,
　No longer would she stay;
But, storming like a fury,
　To her chamber flung away.

She cursed the rascal weaver,
　That had the mantle wrought;
And doubly cursed the froward imp
　Who thither had it brought.

"I had rather live in deserts,
　Beneath the greenwood tree,
Than here, base king, among thy grooms,
　The sport of them and thee."

Sir Kay called forth his lady,
　And bade her to come near:
"Yet dame, if thou be guilty,
　I pray thee now forbear."

This lady, pertly giggling,
　With forward step came on,
And boldly to the little boy
　With fearless face is gone.

When she had taken the mantle,
　With purpose for to wear,
It shrunk up to her shoulder,
　And left her back all bare.

Then every merry knight,
　That was in Arthur's court,
Gibed and laughed and flouted,
　To see that pleasant sport.

Down she threw the mantle,
　No longer bold or gay,
But, with a face all pale and wan,
　To her chamber slunk away.

Then forth came an old knight
　A pattering o'er his creed,
And proffered to the little boy
　Five nobles to his meed:

"And all the time of Christmas
  Plum-porridge shall be thine,
If thou wilt let my lady fair
  Within the mantle shine."

A saint his lady seemed,
  With step demure and slow,
And gravely to the mantle
  With mincing face doth go.

When she the same had taken
  That was so fine and thin,
It shrivelled all about her,
  And showed her dainty skin.

Ah! little did her mincing,
  Or his long prayers bestead;
She had no more hung on her
  Than a tassel and a thread.

Down she threw the mantle,
  With terror and dismay,
And with a face of scarlet
  To her chamber hied away.

Sir Cradock called his lady,
  And bade her to come near:
"Come win this mantle, lady,
  "And do me credit here:

"Come win this mantle, lady,
  For now it shall be thine,
If thou hast never done amiss,
  Since first I made thee mine."

The lady, gently blushing,
  With modest grace came on;
And now to try the wondrous charm
  Courageously is gone.

When she had ta'en the mantle,
  And put it on her back,
About the hem it seemed
  To wrinkle and to crack.

"Lie still," she cried, "O mantle!
    And shame me not for naught;
I'll freely own whate'er amiss
    Or blameful I have wrought

"Once I kissed Sir Cradock
    Beneath the greenwood tree;
Once I kissed Sir Cradock's mouth,
    Before he married me."

When she had thus her shriven,
    And her worst fault had told,
The mantle soon became her,
    Right comely as it should.

Most rich and fair of color,
    Like gold it glittering shone,
And much the knights in Arthur's court
    Admired her every one.

The ballad goes on to tell of two more trials of a similar kind, made by means of a boar's head and a drinking-horn, in both of which the result was equally favorable with the first to Sir Cradock and his lady. It then concludes as follows:

Thus boar's head, horn, and mantle
    Were this fair couple's meed;
And all such constant lovers,
    God send them well to speed.

Percy's Reliques

CHAPTER VIII

LAUNCELOT OF THE LAKE

King Ban, of Brittany, the faithful ally of Arthur, was attacked by his enemy Claudas, and, after a long war, saw himself reduced to the possession of a single fortress, where he was besieged by his enemy. In this extremity, he determined to solicit the assistance of Arthur, and escaped in a dark night, with his wife Helen and his infant son Launcelot, leaving his castle in the hands of his seneschal, who immediately surrendered the place to Claudas. The flames of his burning citadel reached the eyes of the unfortunate monarch during his flight, and he expired with grief. The wretched Helen, leaving her child on the brink of a lake, flew to receive the last sighs of her husband, and on returning perceived the little Launcelot in the arms of a nymph, who, on the approach of the queen, threw herself into the lake with the child. This nymph was Viviane, mistress of the enchanter Merlin, better known by the name of the Lady of the Lake. Launcelot received his appellation from having been educated at the court of this enchantress, whose palace was situated in the midst, not of a real, but, like the appearance which deceives the African traveller, of an imaginary lake, whose deluding resemblance served as a barrier to her residence. Here she dwelt not alone, but in the midst of a numerous retinue and a splendid court of knights and damsels.

The queen, after her double loss, retired to a convent, where she was joined by the widow of Bohort, for this good king had died of grief, on hearing of the death of his brother Ban. His two sons, Lionel and Bohort, were rescued by a faithful knight, and arrived in the shape of greyhounds at the palace of the lake, where, having resumed their natural form, they were educated along with their cousin Launcelot.

The fairy, when her pupil had attained the age of eighteen, conveyed him to the court of Arthur for the purpose of demanding his admission to the honor of knighthood; and at the first appearance of the youthful candidate, the graces of his person, which were not inferior to his courage and skill in arms, made an instantaneous and indelible impression on the heart of Guenever, while her charms inspired him with an equally ardent and constant passion. The mutual attachment of these lovers exerted, from that time forth, an influence over the whole history of Arthur. For the sake of Guenever, Launcelot achieved the conquest of Northumberland, defeated Gallehaut, King of the Marches, who afterwards became his most faithful friend and ally, exposed himself in numberless encounters, and brought hosts of prisoners to the feet of his sovereign.

SIR LAUNCELOT

After King Arthur was come from Rome into England, all the knights of the Table Round resorted unto him and made him many justs and tournaments. And in especial Sir Launcelot of the Lake, in all tournaments and justs and deeds of arms, both for life and death, passed all other knights, and was never overcome, except it were by treason or enchantment; and he increased marvellously in worship, wherefore Queen Guenever had him in great favor, above all other knights. And for certain he loved the queen again above all other ladies; and for her he did many deeds of arms, and saved her from peril, through his noble chivalry. Thus Sir Launcelot rested him long with play and game, and then he thought to prove himself in strange adventures; so he bade his nephew, Sir Lionel, to make him ready—"for we two will seek adventures." So they mounted on their horses, armed at all sights, and rode into a forest, and so into a deep plain. And the weather was hot about noon, and Sir Launcelot had great desire to sleep. Then Sir Lionel espied a great apple-tree that stood by a hedge, and he said: "Brother, yonder is a fair shadow—there may we rest us and our horses." "It is well said," replied Sir Launcelot. So they there alighted, and Sir Launcelot laid him down, and his helm under his head, and soon was asleep passing fast. And Sir Lionel waked while he slept. And presently there came three knights riding as fast as ever they might ride, and there followed them but one knight. And Sir Lionel thought he never saw so great a knight before. So, within a while, this great knight overtook one of those knights and smote him so that he fell to the earth. Then he rode to the second knight and smote him, and so he did to the third knight. Then he alighted down and bound all the three knights fast with their own bridles. When Sir Lionel saw him do thus, he thought to assay him, and made him ready silently, not to awake Sir Launcelot, and rode after the strong knight, and bade him turn. And the other smote Sir Lionel so hard that horse and man fell to the earth; and then he alighted down, and bound Sir Lionel, and threw him across his own horse; and so he served them all four and rode with them away to his own castle. And when he came there, he put them in a deep prison, in which were many more knights in great distress.

Now while Sir Launcelot lay under the apple-tree sleeping, there came by him four queens of great estate. And that the heat should not grieve them, there rode four knights about them, and bare a cloth of green silk, on four spears, betwixt them and the sun. And the queens rode on four white mules.

Thus as they rode they heard by them a great horse grimly neigh. Then they were aware of a sleeping knight that lay all armed under an apple-tree; and as the queens looked on his face, they knew it was Sir Launcelot. Then they began to strive for that knight, and each one said she would have him for her love. "We will not strive," said Morgane le Fay, that was King Arthur's sister, "for I will put an enchantment upon him, that he shall not wake for six hours, and we will take him away to my castle; and then, when he is surely within my hold, I will take the enchantment from him and then let him choose which of us he will have for his love." So the enchantment was cast upon Sir Launcelot. And then they laid him upon his shield, and bare him so on horseback between two knights, and brought him unto the castle and laid him in a chamber, and at night they sent him his supper.

And on the morning came early those four queens, richly dight, and bade him good morning, and he them again. "Sir Knight," they said, "thou must understand thou art our prisoner; and we know thee well, that thou art Sir Launcelot of the Lake, King Ban's son, and that thou art the noblest knight living. And we know well that there can no lady have thy love but one, and that is Queen Guenever; and now thou shalt lose her for ever, and she thee; and therefore it behooveth thee now to choose one of us. I am the Queen Morgane le Fay, and here is the Queen of North Wales, and the Queen of Eastland, and the Queen of the Isles. Now choose one of us which thou wilt have, for if thou choose not, in this prison thou shalt die." "This is a hard case," said Sir Launcelot, "that either I must die, or else choose one of you; yet had I liever to die in this prison with worship than to have one of you for my paramour, for ye be false enchantresses." "Well," said the queens, "is this your answer, that ye will refuse us?" "Yea, on my life it is," said Sir Launcelot. Then they departed, making great sorrow.

Then at noon came a damsel unto him with his dinner and asked him, "What cheer?" "Truly, fair damsel," said Sir Launcelot, "never so ill." "Sir," said she, "if you will be ruled by me, I will help you out of this distress. If ye will promise me to help my father on Tuesday next, who hath made a tournament betwixt him and the king of North Wales; for the last Tuesday my father lost the field." "Fair maiden," said Sir Launcelot, "tell me what is your father's name, and then will I give you an answer." "Sir Knight," she said, "my father is King Bagdemagus." "I know him well," said Sir Launcelot, "for a noble king and a good knight; and, by the faith of my body, I will be ready to do your father and you service at that day."

So she departed, and came on the next morning early and found him ready, and brought him out of twelve locks, and brought him to his own horse, and lightly he saddled him, and so rode forth.

And on the Tuesday next he came to a little wood where the tournament should be. And there were scaffolds and holds, that lords and ladies might look on and give the prize. Then came into the field the King of North Wales, with eightscore helms, and King Bagdemagus came with fourscore helms. And then they couched their spears and came together with a great dash, and there were overthrown at the first encounter twelve of King Bagdemagus's party and six of the King of North Wales's party, and King Bagdemagus's party had the worse.

With that came Sir Launcelot of the Lake, and thrust in with his spear in the thickest of the press; and he smote down five knights ere he held his hand; and he smote down the King of North Wales, and he brake his thigh in that fall. And then the knights of the King of North Wales would just no more; and so the gree was given to King Bagdemagus.

And Sir Launcelot rode forth with King Bagdemagus unto his castle; and there he had passing good cheer, both with the king and with his daughter. And on the morn he took his leave and told the king he would go and seek his brother, Sir Lionel, that went from him when he slept. So he departed, and by adventure he came to the same forest where he was taken sleeping. And in the highway he met a damsel riding on a white palfrey, and they saluted each other. "Fair damsel," said Sir Launcelot, "know ye in this country any adventures?" "Sir Knight," said the damsel, "here are adventures near at hand, if thou durst pursue them." "Why should I not prove adventures?" said Sir Launcelot, "since for that cause came I hither." "Sir," said she, "hereby dwelleth a knight that will not be overmatched for any man I know, except thou overmatch him. His name is Sir Turquine, and, as I understand, he is a deadly enemy of King Arthur, and he has in his prison good knights of Arthur's court threescore and more, that he hath won with his own hands." "Damsel," said Launcelot, "I pray you bring me unto this knight." So she told him, "Hereby, within this mile, is his castle, and by it on the left hand is a ford for horses to drink of, and over that ford there groweth a fair tree, and on that tree hang many shields that good knights wielded aforetime, that are now prisoners; and on the tree hangeth a basin of copper and latten, and if thou strike upon that basin, thou shalt hear tidings." And Sir Launcelot departed, and rode as the damsel had shown him, and shortly he came to the ford and the tree where hung the shields and the basin. And among the shields he saw Sir Lionel's and Sir Hector's shield, besides many others of knights that he knew.

Then Sir Launcelot struck on the basin with the butt of his spear; and long he did so, but he saw no man. And at length he was ware of a great knight that drove a horse before him, and across the horse there lay an armed knight bounden. And as they came near, Sir Launcelot thought he should know the captive knight. Then

Sir Launcelot saw that it was Sir Gaheris, Sir Gawain's brother, a knight of the Table Round. "Now, fair knight," said Sir Launcelot, "put that wounded knight off the horse, and let him rest awhile, and let us two prove our strength. For, as it is told me, thou hast done great despite and shame unto knights of the Round Table; therefore, now, defend thee." "If thou be of the Table Round," said Sir Turquine, "I defy thee and all thy fellowship." "That is overmuch said," said Sir Launcelot.

Then they put their spears in the rests and came together with their horses as fast as they might run. And each smote the other in the middle of their shields, so that their horses fell under them and the knights were both staggered; and as soon as they could clear their horses, they drew out their swords, and came together eagerly, and each gave the other many strong strokes, for neither shield nor harness might withstand their strokes. So, within a while, both had grimly wounds and bled grievously. Then at the last they were breathless both, and stood leaning upon their swords. "Now, fellow," said Sir Turquine, "thou art the stoutest man that ever I met with, and best breathed; and so be it thou be not the knight that I hate above all other knights, the knight that slew my brother, Sir Carados, I will gladly accord with thee; and for thy love I will deliver all the prisoners that I have."

"What knight is he that thou hatest so above others?" "Truly," said Sir Turquine, "his name is Sir Launcelot of the Lake." "I am Sir Launcelot of the Lake, King Ban's son of Benwick, and very knight of the Table Round; and now I defy thee do thy best." "Ah!" said Sir Turquine, "Launcelot, thou art to me the most welcome that ever was knight; for we shall never part till the one of us be dead." And then they hurtled together like two wild bulls, rashing and lashing with their swords and shields, so that sometimes they fell, as it were, headlong. Thus they fought two hours and more, till the ground where they fought was all bepurpled with blood.

Then at the last Sir Turquine waxed sore faint, and gave somewhat aback, and bare his shield full low for weariness. That spied Sir Launcelot, and leapt then upon him fiercely as a lion, and took him by the beaver of his helmet, and drew him down on his knees. And he rased off his helm and smote his neck in sunder.

And Sir Gaheris, when he saw Sir Turquine slain, said, "Fair lord, I pray you tell me your name, for this day I say ye are the best knight in the world, for ye have slain this day in my sight the mightiest man and the best knight except you that ever I saw." "Sir, my name is Sir Launcelot du Lac, that ought to help you of right for King Arthur's sake, and in especial for Sir Gawain's sake, your own dear brother. Now I pray you, that ye go into yonder castle and set free all the prisoners ye find there, for I am sure ye shall find there many knights of the Table Round, and especially my brother Sir Lionel. I pray you greet them all from me, and tell them I bid them take there such stuff as they find; and tell my brother to go unto the court and abide me there, for by the feast of Pentecost I think to be there; but at this time I may not stop, for I have adventures on hand." So he departed, and Sir Gaheris rode into the castle, and took the keys from the porter, and hastily opened the prison door, and let out all the prisoners. There was Sir Kay, Sir Brandeles, and Sir Galynde, Sir Bryan, and Sir Alyduke, Sir Hector de Marys, and Sir Lionel, and many more. And when they saw Sir Gaheris, they all thanked him, for they thought, because he was wounded, that he had slain Sir Turquine. "Not so," said Sir Gaheris; "it was Sir Launcelot that slew him, right worshipfully; I saw it with mine eyes."

Sir Launcelot rode till, at nightfall, he came to a fair castle, and therein he found an old gentlewoman, who lodged him with good will, and there he had good cheer for him and his horse. And when time was, his host brought him to a fair chamber over the gate to his bed. Then Sir Launcelot unarmed him, and set his harness by him, and went to bed, and anon he fell asleep. And soon after, there came one on horseback and knocked at the gate in great haste; and when Sir Launcelot heard this, he arose and looked out of the window, and saw by the moonlight three knights riding after that one man, and all three lashed on him with their swords, and that one knight turned on them knightly again and defended himself. "Truly," said Sir Launcelot, "yonder one knight

will I help, for it is shame to see three knights on one."
Then he took his harness and went out at the window
by a sheet down to the four knights; and he said aloud,
"Turn you knights unto me, and leave your fighting with
that knight." Then the knights left Sir Kay, for it was he
they were upon, and turned unto Sir Launcelot, and
struck many great strokes at Sir Launcelot, and assailed
him on every side. Then Sir Kay addressed him to help
Sir Launcelot, but he said, "Nay, sir, I will none of your
help; let me alone with them." So Sir Kay suffered him
to do his will and stood one side. And within six strokes,
Sir Launcelot had stricken them down.

Then they all cried, "Sir Knight, we yield us unto you."
"As to that," said Sir Launcelot, "I will not take your
yielding unto me. If so be ye will yield you unto Sir
Kay the Seneschal, I will save your lives, but else not."
"Fair knight," then they said, "we will do as thou com-
mandest us." "Then shall ye," said Sir Launcelot, "on
Whitsunday next, go unto the court of King Arthur, and
there shall ye yield you unto Queen Guenever, and say
that Sir Kay sent you thither to be her prisoners."
"Sir," they said, "it shall be done, by the faith of our
bodies"; and then they swore, every knight upon his
sword. And so Sir Launcelot suffered them to depart.

On the morn, Sir Launcelot rose early and left Sir
Kay sleeping; and Sir Launcelot took Sir Kay's armor,
and his shield, and armed him, and went to the stable
and took his horse, and so he departed. Then soon after
arose Sir Kay, and missed Sir Launcelot. And then he
espied that he had taken his armor and his horse. "Now,
by my faith, I know well," said Sir Kay, "that he will
grieve some of King Arthur's knights, for they will deem
that it is I, and will be bold to meet him. But by cause
of his armor, I am sure I shall ride in peace." Then
Sir Kay thanked his host and departed.

Sir Launcelot rode in a deep forest, and there he saw
four knights under an oak, and they were of Arthur's
court. There was Sir Sagramour le Desirus, and Hector
de Marys, and Sir Gawain, and Sir Uwaine. As they spied
Sir Launcelot, they judged by his arms it had been Sir
Kay. "Now, by my faith," said Sir Sagramour, "I will
prove Sir Kay's might"; and got his spear in his hand,

and came towards Sir Launcelot. Therewith Sir Launcelot couched his spear against him and smote Sir Sagramour so sore that horse and man fell both to the earth. Then said Sir Hector, "Now shall ye see what I may do with him." But he fared worse than Sir Sagramour, for Sir Launcelot's spear went through his shoulder and bare him from his horse to the ground. "By my faith," said Sir Uwaine, "yonder is a strong knight, and I fear he hath slain Sir Kay and taken his armor." And therewith Sir Uwaine took his spear in hand and rode toward Sir Launcelot; and Sir Launcelot met him on the plain and gave him such a buffet that he was staggered, and wist not where he was. "Now see I well," said Sir Gawain, "that I must encounter with that knight." Then he adjusted his shield, and took a good spear in his hand, and Sir Launcelot knew him well. Then they let run their horses with all their mights, and each knight smote the other in the middle of his shield. But Sir Gawain's spear broke, and Sir Launcelot charged so sore upon him that his horse fell over backward. Then Sir Launcelot passed by, smiling with himself, and he said, "Good luck be with him that made this spear, for never came a better into my hand." Then the four knights went each to the other and comforted one another. "What say ye to this adventure," said Sir Gawain, "that one spear hath felled us all four?" "I dare lay my head it is Sir Launcelot," said Sir Hector; "I know it by his riding."

And Sir Launcelot rode through many strange countries, till by fortune he came to a fair castle; and as he passed beyond the castle, he thought he heard two bells ring. And then he perceived how a falcon came flying over his head, toward a high elm; and she had long lunys* about her feet, and she flew unto the elm to take her perch, and the lunys got entangled in a bough; and when she would have taken her flight, she hung by the legs fast, and Sir Launcelot saw how she hung, and beheld the fair falcon entangled, and he was sorry for her. Then came a lady out of the castle and cried aloud, "Oh, Launcelot, Launcelot, as thou art the flower of all knights, help me to get my hawk; for if my hawk be

---

* *Lunys*, the string with which the falcon is held.

lost, my lord will slay me, he is so hasty." "What is your lord's name?" said Sir Launcelot. "His name is Sir Phelot, a knight that belongeth to the King of North Wales." "Well, fair lady, since ye know my name and require me of knighthood to help you, I will do what I may to get your hawk; and yet in truth I am an ill climber, and the tree is passing high, and few boughs to help me." And therewith Sir Launcelot alighted and tied his horse to the tree, and prayed the lady to unarm him. And when he was unarmed, he put off his jerkin, and with might and force he clomb up to the falcon, and tied the lunys to a rotten bough, and threw the hawk down with it; and the lady got the hawk in her hand. Then suddenly there came out of the castle her husband, all armed and with his naked sword in his hand, and said, "Oh, Knight Launcelot, now have I got thee as I would," and stood at the boll of the tree to slay him. "Ah, lady!" said Sir Launcelot, "why have ye betrayed me?" "She hath done," said Sir Phelot, "but as I commanded her; and therefore there is none other way but thine hour is come, and thou must die." "That were shame unto thee," said Sir Launcelot; "thou an armed knight to slay a naked man by treason." "Thou gettest none other grace," said Sir Phelot, "and therefore help thyself if thou canst." "Alas!" said Sir Launcelot, "that ever a knight should die weaponless!" And therewith he turned his eyes upward and downward; and over his head he saw a big bough leafless, and he brake it off from the trunk. And then he came lower, and watched how his own horse stood; and suddenly he leapt on the further side of his horse from the knight. Then Sir Phelot lashed at him eagerly, meaning to have slain him. But Sir Launcelot put away the stroke with the big bough and smote Sir Phelot therewith on the side of the head, so that he fell down in a swoon to the ground. Then Sir Launcelot took his sword out of his hand and struck his head from the body. Then said the lady, "Alas! why hast thou slain my husband?" "I am not the cause," said Sir Launcelot, "for with falsehood ye would have slain me, and now it is fallen on yourselves." Thereupon Sir Launcelot got all his armor and put it upon him hastily, for fear of more resort, for the knight's castle was so nigh. And as soon as he might, he took his horse and departed, and thanked God he had escaped that adventure.

And two days before the feast of Pentecost, Sir Launcelot came home; and the king and all the court were passing glad of his coming. And when Sir Gawain, Sir Uwaine, Sir Sagramour, and Sir Hector de Marys saw Sir Launcelot in Sir Kay's armor, then they wist well it was he that smote them down, all with one spear. Then there was laughing and merriment among them; and from time to time came all the knights that Sir Turquine had prisoners, and they all honored and worshipped Sir Launcelot. Then Sir Gaheris said, "I saw all the battle from the beginning to the end," and he told King Arthur all how it was. Then Sir Kay told the king how Sir Launcelot had rescued him, and how he "made the knights yield to me, and not to him." And there they were, all three, and confirmed it all. "And, by my faith," said Sir Kay, "because Sir Launcelot took my harness and left me his, I rode in peace, and no man would have to do with me."

And so at that time Sir Launcelot had the greatest name of any knight of the world, and most was he honored of high and low.

CHAPTER IX

THE ADVENTURE OF THE CART

It befell in the month of May, Queen Guenever called to her knights of the Table Round and gave them warning that early upon the morrow she would ride a maying into the woods and fields beside Westminster; "and I warn you that there be none of you but he be well horsed, and that ye all be clothed in green, either silk or cloth; and I shall bring with me ten ladies, and every knight shall have a lady behind him, and every knight shall have a squire and two yeomen, and all well

horsed." So they made them ready; and these were the
names of the knights: Sir Kay, the seneschal, Sir Agra-
vaine, Sir Brandeles, Sir Sagramour le Desirus, Sir
Dodynas le Sauvage, Sir Ozanna, Sir Ladynas, Sir Per-
sant of Inde, Sir Ironside, and Sir Pelleas; and these ten
knights made them ready, in the freshest manner, to ride
with the queen. So upon the morn they took their horses
with the queen and rode a maying in woods and meadows, as it pleased them, in great joy and delight. Now
there was a knight named Maleagans, son to King
Brademagus, who loved Queen Guenever passing well,
and so had he done long and many years. Now this
knight, Sir Maleagans, learned the queen's purpose, and
that she had no men of arms with her but the ten noble
knights all arrayed in green for maying; so he prepared
him twenty men of arms, and a hundred archers, to take
captive the queen and her knights.

So when the queen had mayed, and all were bedecked
with herbs, mosses, and flowers in the best manner and
freshest, right then came out of a wood Sir Maleagans
with eightscore men well harnessed, and bade the queen
and her knights yield them prisoners. "Traitor knight,"
said Queen Guenever, "what wilt thou do? Wilt thou
shame thyself? Bethink thee how thou art a king's son,
and a knight of the Table Round, and how thou art
about to dishonor all knighthood and thyself." "Be it
as it may," said Sir Maleagans, "know you well, madam,
I have loved you many a year, and never till now could
I get you to such advantage as I do now; and therefore
I will take you as I find you." Then the ten knights of
the Round Table drew their swords, and the other party
run at them with their spears, and the ten knights manfully abode them, and smote away their spears. Then
they lashed together with swords, till several were smitten
to the earth. So when the queen saw her knights thus
dolefully oppressed, and needs must be slain at the last,
then for pity and sorrow she cried, "Sir Maleagans, slay
not my noble knights and I will go with you, upon this
covenant, that they be led with me wheresoever thou
leadest me." "Madame," said Maleagans, "for your sake
they shall be led with you into my own castle, if that
ye will be ruled, and ride with me." Then Sir Male-

agans charged them all that none should depart from the queen, for he dreaded lest Sir Launcelot should have knowledge of what had been done.

Then the queen privily called unto her a page of her chamber that was swiftly horsed, to whom she said, "Go thou when thou seest thy time, and bear this ring unto Sir Launcelot and pray him as he loveth me, that he will see me and rescue me. And spare not thy horse," said the queen, "neither for water nor for land." So the child espied his time, and lightly he took his horse with the spurs, and departed, as fast as he might. And when Sir Maleagans saw him so flee, he understood that it was by the queen's commandment for to warn Sir Launcelot. Then they that were best horsed chased him, and shot at him, but the child went from them all. Then Sir Maleagans said to the queen, "Madam, ye are about to betray me, but I shall arrange for Sir Launcelot that he shall not come lightly at you." Then he rode with her and them all to his castle, in all the haste that they might. And by the way Sir Maleagans laid in ambush the best archers that he had, to wait for Sir Launcelot. And the child came to Westminster, and found Sir Launcelot, and told his message, and delivered him the queen's ring. "Alas!" said Sir Launcelot, "now am I shamed for ever, unless I may rescue that noble lady." Then eagerly he asked his armor, and put it on him, and mounted his horse and rode as fast as he might; and men say he took the water at Westminster Bridge and made his horse swim over Thames unto Lambeth. Then within a while he came to a wood, where was a narrow way; and there the archers were laid in ambush. And they shot at him, and smote his horse, so that he fell. Then Sir Launcelot left his horse and went on foot, but there lay so many ditches and hedges betwixt the archers and him that he might not meddle with them. "Alas! for shame," said Sir Launcelot, "that ever one knight should betray another! But it is an old saw, a good man is never in danger, but when he is in danger of a coward." Then Sir Launcelot went awhile, and he was exceedingly cumbered by his armor, his shield, and his spear, and all that belonged to him. Then by chance there came by him a cart that came thither to fetch wood.

Now at this time carts were little used except for carrying offal and for conveying criminals to execution. But Sir Launcelot took no thought of anything but the necessity of haste for the purpose of rescuing the queen; so he demanded of the carter that he should take him in and convey him as speedily as possible for a liberal reward. The carter consented, and Sir Launcelot placed himself in the cart, and only lamented that with much jolting he made but little progress. Then it happened Sir Gawain passed by, and seeing an armed knight travelling in that unusual way, he drew near to see who it might be. Then Sir Launcelot told him how the queen had been carried off, and how, in hastening to her rescue, his horse had been disabled, and he had been compelled to avail himself of the cart rather than give up his enterprise. Then Sir Gawain said, "Surely it is unworthy of a knight to travel in such sort"; but Sir Launcelot heeded him not.

At nightfall, they arrived at a castle, and the lady thereof came out at the head of her damsels to welcome Sir Gawain. But to admit his companion, whom she supposed to be a criminal, or at least a prisoner, it pleased her not; however, to oblige Sir Gawain, she consented. At supper, Sir Launcelot came near being consigned to the kitchen, and was only admitted to the lady's table at the earnest solicitation of Sir Gawain. Neither would the damsels prepare a bed for him. He seized the first he found unoccupied, and was left undisturbed.

Next morning he saw from the turrets of the castle a train accompanying a lady, whom he imagined to be the queen. Sir Gawain thought it might be so, and became equally eager to depart. The lady of the castle supplied Sir Launcelot with a horse, and they traversed the plain at full speed. They learned from some travellers whom they met that there were two roads which led to the castle of Sir Maleagans. Here therefore the friends separated. Sir Launcelot found his way beset with obstacles, which he encountered successfully, but not without much loss of time. As evening approached, he was met by a young and sportive damsel, who gayly proposed to him a supper at her castle. The knight, who was hungry and weary, accepted the offer, though with no very good grace. He followed the lady to her castle and ate voraciously of her supper, but was quite impenetrable to all her amorous advances. Suddenly the scene changed, and he was assailed by six furious ruffians, whom he dealt with so vigorously that most of them were speedily disabled, when again there was a change, and he found himself alone with his fair hostess, who informed him that she was none other than his guardian fairy, who had but subjected him to tests of his courage and fidelity. The next day the fairy brought him on his road and, before parting, gave him a ring, which she told him would, by its changes of color, disclose to him all enchantments, and enable him to subdue them.

Sir Launcelot pursued his journey, without being much incommoded except by the taunts of travellers, who all seemed to have learned, by some means, his disgraceful drive in the cart. One, more insolent than the rest, had the audacity to interrupt him during dinner and even to risk a battle in support of his pleasantry. Launcelot, after an easy victory, only doomed him to be carted in his turn.

At night, he was received at another castle, with great apparent hospitality, but found himself in the morning in a dungeon and loaded with chains. Consulting his ring and finding that this was an enchantment, he burst his chains, seized his armor in spite of the visionary monsters who attempted to defend it, broke open the gates of the tower, and continued his journey. At length his progress was checked by a wide and rapid torrent, which could only be passed on a narrow bridge, on which a false step would prove his destruction. Launcelot, leading his horse by the bridle and making him swim by his side, passed over the bridge, and was attacked, as soon as he reached the bank, by a lion and a leopard, both of which he slew, and then, exhausted and bleeding, seated himself on the grass and endeavored to bind up his wounds, when he was accosted by Brademagus, the father of Maleagans, whose castle was then in sight, and at no great distance. This king, no less courteous than his son was haughty and insolent, after complimenting Sir Launcelot on the valor and skill he had displayed in the perils of the bridge and the wild beasts, offered him his assistance and informed him that the queen was safe in his castle, but could only be rescued by encountering Maleagans. Launcelot demanded the battle for the next day, and accordingly it took place, at the foot of the tower, and under the eyes of the fair captive. Launcelot was enfeebled by his wounds, and fought not with his usual spirit, and the contest for a time was doubtful; till Guenever exclaimed, "Ah, Launcelot! my knight, truly have I been told that thou art no longer worthy of me!" These words instantly revived the drooping knight; he resumed at once his usual superiority and soon laid at his feet his haughty adversary.

He was on the point of sacrificing him to his resentment when Guenever, moved by the entreaties of Brademagus, ordered him to withhold the blow, and he obeyed. The castle and its prisoners were now at his disposal. Launcelot hastened to the apartment of the queen, threw himself at her feet, and was about to kiss her hand, when she exclaimed, "Ah, Launcelot! why do I see thee again, yet feel thee to be no longer worthy of me, after having been disgracefully drawn about the country in a——" She had not time to finish the phrase, for her lover suddenly started from her, and, bitterly lamenting that he had incurred the displeasure of his sovereign lady, rushed out of the castle, threw his sword and his shield to the right and left, ran furiously into the woods, and disappeared.

It seems that the story of the abominable cart, which haunted Launcelot at every step, had reached the ears of Sir Kay, who had told it to the queen, as a proof that her knight must have been dishonored. But Guenever had full leisure to repent the haste with which she had given credit to the tale. Three days elapsed, during which Launcelot wandered without knowing where he went, till at last he began to reflect that his mistress had doubtless been deceived by misrepresentation, and that it was his duty to set her right. He therefore returned, compelled Maleagans to release his prisoners, and, taking the road by which they expected the arrival of Sir Gawain, had the satisfaction of meeting him the next day; after which the whole company proceeded gaily towards Camelot.

CHAPTER X

THE LADY OF SHALOTT

King Arthur proclaimed a solemn tournament to be held at Winchester. The king, not less impatient than his knights for this festival, set off some days before to superintend the preparations, leaving the queen with her court at Camelot. Sir Launcelot, under pretence of indisposition, remained behind also. His intention was to attend the tournament in disguise; and having communicated his project to Guenever, he mounted his horse, set off without any attendant, and, counterfeiting the feebleness of age, took the most unfrequented road to Winchester, and passed unnoticed as an old knight who was going to be a spectator of the sports. Even Arthur and Gawain, who happened to behold him from the windows of a castle under which he passed, were the dupes of his disguise. But an accident betrayed him. His horse happened to stumble, and the hero, forgetting for a moment his assumed character, recovered the animal with a strength and agility so peculiar to himself that they instantly recognized the inimitable Launcelot. They suffered him, however, to proceed on his journey without interruption, convinced that his extraordinary feats of arms must discover him at the approaching festival.

In the evening, Launcelot was magnificently entertained as a stranger knight at the neighboring castle of Shalott. The lord of this castle had a daughter of exquisite beauty and two sons lately received into the order of knighthood, one of whom was at that time ill in bed and thereby prevented from attending the tournament, for which both brothers had long made preparations. Launcelot offered to attend the other, if he were permitted to borrow the armor of the invalid, and the lord of Shalott, without knowing the name of his guest, being satisfied from his appearance that his son could not have a better assistant in arms, most thankfully accepted the offer. In the meantime the young lady, who had been much struck by the first appearance of the stranger knight, continued to survey him with increased attention, and, before the conclusion of supper, became so deeply enamored of him that, after frequent changes of color and other symptoms which Sir Launcelot could not possibly mistake, she was obliged to retire to her chamber and seek relief in tears. Sir Launcelot hastened to convey to her, by means of her brother, the information that his heart was already disposed of, but that it would be his pride and pleasure to act as her knight at the approaching tournament. The lady, obliged to be satisfied with that courtesy, presented him her scarf to be worn at the tournament.

Launcelot set off in the morning with the young knight, who, on their approaching Winchester, carried him to the castle of a lady, sister to the lord of Shalott, by whom they were hospitably entertained. The next day they put on their armor, which was perfectly plain, and without any device, as was usual to youths during the first year of knighthood, their shields being only painted red, as some color was necessary to enable them to be recognized by their attendants. Launcelot wore on his crest the scarf of the maid of Shalott, and, thus equipped, proceeded to the tournament, where the knights were divided into two companies, the one commanded by Sir Gallehaut, the other by King Arthur. Having surveyed the combat for a short time from without the lists and observed that Sir Gallehaut's party began to give way, they joined the press and attacked the royal knights, the young man choosing such adversaries as were suited to his strength, while his companion selected the principal champions of the Round Table and successively overthrew Gawain, Bohort, and Lionel. The astonishment of the spectators was extreme, for it was thought that no one but Launcelot could possess such invincible force; yet the favor on his crest seemed to preclude the possibility of his being thus disguised, for Launcelot had never been known to wear the badge of any but his sovereign lady. At length, Sir Hector, Launcelot's brother, engaged him and, after a dreadful combat, wounded him dangerously in the head, but was himself completely stunned by a blow on the helmet and felled to the ground, after which the conqueror rode off at full speed, attended by his companion.

They returned to the castle of Shalott, where Launcelot was attended with the greatest care by the good earl, by his two sons, and, above all, by his fair daughter, whose medical skill probably much hastened the period of his recovery. His health was almost completely restored when Sir Hector, Sir Bohort, and Sir Lionel, who, after the return of the court to Camelot, had undertaken the quest of their relation, discovered him walking on the walls of the castle. Their meeting was very joyful; they passed three days in the castle amidst constant festivities and bantered each other on the events of the tournament. Launcelot, though he began by vowing vengeance against the author of his wound, yet ended by declaring that he felt rewarded for the pain by the pride he took in witnessing his brother's extraordinary prowess. He then dismissed them with a message to the queen, promising to follow immediately, it being necessary that he should first take a formal leave of his kind hosts, as well as of the fair maid of Shalott.

The young lady, after vainly attempting to detain him by her tears and solicitations, saw him depart without leaving her any ground for hope.

It was early summer when the tournament took place; but some months had passed since Launcelot's departure, and winter was now near at hand. The health and strength of the Lady of Shalott had gradually sunk, and she felt that she could not live apart from the object of her affections. She left the castle and, descending to the river's brink, placed herself in a boat, which she loosed from its moorings and suffered to bear her down the current towards Camelot.

One morning, as Arthur and Sir Lionel looked from the window of the tower, the walls of which were washed by a river, they descried a boat, richly ornamented and covered with an awning of cloth of gold, which appeared to be floating down the stream without any human guidance. It struck the shore while they watched it, and they hastened down to examine it. Beneath the awning they discovered the dead body of a beautiful woman, in whose features Sir Lionel easily recognized the lovely maid of Shalott. Pursuing their search, they discovered a purse richly embroidered with gold and jewels, and within the purse a letter, which Arthur opened, and found addressed to himself and all the knights of the Round Table, stating that Launcelot of the Lake, the most accomplished of knights and most beautiful of men, but at the same time the most cruel and inflexible, had by his rigor produced the death of the wretched maiden, whose love was no less invincible than his cruelty. The king immediately gave orders for the interment of the lady, with all the honors suited to her rank, at the same time explaining to the knights the history of her affection for Launcelot, which moved the compassion and regret of all.

———

Tennyson has chosen the story of the Lady of Shalott for the subject of a poem. The catastrophe is told thus:

> Under tower and balcony,
> By garden-wall and gallery,
> A gleaming shape she floated by,
> A corse between the houses high,
>   Silent into Camelot.
> Out upon the wharfs they came,
> Knight and burgher, lord and dame,
> And round the prow they read her name,
>   "The Lady of Shalott."
>
> Who is this? and what is here?
> And in the lighted palace near
> Died the sound of royal cheer;
> And they crossed themselves for fear,
>   All the knights at Camelot.
> But Launcelot mused a little space;
> He said, "She has a lovely face;
> God in his mercy lend her grace,
>   The Lady of Shalott."

CHAPTER XI

QUEEN GUENEVER'S PERIL

It happened at this time that Queen Guenever was thrown into great peril of her life. A certain squire who was in her immediate service, having some cause of animosity to Sir Gawain, determined to destroy him by poison at a public entertainment. For this purpose he concealed the poison in an apple of fine appearance, which he placed on the top of several others, and put the dish before the queen, hoping that, as Sir Gawain was the knight of greatest dignity, she would present the apple to him. But it happened that a Scottish knight of high distinction, who arrived on that day, was seated next to the queen, and to him as a stranger she presented the apple, which he had no sooner eaten than he was seized with dreadful pain, and fell senseless. The whole court was, of course, thrown into confusion; the knights rose from table, darting looks of indignation at the wretched queen, whose tears and protestations were unable to remove their suspicions. In spite of all that could be done, the knight died, and nothing remained but to order a magnificent funeral and monument for him, which was done.

Some time after, Sir Mador, brother of the murdered knight, arrived at Arthur's court in quest of him. While hunting in the forest, he by chance came to the spot where the monument was erected, read the inscription, and returned to court determined on immediate and signal vengeance. He rode into the hall, loudly accused the queen of treason, and insisted on her being given up to punishment, unless she should find, by a certain day, a knight hardy enough to risk his life in support of her innocence. Arthur, powerful as he was, did not dare to deny the appeal, but was compelled, with a heavy heart, to accept it, and Mador sternly took his departure, leaving the royal couple plunged in terror and anxiety.

During all this time, Launcelot was absent, and no one knew where he was. He had fled in anger from his fair mistress, upon being reproached by her with his passion for the Lady of Shalott, which she had hastily inferred from his wearing her scarf at the tournament. He took up his abode with a hermit in the forest and resolved to think no more of the cruel beauty, whose conduct he thought must flow from a wish to get rid of him. Yet, calm reflection had somewhat cooled his indignation, and he had begun to wish, though hardly able to hope, for a reconciliation, when the news of Sir Mador's challenge fortunately reached his ears. The intelligence revived his spirits, and he began to prepare with the utmost cheerfulness for a contest which, if successful, would insure him at once the affection of his mistress and the gratitude of his sovereign.

The sad fate of the Lady of Shalott had ere this completely acquitted Launcelot in the queen's mind of all suspicion of his fidelity, and she lamented most grievously her foolish quarrel with him, which now, at her time of need, deprived her of her most efficient champion.

As the day appointed by Sir Mador was fast approaching, it became necessary that she should procure a champion for her defence; and she successively adjured Sir Hector, Sir Lionel, Sir Bohort, and Sir Gawain to undertake the battle. She fell on her knees before them, called Heaven to witness her innocence of the crime alleged against her, but was sternly answered by all that they could not fight to maintain the innocence of one whose act, and the fatal consequences of it, they had seen with their own eyes. She retired, therefore, dejected and disconsolate; but the sight of the fatal pile on which, if guilty, she was doomed to be burned, exciting her to fresh effort, she again repaired to Sir Bohort, threw herself at his feet, and, piteously calling on him for mercy, fell into a swoon. The brave knight was not proof against this. He raised her up and hastily promised that he would undertake her cause, if no other or better champion should present himself. He then summoned his friends and told them his resolution; and as a mortal combat with Sir Mador was a most fearful enterprise, they agreed to accompany him in the morning to the hermitage in the forest, where he proposed to receive absolution from the hermit and to make his peace with Heaven, before he entered the lists. As they approached the hermitage, they espied a knight riding in the forest, whom they at once recognized as Sir Launcelot. Overjoyed at the meeting, they quickly, in answer to his questions, confirmed the news of the queen's imminent danger, and received his instructions to return to court, to comfort her as well as they could, but to say nothing of his intention of undertaking her defence, which he meant to do in the character of an unknown adventurer.

On their return to the castle, they found that mass was finished, and had scarcely time to speak to the queen before they were summoned into the hall to dinner. A general gloom was spread over the countenances of all the guests. Arthur himself was unable to conceal his dejection, and the wretched Guenever, motionless and bathed in tears, sat in trembling expectation of Sir Mador's appearance. Nor was it long ere he stalked into the hall, and with a voice of thunder, rendered more impressive by the general silence, demanded instant justice on the guilty party. Arthur replied with dignity that little of the day was yet spent, and that perhaps a champion might yet be found capable of satisfying his thirst for battle. Sir Bohort now rose from table and, shortly returning in complete armor, resumed his place, after receiving the embraces and thanks of the king, who now began to resume some degree of confidence. Sir Mador, growing impatient, again repeated his denunciations of vengeance and insisted that the combat should no longer be postponed.

In the height of the debate, there came riding into the hall a knight mounted on a black steed and clad in black armor, with his visor down and lance in hand. "Sir," said the king, "is it your will to alight and partake of our cheer?" "Nay, sir," he replied; "I come to save a lady's life. The queen hath ill bestowed her favors and honored many a knight that in her hour of need she should have none to take her part. Thou that darest accuse her of treachery stand forth, for to-day shalt thou need all thy might."

Sir Mador, though surprised, was not appalled by the

stern challenge and formidable appearance of his antagonist, but prepared for the encounter. At the first shock
both were unhorsed. They then drew their swords and
commenced a combat which lasted from noon till evening, when Sir Mador, whose strength began to fail, was
felled to the ground by Launcelot and compelled to sue
for mercy. The victor, whose arm was already raised to
terminate the life of his opponent, instantly dropped his
sword, courteously lifted up the fainting Sir Mador,
frankly confessing that he had never before encountered
so formidable an enemy. The other, with similar courtesy,
solemnly renounced all further projects of vengeance
for his brother's death; and the two knights, now become
fast friends, embraced each other with the greatest cordiality. In the meantime Arthur, having recognized Sir
Launcelot, whose helmet was now unlaced, rushed down
into the lists, followed by all his knights, to welcome and
thank his deliverer. Guenever swooned with joy, and the
place of combat suddenly exhibited a scene of the most
tumultuous delight.

The general satisfaction was still further increased by
the discovery of the real culprit. Having accidentally incurred some suspicion, he confessed his crime, and was
publicly punished in the presence of Sir Mador.

The court now returned to the castle, which, with the
title of "La Joyeuse Garde" bestowed upon it in memory
of the happy event, was conferred on Sir Launcelot by
Arthur, as a memorial of his gratitude.

CHAPTER XII

TRISTRAM AND ISOUDE

Meliadus was King of Leonois, or Lionesse, a country
famous in the annals of romance, which adjoined the
kingdom of Cornwall, but has now disappeared from the
map, having been, it is said, overwhelmed by the ocean.
Meliadus was married to Isabella, sister of Mark, King of

Cornwall. A fairy fell in love with him and drew him away by enchantment while he was engaged in hunting. His queen set out in quest of him, but was taken ill on her journey, and died, leaving an infant son, whom, from the melancholy circumstances of his birth, she called Tristram.

Gouvernail, the queen's squire, who had accompanied her, took charge of the child and restored him to his father, who had at length burst the enchantments of the fairy and returned home.

Meliadus, after seven years, married again, and the new queen, being jealous of the influence of Tristram with his father, laid plots for his life, which were discovered by Gouvernail, who in consequence fled with the boy to the court of the King of France, where Tristram was kindly received, and grew up improving in every gallant and knightly accomplishment, adding to his skill in arms the arts of music and of chess. In particular, he devoted himself to the chase and to all woodland sports, so that he became distinguished above all other chevaliers of the court for his knowledge of all that relates to hunting. No wonder that Belinda, the king's daughter, fell in love with him; but as he did not return her passion, she, in a sudden impulse of anger, excited her father against him, and he was banished the kingdom. The princess soon repented of her act and, in despair, destroyed herself, having first written a most tender letter to Tristram, sending him at the same time a beautiful and sagacious dog, of which she was very fond, desiring him to keep it as a memorial of her. Meliadus was now dead, and as his queen, Tristram's stepmother, held the throne, Gouvernail was afraid to carry his pupil to his native country, and took him to Cornwall, to his Uncle Mark, who gave him a kind reception.

King Mark resided at the castle of Tintadiel, already mentioned in the history of Uther and Iguerne. In this court, Tristram became distinguished in all the exercises incumbent on a knight; nor was it long before he had an opportunity of practically employing his valor and skill. Moraunt, a celebrated champion, brother to the Queen of Ireland, arrived at the court, to demand tribute of King Mark. The knights of Cornwall are in ill repute, in romance, for their cowardice, and they exhibited it on this occasion. King Mark could find no champion who dared to encounter the Irish knight, till his nephew Tristram, who had not yet received the honors of knighthood, craved to be admitted to the order, offering at the same time to fight the battle of Cornwall against the Irish champion. King Mark assented with reluctance; Tristram received the accolade, which conferred knighthood upon him; and the place and time were assigned for the encounter.

Without attempting to give the details of this famous combat, the first and one of the most glorious of Tristram's exploits, we shall only say that the young knight, though severely wounded, cleft the head of Moraunt, leaving a portion of his sword in the wound. Moraunt, half dead with his wound and the disgrace of his defeat, hastened to hide himself in his ship, sailed away with all speed for Ireland, and died soon after arriving in his own country.

The kingdom of Cornwall was thus delivered from its tribute. Tristram, weakened by loss of blood, fell senseless. His friends flew to his assistance. They dressed his wounds, which in general healed readily; but the lance of Moraunt was poisoned, and one wound which it made yielded to no remedies, but grew worse day by day. The surgeons could do no more. Tristram asked permission of his uncle to depart and seek for aid in the kingdom of Loegria (England). With his consent, he embarked, and, after tossing for many days on the sea, was driven by the winds to the coast of Ireland. He landed, full of joy and gratitude that he had escaped the peril of the sea, took his rote,* and began to play. It was a summer evening, and the King of Ireland and his daughter, the beautiful Isoude, were at a window which overlooked the sea. The strange harper was sent for and conveyed to the palace, where, finding that he was in Ireland, whose champion he had lately slain, he concealed his name and called himself Tramtris. The queen undertook his cure and, by a medicated bath, gradually restored him to health. His skill in music and in games occasioned his

---

* A musical instrument.

being frequently called to court, and he became the instructor of the Princess Isoude in minstrelsy and poetry, who profited so well under his care that she soon had no equal in the kingdom, except her instructor.

At this time, a tournament was held, at which many knights of the Round Table, and others, were present. On the first day a Saracen prince, named Palamedes, obtained the advantage over all. They brought him to the court and gave him a feast, at which Tristram, just recovering from his wound, was present. The fair Isoude appeared on this occasion in all her charms. Palamedes could not behold them without emotion and made no effort to conceal his love. Tristram perceived it, and the pain he felt from jealousy taught him how dear the fair Isoude had already become to him.

Next day the tournament was renewed. Tristram, still feeble from his wound, rose during the night, took his arms, and concealed them in a forest near the place of the contest, and, after it had begun, mingled with the combatants. He overthrew all that encountered him, in particular Palamedes, whom he brought to the ground with a stroke of his lance, and then fought him hand to hand, bearing off the prize of the tourney. But his exertions caused his wound to reopen; he bled fast, and in this sad state, yet in triumph, they bore him to the palace. The fair Isoude devoted herself to his relief with an interest which grew more vivid day by day; and her skilful care soon restored him to health.

It happened one day that a damsel of the court, entering the closet where Tristram's arms were deposited, perceived that a part of the sword had been broken off. It occurred to her that the missing portion was like that which was left in the skull of Moraunt, the Irish champion. She imparted her thought to the queen, who compared the fragment taken from her brother's wound with the sword of Tristram, and was satisfied that it was part of the same and that the weapon of Tristram was that which reft her brother's life. She laid her griefs and resentment before the king, who satisfied himself with his own eyes of the truth of her suspicions. Tristram was cited before the whole court, and reproached with having dared to present himself before them after having slain their kinsman. He acknowledged that he had fought with Moraunt to settle the claim for tribute, and said that it was by force of winds and waves alone that he was thrown on their coast. The queen demanded vengeance for the death of her brother; the fair Isoude trembled and grew pale, but a murmur rose from all the assembly that the life of one so handsome and so brave should not be taken for such a cause, and generosity finally triumphed over resentment in the mind of the king. Tristram was dismissed in safety, but commanded to leave the kingdom without delay, and never to return thither under pain of death. Tristram went back, with restored health, to Cornwall.

King Mark made his nephew give him a minute recital of his adventures. Tristram told him all minutely; but when he came to speak of the fair Isoude, he described her charms with a warmth and energy such as none but a lover could display. King Mark was fascinated with the description, and, choosing a favorable time, demanded a boon* of his nephew, who readily granted it. The king made him swear upon the holy reliques that he would fulfil his commands. Then Mark directed him to go to Ireland and obtain for him the fair Isoude to be queen of Cornwall.

Tristram believed it was certain death for him to return to Ireland; and how could he act as ambassador for his uncle in such a cause? Yet, bound by his oath, he hesitated not for an instant. He only took the precaution to change his armor. He embarked for Ireland; but a tempest drove him to the coast of England, near Camelot, where King Arthur was holding his court, attended by the knights of the Round Table, and many others, the most illustrious in the world.

Tristram kept himself unknown. He took part in many

* "Good faith was the very corner-stone of chivalry. Whenever a knight's word was pledged, (it mattered not how rashly,) it was to be redeemed at any price. Hence the sacred obligation of the *boon granted* by a knight to his suppliant. Instances without number occur in romance, in which a knight, by rashly granting an indefinite boon, was obliged to do or suffer something extremely to his prejudice. But it is not in romance alone that we find such singular instances of adherence to an indefinite promise. The history of the times presents authentic transactions equally embarrassing and absurd."—SCOTT, *note to Sir Tristram.*

justs; he fought many combats, in which he covered himself with glory. One day he saw among those recently arrived the King of Ireland, father of the fair Isoude. This prince, accused of treason against his liege sovereign, Arthur, came to Camelot to free himself from the charge. Blaanor, one of the most redoubtable warriors of the Round Table, was his accuser, and Argius, the king, had neither youthful vigor nor strength to encounter him. He must therefore seek a champion to sustain his innocence. But the knights of the Round Table were not at liberty to fight against one another, unless in a quarrel of their own. Argius heard of the great renown of the unknown knight; he also was witness of his exploits. He sought him, and conjured him to adopt his defence, and on his oath declared that he was innocent of the crime of which he was accused. Tristram readily consented and made himself known to the king, who on his part promised to reward his exertions, if successful, with whatever gift he might ask.

Tristram fought with Blaanor, and overthrew him, and held his life in his power. The fallen warrior called on him to use his right of conquest and strike the fatal blow. "God forbid," said Tristram, "that I should take the life of so brave a knight!" He raised him up and restored him to his friends. The judges of the field decided that the King of Ireland was acquitted of the charge against him, and they led Tristram in triumph to his tent. King Argius, full of gratitude, conjured Tristram to accompany him to his kingdom. They departed together and arrived in Ireland; and the queen, forgetting her resentment for her brother's death, exhibited to the preserver of her husband's life nothing but gratitude and good will.

How happy a moment for Isoude, who knew that her father had promised his deliverer whatever boon he might ask! But the unhappy Tristram gazed on her with despair at the thought of the cruel oath which bound him. His magnanimous soul subdued the force of his love. He revealed the oath which he had taken and, with trembling voice, demanded the fair Isoude for his uncle.

Argius consented, and soon all was prepared for the departure of Isoude. Brengwain, her favorite maid of honor, was to accompany her. On the day of departure, the queen took aside this devoted attendant, and told her that she had observed that her daughter and Tristram were attached to one another, and that, to avert the bad effects of this inclination, she had procured from a powerful fairy a potent philter (love-draught), which she directed Brengwain to administer to Isoude and to King Mark on the evening of their marriage.

Isoude and Tristram embarked together. A favorable wind filled the sails and promised them a fortunate voyage. The lovers gazed upon one another and could not repress their sighs. Love seemed to light up all his fires on their lips, as in their hearts. The day was warm; they suffered from thirst. Isoude first complained. Tristram descried the bottle containing the love-draught, which Brengwain had been so imprudent as to leave in sight. He took it, gave some of it to the charming Isoude, and drank the remainder himself. The dog Houdain licked the cup. The ship arrived in Cornwall, and Isoude was married to King Mark. The old monarch was delighted with his bride, and his gratitude to Tristram was unbounded. He loaded him with honors and made him chamberlain of his palace, thus giving him access to the queen at all times.

In the midst of the festivities of the court which followed the royal marriage, an unknown minstrel one day presented himself, bearing a harp of peculiar construction. He excited the curiosity of King Mark by refusing to play upon it till he should grant him a boon. The king having promised to grant his request, the minstrel, who was none other than the Saracen knight, Sir Palamedes, the lover of the fair Isoude, sung to the harp a lay, in which he demanded Isoude as the promised gift. King Mark could not, by the laws of knighthood, withhold the boon. The lady was mounted on her horse and led away by her triumphant lover. Tristram, it is needless to say, was absent at the time and did not return until their departure. When he heard what had taken place, he seized his rote and hastened to the shore, where Isoude and her new master had already embarked. Tristram played upon his rote, and the sound reached the ears of Isoude, who became so deeply affected that Sir Palamedes was induced to return with her to land, that they might see the unknown musician. Tristram watched his opportunity, seized the lady's horse by the bridle, and plunged with her into the forest, tauntingly informing his rival that "what he had got by the harp, he had lost by the rote." Palamedes pursued, and a combat was about to commence, the result of which must have been fatal to one or other of these gallant knights; but Isoude stepped between them and, addressing Palamedes, said, "You tell me that you love me; you will not then deny me the request I am about to make?" "Lady," he replied, "I will perform your bidding." "Leave, then," said she, "this contest, and repair to King Arthur's court, and salute Queen Guenever from me; tell her that there are in the world but two ladies, herself and I, and two lovers, hers and mine; and come thou not in future in any place where I am." Palamedes burst into tears. "Ah, lady," said he, "I will obey you; but I beseech you that you will not for ever steel your heart against me." "Palamedes," she replied, "may I never taste of joy again if I ever quit my first love." Palamedes then went his way. The lovers remained a week in concealment, after which Tristram restored Isoude to her husband, advising him in future to reward minstrels in some other way.

The king showed much gratitude to Tristram, but in the bottom of his heart he cherished bitter jealousy of him. One day Tristram and Isoude were alone together in her private chamber. A base and cowardly knight of the court, named Andret, spied them through a keyhole. They sat at a table of chess, but were not attending to the game. Andret brought the king, having first raised his suspicions, and placed him so as to watch their motions. The king saw enough to confirm his suspicions, and he burst into the apartment with his sword drawn, and had nearly slain Tristram before he was put on his guard. But Tristram avoided the blow, drew his sword, and drove before him the cowardly monarch, chasing him through all the apartments of the palace, giving him frequent blows with the flat of his sword, while he cried in vain to his knights to save him. They were not inclined, or did not dare, to interpose in his behalf.

A proof of the great popularity of the tale of Sir Tristram is the fact that the Italian poets, Boiardo and Ariosto, have founded upon it the idea of the two enchanted fountains, which produced the opposite effects of love and hatred. Boiardo thus describes the fountain of hatred:

> Fair was that fountain, sculptured all of gold,
> With alabaster sculptured, rich and rare;
> And in its basin clear thou might'st behold
> The flowery marge reflected fresh and fair.
> Sage Merlin framed the font,—so legends bear,—
> When on fair Isoude doated Tritram brave,
> That the good errant knight, arriving there,
> Might quaff oblivion in the enchanted wave,
> And leave his luckless love, and 'scape his timeless grave.

> But ne'er the warrior's evil fate allowed
> His steps that fountain's charmed verge to gain,
> Though restless, roving on adventure proud,
> He traversed oft the land and oft the main.

CHAPTER XIII

TRISTRAM AND ISOUDE, CONTINUED

After this affair, Tristram was banished from the kingdom, and Isoude shut up in a tower, which stood on the bank of a river. Tristram could not resolve to depart without some further communication with his beloved, so he concealed himself in the forest till at last he contrived to attract her attention by means of twigs, which he curiously peeled and sent down the stream under her window. By this means many secret interviews were obtained. Tristram dwelt in the forest, sustaining himself by game, which the dog Houdain ran down for him; for this

faithful animal was unequalled in the chase, and knew so
well his master's wish for concealment that, in the pursuit
of his game, he never barked. At length, Tristram departed, but left Houdain with Isoude, as a remembrancer
of him.

Sir Tristram wandered through various countries,
achieving the most perilous enterprises and covering
himself with glory, yet unhappy at the separation from
his beloved Isoude. At length, King Mark's territory was
invaded by a neighboring chieftain, and he was forced to
summon his nephew to his aid. Tristram obeyed the call,
put himself at the head of his uncle's vassals, and drove
the enemy out of the country. Mark was full of gratitude,
and Tristram, restored to favor and to the society of his
beloved Isoude, seemed at the summit of happiness. But
a sad reverse was at hand.

Tristram had brought with him a friend named Pheredin, son of the King of Brittany. This young knight saw
Queen Isoude and could not resist her charms. Knowing
the love of his friend for the queen, and that that love
was returned, Pheredin concealed his own, until his
health failed, and he feared he was drawing near his end.
He then wrote to the beautiful queen that he was dying
for love of her.

The gentle Isoude, in a moment of pity for the friend
of Tristram, returned him an answer so kind and com-
passionate that it restored him to life. A few days afterwards Tristram found this letter. The most terrible jealousy took possession of his soul; he would have slain
Pheredin, who with difficulty made his escape. Then
Tristram mounted his horse and rode to the forest, where
for ten days he took no rest nor food. At length, he was
found by a damsel lying almost dead by the brink of a
fountain. She recognized him and tried in vain to rouse
his attention. At last, recollecting his love for music, she
went and got her harp and played thereon. Tristram was
roused from his reverie; tears flowed; he breathed more
freely; he took the harp from the maiden and sung this
lay, with a voice broken with sobs.

> Sweet I sang in former days,
> Kind love perfected my lays:

Now my art alone displays
The woe that on my being preys.

Charming love, delicious power,
Worshipped from my earliest hour,
Thou who life on all dost shower,
Love! my life thou dost devour.

In death's hour I beg of thee,
Isoude, dearest enemy,
Thou who erst couldst kinder be,
When I'm gone, forget not me.

On my gravestone passers-by
Oft will read, as low I lie,
"Never wight in love could vie
With Tristram, yet she let him die."

Tristram, having finished his lay, wrote it off and gave
it to the damsel, conjuring her to present it to the queen.

Meanwhile, Queen Isoude was inconsolable at the absence of Tristram. She discovered that it was caused by
the fatal letter which she had written to Pheredin. Innocent, but in despair at the sad effects of her letter, she
wrote another to Pheredin, charging him never to see her
again. The unhappy lover obeyed this cruel decree. He
plunged into the forest and died of grief and love in a
hermit's cell.

Isoude passed her days in lamenting the absence and
unknown fate of Tristram. One day her jealous husband, having entered her chamber unperceived, over-
heard her singing the following lay:

My voice to piteous wail is bent,
My harp to notes of languishment;
Ah, love! delightsome days be meant
For happier wights, with hearts content.

Ah, Tristram! far away from me,
Art thou from restless anguish free?
Ah! couldst thou so one moment be,
From her who so much loveth thee?

The king, hearing these words, burst forth in a rage;

but Isoude was too wretched to fear his violence. "You have heard me," she said; "I confess it all. I love Tristram, and always shall love him. Without doubt he is dead, and died for me. I no longer wish to live. The blow that shall finish my misery will be most welcome."

The king was moved at the distress of the fair Isoude, and perhaps the idea of Tristram's death tended to allay his wrath. He left the queen in charge of her women, commanding them to take especial care lest her despair should lead her to do harm to herself.

Tristram, meanwhile, distracted as he was, rendered a most important service to the shepherds by slaying a gigantic robber named Taullas, who was in the habit of plundering their flocks and rifling their cottages. The shepherds, in their gratitude to Tristram, bore him in triumph to King Mark to have him bestow on him a suitable reward. No wonder Mark failed to recognize in the half-clad, wild man before him his nephew Tristram; but grateful for the service the unknown had rendered, he ordered him to be well taken care of, and gave him in charge to the queen and her women. Under such care Tristram rapidly recovered his serenity and his health, so that the romancer tells us he became handsomer than ever. King Mark's jealousy revived with Tristram's health and good looks, and, in spite of his debt of gratitude so lately increased, he again banished him from the court.

Sir Tristram left Cornwall and proceeded into the land of Loegria (England) in quest of adventures. One day, he entered a wide forest. The sound of a little bell showed him that some inhabitant was near. He followed the sound and found a hermit, who informed him that he was in the forest of Arnantes, belonging to the fairy Viviane, the Lady of the Lake, who, smitten with love for King Arthur, had found means to entice him to this forest, where by enchantments she held him a prisoner, having deprived him of all memory of who and what he was. The hermit informed him that all the knights of the Round Table were out in search of the king, and that he (Tristram) was now in the scene of the most grand and important adventures.

This was enough to animate Tristram in the search. He had not wandered far before he encountered a knight of Arthur's court, who proved to be Sir Kay the seneschal, who demanded of him whence he came. Tristram answering, "From Cornwall," Sir Kay did not let slip the opportunity of a joke at the expense of the Cornish knight. Tristram chose to leave him in his error and even confirmed him in it; for, meeting some other knights, Tristram declined to just with them. They spent the night together at an abbey, where Tristram submitted patiently to all their jokes. The seneschal gave the word to his companions that they should set out early next day, and intercept the Cornish knight on his way, and enjoy the amusement of seeing his fright when they should insist on running a tilt with him. Tristram next morning found himself alone; he put on his armor, and set out to continue his quest. He soon saw before him the seneschal and the three knights, who barred the way and insisted on a just. Tristram excused himself a long time; at last, he reluctantly took his stand. He encountered them, one after the other, and overthrew them all four, man and horse, and then rode off, bidding them not to forget their friend, the knight of Cornwall.

Tristram had not ridden far when he met a damsel, who cried out, "Ah, my lord! hasten forward and prevent a horrid treason!" Tristram flew to her assistance and soon reached a spot where he beheld a knight, whom three others had borne to the ground, and were unlacing his helmet in order to cut off his head.

Tristram flew to the rescue and slew with one stroke of his lance one of the assailants. The knight, recovering his feet, sacrificed another to his vengeance, and the third made his escape. The rescued knight then raised the visor of his helmet, and a long white beard fell down upon his breast. The majesty and venerable air of this knight made Tristram suspect that it was none other than Arthur himself, and the prince confirmed his conjecture. Tristram would have knelt before him, but Arthur received him in his arms and inquired his name and country; but Tristram declined to disclose them, on the plea that he was now on a quest requiring secrecy. At this moment, the damsel who had brought Tristram to the rescue darted forward, and, seizing the king's hand, drew from his finger a ring, the gift of the fairy, and by that act dissolved the enchantment. Arthur, having recovered his reason and his memory, offered to Tristram to attach him to his court and to confer honors and dignities upon him; but Tristram declined all and only consented to accompany him till he should see him safe in the hands of his knights. Soon after, Hector de Marys rode up and saluted the king, who on his part introduced him to Tristram as one of the bravest of his knights. Tristram took leave of the king and his faithful follower and continued his quest.

We cannot follow Tristram through all the adventures which filled this epoch of his history. Suffice it to say, he fulfilled on all occasions the duty of a true knight, rescuing the oppressed, redressing wrongs, abolishing evil customs, and suppressing injustice, thus by constant action endeavoring to lighten the pains of absence from her he loved. In the meantime, Isoude, separated from her dear Tristram, passed her days in languor and regret. At length, she could no longer resist the desire to hear some news of her lover. She wrote a letter and sent it by one of her damsels, niece of her faithful Brengwain. One day, Tristram, weary with his exertions, had dismounted and laid himself down by the side of a fountain and fallen asleep. The damsel of Queen Isoude arrived at the same fountain, and recognized Passebreul, the horse of Tristram, and presently perceived his master, asleep. He was thin and pale, showing evident marks of the pain he suffered in separation from his beloved. She awaked him and gave him the letter which she bore, and Tristram enjoyed the pleasure, so sweet to a lover, of hearing from, and talking about, the object of his affections. He prayed the damsel to postpone her return till after the magnificent tournament which Arthur had proclaimed should have taken place, and conducted her to the castle of Persides, a brave and loyal knight, who received her with great consideration.

Tristram conducted the damsel of Queen Isoude to the tournament, and had her placed in the balcony among the ladies of the queen. He then joined the tourney. Nothing could exceed his strength and valor. Launcelot admired him and, by a secret presentiment, declined to dispute the honor of the day with a knight so gallant and so skilful. Arthur descended from the balcony to greet the conqueror; but the modest and devoted Tristram, content with having borne off the prize in the sight of the messenger of Isoude, made his escape with her and disappeared.

The next day, the tourney recommenced. Tristram assumed different armor, that he might not be known; but he was soon detected by the terrible blows that he gave. Arthur and Guenever had no doubt that it was the same knight who had borne off the prize of the day before. Arthur's gallant spirit was roused. After Launcelot of the Lake and Sir Gawain, he was accounted the best knight of the Round Table. He went privately and armed himself, and came into the tourney in undistinguished armor. He ran a just with Tristram, whom he shook in his seat; but Tristram, who did not know him, threw him out of the saddle. Arthur recovered himself, and, content with having made proof of the stranger knight, bade Launcelot finish the adventure and vindicate the honor of the Round Table. Sir Launcelot, at the bidding of the monarch, assailed Tristram, whose lance was already broken in former encounters. But the law of this sort of combat was that the knight, after having broken his lance, must fight with his sword, and must not refuse to meet with his shield the lance of his antagonist. Tristram met Launcelot's charge upon his shield, which that terrible lance could not fail to pierce. It inflicted a wound upon Tristram's side, and, breaking, left the iron in the wound. But Tristram also with his sword smote so vigorously on Launcelot's casque that he cleft it and wounded his head. The wound was not deep, but the blood flowed into his eyes and blinded him for a moment, and Tristram, who thought himself mortally wounded, retired from the field. Launcelot declared to the king that he had never received such a blow in his life before.

Tristram hastened to Gouvernail, his squire, who drew forth the iron, bound up the wound, and gave him immediate ease. Tristram, after the tournament, kept retired in his tent, but Arthur, with the consent of all the knights of the Round Table, decreed him the honors of the second day. But it was no longer a secret that the victor of the two days was the same individual, and

Gouvernail, being questioned, confirmed the suspicions of Launcelot and Arthur that it was no other than Sir Tristram of Leonois, the nephew of the King of Cornwall.

King Arthur, who desired to reward his distinguished valor and knew that his Uncle Mark had ungratefully banished him, would have eagerly availed himself of the opportunity to attach Tristram to his court—all the knights of the Round Table declaring with acclamation that it would be impossible to find a more worthy companion. But Tristram had already departed in search of adventures, and the damsel of Queen Isoude returned to her mistress.

CHAPTER XIV

SIR TRISTRAM'S BATTLE WITH SIR LAUNCELOT

Sir Tristram rode through a forest and saw ten men fighting, and one man did battle against nine. So he rode to the knights and cried to them, bidding them cease their battle, for they did themselves great shame, so many knights to fight against one. Then answered the master of the knights (his name was Sir Breuse sans Pitie, who was at that time the most villanous knight living): "Sir Knight, what have ye to do to meddle with us? If ye be wise, depart on your way as you came, for this knight shall not escape us." "That were pity," said Sir Tristram, "that so good a knight should be slain so cowardly; therefore I warn you I will succor him with all my puissance."

Then Sir Tristram alighted off his horse, because they were on foot, that they should not slay his horse. And he smote on the right hand and on the left so vigorously that well-nigh at every stroke he struck down a knight. At last they fled, with Breuse sans Pitie, into the tower, and shut Sir Tristram without the gate. Then Sir Tristram returned back to the rescued knight and found him sitting under a tree, sore wounded. "Fair knight," said he, "how is it with you?" "Sir Knight," said Sir Palamedes, for he it was, "I thank you of your great goodness, for ye have rescued me from death." "What is your name?" said Sir Tristram. He said, "My name is Sir Palamedes." "Say ye so?" said Sir Tristram; "now know that thou art the man in the world that I most hate; therefore make thee ready, for I will do battle with thee." "What is your name?" said Sir Palamedes. "My name is Sir Tristram, your mortal enemy." "It may be so," said Sir Palamedes; "but you have done overmuch for me this day, that I should fight with you. Moreover, it will be no honor for you to have to do with me, for you are fresh and I am wounded. Therefore, if you will needs have to do with me, assign me a day, and I shall meet you without fail." "You say well," said Sir Tristram; "now I assign you to meet me in the meadow by the river of Camelot, where Merlin set the monument." So they were agreed. Then they departed and took their ways diverse. Sir Tristram passed through a great forest into a plain, till he came to a priory, and there he reposed him with a good man six days.

Then departed Sir Tristram and rode straight into Camelot to the monument of Merlin, and there he looked about him for Sir Palamedes. And he perceived a seemly knight, who came riding against him all in white, with a covered shield. When he came nigh, Sir Tristram said aloud, "Welcome, Sir Knight, and well and truly have you kept your promise." Then they made ready their shields and spears, and came together with all the might of their horses, so fiercely that both the horses and the knights fell to the earth. And as soon as they might, they quitted their horses and struck together with bright swords as men of might, and each wounded the other wonderfully sore, so that the blood ran out upon the grass. Thus they fought for the space of four hours, and never one would speak to the other one word. Then at last spake the white knight and said, "Sir, thou fightest wonderful well, as ever I saw knight; therefore, if it please you, tell me your name." "Why dost thou ask my name?" said Sir Tristram; "art thou not Sir Palamedes?" "No, fair knight," said he, "I am Sir Launcelot of the Lake."

"Alas!" said Sir Tristram, "what have I done? For you are the man of the world that I love best." "Fair knight," said Sir Launcelot, "tell me your name." "Truly," said he, "my name is Sir Tristram de Lionèsse." "Alas! alas!" said Sir Launcelot, "what adventure has befallen me!" And therewith Sir Launcelot kneeled down and yielded him up his sword; and Sir Tristram kneeled down and yielded him up his sword; and so either gave other the degree. And then they both went to the stone, and sat them down upon it, and took off their helms, and each kissed the other a hundred times. And then anon they rode towards Camelot, and on the way they met with Sir Gawain and Sir Gaheris, that had made promise to Arthur never to come again to the court till they had brought Sir Tristram with them.

"Return again," said Sir Launcelot, "for your quest is done; for I have met with Sir Tristram. Lo, here he is in his own person." Then was Sir Gawain glad and said to Sir Tristram, "Ye are welcome." With this came King Arthur, and when he wist there was Sir Tristram, he ran unto him, and took him by the hand, and said, "Sir Tristram, ye are as welcome as any knight that ever came to this court." Then Sir Tristram told the king how he came thither for to have had to do with Sir Palamedes, and how he had rescued him from Sir Breuse sans Pitie and the nine knights. Then King Arthur took Sir Tristram by the hand and went to the Table Round, and Queen Guenever came, and many ladies with her, and all the ladies said with one voice, "Welcome, Sir Tristram." "Welcome," said the knights. "Welcome," said Arthur, "for one of the best of knights, and the gentlest of the world, and the man of most worship; for of all manner of hunting, thou bearest the prize; and of all measures of blowing, thou art the beginning; and of all the terms of hunting and hawking, ye are the inventor; and of all instruments of music, ye are the best skilled; therefore, gentle knight," said Arthur, "ye are welcome to this court." And then King Arthur made Sir Tristram knight of the Table Round with great nobley and feasting as can be thought.

SIR TRISTRAM AS A SPORTSMAN

Tristram is often alluded to by the romancers as the great authority and model in all matters relating to the chase. In the Faery Queene, Tristram, in answer to the inquiries of Sir Calidore, informs him of his name and parentage and concludes:

> All which my days I have not lewdly spent,
> Nor spilt the blossom of my tender years
> In idlesse; but, as was convenient,
> Have trained been with many noble feres
> In gentle thewes, and such like seemly leers;*

> 'Mongst which my most delight hath always been
> To hunt the salvage chace, amongst my peers,·
> Of all that rangeth in the forest green,
> Of which none is to me unknown that yet was seen.

> Ne is there hawk which mantleth on her perch,
> Whether high towering or accosting low,
> But I the measure of her flight do search,
> And all her prey, and all her diet know.
> Such be our joys, which in these forests grow.

CHAPTER XV

THE ROUND TABLE

The famous enchanter, Merlin, had exerted all his skill in fabricating the Round Table. Of the seats which surrounded it, he had constructed thirteen, in memory of the thirteen Apostles. Twelve of these seats only could be occupied, and they only by knights of the highest fame; the thirteenth represented the seat of the traitor Judas. It remained always empty. It was called the *perilous seat*, ever since a rash and haughty Saracen knight

---

* *Feres*, companions; *thewes*, labors; *leers*, learning.

had dared to place himself in it, when the earth opened and swallowed him up.

A magic power wrote upon each seat the name of the knight who was entitled to sit in it. No one could succeed to a vacant seat unless he surpassed in valor and glorious deeds the knight who had occupied it before him; without this qualification, he would be violently repelled by a hidden force. Thus proof was made of all those who presented themselves to replace any companions of the order who had fallen.

One of the principal seats, that of Moraunt of Ireland, had been vacant ten years, and his name still remained over it ever since the time when that distinguished champion fell beneath the sword of Sir Tristram. Arthur now took Tristram by the hand and led him to that seat. Immediately, the most melodious sounds were heard, and exquisite perfumes filled the place; the name of Moraunt disappeared, and that of Tristram blazed forth in light! The rare modesty of Tristram had now to be subjected to a severe task; for the clerks charged with the duty of preserving the annals of the Round Table attended, and he was required by the law of his order to declare what feats of arms he had accomplished to entitle him to take that seat. This ceremony being ended, Tristram received the congratulations of all his companions. Sir Launcelot and Guenever took the occasion to speak to him of the fair Isoude and to express their wish that some happy chance might bring her to the kingdom of Loegria.

While Tristram was thus honored and caressed at the court of King Arthur, the most gloomy and malignant jealousy harassed the soul of Mark. He could not look upon Isoude without remembering that she loved Tristram, and the good fortune of his nephew goaded him to thoughts of vengeance. He at last resolved to go disguised into the kingdom of Loegria, attack Tristram by stealth, and put him to death. He took with him two knights, brought up in his court, who he thought were devoted to him; and, not willing to leave Isoude behind, named two of her maidens to attend her, together with her faithful Brengwain, and made them accompany him.

Having arrived in the neighborhood of Camelot, Mark imparted his plan to his two knights, but they rejected it with horror; nay, more, they declared that they would no longer remain in his service, and left him, giving him reason to suppose that they should repair to the court to accuse him before Arthur. It was necessary for Mark to meet and rebut their accusation; so, leaving Isoude in an abbey, he pursued his way alone to Camelot.

Mark had not ridden far when he encountered a party of knights of Arthur's court, and would have avoided them, for he knew their habit of challenging to a just every stranger knight whom they met. But it was too late. They had seen his armor, and recognized him as a Cornish knight, and at once resolved to have some sport with him. It happened they had with them Daguenet, King Arthur's fool, who, though deformed and weak of body, was not wanting in courage. The knights, as Mark approached, laid their plan that Daguenet should personate Sir Launcelot of the Lake and challenge the Cornish knight. They equipped him in armor belonging to one of their number who was ill, and sent him forward to the cross-road to defy the strange knight. Mark, who saw that his antagonist was by no means formidable in appearance, was not disinclined to the combat; but when the dwarf rode towards him, calling out that he was Sir Launcelot of the Lake, his fears prevailed, he put spurs to his horse, and rode away at full speed, pursued by the shouts and laughter of the party.

Meanwhile, Isoude, remaining at the abbey with her faithful Brengwain, found her only amusement in walking occasionally in a forest adjoining the abbey. There, on the brink of a fountain girdled with trees, she thought of her love, and sometimes joined her voice and her harp in lays reviving the memory of its pains or pleasures. One day, the caitiff knight, Breuse the Pitiless, heard her voice, concealed himself, and drew near. She sang:

> Sweet silence, shadowy bower, and verdant lair,
>   Ye court my troubled spirit to repose,
> Whilst I, such dear remembrance rises there,
>   Awaken every echo with my woes.
>
> Within these woods, by nature's hand arrayed,
>   A fountain springs, and feeds a thousand flowers;

Ah! how my groans do all its murmurs aid!
How my sad eyes do swell it with their showers!

What doth my knight the while? to him is given
A double meed; in love and arms' emprise,
Him the Round Table elevates to heaven!
Tristram! ah me! he hears not Isoude's cries.

Breuse the Pitiless, who like most other caitiffs had felt the weight of Tristram's arm, and hated him accordingly, at hearing his name breathed forth by the beautiful songstress, impelled by a double impulse, rushed forth from his concealment and laid hands on his victim. Isoude fainted, and Brengwain filled the air with her shrieks. Breuse carried Isoude to the place where he had left his horse; but the animal had got away from his bridle, and was at some distance. He was obliged to lay down his fair burden and go in pursuit of his horse. Just then a knight came up, drawn by the cries of Brengwain, and demanded the cause of her distress. She could not speak, but pointed to her mistress lying insensible on the ground.

Breuse had by this time returned, and the cries of Brengwain, renewed at seeing him, sufficiently showed the stranger the cause of the distress. Tristram spurred his horse towards Breuse, who, not unprepared, ran to the encounter. Breuse was unhorsed, and lay motionless, pretending to be dead; but when the stranger knight left him to attend to the distressed damsels, he mounted his horse, and made his escape.

The knight now approached Isoude, gently raised her head, drew aside the golden hair which covered her countenance, gazed thereon for an instant, uttered a cry, and fell back insensible. Brengwain came; her cares soon restored her mistress to life, and then they turned their attention to the fallen warrior. They raised his visor and discovered the countenance of Sir Tristram. Isoude threw herself on the body of her lover and bedewed his face with her tears. Their warmth revived the knight, and Tristram, on awaking, found himself in the arms of his dear Isoude.

It was the law of the Round Table that each knight, after his admission, should pass the next ten days in

quest of adventures, during which time his companions
might meet him in disguised armor and try their strength
with him. Tristram had now been out seven days, and
in that time had encountered many of the best knights
of the Round Table, and acquitted himself with honor.
During the remaining three days, Isoude remained at
the abbey, under his protection, and then set out with
her maidens, escorted by Sir Tristram, to rejoin King
Mark at the court of Camelot.

This happy journey was one of the brightest epochs
in the lives of Tristram and Isoude. He celebrated it
by a lay upon the harp in a peculiar measure, to which
the French give the name of *Triolet*.

> With fair Isoude, and with love,
> Ah! how sweet the life I lead!
> How blest for ever thus to rove,
> With fair Isoude, and with love!
> As she wills, I live and move,
> And cloudless days to days succeed:
> With fair Isoude, and with love,
> Ah! how sweet the life I lead!

> Journeying on from break of day,
> Feel you not fatigued, my fair?
> Yon green turf invites to play;
> Journeying on from day to day,
> Ah! let us to that shade away,
> Were it but to slumber there!
> Journeying on from break of day,
> Feel you not fatigued, my fair?

They arrived at Camelot, where Sir Launcelot received them most cordially. Isoude was introduced to
King Arthur and Queen Guenever, who welcomed her
as a sister. As King Mark was held in arrest under the
accusation of the two Cornish knights, Queen Isoude
could not rejoin her husband, and Sir Launcelot placed
his castle of La Joyeuse Garde at the disposal of his
friends, who there took up their abode.

King Mark, who found himself obliged to confess the
truth of the charge against him, or to clear himself by
combat with his accusers, preferred the former, and King
Arthur, as his crime had not been perpetrated, remitted

the penalty, only enjoining upon him, under pain of his signal displeasure, to lay aside all thoughts of vengeance against his nephew. In the presence of the king and his court, all parties were formally reconciled; Mark and his queen departed for their home, and Tristram remained at Arthur's court.

CHAPTER XVI

SIR PALAMEDES

While Sir Tristram and the fair Isoude abode yet at La Joyeuse Garde, Sir Tristram rode forth one day, without armor, having no weapon but his spear and his sword. And as he rode, he came to a place where he saw two knights in battle, and one of them had gotten the better, and the other lay overthrown. The knight who had the better was Sir Palamedes. When Sir Palamedes knew Sir Tristram, he cried out, "Sir Tristram, now we be met, and ere we depart we will redress our old wrongs." "As for that," said Sir Tristram, "there never yet was Christian man that might make his boast that I ever fled from him, and thou that art a Saracen shalt never say that of me." And therewith Sir Tristram made his horse to run, and with all his might came straight upon Sir Palamedes, and broke his spear upon him. Then he drew his sword and struck at Sir Palamedes six great strokes, upon his helm. Sir Palamedes saw that Sir Tristram had not his armor on, and he marvelled at his rashness and his great folly, and said to himself, "If I meet and slay him, I am shamed wheresoever I go." Then Sir Tristram cried out and said, "Thou coward knight, why wilt thou not do battle with me? For have thou no doubt I shall endure all thy malice." "Ah, Sir Tristram!" said Sir Palamedes, "thou knowest I may not fight with thee for shame; for thou art here naked, and I am armed; now I require that thou answer me a question that I shall ask you." "Tell me what it is," said

Sir Tristram. "I put the case," said Sir Palamedes, "that you were well armed, and I naked as ye be; what would you do to me now, by your true knighthood?" "Ah!" said Sir Tristram, "now I understand thee well, Sir Palamedes; and, as God me bless, what I shall say shall not be said for fear that I have of thee. But if it were so, thou shouldest depart from me, for I would not have to do with thee." "No more will I with thee," said Sir Palamedes, "and therefore ride forth on thy way." "As for that, I may choose," said Sir Tristram, "either to ride or to abide. But, Sir Palamedes, I marvel at one thing—that thou art so good a knight, yet that thou wilt not be christened." "As for that," said Sir Palamedes, "I may not yet be christened, for a vow which I made many years ago; yet in my heart I believe in our Saviour and his mild mother, Mary; but I have yet one battle to do, and when that is done, I will be christened, with a good will." "By my head," said Sir Tristram, "as for that one battle, thou shalt seek it no longer; for yonder is a knight, whom you have smitten down. Now help me to be clothed in his armor, and I will soon fulfil thy vow." "As ye will," said Sir Palamedes, "so shall it be." So they rode both unto that knight that sat on a bank; and Sir Tristram saluted him, and he full weakly saluted him again. "Sir," said Sir Tristram, "I pray you to lend me your whole armor, for I am unarmed and I must do battle with this knight." "Sir," said the hurt knight, "you shall have it, with a right good will." Then Sir Tristram unarmed Sir Galleron, for that was the name of the hurt knight, and he as well as he could helped to arm Sir Tristram. Then Sir Tristram mounted upon his own horse, and in his hand he took Sir Galleron's spear. Thereupon Sir Palamedes was ready, and so they came hurling together, and each smote the other in the midst of their shields. Sir Palamedes' spear broke, and Sir Tristram smote down the horse. Then Sir Palamedes leapt from his horse and drew out his sword. That saw Sir Tristram, and therewith he alighted and tied his horse to a tree. Then they came together as two wild beasts, lashing the one on the other, and so fought more than two hours; and often Sir Tristram smote such strokes at Sir Palamedes that he made him to kneel, and Sir Palamedes broke away Sir Tristram's shield and wounded him. Then Sir Tristram was wroth out of measure, and he rushed to Sir Palamedes and wounded him, passing sore through the shoulder, and by fortune smote Sir Palamedes' sword out of his hand. And if Sir Palamedes had stooped for his sword, Sir Tristram had slain him. Then Sir Palamedes stood and beheld his sword with a full sorrowful heart. "Now," said Sir Tristram, "I have thee at a vantage, as thou hadst me to-day; but it shall never be said, in court, or among good knights, that Sir Tristram did slay any knight that was weaponless; therefore, take thou thy sword, and let us fight this battle to the end." Then spoke Sir Palamedes to Sir Tristram: "I have no wish to fight this battle any more. The offence that I have done unto you is not so great but that, if it please you, we may be friends. All that I have offended is for the love of the queen, La Belle Isoude, and I dare maintain that she is peerless among ladies; and for that offence ye have given me many grievous and sad strokes, and some I have given you again. Wherefore I require you, my lord Sir Tristram, forgive me all that I have offended you, and this day have me unto the next church; and first I will be clean confessed, and after that see you that I be truly baptized, and then we will ride together unto the court of my lord, King Arthur, so that we may be there at the feast of Pentecost." "Now take your horse," said Sir Tristram, "and as you have said, so shall it be done." So they took their horses, and Sir Galleron rode with them. When they came to the church of Carlisle, the bishop commanded to fill a great vessel with water; and when he had hallowed it, he then confessed Sir Palamedes clean, and christened him, and Sir Tristram and Sir Galleron were his godfathers. Then soon after they departed and rode towards Camelot, where the noble King Arthur and Queen Guenever were keeping a court royal. And the king and all the court were glad that Sir Palamedes was christened. Then Sir Tristram returned again to La Joyeuse Garde, and Sir Palamedes went his way.

Not long after these events, Sir Gawain returned from Brittany and related to King Arthur the adventure which befell him in the forest of Brécéliande, how Merlin had there spoken to him and enjoined him to charge the king to go without delay upon the quest of the Holy Greal. While King Arthur deliberated, Tristram determined to enter upon the quest, and the more readily, as it was well known to him that this holy adventure would, if achieved, procure him the pardon of all his sins. He immediately departed for the kingdom of Brittany, hoping there to obtain from Merlin counsel as to the proper course to pursue to insure success.

CHAPTER XVII

SIR TRISTRAM

On arriving in Brittany, Tristram found King Hoel engaged in a war with a rebellious vassal, and hard pressed by his enemy. His best knights had fallen in a late battle, and he knew not where to turn for assistance. Tristram volunteered his aid. It was accepted; and the army of Hoel, led by Tristram and inspired by his example, gained a complete victory. The king, penetrated by the most lively sentiments of gratitude, and having informed himself of Tristram's birth, offered him his daughter in marriage. The princess was beautiful and accomplished, and bore the same name with the Queen of Cornwall; but this one is designated by the romancers as Isoude of the White Hands, to distinguish her from Isoude the Fair.

How can we describe the conflict that agitated the heart of Tristram? He adored the first Isoude, but his love for her was hopeless and not unaccompanied by remorse. Moreover, the sacred quest on which he had now entered demanded of him perfect purity of life. It seemed as if a happy destiny had provided for him, in the charming Princess Isoude of the White Hands, the best security for all his good resolutions. This last reflection determined him. They were married, and passed some months in tranquil happiness at the court of King Hoel. The pleasure which Tristram felt in his wife's society increased day by day. An inward grace seemed to stir within him from the moment when he took the oath to go on the quest of the Holy Greal; it seemed even to triumph over the power of the magic love-potion.

The war, which had been quelled for a time, now burst out anew. Tristram, as usual, was foremost in every danger. The enemy was worsted in successive conflicts, and at last shut himself up in his principal city. Tristram led on the attack of the city. As he mounted a ladder to scale the walls, he was struck on the head by a fragment of rock, which the besieged threw down upon him. It bore him to the ground, where he lay insensible.

As soon as he recovered consciousness, he demanded to be carried to his wife. The princess, skilled in the art of surgery, would not suffer any one but herself to touch her beloved husband. Her fair hands bound up his wounds; Tristram kissed them with gratitude, which began to grow into love. At first, the devoted cares of Isoude seemed to meet with great success; but after a while these flattering appearances vanished, and, in spite of all her care, the malady grew more serious day by day.

In this perplexity, an old squire of Tristram's reminded his master that the Princess of Ireland, afterwards Queen of Cornwall, had once cured him under circumstances quite as discouraging. He called Isoude of the White Hands to him, told her of his former cure, added that he believed that the Queen Isoude could heal him, and that he felt sure that she would come to his relief, if sent for.

Isoude of the White Hands consented that Gesnes, a trusty man and skilful navigator, should be sent to Cornwall. Tristram called him, and, giving him a ring, "Take this," he said, "to the Queen of Cornwall. Tell her that Tristram, near to death, demands her aid. If you succeed in bringing her with you, place white sails to your vessel on your return, that we may know of your success when the vessel first heaves in sight. But if Queen Isoude refuses, put on black sails; they will be the presage of my impending death."

Gesnes performed his mission successfully. King Mark

happened to be absent from his capital, and the queen readily consented to return with the bark to Brittany. Gesnes clothed his vessel in the whitest of sails and sped his way back to Brittany.

Meantime the wound of Tristram grew more desperate day by day. His strength, quite prostrated, no longer permitted him to be carried to the seaside daily, as had been his custom from the first moment when it was possible for the bark to be on the way homeward. He called a young damsel, and gave her in charge to keep watch in the direction of Cornwall, and to come and tell him the color of the sails of the first vessel she should see approaching.

When Isoude of the White Hands consented that the Queen of Cornwall should be sent for, she had not known all the reasons which she had for fearing the influence which renewed intercourse with that princess might have on her own happiness. She had now learned more, and felt the danger more keenly. She thought, if she could only keep the knowledge of the queen's arrival from her husband, she might employ in his service any resources which her skill could supply, and still avert the dangers which she apprehended. When the vessel was seen approaching, with its white sails sparkling in the sun, the damsel, by command of her mistress, carried word to Tristram that the sails were black.

Tristram, penetrated with inexpressible grief, breathed a profound sigh, turned away his face, and said, "Alas, my beloved! we shall never see one another again!" Then he commended himself to God and breathed his last.

The death of Tristram was the first intelligence which the Queen of Cornwall heard on landing. She was conducted, almost senseless, into the chamber of Tristram, and expired holding him in her arms.

Tristram, before his death, had requested that his body should be sent to Cornwall and that his sword, with a letter he had written, should be delivered to King Mark. The remains of Tristram and Isoude were embarked in a vessel, along with the sword, which was presented to the King of Cornwall. He was melted with tenderness when he saw the weapon which slew Moraunt of Ireland—which had so often saved his life, and redeemed the honor of his kingdom. In the letter, Tristram begged pardon of his uncle and related the story of the amorous draught.

Mark ordered the lovers to be buried in his own chapel. From the tomb of Tristram there sprung a vine, which went along the walls, and descended into the grave of the queen. It was cut down three times, but each time sprung up again more vigorous than before, and this wonderful plant has ever since shaded the tombs of Tristram and Isoude.

Spenser introduces Sir Tristram in his Faery Queene. In Book VI, Canto ii, Sir Calidore encounters in the forest a young hunter, whom he thus describes:

> Him steadfastly he marked, and saw to be
> A goodly youth of amiable grace,
> Yet but a slender slip, that scarce did see
> Yet seventeen yeares; but tall and faire of face,
> That sure he deemed him borne of noble race.
> All in a woodman's jacket he was clad
> Of Lincoln greene, belayed with silver lace;
> And on his head an hood with aglets * sprad,
> And by his side his hunter's horne he hanging had.

> Buskins he wore of costliest cordawayne,
> Pinckt upon gold, and paled part per part,†
> As then the guize was for each gentle swayne
> In his right hand he held a trembling dart,
> Whose fellow he before had sent apart;
> And in his left he held a sharp bore-speare,
> With which he wont to launch the salvage heart
> Of many a lyon, and of many a beare,
> That first unto his hand in chase did happen neare.

* *Aglets,* points or tags.

† *Pinckt upon gold, &c.,* adorned with golden points, or eyelets, and regularly intersected with stripes. *Paled,* (in heraldry,) striped.

CHAPTER XVIII

PERCEVAL

The father and two elder brothers of Perceval had fallen in battle or tournaments, and hence, as the last hope of his family, his mother retired with him into a solitary region, where he was brought up in total ignorance of arms and chivalry. He was allowed no weapon but "a lyttel Scots spere," which was the only thing of all "her lordes faire gere" that his mother carried to the wood with her. In the use of this he became so skilful that he could kill with it not only the animals of the chase for her table, but even birds on the wing. At length, however, Perceval was roused to a desire of military renown by seeing in the forest five knights who were in complete armor. He said to his mother, "Mother, what are those yonder?" "They are angels, my son," said she. "By my faith, I will go and become an angel with them." And Perceval went to the road and met them. "Tell me good lad," said one of them, "sawest thou a knight pass this way either to-day or yesterday?" "I know not," said he, "what a knight is." "Such an one as I am," said the knight. "If thou wilt tell me what I ask thee, I will tell thee what thou askest me." "Gladly will I do so," said Sir Owain, for that was the knight's name. "What is this?" demanded Perceval, touching the saddle. "It is a saddle," said Owain. Then he asked about all the accoutrements which he saw upon the men and the horses, and about the arms, and what they were for, and how they were used. And Sir Owain showed him all those things fully. And Perceval in return gave him such information as he had.

Then Perceval returned to his mother and said to her, "Mother, those were not angels, but honorable knights." Then his mother swooned away. And Perceval went to the place where they kept the horses that carried firewood and provisions for the castle, and he took a bony, piebald horse, which seemed to him the strongest of them. And he pressed a pack into the form of a saddle, and with twisted twigs he imitated the trappings which he had seen upon the horses. When he came again to his mother, the countess had recovered from her swoon. "My son," said she, "desirest thou to ride forth?" "Yes, with thy leave," said he. "Go forward then," she said, "to the court of Arthur, where there are the best and the noblest and the most bountiful of men, and tell him thou art Perceval, the son of Pelenore, and ask of him to bestow knighthood on thee. And whenever thou seest a church, repeat there thy pater-noster; and if thou see meat and drink and hast need of them, thou mayest take them. If thou hear an outcry of one in distress, proceed toward it, especially if it be the cry of a woman, and render her what service thou canst. If thou see a fair jewel, win it, for thus shalt thou acquire fame; yet freely give it to another, for thus thou shalt obtain praise. If thou see a fair woman, pay court to her, for thus thou wilt obtain love."

After this discourse, Perceval mounted the horse, and, taking a number of sharp-pointed sticks in his hand, he rode forth. And he rode far in the woody wilderness without food or drink. At last he came to an opening in the wood, where he saw a tent, and as he thought it might be a church, he said his pater-noster to it. And he went towards it; and the door of the tent was open. And Perceval dismounted and entered the tent. In the tent he found a maiden sitting, with a golden frontlet on her forehead and a gold ring on her hand. And Perceval said, "Maiden, I salute you, for my mother told me whenever I met a lady I must respectfully salute her." Perceiving in one corner of the tent some food, two flasks full of wine, and some boar's-flesh roasted, he said, "My mother told me, wherever I saw meat and drink, to take it." And he ate greedily, for he was very hungry. The maiden said, "Sir, thou hadst best go quickly from here, for fear that my friends should come, and evil should befall you." But Perceval said, "My mother told me, wheresoever I saw a fair jewel, to take it," and he took the gold ring from her finger, and put it on his own; and he gave the maiden his own ring in exchange for her's; then he mounted his horse and rode away.

Perceval journeyed on till he arrived at Arthur's court. And it so happened that just at that time an uncourteous knight had offered Queen Guenever a gross insult. For when her page was serving the queen with a golden goblet, this knight struck the arm of the page and dashed the wine in the queen's face and over her stomacher. Then he said, "If any have boldness to avenge this insult to Guenever, let him follow me to the meadow." So the knight took his horse and rode to the meadow, carrying away the golden goblet. And all the household hung down their heads, and no one offered to follow the knight to take vengeance upon him. For it seemed to them that no one would have ventured on so daring an outrage unless he possessed such powers, through magic or charms, that none could be able to punish him. Just then, behold, Perceval entered the hall upon the bony, piebald horse, with his uncouth trappings. In the centre of the hall stood Kay the seneschal. "Tell me, tall man," said Perceval, "is that Arthur yonder?" "What wouldst thou with Arthur?" asked Kay. "My mother told me to go to Arthur and receive knighthood from him." "By my faith," said he, "thou art all too meanly equipped with horse and with arms." Then all the household began to jeer and laugh at him. But there was a certain damsel who had been a whole year at Arthur's court and had never been known to smile. And the king's fool* had said that this damsel would not smile till she had seen him who would be the flower of chivalry. Now this damsel came up to Perceval and told him, smiling, that, if he lived, he would be one of the bravest and best of knights. "Truly," said Kay, "thou art ill taught to remain a year at Arthur's court, with choice of society, and smile on no one, and now before the face of Arthur and all his knights to call such a man as this the flower of knighthood"; and he gave her a box on the ear, that she fell senseless to the ground.

---

* A fool was a common appendage of the courts of those days when this romance was written. A fool was the ornament held in next estimation to a dwarf. He wore a white dress with a yellow bonnet, and carried a bell or *bawble* in his hand. Though called a fool, his words were often weighed and remembered as if there were a sort of oracular meaning in them.

Then said Kay to Perceval, "Go after the knight who went hence to the meadow, overthrow him and recover the golden goblet, and possess thyself of his horse and arms, and thou shalt have knighthood." "I will do so, tall man," said Perceval. So he turned his horse's head towards the meadow. And when he came there, the knight was riding up and down, proud of his strength and valor and noble mien. "Tell me," said the knight, "didst thou see any one coming after me from the court?" "The tall man that was there," said Perceval, "told me to come and overthrow thee, and to take from thee the goblet and thy horse and armor for myself." "Silence!" said the knight; "go back to the court, and tell Arthur either to come himself, or to send some other to fight with me; and unless he do so quickly, I will not wait for him." "By my faith," said Perceval, "choose thou whether it shall be willingly or unwillingly, for I will have the horse and the arms and the goblet." Upon this the knight ran at him furiously and struck him a violent blow with the shaft of his spear, between the neck and the shoulder. "Ha, ha, lad!" said Perceval, "my mother's servants were not used to play with me in this wise; so thus will I play with thee." And he threw at him one of his sharp-pointed sticks, and it struck him in the eye, and came out at the back of his head, so that he fell down lifeless.

"Verily," said Sir Owain, the son of Urien, to Kay the seneschal, "thou wast ill advised to send that madman after the knight, for he must either be overthrown or flee, and either way it will be a disgrace to Arthur and his warriors; therefore will I go to see what has befallen him." So Sir Owain went to the meadow, and he found Perceval trying in vain to get the dead knight's armor off, in order to clothe himself with it. Sir Owain unfastened the armor, and helped Perceval to put it on, and taught him how to put his foot in the stirrup, and use the spur; for Perceval had never used stirrup nor spur, but rode without saddle, and urged on his horse with a stick. Then Owain would have had him return to the court to receive the praise that was his due; but Perceval said, "I will not come to the court till I have encountered the tall man that is there, to revenge the injury he did to the maiden.

But take thou the goblet to Queen Guenever and tell King Arthur that, wherever I am, I will be his vassal and will do him what profit and service I can." And Sir Owain went back to the court and related all these things to Arthur and Guenever and to all the household.

And Perceval rode forward. And he came to a lake, on the side of which was a fair castle, and on the border of the lake he saw a hoary-headed man sitting upon a velvet cushion, and his attendants were fishing in the lake. When the hoary-headed man beheld Perceval approaching, he arose and went into the castle. Perceval rode to the castle, and the door was open, and he entered the hall. And the hoary-headed man received Perceval courteously, and asked him to sit by him on the cushion. When it was time, the tables were set, and they went to meat. And when they had finished their meat, the hoary-headed man asked Perceval if he knew how to fight with the sword. "I know not," said Perceval, "but were I to be taught, doubtless I should." And the hoary-headed man said to him, "I am thy uncle, thy mother's brother; I am called King Pecheur.* Thou shalt remain with me a space, in order to learn the manners and customs of different countries, and courtesy and noble bearing. And this do thou remember, If thou seest aught to cause thy wonder, ask not the meaning of it; if no one has the courtesy to inform thee, the reproach will not fall upon thee, but upon me that am thy teacher." While Perceval and his uncle discoursed together, Perceval beheld two youths enter the hall, bearing a golden cup and a spear of mighty size, with blood dropping from its point to the ground. And when all the company saw this, they began to weep and lament. But for all that, the man did not break off his discourse with Perceval. And as he did not tell him the meaning of what he saw, he forbore to ask him concerning it. Now the cup that Perceval saw was the Sangreal, and the spear the sacred spear; and afterwards King Pecheur removed with those sacred relics into a far country.

*   *   *   *   *

One evening Perceval entered a valley and came to a

* The word means both *fisher* and *sinner*.

hermit's cell; and the hermit welcomed him gladly, and there he spent the night. And in the morning he arose, and when he went forth, behold! a shower of snow had fallen in the night, and a hawk had killed a wild-fowl in front of the cell. And the noise of the horse had scared the hawk away, and a raven alighted on the bird. And Perceval stood and compared the blackness of the raven and the whiteness of the snow and the redness of the blood to the hair of the lady that best he loved, which was blacker than jet, and to her skin, which was whiter than the snow, and to the two red spots upon her cheeks, which were redder than the blood upon the snow.

Now Arthur and his household were in search of Perceval, and by chance they came that way. "Know ye," said Arthur, "who is the knight with the long spear that stands by the brook up yonder?" "Lord," said one of them, "I will go and learn who he is." So the youth came to the place where Perceval was and asked him what he did thus and who he was. But Perceval was so intent upon his thought that he gave him no answer. Then the youth thrust at Perceval with his lance, and Perceval turned upon him and struck him to the ground. And when the youth returned to the king and told how rudely he had been treated, Sir Kay said, "I will go myself." And when he greeted Perceval and got no answer, he spoke to him rudely and angrily. And Perceval thrust at him with his lance and cast him down so that he broke his arm and his shoulder-blade. And while he lay thus stunned, his horse returned back at a wild and prancing pace.

Then said Sir Gawain, surnamed the Golden-Tongued, because he was the most courteous knight in Arthur's court: "It is not fitting that any should disturb an honorable knight from his thought unadvisedly; for either he is pondering some damage that he has sustained, or he is thinking of the lady whom best he loves. If it seem well to thee, lord, I will go and see if this knight has changed from his thought, and if he has, I will ask him courteously to come and visit thee."

And Perceval was resting on the shaft of his spear, pondering the same thought, and Sir Gawain came to him, and said: "If I thought it would be as agreeable to thee as it would be to me, I would converse with thee. I have also a message from Arthur unto thee, to pray thee to come and visit him. And two men have been before on this errand." "That is true," said Perceval; "and un-courteously they came. They attacked me, and I was an-noyed thereat." Then he told him the thought that oc-cupied his mind, and Gawain said, "This was not an ungentle thought, and I should marvel if it were pleasant for thee to be drawn from it." Then said Perceval, "Tell me, is Sir Kay in Arthur's court?" "He is," said Gawain; "and truly, he is the knight who fought with thee last." "Verily," said Perceval, "I am not sorry to have thus avenged the insult to the smiling maiden." Then Perceval told him his name and said, "Who art thou?" And he re-plied, "I am Gawain." "I am right glad to meet thee," said Perceval, "for I have everywhere heard of thy prow-ess and uprightness; and I solicit thy fellowship." "Thou shalt have it, by my faith; and grant me thine," said he. "Gladly will I do so," answered Perceval.

So they went together to Arthur and saluted him. "Be-hold, lord," said Gawain, "him whom thou hast sought so long." "Welcome unto thee, Chieftain," said Arthur. And hereupon there came the queen and her hand-maidens, and Perceval saluted them. And they were re-joiced to see him, and bade him welcome. And Arthur did him great honor and respect, and they returned to-wards Caerleon.

CHAPTER XIX

THE SANGREAL, OR HOLY GRAAL

The Sangreal was the cup from which our Saviour drank at his last supper. He was supposed to have given it to Joseph of Arimathea, who carried it to Europe, to-gether with the spear with which the soldier pierced the Saviour's side. From generation to generation, one of the descendants of Joseph of Arimathea had been devoted to the guardianship of these precious relics; but on the sole condition of leading a life of purity in thought, word, and deed. For a long time the Sangreal was visible to all pilgrims, and its presence conferred blessings upon the land in which it was preserved. But, at length, one of those holy men to whom its guardianship had descended so far forgot the obligation of his sacred office as to look with unhallowed eye upon a young female pilgrim whose robe was accidentally loosened as she knelt before him. The sacred lance instantly punished his frailty, spontaneously falling upon him and inflicting a deep wound. The marvellous wound could by no means be healed, and the guardian of the Sangreal was ever after called "Le Roi Pecheur"—the Sinner King. The Sangreal withdrew its visible presence from the crowds who came to worship, and an iron age succeeded to the happiness which its presence had diffused among the tribes of Britain.

We have told in the history of Merlin how that great prophet and enchanter sent a message to King Arthur by Sir Gawain, directing him to undertake the recovery of the Sangreal, informing him at the same time that the knight who should accomplish that sacred quest was already born, and of a suitable age to enter upon it. Sir Gawain delivered his message, and the king was anxiously revolving in his mind how best to achieve the enterprise when, at the vigil of Pentecost, all the fellowship of the Round Table being met together at Camelot, as they sat at meat, suddenly there was heard a clap of thunder, and then a bright light burst forth, and every knight, as he looked on his fellow, saw him, in seeming, fairer than ever before. All the hall was filled with sweet odors, and every knight had such meat and drink as he best loved. Then there entered into the hall the Holy Graal, covered with white samite, so that none could see it, and it passed through the hall suddenly, and disappeared. During this time no one spoke a word, but when they had recovered breath to speak, King Arthur said, "Certainly we ought greatly to thank the Lord for what he hath showed us this day." Then Sir Gawain rose up and made a vow that for twelve months and a day he would seek the Sangreal, and not return till he had seen it, if so he might speed. When they of the Round Table heard Sir

Gawain say so, they arose, the most part of them, and vowed the same. When King Arthur heard this, he was greatly displeased, for he knew well that they might not gainsay their vows. "Alas!" said he to Sir Gawain, "you have nigh slain me with the vow and promise that ye have made, for ye have bereft me of the fairest fellowship that ever were seen together in any realm of the world; for when they shall depart hence, I am sure that all shall never meet more in this world."

SIR GALAHAD

At that time there entered the hall a good old man, and with him he brought a young knight, and these words he said: "Peace be with you, fair lords." Then the old man said unto King Arthur, "Sir, I bring you here a young knight that is of kings' lineage, and of the kindred of Joseph of Arimathea, being the son of Dame Elaine, the daughter of King Pelles, king of the foreign country." Now the name of the young knight was Sir Galahad, and he was the son of Sir Launcelot du Lac; but he had dwelt with his mother, at the court of King Pelles, his grandfather, till now he was old enough to bear arms, and his mother had sent him in the charge of a holy hermit to King Arthur's court. Then Sir Launcelot beheld his son and had great joy of him. And Sir Bohort told his fellows, "Upon my life, this young knight shall come to great worship." The noise was great in all the court, so that it came to the queen. And she said, "I would fain see him, for he must needs be a noble knight, for so is his father." And the queen and her ladies all said that he resembled much unto his father; and he was seemly and demure as a dove, with all manner of good features, that in the whole world men might not find his match. And King Arthur said, "God make him a good man, for beauty faileth him not, as any that liveth."

Then the hermit led the young knight to the Siege Perilous; and he lifted up the cloth and found there letters that said, "This is the seat of Sir Galahad, the good knight"; and he made him sit in that seat. And all the knights of the Round Table marvelled greatly at Sir Gal-

ahad, seeing him sit securely in that seat, and said,
"This is he by whom the Sangreal shall be achieved, for
there never sat one before in that seat without being
mischieved."

On the next day, the king said, "Now, at this quest of
the Sangreal shall all ye of the Round Table depart, and
never shall I see you again altogether; therefore I will
that ye all repair to the meadow of Camelot, for to just
and tourney yet once more before ye depart." But all the
meaning of the king was to see Sir Galahad proved. So
then were they all assembled in the meadow. Then Sir
Galahad, by request of the king and queen, put on his
harness and his helm, but shield would he take none for
any prayer of the king. And the queen was in a tower,
with all her ladies, to behold that tournament. Then Sir
Galahad rode into the midst of the meadow; and there
he began to break spears marvellously, so that all men
had wonder of him, for he surmounted all knights that
encountered with him, except two, Sir Launcelot and Sir
Perceval. Then the king, at the queen's request, made
him to alight and presented him to the queen; and she
said, "Never two men resembled one another more than
he and Sir Launcelot, and therefore it is no marvel that
he is like him in prowess."

Then the king and the queen went to the minster, and
the knights followed them. And after the service was
done, they put on their helms and departed, and there
was great sorrow. They rode through the streets of
Camelot, and there was weeping of the rich and poor;
and the king turned away, and might not speak for weeping. And so they departed, and every knight took the
way that him best liked.

Sir Galahad rode forth without shield, and rode four
days, and found no adventure. And on the fourth day
he came to a white abbey; and there he was received with
great reverence and led to a chamber. He met there two
knights, King Bagdemagus and Sir Uwaine, and they made
of him great solace. "Sirs," said Sir Galahad, "what adventure brought you hither?" "Sir," said they, "it is told
us that within this place is a shield, which no man may
bear unless he be worthy; and if one unworthy should
attempt to bear it, it shall surely do him a mischief."

Then King Bagdemagus said, "I fear not to bear it, and that shall ye see to-morrow."

So on the morrow they arose and heard mass; then King Bagdemagus asked where the adventurous shield was. Anon a monk led him behind an altar, where the shield hung, as white as snow; but in the midst there was a red cross. Then King Bagdemagus took the shield and bare it out of the minster; and he said to Sir Galahad, "If it please you, abide here till ye know how I shall speed."

Then King Bagdemagus and his squire rode forth; and when they had ridden a mile or two, they saw a goodly knight come towards them, in white armor, horse and all; and he came as fast as his horse might run, with his spear in the rest; and King Bagdemagus directed his spear against him, and broke it upon the white knight, but the other struck him so hard that he broke the mails and thrust him through the right shoulder, for the shield covered him not, and so he bare him from his horse. Then the white knight turned his horse and rode away.

Then the squire went to King Bagdemagus and asked him whether he were sore wounded or not. "I am sore wounded," said he, "and full hardly shall I escape death." Then the squire set him on his horse and brought him to an abbey; and there he was taken down softly, and unarmed, and laid in a bed, and his wound was looked to, for he lay there long, and hardly escaped with his life. And the squire brought the shield back to the abbey.

The next day Sir Galahad took the shield, and within a while he came to the hermitage, where he met the white knight, and each saluted the other courteously. "Sir," said Sir Galahad, "can you tell me the marvel of the shield?" "Sir," said the white knight, "that shield belonged of old to the gentle knight, Joseph of Arimathea; and when he came to die, he said, 'Never shall man bear this shield about his neck but he shall repent it, unto the time that Sir Galahad the good knight bear it, the last of my lineage, the which shall do many marvellous deeds.' " And then the white knight vanished away.

SIR GAWAIN

After Sir Gawain departed, he rode many days, both towards and forward, and at last he came to the abbey where Sir Galahad took the white shield. And they told Sir Gawain of the marvellous adventure that Sir Galahad had done. "Truly," said Sir Gawain, "I am not happy that I took not the way that he went, for, if I may meet with him, I will not part from him lightly, that I may partake with him all the marvellous adventures which he shall achieve." "Sir," said one of the monks, "he will not be your fellowship." "Why?" said Sir Gawain. "Sir," said he, "because ye be sinful, and he is blissful." Then said the monk, "Sir Gawain, thou must do penance for thy sins." "Sir, what penance shall I do?" "Such as I will show," said the good man. "Nay," said Sir Gawain, "I will do no penance, for we knights adventurous often suffer great woe and pain." "Well," said the good man, and he held his peace. And Sir Gawain departed.

Now it happened, not long after this, that Sir Gawain and Sir Hector rode together, and they came to a castle where was a great tournament. And Sir Gawain and Sir Hector joined themselves to the party that seemed the weaker, and they drove before them the other party. Then suddenly came into the lists a knight, bearing a white shield with a red cross, and by adventure he came by Sir Gawain, and he smote him so hard that he clave his helm and wounded his head, so that Sir Gawain fell to the earth. When Sir Hector saw that, he knew that the knight with the white shield was Sir Galahad, and he thought it no wisdom to abide him, and also for natural love, that he was his uncle. Then Sir Galahad retired privily, so that none knew where he had gone. And Sir Hector raised up Sir Gawain and said, "Sir, me seemeth your quest is done." "It is done," said Sir Gawain; "I shall seek no further." Then Gawain was borne into the castle, and unarmed, and laid in a rich bed, and a leech found to search his wound. And Sir Gawain and Sir Hector abode together, for Sir Hector would not away till Sir Gawain were whole.

CHAPTER XX

SIR LAUNCELOT

Sir Launcelot rode overthwart and endlong in a wide forest, and held no path but as wild adventure led him. And at last he came to a stone cross. Then Sir Launcelot looked round him and saw an old chapel. So he tied his horse to a tree, and put off his shield, and hung it upon a tree; and then he went unto the chapel and looked through a place where the wall was broken. And within he saw a fair altar, full richly arrayed with cloth of silk; and there stood a fair candlestick, which bare six great candles, and the candlestick was of silver. When Sir Launcelot saw this sight, he had a great wish to enter the chapel, but he could find no place where he might enter. Then was he passing heavy and dismayed. And he returned and came again to his horse, and took off his saddle and his bridle, and let him pasture; and unlaced his helm, and ungirded his sword, and laid him down to sleep upon his shield before the cross.

And as he lay, half waking and half sleeping, he saw come by him two palfreys, both fair and white, which bare a litter, on which lay a sick knight. And when he was nigh the cross, he there abode still. And Sir Launcelot heard him say, "O sweet Lord, when shall this sorrow leave me, and when shall the holy vessel come by me whereby I shall be healed?" And thus a great while complained the knight, and Sir Launcelot heard it. Then Sir Launcelot saw the candlestick, with the lighted tapers, come before the cross, but he could see nobody that brought it. Also there came a salver of silver and the holy vessel of the Sangreal; and therewithal the sick knight sat him upright, and held up both his hands, and said, "Fair, sweet Lord, which is here within the holy vessel, take heed to me, that I may be whole of this great malady." And therewith, upon his hands and upon his knees, he went so nigh that he touched the holy vessel and kissed it. And anon he was whole. Then the holy vessel went into the chapel again, with the candlestick and the light, so that Sir Launcelot wist not what became of it.

Then the sick knight rose up and kissed the cross; and anon, his squire brought him his arms and asked his lord how he did. "I thank God right heartily," said he, "for, through the holy vessel, I am healed. But I have great marvel of this sleeping knight, who hath had neither grace nor power to awake during the time that the holy vessel hath been here present." "I dare it right well say," said the squire, "that this same knight is stained with some manner of deadly sin, whereof he was never confessed." So they departed.

Then anon Sir Launcelot waked, and set himself upright, and bethought him of what he had seen, and whether it were dreams or not. And he was passing heavy, and wist not what to do. And he said: "My sin and my wretchedness hath brought me into great dishonor. For when I sought worldly adventures and worldly desires, I ever achieved them, and had the better in every place, and never was I discomfited in any quarrel, were it right or wrong. And now I take upon me the adventure of holy things, I see and understand that mine old sin hindereth me, so that I had no power to stir nor to speak when the holy blood appeared before me." So thus he sorrowed till it was day, and heard the fowls of the air sing. Then was he somewhat comforted.

Then he departed from the cross into the forest. And there he found a hermitage, and a hermit therein, who was going to mass. So when mass was done, Sir Launcelot called the hermit to him and prayed him for charity to hear his confession. "With a good will," said the good man. And then he told that good man all his life, and how he had loved a queen unmeasurably many years. "And all my great deeds of arms that I have done, I did the most part for the queen's sake, and for her sake would I do battle, were it right or wrong, and never did I battle all only for God's sake, but for to win worship, and to cause me to be better beloved; and little or naught I thanked God for it. I pray you counsel me."

"I will counsel you," said the hermit, "if ye will insure me that ye will never come in that queen's fellowship as much as ye may forbear." And then Sir Launcelot promised the hermit, by his faith, that he would no more come in her company. "Look that your heart and your mouth accord," said the good man, "and I shall insure you that ye shall have more worship than ever ye had."

Then the good man enjoined Sir Launcelot such penance as he might do, and he assoiled Sir Launcelot and made him abide with him all that day. And Sir Launcelot repented him greatly.

SIR PERCEVAL

Sir Perceval departed and rode till the hour of noon; and he met in a valley about twenty men of arms. And when they saw Sir Perceval, they asked him whence he was; and he answered, "Of the court of King Arthur." Then they cried all at once, "Slay him." But Sir Perceval smote the first to the earth, and his horse upon him. Then seven of the knights smote upon his shield all at once, and the remnant slew his horse, so that he fell to the earth. So had they slain him or taken him, had not the good knight Sir Galahad, with the red cross, come there by adventure. And when he saw all the knights upon one, he cried out, "Save me that knight's life." Then he rode toward the twenty men of arms as fast as his horse might drive, with his spear in the rest, and smote the foremost horse and man to the earth. And when his spear was broken, he set his hand to his sword and smote on the right hand and on the left, that it was marvel to see; and at every stroke he smote down one, or put him to rebuke, so that they would fight no more, but fled to a thick forest, and Sir Galahad followed them. And when Sir Perceval saw him chase them so, he made great sorrow that his horse was slain. And he wist well it was Sir Galahad. Then he cried aloud, "Ah, fair knight, abide, and suffer me to do thanks unto thee; for right well have ye done for me." But Sir Galahad rode so fast that at last he passed out of his sight. When Sir Perceval saw that he would not turn, he said, "Now am I a very wretch, and most unhappy above all other knights." So in this sorrow he abode all that day till it was night; and then he was faint, and laid him down and slept till midnight; and then he awaked and saw before him a woman, who said unto him, "Sir Perceval, what dost thou here?" He answered, "I do neither good, nor great ill." "If thou wilt promise me," said she, "that thou wilt fulfil my will when I summon thee, I will lend thee my own horse, which shall bear thee whither thou wilt." Sir Perceval was glad of her proffer and insured her to fulfil all her desire. "Then abide me here, and I will go fetch you a horse." And so she soon came again and brought a horse with her that was inky black. When Perceval beheld that horse, he marvelled, it was so great and so well appar- elled. And he leapt upon him and took no heed of him- self. And he thrust him with his spurs, and within an hour and less he bare him four days' journey thence, until he came to a rough water, which roared, and his horse would have borne him into it. And when Sir Perceval came nigh the brim and saw the water so boisterous, he doubted to overpass it. And then he made the sign of the cross on his forehead. When the fiend felt him so charged, he shook off Sir Perceval and went into the water crying and roaring; and it seemed unto him that the water burned. Then Sir Perceval perceived it was a fiend that would have brought him unto his perdition. Then he commended himself unto God and prayed our Lord to keep him from all such temptations; and so he prayed all that night till it was day. Then he saw that he was in a wild place that was closed with the sea nigh all about. And Sir Perceval looked forth over the sea and saw a ship come sailing towards him; and it came and stood still under the rock. And when Sir Per- ceval saw this, he hied him thither and found the ship covered with silk; and therein was a lady of great beauty, and clothed so richly that none might be better.

And when she saw Sir Perceval, she saluted him, and Sir Perceval returned her salutation. Then he asked her of her country and her lineage. And she said, "I am a gentlewoman that am disinherited, and was once the rich- est woman of the world." "Damsel," said Sir Perceval,

"who hath disinherited you? for I have great pity of you."
"Sir," said she, "my enemy is a great and powerful lord,
and aforetime he made much of me, so that of his favor
and of my beauty I had a little pride more than I ought
to have had. Also, I said a word that pleased him not.
So he drove me from his company and from mine heritage. Therefore I know no good knight nor good man but
I get him on my side if I may. And, for that I know that
thou art a good knight, I beseech thee to help me."

Then Sir Perceval promised her all the help that he
might, and she thanked him.

And at that time the weather was hot, and she called
to her a gentlewoman and bade her bring forth a pavilion.
And she did so and pitched it upon the gravel. "Sir,"
said she, "now may ye rest you in this heat of the day."
Then he thanked her, and she put off his helm and his
shield, and there he slept a great while. Then he awoke
and asked her if she had any meat, and she said yea,
and so there was set upon the table all manner of meats
that he could think on. Also he drank there the strongest wine that ever he drank, and therewith he was a little
chafed more than he ought to be. With that he beheld
the lady, and he thought she was the fairest creature that
ever he saw. And then Sir Perceval proffered her love
and prayed her that she would be his. Then she refused
him in a manner, for the cause he should be the more
ardent on her, and ever he ceased not to pray her of
love. And when she saw him well enchafed, then she
said, "Sir Perceval, wit you well I shall not give ye my
love, unless you swear from henceforth you will be my
true servant and do nothing but that I shall command
you. Will you insure me this, as ye be a true knight?"
"Yea," said he, "fair lady, by the faith of my body." And
as he said this, by adventure and grace, he saw his sword
lie on the ground naked, in whose pommel was a red
cross, and the sign of the crucifix thereon. Then he
made the sign of the cross on his forehead, and therewith
the pavilion shrivelled up and changed into a smoke and
a black cloud. And the damsel cried aloud and hasted
into the ship, and so she went with the wind roaring and
yelling that it seemed all the water burned after her.
Then Sir Perceval made great sorrow and called himself

a wretch, saying, "How nigh was I lost!" Then he took his arms and departed thence.

CHAPTER XXI

THE SANGREAL, CONTINUED

SIR BOHORT

When Sir Bohort departed from Camelot, he met with a religious man, riding upon an ass; and Sir Bohort saluted him. "What are ye?" said the good man. "Sir," said Sir Bohort, "I am a knight that fain would be counselled in the quest of the Sangreal." So rode they both together till they came to a hermitage; and there he prayed Sir Bohort to dwell that night with him. So he alighted, and put away his armor, and prayed him that he might be confessed. And they went both into the chapel, and there he was clean confessed. And they ate bread and drank water together. "Now," said the good man, "I pray thee that thou eat none other till thou sit at the table where the Sangreal shall be." "Sir," said Sir Bohort, "but how know ye that I shall sit there?" "Yea," said the good man, "that I know well; but there shall be few of your fellows with you." Then said Sir Bohort, "I agree me thereto." And the good man, when he had heard his confession, found him in so pure a life and so stable that he marvelled thereof.

On the morrow, as soon as the day appeared, Sir Bohort departed thence and rode into a forest unto the hour of midday. And there befell him a marvellous adventure. For he met, at the parting of two ways, two knights that led Sir Lionel, his brother, all naked, bound upon a strong hackney, and his hands bound before his breast; and each of them held in his hand thorns wherewith they went beating him, so that he was all bloody before and behind; but he said never a word, but, as he was great of heart, he suffered all that they did to him

as though he had felt none anguish. Sir Bohort prepared
to rescue his brother. But he looked on the other side of
him and saw a knight dragging along a fair gentlewoman,
who cried out, "Saint Mary! succor your maid!" And
when she saw Sir Bohort, she called to him and said, "By
the faith that ye owe to knighthood, help me!" When Sir
Bohort heard her say thus, he had such sorrow that he
wist not what to do. "For if I let my brother be, he must
be slain, and that would I not for all the earth; and if I
help not the maid, I am shamed for ever." Then lift he
up his eyes and said, weeping, "Fair Lord, whose liege-
man I am, keep Sir Lionel, my brother, that none of these
knights slay him, and for pity of you, and our Lady's
sake, I shall succor this maid."

Then he cried out to the knight, "Sir Knight, lay your
your hand off that maid, or else ye be but dead." Then
the knight set down the maid, and took his shield, and
drew out his sword. And Sir Bohort smote him so hard
that it went through his shield and habergeon, on the left
shoulder, and he fell down to the earth. Then came Sir
Bohort to the maid, "Ye be delivered of this knight this
time." "Now," said she, "I pray you lead me there where
this knight took me." "I shall gladly do it," said Sir Bohort. So he took the horse of the wounded knight, and
set the gentlewoman upon it, and brought her there
where she desired to be. And there he found twelve
knights seeking after her; and when she told them how
Sir Bohort had delivered her, they made great joy, and
besought him to come to her father, a great lord, and he
should be right welcome. "Truly," said Sir Bohort, "that
may not be; for I have a great adventure to do." So he
commended them to God and departed.

Then Sir Bohort rode after Sir Lionel, his brother, by
the trace of their horses. Thus he rode seeking, a great
while. Then he overtook a man clothed in a religious
clothing, who said, "Sir Knight, what seek ye?" "Sir,"
said Sir Bohort, "I seek my brother, that I saw within a
little space beaten of two knights." "Ah, Sir Bohort,
trouble not thyself to seek for him, for truly he is dead."
Then he showed him a new-slain body, lying in a thick
bush; and it seemed him that it was the body of Sir Lionel. And then he made such sorrow that he fell to the

ground in a swoon, and lay there long. And when he came to himself again, he said, "Fair brother, since the fellowship of you and me is sundered, shall I never have joy again; and now He that I have taken for my master, He be my help!" And when he had said thus, he took up the body in his arms and put it upon the horse. And then he said to the man, "Canst thou tell me the way to some chapel, where I may bury this body?" "Come on," said the man, "here is one fast by." And so they rode till they saw a fair tower, and beside it a chapel. Then they alighted both and put the body into a tomb of marble.

Then Sir Bohort commended the good man unto God and departed. And he rode all that day and harbored with an old lady. And on the morrow he rode unto the castle in a valley, and there he met with a yeoman. "Tell me," said Sir Bohort, "knowest thou of any adventure?" "Sir," said he, "here shall be, under this castle, a great and marvellous tournament." Then Sir Bohort thought to be there, if he might meet with any of the fellowship that were in quest of the Sangreal; so he turned to a hermitage that was on the border of the forest. And when he was come thither, he found there Sir Lionel his brother, who sat all armed at the entry of the chapel door. And when Sir Bohort saw him, he had great joy, and he alighted off his horse and said, "Fair brother, when came ye hither?" As soon as Sir Lionel saw him he said, "Ah, Sir Bohort, make ye no false show, for, as for you, I might have been slain, for ye left me in peril of death to go succor a gentlewoman; and for that misdeed I now insure you but death, for ye have right well deserved it." When Sir Bohort perceived his brother's wrath, he kneeled down to the earth and cried him mercy, holding up both his hands, and prayed him to forgive him. "Nay," said Sir Lionel, "thou shalt have but death for it, if I have the upper hand; therefore leap upon thy horse and keep thyself, and if thou do not, I will run upon thee there as thou standest on foot, and so the shame shall be mine, and the harm thine, but of that I reck not." When Sir Bohort saw that he must fight with his brother or else die, he wist not what to do. Then his heart counselled him not so to do, inasmuch as Sir Lionel was his elder brother, wherefore he ought to bear him reverence. Yet kneeled he down before Sir Lionel's horse's feet, and said, "Fair brother, have mercy upon me and slay me not." But Sir Lionel cared not, for the fiend had brought him in such a will that he should slay him. When he saw that Sir Bohort would not rise to give him battle, he rushed over him, so that he smote him with his horse's feet to the earth, and hurt him sore, that he swooned of distress. When Sir Lionel saw this, he alighted from his horse for to have smitten off his head; and so he took him by the helm, and would have rent it from his head. But it happened that Sir Colgrevance, a knight of the Round Table, came at that time thither, as it was our Lord's will; and then he beheld how Sir Lionel would have slain his brother, and he knew Sir Bohort, whom he loved right well. Then leapt he down from his horse, and took Sir Lionel by the shoulders, and drew him strongly back from Sir Bohort, and said, "Sir Lionel, will ye slay your brother?" "Why," said Sir Lionel, "will ye stay me? If ye interfere in this, I will slay you, and him after." Then he ran upon Sir Bohort, and would have smitten him; but Sir Colgrevance ran between them and said, "If ye persist to do so any more, we two shall meddle together." Then Sir Lionel defied him and gave him a great stroke through the helm. Then he drew his sword, for he was a passing good knight, and defended himself right manfully. So long endured the battle that Sir Bohort rose up all anguishly and beheld Sir Colgrevance, the good knight, fight with his brother for his quarrel. Then was he full sorry and heavy, and thought that, if Sir Colgrevance slew him that was his brother, he should never have joy, and if his brother slew Sir Colgrevance, the shame should ever be his.

Then would he have risen for to have parted them, but he had not so much strength to stand on his feet; so he staid so long that Sir Colgrevance had the worse, for Sir Lionel was of great chivalry and right hardy. Then cried Sir Colgrevance, "Ah, Sir Bohort, why come ye not to bring me out of peril of death, wherein I have put me to succor you?" With that, Sir Lionel smote off his helm and bore him to the earth. And when he had slain Sir Colgrevance, he ran upon his brother as a fiendly man and gave him such a stroke that he made him stoop. And he that was full of humility prayed him, "For God's sake leave this battle, for if it befell, fair brother, that I slew you, or ye me, we should be dead of that sin." "Pray ye not me for mercy," said Sir Lionel. Then Sir Bohort, all weeping, drew his sword and said, "Now God have mercy upon me, though I defend my life against my brother." With that Sir Bohort lifted up his sword, and would have stricken his brother. Then heard he a voice that said, "Flee, Sir Bohort, and touch him not." Right so alighted a cloud between them, in the likeness of a fire, and a marvellous flame, so that they both fell to the earth and lay there a great while in a swoon. And when they came to themselves, Sir Bohort saw that his brother had no harm; and he was right glad, for he dread sore that God had taken vengeance upon him. Then Sir Lionel said to his brother, "Brother, forgive me, for God's sake, all that I have trespassed against you." And Sir Bohort answered, "God forgive it thee, and I do."

With that Sir Bohort heard a voice say, "Sir Bohort, take thy way anon, right to the sea, for Sir Perceval abideth thee there." So Sir Bohort departed and rode the nearest way to the sea. And, at last, he came to an abbey that was nigh the sea. That night he rested him there, and in his sleep there came a voice unto him and bade him go to the seashore. He started up, and made the sign of the cross on his forehead, and armed himself, and made ready his horse and mounted him, and at a broken wall he rode out, and came to the seashore. And there he found a ship, covered all with white samite. And he entered into the ship; but it was anon so dark that he might see no man, and he laid him down and slept till it was day. Then he awaked and saw in the middle of the ship a knight all armed, save his helm. And then he knew it was Sir Perceval de Galis, and each made of other right great joy. Then said Sir Perceval, "We lack nothing now but the good knight Sir Galahad."

SIR LAUNCELOT, RESUMED

It befell upon a night Sir Launcelot arrived before a castle, which was rich and fair. And there was a postern that opened towards the sea, and was open without any keeping, save two lions kept the entry; and the moon shined clear. Anon Sir Launcelot heard a voice that said, "Launcelot, enter into the castle, where thou shalt see a great part of thy desire." So he went unto the gate and saw the two lions; then he set hands to his sword and drew it. Then there came suddenly, as it were, a stroke upon the arm, so sore that the sword fell out of his hand, and he heard a voice that said, "Oh, man of evil faith, wherefore believest thou more in thy armor than in thy Maker?" Then said Sir Launcelot, "Fair Lord, I thank thee of thy great mercy, that thou reprovest me of my misdeed; now see I well that thou holdest me for thy servant." Then he made a cross on his forehead and came to the lions; and they made semblance to do him harm, but he passed them without hurt, and entered into the castle, and he found no gate nor door but it was open. But at the last he found a chamber whereof the door was shut; and he set his hand thereto, to have opened it, but he might not. Then he listened and heard a voice which sung so sweetly that it seemed none earthly thing; and the voice said, "Joy and honor be to the Father of heaven." Then Sir Launcelot kneeled down before the chamber, for well he wist that there was the Sangreal in that chamber. Then said he, "Fair, sweet Lord, if ever I did anything that pleased thee, for thy pity show me something of that which I seek." And with that he saw the chamber door open, and there came out a great clearness, that the house was as bright as though all the torches of the world had been there. So he came to the chamber door, and would have entered; and anon a voice said unto him, "Stay, Sir Launcelot, and enter not." And he withdrew him back, and was right heavy in his mind. Then looked he in the midst of the chamber, and saw a table of silver, and the holy vessel, covered with red samite, and many angels about it; whereof one held a candle of wax burning, and another held a cross and the ornaments of the altar. Then, for very wonder and thankfulness, Sir Launcelot forgot himself, and he stepped forward and entered the chamber. And suddenly a breath that seemed intermixed with fire smote him so sore in the visage that therewith he fell to the ground, and had no power to rise. Then felt he many hands about him, which took him up and bare him out of the chamber, without any amending of his swoon, and left him there, seeming dead to all the people. So on the morrow, when it was fair daylight and they within were arisen, they found Sir Launcelot lying before the chamber door. And they looked upon him and felt his pulse, to know if there were any life in him. And they found life in him, but he might neither stand nor stir any member that he had. So they took him, and bare him into a chamber, and laid him upon a bed, far from all folk, and there he lay many days. Then the one said he was alive, and others said nay. But said an old man, "He is as full of life as the mightiest of you all, and therefore I counsel you that he be well kept till God bring him back again." And after twenty-four days he opened his eyes; and when he saw folk, he made great sorrow and said, "Why have ye wakened me? for I was better at ease than I am now." "What have ye seen?" said they about him. "I have seen," said he, "great marvels that no tongue can tell, and more than any heart can think." Then they said, "Sir, the quest of the Sangreal is achieved right now in you, and never shall ye see more of it than ye have seen." "I thank God," said Sir Launcelot, "of his great mercy, for that I have seen, for it sufficeth me." Then he rose up and clothed himself; and when he was so arrayed, they marvelled all, for they knew it was Sir Launcelot the good knight. And, after four days, he took his leave of the lord of the castle, and of all the fellowship that were there, and thanked them for their great labor and care of him. Then he departed and turned to Camelot, where he found King Arthur and Queen Guenever; but many of the knights of the Round Table were slain and destroyed, more than half. Then all the court was passing glad of Sir Launcelot; and he told the king all his adventures that had befallen him since he departed.

SIR GALAHAD

Now, when Sir Galahad had rescued Perceval from the twenty knights, he rode into a vast forest, wherein he abode many days. Then he took his way to the sea, and it befell him that he was benighted in a hermitage. And the good man was glad when he saw he was a knight-errant. And when they were at rest, there came a gentle-woman knocking at the door; and the good man came to the door to wit what she would. Then she said, "I would speak with the knight which is with you." Then Galahad went to her and asked her what she would. "Sir Gala-had," said she, "I will that ye arm you, and mount upon your horse, and follow me; for I will show you the high-est adventure that ever knight saw." Then Galahad armed himself, and commended himself to God, and bade the damsel go before, and he would follow where she led.

So she rode as fast as her palfrey might bear her, till she came to the sea; and there they found the ship where Sir Bohort and Sir Perceval were, who cried from the ship, "Sir Galahad, you are welcome; we have awaited you long." And when he heard them, he asked the damsel who they were. "Sir," said she, "leave your horse here, and I shall leave mine, and we will join our-selves to their company." So they entered into the ship, and the two knights received them both with great joy. For they knew the damsel, that she was Sir Perceval's sister. Then the wind arose and drove them through the sea all that day and the next, till the ship arrived be-tween two rocks, passing great and marvellous; but there they might not land, for there was a whirlpool; but there was another ship, and upon it they might go without danger. "Go we thither," said the gentlewoman, "and there shall we see adventures, for such is our Lord's will." Then Sir Galahad blessed him and entered therein, and then next the gentlewoman, and then Sir Bohort and Sir Perceval. And when they came on board, they found there the table of silver and the Sangreal, which was covered with red samite. And they made great rev-erence thereto, and Sir Galahad prayed a long time to our Lord, that at what time he should ask to pass out of this world, he should do so; and a voice said to him, "Galahad, thou shalt have thy request; and when thou askest the death of thy body, thou shalt have it, and then shalt thou find the life of thy soul."

And anon the wind drove them across the sea, till they came to the city of Sarras. Then took they out of the ship the table of silver, and Sir Perceval and Sir Bohort took it before, and Sir Galahad came behind, and right so they went to the city. And at the gate of the city they saw an old man, a cripple. Then Galahad called him and bade him help to bear this heavy thing. "Truly," said the old man, "it is ten years since I could not go but with crutches." "Care thou not," said Sir Galahad, "but arise up and show thy good will." Then the old man rose up, and assayed, and found himself as whole as ever he was; and he ran to the table and took one part with Sir Galahad.

When they came to the city, it chanced that the king was just dead, and all the city was dismayed, and wist not who might be their king. Right so, as they were in council, there came a voice among them and bade them choose the youngest knight of those three to be their king. So they made Sir Galahad king, by all the assent of the city. And when he was made king, he commanded to make a chest of gold and of precious stones, to hold the holy vessel. And every day the three companions would come before it and make their prayers.

Now, at the year's end, and the same day of the year that Sir Galahad received the crown, he got up early, and, with his fellows, came to where the holy vessel was; and they saw one kneeling before it that had about him a great fellowship of angels; and he called Sir Galahad and said, "Come, thou servant of the Lord, and thou shalt see what thou hast much desired to see." And Sir Galahad's mortal flesh trembled right hard when he began to behold the spiritual things. Then said the good man, "Now wottest thou who I am?" "Nay," said Sir Galahad. "I am Joseph of Arimathea, whom our Lord hath sent here to thee, to bear thee fellowship." Then Sir Galahad held up his hands towards heaven and said, "Now, blessed Lord, would I not longer live, if it might please thee." And when he had said these words, Sir Galahad went to Sir Perceval and to Sir Bohort, and kissed them, and commended them to God. And then he kneeled down before the table, and made his prayers, and suddenly his soul departed, and a great multitude of angels bare his soul up to heaven, so as the two fellows could well behold it. Also they saw come from heaven a hand, but they saw not the body; and the hand came right to the vessel and bare it up to heaven. Since then was there never one so hardy as to say that he had seen the Sangreal on earth any more.

CHAPTER XXII

SIR AGRIVAIN'S TREASON

When Sir Perceval and Sir Bohort saw Sir Galahad dead, they made as much sorrow as ever did two men. And if they had not been good men, they might have fallen into despair. As soon as Sir Galahad was buried, Sir Perceval retired to a hermitage out of the city and took a religious clothing; and Sir Bohort was always with him, but did not change his secular clothing, because he purposed to return to the realm of Loegria. Thus a year and two months lived Sir Perceval in the hermitage a full holy life, and then passed out of this world, and Sir Bohort buried him by his sister and Sir Galahad. Then Sir Bohort armed himself, and departed from Sarras, and entered into a ship, and sailed to the kingdom of Loegria, and in due time arrived safe at Camelot, where the king was. Then was there great joy made of him in the whole court, for they feared he had been dead. Then the king made great clerks to come before him, that they should chronicle of the high adventures of the good knights. And Sir Bohort told him of the adventures that had befallen him and his two fellows, Sir Perceval and Sir Galahad. And Sir Launcelot told the adventures of the Sangreal that he had seen.

All this was made in great books and put up in the church at Salisbury.

So King Arthur and Queen Guenever made great joy of the remnant that were come home, and chiefly of Sir Launcelot and Sir Bohort. Then Sir Launcelot began to resort unto Queen Guenever again, and forgot the promise that he made in the quest; so that many in the court spoke of it, and in especial Sir Agrivain, Sir Gawain's brother, for he was ever open-mouthed. So it happened Sir Gawain and all his brothers were in King Arthur's chamber, and then Sir Agrivain said thus openly, "I marvel that we all are not ashamed to see and to know so noble a knight as King Arthur so to be shamed by the conduct of Sir Launcelot and the queen." Then spoke Sir Gawain and said, "Brother, Sir Agrivain, I pray you and charge you move not such matters any more before me, for be ye assured I will not be of your counsel." "Neither will we," said Sir Gaheris and Sir Gareth. "Then will I," said Sir Modred. "I doubt you not," said Sir Gawain, "for to all mischief ever were ye prone; yet I would that ye left all this, for I know what will come of it." "Fall of it what fall may," said Sir Agrivain, "I will disclose it to the king." With that came to them King Arthur. "Now, brothers, hold your peace," said Sir Gawain. "We will not," said Sir Agrivain. Then said Sir Gawain, "I will not hear your tales, nor be of your counsel." "No more will I," said Sir Gareth and Sir Gaheris, and therewith they departed, making great sorrow.

Then Sir Agrivain told the king all that was said in the court of the conduct of Sir Launcelot and the queen, and it grieved the king very much. But he would not believe it to be true without proof. So Sir Agrivain laid a plot to entrap Sir Launcelot and the queen, intending to take them together unawares. Sir Agrivain and Sir Modred led a party for this purpose, but Sir Launcelot escaped from them, having slain Sir Agrivain and wounded Sir Modred. Then Sir Launcelot hastened to his friends, and told them what had happened, and withdrew with them to the forest; but he left spies to bring him tidings of whatever might be done.

So Sir Launcelot escaped, but the queen remained in

the king's power, and Arthur could no longer doubt of
her guilt. And the law was such in those days that they
who committed such crimes, of what estate or condition
soever they were, must be burned to death, and so it
was ordained for Queen Guenever. Then said King Arthur to Sir Gawain, "I pray you make you ready, in
your best armor, with your brethren, Sir Gaheris and Sir
Gareth, to bring my queen to the fire, there to receive
her death." "Nay, my most noble lord," said Sir Gawain,
"that will I never do; for know thou well, my heart will
never serve me to see her die, and it shall never be
said that I was of your counsel in her death." Then the
king commanded Sir Gaheris and Sir Gareth to be there,
and they said, "We will be there, as ye command us,
sire, but in peaceable wise, and bear no armor upon us."

So the queen was led forth, and her ghostly father
was brought to her to shrive her, and there was weeping and wailing of many lords and ladies. And one went
and told Sir Launcelot that the queen was led forth to
her death. Then Sir Launcelot and the knights that were
with him fell upon the troop that guarded the queen,
and dispersed them, and slew all who withstood them.
And in the confusion, Sir Gareth and Sir Gaheris were
slain, for they were unarmed and defenceless. And Sir
Launcelot carried away the queen to his castle of La
Joyeuse Garde.

Then there came one to Sir Gawain and told him
how that Sir Launcelot had slain the knights and carried away the queen. "O Lord, defend my brethren!"
said Sir Gawain. "Truly," said the man, "Sir Gareth and
Sir Gaheris are slain." "Alas!" said Sir Gawain, "now
is my joy gone." And then he fell down and swooned,
and long he lay there as he had been dead.

When he arose out of his swoon, Sir Gawain ran to
the king, crying, "Oh, King Arthur, mine uncle, my
brothers are slain." Then the king wept and he both.
"My king, my lord, and mine uncle," said Sir Gawain,
"bear witness now that I make you a promise that I
shall hold by my knighthood, that from this day I
will never fail Sir Launcelot until the one of us have
slain the other. I will seek Sir Launcelot throughout
seven kings' realms, but I shall slay him or he shall

slay me." "Ye shall not need to seek him," said the
king, "for as I hear, Sir Launcelot will abide me and
you in the Joyeuse Garde; and much people draweth
unto him, as I hear say." "That may I believe," said
Sir Gawain; "but, my lord, summon your friends, and
I will summon mine." "It shall be done," said the king.
So then the king sent letters and writs throughout all
England, both in the length and breadth, to summon all
his knights. And unto Arthur drew many knights, dukes,
and earls, so that he had a great host. Thereof heard
Sir Launcelot, and collected all whom he could; and
many good knights held with him, both for his sake and
for the queen's sake. But King Arthur's host was too
great for Sir Launcelot to abide him in the field; and he
was full loath to do battle against the king. So Sir Launcelot drew him to his strong castle, with all manner of
provisions. Then came King Arthur with Sir Gawain, and
laid siege all about La Joyeuse Garde, both the town
and the castle; but in no wise would Sir Launcelot ride
out of his castle, neither suffer any of his knights to
issue out, until many weeks were past.

Then it befell upon a day in harvest-time, Sir Launcelot looked over the wall and spoke aloud to King Arthur and Sir Gawain, "My lords both, all is in vain that
ye do at this siege, for here ye shall win no worship,
but only dishonor; for if I list to come out, and my
good knights, I shall soon make an end of this war."
"Come forth," said Arthur, "if thou darest, and I promise thee I shall meet thee in the midst of the field."
"God forbid me," said Sir Launcelot, "that I should encounter with the most noble king that made me knight."
"Fie upon thy fair language," said the king, "for know
thou well I am thy mortal foe, and ever will be to my
dying day." And Sir Gawain said, "What cause hadst
thou to slay my brother, Sir Gaheris, who bore no arms
against thee, and Sir Gareth, whom thou madest knight,
and who loved thee more than all my kin? Therefore
know thou well I shall make war to thee all the while
that I may live."

When Sir Bohort, and Sir Hector de Marys, and Sir
Lionel heard this outcry, they called to them Sir Palamedes, and Sir Saffire his brother, and Sir Lawayn, with

many more, and all went to Sir Launcelot. And they said, "My lord, Sir Launcelot, we pray you, if you will have our service, keep us no longer within these walls, for know well all your fair speech and forbearance will not avail you." "Alas!" said Sir Launcelot, "to ride forth and to do battle I am full loath." Then he spake again unto the king and Sir Gawain, and willed them to keep out of the battle; but they despised his words. So then Sir Launcelot's fellowship came out of the castle, in full good array. And always Sir Launcelot charged all his knights, in any wise, to save King Arthur and Sir Gawain.

Then came forth Sir Gawain from the king's host, and offered combat, and Sir Lionel encountered with him, and there Sir Gawain smote Sir Lionel through the body, that he fell to the earth as if dead. Then there began a great conflict, and much people were slain; but ever Sir Launcelot did what he might to save the people on King Arthur's party, and ever King Arthur followed Sir Launcelot to slay him; but Sir Launcelot suffered him, and would not strike again. Then Sir Bohort encountered with King Arthur and smote him down; and he alighted, and drew his sword, and said to Sir Launcelot, "Shall I make an end of this war?" for he meant to have slain King Arthur. "Not so," said Sir Launcelot, "touch him no more, for I will never see that most noble king that made me knight either slain or shamed"; and therewith Sir Launcelot alighted off his horse, and took up the king, and horsed him again, and said thus: "My lord Arthur, for God's love, cease this strife." And King Arthur looked upon Sir Launcelot, and the tears burst from his eyes, thinking on the great courtesy that was in Sir Launcelot more than in any other man; and therewith the king rode his way. Then anon both parties withdrew to repose them, and buried the dead.

But the war continued, and it was noised abroad through all Christendom, and at last it was told afore the Pope; and he, considering the great goodness of King Arthur and of Sir Launcelot, called unto him a noble clerk, which was the Bishop of Rochester, who was then in his dominions, and sent him to King Arthur, charging him that he take his queen, dame Guenever, unto him again and make peace with Sir Launcelot.

So, by means of this bishop, peace was made for the space of one year; and King Arthur received back the queen, and Sir Launcelot departed from the kingdom with all his knights and went to his own country. So they shipped at Cardiff and sailed unto Benwick, which some men call Bayonne. And all the people of those lands came to Sir Launcelot and received him home right joyfully. And Sir Launcelot stablished and garnished all his towns and castles, and he greatly advanced all his noble knights, Sir Lionel and Sir Bohort, and Sir Hector de Marys, Sir Blamor, Sir Lawayn, and many others, and made them lords of lands and castles; till he left himself no more than any one of them.

But when the year was passed, King Arthur and Sir Gawain came with a great host, and landed upon Sir Launcelot's lands, and burnt and wasted all that they might overrun. Then spake Sir Bohort and said, "My lord, Sir Launcelot, give us leave to meet them in the field, and we shall make them rue the time that ever they came to this country." Then said Sir Launcelot, "I am full loath to ride out with my knights for shedding of Christian blood; so we will yet a while keep our walls, and I will send a messenger unto my lord Arthur, to propose a treaty; for better is peace than always war." So Sir Launcelot sent forth a damsel, and a dwarf with her, requiring King Arthur to leave his warring upon his lands; and so she started on a palfrey, and the dwarf ran by her side. And when she came to the pavilion of King Arthur, she alighted, and there met her a gentle knight, Sir Lucan the butler, and said, "Fair damsel, come ye from Sir Launcelot du Lac?" "Yea, sir," she said, "I come hither to speak with the king." "Alas!" said Sir Lucan, "my lord Arthur would be reconciled to Sir Launcelot, but Sir Gawain will not suffer him." And with this, Sir Lucan led the damsel to the king, where he sat with Sir Gawain, to hear what she would say. So when she had told her tale, the tears ran out of the king's eyes; and all the lords were forward to advise the king to be accorded with Sir Launcelot, save only Sir Gawain; and he said, "My lord, mine uncle, what will ye do? Will you now turn back, now you are so far advanced upon your journey? If ye do, all the world will speak shame of you." "Nay," said King Arthur, "I will do as ye advise me; but do thou give the damsel her answer, for I may not speak to her for pity."

Then said Sir Gawain, "Damsel, say ye to Sir Launcelot that it is waste labor to sue to mine uncle for peace, and say that I, Sir Gawain, send him word that I promise him, by the faith I owe unto God and to knighthood, I shall never leave him till he have slain me or I him." So the damsel returned, and when Sir Launcelot had heard this answer, the tears ran down his cheeks.

Then it befell on a day Sir Gawain came before the gates, armed at all points, and cried with a loud voice, "Where art thou now, thou false traitor, Sir Launcelot? Why hidest thou thyself within holes and walls like a coward? Look out now, thou traitor knight, and I will avenge upon thy body the death of my three brethren." All this language heard Sir Launcelot, and the knights which were about him; and they said to him, "Sir Launcelot, now must ye defend you like a knight, or else be shamed for ever, for you have slept overlong and suffered overmuch." Then Sir Launcelot spake on high unto King Arthur and said, "My lord Arthur, now I have forborne long, and suffered you and Sir Gawain to do what ye would, and now must I needs defend myself, inasmuch as Sir Gawain hath appealed me of treason." Then Sir Launcelot armed him and mounted upon his horse, and the noble knights came out of the city, and the host without stood all apart; and so the covenant was made that no man should come near the two knights, nor deal with them, till one were dead or yielded.

Then Sir Launcelot and Sir Gawain departed a great way asunder, and then they came together with all their horses' might, and each smote the other in the middle of their shields, but neither of them was unhorsed, but their horses fell to the earth. And then they leapt from their horses, and drew their swords, and gave many sad strokes, so that the blood burst out in many places. Now Sir Gawain had this gift from a holy man, that every day in the year, from morning to noon, his strength was increased threefold, and then it fell again to its natural measure. Sir Launcelot was aware of this, and therefore, during the three hours that Sir Gawain's strength was at the height, Sir Launcelot covered himself with his shield and kept his might in reserve. And during that time, Sir Gawain gave him many sad brunts, that all the knights that looked on marvelled how Sir Launcelot might endure them. Then, when it was past noon, Sir Gawain had only his own might; and when Sir Launcelot felt him so brought down, he stretched himself up, and doubled his strokes, and gave Sir Gawain such a buffet that he fell down on his side; and Sir Launcelot drew back and would strike no more. "Why withdrawest thou, false traitor?" then said Sir Gawain; "now turn again and slay me, for if thou leave me thus, when I am whole again, I shall do battle with thee again." "I shall endure you, sir, by God's grace," said Sir Launcelot, "but know thou well, Sir Gawain, I will never smite a felled knight." And so Sir Launcelot went into the city, and Sir Gawain was borne into King Arthur's pavilion, and his wounds were looked to.

Thus the siege endured, and Sir Gawain lay helpless near a month; and when he was near recovered, came tidings unto King Arthur that made him return with all his host to England.

CHAPTER XXIII

MORTE D'ARTHUR

Sir Modred was left ruler of all England, and he caused letters to be written, as if from beyond sea, that King Arthur was slain in battle. So he called a Parliament and made himself be crowned king; and he took the queen, Guenever, and said plainly that he would wed her, but she escaped from him and took refuge in the Tower of London. And Sir Modred went and laid siege about the Tower of London, and made great assaults thereat, but all might not avail him. Then came word to Sir Modred that King Arthur had raised the siege of Sir Launcelot, and was coming home. Then Sir

Modred summoned all the barony of the land; and much people drew unto Sir Modred, and said they would abide with him for better and for worse; and he drew a great host to Dover, for there he heard say that King Arthur would arrive.

And as Sir Modred was at Dover with his host, came King Arthur, with a great number of ships and galleys, and there was Sir Modred awaiting upon the landing. Then was there launching of great boats and small, full of noble men of arms, and there was much slaughter of gentle knights on both parts. But King Arthur was so courageous, there might no manner of knights prevent him to land, and his knights fiercely followed him; and so they landed, and put Sir Modred aback so that he fled, and all his people. And when the battle was done, King Arthur commanded to bury his people that were dead. And then was noble Sir Gawain found, in a great boat, lying more than half dead. And King Arthur went to him and made sorrow out of measure. "Mine uncle," said Sir Gawain, "know thou well my death-day is come, and all is through mine own hastiness and wilfulness, for I am smitten upon the old wound which Sir Launcelot gave me, of the which I feel I must die. And had Sir Launcelot been with you as of old, this war had never begun, and of all this I am the cause." Then Sir Gawain prayed the king to send for Sir Launcelot and to cherish him above all other knights. And so, at the hour of noon, Sir Gawain yielded up his spirit, and then the king bade inter him in a chapel within Dover Castle; and there all men may see the skull of him, and the same wound is seen that Sir Launcelot gave him in battle.

Then was it told the king that Sir Modred had pitched his camp upon Barrendown; and the king rode thither, and there was a great battle betwixt them, and King Arthur's party stood best, and Sir Modred and his party fled unto Canterbury.

And there was a day assigned betwixt King Arthur and Sir Modred that they should meet upon a down beside Salisbury, and not far from the seaside, to do battle yet again. And at night, as the king slept, he dreamed a wonderful dream. It seemed him verily that there came Sir Gawain unto him, with a number of fair ladies with him. And when King Arthur saw him, he said, "Welcome, my sister's son; I weened thou hadst been dead; and now I see thee alive, great is my joy. But, oh, fair nephew, what be these ladies that hither be come with you?" "Sir," said Sir Gawain, "all these be ladies for whom I have fought when I was a living man; and because I did battle for them in righteous quarrel, they have given me grace to bring me hither unto you, to warn you of your death, if ye fight to-morrow with Sir Modred. Therefore, take ye treaty and proffer you largely for a month's delay; for within a month shall come Sir Launcelot and all his noble knights, and rescue you worshipfully, and slay Sir Modred and all that hold with him." And then Sir Gawain and all the ladies vanished. And anon the king called to fetch his noble lords and wise bishops unto him. And when they were come, the king told them his vision and what Sir Gawain had told him. Then the king sent Sir Lucan the butler, and Sir Bedivere, with two bishops, and charged them in any wise to take a treaty for a month and a day with Sir Modred. So they departed and came to Sir Modred; and so, at the last, Sir Modred was agreed to have Cornwall and Kent, during Arthur's life, and all England after his death.

Then was it agreed that King Arthur and Sir Modred should meet betwixt both their hosts, and each of them should bring fourteen persons, and then and there they should sign the treaty. And when King Arthur and his knights were prepared to go forth, he warned all his host, "If so be ye see any sword drawn, look ye come on fiercely, and slay whomsoever withstandeth, for I in no wise trust that traitor, Sir Modred." In like wise Sir Modred warned his host. So they met, and were agreed and accorded thoroughly. And wine was brought, and they drank. Right then came an adder out of a little heath-bush, and stung a knight on the foot. And when the knight felt him sting, he looked down and saw the adder, and then he drew his sword to slay the adder, and thought of no other harm. And when the host on both sides saw that sword drawn, they blew trumpets and horns, and shouted greatly. And King Arthur took his horse, and rode to his party, saying, "Alas, this unhappy day!" And Sir Modred did in like wise. And never was there a more doleful battle in Christian land. And ever King Arthur rode throughout the battle, and did full nobly, as a worthy king should, and Sir Modred that day did his devoir and put himself in great peril. And thus they fought all the long day, till the most of all the noble knights lay dead upon the ground. Then the king looked about him and saw of all his host were left alive but two knights, Sir Lucan the butler and Sir Bedivere his brother, and they were full sore wounded.

Then King Arthur saw where Sir Modred leaned upon his sword among a great heap of dead men. "Now give me my spear," said Arthur unto Sir Lucan, "for yonder I espy the traitor that hath wrought all this woe." "Sir, let him be," said Sir Lucan; "for if ye pass this unhappy day, ye shall be right well revenged upon him. Remember what the sprite of Sir Gawain told you, and leave off now, for ye have won the field; and if ye leave off now, this evil day of destiny is past." "Betide me life, betide me death," said King Arthur, "he shall not now escape my hands." Then the king took his spear in both hands and ran towards Sir Modred, crying, "Traitor, now is thy death-day come." And there King Arthur smote Sir Modred under the shield, with a thrust of his spear through the body. And when Sir Modred felt that he had his death-wound, with the might that he had he smote King Arthur, with his sword holden in both his hands, on the side of the head, that the sword pierced the helmet and the brain-pan; and then Sir Modred fell stark dead upon the earth. And the noble Arthur fell in a swoon to the earth. And Sir Lucan the butler and Sir Bedivere raised him up and gently led him betwixt them both to a little chapel not far from the seaside. And when the king was there, he thought him well eased. Then heard they people cry in the field. And Sir Lucan went to see what that cry betokened, and he saw by the moonlight that pillers and robbers were come to rob the dead. And he returned and said to the king, "By my rede, it is best that we bring you to some town." "I would it were so," said the king. And when the king tried to go, he fainted. Then Sir Lucan took up the king on the one part, and Sir Bedivere on the other part;

and, in the lifting, Sir Lucan fell in a swoon to the earth, for he was grievously wounded. And then the noble knight's heart burst. And when the king awoke, he beheld Sir Lucan, how he lay foaming at the mouth, and speechless. "Alas!" said the king, "this is to me a full heavy sight, to see this noble duke so die for my sake; for he would have holpen me that had more need of help then I, and he would not complain, his heart was so set to help me." Then Sir Bedivere wept for his brother. "Leave this mourning and weeping," said the king, "for wit thou well, if I might live myself, the death of Sir Lucan would grieve me evermore; but my time hieth fast. Therefore," said Arthur unto Sir Bedivere, "take thou Excalibar, my good sword, and go with it to yonder waterside; and when thou comest there, I charge thee throw my sword in that water, and come again and tell me what thou there seest." "My lord," said Sir Bedivere, "your commandment shall be done." So Sir Bedivere departed, and by the way he beheld that noble sword, that the pommel and the haft were all of precious stones; and then he said to himself, "If I throw this rich sword into the water, no good shall come thereof, but only harm and loss." And then Sir Bedivere hid Excalibar under a tree. And so, as soon as he might, he came again unto the king. "What sawest thou there?" said the king. "Sir," he said, "I saw nothing." "Alas! thou hast deceived me," said the king. "Go thou lightly again, and as thou love me, spare not to throw it in." Then Sir Bedivere went again and took the sword in his hand to throw it; but again it beseemed him but sin and shame to throw away that noble sword, and he hid it away again, and returned, and told the king he had done his commandment. "What sawest thou there?" said the king. "Sir," he said, "I saw nothing but waters deep and waves wan." "Ah, traitor untrue!" said King Arthur, "now hast thou betrayed me twice. And yet thou art named a noble knight, and hast been lief and dear to me. But now go again, and do as I bid thee, for thy long tarrying putteth me in jeopardy of my life." Then Sir Bedivere went to the sword, and lightly took it up, and went to the waterside, and he bound the girdle about the hilt, and then he threw the sword as far into the water as he might. And there came an arm and a hand out of the water, and met it, and caught it, and shook it thrice and brandished it, and then vanished away the hand with the sword in the water.

Then Sir Bedivere came again to the king and told him what he saw. "Help me hence," said the king, "for I fear I have tarried too long." Then Sir Bedivere took the king on his back, and so went with him to that water-side; and when they came there, even fast by the bank, there rode a little barge with many fair ladies in it, and among them was a queen; and all had black hoods, and they wept and shrieked when they saw King Arthur.

"Now put me in the barge," said the king. And there received him three queens with great mourning, and in one of their laps King Arthur laid his head. And the queen said, "Ah, dear brother, why have ye tarried so long? Alas! this wound on your head hath caught over-much cold." And then they rowed from the land, and Sir Bedivere beheld them go from him. Then he cried: "Ah, my lord Arthur, will ye leave me here alone among mine enemies?" "Comfort thyself," said the king, "for in me is no further help; for I will to the Isle of Avalon, to heal me of my grievous wound." And as soon as Sir Bedivere had lost sight of the barge, he wept and wailed; then he took the forest, and went all that night, and in the morning he was ware of a chapel and a hermitage.

Then went Sir Bedivere thither; and when he came into the chapel, he saw where lay a hermit on the ground, near a tomb that was newly graven. "Sir," said Sir Bedivere, "what man is there buried that ye pray so near unto?" "Fair son," said the hermit, "I know not verily. But this night there came a number of ladies, and brought hither one dead, and prayed me to bury him." "Alas!" said Sir Bedivere, "that was my lord, King Arthur." Then Sir Bedivere swooned; and when he awoke, he prayed the hermit he might abide with him, to live with fasting and prayers. "Ye are welcome," said the hermit. So there bode Sir Bedivere with the hermit; and he put on poor clothes and served the hermit full lowly in fasting and in prayers.

Thus of Arthur I find never more written in books that be authorized, nor more of the very certainty of his death; but thus was he led away in a ship, wherein were three queens; the one was King Arthur's sister, Queen Morgane le Fay; the other was Viviane, the Lady of the Lake; and the third was the Queen of North Galis. And this tale Sir Bedivere, knight of the Table Round, made to be written.

Yet some men say that King Arthur is not dead, but hid away into another place, and men say that he shall come again and reign over England. But many say that there is written on his tomb this verse:

Hic jacet Arthurus, Rex quondam, Rexque futurus.
Here Arthur lies, King once and King to be.

And when Queen Guenever understood that King Arthur was slain, and all the noble knights with him, she stole away, and five ladies with her; and so she went to Almesbury, and made herself a nun, and ware white clothes and black, and took great penance as ever did sinful lady, and lived in fasting, prayers, and alms-deeds. And there she was abbess and ruler of the nuns. Now turn we from her and speak of Sir Launcelot of the Lake.

When Sir Launcelot heard in his country that Sir Modred was crowned King of England, and made war against his own uncle, King Arthur, then was Sir Launcelot wroth out of measure, and said to his kinsmen: "Alas that double traitor, Sir Modred! Now it repenteth me that ever he escaped out of my hands." Then Sir Launcelot and his fellows made ready in all haste, with ships and galleys, to pass into England; and so he passed over till he came to Dover, and there he landed with a great army. Then Sir Launcelot was told that King Arthur was slain. "Alas!" said Sir Launcelot, "this is the heaviest tidings that ever came to me." Then he called the kings, dukes, barons, and knights and said thus: "My fair lords, I thank you all for coming into this country with me, but we came too late, and that shall repent me while I live. But since it is so," said Sir Launcelot, "I will myself ride and seek my lady, Queen Guenever, for I have heard say she hath fled into the west; therefore ye shall abide me here fifteen days, and if I come not within that time, then take your ships and your host and depart into your country."

So Sir Launcelot departed and rode westerly, and there he sought many days; and at last he came to a nunnery, and was seen of Queen Guenever as he walked in the cloister; and when she saw him, she swooned away. And when she might speak, she bade him to be called to her. And when Sir Launcelot was brought to her, she said: "Sir Launcelot, I require thee and beseech thee, for all the love that ever was betwixt us, that thou never see me more, but return to thy kingdom and take thee a wife, and live with her with joy and bliss; and pray for me to my Lord that I may get my soul's health." "Nay, madam," said Sir Launcelot, "wit you well that I shall never do; but the same destiny that ye have taken you to will I take me unto, for to please and serve God." And so they parted, with tears and much lamentation; and the ladies bare the queen to her chamber, and Sir Launcelot took his horse and rode away, weeping.

And at last Sir Launcelot was ware of a hermitage and a chapel, and then he heard a little bell ring to mass; and thither he rode and alighted, and tied his horse to the gate, and heard mass. And he that sang the mass was the hermit with whom Sir Bedivere had taken up his abode; and Sir Bedivere knew Sir Launcelot, and they spake together after mass. But when Sir Bedivere had told his tale, Sir Launcelot's heart almost burst for sorrow. Then he kneeled down, and prayed the hermit to shrive him, and besought that he might be his brother. Then the hermit said, "I will gladly"; and then he put a habit upon Sir Launcelot, and there he served God day and night, with prayers and fastings.

And the great host abode at Dover till the end of the fifteen days set by Sir Launcelot, and then Sir Bohort made them to go home again to their own country; and Sir Bohort, Sir Hector de Marys, Sir Blamor, and many others, took on them to ride through all England to seek Sir Launcelot. So Sir Bohort by fortune rode until he came to the same chapel where Sir Launcelot was; and when he saw Sir Launcelot in that manner of clothing, he prayed the hermit that he might be in that same. And so there was a habit put upon him, and there he lived in prayers and fasting. And within half a year came others of the knights, their fellows, and took such a habit as Sir Launcelot and Sir Bohort had. Thus they endured in great penance six years.

And upon a night there came a vision to Sir Launcelot, and charged him to haste him toward Almesbury, and "by the time thou come there, thou shalt find Queen Guenever dead." Then Sir Launcelot rose up early and told the hermit thereof. Then said the hermit, "It were well that ye disobey not this vision." And Sir Launcelot took his seven companions with him, and on foot they went from Glastonbury to Almesbury, which is more than thirty miles. And when they were come to Almesbury, they found that Queen Guenever died but half an hour before. Then Sir Launcelot saw her visage, but he wept not greatly, but sighed. And so he did all the observance of the service himself, both the "dirige" at night, and at morn he sang mass. And there was prepared an horse-bier, and Sir Launcelot and his fellows followed the bier on foot from Almesbury until they came to Glastonbury; and she was wrapped in cered clothes and laid in a coffin of marble. And when she was put in the earth, Sir Launcelot swooned, and lay long as one dead.

And Sir Launcelot never after ate but little meat, nor drank, but continually mourned. And within six weeks Sir Launcelot fell sick; and he sent for the hermit and all his true fellows and said, "Sir Hermit, I pray you give me all my rights that a Christian man ought to have." "It shall not need," said the hermit and all his fellows; "it is but heaviness of your blood, and to-morrow morn you shall be well." "My fair lords," said Sir Launcelot, "my careful body will into the earth; I have warning more than now I will say; therefore give me my rights." So when he was houseled and aneled, and had all that a Christian man ought to have, he prayed the hermit that his fellows might bear his body to Joyous Garde. (Some men say it was Alnwick, and some say it was Bamborough.) "It repenteth me sore," said Sir Launcelot, "but I made a vow aforetime that in Joyous Garde I would be buried." Then there was weeping and wringing of hands among his fellows. And that night Sir Launcelot died; and when Sir Bohort and his fellows came to his bedside the next morning, they found him stark dead; and he lay as if he had smiled, and the sweetest savor all about him that ever they knew.

And they put Sir Launcelot into the same horse-bier that Queen Guenever was laid in, and the hermit and they all together went with the body till they came to Joyous Garde. And there they laid his corpse in the body of the quire and sang and read many psalms and prayers over him. And ever his visage was laid open and naked, that all folks might behold him. And right thus, as they were at their service, there came Sir Hector de Maris, that had seven years sought Sir Launcelot, his brother, through all England, Scotland, and Wales. And when Sir Hector heard such sounds in the chapel of Joyous Garde, he alighted and came into the quire. And all they knew Sir Hector. Then went Sir Bohort and told him how there lay Sir Launcelot his brother dead. Then Sir Hector threw his shield, his sword, and helm from him. And when he beheld Sir Launcelot's visage, it were hard for any tongue to tell the doleful complaints he made for his brother. "Ah, Sir Launcelot!" he said, "there thou liest. And now I dare to say thou wert never matched of none earthly knight's hand. And thou wert the courteousest knight that ever bare shield; and thou wert the truest friend to thy lover that ever bestrode horse; and thou wert the truest lover, of a sinful man, that ever loved woman; and thou wert the kindest man that ever struck with sword. And thou wert the goodliest person that ever came among press of knights. And thou wert the meekest man, and the gentlest, that ever ate in hall among ladies. And thou wert the sternest knight to thy mortal foe that ever put spear in the rest." Then there was weeping and dolor out of measure. Thus they kept Sir Launcelot's corpse fifteen days, and then they buried it with great devotion.

Then they went back with the hermit to his hermitage. And Sir Bedivere was there ever still hermit to his life's end. And Sir Bohort, Sir Hector, Sir Blamor, and Sir Bleoberis went into the Holy Land. And these four knights did many battles upon the miscreants, the Turks; and there they died upon a Good Friday, as it pleased God.

Thus endeth this noble and joyous book, entitled La Morte d'Arthur; notwithstanding it treateth of the birth, life, and acts of the said King Arthur, and of his noble Knights of the Round Table, their marvellous enquests and adventures, the achieving of the Sangreal, and, in the end, la Morte d'Arthur, with the dolorous death and departing out of this world of them all. Which book was reduced into English by Sir Thomas Mallory, Knight, and divided into twenty-one books, chaptered and imprinted and finished in the Abbey Westmestre, the last day of July, the year of our Lord MCCCCLXXXV.

Caxton me fieri fecit.

PART TWO

THE MABINOGION

CHAPTER I

This famous story was called the *Mabinogion* by its first translator from Welsh into English, Lady Charlotte Guest (1812–1895). The thirteen stories were first told by a medieval storyteller in Wales, a bard who had memorized three hundred fifty such stories. Such a bard was member of an order of minor nobility, often attached to the court of a lord as the court historian. The stories we now read, ancient accounts first written down in the thirteenth century, take us back to the British Heroic Age of King Arthur: A.D. 500–600.

While the dispute rages again today (as it has raged pro and con, century after century) as to whether King Arthur was historical, other persons whose stories are told in the *Mabinogion* clearly were. They have been proven so by Welsh scholars. While there are several "Arthur" stories of megalithic graves in Wales, the tomb of the great Welsh poet Taliesin, in Dyfed, South Wales, is well known, as is his poetry. When gravediggers tried to recover his skeleton, however, they were frightened away by thunder and lightning. Archaeologists were more fortunate in recovering a woman's skeleton from the tomb of the beloved Welsh Princess Bronwen. Her square grave lies on the Alaw River bank on the island of Anglesey, North Wales (*Gwynedd*).[1] Several other personages in the stories, King Urien Rheged, for example, not only were historical, but are beloved in Wales today—as is King Arthur. For wonder, charm, and pure delight, no other collection of stories surpasses the *Mabinogion*.

Everyone in Wales today claims King Arthur as "Once and Future King." In southeastern Wales there still stand churches founded by Merlin himself; his grave lies in the Llandaf cathedral, where he is known by his Welsh and Latin names: Saint Dyfrig (Dubricius). During Merlin's lifetime the Celtic countries (north and western Britain and Ireland) worshipped under their own Celtic Church. Wales did not join the Church of Rome until the year A.D. 777, but Celtic-speaking representatives had attended church councils at Arles (France) in A.D. 314, and Rimini (Italy) in 359. Their system of Christianity came directly from Jerusalem and Constantinople (as King Arthur claims) and was monastic. Thus, Perceval became the last King of the Holy Grail. King Arthur, whom Merlin is believed to have crowned, was an earlier Grail King.

Today the Celtic peoples live in Great Britain, but speak some of their original languages: Brythonic (Welsh), Gaelic, and Cornish. Even though the Manx language is no longer spoken, the Bible in Manx was published recently, and also a new English–Manx dictionary. A recent book places the Grail Castle of King Arthur and King Perceval on Saint Patrick's Isle, near the west coast of the Isle of Man. Such books continue the heritage of the Celtic peoples (Cornish, Welsh, Breton, Scottish, Irish, and Manx), who were conquered by the Anglo-Saxons.[2]

We seldom realize that a story like "The Lady of the Fountain" in the *Mabinogion* is even older than the days of King Arthur, the British (or Celtic) Heroic Age. Technically speaking, "The Lady of the Fountain" is a *tale* and very similar to any fairy tale.

In Moscow in 1928 a noted Russian academician, Vladimir J. A. Propp, published a book on the structure, or morphology, of the fairy tale. His book was translated into French by Claude Ligny in 1970 and called *Morphologie du conte* (*Morphology of the Tale*). His formalist argument supports a novel theory: *that the fairy tale and the historical chronicle of ancient times are different accounts originating from the same event in the past.* Propp suggests a more serious consideration of stories such as those collected in the *Mabinogion*—a reconsideration of tales as actual history. Other scholars, like myself, in such books as *Ancient Myths* (Penguin, New York, 1994), have proposed that myths be viewed as records of ancient religious ceremonies.

In the 1960s the French novelist and literary scholar Michel Butor pointed out in an essay, "On Fairy Tales," that the "fairies" of our folk tales were once the gods and goddesses of old religions. Their morality, wrote Butor, is clear (good vs. evil, king vs. giant, rescuer vs. murderer) and their world is one where even a lowly woodcutter can become a great prince. Some things continue in our modern world: The fairy tale warns girls of their inequality, teaching adolescents what to expect from modern society.[3] Both the professor, Propp, and the artist, Butor, stress the significance and the importance of the fairy tale for our lives.

Every fairy tale has a standard format. We first meet the parents of a youth, our future hero. He faces a task—a problem which he is to solve—adolescents face that situation in school every day. The youngster must then leave home on a quest, which involves a departure or farewell, a separation from caring parents or rulers, and a series of fearsome adventures, including combat of some sort. The first hero may be stumped, or defeated along the journey, so the reader realizes he is an alternate and not the real champion.

Easily following the track of the secondary hero, the real heroic winner proceeds jauntily along the path marked out by his predecessor. En route, however, he alone receives an unexpected boon. He is met by an often unidentified personage who presents him with a gift that turns out to be magical—a talisman, for example. The most renowned Arthurian hero, Lancelot, has a defect of falling ill and even going mad in the forest alone. In his case the mysterious personage is an unknown woman. She administers a medication to Lancelot, and he recovers. The great Lancelot completes all his heroic missions—until the last one, of course. The mythological/historical hero like Lancelot of the Lake continues the series of tests until his lack is removed, and the evil is overcome. We then have the last parts of this mythological design: the return of the hero followed by his wedding to the Princess. The hero of the *Mabinogion,* says the author Caitlin Matthews, weds the "Sovereignty of Britain," no less.[4]

If we now apply the conclusions of Propp to "The Lady of the Fountain," we shall see that like every other tale, it contains the same seven characters: King, Queen, Secondary Hero, Primary Hero, Antagonist, Donor, and Princess. The mythological pattern rises from the text:

I. King
II. Queen
III. Kynon = Hero #1
  Adventures:
    1. Black man of the mound
    2. Persons at the castle
    3. Fountain (thunder, birds)
IV. Owain, son of King Urien Rheged = the real Hero
  Adventures repeated:
    1. Persons at the castle
    2. Fountain
V. Combat and Death of the Mystery Antagonist
VI. The Donor Luned, a yellow maiden, gives Owain or shows him
    1. The talisman (ring? stone?)
    2. The "horseblock" (*perron*), or entrance to the Otherworld
VII. The Princess (Lady of the Castle) whom Owain weds:
    1. The wedding
    2. The aftermath: Owain hears that he has only a six-year tenure.

This thirteenth-century Welsh story is a translation/adaptation of a twelfth-century account by the most famous French writer on King Arthur, Chrétien de Troyes, who was commissioned by the Countess Marie de Champagne, daughter of Queen Eleanor of England. Though closer to Roman religious ritual himself, Chrétien makes his source apparent to any reader with a Latin dictionary. The key is the Donor named "Moon," Luned in the Welsh, Lunette in the Old French of Chrétien: Our story is an account of a pre-Christian ceremony, the worship of the Moon Goddess Diana, the Roman equivalent of the Greek Moon Goddess Artemis (see Bulfinch's *The Age of Fable*). *Diana* is her name on earth. By association, she is also called *Luna,* or *Luned,* or *Lunette,* when she orbits the earth overhead. In the Otherworld, however, she is the dire Hecate, whose male priests all die one after another.

The worship of Diana occurred, as the tale has it, in a forest grove, beside a small lake (or "fountain"). Her temple outside Rome was therefore called *Nemorensis* (of the woodland grove). The King of the Grove was her male priest, killed by a new hero every six years—when his strength had failed and he was no longer able to defend

Diana's shrine against younger challengers. Quite a wedding present!

This story by Chrétien and its adaptation in the *Mabinogion* refer back to the real temple of the moon goddess Diana, daughter of Jove (Jupiter). The French hero's name was Yvain, Owain in Brythonic. The lake and grove were in the Roman town of Aricia on the Appian Way (the main road north) sixteen miles from Rome, in the area called Latium. The town is called La Riccia today.

The Roman conqueror Julius Caesar once owned a villa there. He had conquered Britain in 55 B.C. and written a book about it. His book contains the earliest descriptions of the Gauls and other Celtic peoples: *Commentaries on the Gallic War* (*De bello gallico*). Rome ruled Britain for about five hundred years, or until the lifetime of King Arthur (*c.*475–542), say the Welsh Annals.[5]

NOTES

1. Chris Barber's *Mysterious Wales,* Granada (London, 1983), p. 33. The site is called Bedd (Grave) Bronwen. See Bedd Taliesin, p. 44; Arthur's Stone, p. 130. Or see *The Penguin Guide to Prehistoric England and Wales* by James Dyer, which includes road maps to such sites, Penguin (New York, 1981).

2. *Fargher's English–Manx Dictionary,* ed. by Brian Stowell and Ian Faulds, Shearwater Press (Douglas, Isle of Man, 1979); *Bible Chaserick Yn Lught Thie,* Shearwater Press (Onchan, Isle of Man, 1979); *King Arthur* (1986–94) and *Merlin* (1987–94), Norma Lorre Goodrich.

3. *Inventory: Essays by Michel Butor,* ed. and foreword by Richard Howard. See "On Fairy Tales," pp. 211–23, Simon and Schuster (New York, 1968).

4. *Arthur and the Sovereignty of Britain: King and Goddess in "The Mabinogion,"* Penguin (London, 1989).

5. See also *The Mabinogion,* ed. by Gwyn Jones and Thomas Jones, Dutton (New York, 1974); and seven poems by Taliesin, two in praise of Kynon (Cynan) and Urien in *The Earliest Welsh Poetry,* tr. by Joseph P. Clancy, Macmillan (London, 1970). See also *Chrétien de Troyes: Yvain ou Le Chevalier au lion,* a modernization of Chrétien's version into prose by André Mary, introduction and notes by Julian Harris, Dell (New York, 1963).

CHAPTER II

THE LADY OF THE FOUNTAIN

KYNON'S ADVENTURE

King Arthur was at Caerleon upon Usk; and one day he sat in his chamber, and with him were Owain the son of Urien, and Kynon the son of Clydno, and Kay the son of Kyner, and Guenever and her handmaidens at needlework by the window. In the centre of the chamber King Arthur sat, upon a seat of green rushes,* over which was spread a covering of flame-colored satin, and a cushion of red satin was under his elbow.

Then Arthur spoke. "If I thought you would not disparage me," said he, "I would sleep while I wait for my repast; and you can entertain one another with relating tales, and can obtain a flagon of mead and some meat from Kay." And the king went to sleep. And Kynon the son of Clydno asked Kay for that which Arthur had promised them. "I too will have the good tale which he promised me," said Kay. "Nay," answered Kynon; "fairer will it be for thee to fulfil Arthur's behest in the first place, and then we will tell thee the best tale that we know." So Kay went to the kitchen and to the mead-cellar, and returned, bearing a flagon of mead, and a golden goblet, and a handful of skewers, upon which were broiled collops of meat. Then they ate the collops and began to drink the mead. "Now," said Kay, "it is time for you to give me my story." "Kynon," said Owain, "do thou pay to Kay the tale that is his due." "I will do so," answered Kynon.

"I was the only son of my mother and father, and I

---

* The use of green rushes in apartments was by no means peculiar to the court of Caerleon upon Usk. Our ancestors had a great predilection for them, and they seem to have constituted an essential article, not only of comfort, but of luxury. The custom of strewing the floor with rushes is well known to have existed in England during the Middle Ages, and also in France.

was exceedingly aspiring, and my daring was very great. I thought there was no enterprise in the world too mighty for me; and after I had achieved all the adventures that were in my own country, I equipped myself and set forth to journey through deserts and distant regions. And at length it chanced that I came to the fairest valley in the world, wherein were trees all of equal growth; and a river ran through the valley, and a path was by the side of the river. And I followed the path until midday and continued my journey along the remainder of the valley until the evening; and at the extremity of a plain, I came to a large and lustrous castle, at the foot of which was a torrent. And I approached the castle, and there I beheld two youths with yellow curling hair, each with a frontlet of gold upon his head, and clad in a garment of yellow satin; and they had gold clasps upon their insteps. In the hand of each of them was an ivory bow, strung with the sinews of the stag, and their arrows and their shafts were of the bone of the whale and were winged with peacock's feathers. The shafts also had golden heads. And they had daggers with blades of gold and with hilts of the bone of the whale. And they were shooting at a mark.

"And a little away from them I saw a man in the prime of life, with his beard newly shorn, clad in a robe and mantle of yellow satin, and round the top of his mantle was a band of gold lace. On his feet were shoes of variegated leather,* fastened by two bosses of gold. When I saw him, I went towards him and saluted him; and such was his courtesy that he no sooner received my greeting than he returned it. And he went with me towards the castle. Now there were no dwellers in the castle, except those who were in one hall. And there I saw four and twenty damsels embroidering satin at a window. And this I tell thee, Kay, that the least fair of them was fairer than the fairest maid thou didst ever behold in the island of Britain; and the least lovely of them was more lovely than Guenever, the wife of Arthur, when she appeared loveliest, at the feast of Easter. They rose

---

* Cordwal is the word in the original, and from the manner in which it is used it is evidently intended for the French Cordouan or Cordovan leather, which derived its name from Cordova, where it was manufactured. From this comes also our English word *cordwainer*.

up at my coming, and six of them took my horse and
divested me of my armor, and six others took my
arms and washed them in a vessel till they were perfectly bright. And the third six spread cloths upon the tables
and prepared meat. And the fourth six took off my
soiled garments and placed others upon me, namely, an
under vest and a doublet of fine linen, and a robe and a
surcoat, and a mantle of yellow satin, with a broad gold
band upon the mantle. And they placed cushions both
beneath and around me, with coverings of red linen.
And I sat down. Now the six maidens who had taken
my horse unharnessed him as well, as if they had been
the best squires in the island of Britain.

"Then, behold, they brought bowls of silver, wherein
was water to wash, and towels of linen, some green and
some white; and I washed. And in a little while the man
sat down at the table. And I sat next to him, and below
me sat all the maidens, except those who waited on us.
And the table was of silver, and the cloths upon the table
were of linen. And no vessel was served upon the table
that was not either of gold or of silver or of buffalo-horn.
And our meat was brought to us. And verily, Kay, I saw
there every sort of meat and every sort of liquor that I
ever saw elsewhere; but the meat and the liquor were
better served there than I ever saw them in any other
place.

"Until the repast was half over, neither the man nor
any one of the damsels spoke a single word to me; but
when the man perceived that it would be more agreeable for me to converse than to eat any more, he began
to inquire of me who I was. Then I told the man who I
was, and what was the cause of my journey, and said
that I was seeking whether any one was superior to me,
or whether I could gain the mastery over all. The man
looked upon me, and he smiled and said, 'If I did not
fear to do thee a mischief, I would show thee that which
thou seekest.' Then I desired him to speak freely. And
he said: 'Sleep here to-night, and in the morning arise
early and take the road upwards through the valley,
until thou reachest the wood. A little way within the
wood thou wilt come to a large sheltered glade, with a
mound in the centre. And thou wilt see a black man of

great stature on the top of the mound. He has but one foot, and one eye in the middle of his forehead. He is the wood-ward of that wood. And thou wilt see a thousand wild animals grazing around him. Inquire of him the way out of the glade, and he will reply to thee briefly and will point out the road by which thou shalt find that which thou art in quest of.'

"And long seemed that night to me. And the next morning I arose and equipped myself, and mounted my horse, and proceeded straight through the valley to the wood, and at length I arrived at the glade. And the black man was there, sitting upon the top of the mound; and I was three times more astonished at the number of wild animals that I beheld than the man had said I should be. Then I inquired of him the way, and he asked me roughly whither I would go. And when I had told him who I was and what I sought, 'Take,' said he, 'that path that leads towards the head of the glade, and there thou wilt find an open space like to a large valley, and in the midst of it a tall tree. Under this tree is a fountain, and by the side of the fountain a marble slab, and on the marble slab a silver bowl, attached by a chain of silver, that it may not be carried away. Take the bowl and throw a bowlful of water on the slab. And if thou dost not find trouble in that adventure, thou needest not seek it during the rest of thy life.'

"So I journeyed on until I reached the summit of the steep. And there I found everything as the black man had described it to me. And I went up to the tree, and beneath it I saw the fountain, and by its side the marble slab, and the silver bowl fastened by the chain. Then I took the bowl and cast a bowlful of water upon the slab. And immediately I heard a mighty peal of thunder, so that heaven and earth seemed to tremble with its fury. And after the thunder came a shower; and of a truth I tell thee, Kay, that it was such a shower as neither man nor beast could endure and live. I turned my horse's flank towards the shower, and placed the beak of my shield over his head and neck, while I held the upper part of it over my own neck. And thus I withstood the shower. And presently the sky became clear, and with that, behold, the birds lighted upon the tree, and sang.

And truly, Kay, I never heard any melody equal to that, either before or since. And when I was most charmed with listening to the birds, lo! a chiding voice was heard of one approaching me and saying: 'Oh, knight, what has brought thee hither? What evil have I done to thee that thou shouldst act towards me and my possessions as thou hast this day? Dost thou not know that the shower to-day has left in my dominions neither man nor beast alive that was exposed to it?' And thereupon, behold, a knight on a black horse appeared, clothed in jetblack velvet and with a tabard of black linen about him. And we charged each other, and, as the onset was furious, it was not long before I was overthrown. Then the knight passed the shaft of his lance through the bridlerein of my horse and rode off with the two horses, leaving me where I was. And he did not even bestow so much notice upon me as to imprison me, nor did he despoil me of my arms. So I returned along the road by which I had come. And when I reached the glade where the black man was, I confess to thee, Kay, it is a marvel that I did not melt down into a liquid pool, through the shame that I felt at the black man's derision. And that night I came to the same castle where I had spent the night preceding. And I was more agreeably entertained that night than I had been the night before. And I conversed freely with the inmates of the castle; and none of them alluded to my expedition to the fountain, neither did I mention it to any. And I remained there that night. When I arose on the morrow, I found ready saddled a dark bay palfrey, with nostrils as red as scarlet. And after putting on my armor and leaving there my blessing, I returned to my own court. And that horse I still possess, and he is in the stable yonder. And I declare that I would not part with him for the best palfrey in the island of Britain.

"Now, of a truth, Kay, no man ever before confessed to an adventure so much to his own discredit; and, verily, it seems strange to me that neither before nor since have I heard of any person who knew of this adventure, and that the subject of it should exist within King Arthur's dominions without any other person lighting upon it."

CHAPTER III

OWAIN'S ADVENTURE *

"Now," quoth Owain, "would it not be well to go and endeavor to discover that place?"

"By the hand of my friend," said Kay, "often dost thou utter that with thy tongue which thou wouldest not make good with thy deeds."

"In very truth," said Guenever, "it were better thou wert hanged, Kay, than to use such uncourteous speech towards a man like Owain."

"By the hand of my friend, good lady," said Kay, "thy praise of Owain is not greater than mine."

With that Arthur awoke and asked if he had not been sleeping a little.

"Yes, lord," answered Owain, "thou hast slept awhile."

"Is it time for us to go to meat?"

"It is, lord," said Owain.

Then the horn for washing was sounded, and the king and all his household sat down to eat. And when the meal was ended, Owain withdrew to his lodging and made ready his horse and his arms.

On the morrow, with the dawn of day, he put on his armor, and mounted his charger, and travelled through

---

* Amongst all the characters of early British history, none is more interesting, or occupies a more conspicuous place, than the hero of this tale. Urien, his father, was Prince of Rheged, a district comprising the present Cumberland and part of the adjacent country. His valor, and the consideration in which he was held, are a frequent theme of Bardic song, and form the subject of several very spirited odes by Taliesin. Among the Triads there is one relating to him; it is thus translated:

"Three Knights of Battle were in the court of Arthur: Cadwr the Earl of Cornwall, Launcelot du Lac, and Owain the son of Urien. And this was their characteristic,—that they would not retreat from battle, neither for spear, nor for arrow, nor for sword. And Arthur never had shame in battle the day he saw their faces there. And they were called the Knights of Battle."

distant lands and over desert mountains. And at length he arrived at the valley which Kynon had described to him, and he was certain that it was the same that he sought. And journeying along the valley, by the side of the river, he followed its course till he came to the plain, and within sight of the castle. When he approached the castle, he saw the youths shooting with their bows, in the place where Kynon had seen them, and the yellow man, to whom the castle belonged, standing hard by. And no sooner had Owain saluted the yellow man than he was saluted by him in return.

And he went forward towards the castle, and there he saw the chamber; and when he had entered the chamber, he beheld the maidens working at satin embroidery, in chains of gold. And their beauty and their comeliness seemed to Owain far greater than Kynon had represented to him. And they arose to wait upon Owain, as they had done to Kynon. And the meal which they set before him gave even more satisfaction to Owain than it had done to Kynon.

About the middle of the repast, the yellow man asked Owain the object of his journey. And Owain made it known to him and said, "I am in quest of the knight who guards the fountain." Upon this the yellow man smiled and said that he was as loath to point out that adventure to him as he had been to Kynon. However, he described the whole to Owain, and they retired to rest.

The next morning Owain found his horse made ready for him by the damsels, and he set forward and came to the glade where the black man was. And the stature of the black man seemed more wonderful to Owain than it had done to Kynon; and Owain asked of him his road, and he showed it to him. And Owain followed the road till he came to the green tree; and he beheld the fountain, and the slab beside the fountain, with the bowl upon it. And Owain took the bowl and threw a bowlful of water upon the slab. And, lo! the thunder was heard, and after the thunder came the shower, more violent than Kynon had described, and after the shower the sky became bright. And immediately the birds came and settled upon the tree and sang. And when their song was most pleasing to Owain, he beheld a knight coming to-

wards him through the valley; and he prepared to receive
him and encountered him violently. Having broken both
their lances, they drew their swords and fought blade to
blade. Then Owain struck the knight a blow through his
helmet, head-piece, and visor, and through the skin, and
the flesh, and the bone, until it wounded the very brain.
Then the black knight felt that he had received a mortal
wound, upon which he turned his horse's head and fled.
And Owain pursued him and followed close upon him,
although he was not near enough to strike him with his
sword. Then Owain descried a vast and resplendent castle; and they came to the castle gate. And the black
knight was allowed to enter, and the portcullis was let
fall upon Owain; and it struck his horse behind the saddle, and cut him in two, and carried away the rowels of
the spurs that were upon Owain's heels. And the portcullis descended to the floor. And the rowels of the spurs
and part of the horse were without, and Owain with the
other part of the horse remained between the two gates,
and the inner gate was closed, so that Owain could not
go thence; and Owain was in a perplexing situation. And
while he was in this state, he could see through an aper-
ture in the gate a street facing him, with a row of houses
on each side. And he beheld a maiden, with yellow, curling hair, and a frontlet of gold upon her head; and she
was clad in a dress of yellow satin, and on her feet were
shoes of variegated leather. And she approached the gate
and desired that it should be opened. "Heaven knows,
lady," said Owain, "it is no more possible for me to open
to thee from hence than it is for thee to set me free."
And he told her his name and who he was. "Truly," said
the damsel, "it is very sad that thou canst not be released; and every woman ought to succor thee, for I
know there is no one more faithful in the service of ladies
than thou. Therefore," quoth she, "whatever is in my
power to do for thy release, I will do it. Take this ring
and put it on thy finger, with the stone inside thy hand,
and close thy hand upon the stone. And as long as thou
concealest it, it will conceal thee. When they come forth
to fetch thee, they will be much grieved that they cannot
find thee. And I will await thee on the horseblock yonder, and thou wilt be able to see me, though I cannot

see thee. Therefore, come and place thy hand upon my shoulder, that I may know that thou art near me. And by the way that I go hence, do thou accompany me."

Then the maiden went away from Owain, and he did all that she had told him. And the people of the castle came to seek Owain to put him to death; and when they found nothing but the half of his horse, they were sorely grieved.

And Owain vanished from among them, and went to the maiden, and placed his hand upon her shoulder; whereupon she set off, and Owain followed her, until they came to the door of a large and beautiful chamber, and the maiden opened it, and they went in. And Owain looked around the chamber, and behold, there was not a single nail in it that was not painted with gorgeous colors, and there was not a single panel that had not sundry images in gold portrayed upon it.

The maiden kindled a fire, and took water in a silver bowl, and gave Owain water to wash. Then she placed before him a silver table inlaid with gold, upon which was a cloth of yellow linen, and she brought him food. And, of a truth, Owain never saw any kind of meat that was not there in abundance, but it was better cooked there than he had ever found it in any other place. And there was not one vessel from which he was served that was not of gold or of silver. And Owain ate and drank until late in the afternoon, when, lo! they heard a mighty clamor in the castle, and Owain asked the maiden what it was. "They are administering extreme unction," said she, "to the nobleman who owns the castle." And she prepared a couch for Owain which was meet for Arthur himself, and Owain went to sleep.

And a little after daybreak he heard an exceeding loud clamor and wailing, and he asked the maiden what was the cause of it. "They are bearing to the church the body of the nobleman who owned the castle."

And Owain rose up, and clothed himself, and opened a window of the chamber, and looked towards the castle; and he could see neither the bounds nor the extent of the hosts that filled the streets. And they were fully armed; and a vast number of women were with them, both on horseback and on foot, and all the ecclesiastics in the city singing. In the midst of the throng he beheld the bier, over which was a veil of white linen; and wax tapers were burning beside and around it; and none that supported the bier was lower in rank than a powerful baron.

Never did Owain see an assemblage so gorgeous with silk * and satin. And, following the train, he beheld a lady with yellow hair falling over her shoulders, and stained with blood; and about her a dress of yellow satin, which was torn. Upon her feet were shoes of variegated leather. And it was a marvel that the ends of her fingers were not bruised from the violence with which she smote her hands together. Truly, she would have been the fairest lady Owain ever saw, had she been in her usual guise. And her cry was louder than the shout of the men or the clamor of the trumpets. No sooner had he beheld the lady than he became inflamed with her love, so that it took entire possession of him.

Then he inquired of the maiden who the lady was. "Heaven knows," replied the maiden, "she is the fairest, and the most chaste, and the most liberal, and the most noble of women. She is my mistress, and she is called the Countess of the Fountain, the wife of him whom thou didst slay yesterday." "Verily," said Owain, "she is the woman that I love best." "Verily," said the maiden, "she shall also love thee, not a little."

Then the maiden prepared a repast for Owain, and truly he thought he had never before so good a meal, nor was he ever so well served. Then she left him and went towards the castle. When she came there, she found nothing but mourning and sorrow; and the countess in her chamber could not bear the sight of any one through grief. Luned, for that was the name of the maiden, sa-

---

* Before the sixth century, all the silk used by Europeans had been brought to them by the Seres, the ancestors of the present Boukharians, whence it derived its Latin name of Serica. In 551, the silkworm was brought by two monks to Constantinople; but the manufacture of silk was confined to the Greek empire till the year 1130, when Roger, King of Sicily, returning from a crusade, collected some manufacturers from Athens and Corinth and established them at Palermo, whence the trade was gradually disseminated over Italy. The varieties of silk stuffs known at this time were velvet, satin (which was called *samite*), and taffety (called *cendal* or *sendall*), all of which were occasionally stitched with gold and silver.

luted her, but the countess answered her not. And the maiden bent down towards her and said, "What aileth thee, that thou answerest no one to-day?" "Luned," said the countess, "what change hath befallen thee, that thou hast not come to visit me in my grief. It was wrong in thee, and I so sorely afflicted." "Truly," said Luned, "I thought thy good sense was greater than I find it to be. Is it well for thee to mourn after that good man, or for anything else that thou canst not have?" "I declare to Heaven," said the countess, "that in the whole world there is not a man equal to him." "Not so," said Luned, "for an ugly man would be as good as, or better than, he." "I declare to Heaven," said the countess, "that were it not repugnant to me to put to death one whom I have brought up, I would have thee executed, for making such a comparison to me. As it is, I will banish thee." "I am glad," said Luned, "that thou hast no other cause to do so than that I would have been of service to thee, where thou didst not know what was to thine advantage. Henceforth, evil betide whichever of us shall make the first advance towards reconciliation to the other, whether I should seek an invitation from thee, or thou of thine own accord shouldst send to invite me."

With that Luned went forth; and the countess arose and followed her to the door of the chamber, and began coughing loudly. And when Luned looked back, the countess beckoned to her, and she returned to the countess. "In truth," said the countess, "evil is thy disposition; but if thou knowest what is to my advantage, declare it to me." "I will do so," said she.

"Thou knowest that, except by warfare and arms, it is impossible for thee to preserve thy possessions; delay not, therefore, to seek some one who can defend them." "And how can I do that?" said the countess. "I will tell thee," said Luned; "unless thou canst defend the fountain, thou canst not maintain thy dominions; and no one can defend the fountain except it be a knight of Arthur's household. I will go to Arthur's court, and ill betide me if I return not thence with a warrior who can guard the fountain as well as, or even better than, he who defended it formerly." "That will be hard to perform," said the countess. "Go, however, and make proof of that which thou hast promised."

Luned set out under the pretence of going to Arthur's court; but she went back to the mansion where she had left Owain, and she tarried there as long as it might have taken her to travel to the court of King Arthur and back. And at the end of that time she apparelled herself and went to visit the countess. And the countess was much rejoiced when she saw her, and inquired what news she brought from the court. "I bring thee the best of news," said Luned, "for I have compassed the object of my mission. When wilt thou that I should present to thee the chieftain who has come with me hither?" "Bring him here to visit me to-morrow," said the countess, "and I will cause the town to be assembled by that time."

And Luned returned home. And the next day, at noon, Owain arrayed himself in a coat and a surcoat, and a mantle of yellow satin, upon which was a broad band of gold lace; and on his feet were high shoes of variegated leather, which were fastened by golden clasps, in the form of lions. And they proceeded to the chamber of the countess.

Right glad was the countess of their coming. And she gazed steadfastly upon Owain and said, "Luned, this knight has not the look of a traveller." "What harm is there in that, lady?" said Luned. "I am certain," said the countess, "that no other man than this chased the soul from the body of my lord." "So much the better for thee, lady," said Luned, "for had he not been stronger than thy lord, he could not have deprived him of life. There is no remedy for that which is past, be it as it may." "Go back to thine abode," said the countess, "and I will take counsel."

The next day the countess caused all her subjects to assemble, and showed them that her earldom was left defenceless, and that it could not be protected but with horse and arms and military skill. "Therefore," said she, "this is what I offer for your choice: either let one of you take me, or give your consent for me to take a husband from elsewhere to defend my dominions."

So they came to the determination that it was better that she should have permission to marry some one from elsewhere; and thereupon she sent for the bishops and archbishops to celebrate her nuptials with Owain. And the men of the earldom did Owain homage.

And Owain defended the fountain with lance and sword. And this is the manner in which he defended it. Whensoever a knight came there, he overthrew him and sold him for his full worth. And what he thus gained he divided among his barons and his knights, and no man in the whole world could be more beloved than he was by his subjects. And it was thus for the space of three years.*

CHAPTER IV

THE LADY OF THE FOUNTAIN, CONTINUED

GAWAIN'S ADVENTURE

It befell that, as Gawain went forth one day with King Arthur, he perceived him to be very sad and sorrowful. And Gawain was much grieved to see Arthur in this state, and he questioned him, saying, "Oh, my lord, what has befallen thee?" "In sooth, Gawain," said Arthur, "I am grieved concerning Owain, whom I have lost these three years; and I shall certainly die if the fourth year pass without my seeing him. Now I am sure that it is through the tale which Kynon, the son of Clydno, related, that I have lost Owain." "There is no need for thee," said Gawain, "to summon to arms thy whole dominions on this account, for thou thyself, and the men of thy house-

---

* There exists an ancient poem, printed among those of Taliesin, called the Elegy of Owain ap Urien, and containing several very beautiful and spirited passages. It commences:

"The soul of Owain ap Urien,
    May its Lord consider its exigencies!
    Reged's chief the green turf covers."

In the course of this Elegy, the bard, alluding to the incessant warfare with which this chieftain harassed his Saxon foes, exclaims:

"Could England sleep with the light upon her eyes!"

hold, will be able to avenge Owain if he be slain, or to
set him free if he be in prison; and, if alive, to bring him
back with thee." And it was settled according to what
Gawain had said.

Then Arthur and the men of his household prepared to
go and seek Owain. And Kynon, the son of Clydno, acted
as their guide. And Arthur came to the castle where
Kynon had been before. And when he came there, the
youths were shooting in the same place, and the yellow
man was standing hard by. When the yellow man saw
Arthur, he greeted him and invited him to the castle. And
Arthur accepted his invitation, and they entered the
castle together. And great as was the number of his
retinue, their presence was scarcely observed in the castle, so vast was its extent. And the maidens rose up to
wait on them. And the service of the maidens appeared to
them all to excel any attendance they had ever met with;
and even the pages, who had charge of the horses, were
no worse served that night than Arthur himself would
have been in his own palace.

The next morning, Arthur set out thence, with Kynon
for his guide, and came to the place where the black man
was. And the stature of the black man was more surpris-
ing to Arthur than it had been represented to him. And
they came to the top of the wooded steep, and traversed
the valley, till they reached the green tree, where they
saw the fountain and the bowl and the slab. And upon
that Kay came to Arthur and spoke to him. "My lord,"
said he, "I know the meaning of all this, and my request
is that thou wilt permit me to throw the water on the
slab and to receive the first adventure that may befall."
And Arthur gave him leave.

Then Kay threw a bowlful of water upon the slab, and
immediately there came the thunder, and after the thunder the shower. And such a thunder-storm they had never
known before. After the shower had ceased, the sky
became clear, and on looking at the tree, they beheld it
completely leafless. Then the birds descended upon the
tree. And the song of the birds was far sweeter than any
strain they had ever heard before. Then they beheld a
knight, on a coal-black horse, clothed in black satin,
coming rapidly towards them. And Kay met him and

encountered him, and it was not long before Kay was overthrown. And the knight withdrew. And Arthur and his host encamped for the night.

And when they arose in the morning, they perceived the signal of combat upon the lance of the knight. Then, one by one, all the household of Arthur went forth to combat the knight, until there was not one that was not overthrown by him, except Arthur and Gawain. And Arthur armed himself to encounter the knight. "Oh, my lord," said Gawain, "permit me to fight with him first." And Arthur permitted him. And he went forth to meet the knight, having over himself and his horse a satin robe of honor, which had been sent him by the daughter of the Earl of Rhangyr, and in this dress he was not known by any of the host. And they charged each other and fought all that day until the evening. And neither of them was able to unhorse the other. And so it was the next day; they broke their lances in the shock, but neither of them could obtain the mastery.

And the third day they fought with exceeding strong lances. And they were incensed with rage and fought furiously, even until noon. And they gave each other such a shock that the girths of their horses were broken, so that they fell over their horses' cruppers to the ground. And they rose up speedily, and drew their swords, and resumed the combat. And all they that witnessed their encounter felt assured that they had never before seen two men so valiant or so powerful. And had it been midnight, it would have been light, from the fire that flashed from their weapons. And the knight gave Gawain a blow that turned his helmet from off his face, so that the knight saw that it was Gawain. Then Owain said, "My lord Gawain, I did not know thee for my cousin, owing to the robe of honor that enveloped thee; take my sword and my arms." Said Gawain, "Thou, Owain, art the victor; take thou my sword." And with that Arthur saw that they were conversing, and advanced towards them. "My lord Arthur," said Gawain, "here is Owain, who has vanquished me, and will not take my arms." "My lord," said Owain, "it is he that has vanquished me, and he will not take my sword." "Give me your swords," said Arthur, "and then neither of you has vanquished the other." Then

Owain put his arms round Arthur's neck, and they embraced. And all the host hurried forward to see Owain and to embrace him. And there was nigh being a loss of life, so great was the press.

And they retired that night, and the next day Arthur prepared to depart. "My lord," said Owain, "this is not well of thee. For I have been absent from thee these three years, and during all that time, up to this very day, I have been preparing a banquet for thee, knowing that thou wouldst come to seek me. Tarry with me, therefore, until thou and thy attendants have recovered the fatigues of the journey and have been anointed."

And they all proceeded to the castle of the Countess of the Fountain, and the banquet which had been three years preparing was consumed in three months. Never had they a more delicious or agreeable banquet. And Arthur prepared to depart. Then he sent an embassy to the countess to beseech her to permit Owain to go with him, for the space of three months, that he might show him to the nobles and the fair dames of the island of Britain. And the countess gave her consent, although it was very painful to her. So Owain came with Arthur to the island of Britain. And when he was once more amongst his kindred and friends, he remained three years, instead of three months, with them.

THE ADVENTURE OF THE LION

And as Owain one day sat at meat, in the city of Caerleon upon Usk, behold a damsel entered the hall, upon a bay horse,* with a curling mane, and covered

---

* The custom of riding into a hall while the lord and his guests sat at meat, might be illustrated by numerous passages of ancient romance and history. But a quotation from Chaucer's beautiful and half-told tale of Cambuscan is sufficient:

"And so befell that after the thriddle cours,
While that this king sat thus in his nobley,
Herking his minstralles thir thinges play,
Beforne him at his bord deliciously,
In at the halle door all sodenly
Ther came a knight upon a stede of bras,
And in his hond a brod mirrour of glas;

with foam; and the bridle, and as much as was seen of the saddle, were of gold. And the damsel was arrayed in a dress of yellow satin. And she came up to Owain and took the ring from off his hand. "Thus," said she, "shall be treated the deceiver, the traitor, the faithless, the disgraced, and the beardless." And she turned her horse's head and departed.

Then his adventure came to Owain's remembrance, and he was sorrowful. And having finished eating, he went to his own abode and made preparations that night. And the next day he arose, but did not go to the court, nor did he return to the Countess of the Fountain, but wandered to the distant parts of the earth and to uncultivated mountains. And he remained there until all his apparel was worn out, and his body was wasted away, and his hair was grown long. And he went about with the wild beasts, and fed with them, until they became familiar with him. But at length he became so weak that he could no longer bear them company. Then he descended from the mountains to the valley, and came to a park, that was the fairest in the world and belonged to a charitable lady.

One day, the lady and her attendants went forth to walk by a lake that was in the middle of the park. And they saw the form of a man, lying as if dead. And they were terrified. Nevertheless they went near him and touched him, and they saw that there was life in him. And the lady returned to the castle, and took a flask full of precious ointment, and gave it to one of her maidens. "Go with this," said she, "and take with thee yonder horse, and clothing, and place them near the man we saw just now; and anoint him with this balsam near his heart; and if there is life in him, he will revive, through the efficiency of this balsam. Then watch what he will do."

And the maiden departed from her, and went and poured of the balsam upon Owain, and left the horse and the garments hard by, and went a little way off and

---

Upon his thombe he had of gold a ring,
And by his side a naked sword hanging;
And up he rideth to the highe bord.
In all the halle ne was ther spoke a word,
For mervaille of this knight; him to behold
Full besily they waiten, young and old."

hid herself to watch him. In a short time, she saw him begin to move; and he rose up, and looked at his person, and became ashamed of the unseemliness of his appearance. Then he perceived the horse and the garments that were near him. And he clothed himself and, with difficulty, mounted the horse. Then the damsel discovered herself to him and saluted him. And he and the maiden proceeded to the castle, and the maiden conducted him to a pleasant chamber, and kindled a fire, and left him.

And he stayed at the castle three months, till he was restored to his former guise, and became even more comely than he had ever been before. And Owain rendered signal service to the lady, in a controversy with a powerful neighbor, so that he made ample requital to her for her hospitality; and he took his departure.

And as he journeyed he heard a loud yelling in a wood. And it was repeated a second and a third time. And Owain went towards the spot and beheld a huge craggy mound, in the middle of the wood, on the side of which was a gray rock. And there was a cleft in the rock, and a serpent was within the cleft. And near the rock stood a black lion, and every time the lion sought to go thence, the serpent darted towards him to attack him. And Owain unsheathed his sword and drew near to the rock; and as the serpent sprung out, he struck him with his sword and cut him in two. And he dried his sword and went on his way as before. But behold the lion followed him, and played about him, as though it had been a greyhound that he had reared.

They proceeded thus throughout the day, until the evening. And when it was time for Owain to take his rest, he dismounted and turned his horse loose in a flat and wooded meadow. And he struck fire, and when the fire was kindled, the lion brought him fuel enough to last for three nights. And the lion disappeard. And presently the lion returned, bearing a fine large roebuck. And he threw it down before Owain, who went towards the fire with it.

And Owain took the roebuck, and skinned it, and placed collops of its flesh upon skewers round the fire. The rest of the buck he gave to the lion to devour. While he was so employed, he heard a deep groan near him, and

a second, and a third. And the place whence the groans
proceeded was a cave in the rock; and Owain went near
and called out to know who it was that groaned so piteously. And a voice answered, "I am Luned, the hand-
maiden of the Countess of the Fountain." "And what
dost thou here?" said he. "I am imprisoned," said she,
"on account of the knight who came from Arthur's court
and married the countess. And he staid a short time with
her, but he afterwards departed for the court of Arthur,
and has not returned since. And two of the countess's
pages traduced him and called him a deceiver. And because I said I would vouch for it he would come before
long and maintain his cause against both of them, they
imprisoned me in this cave and said that I should be put
to death, unless he came to deliver me, by a certain day;
and that is no further off than to-morrow, and I have no
one to send to seek him for me. His name is Owain, the
son of Urien." "And art thou certain that if that knight
knew all this, he would come to thy rescue?" "I am most
certain of it," said she.

When the collops were cooked, Owain divided them
into two parts, between himself and the maiden, and
then Owain laid himself down to sleep; and never did
sentinel keep stricter watch over his lord than the lion
that night over Owain.

And the next day there came the two pages with a
great troop of attendants to take Luned from her cell
and put her to death. And Owain asked them what charge
they had against her. And they told him of the compact
that was between them; as the maiden had done the night
before. "And," said they, "Owain has failed her, therefore we are taking her to be burnt." "Truly," said Owain,
"he is a good knight, and if he knew that the maiden
was in such peril, I marvel that he came not to her rescue.
But if you will accept me in his stead, I will do battle
with you." "We will," said the youths.

And they attacked Owain, and he was hard beset by
them. And with that, the lion came to Owain's assistance, and they two got the better of the young men. And
they said to him, "Chieftain, it was not agreed that we
should fight save with thyself alone, and it is harder for
us to contend with yonder animal than with thee." And

Owain put the lion in the place where Luned had been imprisoned, and blocked up the door with stones. And he went to fight with the young men as before. But Owain had not his usual strength, and the two youths pressed hard upon him. And the lion roared incessantly at seeing Owain in trouble. And he burst through the wall, until he found a way out, and rushed upon the young men and instantly slew them. So Luned was saved from being burned.

Then Owain returned with Luned to the castle of the Lady of the Fountain. And when he went thence, he took the countess with him to Arthur's court, and she was his wife as long as she lived.

CHAPTER V

GERAINT, THE SON OF ERBIN

Arthur was accustomed to hold his court at Caerleon upon Usk. And there he held it seven Easters and five Christmases. And once upon a time he held his court there at Whitsuntide. For Caerleon was the place most easy of access in his dominions, both by sea and by land. And there were assembled nine crowned kings, who were his tributaries, and likewise earls and barons. For they were his invited guests at all the high festivals, unless they were prevented by any great hindrance. And when he was at Caerleon holding his court, thirteen churches were set apart for mass. And thus they were appointed: one church for Arthur and his kings, and his guests; and the second for Guenever and her ladies; and the third for the steward of the household and the suitors; and the fourth for the Franks and the other officers; and the other nine churches were for the nine masters of the household, and chiefly for Gawain, for he, from the eminence of his warlike fame and from the nobleness of his birth, was the most exalted of the nine. And there was no other ar-

rangement respecting the churches than that which we
have here mentioned.

And on Whit-Tuesday, as the king sat at the banquet,
lo, there entered a tall, fair-headed youth, clad in a coat
and surcoat of satin, and a golden-hilted sword about his
neck, and low shoes of leather upon his feet. And he came
and stood before Arthur. "Hail to thee, lord," said he.
"Heaven prosper thee," he answered, "and be thou welcome." "Dost thou bring any new tidings?" "I do, lord,"
he said. "I am one of thy foresters, lord, in the forest of
Dean, and my name is Madoc, son of Turgadarn. In the
forest I saw a stag, the like of which beheld I never yet."
"What is there about him," asked Arthur, "that thou
never yet didst see his like?" He is of pure white, lord,
and he does not herd with any other animal, through
stateliness and pride, so royal is his bearing. And I come
to seek thy counsel, lord, and to know thy will concerning him." "It seems best to me," said Arthur, "to go and
hunt him to-morrow at break of day, and to cause general notice thereof to be given to-night, in all quarters of
the court." And Arryfuerys was Arthur's chief huntsman,
and Arelivri his chief page. And all received notice; and
thus it was arranged.

Then Guenever said to Arthur, "Wilt thou permit me,
lord, to go to-morrow to see and hear the hunt of the
stag of which the young man spoke?" "I will gladly," said
Arthur. And Gawain said to Arthur, "Lord, if it seem
well to thee, permit that into whose hunt soever the stag
shall come, that one, be he a knight or one on foot, may
cut off his head, and give it to whom he pleases, whether
to his own lady-love, or to the lady of his friend." "I
grant it gladly," said Arthur, "and let the steward of the
household be chastised, if all things are not ready to-
morrow for the chase."

And they passed the night with songs, and diversions,
and discourse, and ample entertainment. And when it
was time for them all to go to sleep, they went. And
when the next day came, they arose. And Arthur called
the attendants who guarded his couch. And there were
four pages whose names were Cadyrnerth, the son of
Gandwy, and Ambreu, the son of Bedwor, and Amhar,
the son of Arthur, and Goreu, the son of Custennin. And

these men came to Arthur, and saluted him, and arrayed him in his garments. And Arthur wondered that Guenever did not awake, and the attendants wished to awaken her. "Disturb her not," said Arthur, "for she had rather sleep than go to see the hunting."

Then Arthur went forth, and he heard two horns sounding, one from near the lodging of the chief huntsman, and the other from near that of the chief page. And the whole assembly of the multitudes came to Arthur, and they took the road to the forest.

And after Arthur had gone forth from the palace, Guenever awoke, and called to her maidens, and apparelled herself. "Maidens," said she, "I had leave last night to go and see the hunt. Go one of you to the stable and order hither a horse such as a woman may ride." And one of them went, and she found but two horses in the stable; and Guenever and one of her maidens mounted them, and went through the Usk, and followed the track of the men and the horses. And as they rode thus, they heard a loud and rushing sound; and they looked behind them and beheld a knight upon a hunter foal of mighty size. And the rider was a fair-haired youth, bare-legged, and of princely mien; and a golden-hilted sword was at his side, and a robe and a surcoat of satin were upon him, and two low shoes of leather upon his feet; and around him was a scarf of blue purple at each corner of which was a golden apple. And his horse stepped stately, and swift, and proud; and he overtook Guenever and saluted her. "Heaven prosper thee, Geraint," said she; "and why didst thou not go with thy lord to hunt?" "Because I knew not when he went," said he. "I marvel, too," said she, "how he could go, unknown to me. But thou, oh, young man, art the most agreeable companion I could have in the whole kingdom; and it may be I shall be more amused with the hunting than they; for we shall hear the horns when they sound, and we shall hear the dogs when they are let loose and begin to cry."

So they went to the edge of the forest, and there they stood. "From this place," said she, "we shall hear when the dogs are let loose." And thereupon they heard a loud noise; and they looked towards the spot whence it came, and they beheld a dwarf riding upon a horse, stately

and foaming and prancing and strong and spirited. And
in the hand of the dwarf was a whip. And near the dwarf
they saw a lady upon a beautiful white horse, of steady
and stately pace; and she was clothed in a garment of
gold brocade. And near her was a knight upon a war-
horse of large size, with heavy and bright armor both
upon himself and upon his horse. And truly they never
before saw a knight, or a horse, or armor of such remarkable size.

"Geraint," said Guenever, "knowest thou the name of
that tall knight yonder?" "I know him not," said he, "and
the strange armor that he wears prevents my either seeing
his face or his features." "Go, maiden," said Guenever,
"and ask the dwarf who that knight is." Then the maiden
went up to the dwarf; and she inquired of the dwarf who
the knight was. "I will not tell thee," he answered. "Since
thou art so churlish," said she, "I will ask him, himself."
"Thou shalt not ask him, by my faith," said he. "Wherefore not?" said she. "Because thou art not of honor sufficient to befit thee to speak to my lord." Then the maiden
turned her horse's head towards the knight, upon which
the dwarf struck her with the whip that was in his
hand across the face and the eyes, so that the blood
flowed forth. And the maiden returned to Guenever, complaining of the hurt she had received. "Very rudely has
the dwarf treated thee," said Geraint, and he put his
hand upon the hilt of his sword. But he took counsel
with himself, and considered that it would be no vengeance for him to slay the dwarf, and to be attacked
unarmed by the armed knight; so he refrained.

"Lady," said he, "I will follow him, with thy permission, and at last he will come to some inhabited place,
where I may have arms, either as a loan or for a pledge,
so that I may encounter the knight." "Go," said she,
"and do not attack him until thou hast good arms; and I
shall be very anxious concerning thee, until I hear tidings
of thee." "If I am alive," said he, "thou shalt hear tidings
of me by to-morrow afternoon"; and with that he departed.

And the road they took was below the palace of Caerleon and across the ford of the Usk; and they went
along a fair and even and lofty ridge of ground, until

they came to a town, and at the extremity of the town
they saw a fortress and a castle. And as the knight
passed through the town, all the people arose and saluted him, and bade him welcome. And when Geraint
came into the town, he looked at every house to see if he
knew any of those whom he saw. But he knew none,
and none knew him, to do him the kindness to let him
have arms, either as a loan or for a pledge. And every
house he saw was full of men, and arms, and horses.
And they were polishing shields, and burnishing swords,
and washing armor, and shoeing horses. And the knight
and the lady and the dwarf rode up to the castle, that
was in the town, and every one was glad in the castle.
And from the battlements and the gates they risked their
necks, through their eagerness to greet them and to show
their joy.

Geraint stood there to see whether the knight would
remain in the castle; and when he was certain that he
would do so, he looked around him. And at a little distance from the town he saw an old palace in ruins, wherein was a hall that was falling to decay. And as he knew
not any one in the town, he went towards the old palace.
And when he came near to the palace, he saw a hoary-
headed man standing by it, in tattered garments. And
Geraint gazed steadfastly upon him. Then the hoary-
headed man said to him, "Young man, wherefore art
thou thoughtful?" "I am thoughtful," said he, "because I
know not where to pass the night." "Wilt thou come forward this way, Chieftain," said he, "and thou shalt have
of the best that can be procured for thee." So Geraint
went forward. And the hoary-headed man led the way
into the hall. And in the hall he dismounted, and he left
there his horse. Then he went on to the upper chamber
with the hoary-headed man. And in the chamber he
beheld an old woman sitting on a cushion, with old, worn-
out garments upon her; yet it seemed to him that she
must have been comely when in the bloom of youth.
And beside her was a maiden, upon whom were a vest
and a veil that were old and beginning to be worn out.
And truly he never saw a maiden more full of comeliness and grace and beauty than she. And the hoary-
headed man said to the maiden, "There is no attendant

for the horse of this youth but thyself." "I will render the best service I am able," said she, "both to him and to his horse." And the maiden disarrayed the youth, and then she furnished his horse with straw and with corn; and then she returned to the chamber. And the hoary-headed man said to the maiden, "Go to the town and bring hither the best that thou canst find, both of food and of liquor." "I will gladly, lord," said she. And to the town went the maiden. And they conversed together while the maiden was at the town. And, behold, the maiden came back, and a youth with her, bearing on his back a costrel full of good purchased mead and a quarter of a young bullock. And in the hands of the maiden was a quantity of white bread, and she had some manchet bread in her veil, and she came into the chamber. "I could not obtain better than this," said she, "nor with better should I have been trusted." "It is good enough," said Geraint. And they caused the meat to be boiled; and when their food was ready, they sat down. And it was in this wise. Geraint sat between the hoary-headed man and his wife, and the maiden served them. And they ate and drank.

And when they had finished eating, Geraint talked with the hoary-headed man, and he asked him in the first place to whom belonged the palace that he was in. "Truly," said he, "it was I that built it, and to me belonged the city and the castle which thou sawest." "Alas!" said Geraint, "how is it that thou hast lost them now?" "I lost a great earldom as well as these," said he, "and this is how I lost them. I had a nephew, the son of my brother, and I took care of his possessions; but he was impatient to enter upon them, so he made war upon me and wrested from me not only his own, but also my estates, except this castle." "Good sir," said Geraint, "wilt thou tell me wherefore came the knight and the lady and the dwarf just now into the town, and what is the preparation which I saw, and the putting of arms in order?" "I will do so," said he. "The preparations are for the game that is to be held to-morrow by the young earl, which will be on this wise. In the midst of a meadow which is here, two forks will be set up, and upon the two forks a silver rod, and upon the silver rod a sparrow-hawk, and for the sparrow-hawk there will be a tournament. And to the tournament will go all the array thou didst see in the city, of men and of horses and of arms. And with each man will go the lady he loves best; and no man can joust for the sparrow-hawk, except the lady he loves best be with him. And the knight that thou sawest has gained the sparrow-hawk these two years; and if he gains it the third year, he will be called the Knight of the Sparrow-hawk from that time forth." "Sir," said Geraint, "what is thy counsel to me concerning this knight, on account of the insult which the maiden of Guenever received from the dwarf?" And Geraint told the hoary-headed man what the insult was that the maiden had received. "It is not easy to counsel thee, inasmuch as thou hast neither dame nor maiden belonging to thee, for whom thou canst joust. Yet I have arms here, which thou couldst have, and there is my horse also, if he seem to thee better than thine own." "Ah, sir," said he, "Heaven reward thee! But my own horse, to which I am accustomed, together with thine arms, will suffice me. And if, when the appointed time shall come to-morrow, thou wilt permit me, sir, to challenge for yonder maiden that is thy daughter, I will engage, if I escape from the tournament, to love the maiden as long as I live." "Gladly will I permit thee," said the hoary-headed man; "and since thou dost thus resolve, it is necessary that thy horse and arms should be ready to-morrow at break of day. For then the Knight of the Sparrow-hawk will make proclamation, and ask the lady he loves best to take the sparrow-hawk; and if any deny it to her, by force will he defend her claim. And therefore," said the hoary-headed man, "it is needful for thee to be there at daybreak, and we three will be with thee." And thus was it settled.

And at night they went to sleep. And before the dawn, they arose and arrayed themselves; and by the time that it was day, they were all four in the meadow. And there was the Knight of the Sparrow-hawk making the proclamation, and asking his lady-love to take the sparrow-hawk. "Take it not," said Geraint, "for here is a maiden who is fairer, and more noble, and more comely, and who has a better claim to it than thou." Then said the knight, "If thou maintainest the sparrow-hawk to be due to her, come forward and do battle with me." And Geraint went

forward to the top of the meadow, having upon himself
and upon his horse armor which was heavy and rusty,
and of uncouth shape. Then they encountered each other,
and they broke a set of lances; and they broke a second
set, and a third. And when the earl and his company saw
the Knight of the Sparrow-hawk gaining the mastery,
there was shouting and joy and mirth amongst them; and
the hoary-headed man and his wife and his daughter were
sorrowful. And the hoary-headed man served Geraint
with lances as often as he broke them, and the dwarf
served the Knight of the Sparrow-hawk. Then the hoary-
headed man said to Geraint, "Oh, chieftain, since no
other will hold with thee, behold, here is the lance which
was in my hand on the day when I received the honor of
knighthood, and from that time to this I never broke it,
and it has an excellent point." Then Geraint took the
lance, thanking the hoary-headed man. And thereupon
the dwarf also brought a lance to his lord. "Behold, here
is a lance for thee, not less good than his," said the
dwarf. "And bethink thee that no knight ever withstood
thee so long as this one has done." "I declare to Heaven,"
said Geraint, "that unless death takes me quickly hence,
he shall fare never the better for thy service." And
Geraint pricked his horse towards him from afar,
and, warning him, he rushed upon him, and gave him a
blow so severe, and furious, and fierce, upon the face of
his shield, that he cleft it in two, and broke his armor, and
burst his girths, so that both he and his saddle were
borne to the ground over the horse's crupper. And
Geraint dismounted quickly. And he was wroth, and he
drew his sword and rushed fiercely upon him. Then the
knight also arose and drew his sword against Geraint. And
they fought on foot with their swords until their arms
struck sparks of fire like stars from one another; and thus
they continued fighting until the blood and sweat obscured the light from their eyes. At length Geraint called
to him all his strength, and struck the knight upon the
crown of his head, so that he broke all his head-armor,
and cut through all the flesh and the skin, even to the
skull, until he wounded the bone.

Then the knight fell upon his knees, and cast his sword
from his hand, and besought mercy from Geraint. "Of a

truth," said he, "I relinquish my overdaring and my pride and crave thy mercy; and unless I have time to commit myself to Heaven for my sins, and to talk with a priest, thy mercy will avail me little." "I will grant thee grace upon this condition," said Geraint; "that thou go to Guenever, the wife of Arthur, to do her satisfaction for the insult which her maiden received from thy dwarf. Dismount not from the time thou goest hence until thou comest into the presence of Guenever, to make her what atonement shall be adjudged at the court of Arthur." "This will I do gladly; and who art thou?" "I am Geraint, the son of Erbin; and declare thou also who thou art." "I am Edeyrn, the son of Nudd." Then he threw himself upon his horse and went forward to Arthur's court; and the lady he loved best went before him and the dwarf, with much lamentation.

Then came the young earl and his hosts to Geraint, and saluted him, and bade him to his castle. "I may not go," said Geraint; "but where I was last night, there will I be to-night also." "Since thou wilt none of my inviting, thou shalt have abundance of all that I can command for thee; and I will order ointment for thee, to recover thee from thy fatigues and from the weariness that is upon thee." "Heaven reward thee," said Geraint, "and I will go to my lodging." And thus went Geraint and Earl Ynywl, and his wife and his daughter. And when they reached the old mansion, the household servants and attendants of the young earl had arrived, and had arranged all the apartments, dressing them with straw and with fire; and in a short time the ointment was ready, and Geraint came there, and they washed his head. Then came the young earl, with forty honorable knights from among his attendants, and those who were bidden to the tournament. And Geraint came from the anointing. And the earl asked him to go to the hall to eat. "Where is the Earl Ynywl," said Geraint, "and his wife and his daughter?" "They are in the chamber yonder," said the earl's chamberlain, "arraying themselves in garments which the earl has caused to be brought for them." "Let not the damsel array herself," said he, "except in her vest and her veil, until she come to the court of Arthur, to be clad by Guenever in such garments as she may choose." So the maiden did not array herself.

Then they all entered the hall, and they washed, and sat down to meat. And thus were they seated. On one side of Geraint sat the young earl, and Earl Ynywl beyond him, and on the other side of Geraint was the maiden and her mother. And after these all sat according to their precedence in honor. And they ate. And they were served abundantly, and they received a profusion of divers kinds of gifts. Then they conversed together. And the young earl invited Geraint to visit him next day. "I will not, by Heaven," said Geraint. "To the court of Arthur will I go with this maiden to-morrow. And it is enough for me, as long as Earl Ynywl is in poverty and trouble; and I go chiefly to seek to add to his maintenance." "Ah, Chieftain," said the young earl, "it is not by my fault that Earl Ynywl is without his possessions." "By my faith," said Geraint, "he shall not remain without them, unless death quickly takes me hence." "Oh, Chieftain," said he, "with regard to the disagreement between me and Ynywl, I will gladly abide by thy counsel, and agree to what thou mayest judge right between us." "I but ask thee," said Geraint, "to restore to him what is his, and what he should have received from the time he lost his possessions even until this day." "That will I do, gladly, for thee," answered he. "Then," said Geraint, "whosoever is here who owes homage to Ynywl, let him come forward and perform it on the spot." And all the men did so; and by that treaty they abided. And his castle, and his town, and all his possessions were restored to Ynywl. And he received back all that he had lost, even to the smallest jewel.

Then spoke Earl Ynywl to Geraint. "Chieftain," said he, "behold the maiden for whom thou didst challenge at the tournament; I bestow her upon thee." "She shall go with me," said Geraint, "to the court of Arthur, and Arthur and Guenever, they shall dispose of her as they will." And the next day they proceeded to Arthur's court. So far concerning Geraint.

CHAPTER VI

GERAINT, THE SON OF ERBIN, CONTINUED

Now this is how Arthur hunted the stag. The men and the dogs were divided into hunting-parties, and the dogs were let loose upon the stag. And the last dog that was let loose was the favorite dog of Arthur; Cavall was his name. And he left all the other dogs behind him and turned the stag. And at the second turn the stag came toward the hunting-party of Arthur. And Arthur set upon him; and before he could be slain by any other, Arthur cut off his head. Then they sounded the death-horn for slaying, and they all gathered round.

Then came Kadyriath to Arthur and spoke to him. "Lord," said he, "behold, yonder is Guenever, and none with her save only one maiden." "Command Gildas, the son of Caw, and all the scholars of the court," said Arthur, "to attend Guenever to the palace." And they did so.

Then they all set forth, holding converse together concerning the head of the stag, to whom it should be given. One wished that it should be given to the lady best beloved by him, and another to the lady whom he loved best. And so they came to the palace. And when Arthur and Guenever heard them disputing about the head of the stag, Guenever said to Arthur: "My lord, this is my counsel concerning the stag's head; let it not be given away until Geraint, the son of Erbin, shall return from the errand he is upon." And Guenever told Arthur what that errand was. "Right gladly shall it be so," said Arthur. And Guenever caused a watch to be set upon the ramparts for Geraint's coming. And after midday they beheld an unshapely little man upon a horse, and after him a dame or a damsel, also on horseback, and after her a knight of large stature, bowed down, and hanging his head low and sorrowfully, and clad in broken and worthless armor.

229

And before they came near to the gate, one of the watch went to Guenever and told her what kind of people they saw, and what aspect they bore. "I know not who they are," said he. "But *I* know," said Guenever; "this is the knight whom Geraint pursued, and methinks that he comes not here by his own free will. But Geraint has overtaken him and avenged the insult to the maiden to the uttermost." And thereupon, behold, a porter came to the spot where Guenever was. "Lady," said he, "at the gate there is a knight, and I saw never a man of so pitiful an aspect to look upon as he. Miserable and broken is the armor that he wears, and the hue of blood is more conspicuous upon it than its own color." "Knowest thou his name?" said she. "I do," said he; "he tells me that he is Edeyrn, the son of Nudd." Then she replied, "I know him not."

So Guenever went to the gate to meet him, and he entered. And Guenever was sorry when she saw the condition he was in, even though he was accompanied by the churlish dwarf. Then Edeyrn saluted Guenever. "Heaven protect thee," said she. "Lady," said he, "Geraint, the son of Erbin, thy best and most valiant servant, greets thee." "Did he meet with thee?" she asked. "Yes," said he, "and it was not to my advantage; and that was not his fault, but mine, lady. And Geraint greets thee well; and in greeting thee he compelled me to come hither to do thy pleasure for the insult which thy maiden received from the dwarf." "Now where did he overtake thee?" "At the place where we were jousting and contending for the sparrow-hawk, in the town which is now called Cardiff. And it was for the avouchment of the love of the maiden, the daughter of Earl Ynywl, that Geraint jousted at the tournament. And thereupon we encountered each other, and he left me, lady, as thou seest." "Sir," said she, "when thinkest thou that Geraint will be here?" "To-morrow, lady, I think he will be here with the maiden."

Then Arthur came to them. And he saluted Arthur, and Arthur gazed a long time upon him, and was amazed to see him thus. And thinking that he knew him, he inquired of him, "Art thou Edeyrn, the son of Nudd?" "I am, lord," said he, "and I have met with much trouble and received wounds unsupportable." Then he told Arthur all his adventure. "Well," said Arthur, "From what I hear, it behooves Guenever to be merciful towards thee." "The mercy which thou desirest, lord," said she, "will I grant to him, since it is as insulting to thee that an insult should be offered to me as to thyself." "Thus will it be best to do," said Arthur; "let this man have medical care until it be known whether he may live. And if he live, he shall do such satisfaction as shall be judged best by the men of the court. And if he die, too much will be the death of such a youth as Edeyrn for an insult to a maiden." "This pleases me," said Guenever. And Arthur caused Morgan Tud to be called to him. He was the chief physician. "Take with thee Edeyrn, the son of Nudd, and cause a chamber to be prepared for him, and let him have the aid of medicine as thou wouldest do unto myself, if I were wounded; and let none into his chamber to molest him, but thyself and thy disciples, to administer to him remedies." "I will do so, gladly, lord," said Morgan Tud. Then said the steward of the household, "Whither is it right, lord, to order the maiden?" "To Guenever and her handmaidens," said he. And the steward of the household so ordered her.

The next day came Geraint towards the court; and there was a watch set on the ramparts by Guenever, lest he should arrive unawares. And one of the watch came to Guenever. "Lady," said he, "methinks that I see Geraint, and a maiden with him. He is on horseback, but he has his walking gear upon him, and the maiden appears to be in white, seeming to be clad in a garment of linen." "Assemble all the women," said Guenever, "and come to meet Geraint, to welcome him, and wish him joy." And Guenever went to meet Geraint and the maiden. And when Geraint came to the place where Guenever was, he saluted her. "Heaven prosper thee," said she, "and welcome to thee." "Lady," said he, "I earnestly desired to obtain thee satisfaction, according to thy will; and, behold, here is the maiden through whom thou hadst thy revenge." "Verily," said Guenever, "the welcome of Heaven be unto her; and it is fitting that we should receive her joyfully." Then they went in and dismounted. And Geraint came to where Arthur was and saluted him.

"Heaven protect thee," said Arthur, "and the welcome of Heaven be unto thee. And inasmuch as thou hast vanquished Edeyrn, the son of Nudd, thou hast had a prosperous career." "Not upon me be the blame," said Geraint; "it was through the arrogance of Edeyrn, the son of Nudd, himself, that we were not friends." "Now," said Arthur, "where is the maiden for whom I heard thou didst give challenge?" "She is gone with Guenever to her chamber." Then went Arthur to see the maiden. And Arthur, and all his companions, and his whole court, were glad concerning the maiden. And certain were they all, that, had her array been suitable to her beauty, they had never seen a maid fairer than she. And Arthur gave away the maiden to Geraint. And the usual bond made between two persons was made between Geraint and the maiden, and the choicest of all Guenever's apparel was given to the maiden; and thus arrayed, she appeared comely and graceful to all who beheld her. And that day and the night were spent in abundance of minstrelsy, and ample gifts of liquor, and a multitude of games. And when it was time for them to go to sleep, they went. And in the chamber where the couch of Arthur and Guenever was, the couch of Geraint and Enid was prepared. And from that time she became his wife. And the next day Arthur satisfied all the claimants upon Geraint with bountiful gifts. And the maiden took up her abode in the palace, and she had many companions, both men and women, and there was no maiden more esteemed than she in the island of Britain.

Then spake Guenever. "Rightly did I judge," said she, "concerning the head of the stag, that it should not be given to any until Geraint's return; and behold, here is a fit occasion for bestowing it. Let it be given to Enid, the daughter of Ynywl, the most illustrious maiden. And I do not believe that any will begrudge it her, for between her and every one here there exists nothing but love and friendship." Much applauded was this by them all, and by Arthur also. And the head of the stag was given to Enid. And thereupon her fame increased, and her friends became more in number than before. And Geraint from that time forth loved the hunt, and the tournament, and hard encounters; and he came victorious from them all.

And a year, and a second, and a third, he proceeded thus, until his fame had flown over the face of the kingdom.

And, once upon a time, Arthur was holding his court at Caerleon upon Usk; and behold, there came to him ambassadors, wise and prudent, full of knowledge and eloquent of speech, and they saluted Arthur. "Heaven prosper you!" said Arthur; "and whence do you come?" "We come, lord," said they, "from Cornwall; and we are ambassadors from Erbin, the son of Custennin, thy uncle, and our mission is unto thee. And he greets thee well, as an uncle should greet his nephew and as a vassal should greet his lord. And he represents unto thee that he waxes heavy and feeble, and is advancing in years. And the neighboring chiefs, knowing this, grow insolent towards him and covet his land and possessions. And he earnestly beseeches thee, lord, to permit Geraint his son to return to him, to protect his possessions, and to become acquainted with his boundaries. And unto him he represents that it were better for him to spend the flower of his youth and the prime of his age in preserving his own boundaries than in tournaments which are productive of no profit, although he obtains glory in them."

"Well," said Arthur, "go and divest yourselves of your accoutrements, and take food, and refresh yourselves after your fatigues; and before you go from hence, you shall have an answer." And they went to eat. And Arthur considered that it would go hard with him to let Geraint depart from him and from his court; neither did he think it fair that his cousin should be restrained from going to protect his dominions and his boundaries, seeing that his father was unable to do so. No less was the grief and regret of Guenever, and all her women, and all her damsels, through fear that the maiden would leave them. And that day and that night were spent in abundance of feasting. And Arthur told Geraint the cause of the mission and of the coming of the ambassadors to him out of Cornwall. "Truly," said Geraint, "be it to my advantage or disadvantage, lord, I will do according to thy will concerning this embassy." "Behold," said Arthur, "though it grieves me to part with thee, it is my counsel that thou go to dwell in thine own dominions, and to defend thy boundaries, and take with thee to accompany thee as many as thou wilt of those thou lovest best among my faithful ones, and among thy friends, and among thy companions in arms." "Heaven reward thee! and this will I do," said Geraint. "What discourse," said Guenever, "do I hear between you? Is it of those who are to conduct Geraint to his country?" "It is," said Arthur. "Then is it needful for me to consider," said she, "concerning companions and a provision for the lady that is with me." "Thou wilt do well," said Arthur.

And that night they went to sleep. And the next day the ambassadors were permitted to depart, and they were told that Geraint should follow them. And on the third day, Geraint set forth, and many went with him— Gawain, the son of Gwyar; and Riogoned, the son of the King of Ireland; and Ondyaw, the son of the Duke of Burgundy; Gwilim, the son of the ruler of the Franks; Howel, the son of the Earl of Brittany; Perceval, the son of Evrawk; Gwyr, a judge in the court of Arthur; Bedwyr, the son of Bedrawd; Kai, the son of Kyner; Odyar, the Frank; and Edeyrn, the son of Nudd. Said Geraint, "I think I shall have enough of knighthood with me." And they set forth. And never was there seen a fairer host journeying towards the Severn. And on the other side of the Severn were the nobles of Erbin, the son of Custennin, and his foster-father at their head, to welcome Geraint with gladness; and many of the women of the court, with his mother, came to receive Enid, the daughter of Ynywl, his wife. And there was great rejoicing and gladness throughout the whole court, and through all the country, concerning Geraint, because of the greatness of their love to him, and of the greatness of the fame which he had gained since he went from amongst them, and because he was come to take possession of his dominions and to preserve his boundaries. And they came to the court. And in the court they had ample entertainment, and a multitude of gifts, and abundance of liquor, and a sufficiency of service, and a variety of games. And to do honor to Geraint, all the chief men of the country were invited that night to visit him. And they passed that day and that night in the utmost enjoyment. And at dawn next day Erbin arose and summoned to him Geraint and the noble persons who had borne him company. And he said to Geraint: "I am a feeble and an aged man, and whilst I was able to maintain the dominion for thee and for myself, I did so. But thou art young and in the flower of thy vigor and of thy youth. Henceforth do thou preserve thy possessions." "Truly," said Geraint, "with my consent thou shalt not give the power over thy dominions at this time into my hands, and thou shalt not take me from Arthur's court." "Into thy hands will I give them," said Erbin, "and this day also shalt thou receive the homage of thy subjects."

Then said Gawain, "It were better for thee to satisfy those who have boons to ask, to-day, and to-morrow thou canst receive the homage of thy dominions." So all that had boons to ask were summoned into one place. And Kadyraith came to them to know what were their requests. And every one asked that which he desired. And the followers of Arthur began to make gifts, and immediately the men of Cornwall came and gave also. And they were not long in giving, so eager was every one to bestow gifts. And of those who came to ask gifts, none departed unsatisfied. And that day and that night were spent in the utmost enjoyment.

And the next day at dawn, Erbin desired Geraint to send messengers to the men to ask them whether it was displeasing to them that he should come to receive their homage, and whether they had anything to object to him. Then Geraint sent ambassadors to the men of Cornwall to ask them this. And they all said that it would be the fulness of joy and honor to them for Geraint to come and receive their homage. So he received the homage of such as were there. And the day after, the followers of Arthur intended to go away. "It is too soon for you to go away yet," said he; "stay with me until I have finished receiving the homage of my chief men, who have agreed to come to me." And they remained with him until he had done so. Then they set forth towards the court of Arthur. And Geraint went to bear them company, and Enid also, as far as Diganwy; there, they parted. And Ondyaw, the son of the Duke of Burgundy, said to Geraint, "Go, now, and visit the uttermost parts of thy dominions, and see well to the boundaries of thy territories; and if thou hast any trouble respecting them, send unto thy companions." "Heaven reward thee!" said Geraint; "and this will I do." And Geraint journeyed to the uttermost parts of his dominions. And experienced guides, and the chief men of his country, went with him. And the furthermost point that they showed him he kept possession of.

CHAPTER VII

GERAINT, THE SON OF ERBIN, CONTINUED

Geraint, as he had been used to do when he was at Arthur's court, frequented tournaments. And he became acquainted with valiant and mighty men, until he had gained as much fame there as he had formerly done elsewhere. And he enriched his court, and his companions, and his nobles, with the best horses and the best arms, and with the best and most valuable jewels, and he ceased not until his fame had flown over the face of the whole kingdom. When he knew that it was thus, he began to love ease and pleasure, for there was no one who was worth his opposing. And he loved his wife, and liked to continue in the palace, with minstrelsy and diversions. So he began to shut himself up in the chamber of his wife, and he took no delight in anything besides, insomuch that he gave up the friendship of his nobles, together with his hunting and his amusements, and lost the hearts of all the host in his court. And there was murmuring and scoffing concerning him among the inhabitants of the palace, on account of his relinquishing so completely their companionship for the love of his wife. These tidings came to Erbin. And when Erbin had heard these things, he spoke unto Enid and inquired of her whether it was she that had caused Geraint to act thus, and to forsake his people and his hosts. "Not I, by my confession unto Heaven," said she; "there is nothing more hateful unto me than this." And she knew not what she should do, for, although it was hard for her to own this to Geraint, yet was it not more easy for her to listen to what she heard, without warning Geraint concerning it. And she was very sorrowful.

One morning in the summer-time they were upon their couch, and Geraint lay upon the edge of it. And Enid was without sleep in the apartment, which had windows of glass; * and the sun shone upon the couch. And the clothes had slipped from off his arms and his breast, and he was asleep. Then she gazed upon the marvellous beauty of his appearance, and she said, "Alas! and am I the cause that these arms and this breast have lost their glory, and the warlike fame which they once so richly enjoyed!" As she said this, the tears dropped from her eyes, and they fell upon his breast. And the tears she shed, and the words she had spoken, awoke him. And another thing contributed to awaken him, and that was the idea that it was not in thinking of him that she spoke thus, but that it was because she loved some other man more than him, and that she wished for other society. Thereupon Geraint was troubled in his mind, and he called his squire; and when he came to him, "Go quickly," said he, "and prepare my horse and my arms, and make them ready. And do thou arise," said he to Enid, "and apparel thyself; and cause thy horse to be accoutred, and clothe thee in the worst riding-dress that thou hast in thy possession. And evil betide me," said he, "if thou returnest here until thou knowest whether I have lost my strength so completely as thou didst say. And if it be so, it will then be easy for thee to seek the society thou didst wish for of him of whom thou wast thinking." So she arose and clothed herself in her meanest garments. "I know nothing, lord," said she, "of thy meaning." "Neither wilt thou know at this time," said he.

Then Geraint went to see Erbin. "Sir," said he, "I am going upon a quest, and I am not certain when I may come back. Take heed, therefore, unto thy possessions

* The terms of admiration in which the older writers invariably speak of *glass windows* would be sufficient proof, if other evidence were wanting, how rare an article of luxury they were in the houses of our ancestors. They were first introduced in ecclesiastical architecture, to which they were for a long time confined. Glass is said not to have been employed in domestic architecture before the fourteenth century.

until my return." "I will do so," said he; "but it is strange
to me that thou shouldst go so suddenly. And who will
proceed with thee, since thou art not strong enough to
traverse the land of Loegyr alone?" "But one person only
will go with me." "Heaven counsel thee, my son," said
Erbin, "and may many attach themselves to thee in
Loegyr." Then went Geraint to the place where his horse
was, and it was equipped with foreign armor, heavy and
shining. And he desired Enid to mount her horse, and to
ride forward, and to keep a long way before him. "And
whatever thou mayest see, and whatever thou mayest
hear concerning me," said he, "do thou not turn back.
And unless I speak unto thee, say not thou one word
either." So they set forward. And he did not choose the
pleasantest and most frequented road, but that which was
the wildest, and most beset by thieves and robbers and
venomous animals.

And they came to a high-road, which they followed till
they saw a vast forest; and they saw four armed horsemen come forth from the forest. When the armed men
saw them, they said one to another, "Here is a good occasion for us to capture two horses and armor, and a
lady likewise; for this we shall have no difficulty in doing
against yonder single knight, who hangs his head so pen-
sively and heavily." Enid heard this discourse, and she
knew not what she should do through fear of Geraint,
who had told her to be silent. "The vengeance of Heaven
be upon me," said she, "if I would not rather receive my
death from his hand than from the hand of any other;
and though he should slay me, yet will I speak to him, lest
I should have the misery to witness his death." So she
waited for Geraint until he came near to her. "Lord," said
she, "didst thou hear the words of those men concerning
thee?" Then he lifted up his eyes, and looked at her
angrily. "Thou hadst only," said he, "to hold thy peace,
as I bade thee. I wish but for silence, and not for warning.
And though thou shouldst desire to see my defeat and my
death by the hands of those men, yet do I feel no dread."
Then the foremost of them couched his lance and
rushed upon Geraint. And he received him, and that
not feebly. But he let the thrust go by him, while he
struck the horseman upon the centre of his shield,

in such a manner that his shield was split and his armor broken, so that a cubit's length of the shaft of Geraint's lance passed through his body, and sent him to the earth, the length of the lance over his horse's crupper. Then the second horseman attacked him furiously, being wroth at the death of his companion. But with one thrust Geraint overthrew him also and killed him as he had done the other. Then the third set upon him, and he killed him in like manner. And thus also he slew the fourth. Sad and sorrowful was the maiden as she saw all this. Geraint dismounted his horse, and took the arms of the men he had slain, and placed them upon their saddles and tied together the reins of their horses; and he mounted his horse again. "Behold what thou must do," said he; "take the four horses, and drive them before thee, and proceed forward as I bade thee just now. And say not one word unto me, unless I speak first unto thee. And I declare unto Heaven," said he, "if thou doest not thus, it will be to thy cost." "I will do as far as I can, lord," said she, "according to thy desire."

So the maiden went forward, keeping in advance of Geraint, as he had desired her; and it grieved him as much as his wrath would permit to see a maiden so illustrious as she having so much trouble with the care of the horses. Then they reached a wood, and it was both deep and vast, and in the wood night overtook them. "Ah, maiden," said he, "it is vain to attempt proceeding forward." "Well, lord," said she, "whatever thou wishest, we will do. "It will be best for us," he answered, "to rest and wait for the day, in order to pursue our journey." "That will we, gladly," said she. And they did so. Having dismounted himself, he took her down from her horse. "I cannot by any means refrain from sleep, through weariness," said he; "do thou therefore watch the horses, and sleep not." "I will, lord," said she. Then he went to sleep in his armor and thus passed the night, which was not long at that season. And when she saw the dawn of day appear, she looked around her to see if he were waking, and thereupon he woke. Then he arose and said unto her, "Take the horses and ride on, and keep straight on as thou didst yesterday." And they left the wood, and they came to an open country, with meadows on one hand,

and mowers mowing the meadows. And there was a river before them, and the horses bent down and drank of the water. And they went up out of the river by a lofty steep; and there they met a slender stripling with a satchel about his neck, and they saw that there was something in the satchel, but they knew not what it was. And he had a small blue pitcher in his hand, and a bowl on the mouth of the pitcher. And the youth saluted Geraint. "Heaven prosper thee!" said Geraint; "and whence dost thou come?" "I come," said he, "from the city that lies before thee. My lord," he added, "will it be displeasing to thee if I ask whence thou comest also?" "By no means; through yonder wood did I come." "Thou camest not through the wood to-day." "No," he replied; "we were in the wood last night." "I warrant," said the youth, "that thy condition there last night was not the most pleasant, and that thou hadst neither meat nor drink." "No, by my faith," said he. "Wilt thou follow my counsel," said the youth, "and take thy meal from me?" "What sort of meal?" he inquired. "The breakfast which is sent for yonder mowers, nothing less than bread and meat and wine; and if thou wilt, sir, they shall have none of it." "I will," said he, "and Heaven reward thee for it."

So Geraint alighted, and the youth took the maiden from off her horse. Then they washed and took their repast. And the youth cut the bread in slices, and gave them drink, and served them withal. And when they had finished, the youth arose and said to Geraint, "My lord, with thy permission, I will now go and fetch some food for the mowers." "Go first to the town," said Geraint, "and take a lodging for me in the best place that thou knowest, and the most commodious one for the horses; and take thou whichever horse and arms thou choosest, in payment for thy service and thy gift." "Heaven reward thee, lord!" said the youth; "and this would be ample to repay services much greater than those I have rendered unto thee." And to the town went the youth, and he took the best and the most pleasant lodgings that he knew; and after that he went to the palace, having the horse and armor with him, and proceeded to the place where the earl was, and told him all his adventure. "I go now, lord," said he, "to meet the knight and to conduct him to his lodging." "Go, gladly," said the earl; "and right joyfully shall he be received here, if he so come." And the youth went to meet Geraint, and told him that he would be received gladly by the earl in his own palace; but he would go only to his lodgings. And he had a goodly chamber, in which was plenty of straw and drapery, and a spacious and commodious place he had for the horses; and the youth prepared for them plenty of provender. After they had disarrayed themselves, Geraint spoke thus to Enid: "Go," said he, "to the other side of the chamber, and come not to this side of the house; and thou mayst call to thee the woman of the house, if thou wilt." "I will do, lord," said she, "as thou sayest." Thereupon the man of the house came to Geraint and welcomed him. And after they had eaten and drank, Geraint went to sleep, and so did Enid also.

In the evening, behold, the earl came to visit Geraint, and his twelve honorable knights with him. And Geraint rose up and welcomed him. Then they all sat down according to their precedence in honor. And the earl conversed with Geraint and inquired of him the object of his journey. "I have none," he replied, "but to seek adventures and to follow my own inclination." Then the earl cast his eye upon Enid, and he looked at her steadfastly. And he thought he had never seen a maiden fairer or more comely than she. And he set all his thoughts and his affections upon her. Then he asked of Geraint, "Have I thy permission to go and converse with yonder maiden, for I see that she is apart from thee?" "Thou hast it gladly," said he. So the Earl went to the place where the maiden was and spake with her. "Ah! maiden," said he, "it cannot be pleasant to thee to journey with yonder man." "It is not unpleasant to me," said she. "Thou hast neither youths nor maidens to serve thee," said he. "Truly," she replied, "it is more pleasant for me to follow yonder man than to be served by youths and maidens." "I will give thee good counsel," said he: "all my earldom will I place in thy possession, if thou wilt dwell with me." "That will I not, by Heaven," she said; "yonder man was the first to whom my faith was ever pledged; and shall I prove inconstant to him?" "Thou art in the wrong," said the earl; "if I slay the man yonder, I can keep thee with me as long as I choose; and when thou no longer pleasest me, I can turn thee away. But if thou goest with me by thy own good will, I protest that our union shall continue as long as I remain alive." Then she pondered those words of his, and she considered that it was advisable to encourage him in his request. "Behold then, Chieftain, this is most expedient for thee to do to save me from all reproach; come here to-morrow and take me away as though I knew nothing thereof." "I will do so," said he. So he arose and took his leave, and went forth with his attendants. And she told not then to Geraint any of the conversation which she had had with the earl, lest it should rouse his anger and cause him uneasiness and care.

And at the usual hour they went to sleep. And at the beginning of the night Enid slept a little; and at midnight she arose and placed all Geraint's armor together, so that it might be ready to put on. And although fearful of her errand, she came to the side of Geraint's bed; and she spoke to him softly and gently, saying, "My lord, arise, and clothe thyself, for these were the words of the earl to me, and his intention concerning me." So she told Geraint all that had passed. And although he was wroth with her, he took warning and clothed himself. And she lighted a candle that he might have light to do so. "Leave there the candle," said he, "and desire the man of the house to come here." Then she went, and the man of the house came to him. "Dost thou know how much I owe thee?" asked Geraint. "I think thou owest but little." "Take the three horses, and the three suits of armor." "Heaven reward thee, Lord," said he, "but I spent not the value of one suit of armor upon thee." "For that reason," said he, "thou wilt be the richer. And now, wilt thou come to guide me out of the town?" "I will gladly," said he; "and in which direction dost thou intend to go?" "I wish to leave the town by a different way from that by which I entered it." So the man of the lodgings accompanied him as far as he desired. Then he bade the maiden to go on before him, and she did so and went straight forward, and his host returned home.

And Geraint and the maiden went forward along the high-road. And as they journeyed thus, they heard an exceeding loud wailing near to them. "Stay thou here," said he, "and I will go and see what is the cause of this wailing." "I will," said she. Then he went forward into an open glade that was near the road. And in the glade he saw two horses, one having a man's saddle, and the other a woman's saddle upon it. And behold, there was a knight lying dead in his armor, and a young damsel in a riding-dress standing over him lamenting. "Ah, lady," said Geraint, "what hath befallen thee?" "Behold," she answered, "I journeyed here with my beloved husband, when lo! three giants came upon us, and without any cause in the world, they slew him." "Which way went they hence?" said Geraint. "Yonder by the high-road," she replied. So he returned to Enid. "Go," said he, "to the lady that is below yonder, and await me there till I come." She was sad when he ordered her to do thus, but nevertheless she went to the damsel, whom it was ruth to hear, and she felt certain Geraint would never return.

Meanwhile Geraint followed the giants and overtook them. And each of them was greater in stature than three other men, and a huge club was on the shoulder of each. Then he rushed upon one of them and thrust his lance through his body. And having drawn it forth again, he pierced another of them through likewise. But the third turned upon him and struck him with his club so that he split his shield and crushed his shoulder. But Geraint drew his sword and gave the giant a blow on the crown of his head, so severe, and fierce, and violent, that his head and his neck were split down to his shoulders and he fell dead. So Geraint left him thus and returned to Enid. And when he reached the place where she was, he fell down lifeless from his horse. Piercing and loud and thrilling was the cry that Enid uttered. And she came and stood over him where he had fallen. And at the sound of her cries came the Earl of Limours, and they who journeyed with him, whom her lamentations brought out of their road. And the earl said to Enid, "Alas, lady, what hath befallen thee?" "Ah, good sir," said she, "the only man I have loved, or ever shall love, is slain." Then he said to the other, "And what is the cause of thy grief?" "They have slain my beloved husband also," said she. "And who was it that slew them?" "Some giants," she answered, "slew my best-beloved, and the other knight went in pursuit of them and came back in the state thou seest." The earl caused the knight that was dead to be buried, but he thought that there still remained some life in Geraint; and to see if he yet would live, he had him carried with him in the hollow of his shield, and upon a bier. And the two damsels went to the court; and when they arrived there, Geraint was placed upon a little couch in front of the table that was in the hall. Then they all took off their travelling-gear, and the earl besought Enid to do the same and to clothe herself in other garments. "I will not, by Heaven," said she. "Ah, lady," said he, "be not so sorrowful for this matter." "It were hard to persuade me to be otherwise," said she. "I will act towards thee in such wise that thou needest not be sorrowful, whether yonder knight live or die. Behold, a good earldom, together with myself, will I bestow upon thee; be therefore happy and joyful." "I declare to Heaven," said she, "that henceforth I shall never be joyful while I live." "Come," said he, "and eat." "No, by Heaven, I will not." "But by Heaven, thou shalt," said he. So he took her with him to the table against her will, and many times desired her to eat. "I call Heaven to witness," said she, "that I will not eat until the man that is upon yonder bier shall eat likewise." "Thou canst not fulfil that," said the earl; "yonder man is dead already." "I will prove that I can," said she. Then he offered her a goblet of liquor. "Drink this goblet," he said, "and it will cause thee to change thy mind." "Evil betide me," she answered, "if I drink aught until he drink also." "Truly," said the earl, "it is of no more avail for me to be gentle with thee than ungentle." And he gave her a box in the ear. Thereupon she raised a loud and piercing shriek, and her lamentations were much greater than they had been before; for she considered in her mind that, had Geraint been alive, he durst not have struck her thus. But, behold, at the sound of her cry, Geraint revived from his swoon, and he sat up on the bier; and finding his sword in the hollow of his shield, he rushed to the place where the earl was and struck him a fiercely wounding, severely venomous, and sternly smiting blow upon the crown of his head, so that he clove him in twain, until his sword was staid by the table. Then all left the board and fled away. And this was not so much through fear of the living as through the dread they felt at seeing the dead man rise up to slay them. And Geraint looked upon Enid, and he was grieved for two causes; one was to see that Enid had lost her color and her wonted aspect; and the other, to know that she was in the right. "Lady," said he, "knowest thou where our horses are?" "I know, lord, where thy horse is," she replied, "but I know not where is the other. Thy horse is in the house yonder." So he went to the house, and brought forth his horse, and mounted him, and took up Enid, and placed her upon the horse with him. And he rode forward. And their road lay between two hedges; and the night was gaining on the day. And lo! they saw behind them the shafts of spears betwixt them and the sky, and they heard the tramping of horses and the noise of a host approaching. "I hear something following us," said he, "and I will put thee on the other side of the hedge." And thus he did. And thereupon, behold, a knight pricked towards him and couched his lance. When Enid saw this, she cried out, saying, "Oh, Chieftain, whoever thou art, what renown wilt thou gain by slaying a dead man?" "O Heaven!" said he, "is it Geraint?" "Yes, in truth," said she; "and who art thou?" "I am Gwiffert Petit," said he, "thy husband's ally, coming to thy assistance, for I heard that thou wast in trouble. Come with me to the court of a son-in-law of my sister, which is near here, and thou shalt have the best medical assistance in the kingdom." "I will do so gladly," said Geraint. And Enid was placed upon the horse of one of Gwiffert's squires, and they went forward to the baron's palace. And they were received there with gladness, and they met with hospitality and attention. The next morning they went to seek physicians; and it was not long before they came, and they attended Geraint until he was perfectly well. And while Geraint was under medical care, Gwiffert caused his armor to be repaired, until it was as good as it had ever been. And they remained there a month and a fortnight. Then they separated, and Geraint went towards his own dominions, and thenceforth he reigned prosperously, and his warlike fame and splendor lasted with renown and honor both to him and to Enid,* from that time forward.

CHAPTER VIII

PWYLL, PRINCE OF DYVED

Once upon a time, Pwyll was at Narberth, his chief palace, where a feast had been prepared for him, and with him was a great host of men. And after the first meal, Pwyll arose to walk; and he went to the top of a mound that was above the palace, and was called Gorsedd Arberth. "Lord," said one of the court, "it is peculiar to the mound that whosoever sits upon it cannot go thence without either receiving wounds or blows, or else seeing a wonder." "I fear not to receive wounds or blows," said Pwyll; "But as to the wonder, gladly would I see it. I will therefore go and sit upon the mound."

And upon the mound he sat. And while he sat there, they saw a lady, on a pure white horse of large size, with a garment of shining gold around her, coming along the highway that led from the mound. "My men," said Pwyll, "is there any among you who knows yonder lady?" "There is not, lord," said they. "Go one of you and meet her, that we may know who she is." And one of them arose, and as he came upon the road to meet her, she passed by; and he followed as fast as he could, being on foot, and the greater was his speed, the further was

* Throughout the broad and varied region of romance, it would be difficult to find a character of greater simplicity and truth than that of Enid, the daughter of Earl Ynywl. Conspicuous for her beauty and noble bearing, we are at a loss whether more to admire the patience with which she bore all the hardships she was destined to undergo, or the constancy and affection which finally achieved the triumph she so richly deserved.

The character of Enid is admirably sustained through the whole tale; and as it is more natural, because less overstrained, so perhaps it is even more touching, than that of Griselda, over which, however, Chaucer has thrown a charm that leads us to forget the improbability of her story.

she from him. And when he saw that it profited him nothing to follow her, he returned to Pwyll and said unto him, "Lord, it is idle for any one in the world to follow her on foot." "Verily," said Pwyll, "go unto the palace, and take the fleetest horse that thou seest, and go after her."

And he took a horse and went forward. And he came to an open, level plain and put spurs to his horse, and the more he urged his horse, the further was she from him. And he returned to the place where Pwyll was and said, "Lord, it will avail nothing for any one to follow yonder lady. I know of no horse in these realms swifter than this, and it availed me not to pursue her." "Of a truth," said Pwyll, "there must be some illusion here; let us go towards the palace." So to the palace they went and spent the day.

And the next day they amused themselves until it was time to go to meat. And when meat was ended, Pwyll said, "Where are the hosts that went yesterday to the top of the mound?" "Behold, lord, we are here," said they. "Let us go," said he, "to the mound and sit there. And do thou," said he to the page who tended his horse, "saddle my horse well, and hasten with him to the road, and bring also my spurs with thee." And the youth did thus. And they went and sat upon the mound; and ere they had been there but a short time, they beheld the lady coming by the same road, and in the same manner, and at the same pace. "Young man," said Pwyll, "I see the lady coming; give me my horse." And before he had mounted his horse she passed him. And he turned after her and followed her. And he let his horse go bounding playfully, and thought that he should soon come up with her. But he came no nearer to her than at first. Then he urged his horse to his utmost speed, yet he found that it availed not. Then said Pwyll, "Oh, maiden, for the sake of him whom thou best lovest, stay for me." "I will stay gladly," said she; "and it were better for thy horse hadst thou asked it long since." So the maiden stopped; and she threw back that part of her headdress which covered her face. Then he thought that the beauty of all the maidens and all the ladies that he had ever seen was as nothing compared to her beauty. "Lady," he said, "wilt thou tell me aught concerning thy purpose?" "I will tell thee," said

she; "my chief quest was to see thee." "Truly," said
Pwyll, "this is to me the most pleasing quest on which
thou couldst have come; and wilt thou tell me who thou
art?" "I will tell thee, lord," said she. "I am Rhiannon, the
daughter of Heveydd, and they sought to give me to a
husband against my will. But no husband would I have,
and that because of my love for thee; neither will I yet
have one, unless thou reject me; and hither have I come
to hear thy answer." "By Heaven," said Pwyll, "behold,
this is my answer. If I might choose among all the ladies
and damsels in the world, thee would I choose." "Verily,"
said she, "if thou art thus minded, make a pledge to meet
me ere I am given to another." "The sooner I may do so,
the more pleasing will it be to me," said Pwyll; "and
wheresoever thou wilt, there will I meet with thee." "I
will that thou meet me this day twelvemonth at the palace
of Heveydd." "Gladly," said he, "will I keep this tryst."
So they parted, and he went back to his hosts and to
them of his household. And whatsoever questions they
asked him respecting the damsel, he always turned the
discourse upon other matters.

And when a year from that time was gone, he caused
a hundred knights to equip themselves and to go with
him to the palace of Heveydd. And he came to the palace,
and there was great joy concerning him, with much con-
course of people, and great rejoicing, and vast preparations for his coming. And the whole court was placed
under his orders.

And the hall was garnished, and they went to meat,
and thus did they sit: Heveydd was on one side of Pwyll,
and Rhiannon on the other; and all the rest according to
their rank. And they ate, and feasted, and talked one
with another. And at the beginning of the carousal after
the meat, there entered a tall, auburn-haired youth, of
royal bearing, clothed in a garment of satin. And when he
came into the hall, he saluted Pwyll and his companions.
"The greeting of Heaven be unto thee," said Pwyll;
"come thou and sit down." "Nay," said he, "a suitor am
I, and I will do my errand." "Do so, willingly," said
Pwyll. "Lord," said he, "my errand is unto thee, and it is
to crave a boon of thee that I come." "What boon soever thou mayest ask of me, so far as I am able, thou

shalt have." "Ah!" said Rhiannon, "wherefore didst thou
give that answer?" "Has he not given it before the presence
of these nobles?" asked the youth. "My soul," said Pwyll,
"what is the boon thou askest?" "The lady whom best I
love is to be thy bride this night; I come to ask her of
thee, with the feast and the banquet that are in this
place." And Pwyll was silent, because of the promise
which he had given. "Be silent as long as thou wilt," said
Rhiannon, "never did man make worse use of his wits
than thou hast done." "Lady," said he, "I knew not who
he was." "Behold, this is the man to whom they would
have given me against my will," said she; "and he is Gawl,
the son of Clud, a man of great power and wealth, and
because of the word thou hast spoken, bestow me upon
him, lest shame befall thee." "Lady," said he, "I understand not thy answer; never can I do as thou sayest."
"Bestow me upon him," said she, "and I will cause that
I shall never be his." "By what means will that be?"
asked Pwyll. Then she told him the thought that was in
her mind. And they talked long together. Then Gawl said,
"Lord, it is meet that I have an answer to my request."
"As much of that thou hast asked as it is in my power to
give, thou shalt have," replied Pwyll. "My soul," said
Rhiannon unto Gawl, "as for the feast and the banquet
that are here, I have bestowed them upon the men of
Dyved, and the household and the warriors that are with
us. These can I not suffer to be given to any. In a year
from to-night, a banquet shall be prepared for thee in this
palace, that I may become thy bride."

So Gawl went forth to his possessions, and Pwyll went
also back to Dyved. And they both spent that year until
it was the time for the feast at the palace of Heveydd.
Then Gawl, the son of Clud, set out to the feast that was
prepared for him; and he came to the palace, and was received there with rejoicing. Pwyll, also, the chief of Dyved,
came to the orchard with a hundred knights, as Rhiannon
had commanded him. And Pwyll was clad in coarse and
ragged garments and wore large, clumsy old shoes upon
his feet. And when he knew that the carousal after the
meat had begun, he went toward the hall; and when he
came into the hall, he saluted Gawl, the son of Clud,
and his company, both men and women. "Heaven prosper

thee," said Gawl, "and friendly greeting be unto thee!"
"Lord," said he, "may Heaven reward thee! I have an
errand unto thee." "Welcome be thine errand, and if
thou ask of me that which is right, thou shalt have it
gladly." "It is fitting," answered he; "I crave but from
want, and the boon I ask is to have this small bag that
thou seest filled with meat." "A request within reason is
this," said he, "and gladly shalt thou have it. Bring him
food." A great number of attendants arose and began to
fill the bag; but for all they put into it, it was no fuller
than at first. "My soul," said Gawl, "will thy bag ever be
full?" "It will not, I declare to Heaven," said he, "for all
that may be put into it, unless one possessed of lands,
and domains, and treasure, shall arise and tread down
with both his feet the food that is within the bag, and
shall say, 'Enough has been put therein.' " Then said
Rhiannon unto Gawl, the son of Clud, "Rise up quickly."
"I will willingly arise," said he. So he rose up and put his
two feet into the bag. And Pwyll turned up the sides of
the bag, so that Gawl was over his head in it. And he
shut it up quickly, and slipped a knot upon the thongs,
and blew his horn. And thereupon, behold, his knights
came down upon the palace. And they seized all the
host that had come with Gawl and cast them into his
own prison. And Pwyll threw off his rags, and his old
shoes, and his tattered array. And as they came in,
every one of Pwyll's knights struck a blow upon the bag,
and asked, "What is here?" "A badger," said they. And
in this manner they played, each of them striking the bag,
either with his foot or with a staff. And thus played they
with the bag. And then was the game of Badger in the Bag
first played.

"Lord," said the man in the bag, "if thou wouldst but
hear me, I merit not to be slain in a bag." Said Heveydd,
"Lord, he speaks truth; it were fitting that thou listen to
him, for he deserves not this." "Verily," said Pwyll, "I will
do thy counsel concerning him." "Behold, this is my counsel then," said Rhiannon. "Thou art now in a position in
which it behooves thee to satisfy suitors and minstrels.
Let him give unto them in thy stead, and take a pledge
from him that he will never seek to revenge that which
has been done to him. And this will be punishment

enough." "I will do this gladly," said the man in the bag.
"And gladly will I accept it," said Pwyll, "since it is the
counsel of Heveydd and Rhiannon. Seek thyself sureties."
"We will be for him," said Heveydd, "until his men be
free to answer for him." And upon this he was let out
of the bag, and his liegemen were liberated. "Verily,
lord," said Gawl, "I am greatly hurt, and I have many
bruises. With thy leave I will go forth. I will leave nobles
in my stead to answer for me in all that thou shalt require." "Willingly," said Pwyll, "mayest thou do thus."
So Gawl went to his own possessions.

And the hall was set in order for Pwyll and the men
of his host, and for them also of the palace, and they
went to the tables and sat down. And as they had sat
that time twelvemonth, so sat they that night. And they
ate, and feasted, and spent the night in mirth and tran-
quillity. And the time came that they should sleep, and
Pwyll and Rhiannon went to their chamber.

And next morning at break of day, "My lord," said
Rhiannon, "arise and begin to give thy gifts unto the
minstrels. Refuse no one to-day that may claim thy
bounty." "Thus shall it be gladly," said Pwyll, "both
to-day and every day while the feast shall last." So Pwyll
arose, and he caused silence to be proclaimed, and desired all the suitors and minstrels to show and to point
out what gifts they desired. And this being done, the
feast went on, and he denied no one while it lasted. And
when the feast was ended, Pwyll said unto Heveydd, "My
lord, with thy permission, I will set out for Dyved to-
morrow." "Certainly," said Heveydd; "may Heaven prosper thee! Fix also a time when Rhiannon shall follow
thee." "By Heaven," said Pwyll, "we will go hence together." "Willest thou this, lord?" said Heveydd. "Yes,
lord," answered Pwyll.

And the next day they set forward towards Dyved
and journeyed to the palace of Narberth, where a feast
was made ready for them. And there came to them great
numbers of the chief men and the most noble ladies of
the land, and of these there were none to whom Rhiannon
did not give some rich gift, either a bracelet, or a ring,
or a precious stone. And they ruled the land prosperously
that year and the next.

CHAPTER IX

BRANWEN, THE DAUGHTER OF LLYR

Bendigeid Vran, the son of Llyr, was the crowned king of this island, and he was exalted from the crown of London. And one afternoon he was at Harlech, in Ardudwy, at his court; and he sat upon the rock of Harlech, looking over the sea. And with him were his brother, Manawyddan, the son of Llyr, and his brothers by the mother's side, Nissyen and Evnissyen, and many nobles likewise, as was fitting to see around a king. His two brothers by the mother's side were the sons of Euroswydd, and one of these youths was a good youth, and of gentle nature, and would make peace between his kindred, and cause his family to be friends when their wrath was at the highest, and this one was Nissyen; but the other would cause strife between his two brothers when they were most at peace. And as they sat thus, they beheld thirteen ships coming from the south of Ireland and making towards them; and they came with a swift motion, the wind being behind them; and they neared them rapidly. "I see ships afar," said the king, "coming swiftly towards the land. Command the men of the court that they equip themselves, and go and learn their intent." So the men equipped themselves and went down towards them. And when they saw the ships near, certain were they that they had never seen ships better furnished. Beautiful flags of satin were upon them. And, behold, one of the ships outstripped the others, and they saw a shield lifted up above the side of the ship, and the point of the shield was upwards, in token of peace. And the men drew near, that they might hold converse. Then they put out boats and came towards the land. And they saluted the king. Now the king could hear them from the place where he was upon the rock above their heads. "Heaven prosper you," said he, "and be ye welcome! To whom do these ships belong, and who is the chief amongst

you?" "Lord," said they, "Matholch, King of Ireland, is
here, and these ships belong to him." "Wherefore comes
he?" asked the king, "and will he come to the land?" "He
is a suitor unto thee, lord," said they, "and he will not
land unless he have his boon." "And what may that be?"
inquired the king. "He desires to ally himself, lord, with
thee," said they, "and he comes to ask Branwen, the
daughter of Llyr, that, if it seem well to thee, the Island
of the Mighty* may be leagued with Ireland, and both
become more powerful." "Verily," said he, "let him
come to land, and we will take counsel thereupon." And
this answer was brought to Matholch. "I will go willingly," said he. So he landed, and they received him
joyfully; and great was the throng in the palace that
night, between his hosts and those of the court; and next
day they took counsel, and they resolved to bestow Branwen upon Matholch. Now she was one of the three
chief ladies of this island, and she was the fairest damsel in the world.

And they fixed upon Aberfraw as the place where she
should become his bride. And they went thence, and towards Aberfraw the hosts proceeded, Matholch and his
host in their ships, Bendigeid Vran and his host by land,
until they came to Aberfraw. And at Aberfraw they began
the feast and sat down. And thus sat they: the King of the
Island of the Mighty and Manawyddan, the son
of Llyr, on one side, and Matholch on the other side,
and Branwen, the daughter of Llyr, beside him. And
they were not within a house, but under tents. No house
could ever contain Bendigeid Vran. And they began the
banquet, and caroused, and discoursed. And when it
was more pleasing to them to sleep than to carouse, they
went to rest, and Branwen became Matholch's bride.

And next day they arose, and all they of the court and
the officers began to equip, and to range the horses and
the attendants, and they ranged them in order as far as
the sea.

And, behold, one day Evnissyen, the quarrelsome man,
of whom it is spoken above, came by chance into the
place where the horses of Matholch were, and asked whose

* The Island of the Mighty is one of the many names bestowed upon
Britain by the Welsh.

horses they might be. "They are the horses of Matholch, King of Ireland, who is married to Branwen, thy sister; his horses are they." "And is it thus they have done with a maiden such as she, and moreover my sister, bestowing her without my consent? They could have offered no greater insult to me than this," said he. And thereupon he rushed under the horses, and cut off their lips at the teeth, and their ears close to their heads, and their tails close to their backs; and he disfigured the horses and rendered them useless.

And they came with these tidings unto Matholch, saying that the horses were disfigured and injured, so that not one of them could ever be of any use again. "Verily, lord," said one, "it was an insult unto thee, and as such was it meant." "Of a truth, it is a marvel to me that, if they desire to insult me, they should have given me a maiden of such high rank, and so much beloved of her kindred, as they have done." "Lord," said another, "thou seest that thus it is, and there is nothing for thee to do but to go to thy ships." And thereupon towards his ships he set out.

And tidings came to Bendigeid Vran that Matholch was quitting the court without asking leave, and messengers were sent to inquire of him wherefore he did so. And the messengers that went were Iddic, the son of Anarawd, and Heveyd Hir. And these overtook him and asked of him what he designed to do and wherefore he went forth. "Of a truth," said he, "if I had known, I had not come hither. I have been altogether insulted; no one had ever worse treatment than I have had here." "Truly, lord, it was not the will of any that are of the court," said they, "nor of any that are of the council, that thou shouldst have received this insult; and as thou hast been insulted, the dishonor is greater unto Bendigeid Vran than unto thee." "Verily," said he, "I think so. Nevertheless, he cannot recall the insult." These men returned with that answer to the place where Bendigeid Vran was, and they told him what reply Matholch had given them. "Truly," said he, "there are no means by which we may prevent his going away at enmity with us that we will not take." "Well, lord," said they, "send after him another embassy." "I will do so," said he.

"Arise, Manawyddan, son of Llyr, and Heveyd Hir, and go after him, and tell him that he shall have a sound horse for every one that has been injured. And beside that, as an atonement for the insult, he shall have a staff of silver as large and as tall as himself, and a plate of gold of the breadth of his face. And show unto him who it was that did this, and that it was done against my will; but that he who did it is my brother, and therefore it would be hard for me to put him to death. And let him come and meet me," said he, "and we will make peace in any way he may desire."

The embassy went after Matholch and told him all these sayings in a friendly manner; and he listened thereunto. "Men," said he, "I will take counsel." So to the council he went. And in the council they considered that, if they should refuse this, they were likely to have more shame rather than to obtain so great an atonement. They resolved, therefore, to accept it, and they returned to the court in peace.

Then the pavilions and the tents were set in order, after the fashion of a hall; and they went to meat, and as they had sat at the beginning of the feast, so sat they there. And Matholch and Bendigeid Vran began to discourse; and, behold, it seemed to Bendigeid Vran, while they talked, that Matholch was not so cheerful as he had been before. And he thought that the chieftain might be sad because of the smallness of the atonement which he had for the wrong that had been done him. "Oh, man," said Bendigeid Vran, "thou dost not discourse to-night so cheerfully as thou wast wont. And if it be because of the smallness of the atonement, thou shalt add thereunto whatsoever thou mayest choose, and to-morrow I will pay thee for the horses." "Lord," said he, "Heaven reward thee!" "And I will enhance the atonement," said Bendigeid Vran, "for I will give unto thee a caldron, the property of which is, that if one of thy men be slain to-day, and be cast therein, to-morrow he will be as well as ever he was at the best, except that he will not regain his speech." And thereupon he gave him great thanks, and very joyful was he for that cause.

That night they continued to discourse as much as they would, and had minstrelsy and carousing; and when it was more pleasant to them to sleep than to sit longer, they went to rest. And thus was the banquet carried on with joyousness; and when it was finished, Matholch journeyed towards Ireland, and Branwen with him; and they went from Aber Menei with thirteen ships and came to Ireland. And in Ireland was there great joy because of their coming. And not one great man nor noble lady visited Branwen unto whom she gave not either a clasp or a ring, or a royal jewel to keep, such as it was honorable to be seen departing with. And in these things she spent that year in much renown, and she passed her time pleasantly, enjoying honor and friendship. And in due time a son was born unto her, and the name that they gave him was Gwern, the son of Matholch, and they put the boy out to be nursed in a place where were the best men of Ireland.

And, behold, in the second year a tumult arose in Ireland, on account of the insult which Matholch had received in Wales, and the payment made him for his horses. And his foster-brothers, and such as were nearest to him, blamed him openly for that matter. And he might have no peace by reason of the tumult, until they should revenge upon him this disgrace. And the vengeance which they took was to drive away Branwen from the same chamber with him and to make her cook for the court; and they caused the butcher, after he had cut up the meat, to come to her and give her every day a blow on the ear; and such they made her punishment.

"Verily, lord," said his men to Matholch, "forbid now the ships and the ferry-boats, and the coracles, that they go not into Wales, and such as come over from Wales hither, imprison them, that they go not back for this thing to be known there." And he did so; and it was thus for no less than three years.

And Branwen reared a starling in the cover of the kneading-trough, and she taught it to speak, and she taught the bird what manner of man her brother was. And she wrote a letter of her woes, and the despite with which she was treated, and she bound the letter to the root of the bird's wing, and sent it towards Wales. And the bird came to that island; and one day it found Bendigeid Vran at Caer Seciont in Arvon, conferring there, and it alighted upon his shoulder, and ruffled its feathers, so that the letter was seen, and they knew that the bird had been reared in a domestic manner.

Then Bendigeid Vran took the letter and looked upon it. And when he had read the letter, he grieved exceedingly at the tidings of Branwen's woes. And immediately he began sending messengers to summon the island together. And he caused sevenscore and four of his chief men to come unto him, and he complained to them of the grief that his sister endured. So they took counsel. And in the counsel they resolved to go to Ireland and to leave seven men as princes at home, and Caradoc,* the son of Bran, as the chief of them.

Bendigeid Vran, with the host of which we spoke, sailed towards Ireland; and it was not far across the sea, and he came to shoal water. Now the swineherds of Matholch were upon the seashore, and they came to Matholch. "Lord," said they, "greeting be unto thee." "Heaven protect you!" said he; "have you any news?" "Lord," said they, "we have marvellous news. A wood have we seen upon the sea, in a place where we never yet saw a single tree." "This is indeed a marvel," said he; "saw you aught else?" "We saw, lord," said they, "a vast mountain beside the wood, which moved, and there was a lofty ridge on the top of the mountain, and a lake on each side of the ridge. And the wood, and the mountain, and all these things, moved." "Verily," said he, "there is none who can know aught concerning this unless it be Branwen."

Messengers then went unto Branwen. "Lady," said they, "what thinkest thou that this is?" "The men of the Island of the Mighty, who have come hither on hearing of my ill treatment and of my woes." "What is the forest that is seen upon the sea?" asked they. "The yards and the masts of ships," she answered. "Alas!" said they; "what is the mountain that is seen by the side of the ships?" "Bendigeid Vran, my brother," she replied, "coming to shoal water, and he is wading to the land." "What is the lofty ridge, with the lake on each side thereof?" "On looking towards this island he is wroth, and his two

---
* Caractacus.

eyes on each side of his nose are the two lakes on each side of the ridge."

The warriors and chief men of Ireland were brought together in haste, and they took counsel. "Lord," said the neighbors unto Matholch, "there is no other counsel than this alone. Thou shalt give the kingdom to Gwern, the son of Branwen his sister, as a compensation for the wrong and despite that have been done unto Branwen. And he will make peace with thee." And in the council it was resolved that this message should be sent to Bendigeid Vran, lest the country should be destroyed. And this peace was made. And Matholch caused a great house to be built for Bendigeid Vran and his host. Thereupon came the hosts into the house. The men of the island of Ireland entered the house on the one side, and the men of the Island of the Mighty on the other. And as soon as they had sat down, there was concord between them; and the sovereignty was conferred upon the boy. When the peace was concluded, Bendigeid Vran called the boy unto him, and from Bendigeid Vran the boy went unto Manawyddan, and he was beloved by all that beheld him. And from Manawyddan the boy was called by Nissyen, the son of Euroswydd, and the boy went unto him lovingly. "Wherefore," said Evnissyen, "comes not my nephew, the son of my sister, unto me? Though he were not King of Ireland, yet willingly would I fondle the boy." "Cheerfully let him go to thee," said Bendigeid Vran; and the boy went unto him cheerfully. "By my confession to Heaven," said Evnissyen in his heart, "unthought of is the slaughter that I will this instant commit."

Then he arose and took up the boy, and before any one in the house could seize hold of him he thrust the boy headlong into the blazing fire. And when Branwen saw her son burning in the fire, she strove to leap into the fire also, from the place where she sat between her two brothers. But Bendigeid Vran grasped her with one hand, and his shield with the other. Then they all hurried about the house, and never was there made so great a tumult by any host in one house as was made by them, as each man armed himself. And while they all sought their arms Bendigeid Vran supported Branwen between his shield and his shoulder. And they fought.

Then the Irish kindled a fire under the caldron of renovation, and they cast the dead bodies into the caldron until it was full; and the next day they came forth fighting men, as good as before, except that they were not able to speak. Then when Evnissyen saw the dead bodies of the men of the Island of the Mighty nowhere resuscitated, he said in his heart, "Alas! woe is me, that I should have been the cause of bringing the men of the Island of the Mighty into so great a strait. Evil betide me if I find not a deliverance therefrom." And he cast himself among the dead bodies of the Irish; and two unshod Irishmen came to him and, taking him to be one of the Irish, flung him into the caldron. And he stretched himself out in the caldron, so that he rent the caldron into four pieces and burst his own heart also.

In consequence of this, the men of the Island of the Mighty obtained such success as they had; but they were not victorious, for only seven men of them all escaped, and Bendigeid Vran himself was wounded in the foot with a poisoned dart. Now the men that escaped were Pryderi, Manawyddan, Taliesin, and four others.

And Bendigeid Vran commanded them that they should cut off his head. "And take you my head," said he, "and bear it even unto the White Mount in London, and bury it there with the face towards France. And so long as it lies there, no enemy shall ever land on the island." So they cut off his head, and these seven went forward therewith. And Branwen was the eighth with them. And they came to land on Aber Alaw, and they sat down to rest. And Branwen looked towards Ireland, and towards the Island of the Mighty, to see if she could descry them. "Alas!" said she, "woe is me that I was ever born; two islands have been destroyed because of me." Then she uttered a groan, and there broke her heart. And they made her a four-sided grave and buried her upon the banks of the Alaw.

Then the seven men journeyed forward, bearing the head with them; and as they went, behold there met them a multitude of men and women. "Have you any tidings?" said Manawyddan. "We have none," said they, "save that Caswallawn,* the son of Beli, has conquered

* Cassivellaunus.

the Island of the Mighty, and is crowned king in London." "What has become," said they, "of Caradoc, the son of Bran, and the seven men who were left with him in this island?" "Caswallawn came upon them and slew six of the men, and Caradoc's heart broke for grief thereof." And the seven men journeyed on towards London, and they buried the head in the White Mount, as Bendigeid Vran had directed them.†

CHAPTER X

MANAWYDDAN

Pwyll and Rhiannon had a son, whom they named Pryderi. And when he was grown up, Pwyll, his father, died. And Pryderi married Kicva, the daughter of Gwynn Gloy.

Now Manawyddan returned from the war in Ireland, and he found that his cousin had seized all his possessions, and much grief and heaviness came upon him. "Alas! woe is me!" he exclaimed; "there is none save myself without a home and a resting-place." "Lord," said Pryderi, "be not so sorrowful. Thy cousin is King of the Island of the Mighty, and though he has done thee wrong, thou hast never been a claimant of land or possessions." "Yea," answered he, "but although this man is my cousin, it grieveth me to see any one in the place of my brother, Bendigeid Vran; neither can I be happy in the same dwelling with him." "Wilt thou follow the counsel of another?" said Pryderi. "I stand in need of counsel," he answered, "and what may that counsel be?" "Seven cantrevs belong unto me," said Pryderi, "wherein Rhiannon, my mother, dwells. I will bestow her upon thee, and the seven cantrevs with her; and though thou hadst no

† There is a Triad upon the story of the head buried under the White Tower of London, as a charm against invasion. Arthur, it seems, proudly disinterred the head, preferring to hold the island by his own strength alone.

possessions but those cantrevs only, thou couldst not have any fairer than they. Do thou and Rhiannon enjoy them, and if thou desire any possessions, thou wilt not despise these." "I do not, chieftain," said he. "Heaven reward thee for thy friendship! I will go with thee to seek Rhiannon and to look at thy possessions." "Thou wilt do well," he answered; "and I believe that thou didst never hear a lady discourse better than she, and when she was in her prime, none was ever fairer. Even now her aspect is not uncomely."

They set forth, and, however long the journey, they came at last to Dyved; and a feast was prepared for them by Rhiannon and Kicva. Then began Manawyddan and Rhiannon to sit and to talk together; and his mind and his thoughts became warmed towards her, and he thought in his heart he had never beheld any lady more fulfilled of grace and beauty than she. "Pryderi," said he, "I will that it be as thou didst say." "What saying was that?" asked Rhiannon. "Lady," said Pryderi, "I did offer thee as a wife to Manawyddan, the son of Llyr." "By that will I gladly abide," said Rhiannon. "Right glad am I also," said Manawyddan; "may Heaven reward him who hath shown unto me friendship so perfect as this!"

And before the feast was over, she became his bride. Said Pryderi, "Tarry ye here the rest of the feast, and I will go into England to tender my homage unto Caswallawn, the son of Beli." "Lord," said Rhiannon, "Caswallawn is in Kent; thou mayest therefore tarry at the feast and wait until he shall be nearer." "We will wait," he answered. So they finished the feast. And they began to make the circuit of Dyved, and to hunt, and to take their pleasure. And as they went through the country, they had never seen lands more pleasant to live in, nor better hunting-grounds, nor greater plenty of honey and fish. And such was the friendship between these four that they would not be parted from each other by night nor by day.

And in the midst of all this he went to Caswallawn at Oxford and tendered his homage; and honorable was his reception there, and highly was he praised for offering his homage.

And after his return, Pryderi and Manawyddan feasted

and took their ease and pleasure. And they began a feast at Narberth, for it was the chief palace. And when they had ended the first meal, while those who served them ate, they arose, and went forth, and proceeded to the Gorsedd, that is, the Mound of Narberth, and their retinue with them. And as they sat thus, behold, a peal of thunder, and with the violence of the thunder-storm, lo! there came a fall of mist so thick that not one of them could see the other. And after the mist, it became light all around. And when they looked towards the place where they were wont to see cattle and herds and dwellings, they saw nothing now, neither house, nor beast, nor smoke, nor fire, nor man, nor dwelling, but the buildings of the court empty, and desert, and uninhabited, without either man or beast within them. And truly all their companions were lost to them, without their knowing aught of what had befallen them, save those four only.

"In the name of Heaven," said Manawyddan, "where are they of the court, and all my host beside? Let us go and see."

So they came to the castle and saw no man, and into the hall, and to the sleeping-place, and there was none; and in the mead-cellar and in the kitchen, there was naught but desolation. Then they began to go through the land and all the possessions that they had; and they visited the houses and dwellings and found nothing but wild beasts. And when they had consumed their feast and all their provisions, they fed upon the prey they killed in hunting and the honey of the wild swarms.

And one morning Pryderi and Manawyddan rose up to hunt, and they ranged their dogs and went forth. And some of the dogs ran before them and came to a bush which was near at hand; but as soon as they were come to the bush, they hastily drew back and returned to the men, their hair bristling up greatly. "Let us go near to the bush," said Pryderi, "and see what is in it." And as they came near, behold, a wild boar of a pure white color rose up from the bush. Then the dogs, being set on by the men, rushed towards him; but he left the bush, and fell back a little way from the men, and made a stand against the dogs, without retreating from them, until the men had come near. And when the men came up, he fell back a second time and betook him to flight. Then they pursued the boar until they beheld a vast and lofty castle, all newly built, in a place where they had never before seen either stone or building. And the boar ran swiftly into the castle, and the dogs after him. Now when the boar and the dogs had gone into the castle, the men began to wonder at finding a castle in a place where they had never before seen any building whatsoever. And from the top of the Gorsedd they looked and listened for the dogs. But so long as they were there, they heard not one of the dogs, nor aught concerning them.

"Lord," said Pryderi, "I will go into the castle to get tidings of the dogs." "Truly," he replied, "thou wouldst be unwise to go into this castle, which thou hast never seen till now. If thou wouldst follow my counsel, thou wouldst not enter therein. Whosoever has cast a spell over this land has caused this castle to be here." "Of a truth," answered Pryderi, "I cannot thus give up my dogs." And for all the counsel that Manawyddan gave him, yet to the castle he went.

When he came within the castle, neither man nor beast, nor boar, nor dogs, nor house, nor dwelling, saw he within it. But in the centre of the castle-floor, he beheld a fountain with marble-work around it, and on the margin of the fountain a golden bowl upon a marble slab, and chains hanging from the air, to which he saw no end.

And he was greatly pleased with the beauty of the gold and with the rich workmanship of the bowl, and he went up to the bowl and laid hold of it. And when he had taken hold of it, his hands stuck to the bowl, and his feet to the slab on which the bowl was placed; and all his joyousness forsook him, so that he could not utter a word. And thus he stood.

And Manawyddan waited for him till near the close of the day. And late in the evening, being certain that he should have no tidings of Pryderi or the dogs, he went back to the palace. And as he entered, Rhiannon looked at him. "Where," said she, "are thy companion and thy dogs?" "Behold," he answered, "the adventure that has befallen me." And he related it all unto her. "An evil companion hast thou been," said Rhiannon, "and a good companion hast thou lost." And with that word she went out and proceeded towards the castle, according to the direction which he gave her. The gate of the castle she found open. She was nothing daunted, and she went in. And as she went in, she perceived Pryderi laying hold of the bowl, and she went towards him. "Oh, my lord," said she, "what dost thou here?" And she took hold of the bowl with him; and as she did so, her hands also became fast to the bowl, and her feet to the slab, and she was not able to utter a word. And with that, as it became night, lo! there came thunder upon them, and a fall of mist; and thereupon the castle vanished, and they with it.

When Kicva, the daughter of Glynn Gloy, saw that there was no one in the palace but herself and Manawyddan, she sorrowed so that she cared not whether she lived or died. And Manawyddan saw this. "Thou art in the wrong," said he, "if through fear of me thou grievest thus. I call Heaven to witness that thou hast never seen friendship more pure than that which I will bear thee, as long as Heaven will that thou shouldst be thus. I declare to thee, that, were I in the dawn of youth, I would keep my faith unto Pryderi, and unto thee also will I keep it. Be there no fear upon thee, therefore." "Heaven reward thee!" she said; "and that is what I deemed of thee." And the damsel thereupon took courage, and was glad.

"Truly, lady," said Manawyddan, "it is not fitting for us to stay here; we have lost our dogs, and cannot get food. Let us go into England; it is easiest for us to find support there." "Gladly, lord," said she, "we will do so." And they set forth together to England.

"Lord," said she, "what craft wilt thou follow? Take up one that is seemly." "None other will I take," answered he, "but that of making shoes." "Lord," said she, "such a craft becomes not a man so nobly born as thou." "By that, however, will I abide," said he. "I know nothing thereof," said Kicva. "But I know," answered Manawyddan, "and I will teach thee to stitch. We will not attempt to dress the leather, but we will buy it ready dressed and will make the shoes from it."

So they went into England and went as far as Hereford; and they betook themselves to making shoes. And he began by buying the best cordwain that could be had in the town, and none other would he buy. And he associated himself with the best goldsmith in the town and caused him to make clasps for the shoes and to gild the clasps; and he marked how it was done until he learned the method. And therefore is he called one of the three makers of gold shoes. And when they could be had from him, not a shoe nor hose was bought of any of the cordwainers in the town. But when the cordwainers perceived that their gains were failing (for as Manawyddan shaped the work, so Kicva stitched it), they came together, and took counsel, and agreed that they would slay them. And he had warning thereof, and it was told him how the cordwainers had agreed together to slay him.

"Lord," said Kicva, "wherefore should this be borne from these boors?" "Nay," said he, "we will go back unto Dyved." So towards Dyved they set forth.

Now Manawyddan, when he set out to return to Dyved, took with him a burden of wheat. And he proceeded towards Narberth, and there he dwelt. And never was he better pleased than when he saw Narberth again, and the lands where he had been wont to hunt with Pryderi and with Rhiannon. And he accustomed himself to fish and to hunt the deer in their covert. And then he began to prepare some ground, and he sowed a croft, and a second, and a third. And no wheat in the world ever sprung up better. And the three crofts prospered with perfect growth, and no man ever saw fairer wheat than it.

And thus passed the seasons of the year, until the harvest came. And he went to look at one of his crofts, and, behold, it was ripe. "I will reap this to-morrow," said he. And that night he went back to Narberth, and on the morrow, in the gray dawn, he went to reap the croft; and when he came there, he found nothing but the bare straw. Every one of the ears of the wheat was cut off from the stalk, and all the ears carried entirely away, and nothing but the straw left. And at this he marvelled greatly.

Then he went to look at another croft, and, behold,

that also was ripe. "Verily," said he, "this will I reap to-morrow." And on the morrow he came with the intent to reap it; and when he came there, he found nothing but the bare straw. "O gracious Heaven!" he exclaimed, "I know that whosoever has begun my ruin is completing it, and has also destroyed the country with me."

Then he went to look at the third croft; and when he came there, finer wheat had there never been seen, and this also was ripe. "Evil betide me," said he, "if I watch not here to-night. Whoever carried off the other corn will come in like manner to take this, and I will know who it is." And he told Kicva all that had befallen. "Verily," said she, "what thinkest thou to do?" "I will watch the croft to-night," said he. And he went to watch the croft.

And at midnight, he heard something stirring among the wheat; and he looked, and behold, the mightiest host of mice in the world, which could neither be numbered nor measured. And he knew not what it was until the mice had made their way into the croft, and each of them, climbing up the straw, and bending it down with its weight, had cut off one of the ears of wheat and had carried it away, leaving there the stalk; and he saw not a single straw there that had not a mouse to it. And they all took their way, carrying the ears with them.

In wrath and anger did he rush upon the mice; but he could no more come up with them than if they had been gnats or birds of the air, except one only, which, though it was but sluggish, went so fast that a man on foot could scarce overtake it. And after this one he went, and he caught it, and put it in his glove, and tied up the opening of the glove with a string, and kept it with him, and returned to the palace. Then he came to the hall where Kicva was, and he lighted a fire, and hung the glove by the string upon a peg. "What hast thou there, lord?" said Kicva. "A thief," said he, "that I found robbing me." "What kind of a thief may it be, lord, that thou couldst put into thy glove?" said she. Then he told her how the mice came to the last of the fields in his sight. "And one of them was less nimble than the rest, and is now in my glove; to-morrow I will hang it." "My lord," said she, "this is marvellous; but yet it would be unseemly for a man of dignity like thee to be hanging such a reptile as this." "Woe betide me," said he, "if I would not hang them all, could I catch them, and such as I have I will hang." "Verily, lord," said she, "there is no reason that I should succor this reptile, except to prevent discredit unto thee. Do therefore, lord, as thou wilt."

Then he went to the Mound of Narberth, taking the mouse with him. And he set up two forks on the highest part of the mound. And while he was doing this, behold, he saw a scholar coming towards him, in old and poor and tattered garments. And it was now seven years since he had seen in that place either man or beast, except those four persons who had remained together until two of them were lost.

"My lord," said the scholar, "good day to thee." "Heaven prosper thee, and my greeting be unto thee! And whence dost thou come, scholar?" asked he. "I come, lord, from singing in England; and wherefore dost thou inquire?" "Because for the last seven years," answered he, "I have seen no man here save four secluded persons, and thyself this moment." "Truly, lord," said he, "I go through this land unto mine own. And what work art thou upon, lord?" "I am hanging a thief that I caught robbing me," said he. "What manner of thief is that?" asked the scholar. "I see a creature in thy hand like unto a mouse, and ill does it become a man of rank equal to thine to touch a reptile such as this. Let it go forth free." "I will not let it go free, by Heaven," said he; "I caught it robbing me, and the doom of a thief will I inflict upon it, and I will hang it." "Lord," said he, "rather than see a man of rank equal to thine at such a work as this, I would give thee a pound, which I have received as alms, to let the reptile go forth free." "I will not let it go free," said he, "neither will I sell it." "As thou wilt, lord," he answered; "I care naught." And the scholar went his way.

And as he was placing the cross-beam upon the two forks, behold, a priest came towards him, upon a horse covered with trappings. "Good day to thee, lord," said he. "Heaven prosper thee!" said Manawyddan; "thy blessing." "The blessing of Heaven be upon thee! And what, lord, art thou doing?" "I am hanging a thief that I caught robbing me," said he. "What manner of thief, lord?" asked he. "A creature," he answered, "in form of a mouse. It has been robbing me, and I am inflicting upon it the doom of a thief." "Lord," said he, "rather than see thee touch this reptile, I would purchase its freedom." "By my confession to Heaven, neither will I sell it nor set it free." "It is true, lord, that it is worth nothing to buy; but rather than see thee defile thyself by touching such a reptile as this, I will give thee three pounds to let it go." "I will not, by Heaven," said he, "take any price for it. As it ought, so shall it be hanged." And the priest went his way.

Then he noosed the string around the mouse's neck, and as he was about to draw it up, behold, he saw a bishop's retinue, with his sumpter-horses and his attendants. And the bishop himself came towards him. And he stayed his work. "Lord Bishop," said he, "thy blessing." "Heaven's blessing be unto thee!" said he. "What work art thou upon?" "Hanging a thief that I caught robbing me," said he. "Is not that a mouse that I see in thy hand?" "Yes," answered he, "and she has robbed me." "Ay," said he, "since I have come at the doom of this reptile, I will ransom it of thee. I will give thee seven pounds for it, and that rather than see a man of rank equal to thine destroying so vile a reptile as this. Let it loose, and thou shalt have the money." "I declare to Heaven that I will not let it loose." "If thou wilt not loose it for this, I will give thee four and twenty pounds of ready money to set it free." "I will not set it free, by Heaven, for as much again," said he. "If thou wilt not set it free for this, I will give thee all the horses that thou seest in this plain, and the seven loads of baggage, and the seven horses that they are upon." "By Heaven, I will not," he replied. "Since for this thou wilt not set it free, do so at what price soever thou wilt." "I will that Rhiannon and Pryderi be free," said he. "That thou shalt have," he answered. "Not yet will I loose the mouse, by Heaven." "What then wouldst thou?" "That the charm and the illusion be removed from the seven cantrevs of Dyved." "This shalt thou have also; set therefore the mouse free." "I will not set it free, by Heaven," said he,

"till I know who the mouse may be." "She is my wife."
"Wherefore came she to me?" "To despoil thee," he answered. "I am Lloyd, the son of Kilwed, and I cast the
charm over the seven cantrevs of Dyved. And it was to
avenge Gawl, the son of Clud, from the friendship I had
towards him, that I cast the charm. And upon Pryderi
did I avenge Gawl, the son of Clud, for the game of
Badger in the Bag, that Pwyll, the son of Auwyn, played
upon him. And when it was known that thou wast come
to dwell in the land, my household came and besought
me to transform them into mice, that they might destroy
thy corn. And they went the first and the second night
and destroyed thy two crops. And the third night came
unto me my wife and the ladies of the court and besought me to transform them. And I transformed them.
Now she is not in her usual health. And had she been in
her usual health, thou wouldst not have been able to
overtake her; but since this has taken place, and she
has been caught, I will restore to thee Pryderi and Rhiannon, and I will take the charm and illusion from off
Dyved. Set her therefore free." "I will not set her free
yet." "What wilt thou more?" he asked. "I will that
there be no more charm upon the seven cantrevs of
Dyved, and that none shall be put upon it henceforth;
moreover, that vengeance be never taken for this, either
upon Pryderi or Rhiannon, or upon me." "All this shalt
thou have. And truly thou hast done wisely in asking
this. Upon thy head would have lit all this trouble."
"Yea," said he, "for fear thereof was it that I required
this." "Set now my wife at liberty." "I will not," said he,
"until I see Pryderi and Rhiannon with me free." "Behold, here they come," he answered.

And thereupon, behold, Pryderi and Rhiannon. And
he rose up to meet them, and greeted them, and sat
down beside them. "Ah, Chieftain, set now my wife at
liberty," said the bishop. "Hast thou not received all
thou didst ask?" "I will release her, gladly," said he.
And thereupon he set her free.

Then he struck her with a magic wand, and she was
changed back into a young woman, the fairest ever seen.

"Look round upon thy land," said he, "and thou wilt
see it all tilled and peopled as it was in its best estate."

And he rose up and looked forth. And when he looked he saw all the lands tilled, and full of herds and dwellings. And thus ends this portion of the Mabinogi.

The following allusions to the preceding story are found in a letter of the poet Southey to John Rickman, Esq., dated June 6th, 1802:

You will read the Mabinogeon, concerning which I ought to have talked to you. In the last, that most odd and Arabian-like story of the mouse, mention is made of a begging scholar, that helps to the date; but where did the Cymri get the imagination that could produce such a tale? That enchantment of the basin hanging by the chain from heaven is in the wildest spirit of the Arabian Nights. I am perfectly astonished that such fictions should exist in Welsh. They throw no light on the origin of romance, everything being utterly dissimilar to what we mean by that term, but they do open a new world of fiction; and if the date of their language be fixed about the twelfth or thirteenth century, I cannot but think the mythological substance is of far earlier date; very probably brought from the East by some of the first settlers or conquerors.

CHAPTER XI

KILWICH AND OLWEN

Kilydd, the son of Prince Kelyddon, desired a wife as a helpmate, and the wife that he chose was Goleudid, the daughter of Prince Anlawd. And after their union, the people put up prayers that they might have an heir. And they had a son through the prayers of the people, and called his name Kilwich.

After this the boy's mother, Goleudid, the daughter of Prince Anlawd, fell sick. Then she called her husband to her and said to him, "Of this sickness I shall die, and thou wilt take another wife. Now wives are the gift of the Lord, but it would be wrong for thee to harm thy son. Therefore I charge thee that thou take not a wife until thou see a briar with two blossoms upon my grave." And this he promised her. Then she besought him to dress her grave every year, that no weeds might grow thereon. So the queen died. Now the king sent an attendant every morning to see if anything were growing upon the grave. And, at the end of the seventh year, they neglected that which they had promised to the queen.

One day the king went to hunt; and he rode to the place of burial, to see the grave, and to know if it were time that he should take a wife: and the king saw the briar. And when he saw it, the king took counsel where he should find a wife. Said one of his counsellors, "I know a wife that will suit thee well; and she is the wife of King Doged." And they resolved to go to seek her; and they slew the king and brought away his wife. And they conquered the king's lands. And he married the widow of King Doged, the sister of Yspadaden Penkawr.

And one day his stepmother said to Kilwich, "It were well for thee to have a wife." "I am not yet of an age to wed," answered the youth. Then said she unto him, "I declare to thee that it is thy destiny not to be suited with a wife until thou obtain Olwen, the daughter of Yspadaden Penkawr." And the youth blushed, and the love of the maiden diffused itself through all his frame, although he had never seen her. And his father inquired of him, "What has come over thee, my son, and what aileth thee?" "My stepmother has declared to me that I shall never have a wife until I obtain Olwen, the daughter of Yspadaden Penkawr." "That will be easy for thee," answered his father. "Arthur is thy cousin. Go, therefore, unto Arthur, to cut thy hair, and ask this of him as a boon."

And the youth pricked forth upon a steed with head dappled gray, four winters old, firm of limb, with shell-formed hoofs, having a bridle of linked gold on his head, and upon him a saddle of costly gold. And in the youth's hand were two spears of silver, sharp, well-tempered, headed with steel, three ells in length, of an edge to wound the wind and cause blood to flow, and swifter than the fall of the dew-drop from the blade of reed-grass, when the dew of June is at the heaviest. A gold-hilted sword was upon his thigh, the blade of which was gilded, bearing a cross of inlaid gold of the hue of the lightning of heaven. His war-horn was of ivory. Before him were two brindled, white-breasted greyhounds, having strong collars of rubies about their necks, reaching from the shoulder to the ear. And the one that was upon the left side bounded across to the right side, and the one on the right to the left, and, like two sea-swallows, sported around him. And his courser cast up four sods, with his four hoofs, like four swallows in the air, about his head, now above, now below. About him was a four-cornered cloth of purple, and an apple of gold was at each corner, and every one of the apples was of the value of an hundred kine. And there was precious gold of the value of three hundred kine upon his shoes and upon his stirrups, from his knee to the tip of his toe. And the blade of grass bent not beneath him, so light was his courser's tread, as he journeyed towards the gate of Arthur's palace.

Spoke the youth: "Is there a porter?" "There is; and if thou holdest not thy peace, small will be thy welcome. I am Arthur's porter every first day of January." "Open the portal." "I will not open it." "Wherefore not?" "The knife is in the meat, and the drink is in the horn, and there is revelry in Arthur's hall; and none may enter therein but the son of a king of a privileged country, or a craftsman bringing his craft. But there will be refreshment for thy dogs and for thy horse; and for thee there will be collops cooked and peppered, and luscious wine, and mirthful songs; and food for fifty men shall be brought unto thee in the guest-chamber, where the stranger and the sons of other countries eat, who come not into the precincts of the palace of Arthur. Thou wilt fare no worse there than thou wouldst with Arthur in the court. A lady shall smooth thy couch and shall lull thee with songs; and early to-morrow morning, when the gate is open for the multitude that came hither to-day, for thee shall it be opened first, and thou mayest sit in the place that thou shalt choose in Arthur's hall, from the upper end to the lower." Said the youth: "That

will I not do. If thou openest the gate, it is well. If thou
dost not open it, I will bring disgrace upon thy lord and
evil report upon thee. And I will set up three shouts at
this very gate, than which none were ever heard more
deadly." "What clamor soever thou mayest make," said
Glewlwyd the porter, "against the laws of Arthur's
palace, shalt thou not enter therein, until I first go and
speak with Arthur."

Then Glewlwyd went into the hall. And Arthur said to
him, "Hast thou news from the gate?" "Half of my
life is passed," said Glewlwyd, "and half of thine. I was
heretofore in Kaer Se and Asse, in Sach and Salach, in
Lotor and Fotor, and I have been in India the Great
and India the Lesser, and I have also been in Europe
and Africa, and in the islands of Corsica, and I was
present when thou didst conquer Greece in the East.
Nine supreme sovereigns, handsome men, saw we there,
but never did I behold a man of equal dignity with him
who is now at the door of the portal." Then said Arthur:
"If walking thou didst enter here, return thou running. It
is unbecoming to keep such a man as thou sayest he is in
the wind and the rain." Said Kay: "By the hand of my
friend, if thou wouldst follow my counsel, thou wouldst
not break through the laws of the court because of him."
"Not so, blessed Kay," said Arthur; "it is an honor to us
to be resorted to, and the greater our courtesy, the
greater will be our renown and our fame and our glory."

And Glewlwyd came to the gate and opened the gate
before Kilwich; and although all dismounted upon the
horse-block at the gate, yet did he not dismount, but he
rode in upon his charger. Then said he, "Greeting be unto
thee, sovereign ruler of this island, and be this greeting
no less unto the lowest than unto the highest, and be it
equally unto thy guests, and thy warriors, and thy
chieftains; let all partake of it as completely as thyself.
And complete be thy favor, and thy fame, and thy glory,
throughout all this island." "Greeting unto thee also,"
said Arthur; "sit thou between two of my warriors, and
thou shalt have minstrels before thee, and thou shalt enjoy the privileges of a king born to a throne, as long as
thou remainest here. And when I dispense my presents
to the visitors and strangers in this court, they shall be

in thy hand at my commencing." Said the youth, "I came not here to consume meat and drink; but if I obtain the boon that I seek, I will requite it thee, and extol thee; but if I have it not, I will bear forth thy dispraise to the four quarters of the world, as far as thy renown has extended." Then said Arthur, "Since thou wilt not remain here, Chieftain, thou shalt receive the boon, whatsoever thy tongue may name, as far as the wind dries, and the rain moistens, and the sun revolves, and the sea encircles, and the earth extends; save only my ship Prydwen, and my mantle, and Caleburn, my sword, and Rhongomyant, my lance, and Guenever, my wife. By the truth of Heaven, thou shalt have it cheerfully, name what thou wilt." "I would that thou bless my hair," said he. "That shall be granted thee."

And Arthur took a golden comb, and scissors whereof the loops were of silver, and he combed his hair. And Arthur inquired of him who he was; "for my heart warms unto thee, and I know that thou art come of my blood. Tell me, therefore, who thou art." "I will tell thee," said the youth. "I am Kilwich, the son of Kilydd, the son of Prince Kelyddon, by Goleudyd my mother, the daughter of Prince Anlawd." "That is true," said Arthur; "thou art my cousin. Whatsoever boon thou mayest ask, thou shalt receive, be it what it may that thy tongue shall name." "Pledge the truth of Heaven and the faith of thy kingdom thereof." "I pledge it thee gladly." "I crave of thee, then, that thou obtain for me Olwen, the daughter of Yspadaden Penkawr, to wife; and this boon I likewise seek at the hands of thy warriors. I seek it from Kay and from Bedwyr; and from Gwynn, the son of Nudd, and Gadwy, the son of Geraint, and Prince Flewddur Flam, and Iona, King of France, and Sel, the son of Selgi, and Taliesin, the chief of the bards, and Geraint, the son of Erbin, Garanwyn, the son of Kay, and Amren, the son of Bedwyr, Ol, the son of Olwyd, Bedwin, the bishop, Guenever, the chief lady, and Guenhywach, her sister, Morved, the daughter of Urien, and Gwenlian Deg, the majestic maiden, Creiddylad,*

---

* Creiddylad is no other than Shakespeare's Cordelia, whose father, King Lear, is by the Welsh authorities called indiscriminately Llyr or Lludd. All the old chroniclers give the story of her devotion to

the daughter of Lludd, the constant maiden, and Ewaedan, the daughter of Kynvelyn,* the half-man." All these did Kilwich, the son of Kilydd, adjure to obtain his boon.

Then said Arthur, "Oh, Chieftain, I have never heard of the maiden of whom thou speakest, nor of her kindred, but I will gladly send messengers in search of her. Give me time to seek her." And the youth said, "I will willingly grant from this night to that at the end of the year to do so." Then Arthur sent messengers to every land within his dominions to seek for the maiden, and at the end of the year Arthur's messengers returned without having gained any knowledge or intelligence concerning Olwen, more than on the first day. Then said Kilwich, "Every one has received his boon, and I yet lack mine. I will depart and bear away thy honor with me." Then said Kay, "Rash Chieftain! dost thou reproach Arthur? Go with us, and we will not part until thou dost either confess that the maiden exists not in the world, or until we obtain her." Thereupon Kay rose up. And Arthur called Bedwyr, who never shrank from any enterprise upon which Kay was bound. None were equal to him in swiftness throughout this island except Arthur alone; and although he was one-handed, three warriors could not shed blood faster than he on the field of battle.

And Arthur called to Kyndelig, the guide, "Go thou upon this expedition with the chieftain." For as good a guide was he in a land which he had never seen as he was in his own.

---

* The Welsh have a fable on the subject of the half-man, taken to be illustrative of the force of habit. In this allegory Arthur is supposed to be met by a sprite, who appears at first in a small and indistinct form, but who, on approaching nearer, increases in size, and, assuming the semblance of half a man, endeavors to provoke the king to wrestle. Despising his weakness, and considering that he should gain no credit by the encounter, Arthur refuses to do so and delays the contest until at length the half-man (Habit) becomes so strong that it requires his utmost efforts to overcome him.

---

her aged parent, but none of them seem to have been aware that she is destined to remain with him till the day of doom, whilst Gwyn ap Nudd, the king of the fairies, and Gwythyr ap Greidiol, fight for her every first of May, and whichever of them may be fortunate enough to be the conqueror at that time will obtain her as his bride.

He called Gurhyr Gwalstat, because he knew all tongues.

He called Gawain, the son of Gwyar, because he never returned home without achieving the adventure of which he went in quest.

And Arthur called Meneu, the son of Teirgwed, in order that, if they went into a savage country, he might cast a charm and an illusion over them, so that none might see them, whilst they could see every one.

They journeyed until they came to a vast open plain, wherein they saw a great castle, which was the fairest of the castles of the world. And when they came before the castle, they beheld a vast flock of sheep. And upon the top of a mound there was a herdsman keeping the sheep. And a rug made of skins was upon him, and by his side was a shaggy mastiff, larger than a steed nine winters old.

Then said Kay, "Gurhyr Gwalstat, go thou and salute yonder man." "Kay," said he, "I engaged not to go further than thou thyself." "Let us go then together," answered Kay. Said Meneu, "Fear not to go thither, for I will cast a spell upon the dog, so that he shall injure no one." And they went up to the mound whereon the herdsman was, and they said to him, "How dost thou fare, herdsman?" "Not less fair be it to you than to me." "Whose are the sheep that thou dost keep, and to whom does yonder castle belong?" "Stupid are ye, truly! not to know that this is the castle of Yspadaden Penkawr. And ye also, who are ye?" "We are an embassy from Arthur, come to seek Olwen, the daughter of Yspadaden Penkawr." "Oh, men! the mercy of Heaven be upon you; do not that for all the world. None who ever came hither on this quest has returned alive." And the herdsman rose up. And as he rose, Kilwich gave unto him a ring of gold. And he went home and gave the ring to his spouse to keep. And she took the ring when it was given her, and she said, "Whence came this ring, for thou art not wont to have good fortune." "Oh, wife, him to whom this ring belonged thou shalt see here this evening." "And who is he?" asked the woman. "Kilwich, the son of Kilydd, by Goleudid, the daughter of Prince Anlawd, who is come to seek Olwen as his wife." And when she heard that, she had joy that her nephew, the son of her sister, was coming to her, and sorrow, because she had never known any one depart alive who had come on that quest.

And the men went forward to the gate of the herdsman's dwelling. And when she heard their footsteps approaching, she ran out with joy to meet them. And Kay snatched a billet out of the pile. And when she met them, she sought to throw her arms about their necks. And Kay placed the log between her two hands, and she squeezed it so that it became a twisted coil. "Oh, woman," said Kay, "if thou hadst squeezed me thus, none could ever again have set their affections on me. Evil love were this." They centered into the house and were served; and soon after, they all went forth to amuse themselves. Then the woman opened a stone chest that was before the chimney-corner, and out of it arose a youth with yellow, curling hair. Said Gurhyr, "It is a pity to hide this youth. I know that it is not his own crime that is thus visited upon him." "This is but a remnant," said the woman. "Three and twenty of my sons has Yspadaden Penkawr slain, and I have no more hope of this one than of the others." Then said Kay, "Let him come and be a companion with me, and he shall not be slain unless I also am slain with him." And they ate. And the woman asked them, "Upon what errand come you here?" "We come to seek Olwen for this youth." Then said the woman, "In the name of Heaven, since no one from the castle hath yet seen you, return again whence you came." "Heaven is our witness, that we will not return until we have seen the maiden. Does she ever come hither, so that she may be seen?" "She comes here every Saturday to wash her head, and in the vessel where she washes she leaves all her rings, and she never either comes herself or sends any messengers to fetch them." "Will she come here if she is sent to?" "Heaven knows that I will not destroy my soul, nor will I betray those that trust me; unless you will pledge me your faith that you will not harm her, I will not send to her." "We pledge it," said they. So a message was sent, and she came.

The maiden was clothed in a robe of flame-colored silk, and about her neck was a collar of ruddy gold, on which were precious emeralds and rubies. More yellow was her head than the flower of the broom,* and her skin was whiter than the foam of the wave, and fairer were her hands and her fingers than the blossoms of the wood-anemone amidst the spray of the meadow fountain. The eye of the trained hawk was not brighter than hers. Her bosom was more snowy than the breast of the white swan, her cheek was redder than the reddest roses. Whoso beheld her was filled with her love. Four white trefoils sprung up wherever she trod. And therefore was she called Olwen.

She entered the house and sat beside Kilwich upon the foremost bench; and as soon as he saw her, he knew her. And Kilwich said unto her, "Ah! maiden, thou art she whom I have loved; come away with me, lest they speak evil of thee and of me. Many a day have I loved thee." "I cannot do this, for I have pledged my faith to my father not to go without his counsel, for his life will last only until the time of my espousals. Whatever is to be, must be. But I will give thee advice, if thou wilt take it. Go, ask me of my father, and that which he shall require of thee, grant it, and thou wilt obtain me; but if thou deny him anything, thou wilt not obtain me, and it will be well for thee if thou escape with thy life." "I promise all this, if occasion offer," said he.

She returned to her chamber, and they all rose up and followed her to the castle. And they slew the nine porters, that were at the nine gates, in silence. And they slew the nine watch-dogs without one of them barking. And they went forward to the hall.

"The greeting of Heaven and of man be unto thee, Yspadaden Penkawr," said they. "And you, wherefore come you?" "We come to ask thy daughter Olwen for Kilwich, the son of Kilydd, the son of Prince Kelyddon." "Where are my pages and my servants? Raise up the forks beneath my two eyebrows, which have fallen over

* The romancers dwell with great complacency on the fair hair and delicate complexion of their heroines. This taste continued for a long time, and to render the hair light was an object of education. Even when wigs came into fashion, they were all flaxen. Such was the color of the hair of the Gauls and of their German conquerors. It required some centuries to reconcile their eyes to the swarthy beauties of their Spanish and Italian neighbors.

my eyes, that I may see the fashion of my son-in-law."
And they did so. "Come hither to-morrow, and you shall
have an answer."

They rose to go forth, and Yspadaden Penkawr seized
one of the three poisoned darts that lay beside him and
threw it after them. And Bedwyr caught it, and flung it,
and pierced Yspadaden Penkawr grievously with it
through the knee. Then he said, "A cursed ungentle son-
in-law, truly! I shall ever walk the worse for his rude-
ness and shall ever be without a cure. This poisoned iron
pains me like the bite of a gad-fly. Cursed be the smith
who forged it, and the anvil on which it was wrought! So
sharp is it!"

That night also they took up their abode in the house
of the herdsman. The next day, with the dawn, they arrayed themselves, and proceeded to the castle, and entered the hall; and they said, "Yspadaden Penkawr, give
us thy daughter in consideration of her dower and her
maiden fee, which we will pay to thee, and to her two
kinswomen likewise." Then he said, "Her four-grand-
mothers and her four great-grandsires are yet alive; it is
needful that I take counsel of them." "Be it so," they
answered; "we will go to meat." As they rose up, he
took the second dart that was beside him and cast it
after them. And Meneu, the son of Gawedd, caught it,
and flung it back at him, and wounded him in the center
of the breast. "A cursed ungentle son-in-law, truly!" said
he; "the hard iron pains me like the bite of a horse-leech.
Cursed be the hearth whereon it was heated and the
smith who formed it! So sharp is it! Henceforth, whenever I go up hill, I shall have a scant in my breath, and
a pain in my chest, and I shall often loathe my food."
And they went to meat.

And the third day they returned to the palace. And
Yspadaden Penkawr said to them, "Shoot not at me
again unless you desire death. Where are my attendants?
Lift up the forks of my eyebrows, which have fallen
over my eyeballs, that I may see the fashion of my son-
in-law." Then they arose, and, as they did so, Yspadaden
Penkawr took the third poisoned dart and cast it at
them. And Kilwich caught it, and threw it vigorously,
and wounded him through the eyeball. "A cursed un-

gentle son-in-law, truly! As long as I remain alive, my eyesight will be the worse. Whenever I go against the wind, my eyes will water; and peradventure my head will burn, and I shall have a giddiness every new moon. Like the bite of a mad dog is the stroke of this poisoned iron. Cursed be the fire in which it was forged!" And they went to meat.

And the next day they came again to the palace, and they said, "Shoot not at us any more, unless thou desirest such hurt and harm and torture as thou now hast, and even more." Said Kilwich, "Give me thy daughter; and if thou wilt not give her, thou shalt receive thy death because of her." "Where is he that seeks my daughter? Come hither where I may see thee." And they placed him a chair face to face with him.

Said Yspadaden Penkawr, "Is it thou that seekest my daughter?"

"It is I," answered Kilwich.

"I must have thy pledge that thou wilt not do towards me otherwise than is just; and when I have gotten that which I shall name, my daughter thou shalt have."

"I promise thee that, willingly," said Kilwich; "name what thou wilt."

"I will do so," said he. "Seest thou yonder red tilled ground?"

"I see it."

"When first I met the mother of this maiden, nine bushels of flax were sown therein, and none has yet sprung up, white nor black. I require to have the flax to sow in the new land yonder, that when it grows up it may make a white wimple for my daughter's head on the day of thy wedding."

"It will be easy for me to compass this, although thou mayest think it will not be easy."

"Though thou get this, there is yet that which thou wilt not get—the harp of Teirtu, to play to us that night. When a man desires that it should play, it does so of itself; and when he desires that it should cease, it ceases. And this he will not give of his own free will, and thou wilt not be able to compel him."

"It will be easy for me to compass this, although thou mayest think that it will not be easy."

"Though thou get this, there is yet that which thou wilt not get. I require thee to get me for my huntsman Mabon, the son of Modron. He was taken from his mother when three nights old, and it is not known where he now is, nor whether he is living or dead."

"It will be easy for me to compass this, although thou mayest think it will not be easy."

"Though thou get this, there is yet that which thou wilt not get—the two cubs of the wolf Gast Rhymhi; no leash in the world will hold them, but a leash made from the beard of Dillus Varwawc, the robber. And the leash will be of no avail unless it be plucked from his beard while he is alive. While he lives, he will not suffer this to be done to him, and the leash will be of no use should he be dead, because it will be brittle."

"It will be easy for me to compass this, although thou mayest think it will not be easy."

"Though thou get this, there is yet that which thou wilt not get—the sword of Gwernach the Giant; of his own free will he will not give it, and thou wilt never be able to compel him."

"It will be easy for me to compass this, although thou mayest think it will not be easy."

"Though thou get this, there is yet that which thou wilt not get. Difficulties shalt thou meet with, and nights without sleep, in seeking this, and if thou obtain it not, neither shalt thou obtain my daughter."

"Horses shall I have, and chivalry; and my lord and kinsman, Arthur, will obtain for me all these things. And I shall gain thy daughter, and thou shalt lose thy life."

"Go forward. And thou shalt not be chargeable for food or raiment for my daughter while thou art seeking these things; and when thou hast compassed all these marvels, thou shalt have my daughter for thy wife."

CHAPTER XII

KILWICH AND OLWEN, CONTINUED

All that day they journeyed, until the evening, and then they beheld a vast castle, which was the largest in the world. And lo! a black man, larger than three of the men of this world, came out from the castle. And they spoke unto him, and said, "Oh, man, whose castle is that?" "Stupid are ye, truly, O men! There is no one in the world that does not know that this is the castle of Gwernach the Giant." "What treatment is there for guests and strangers that alight in that castle?" "Oh, Chieftain, Heaven protect thee! No guest ever returned thence alive, and no one may enter therein unless he brings with him his craft."

Then they proceeded towards the gate. Said Gurhyr Gwalstat, "Is there a porter?" "There is; wherefore dost thou call?" "Open the gate." "I will not open it." "Wherefore wilt thou not?" "The knife is in the meat, and the drink is in the horn, and there is revelry in the hall of Gwernach the Giant; and except for a craftsman who brings his craft, the gate will not be opened to-night." "Verily, porter," then said Kay, "my craft bring I with me." "What is thy craft?" "The best burnisher of swords am I in the world." "I will go and tell this unto Gwernach the Giant, and I will bring thee an answer."

So the porter went in, and Gwernach said to him, "Hast thou news from the gate?" "I have. There is a party at the door of the gate who desire to come in." "Didst thou inquire of them if they possessed any art?" "I did inquire," said he, "and one told me that he was well skilled in the burnishing of swords." "We have need of him then. For some time have I sought for some one to polish my sword, and could find no one. Let this man enter, since he brings with him his craft."

The porter thereupon returned and opened the gate. And Kay went in by himself, and he saluted Gwernach the

Giant. And a chair was placed for him opposite to Gwernach. And Gwernach said to him, "Oh, man, is it true
that is reported of thee, that thou knowest how to bur-
nish swords?" "I know full well how to do so," answered Kay. Then was the sword of Gwernach brought
to him. And Kay took a blue whetstone from under his
arm, and asked whether he would have it burnished white
or blue. "Do with it as it seems good to thee, or as thou
wouldst if it were thine own." Then Kay polished one half
of the blade, and put it in his hand. "Will this please thee?"
asked he. "I would rather than all that is in my dominions
that the whole of it were like this. It is a marvel to me
that such a man as thou should be without a companion."
"Oh, noble sir, I have a companion, albeit he is not skilled
in this art." "Who may he be?" "Let the porter go forth,
and I will tell him whereby he may know him. The head
of his lance will leave its shaft, and draw blood from the
wind, and will descend upon its shaft again." Then the
gate was opened, and Bedwyr entered. And Kay said,
"Bedwyr is very skilful, though he knows not this art."

And there was much discourse among those who were
without, because that Kay and Bedwyr had gone in. And
a young man who was with them, the only son of the
herdsman, got in also; and he contrived to admit all the
rest, but they kept themselves concealed.

The sword was now polished, and Kay gave it unto the
hand of Gwernach the Giant, to see if he were pleased
with his work. And the giant said, "The work is good;
I am content therewith." Said Kay, "It is thy scabbard that
hath rusted thy sword; give it to me, that I may take out
the wooden sides of it and put in new ones." And he took
the scabbard from him, and the sword in the other
hand. And he came and stood over against the giant, as
if he would have put the sword into the scabbard;
and with it he struck at the head of the giant, and cut
off his head at one blow. Then they despoiled the castle, and took from it what goods and jewels they would.
And they returned to Arthur's court, bearing with them
the sword of Gwernach the Giant.

And when they told Arthur how they had sped, Arthur
said, "It is a good beginning." Then they took counsel,
and said, "Which of these marvels will it be best for us

to seek next?" "It will be best," said one, "to seek Mabon, the son of Modron; and he will not be found unless we first find Eidoel, the son of Aer, his kinsman." Then Arthur rose up, and the warriors of the island of Britain with him, to seek for Eidoel; and they proceeded until they came to the castle of Glivi, where Eidoel was imprisoned. Glivi stood on the summit of his castle, and he said, "Arthur, what requirest thou of me, since nothing remains to me in this fortress, and I have neither joy nor pleasure in it, neither wheat nor oats? Seek not, therefore, to do me harm." Said Arthur, "Not to injure thee came I hither, but to seek for the prisoner that is with thee." "I will give thee my prisoner, though I had not thought to give him up to any one, and therewith shalt thou have my support and my aid."

His followers said unto Arthur, "Lord, go thou home, thou canst not proceed with thy host in quest of such small adventures as these." Then said Arthur, "It were well for thee, Gurhyr Gwalstat, to go upon this quest, for thou knowest all languages, and art familiar with those of the birds and the beasts. Thou, Eidoel, oughtest likewise to go with thy men in search of thy cousin. And as for you, Kay and Bedwyr, I have hope of whatever adventure ye are in quest of, that ye will achieve it. Achieve ye this adventure for me."

They went forward until they came to the Ousel of Cilgwri. And Gurhyr adjured her, saying, "Tell me if thou knowest aught of Mabon, the son of Modron, who was taken when three nights old from between his mother and the wall?" And the Ousel answered, "When I first came here, there was a smith's anvil in this place, and I was then a young bird; and from that time no work has been done upon it, save the pecking of my beak every evening; and now there is not so much as the size of a nut remaining thereof; yet during all that time I have never heard of the man for whom you inquire. Nevertheless, I will do that which it is fitting that I should for an embassy from Arthur. There is a race of animals who were formed before me, and I will be your guide to them."

So they proceeded to the place where was the Stag of Redynvre. "Stag of Redynvre, behold, we are come to thee, an embassy from Arthur, for we have not heard of any animal older than thou. Say, knowest thou aught of Mabon, the son of Modron, who was taken from his mother when three nights old?" The Stag said, "When first I came hither there was a plain all around me, without any trees save one oak sapling, which grew up to be an oak with an hundred branches; and that oak has since perished, so that now nothing remains of it but the withered stump; and from that day to this I have been here, yet have I never heard of the man for whom you inquire. Nevertheless, being an embassy from Arthur, I will be your guide to the place where there is an animal which was formed before I was, and the oldest animal in the world, and the one that has travelled most, the Eagle of Gwern Abwy."

Gurhyr said, "Eagle of Gwern Abwy, we have come to thee, an embassy from Arthur, to ask thee if thou knowest aught of Mabon, the son of Modron, who was taken from his mother when he was three nights old?" The Eagle said, "I have been here for a great space of time, and when I first came hither, there was a rock here from the top of which I pecked at the stars every evening; and it has crumbled away, and now it is not so much as a span high. All that time I have been here, and I have never heard of the man for whom you inquire, except once when I went in search of food as far as Llyn Llyw. And when I came there, I struck my talons into a salmon, thinking he would serve me as food for a long time. But he drew me into the water, and I was scarcely able to escape from him. After that I made peace with him. And I drew fifty fish-spears out of his back and relieved him. Unless he know something of him whom you seek, I cannot tell who may. However, I will guide you to the place where he is."

So they went thither; and the Eagle said, "Salmon of Llyn Llyw, I have come to thee with an embassy from Arthur, to ask thee if thou knowest aught of Mabon, the son of Modron, who was taken away at three nights old from his mother." "As much as I know I will tell thee. With every tide I go along the river upward, until I come near to the walls of Gloucester, and there have I found such wrong as I never found elsewhere; and to the end that ye may give credence thereto, let one of you go thither upon each of my two shoulders." So Kay and Gurhyr Gwalstat went upon the two shoulders of the Salmon, and they proceeded until they came unto the wall of the prison; and they heard a great wailing and lamenting from the dungeon. Said Gurhyr, "Who is it that laments in this house of stone?" "Alas! it is Mabon, the son of Modron, who is here imprisoned; and no imprisonment was ever so grievous as mine." "Hast thou hope of being released for gold or for silver, or for any gifts of wealth, or through battle and fighting?" "By fighting will whatever I may gain be obtained."

Then they went thence, and returned to Arthur, and they told him where Mabon, the son of Modron, was imprisoned. And Arthur summoned the warriors of the island, and they journeyed as far as Gloucester, to the place where Mabon was in prison. Kay and Bedwyr went upon the shoulders of the fish, whilst the warriors of Arthur attacked the castle. And Kay broke through the wall into the dungeon and brought away the prisoner upon his back, whilst the fight was going on between the warriors. And Arthur returned home, and Mabon with him at liberty.

On a certain day as Gurhyr Gwalstat was walking over a mountain, he heard a wailing and a grievous cry. And when he heard it, he sprung forward and went towards it. And when he came there, he saw a fire burning among the turf, and an ant-hill nearly surrounded with the fire. And he drew his sword and smote off the ant-hill close to the earth, so that it escaped being burned in the fire. And the ants said to him, "Receive from us the blessing of Heaven, and that which no man can give, we will give thee." Then they fetched the nine bushels of flax-seed which Yspadaden Penkawr had required of Kilwich, and they brought the full measure, without lacking any, except one flax-seed, and that the lame pismire brought in before night.

Then said Arthur, "Which of the marvels will it be best for us to seek next?" "It will be best to seek for the two cubs of the wolf Gast Rhymhi."

"Is it known," said Arthur, "where she is?" "She is in Aber Cleddyf," said one. Then Arthur went to the house of Tringad, in Aber Cleddyf, and he inquired of him whether he had heard of her there. "She has often slain my herds, and she is there below in a cave in Aber Cleddyf."

Then Arthur went in his ship Prydwen by sea, and the others went by land to hunt her. And they surrounded her and her two cubs, and took them, and carried them away.

As Kay and Bedwyr sat on a beacon-cairn on the summit of Plinlimmon, in the highest wind that ever was, they looked around them and saw a great smoke, afar off. Then said Kay, "By the hand of my friend, yonder is the fire of a robber." Then they hastened towards the smoke, and they came so near to it that they could see Dillus Varwawc scorching a wild boar. "Behold, yonder is the greatest robber that ever fled from Arthur," said Bedwyr to Kay. "Dost thou know him?" "I do know him," answered Kay; "he is Dillus Varwawc, and no leash in the world will be able to hold the cubs of Gast Rhymhi, save a leash made from the beard of him thou seest yonder. And even that will be useless unless his beard be plucked out alive, with wooden tweezers; for if dead it will be brittle." "What thinkest thou that we should do concerning this?" said Bedwyr. "Let us suffer him," said Kay, "to eat as much as he will of the meat, and after that he will fall asleep." And during that time they employed themselves in making the wooden tweezers. And when Kay knew certainly that he was asleep, he made a pit under his feet, and he struck him a violent blow, and squeezed him into the pit. And there they twitched out his beard completely with the wooden tweezers, and after that they slew him altogether. And from thence they went, and took the leash made of Dillus Varwawc's beard, and they gave it into Arthur's hand.

Thus they got all the marvels that Yspadaden Penkawr had required of Kilwich; and they set forward and took the marvels to his court. And Kilwich said to Yspadaden Penkawr, "Is thy daughter mine now?" "She is thine," said he, "but therefore needest thou not thank me, but Arthur, who hath accomplished this for thee." Then Goreu, the son of Custennin, the herdsman, whose brothers Yspadaden Penkawr had slain, seized him by the hair of his head, and dragged him after him to the keep, and cut off his head, and placed it on a stake on the citadel. Then they took possession of his castle and of his treasures. And that night Olwen became Kilwich's bride, and she continued to be his wife as long as she lived.

CHAPTER XIII

TALIESIN

Gwyddno Garanhir was sovereign of Gwaelod, a territory bordering on the sea. And he possessed a weir upon the strand between Dyvi and Aberystwyth, near to his own castle, and the value of a hundred pounds was taken in that weir every May eve. And Gwyddno had an only son named Elphin, the most hapless of youths and the most needy. And it grieved his father sore, for he thought that he was born in an evil hour. By the advice of his council, his father had granted him the drawing of the weir that year, to see if good luck would ever befall him, and to give him something wherewith to begin the world. And this was on the twenty-ninth of April.

The next day, when Elphin went to look, there was nothing in the weir but a leathern bag upon a pole of the weir. Then said the weir-ward unto Elphin, "All thy ill luck aforetime was nothing to this; and now thou hast destroyed the virtues of the weir, which always yielded the value of a hundred pounds every May eve; and to-night there is nothing but this leathern skin within it." "How now," said Elphin, "there may be therein the value of a hundred pounds." Well! they took up the leathern bag, and he who opened it saw the forehead of an infant, the fairest that ever was seen; and he said, "Behold, a radiant brow!" (in the Welsh language, *taliesin*). "Taliesin be he called," said Elphin. And he lifted the bag in his arms, and, lamenting his bad luck, placed the boy sorrowfully behind him. And he made his horse amble gently, that before had been trotting, and he carried him as softly as if he had been sitting in the easiest chair in the world. And presently the boy made a Consolation and praise to Elphin; and the Consolation was as you may here see.

> Fair Elphin, cease to lament!
> Never in Gwyddno's weir
> Was there such good luck as this night.
> Being sad will not avail;
> Better to trust in God than to forebode ill;
> Weak and small as I am,
> On the foaming beach of the ocean,
> In the day of trouble I shall be
> Of more service to thee than three hundred salmon.

This was the first poem that Taliesin ever sung, being to console Elphin in his grief for that the produce of the weir was lost, and what was worse, that all the world would consider that it was through his fault and ill luck. Then Elphin asked him what he was, whether man or spirit. And he sung thus:

> I have been formed a comely person;
> Although I am but little, I am highly gifted;
> Into a dark leathern bag I was thrown,
> And on a boundless sea I was sent adrift.
> From seas and from mountains
> God brings wealth to the fortunate man.

Then came Elphin to the house of Gwyddno, his father, and Taliesin with him. Gwyddno asked him if he had had a good haul at the weir, and he told him that he had got that which was better than fish. "What was that?" said Gwyddno. "A bard," said Elphin. Then said Gwyddno, "Alas! what will he profit thee?" And Taliesin himself replied and said, "He will profit him more than the weir ever profited thee." Asked Gwyddno, "Art thou able to speak, and thou so little?" And Taliesin answered him, "I am better able to speak than thou to question me." "Let me hear what thou canst say," quoth Gwyddno. Then Taliesin sang:

Three times have I been born, I know by meditation;
All the sciences of the world are collected in my breast,
For I know what has been, what hereafter will occur.

Elphin gave his haul to his wife, and she nursed him
tenderly and lovingly. Thenceforward, Elphin increased
in riches more and more, day after day, and in love
and favor with the king; and there abode Taliesin until he
was thirteen years old, when Elphin, son of Gwyddno,
went by a Christmas invitation to his uncle, Maelgan
Gwynedd, who held open court at Christmas-tide in the
castle of Dyganwy, for all the number of his lords of
both degrees, both spiritual and temporal, with a vast
and thronged host of knights and squires. And one arose
and said, "Is there in the whole world a king so great
as Maelgan, or one on whom Heaven has bestowed so
many gifts as upon him—form, and beauty, and meek-
ness, and strength, besides all the powers of the soul?"
And together with these they said that Heaven had
given one gift that exceeded all the others, which
was the beauty, and grace, and wisdom, and modesty
of his queen, whose virtues surpassed those of all the ladies and noble maidens throughout the whole kingdom.
And with this they put questions one to another: Who
had braver men? Who had fairer or swifter horses or greyhounds? Who had more skilful or wiser bards than
Maelgan?

When they had all made an end of their praising the
king and his gifts, it befell that Elphin spoke on this wise.
"Of a truth, none but a king may vie with a king; but
were he not a king, I would say that my wife was as
virtuous as any lady in the kingdom, and also that I have
a bard who is more skilful than all the king's bards."
In a short space some of his fellows told the king all the
boastings of Elphin; and the king ordered him to be
thrown into a strong prison, until he might show the truth
as to the virtues of his wife and the wisdom of his bard.

Now when Elphin had been put in a tower of the
castle, with a thick chain about his feet (it is said that it
was a silver chain, because he was of royal blood), the
king, as the story relates, sent his son Rhun to inquire
into the demeanor of Elphin's wife. Now Rhun was the

most graceless man in the world, and there was neither wife nor maiden with whom he held converse, but was evil spoken of. While Rhun went in haste towards Elphin's dwelling, being fully minded to bring disgrace upon his wife, Taliesin told his mistress how that the king had placed his master in durance in prison, and how that Rhun was coming in haste to strive to bring disgrace upon her. Wherefore he caused his mistress to array one of the maids of her kitchen in her apparel; which the noble lady gladly did, and she loaded her hands with the best rings that she and her husband possessed.

In this guise, Taliesin caused his mistress to put the maiden to sit at the board in her room at supper; and he made her to seem as her mistress and the mistress to seem as the maid. And when they were in due time seated at their supper, in the manner that has been said, Rhun suddenly arrived at Elphin's dwelling, and was received with joy, for the servants knew him; and they brought him to the room of their mistress, in the semblance of whom the maid rose up from supper and welcomed him gladly. And afterwards she sat down to supper again, and Rhun with her. Then Rhun began jesting with the maid, who still kept the semblance of her mistress. And verily this story shows that the maiden became so intoxicated that she fell asleep; and the story relates that it was a powder that Rhun put into the drink, that made her sleep so soundly that she never felt it when he cut off from her hand her little finger, whereon was the signet ring of Elphin, which he had sent to his wife as a token a short time before. And Rhun returned to the king with the finger and the ring as a proof, to show that he had cut it off from her hand without her awaking from her sleep of intemperance.

The king rejoiced greatly at these tidings, and he sent for his councillors, to whom he told the whole story from the beginning. And he caused Elphin to be brought out of prison, and he chided him because of his boast. And he spake on this wise: "Elphin, be it known to thee beyond a doubt that it is but folly for a man to trust in the virtues of his wife further than he can see her; and that thou mayest be certain of thy wife's vileness, behold her finger, with thy signet ring upon it, which was cut from her

hand last night, while she slept the sleep of intoxication."
Then thus spake Elphin: "With thy leave, mighty king, I
I cannot deny my ring, for if it is known of many; but
verily I assert that the finger around which it is was
never attached to the hand of my wife; for in truth and
certainty there are three notable things pertaining to it,
none of which ever belonged to any of my wife's
fingers. The first of the three is that it is certainly known
to me that this ring would never remain upon her thumb,
whereas you can plainly see that it is hard to draw it over
the joint of the little finger of the hand whence this was
cut. The second thing is, that my wife has never let pass
one Saturday since I have known her without paring her
nails before going to bed, and you can see fully that the
nail of this little finger has not been pared for a
month. The third is, truly, that the hand whence this finger came was kneading rye dough within three days before the finger was cut therefrom, and I can assure
your Highness that my wife has never kneaded rye dough
since my wife she has been."

The king was mightily wroth with Elphin for so stoutly
withstanding him, respecting the goodness of his wife;
wherefore he ordered him to prison a second time, saying
that he should not be loosed thence until he had proved
the truth of his boast, as well concerning the wisdom of
his bard as the virtues of his wife.

In the meantime, his wife and Taliesin remained joyful
at Elphin's dwelling. And Taliesin showed his mistress how
that Elphin was in prison because of them; but he bade her
be glad, for that he would go to Maelgan's court to free
his master. So he took leave of his mistress and came to
the court of Maelgan, who was going to sit in his hall and
dine in his royal state, as it was the custom in those
days for kings and princes to do at every chief feast. As
soon as Taliesin entered the hall, he placed himself in a
quiet corner, near the place where the bards and the
minstrels were wont to come, in doing their service and
duty to the king, as is the custom at the high festivals,
when the bounty is proclaimed. So, when the bards
and the heralds came to cry largess and to proclaim the
power of the king and his strength, at the moment when
they passed by the corner wherein he was crouching,

Taliesin pouted out his lips after them and played "Blerwm, blerwm!" with his finger upon his lips. Neither took they much notice of him as they went by, but proceeded forward till they came before the king, unto whom they made their obeisance with their bodies, as they were wont, without speaking a single word, but pouting out their lips and making mouths at the king, playing "Blerwm, blerwm!" upon their lips with their fingers, as they had seen the boy do. This sight caused the king to wonder, and to deem within himself that they were drunk with many liquors. Wherefore he commanded one of his lords, who served at the board, to go to them and desire them to collect their wits, and to consider where they stood, and what it was fitting for them to do. And this lord did so gladly. But they ceased not from their folly any more than before. Whereupon he sent to them a second time, and a third, desiring them to go forth from the hall. At the last the king ordered one of his squires to give a blow to the chief of them, named Heinin Vardd; and the squire took a broom and struck him on the head, so that he fell back in his seat. Then he arose, and went on his knees, and besought leave of the king's grace to show that this their fault was not through want of knowledge, neither through drunkenness, but by the influence of some spirit that was in the hall. And he spoke on this wise: "Oh, honorable king, be it known to your grace that not from the strength of drink, or of too much liquor, are we dumb, but through the influence of a spirit that sits in the corner yonder, in the form of a child." Forthwith the king commanded the squire to fetch him; and he went to the nook where Taliesin sat and brought him before the king, who asked him what he was and whence he came. And he answered the king in verse:

Primary chief bard am I to Elphin,
And my native country is the region of the summer stars;
I have been in Asia with Noah in the ark,
I have seen the destruction of Sodom and Gomorrah,
I was in India when Rome was built,
I have now come here to the remnant of Troia.

When the king and his nobles had heard the song, they

wondered much, for they had never heard the like from a
boy so young as he. And when the king knew that he was
the bard of Elphin, he bade Heinin, his first and wisest
bard, to answer Taliesin and to strive with him. But when
he came, he could do no other than play "Blerwm!" on
his lips; and when he sent for the others of the four
and twenty bards, they all did likewise, and could do no
other. And Maelgan asked the boy Taliesin what was his
errand, and he answered him in song:

> Elphin, the son of Gwyddno,
> Is in the land of Artro,
> Sccured by thirteen locks,
> For praising his instructor.
> Therefore I, Taliesin,
> Chief of the bards of the west,
> Will loosen Elphin
> Out of a golden fetter.

Then he sang to them a riddle:

> Discover thou what is
> The strong creature from before the flood,
> Without flesh, without bone,
> Without vein, without blood,
> Without head, without feet;
> It will neither be older nor younger
> Than at the beginning.
> Behold how the sea whitens
> When first it comes,
> When it comes from the south,
> When it strikes on coasts.
> It is in the field, it is in the wood,
> But the eye cannot perceive it.
> One Being has prepared it,
> By a tremendous blast,
> To wreak vengeance
> On Maelgan Gwynedd.

While he was thus singing his verse, there arose a
mighty storm of wind, so that the king and all his nobles
thought that the castle would fall upon their heads.
And the king caused them to fetch Elphin in haste from
his dungeon, and placed him before Taliesin. And it is said

that immediately he sung a verse, so that the chains opened from about his feet.

After that, Taliesin brought Elphin's wife before them and showed that she had not one finger wanting. And in this manner did he set his master free from prison, and protect the innocence of his mistress, and silence the bards so that not one of them dared to say a word. Right glad was Elphin, right glad was Taliesin.

PART THREE

THE KNIGHTS OF ENGLISH HISTORY[1]

CHAPTER XXXIII

KING RICHARD AND THE THIRD CRUSADE

The Crusades were the mightiest, or rather, the most ambitious undertaking of the chivalry of Europe. From the year 1096, for more than a century the knights of all countries looked to the Holy Land as a field for winning their spurs and obtaining pardon of their sins. And it is most natural that in giving a picture of English chivalry as it is shown in history that we should give a description of King Richard's exploits in Palestine.

In the last decade of the twelfth century, Richard I of England took the cross, which had come to him as a sort of legacy from his father, and sailed for Antioch, which was being besieged by the Christians, to assist in the war in the Holy Land. At the same time Philip Augustus of France and Frederick Barbarossa joined the Crusaders. Frederick was drowned in a river of Cilicia, and his force had so dwindled that when they reached Antioch hardly a tenth of the number were left that had started. Philip of France reached Antioch with his army, and there, as we shall learn later, he fought with the Turk and quarreled with the Christian for a time, until he finally set sail for

France without having accomplished the capture of the Holy City. As for Richard, he was not more successful, and although his deeds were so glorious as to cover him with honor, he was obliged to return home, leaving Jerusalem still in the hands of infidels.

THE EXPLOITS OF KING RICHARD

Now as the ships were proceeding, some being before others, two of the three first, driven by the violence of the winds, were broken on the rocks near the port of Cyprus; the third, which was English, more speedy than they, having turned back into the deep, escaped the peril. Almost all the men of both ships got away alive to land, many of whom the hostile Cypriotes slew, some they took captive, some, taking refuge in a certain church, were besieged. Whatever also in the ships was cast up by the sea fell a prey to the Cypriotes. The prince also of that island coming up, received for his share the gold and the arms; and he caused the shore to be guarded by all the armed force he could summon together, that he might not permit the fleet which followed to approach, lest the king should take again what had been thus stolen from him. Above the port was a strong city, and upon a natural rock, a high and fortified castle. The whole of that nation was warlike and accustomed to live by theft. They placed beams and planks at the entrance of the port, across the passage, the gates, and entrances; and the whole land with one mind prepared themselves for a conflict with the English. God so willed that the cursed people should receive the reward of their evil deeds by the hands of one who would not spare. The third English ship, in which the women, having cast out their anchors, rode out at sea, and watched all things from opposite, to report the misfortunes to the king,[2] lest haply, being ignorant of the loss and disgrace, he should pass the place unavenged. The next line of the king's ships came up after the other, and they are stopped at the first. A full report reached the king, who, sending heralds to the lord of the island, and obtaining no satisfaction, commanded his entire army to arm, from the first even to the last, and to get out of the great ships into the galleys and boats, and follow him to the shore. What he commanded was immediately performed; they came in arms to the port. The king, being armed, leaped first from the galley and gave the first blow in the war; but before he was able to strike a second, he had three thousand of his followers with him striking away at his side. All the timber that had been placed as a barricade in the port was cast down instantly, and the brave fellows went up into the city as ferocious as lionesses are wont to be when robbed of their young. The fight was carried on manfully against them, numbers fell wounded on both sides, and the swords of both parties were made drunk with blood. The Cypriotes are vanquished, the city is taken, with the castle besides; whatever the victors choose is ransacked; and the lord of the island is himself taken and brought to the king. He, being taken, supplicates and obtains pardon; he offers homage to the king, and it is received; and he swears, though unasked, that henceforth he will hold the island of him as his liege lord, and will open all the castles of the land to him, and make satisfaction for the damage already done; and further, bring presents of his own. On being dismissed after the oath, he is commanded to fulfil the conditions in the morning.

That night the king remained peaceably in the castle; and his newly sworn vassal, flying, retired to another castle and caused the whole of the men of the land, who were able to bear arms, to be summoned to repair to him, and so they did. The king of Jerusalem, however, that same night landed in Kyprus, that he might assist the king and salute him, whose arrival he had desired above that of any other in the whole world. On the morrow the lord of Cyprus was sought for and found to have fled. The king, seeing that he was abused, and having been informed where he was, directed the King of Jerusalem to follow the traitor by land with the best of the army, while he conducted the other part by water, intending to be in the way that he might not escape by sea. The divisions reassembled around the city in which he had taken refuge, and he, having sallied out against the king, fought with the English, and the battle was carried on sharply by both sides. The English would that day have been beaten had they not fought under the command of King Richard. They at length obtained a dear-bought victory, the Cypriote flies, and the castle is taken. The kings pursue him as before, the one by land and the other by water, and he is besieged in the third castle. Its walls are cast down by engines hurling huge stones; he, being overcome, promises to surrender, if only he might not be put in iron fetters. The king consents to the prayers of the supplicant, and caused silver shackles to be made for him. The prince of the pirates being thus taken, the king traversed the whole island, and took all its castles, and placed his constables in each, and constituted justiciaries and sheriffs, and the whole land was subjected to him in everything just like England. The gold, and the silks, and the jewels from the treasuries that were broken open, he retained for himself; the silver and victuals he gave to the army. To the King of Jerusalem also he made a handsome present out of the booty.

The king, proceeding thence, came to the siege of Acre, and was welcomed by the besiegers with as great a joy as if it had been Christ that had come again on earth to restore the kingdom of Israel. The King of the French had arrived at Acre first, and was very highly esteemed by the natives; but on Richard's arrival, he became obscured and without consideration, just as the moon is wont to relinquish her lustre at the rising of the sun.

The King of the English, unused to delay, on the third day of his arrival at the siege, caused his wooden fortress, which he had called "Mate Grifun," when it was made in Sicily, to be built and set up, and before the dawn of the fourth day the machine stood erect by the walls of Acre, and from its height looked down upon the city lying beneath it; and there were thereon by sunrise archers casting missiles without intermission on the Turks and Thracians. Engines also for casting stones, placed in convenient positions, battered the walls with frequent volleys. More important than these, the sappers, making themselves a way beneath the ground, undermined the foundation of the walls; while soldiers, bearing shields, having planted ladders, sought an entrance over the ramparts.

The king himself was running up and down through the ranks, directing some, reproving some, and urging others, and thus was he everywhere present with every one of them, so that whatever they all did ought properly to be ascribed to him. The King of the French also did not lightly assail them, making as bold an assault as he could on the tower of the city which is called Cursed.

The renowned Carracois and Mestocus, after Saladin the most powerful princes of the heathen, had at that time the charge of the besieged city, who, after a contest of many days, promised by their interpreters the surrender of the city and a ransom for their heads; but the King of the English desired to subdue their obstinacy by force; and wished that the vanquished should pay their heads for the ransom of their bodies, but by the mediation of the King of the French, their life and indemnity of limbs only was accorded, if, after the surrender of the city and yielding of everything they possessed, the Holy Cross should be given up.

All the heathen warriors in Acre were chosen men and were in number nine thousand; many of whom, swallowing many gold coins, made a purse of their stomachs, because they foresaw that whatever they had of any value would be turned against them, even against themselves, if they should again oppose the cross, and would only fall a prey to the victors. So all of them came out before the kings entirely disarmed, and outside the city, without money, are given into custody; and the kings, with triumphal banners, having entered the city, divided the whole with all its stores into two parts between themselves and their soldiers; the pontiff's seat alone its bishop received by their united gift. The captives being divided, Mestocus fell by lot to the portion of the King of the English, and Carracois, as a drop of cold water, fell into the mouth of the thirsty Philip, King of the French.

Messengers on the part of the captives having been sent to Saladin for their ransom, when the heathen could by no entreaty be moved to restore the Holy Cross, the King of the English beheaded all his, with the exception of Mestocus only, who on account of his nobility was spared, and declared openly, without any ceremony, that he would act in the same way towards Saladin himself.

The King of the English, then, having sent for the commanders of the French, proposed that in the first place they should conjointly attempt Jerusalem itself; but the dissuasion of the French discouraged the hearts of both parties, dispirited the troops, and restrained the king, thus destitute of men, from his intended march on that metropolis. The king, troubled at this, though not despairing, from that day forth separated his army from the French, and directing his arms to the storming of castles along the seashore, he took every fortress that came in his way from Tyre to Ascalon, though after hard fighting and deep wounds.[3]

On the Saturday, the eve of the Nativity of the blessed Virgin Mary, at earliest dawn, our men armed themselves with great care to receive the Turks, who were known to have preceded their march, and whose insolence nothing but a battle could check. The enemy had ranged themselves in order, drawing gradually nearer and nearer; and our men also took the utmost care to place themselves in as good order as possible. King Richard, who was most experienced in military affairs, arranged the army in squadrons and directed who should march in front and who in the rear. He divided the army into twelve companies, and these again into five divisions, marshalled according as the men ranked in military discipline; and none could be found more warlike, if they had only had confidence in God, who is the giver of all good things. On that day the Templars formed the first rank, and after them came, in due order, the Bretons and men of Anjou; then followed King Guy, with the men of Pictou; and in the fourth line were the Normans and English, who had the care of the royal standard, and last of all marched the Hospitallers: this line was composed of chosen warriors, divided into companies. They kept together so closely that an apple, if thrown, would not have fallen to the ground without touching a man or a horse; and the army stretched from the army of Saracens to the seashore. There you might have seen their most appropriate distinctions—standards, and ensigns of various forms, and hardy soldiers, fresh and full of spirits, and well fitted for war. Henry, Count of Champagne, kept guard on the mountainside and maintained a constant lookout on the flank; the foot-soldiers, bowmen, and arbalesters were on the outside, and the rear of the army was closed by the post horses and wagons, which carried provisions and other things, and journeyed along between the army and the sea, to avoid an attack from the enemy.

This was the order of the army, as it advanced gradually, to prevent separation; for the less close the line of battle, the less effective was it for resistance. King Richard and the Duke of Burgundy, with a chosen retinue of warriors, rode up and down, narrowly watching the position and manner of the Turks, to correct anything in their own troops, if they saw occasion, for they had need, at that moment, of the utmost circumspection.

It was now nearly nine o'clock, when there appeared a large body of the Turks, ten thousand strong, coming down upon us at full charge and throwing darts and arrows as far as they could, while they mingled their voices in one horrible yell. There followed after them an infernal race of men, of black color, and bearing a suitable appellation, expressive of their blackness. With them also were the Saracens, who live in the desert, called Bedouins;[4] they are a savage race of men, blacker than soot; they fight on foot, and carry a bow, quiver, and round shield, and are a light and active race. These men dauntlessly attacked our army. Beyond these might be seen the well-arranged phalanxes of the Turks, with ensigns fixed to their lances, and standards and banners of separate distinctions. Their army was divided into troops, and the troops into companies, and their numbers seemed to exceed twenty thousand. They came on with irresistible charge, on horses swifter than eagles, and urged on like lightning to attack our men; and as they advanced, they raised a cloud of dust, so that the air was darkened. In front came certain of their admirals, as it was their duty, with clarions and trumpets; some had horns, others had pipes and timbrels, gongs, cymbals, and other instruments, producing a horrible noise and clamor. The earth vibrated from the loud and discordant sounds, so that the crash of thunder could not be heard amidst the tumultuous noise of horns and trumpets. They did this to excite their spirit and courage, for the more violent their clamor became, the more bold were they for the fray. Thus the impious Turks threatened us, both on the side towards the sea and from the side of the land; and for the space of two miles not so much earth as could be taken up in one hand could be seen, on account of the hostile Turks who covered it. Oh, how obstinately they pressed on and continued their stubborn attacks, so that our men suffered severe loss of their horses, which were killed by their darts and arrows. Oh, how useful to us on that day were our arbalesters and bowmen, who closed the extremities of the lines, and did their best to repel the obstinate Turks.

The enemy came rushing down, like a torrent, to the attack; and many of our arbalesters, unable to restrain the weight of their terrible and calamitous charge, threw away their arms, and, fearing lest they should be shut out, took refuge, in crowds, behind the dense lines of the army; yielding through fear of death to sufferings which they could not support. Those whom shame forbade to yield, or the hope of an immortal crown sustained, were animated with greater boldness and courage to persevere in the contest, and fought with indefatigable valor face to face against the Turks, whilst they at the same time receded step by step, and so reached their retreat. The whole of that day, on account of the Turks pressing them closely from behind, they faced around and went on skirmishing, rather than proceeding on their march.

Oh, how great was the strait they were in on that day! How great was their tribulation! when some were affected with fears, and no one had such confidence or spirit as not to wish, at that moment, he had finished his pilgrimage and had returned home, instead of standing with trembling heart the chances of a doubtful battle. In truth our people, so few in number, were so hemmed in by the multitudes of the Saracens that they had no means of escape, if they tried; neither did they seem to have valor sufficient to withstand so many foes—nay, they were shut in like a flock of sheep in the jaws of

wolves, with nothing but the sky above and the enemy
all around them. O Lord God! what feelings agitated that
weak flock of Christ! straitened by such a perplexity,
whom the enemy pressed with such unabating vigor, as if
they would pass them through a sieve. What army was
ever assailed by so mighty a force? There you might
have seen our troopers, having lost their chargers,
marching on foot with the footmen, or casting missiles
from the arbalests, or arrows from bows, against the
enemy, and repelling their attacks in the best manner
they were able. The Turks, skilled in the bow, pressed
unceasingly upon them; it rained darts; the air was
filled with the shower of arrows, and the brightness of
the sun was obscured by the multitude of missiles, as if
it had been darkened by a fall of winter's hail or snow.
Our horses were pierced by the darts and arrows, which
were so numerous that the whole face of the earth
around was covered with them, and if any one wished
to gather them up, he might take twenty of them in his
hand at a time.

The Turks pressed with such boldness that they nearly
crushed the Hospitallers;[5] on which the latter sent word
to King Richard that they could not withstand the violence of the enemy's attack, unless he would allow their
knights to advance at full charge against them. This the
king dissuaded them from doing, but advised them to
keep in a close body; they therefore persevered and kept
together, though scarcely able to breathe for the pressure. By these means they were able to proceed on their
way, though the heat happened to be very great on that
day; so that they labored under two disadvantages—the
hot weather and the attacks of the enemy. These approved martyrs of Christ sweated in the contest; and
he who could have seen them closed up in a narrow
space, so patient under the heat and toil of the day and
the attacks of the enemy, who exhorted each other to
destroy the Christians, could not doubt in his mind that
it augured ill to our success from their straitened and
perilous position, hemmed in as they were by so large
a multitude; for the enemy thundered at their backs as if
with mallets, so that, having no room to use their bows,
they fought hand to hand with swords, lances, and

clubs; and the blows of the Turks, echoing from their metal armor, resounded as if they had been struck upon an anvil. They were now tormented with the heat, and no rest was allowed them. The battle fell heavy on the extreme line of the Hospitallers, the more so as they were unable to resist, but moved forward with patience under their wounds, returning not even a word for the blows which fell upon them, and advancing on their way because they were not able to bear the weight of the contest.

Then they pressed on for safety upon the centre of the army which was in front of them, to avoid the fury of the enemy who harassed them in the rear. Was it wonderful that no one could withstand so continuous an attack, when he could not even return a blow to the numbers who pressed on him? The strength of all paganism had gathered together from Damascus and Persia, from the Mediterranean to the East; there was not left in the uttermost recesses of the earth one man of fame or power, one nation's valor, or one bold soldier, whom the sultan had not summoned to his aid, either by entreaty, by money, or by authority, to crush the Christian race; for he presumed to hope he could blot them from the face of the earth; but his hopes were vain, for their numbers were sufficient, through the assistance of God, to effect their purpose. The flower of the chosen youth and soldiers of Christendom had indeed assembled together, and were united in one body, like ears of corn on their stalks, from every region of the earth; and if they had been utterly destroyed, there is no doubt that there were some left to make resistance.

A cloud of dust obscured the air as our men marched on; and, in addition to the heat, they had an enemy pressing them in the rear, insolent and rendered obstinate by the instigation of the devil. Still the Christians proved good men, and secure in their unconquerable spirit, kept constantly advancing, while the Turks threatened them without ceasing in the rear; but their blows fell harmless upon the defensive armor, and this caused the Turks to slacken in courage at the failure of their attempts, and they began to murmur in whispers of disappointment, crying out in their rage, "that our peo-

306 THE AGE OF CHIVALRY

ple were made of iron and would yield to no blow."
Then the Turks, about twenty thousand strong, rushed
again upon our men pell-mell, annoying them in every
possible manner; when, as if overcome by their savage
fury, brother Garnier de Napes, one of the Hospitallers,
suddenly exclaimed with a loud voice, "O excellent St.
George! will you leave us to be thus put to confusion?
The whole of Christendom is now on the point of perish-
ing, because it fears to return a blow against this impious race."

Upon this the master of the Hospitallers went to the
king and said to him, "My lord the king, we are violently pressed by the enemy, and are in danger of eternal
infamy, as if we did not dare to return their blows; we
are each of us losing our horses one after another, and
why should we bear with them any further?" To whom
the king replied, "Good master, it is you who must sustain their attack; no one can be everywhere at once."
On the master returning, the Turks again made a fierce
attack on them from the rear, and there was not a
prince or count amongst them but blushed with shame,
and they said to each other, "Why do we not charge
them at full gallop? Alas! alas! we shall forever deserve
to be called cowards, a thing which never happened to
us before, for never has such a disgrace befallen so great
an army, even from unbelievers. Unless we defend our-
selves by immediately charging the enemy, we shall gain
everlasting scandal, and so much the greater the longer
we delay to fight." Oh, how blind is human fate! On
what slippery points it stands! Alas, on how uncertain
wheels doth it advance, and with what ambiguous success doth it unfold the course of human things! A countless multitude of the Turks would have perished if the
aforesaid attempt had been orderly conducted; but to
punish us for our sins, as it is believed, the potter's
ware produces a paltry vessel instead of the grand design which he had conceived. For when they were
treating on this point, and had come to the same decision
about charging the enemy, two knights, who were impatient of delay, put everything in confusion. It had been
resolved by common consent that the sounding of six
trumpets in three different parts of the army should be a

signal for a charge, viz., two in front, two in the rear, and two in the middle, to distinguish the sounds from those of the Saracens and to mark the distance of each. If these orders had been attended to, the Turks would have been utterly discomfited; but from the too great haste of the aforesaid knights, the success of the affair was marred.

They rushed at full gallop upon the Turks, and each of them prostrated his man by piercing him through with his lance. One of them was the marshal of the Hospitallers, the other was Baldwin de Carreo, a good and brave man, and the companion of King Richard, who had brought him in his retinue.[6] When the other Christians observed these two rushing forward, and heard them calling with a clear voice on St. George for aid, they charged the Turks in a body with all their strength; then the Hospitallers, who had been distressed all day by their close array, following the two soldiers, charged the enemy in troops, so that the van of the army became the rear from their position in the attack, and the Hospitallers, who had been the last, were the first to charge.

The Count of Champagne also burst forward with his chosen company, and James d'Avennes with his kinsmen, and also Robert Count of Dreux, the Bishop of Beauvais and his brother, as well as the Earl of Leicester, who made a fierce charge on the left towards the sea. Why need we name each? Those who were in the first line of the rear made a united and furious charge; after them the men of Poictou, the Bretons, and the men of Anjou, rushed swiftly onward, and then came the rest of the army in a body: each troop showed its valor, and boldly closed with the Turks, transfixing them with their lances, and casting them to the ground. The sky grew black with the dust that was raised in the confusion of that encounter. The Turks, who had purposely dismounted from their horses in order to take better aim at our men with their darts and arrows, were slain on all sides in that charge, for on being prostrated by the horse-soldiers, they were beheaded by the foot-men. King Richard, on seeing his army in motion and in encounter with the Turks, flew rapidly on his horse at full speed through the Hospitallers, who had led the charge, and to whom

he was bringing assistance with all his retinue, and broke
into the Turkish infantry, who were astonished at his
blows and those of his men, and gave way to the right
and to the left.

Then might be seen numbers prostrated on the ground,
horses without their riders in crowds, the wounded lamenting with groans their hard fate, and others drawing
their last breath, weltering in their gore, and many lay
headless, whilst their lifeless forms were trodden under
foot both by friend and foe. Oh, how different are the
speculations of those who meditate amidst the columns
of the cloister from the fearful exercise of war! There
the king, the fierce, the extraordinary king, cut down
the Turks in every direction, and none could escape the
force of his arm, for wherever he turned, brandishing
his sword, he carved a wide path for himself; and as he
advanced and gave repeated strokes with his sword, cutting them down like a reaper with his sickle, the rest,
warned by the sight of the dying, gave him more ample
space, for the corpses of the dead Turks which lay on
the face of the earth extended over half a mile. In fine,
the Turks were cut down, the saddles emptied of their
riders, and the dust which was raised by the conflict of
the combatants proved very hurtful to our men, for on
becoming fatigued from slaying so many, when they were
retiring to take fresh air, they could not recognize each
other on account of the thick dust, and struck their
blows indiscriminately to the right and to the left; so
that, unable to distinguish friend from foe, they took
their own men for enemies and cut them down without
mercy. Then the Christians pressed hard on the Turks,
the latter gave way before them: but for a long time
the battle was doubtful; they still exchanged blows, and
either party strove for the victory; on both sides were
seen some retreating, covered with wounds, while others
fell slain to the ground.

Oh, how many banners and standards of different
forms, and pennons and many-colored ensigns, might
there be seen torn and fallen on the earth; swords of
proved steel, and lances made of cane with iron heads,
Turkish bows, and maces bristling with sharp teeth, darts
and arrows covering the ground, and missiles enough to

load twenty wagons or more! There lay the headless
trunks of the Turks who had perished, whilst others retained their courage for a time until our men increased
in strength, when some of them concealed themselves in
the copses, some climbed up trees, and, being shot with
arrows, fell with a fearful groan to the earth; others,
abandoning their horses, betook themselves by slippery
footpaths to the seaside and tumbled headlong into the
waves from the precipitous cliffs that were five poles in
height. The rest of the enemy were repulsed in so wonderful a manner that for the space of two miles nothing
could be seen but fugitives, although they had before
been so obstinate and fierce and puffed up with pride;
but by God's grace their pride was humbled, and they
continued still to fly, for when our men ceased the pursuit, fear alone added wings to their feet. Our army
had been ranged in divisions when they attacked the
Turks; the Normans and English also, who had the care
of the standard, came up slowly towards the troops
which were fighting with the Turks—for it was very
difficult to disperse the enemy's strength, and they
stopped at a short distance therefrom, that all might
have a rallying point. On the conclusion of the slaughter
our men paused; but the fugitives, to the number of
twenty thousand, when they saw this, immediately recovering their courage and armed with maces, charged
the hindmost of those who were retiring and rescued
some from our men who had just struck them down.

Oh, how dreadfully were our men then pressed! For
the darts and arrows, thrown at them as they were falling back, broke the heads, arms, and other limbs of our
horsemen, so that they bent, stunned, to their saddle-
bows; but having quickly regained their spirits and resumed their strength, and thirsting for vengeance with
greater eagerness, like a lioness when her whelps are
stolen, they charged the enemy and broke through them
like a net. Then you might have seen the horses with
their saddles displaced, and the Turks, who had but just
now fled, returning, and pressing upon our people with
the utmost fury; every cast of their darts would have
told, had our men kept marching and not stood still in a
compact, immovable body. The commander of the Turks

was an admiral named Tekedmus, a kinsman of the sultan, having a banner with a remarkable device; namely, that of a pair of breeches carved thereon, a symbol well known to his men. He was a most cruel persecutor and a persevering enemy of the Christians; and he had under his command seven hundred chosen Turks of great valor, of the household troops of Saladin, each of whose companies bore a yellow banner with pennons of a different color. These men, coming at full charge, with clamor and haughty bearing, attacked our men, who were turning off from them towards the standard, cutting at them, and piercing them severely, so that even the firmness of our chiefs wavered under the weight of the pressure; yet our men remained immovable, compelled to repel force by force. And the conflict grew thicker, the blows were redoubled, and the battle waxed fiercer than before: the one side labored to crush, the other to repel; both exerted their strength, and although our men were by far the fewest in numbers, they made havoc of great multitudes of the enemy; and that portion of the army which thus toiled in the battle could not return to the standard with ease, on account of the immense mass which pressed upon them so severely; for thus hemmed in, they began to flag in courage, and but few dared to renew the attack of the enemy. In truth, the Turks were furious in the assault, and greatly distressed our men, whose blood poured forth in a stream beneath their blows. On perceiving them reel and give way, William de Barris, a renowned knight, breaking through the ranks, charged the Turks with his men; and such was the vigor of the onset that some fell by the edge of his sword, while others only saved themselves by rapid flight. For all that, the king, mounted on a bay Cyprian steed, which had not its match, bounded forward in the direction of the mountains, and scattered those he met on all sides; for the enemy fled from his sword and gave way, while helmets tottered beneath it, and sparks flew forth from its strokes. So great was the fury of his onset, and so many and deadly his blows that day, in his conflict with the Turks, that in a short space of time the enemy were all scattered, and allowed our army to proceed; and thus our men, having suffered somewhat, at last returned to the standard and proceeded on their march as far as Arsur, and there they pitched their tents outside its walls.

While they were thus engaged, a large body of the Turks made an attack on the extreme rear of our army. On hearing the noise of the assailants, King Richard, encouraging his men to battle, rushed at full speed, with only fifteen companions, against the Turks, crying out, with a loud voice, "Aid us, O God! and the Holy Sepulchre!" and this he exclaimed a second and a third time; and when our men heard it, they made haste to follow him, and attacked, routed, and put them to flight, pursuing them as far as Arsur, whence they had first come out, cutting them down and subduing them. Many of the Turks fell there also. The king returned thence from the slaughter of the fugitives to his camp; and the men, overcome with the fatigue and exertions of the day, rested quietly that night.

Whoever was greedy of gain and wished to plunder the booty, returned to the place of battle and loaded himself to his heart's desire; and those who returned from thence reported that they had counted thirty-two Turkish chiefs who were found slain on that day, and whom they supposed to be men of great influence and power from the splendor of their armor and the costliness of their apparel. The Turks also made search for them to carry them away as being of the most importance; and besides these the Turks carried off seven thousand mangled bodies of those who were next in rank, besides of the wounded, who went off in straggling parties and, when their strength failed, lay about the fields and died. But, by the protection of God, we did not lose a tenth, nor a hundredth part so many as fell in the Turkish army. Oh, the disasters of that day! Oh, the trials of the warriors! for the tribulations of the just are many. Oh, mournful calamity and bitter distress. How great must have been the blackness of our sins to require so fiery an ordeal to purify it, for if we had striven to overcome the urgent necessity by pious long-suffering, and without a murmur, the sense of our obligations would have been deeper.

And again the Christians were put in great peril, in

the following manner. At the siege of Joppa, a certain depraved set of men among the Saracens, called Mene-lones of Aleppo and Cordivi, an active race, met to-gether to consult what should be done in the existing state of things. They spoke of the scandal which lay against them, that so small an army, without horses, had driven them out of Joppa, and they reproached themselves with cowardice and shameful baseness, and arrogantly made a compact among themselves that they would seize King Richard in his tent, and bring him before Saladin, from whom they would receive a most munificent reward.

So they prepared themselves in the middle of the night to surprise the king, and sallied forth armed, by the light of the moon, conversing with one another about the object they had in hand. O hateful race of un-believers! They are anxiously bent upon seizing Christ's steadfast soldier while he is asleep. They rush on in numbers to seize him, unarmed and apprehensive of no danger. They were not far from his tent, and were pre-paring to lay hands on him, when, lo! the God of mercy, who never neglects those who trust in Him, and acts in a wonderful manner even to those who know Him not, sent the spirit of discord among the aforesaid Cordivi and Menelones. The Cordivi said, "You shall go in on foot to take the king and his followers, whilst we will remain on horseback to prevent their escaping into the castle." But the Menelones replied, "Nay, it is your place to go in on foot, because our rank is higher than yours; but this serv-ice on foot belongs to your rather than us." Whilst thus the two parties were contending which of them were the greatest, their combined dispute caused much delay; and when at last they came to a decision how their nefarious attempt should be achieved, the dawn of the day appeared, viz., the Wednesday next following the feast of St. Peter *ad vincula.* But now by the providence of God, who had decreed that his holy champion should not be seized whilst asleep by the infidels, a certain Genoese was led by the divine impulse to go out early in the morning into the fields, where he was alarmed by the noise of men and horses advancing, and returned speedily, but just had time to see helmets reflecting back the light which now fell upon them. He immediately rushed with speed into the camp, calling out, "To arms! to arms!" The king was awakened by the noise, and leaping startled from his bed, put on his impenetrable coat of mail and summoned his men to the rescue.

God of all mercies! Lives there a man who would not be shaken by such a sudden alarm? The enemy rushed unawares, armed against unarmed, many against few, for our men had no time to arm or even to dress themselves. The king himself, therefore, and many others with him, on the urgency of the moment, proceeded without their cuishes to the fight, some even without their breeches, and they armed themselves in the best manner they could, though they were going to fight the whole day. Whilst our men were thus arming in haste, the Turks drew near, and the king mounted his horse, with only ten other knights with him. These alone had horses, and some even of them had base and impotent horses, unused to arms; the common men were drawn skilfully out in ranks and troops, with each a captain to command them. The knights were posted nearer to the sea, having the church of St. Nicholas on the left, because the Turks had directed their principal attack on that quarter, and the Pisans and Genoese were posted beyond the suburban gardens, having other troops mingled with them. Oh, who could fully relate the terrible attacks of the infidels? The Turks at first rushed on with horrid yells, hurling their javelins and shooting their arrows. Our men prepared themselves as they best could to receive their furious attack, each fixing his right knee in the ground, that so they might the better hold together and maintain their position; whilst there the thighs of their left legs were bent, and their left hands held their shields or bucklers; stretched out before them in their right hands they held their lances, of which the lower ends were fixed in the ground, and their iron heads pointed threateningly towards the enemy.

Between every two of the men who were thus covered with their shields, the king, versed in arms, placed an arbalester, and another behind him to stretch the arbalest as quickly as possible, so that the man in front might discharge his shot whilst the other was loading. This was found to be of much benefit to our men, and did much harm to the enemy. Thus everything was prepared as well as the shortness of the time allowed, and our little army was drawn up in order. The king ran along the ranks and exhorted every man to be grave and not to flinch. "Courage, my brave men," said he; "and let not the attack of the enemy disturb you. Bear up against the powers of fortune, and you will rise above them. Everything may be borne by brave men; adversity sheds a light upon the virtues of mankind, as certainly as prosperity casts over them a shade; there is no room for flight, for the enemy surround us, and to attempt to flee is to provoke certain death. Be brave, therefore, and let the urgency of the case sharpen up your valor; brave men should either conquer nobly or gloriously die. Martyrdom is a boon which we should receive with willing mind; but before we die, let us, whilst still alive, do what we may to avenge our deaths, giving thanks to God that it has been our lot to die martyrs. This will be the end of our labors, the termination of our life and of our battles." These words were hardly spoken when the hostile army rushed with ferocity upon them, in seven troops, each of which contained about a thousand horse. Our men received their attack with their right feet planted firm against the sand, and remained immovable. Their lances formed a wall against the enemy, who would have assuredly broken through, if our men had in the least given way.

The first line of the Turks, perceiving, as they advanced, that our men stood immovable, recoiled a little, when our men plied them with a shower of missiles, slaying large numbers of men and horses. Another line of Turks at once came on in like manner, and were again encountered and driven back. In this way the Turks came on like a whirlwind, again and again, making the appearance of an attack, that our men might be induced to give way, and when they were close up they turned their horses off in another direction. The king and his knights, who were on horseback, perceiving this, put spurs to their horses, and charged into the middle of the enemy, upsetting them right and left and piercing a large number through the body with their lances; at last they pulled up their horses, because they found that they had penetrated entirely through the Turkish lines. The king, now looking about him, saw the noble Earl of Leicester fallen from his horse, and fighting bravely on foot. No sooner did he see this than he rushed to his rescue, snatched him out of the hands of the enemy, and replaced him on his horse. What a terrible combat was then waged! A multitude of Turks advanced and used every exertion to destroy our small army; vexed at our success, they rushed toward the royal standard of the lion, for they would rather have slain the king than a thousand others. In the midst of the mêlée, the king saw Ralph de Mauleon dragged off prisoner by the Turks, and spurring his horse to speed, in a moment released him from their hands and restored him to the army; for the king was a very giant in the battle, and was everywhere in the field—now here, now there, wherever the attacks of the Turks raged the hottest. So bravely did he fight that there was no one, however gallant, that would not readily and deservedly yield to him the preeminence. On that day he performed the most gallant deeds on the furious army of the Turks and slew numbers with his sword, which shone like lightning; some of them were cloven in two, from their helmet to their teeth, whilst others lost their heads, arms, and other members, which were lopped off at a single blow. While the king was thus laboring with incredible exertions in the fight, a Turk advanced towards him, mounted on a foaming steed. He had been sent by Saphadin of Archadia, brother to Saladin, a liberal and munificent man, if he had not rejected the Christian faith. This man now sent to the king, as a token of his well-known honorable character, two noble horses, requesting him earnestly to accept them and make use of them, and if he returned safe and sound out of that battle, to remember the gift and recompense it in any manner he pleased. The king readily received the present and afterwards nobly recompensed the giver. Such is bravery, cognizable even in an enemy; since a Turk, who was our bitter foe, thus honored the king for his distinguished valor. The king, especially at such a moment of need, protested that he would have taken any number of horses equally good from any one even more a foe than Saphadin, so necessary were they to him at that moment. Fierce now raged the fight, when such numbers attacked so few; the whole earth was covered with the javelins and arrows of the unbelievers; they threw them, several at a time, at our men, of whom many were wounded. Thus the weight of battle fell heavier upon us than before, and the galley-men withdrew in the galleys which brought them; and so, in their anxiety to be safe, they sacrificed their character for bravery. Meanwhile a shout was raised by the Turks, as they strove who should first occupy the town, hoping to slay those of our men whom they should find within. The king, hearing the clamor, taking with him only two knights and two crossbowmen, met three Turks, nobly caparisoned, in one of the principal streets. Rushing bravely upon them, he slew the riders in his own royal fashion and made booty of two horses. The rest of the Turks who were found in the town were put to the rout in spite of their resistance, and dispersing in different directions, sought to make their escape, even where there was no regular road. The king also commanded the parts of the walls which were broken down to be made good, and placed sentinels to keep watch lest the town should be again attacked.

These matters settled, the king went down to the shore, where many of our men had taken refuge on board the galleys. These the king exhorted by the most cogent arguments to return to the battle and share with the rest whatever might befall them. Leaving five men as guards on board each galley, the king led back the rest to assist his hard-pressed army; and he no sooner arrived than with all his fury he fell upon the thickest ranks of the enemy, driving them back and routing them, so that even those who were at a distance and untouched by him were overwhelmed by the throng of the troops as they retreated. Never was there such an attack made by an individual. He pierced into the middle of the hostile army and performed the deeds of a brave and distinguished warrior. The Turks at once closed upon him and tried to overwhelm him. In the meantime, our men, losing sight of the king, were fearful lest he should have been slain, and when one of them proposed that they should advance to find him, our lines could hardly contain themselves. But if by any chance the disposition of our troops had been broken, without doubt they would all have been destroyed. What, however, was to be thought of the king, who was hemmed in by the enemy, a single man opposed to so many thousands? The hand of the writer faints to see it, and the mind of the reader to hear it. Who ever heard of such a man? His bravery was ever of the highest order; no adverse storm could sink it; his valor was ever becoming, and if we may from a few instances judge of many, it was ever indefatigable in war. Why then do we speak of the valor of Antæus, who regained his strength every time he touched his mother earth, for Antæus perished when he was lifted up from earth in the long wrestling match.[7] The body of Achilles also, who slew Hector, was invulnerable, because he was dipped in the Stygian waves; yet Achilles was mortally wounded in the very part by which he was held when they dipped him. Likewise Alexander, the Macedonian, who was stimulated by ambition to subjugate the whole world, undertook a most difficult enterprise and, with a handful of choice soldiers, fought many celebrated battles, but the chief part of his valor consisted of the excellence of his soldiers. In the same manner the brave Judas Maccabeus, of whom all the world discoursed, performed many wonderful deeds worthy forever to be remembered, but when he was abandoned by his soldiers in the midst of a battle, with thousands of enemies to oppose him, he was slain, together with his brothers. But King Richard, inured to battle from his tenderest years, and to whom even famous Roland could not be considered equal, remained invincible, even in the midst of the enemy; and his body, as if it were made of brass, was impenetrable to any kind of weapon. In his right hand he brandished his sword, which in its rapid descent broke the ranks on either side of him. Such was his energy amid that host of Turks that, fearing nothing, he destroyed all around him, mowing men down with his scythe as reapers mow down the corn with their sickles. Who could describe his deeds? Whoever felt one of his blows had no need of a second. Such was the energy of his courage that it seemed to rejoice at having found an occasion to display itself. The sword wielded by his powerful hand cut down men and horses alike, cleaving them to the middle. The more he was himself separated from his men, and the more the enemy sought to overwhelm him, the more did his valor shine conspicuous. Among other brave deeds which he performed on that occasion he slew by one marvellous stroke an admiral, who was conspicuous above the rest of the enemy by his rich caparisons. This man by his gestures seemed to say that he was going to do something wonderful, and whilst he reproached the rest with cowardice, he put spurs to his horse and charged full against the king, who, waving his sword as he saw him coming, smote off at a single blow not only his head, but his shoulder and right arm. The Turks were terror-struck at the sight, and, giving way on all sides, scarcely dared to shoot at him from a distance with their arrows.

The king now returned, safe and unhurt, to his friends and encouraged them more than ever with the hope of victory. How were their minds raised from despair when they saw him coming safe out of the enemy's ranks! They knew not what had happened to him, but they knew that without him all the hopes of the Christian army would be in vain. The king's person was stuck all over with javelins, like a deer pierced by the hunters, and the trappings of his horse were thickly covered with arrows. Thus, like a brave soldier, he returned from the contest, and a bitter contest it was, for it had lasted from the morning sun to the setting sun. It may seem wonderful and even incredible that so small a body of men endured so long a conflict; but by God's mercy we cannot doubt the truth of it, for in that battle only one or two of our men were slain. But the number of the Turkish horses that lay dead on the field is said to have exceeded fifteen hundred; and of the Turks themselves, more than seven hundred were killed, and yet they did not carry back King Richard, as they had boasted, as a present to Saladin; but, on the contrary, he and his horse performed so many deeds of valor in the sight of the Turks that the enemy shuddered to behold him.

In the meantime, our men having by God's grace escaped destruction, the Turkish army returned to Saladin, who is said to have ridiculed them by asking where

Melech Richard was, for they had promised to bring him a prisoner? "Which of you," continued he, "first seized him, and where is he? Why is he not produced?" To whom one of the Turks that came from the furthest countries of the earth replied, "In truth, my lord, Melech Richard, about whom you ask, is not here; we have never heard since the beginning of the world that there ever was such a knight, so brave and so experienced in arms. In every deed of arms he is ever the foremost; in deeds he is without a rival, the first to advance and the last to retreat; we did our best to seize him, but in vain, for no man can escape from his sword; his attack is dreadful; to engage with him is fatal, and his deeds are beyond human nature."

CHAPTER XXXIV

ROBIN HOOD OF SHERWOOD FOREST

In this our spacious isle I think there is not one,
But he of ROBIN HOOD hath heard and Little John;
And to the end of time the tales shall ne'er be done
Of Scarlock, George a Green, and Much the miller's son,
Of Tuck, the merry friar, which many a sermon made
In praise of ROBIN HOOD, his outlaws and their trade.
                                                    DRAYTON[8]

Every reader of Ivanhoe, at the mention of Richard the Crusader, will be reminded of Robin Hood, the noble outlaw of Sherwood Forest, and his band of merry bowmen. With these we next concern ourselves, and if the reader will pardon the dry outlines of the historian before proceeding to the more interesting and imaginative story of the ballad-singer, we will at first state what so careful an antiquary as Mr. Ritson considers to be truly trustworthy in Robin Hood's history.

Robin Hood was born at Locksley, in the county of Nottingham, in the reign of King Henry II, and about the year of Christ 1160. His extraction was noble, and his true name Robert Fitzooth, which vulgar pronunciation easily corrupted into Robin Hood. He is frequently styled, and commonly reputed to have been, Earl of Huntingdon, a title to which, in the latter part of his life at least, he actually appears to have had some sort of pretension. In his youth he is reported to have been of a wild and extravagant disposition, insomuch that, his inheritance being consumed or forfeited by his excesses, and his person outlawed for debt, either from necessity or choice he sought an asylum in the woods and forests, with which immense tracts, especially in the northern part of the kingdom, were at that time covered. Of these he chiefly affected Barnsdale, in Yorkshire; Sherwood in Nottinghamshire; and, according to some, Plompton Park in Cumberland. Here he either found, or was afterwards joined by, a number of persons in similar circumstances, who appear to have considered and obeyed him as their chief or leader. . . . Having for a long series of years maintained a sort of independent sovereignty, and set kings, judges, and magistrates at defiance, a proclamation was published, offering a considerable reward for bringing him in either dead or alive; which, however, seems to have been productive of no greater success than former attempts for that purpose. At length, the infirmities of old age increasing upon him, and desirous to be relieved, in a fit of sickness, by being let blood, he applied for that purpose to the prioress of Kirkley nunnery in Yorkshire, his relative (women, and particularly religious women, being in those times somewhat better skilled in surgery than the sex is at present), by whom he was treacherously suffered to bleed to death. This event happened on the 18th November, 1247, being the thirty-first year of King Henry III; and if the date assigned to his birth be correct, about the eighty-seventh year of his age. He was interred under some trees at a short distance from the house, a stone being placed over his grave, with an inscription to his memory.

There are some who will have it that Robin Hood was not alive in the reign of Richard I, and who will have it that he preferred other forests to Sherwood. But the stories that we have chosen are of the Robin Hood of Sherwood Forest and of King Richard the Lion-hearted.

LITTLE JOHN

The lieutenant of Robin Hood's band was named Little John, not so much from his smallness in stature (for he was seven feet high and more), as for a reason which I shall tell later. And the manner in which Robin Hood, to whom he was very dear, met him was this.

Robin Hood, on one occasion, being hunting with his men and finding the sport to be poor, said: "We have had no sport now for some time. So I go abroad alone. And if I should fall into any peril whence I cannot escape, I will blow my horn that ye may know of it and bear me aid." And with that he bade them adieu and departed alone, having with him his bow and the arrows in his quiver. And passing shortly over a brook by a long bridge, he met at the middle a stranger. And neither of the two would give way to the other. And Robin Hood, being angry, fitted an arrow to his bow and made ready to fire. "Truly," said the stranger at this, "thou art a fine fellow that you must draw your long bow on me who have but a staff by me." "That is just truly," said Robin; "and so I will lay by my bow and get me a staff to try if your deeds be as good as your words." And with that he went into a thicket, and chose him a small ground oak for a staff, and returned to the stranger.

"Now," said he, "I am a match for you, so let us play upon this bridge, and if one should fall in the stream, the other will have the victory." "With all my heart," said the stranger; "I shall not be the first to give out." And with that they began to make great play with their staves. And Robin Hood first struck the stranger such a blow as warmed all his blood, and from that they rattled their sticks as though they had been threshing corn. And finally the stranger gave Robin such a crack on his crown that he broke his head and the blood flowed. But this only urged him the more, so that he attacked the stranger with such vigor that he had like to have made an end of him. But he growing into a fury finally fetched him such a blow that he tumbled him from the bridge into the brook. Whereat the stranger laughed loudly and long and cried out to him, "Where art thou now, I prythee, my good fellow?" And Robin replied, "Thou art truly a brave soul, and I will have no more to do with thee to-day; so our battle is at an end, and I must allow that thou hast won the day." And then wading to the bank he pulled out his horn and blew a blast on it so that the echoes flew throughout the valley. And at that came fifty bold bowmen out of the wood, all clad in green, and they made for Robin Hood, and said William Stukely, "What is the matter, my master? You are wet to the skin." "Truly, nothing is the matter," said Robin, "but that the lad on the bridge has tumbled me into the stream." And on that the archers would have seized the stranger to duck him as well, but Robin Hood forbade them. "No one shall harm thee, friend," said he. "These are all my bowmen, threescore and nine, and if you will be one of us you shall straightway have my livery and accoutrements, fit for a man. What say you?" "With all my heart," said the stranger; "here is my hand on it. My name is John Little, and I will be a good man and true to you." "His name shall be changed," said William Stukely on this. "We will call him Little John, and I will be his godfather."

So they fetched a pair of fat does and some humming strong ale, and there they christened their babe Little John, for he was seven feet high and an ell round at his waist.

FRIAR TUCK

Now Robin Hood had instituted a day of mirth for himself and all his companions, and wagers were laid amongst them who should exceed at this exercise and who at that; some did contend who should jump farthest, some who should throw the bar, some who should be swiftest afoot in a race five miles in length; others there were with which Little John was most delighted, who did strive which of them should draw the strongest bow and be the best marksman. "Let me see," said Little John, "which of you can kill a buck, and who can kill a doe, and who is he can kill a hart, being distant from it by the space of five hundred feet." With that, Robin Hood going before them, they went directly to the forest, where they found good store of game feeding before them. William Scarlock, that drew the strongest bow of them all, did kill a buck, and Little John made choice of a barren fat doe, and the well-directed arrow did enter in the very heart of it; and Midge, the miller's son, did kill a hart above five hundred feet distant from him. The hart falling, Robin Hood stroked him gently on the shoulder and said unto him, "God's blessing on thy heart, I will ride five hundred miles to find a match for thee." William Scarlock, hearing him speak these words, smiled and said unto him, "Master, what needs that? Here is a Curtal Friar* not far off, that for a hundred pound will shoot at what distance yourself will propound, either with Midge or with yourself. An experienced man he is, and will draw a bow with great strength; he will shoot with yourself, and with all the men you have, one after another."

"Sayest thou so, Scarlock?" replied Robin Hood. "By the grace of God I will neither eat nor drink till I see this Friar thou dost speak of." And having prepared himself for his journey, he took Little John and fifty of his best archers with him, whom he bestowed in a convenient place, as he himself thought fitting. This being done, he ran down into the dale, where he found the Curtal Friar walking by the waterside. He no sooner espied him, but presently he took unto him his broadsword and buckler, and put on his head a steel bonnet. The friar, not knowing who he was, or for what intent he came, did presently arm himself to encounter with him. Robin Hood, coming near unto him, alighted from his horse, which he tied to a thorn that grew hard by, and looking wistfully on the friar, said unto him, "Carry me over the water, thou Curtal Friar, or else thy life lies at the stake." The friar made no more ado, but took up Robin Hood and carried

---

* "The Curtal Friar," Dr. Stukely says, "is Cordelier, from the cord or rope which they wore round their waist, to whip themselves with. They were," adds he, "of the Franciscan order. Our friar, however, is undoubtedly so called from his Curtal dogs, or curs, as we now say." *Thoms. Early Prose Romances:* in which, by the way, may be found many of the tales of Robin Hood printed here, and much more beside of interest. [Hale's note, 1884 ed.]

him on his back; deep water he did stride; he spake not so much as one word to him, but having carried him over, he gently laid him down on the side of the bank; which being done, the friar said to Robin Hood, "It is now thy turn; therefore carry me over the water, thou bold fellow, or sure I shall make thee repent it." Robin Hood, to requite the courtesy, took the friar on his back, and not speaking the least word to him, carried him over the water, and laid him gently down on the side of the bank; and turning to him, he spake unto him as at first, and bade him carry him over the water once more, or he should answer it with the forfeit of his life. The friar in a smiling manner took him up, and spake not a word till he came in the midst of the stream, when, being up to the middle and higher, he did shake him from off his shoulders and said unto him, "Now choose thee, bold fellow, whether thou wilt sink or swim."

Robin Hood, being soundly washed, got him up on his feet, and prostrating himself, did swim to a bush of broom on the other side of the bank; and the friar swam to a willow tree which was not far from it. Then Robin Hood, taking his bow in his hand and one of his best arrows, did shoot at the friar, which the friar received in his buckler of steel and said unto him, "Shoot on, thou bold fellow; if thou shootest at me a whole summer's day, I will stand your mark still." "That will I," said Robin Hood, and shot arrow after arrow at him, until he had not an arrow left in his quiver. He then laid down his bow, and drew out his sword, which but two days before had been the death of three men. Now hand to hand they went with sword and buckler; the steel buckler defends whatsoever blow is given; sometimes they make at the head, sometimes at the foot, sometimes at the side; sometimes they strike directly down, sometimes they falsify their blows, and come in foot and arm, with a free thrust at the body; and being ashamed that so long they exercise their unprofitable valor and cannot hurt one another, they multiply their blows, they hack, they hew, they slash, they foam. At last Robin Hood desired the friar to hold his hand, and to give him leave to blow his horn.

"Thou wantest breath to sound it," said the friar;

"take thee a little respite, for we have been five hours at
it by the Fountain Abbey clock." Robin Hood took his
horn from his side, and having sounded it three times,
behold where fifty lusty men, with their bended bows,
came to his assistance. The friar, wondering at it, "Whose
men," said he, "be these?" "They are mine," said Robin
Hood; "what is that to thee?" "False loon," said the
friar; and making a little pause, he desired Robin Hood
to show him the same courtesy which he gave him. "What
is that?" said Robin Hood. "Thou soundest thy horn three
times," said the friar; "let me now but whistle three
times." "Ay, with all my heart," said Robin Hood; "I
were to blame if I should deny thee that courtesy." With
that the friar set his fist to his mouth and whistled three
times so shrilly that the place echoed again with it; and
behold, three and fifty fair ban-dogs (their hairs rising
on their back, betokening their rage) were almost on the
backs of Robin Hood and his companions. "Here is for
every one of thy men a dog," said the friar, "and two for
thee." "That is foul play," said Robin Hood. He had
scarce spoken that word but two dogs came upon him
at once, one before, another behind him, who, although
they could not touch his flesh (his sword had made so
swift a despatch of them), yet they tore his coat into
two pieces. By this time the men had so laid about them
that the dogs began to fly back, and their fury to languish
into barking. Little John did so bestir himself that the
Curtal Friar, admiring at his courage and his nimbleness,
did ask him who he was. He made him answer, "I will
tell the truth, and not lie. I am he who is called Little
John, and do belong to Robin Hood, who hath fought
with thee this day, five hours together; and if thou wilt
not submit unto him, this arrow shall make thee." The
friar, perceiving how much he was overpowered, and that
it was impossible for him to deal with so many at once,
did come to composition with Robin Hood. And the
articles of agreement were these: That the friar should
abandon Fountain Dale and Fountain Abbey, and should
live with Robin Hood, at his place not far from Nottingham, where for saying of mass, he should receive a
noble for every Sunday throughout the year, and for
saying mass on every holy day, a new change of gar-

ment. The friar, contented with these conditions, did seal the agreement. And thus by the courage of Robin Hood and his yeomen, he was enforced at the last to submit, having for seven long years kept Fountain Dale, not all the power thereabouts being able to bring him on his knees.

But Friar Tuck was the only man of the clergy with whom Robin had friendly dealings. As a rule these churchmen fared as did the Bishop of Hereford in the following ballad, which we add for the sake of an example of the manner in which this True History of Robin Hood has come down to us from the year 1245:

THE BISHOP OF HEREFORD'S ENTERTAINMENT BY ROBIN HOOD AND LITTLE JOHN AND THEIR COMPANY, IN MERRY BARNSDALE

SOME they will talk of bold Robin Hood,
    And some of barons bold;
But I'll tell you how he served the Bishop of Hereford,
    When he robbed him of his gold.

As it befell in merry Barnsdale,
    All under the greenwood tree,
The Bishop of Hereford was to come by,
    With all his company.

"Come, kill me a venison," said bold Robin Hood,
    "And dress it by the highway side,
And we will watch the bishop narrowly,
    Lest some other way he should ride."

Robin Hood dressed himself in shepherd's attire,
    With six of his men also;
And, when the Bishop of Hereford came by,
    They about the fire did go.

"O, what is the matter?" then said the bishop,
    "Or for whom do you make this ado?
Or why do you kill the king's ven'son,
    When your company is so few?"

"We are shepherds," said bold Robin Hood,
    "And we keep sheep all the year;
And we are disposed to be merry this day,
    And to kill of the king's fat deer."

"You are brave fellows," said the bishop,
  "And the king of your doings shall know;
Therefore make haste, and come along with me,
  For before the king you shall go."

"O pardon, O pardon," said bold Robin Hood,
  "O pardon, I thee pray;
For it becomes not your lordship's coat
  To take so many lives away."

"No pardon, no pardon," said the bishop,
  "No pardon I thee owe;
Therefore make haste, and come along with me,
  For before the king you shall go."

Then Robin he set his back against a tree,
  And his foot against a thorn,
And from underneath his shepherd's coat
  He pulled out a bugle horn.

He put the little end to his mouth,
  And a loud blast did he blow,
Till threescore and ten of bold Robin's men
  Came running all in a row:

All making obeisance to bold Robin Hood;
  'Twas a comely sight for to see.
"What is the matter, master," said Little John,
  "That you blow so lustily?"

"O here is the Bishop of Hereford,
  And no pardon we shall have."
"Cut off his head, master," said Little John,
  "And throw him into his grave."

"O pardon, O pardon," said the bishop,
  "O pardon, I thee pray;
For if I had known it had been you,
  I'd have gone some other way."

"No pardon, no pardon," said bold Robin Hood,
  "No pardon I thee owe;
Therefore make haste, and come along with me,
  For to merry Barnsdale you shall go."

Then Robin he took the bishop by the hand,
  And led him to merry Barnsdale;

He made him stay and sup with him that night,
    And to drink wine, beer, and ale.

"Call in a reckoning," said the bishop,
    "For methinks it grows wondrous high."
"Send me your purse, master," said Little John,
    "And I'll tell you bye and bye."

Then Little John took the bishop's cloak,
    And spread it upon the ground,
And out of the bishop's portmantua
    He told three hundred pound.

"Here's money enough, master," said Little John,
    "And a comely sight 'tis to see;
It makes me in charity with the bishop,
    Though he heartily loveth not me."

Robin Hood took the bishop by the hand,
    And he caused the music to play;
And he made the old bishop to dance in his boots,
    And glad to get so away.

CHAPTER XXXV

ROBIN HOOD AND HIS ADVENTURES

"They say he is already in the forest of Arden, and a many merry men with him, and there they live like the old Robin Hood of England . . . and fleet the time carelessly as they did in the golden world."–As You Like It.

As has been already said, some of the ballad makers have so far erred from the truth as to represent Robin Hood as being outlawed by Henry VIII, and several stories are told of Queen Katherine's interceding with her husband for the pardon of the bold outlaw.* How-

---

* This seems to have been the opinion of the author from whom we draw the following account of our hero's life—to show how the

ever this may be, it is known that Robin Hood once shot a match on the queen's side against the king's archers, and here is the story:

Robin Hood on one occasion sent a present to Queen Katherine with which she was so pleased that she swore she would be a friend to the noble outlaw as long as she might live. So one day the queen went to her chamber and called to her a page of her company, and bade him make haste and prepare to ride to Nottinghamshire to find Robin Hood in Sherwood Forest; for the queen had made a match with the king, her archers against his archers, and the queen proposed to have Robin Hood and his band to shoot on her side against the king's archers.

Now, as for the page, he started for Nottingham and posted all the way, and inquired on the road for Robin Hood, where he might be, but he could not find any one who could let him know exactly. So he took up his quarters at an inn at Nottingham. And in the room of the inn he sat him down and called for a bottle of Rhenish wine, and he drank the queen's health out of it. Now at

---

doctors will disagree even on a topic as important as Robin Hood:

THE NOBLE BIRTH AND THE ACHIEVEMENTS OF ROBIN HOOD

"Robin Hood was descended from the noble family of the Earl of Huntingdon, and being outlawed by Henry VIII. for many extravagancies and outrages he had committed, he did draw together a company of such bold and licentious persons as himself, who lived for the most part on robberies committed in or near unto Sherwood Forest in Nottinghamshire. He had these always ready at his command, so that if need did require he at the winding of his horn would have fifty or more of them in readiness to assist him. He whom he most affected was called Little John by reason of his low stature, though not inferior to any of them in strength of body and stoutness of spirit. He would not entertain any into his service whom he had not first fought with himself and made sufficient trial of his courage and dexterity how to use his weapons, which was the reason that oftentimes he came home hurt and beaten as he was; which was nevertheless no occasion of the diminution of his love to the person whom he fought with, for ever afterwards he would be the more familiar with him, and better respect him for · it. Many petitions were referred to the king for a pardon for him, which the king (understanding of the many mad pranks he and his associates played) would give no ear unto; but being attended with a considerable guard, did make a progress himself to find out and bring him to condign punishment. At last, by the means and mediation of Queen Katherine the king's wrath was qualified, and his pardon sealed, and he spent his old age in peace, at a house of his own, not far from Nottingham, being generally beloved and respected by all." [Hale's note, 1884 ed.]

his side was sitting a yeoman of the country, clad in Lincoln green, with a long bow in his hand. And he turned to the page and asked him, "What is thy business, my sweet boy, so far in the north country, for methinks you must come from London?" So then the page told him that it was his business to find Robin Hood the outlaw, and for that he asked every yeoman that he met. And he asked his friend if he knew anything which might help him. "Truly," said the yeoman, "that I do. And if you will get to horse early to-morrow morning, I will show you Robin Hood and all his gay yeomen."

So the next morning they got them to horse and rode out into the forest, and the yeoman brought the page to where were Robin Hood and his yeomen. And the page fell down on his knee and said to Robin Hood, "Queen Katherine greets you well by me, and hath sent you this ring as a token. She bids you post up to London town, for that there shall be some sport there in which she has a mind you shall have a hand." And at this Robin took off his mantle of Lincoln green from his back and sent it by the page to Queen Katherine with a promise that he and his band would follow him as soon as they might.

So Robin Hood clothed all his men in Lincoln green and himself in scarlet, and each man wore a black hat with a white feather stuck therein. And thus Robin Hood and his band came up to London. And Robin fell down on his knees before the queen, and she bade him welcome with all his band. For the match between the queen's archers and the king's was to come off the next day in Finsbury fields.

Here first came the king's archers marching with bold bearing, and then came Robin Hood and his archers for the queen. And they laid out the marks there. And the king laid a wager with the queen on the shooting. Now the wager was three hundred tun of Rhenish, and three hundred tun of good English beer, and three hundred fat harts. So then the queen asked if there were any knights with the king who would take her side. But they were unwilling, for said they, "How shall we bet on these men whom we have never seen, when we know Clifton and the rest of the king's archers, and have seen them shoot?" Now this Clifton was one of the king's archers and a great boaster. And when he had reached the shooting field he had cried out, "Measure no marks for us, my lord the king, for we will shoot at the sun and moon." But for all that Robin Hood beat him at the shooting. And the queen asked the Bishop of Herefordshire to back her archers. But he swore by his mitre that he would not bet a single penny on the queen's archers, for he knew them not. "What will you bet against them," asked Robin Hood at this, "since you think our shooting is the worse?" "Truly," said the bishop, "I will bet all the money that may be in my purse," and he pulled it up from where it hung at his side. "What is in your purse?" asked Robin Hood. And the bishop tossed it down on the ground, saying, "Fifteen rose-nobles, and that's an hundred pound." So Robin Hood tossed out a bag beside the bishop's purse on the green.

And with that they began shooting, and shot three bouts, and they came out even; the king's and the queen's. "The next three shots," said the king, "shall pay for all." And so the king's archers shot, and then Robin Hood, and Little John, and Midge the miller's son shot for the queen, and came every man of them nearer the prick in the willow wand than did any of the king's men. So the queen's archers having beaten, Queen Katherine asked a boon of the king, and he granted it. "Give me, I pray you," said the queen, "safe conduct for the archers of my party to come and to go home and to stay in London here some time to enjoy themselves." "I grant it," said the king. "Then you are welcome, Robin Hood," said the queen, "and so is Little John and Midge the miller's son and every one of you." "Is this Robin Hood?" asked the king, "for I had heard that he was killed in a quarrel in the north country." And the bishop too asked, "Is this Robin Hood? If I had known that, I would not have bet a penny with him. He took me one Saturday evening and bound me fast to a tree, and there he made me sing a mass for him and his yeomanry about." "Well, if I did," said Robin Hood, "surely I needed all the masses that I might get for my soul." And with that he and his yeomanry departed, and when their safe conduct was expired they journeyed north again to Sherwood Forest.

ROBIN HOOD AND THE BEGGAR

But Robin Hood, once having supplied himself with good store of money, which he had gotten of the Sheriff of Nottingham, bought him a stout gelding, and riding on him one day towards Nottingham, it was his fortune to meet with a poor beggar. Robin Hood was of a frolic spirit, and no accepter of persons; but observing the beggar to have several sorts of bags, which were fastened to his patched coat, he did ride up to him, and giving him the time of day, he demanded of him what countryman he was. "A Yorkshireman," said the beggar; "and I would desire of you to give me something." "Give thee!" said Robin Hood; "why, I have nothing to give thee. I am a poor ranger in the forest, and thou seemest to be a lusty knave; shall I give thee a good bastinado over thy shoulders?" "Content, content," said the beggar; "I durst lay all my bags to a threaden joust, thou wilt repent it." With that Robin Hood alighted, and the beggar, with his long quarterstaff, so well defended himself, that, let Robin Hood do what he could, he could not come within the beggar, to flash him to a remembrance of his overboldness; and nothing vexed him more than to find that the beggar's staff was as hard and as obdurate as iron itself; but not so Robin Hood's head, for the beggar with all his force did let his staff descend with such a side blow, that Robin Hood, for all his skill, could not defend it, but the blood came trickling down his face, which, turning Robin Hood's courage into revenge and fury, he let fly at him with his trusty sword and doubled blow upon blow; but perceiving that the beggar did hold him so hard to it that one of his blows was but the forerunner of another, and every blow to be almost the Postilion of Death, he cried out to him to hold his hand. "That will I not do," said the beggar, "unless thou wilt resign unto me thy horse, and thy sword, and thy clothes, with all the money thou hast in thy pockets." "The change is uneven," said Robin Hood, "but for once I am content."

So, putting on the beggar's clothes, the beggar was

the gentleman, and Robin Hood was the beggar, who, entering into Nottingham town with his patched coat and several wallets, understood that three brethren were that day to suffer at the gallows, being condemned for killing the king's deer, he made no more ado, but went directly to the sheriff's house, where a young gentleman, seeing him to stand at the door, demanded of him what he would have. Robin Hood returned answer that he came to crave neither meat nor drink, but the lives of those three brothers who were condemned to die. "That cannot be," said the young gentleman, "for they are all this day to suffer according to law, for stealing of the king's deer, and they are already conveyed out of the town to the place of execution." "I will be with them presently," said Robin Hood, and coming to the gallows, he found many making great lamentation for them. Robin Hood did comfort them and assured them they should not die; and blowing his horn, behold on a sudden a hundred brave archers came unto him, by whose help, having released the prisoners, and killed the hangman, and hurt many of the sheriff's officers, they took those who were condemned to die for killing the king's deer along with them, who, being very thankful for the preservation of their lives, became afterwards of the yeomanry of Robin Hood.

ROBIN HOOD AND KING RICHARD

Now King Richard, hearing of the deeds of Robin Hood and his men, wondered much at them, and desired greatly himself to see him and his men as well. So he with a dozen of his lords rode to Nottingham town and there took up his abode. And being at Nottingham, the king one day with his lords put on friars' gowns every one, and rode forth from Fountain Abbey down to Barnsdale. And as they were riding there they saw Robin Hood and all his band standing ready to assail them. The king, being taller than the rest, was thought by Robin to be the abbot. So he made up to him, and seized his horse by the head, and bade him stand. "For," said he, "it is against such knaves as you that I am bound to make war." "But," said the king himself, "we are messengers from the king, who is but a little away, waiting to speak with you." "God save the king," said Robin Hood, "and all his well-wishers. And accursed be every one who may deny his sovereignty." "You are cursing yourself," said the king, "for you are a traitor." "Now," said Robin Hood, "if you were not the king's messenger, I would make you rue that word of yours. I am as true a man to the king as lives. And I never yet injured any honest man and true, but only those who make their living by stealing from others. I have never in my life harmed either husbandman or huntsman. But my chief spite lies against the clergy, who have in these days great power. But I am right glad to have met you here. Come with me, and you shall taste our greenwood cheer." But the king and his lords marvelled, wondering what kind of cheer Robin might provide for them. And Robin took the king's horse by the head and led him towards his tent. "It is because thou comest from the king," said he, "that I use you in this wise; and hadst thou as much gold as ever I had, it should be all of it safe for good King Richard's sake." And with that he took out his horn and blew on it a loud blast. And thereat came marching forth from the wood five score and ten of Robin's followers, and each one bent the knee before Robin Hood. "Surely," thought the king, "it is a goodly sight to see; for they are more humble to their master than my servants are to me. Here may the court learn something from the greenwood." And here they laid a dinner for the king and his lords, and the king swore that he had never feasted better. Then Robin Hood, taking a can of ale, said, "Let us now begin, each man with his can. Here's a health to the king." And they all drank the health to the king, the king himself, as well as another.

And after the dinner they all took their bows and showed the king such archery that the king said he had never seen such men as they in any foreign land. And then said the king to Robin Hood, "If I could get thee a pardon from King Richard, wouldst thou serve the king well in everything?" "Yes, with all my heart," said Robin. And so said all his men.

And with that the king declared himself to them and

said, "I am the king, your sovereign, that is now before you." And at this Robin and all his men fell down on their knees; but the king raised them up, saying to them that he pardoned each one of them, and that they should every one of them be in his service. So the king returned to Nottingham, and with him returned Robin Hood and his men, to the great joy of the townspeople, whom they had for a long time sorely vexed.

And they are gone to London court,
Robin Hood and all his train;
He once was there a noble peer,
And now he's there again.

THE DEATH OF ROBIN HOOD

But Robin Hood returned to Sherwood Forest, and there met his death. For one day, being wounded in a fight, he fled out of the battle with Little John. And being at some distance, Robin Hood said to his lieutenant, "Now truly I cannot shoot even one shot more, for the arrows will not fly. For I am sore wounded. So I will go to my cousin, the abbess, who dwelleth near here in Kirkley Hall, and she shall bleed me, that I may be well again." So Robin Hood left Little John, and he went his way to Kirkley; and reaching the Hall, his strength nearly left him, yet he knocked heavily at the door. And his cousin came down first to let him in. And when she saw him, she knew that it was her cousin Robin Hood, and she received him with a joyful face. Then said Robin, "You see me, my cousin, how weak I am. Therefore I pray you to bleed me, that I may be whole again." And his cousin took him by the hand, and led him into an an upper room, and laid him on a bed, and she bled him. But the treacherous woman tied not up the vein again, but left him so that his life began to flow from him. And he, finding his strength leaving him, thought to escape; but he could not, for the door was locked, and the casement window was so high that he might not leap down from it. Then, knowing that he must die, he reached forth his hand to his bugle horn, which lay by him on the bed. And setting the horn to his mouth, he blew weakly, though with all his strength, three blasts upon it. And Little John, as he sat under the tree in the greenwood, heard his blowing, and he said, "Now must Robin be near death, for his blast is very weak."

And he got up and ran to Kirkley Hall as fast as he might. And coming to the door, he found it locked; but he broke it down and so came to Robin Hood. And coming to the bed, he fell upon his knees and said, "Master, I beg a boon of thee—that thou lettest me burn down Kirkley Hall and all the nunnery." "Nay," quoth Robin Hood; "nay, I cannot grant you your boon; for never in my life did I hurt woman, or man in woman's company, nor shall it be done when I die. But for me, give me my long bow, and I will let fly an arrow, and where you shall find the arrow, there bury me. And make my grave long and broad, that I may rest easily; and place my head upon a green sod, and place my bow at my side." And these words Little John readily promised him, so that Robin Hood was pleased. And they buried him as he had asked, an arrow-shot from Kirkley Hall.

CHAPTER XXXVI

CHEVY CHASE

The Perse out of Northumberlande,
  And a vowe to God mayde he,
That he wold hunte in the mountayns
  Off Chyviat within days thre,
In the mauger of doughtè Dogles,
  And all that ever with him be.
        PERCY: *Reliques of Ancient Poetry*[9]

Scarcely less famous than Robin Hood as a subject for ballad makers was the battle of Chevy Chase. This battle was one of the many struggles rising out of the never-ending border quarrels between Scotland and England, of which poets are never tired of singing. Sometimes the Earl of Douglas, the great Scotch border-lord, would make an incursion into Northumberland, and then to revenge the insult Lord Percy would come riding over the Tweed into Scotland.

In the battle of Chevy Chase it would seem as if Earl Percy was the aggressor. As a matter of fact it mattered little which began the quarrel at any particular time. The feud was ever smouldering, and needed little to make it burst forth.

THE BALLAD OF CHEVY CHASE

GOD prosper long our noble king,
    Our lives and safetyes all;
A woefull hunting once there did
    In Chevy Chase befall.

To drive the deer with hound and horne,
    Erle Percy took his way,
The child may rue that is unborne
    The hunting of that day.

The stout Erle of Northumberland
    A vow to God did make,
His pleasure in the Scottish woods
    Three summer days to take;

The cheefest harts in Chevy Chase
    To kill and bear away.
These tidings to Erle Douglas came,
    In Scotland where he lay,

Who sent Erle Percy present word
    He would prevent his sport.
The English Erle not fearing that,
    Did to the woods resort,

With fifteen hundred bowmen bold;
    All chosen men of might,
Who knew full well in time of neede
    To ayme their shafts aright.

The gallant greyhounds swiftly ran
    To chase the fallow deere:
On Monday they began to hunt
    Ere daylight did appear;

And long before high noon they had
  An hundred fat buckes slaine;
Then having dined the drovyers went
  To rouse the deer again.

The bowmen mustered on the hill,
  Well able to endure;
Their backsides all, with special care,
  That day were guarded sure.

The hounds ran swiftly through the woods,
  The nimble deere to take,
That with their cryes the hills and dales
  An eccho shrill did make.

Lord Percy to the quarry went,
  To view the slaughtered deer;
Quoth he, Erle Douglas promised
  This day to meet me heere;

But if I thought he would not come,
  Noe longer would I stay.
With that a brave young gentleman
  Thus to the Erle did say:—

Loe, yonder doth Erle Douglas come,
  His men in armour bright;
Full twenty hundred Scottish speres
  All marching in our sight;

All men of pleasant Tivydale,
  Fast by the river Tweede:
O cease your sports, Erle Percy said,
  And take your bowes with speede.

And now with me, my countrymen,
  Your courage forth advance;
For there was never champion yett
  In Scotland or in France,

That ever did on horseback come,
  But if my hap it were,
I durst encounter man for man,
  With him to break a spere.

Erle Douglas on his milk-white steede,
  Most like a baron bold,
Rode foremost of his company,
  Whose armour shone like gold.

Show me, sayd he, whose men you be,
  That hunt so boldly heere,
That without my consent doe chase
  And kill my fallow deere.

The first man that did answer make
  Was noble Percy he;
Who sayd, We list not to declare,
  Nor show whose men we be.

Yet we will spend our deerest blood,
  Thy cheefest harts to slay.
The Douglas swore a solempne oathe,
  And thus in rage did say,

Ere thus I will outbraved be,
  One of us two shall dye:
I know thee well, an erle thou art;
  Lord Percy, soe am I.

But trust me, Percy, pittye it were
  And great offence to kill
Any of these our guiltless men,
  For they have done no ill.

Let thou and I the battell trye,
  And set our men aside.
Accurst be he, Erle Percy sayd,
  By whom this is denyed.

Then stept a gallant squier forth,
  Witherington was his name,
Who said, I wold not have it told
  To Henry our king for shame,

That ere my captaine fought on foot
  And I stood looking on.
You be two erles, sayd Witherington,
  And I a squier alone:

Ile doe the best that doe I may,
　　While I have power to stand:
While I have power to wield my sword,
　　Ile fight with hart and hand.

Our English archers bent their bowes
　　Their harts were good and trew;
At the first flight of arrowes sent,
　　Full fourscore Scots they slew.

Yet bides Erle Douglas on the bent,
　　As cheeftain stout and good,
As valiant captain, all unmoved,
　　The shock he firmly stood.

His host he parted had in three,
　　As leader ware and tryd,
And soon his spearmen on his foes
　　Bare down on every side.

To drive the deere with hound and horne,
　　Douglass bade on the bent:
Two captaines moved with mickle might
　　Their speares to shivers went.

Throughout the English archery
　　They dealt full many a wound;
But still our valiant Englishmen
　　All firmly kept their ground:

And throwing straight their bowes away,
　　They grasped their swords so bright:
And now sharp blows, a heavy shower,
On shields and helmets light.

They closed full fast on every side,
　　No slackness there was found;
And many a gallant gentleman
　　Lay gasping on the ground.

O Christ! it was a griefe to see,
　　And likewise for to heare,
The cries of men lying in their gore,
　　And scattered here and there.

At last these two stout erles did meet,
    Like captaines of great might;
Like lyons wood, they layd on lode
    And made a cruell fight:

They fought until they both did sweat,
    With swords of tempered steele;
Until the blood, like drops of rain,
    They trickling down did feele.

Yield thee, Lord Percy, Douglas sayd;
    In faith I will thee bringe,
Where thou shalt high advanced be
    By James our Scottish king:

Thy ransome I will freely give,
    And this report of thee:
Thou art the most courageous knight
    That ever I did see.

Noe, Douglas, quoth Erle Percy then,
    Thy proffer I do scorne;
I will not yield to any Scott,
    That ever yet was borne.

With that there came an arrow keene,
    Out of an English bow,
Which struck Erle Douglas to the heart,
    A deepe and deadly blow:

Who never spake more words than these,
    Fight on, my merry men all;
For why, my life is at an end;
    Lord Percy sees my fall.

Then leaving liffe, Erle Percy tooke
    The dead man by the hand;
And said, Erle Douglas, for thy life
    Wold I have lost my land.

O Christ, my very hart doth bleed
    With sorrow for thy sake;
For sure a more redoubted knight
    Mischance cold never take.

A knight among the Scotts there was
  Who saw Erle Douglas dye,
Who streight in wrath did vow revenge
  Upon the Lord Percy.

Sir Hugh Montgomery was he called,
  Who, with a spear most bright,
Well mounted on a gallant steed,
  Ran fiercely through the fight;

And past the English archers all,
  Without all dread and feare;
And through Earl Percy's body then
  He thrust his hatefull speare;

With such a vehement force and might
  He did his body gore,
The staff ran through the other side
  A large cloth-yard or more.

So thus did both these nobles dye,
  Whose courage none could staine:
An English archer then perceived
  The noble erle was slaine;

He had a bow bent in his hand,
  Made of a trusty tree;
An arrow of a cloth-yard long
  Up to the head drew he:

Against Sir Hugh Montgomery,
  So right the shaft he sett,
The grey goose-wing that was thereon
  In his hart's blood was wett.

This fight did last from break of day
  Till setting of the sun;
For when they rang the evening-bell
  The battle scarce was done.

With stoute Erle Percy there was slaine
  Sir John of Egerton,
Sir Robert Ratcliff, and Sir John,
  Sir James that bold barron:

And with Sir George and stoute Sir James
  Both knights of good account,
Good Sir Ralph Raby there was slaine,
  Whose prowese did surmount.

For Witherington my heart is woe,
  That ever he slain should be;
For when his legs were hewn in two
  He knelt and fought on his knee.

And with Erle Douglas there was slaine
  Sir Hugh Montgomery,
Sir Charles Murray, that from the field
  One foot wold never flee.

Sir Charles Murray, of Ratcliff too,
  His sister's sonne was he;
Sir David Lamb, so well esteem'd,
  Yet savéd cold not be,

And the Lord Maxwell in like case
  Did with Erle Douglass dye:
Of twenty hundred Scottish speres
  Scarce fifty-five did flye.

Of fifteen hundred Englishmen,
  Went home but fifty-three;
The rest were slaine in Chevy Chase,
  Under the greene woode tree.

Next day many widowes come,
  Their husbands to bewayle;
They washed their wounds in brinish teares,
  But all wold not prevayle.

Theyr bodyes, bathed in purple gore,
  They bore with them away;
They kist them dead a thousand times,
  Ere they were cladd in clay.

The newes was brought to Eddenborrow,
  Where Scotland's king did raigne,
That brave Erle Douglas suddenlye
  Was with an arrow slaine.

O heavy newes, King James did say,
  Scotland may witness be,
I have not any captain more
  Of such account as he.

Like tydings to King Henry came,
  Within as short a space,
That Percy of Northumberland
  Was slaine in Chevy Chase:

Now God be with him, said the king,
  Sith it will noe better be;
I trust I have within my realme,
  Five hundred as good as he.

Yet shall not Scotts nor Scotland say,
  But I will vengeance take;
Ile be revengéd on them all
  For brave Erle Percy's sake.

This vow full well the king performed
  After at Humbledowne;
In one day fifty knights were slaine,
  With lords of great renowne;

And of the rest of small account,
  Did many thousands dye:
Thus endeth the hunting of Chevy Chase
  Made by the Erle Percy.

God save our king, and bless this land
  With plentye, joy, and peace;
And grant henceforth that foule debate
  'Twixt noblemen may cease.

CHAPTER XXXVII

THE BATTLE OF OTTERBOURNE

It fell about a Lamass-tide,
When husbands wynn their hay,
The doughty Douglas bound him to ride
In England to take a pray.

Another famous battle in the border-warfare between England and Scotland was fought at Otterbourne. This is a town in Northumberland, and here, as in Chevy Chase, the Douglas and the Percy matched their strength. Earl Douglas was killed in the fight, and Sir Henry Percy, called Hotspur, was taken prisoner.[10] The story as it is told here is from the works of that most entertaining and long-winded historian of chivalry, Sir John Froissart.

We begin *in medias res* with a Scotch foray, in which the Douglas, with the Earl of March and Dunbar and the Earl of Moray, has penetrated as far into England as the city of Durham, and is now returning to Scotland.

The three Scotts lords, having completed the object of their expedition into Durham, lay before Newcastle three days, where there was an almost continual skirmish. The sons of the Earl of Northumberland, from their great courage, were always the first at the barriers, where many valiant deeds were done with lances hand to hand. The Earl of Douglas had a long conflict with Sir Henry Percy, and in it, by gallantry of arms, won his pennon, to the great vexation of Sir Henry and the other English. The Earl of Douglas said, "I will carry this token of your prowess with me to Scotland and place it on the tower of my castle at Dalkeith, that it may be seen from afar." "By Heaven, Earl of Douglas," replied Sir Henry, "you shall not even bear it out of Northumberland: be assured you shall never have this pennon to brag of." "You must come then," answered Earl Douglas, "this night and seek for it. I will fix your pennon before my tent, and shall see if you will venture to take it away."

As it was now late, the skirmish ended, and each party

retired to their quarters to disarm and comfort themselves. They had plenty of everything, particularly flesh meat. The Scots kept up a very strict watch, concluding from the words of Sir Henry Percy they should have their quarters beaten up this night; they were disappointed, for Sir Henry Percy was advised to defer it.

On the morrow the Scots dislodged from before Newcastle; and, taking the road to their own country, they came to a town and castle called Ponclau, of which Sir Raymond de Laval, a very valiant knight of Northumberland, was the lord. They halted there about four o'clock in the morning, and they learned the knight to be within it, and made preparations for the assault. This was done with such courage that the place was won and the knight made prisoner. After they had burnt the town and castle, they marched away for Otterbourne, which was eight English leagues from Newcastle, and there encamped themselves. This day they made no attack; but very early on the morrow their trumpets sounded, and they made ready for the assault, advancing towards the castle, which was tolerably strong and situated among the marshes. They attacked it so long and so unsuccessfully that they were fatigued, and therefore sounded a retreat. When they had retired to their quarters, the chiefs held a council how to act; and the greater part were for decamping on the morrow, without attempting more against the castle, to join their countrymen in the neighborhood of Carlisle. But the Earl of Douglas overruled this by saying, "In despite of Sir Henry Percy, who the day before yesterday declared he would take from me his pennon, that I conquered by fair deeds of arms before Newcastle, I will not return home for two or three days; and we will renew our attack on the castle, for it is to be taken: we shall thus gain double honor, and see if within that time he will come for his pennon; if he do, it shall be well defended." Every one agreed to what Earl Douglas had said; for it was not only honorable, but he was the principal commander; and from affection to him they quietly returned to their quarters. They made huts of trees and branches and strongly fortified themselves. They placed their baggage and servants at the entrance of the marsh on the road to Newcastle, and the cattle they drove into the marsh lands.

I will return to Sir Henry and Sir Ralph Percy, who were greatly mortified that the Earl of Douglas should have conquered their pennon in the skirmish before New-castle. They felt the more for this disgrace because Sir Henry had not kept his word; for he had told the earl that he should never carry his pennon out of England, and this he explained to the knights who were with him in Newcastle. The English imagined the army under the Earl of Douglas to be only the van of the Scots, and that the main body was behind; for which reason those knights who had the most experience in arms, and were best acquainted with warlike affairs, strongly opposed the pro-posal of Sir Henry Percy to pursue them. They said, "Sir, many losses happen in war: if the Earl of Douglas has won your pennon, he has bought it dear enough; for he has come to the gates to seek it, and has been well fought with. Another time you will gain from him as much if not more. We say so, because you know as well as we do that the whole power of Scotland has taken the field. We are not sufficiently strong to offer them battle; and per-haps this skirmish may have been only a trick to draw us out of the town; and if they be, as reported, forty thousand strong, they will surround us and have us at their mercy. It is much better to lose a pennon than two or three hundred knights and squires and leave our country in a defenceless state." This speech checked the eagerness of the two brothers Percy, for they would not act con-trary to the opinion of the council; when other news was brought them by some knights and squires who had followed and observed the Scots, their numbers, dispo-sition, and where they had halted. This was all fully related by knights who had traversed the whole extent of coun-try the Scots had passed through, that they might carry to their lords the most exact information. They thus spoke: "Sir Henry and Sir Ralph Percy, we come to tell you that we have followed the Scottish army and observed all the country where they now are. They first halted at Ponclau and took Sir Raymond de Laval in his castle; thence they went to Otterbourne and took up their quarters for the night. We are ignorant of what they did on the morrow, but they seem to have taken measures for a long stay. We know for certain that their army does not consist of more than three thousand men, including all sorts." Sir Henry Percy on hearing this was greatly rejoiced, and cried out, "To horse! to horse! for by the faith I owe my God, and to my lord and father, I will seek to recover my pennon and to beat up their quarters this night." Such knights and squires in Newcastle as learned this were willing to be of the party, and made themselves ready.

The Bishop of Durham was expected daily at the town; for he had heard of the irruption of the Scots, and that they were before it, in which were the sons of the Earl of Northumberland preparing to offer them combat. The bishop had collected a number of men, and was hastening to their assistance, but Sir Henry Percy would not wait; for he was accompanied by six hundred spears, of knights and squires, and upwards of eight thousand infantry, which he said would be more than enough to fight the Scots, who were but three hundred lances and two thousand others. When they were all assembled, they left Newcastle after dinner and took the field in good array, following the road the Scots had taken, making for Otterbourne, which was eight short leagues distant, but they could not advance very fast, that their infantry might keep up with them.

As the Scots were supping—some indeed had gone to sleep, for they had labored hard during the day at the attack of the castle, and intended renewing it in the cool of the morning—the English arrived, and mistook, at their entrance, the huts of the servants for those of their masters. They forced their way into the camp, which was, however, tolerably strong, shouting out, "Percy! Percy!" In such cases, you may suppose an alarm is soon given, and it was fortunate for the Scots that the English had made their first attack on the servants' quarters, which checked them some little. The Scots, expecting the English, had prepared accordingly; for while the lords were arming themselves, they ordered a body of infantry to join their servants and keep up the skirmish. As their men were armed, they formed themselves under the pennons of the three principal barons, who each had his particular appointment. In the meantime, the night advanced, but it was sufficiently light, for the moon shone, and it was the month of August, when the weather is temperate and serene.

When the Scots were quite ready, and properly arrayed, they left their camp in silence, but did not march to meet the English. They skirted the side of the mountain which was hard by; for, during the preceding day, they had well examined the country round and said among themselves, "Should the English come to beat up our quarters, we will do so and so," and thus settled their plans beforehand, which was the saving of them; for it is of the greatest advantage to men-at-arms when attacked in the night to have previously arranged their mode of defence, and well to have weighed the chance of victory or defeat. The English had soon overpowered their servants; but as they advanced into the camp, they found fresh bodies ready to oppose them and to continue the fight. The Scots, in the meantime, marched along the mountain-side and fell upon the enemy's flank quite unexpectedly, shouting their cries. This was a great surprise to the English, who, however, formed themselves in better order and reinforced that part of their army. The cries of Percy and Douglas resounded on either side.

The battle now raged: great was the pushing of lances, and very many of each party was struck down at the first onset. The English, being more numerous and anxious to defeat the enemy, kept in a compact body and forced the Scots to retire, who were on the point of being discomfited. The Earl of Douglas, being young and impatient to gain renown in arms, ordered his banner to advance, shouting, "Douglas! Douglas!" Sir Henry and Sir Ralph Percy, indignant for the affront the Earl of Douglas had put on them, by conquering their pennon, and desirous of meeting him, hastened to the place from whence the sounds came, calling out, "Percy! Percy!" The two banners met, and many gallant deeds of arms ensued. The English were in superior strength and fought so lustily that they drove back the Scots. Sir Patrick Hepburn and his son of the same name did honor to their knighthood and country by their gallantry, under the banner of Douglas, which would have been conquered but for the vigorous defence they made; and this circumstance not only contributed to their personal credit, but the memory of it is continued with honor to their descendants.

The knights and squires of either party were anxious to continue the combat with vigor as long as their spears might be capable of holding. Cowardice was there unknown, and the most splendid courage was everywhere exhibited by the gallant youths of England and Scotland; they were so closely intermixed that the archers' bows were useless, and they fought hand to hand, without either battalion giving way. The Scots behaved most valiantly, for the English were three to one. I do not mean to say the English did not acquit themselves well; for they would sooner be slain or made prisoners in battle than reproached with flight. As I before mentioned, the two banners of Douglas and Percy met, and the men-at-arms under each exerted themselves by every means to gain the victory; but the English, at this attack, were so much the stronger, that the Scots were driven back. The Earl of Douglas, who was of a high spirit, seeing his men repulsed, seized a battle-axe with both his hands, like a gallant knight, and, to rally his men, dashed into the midst of his enemies and gave such blows on all around him that no one could withstand them, but all made way for him on every side; for there was none so well armed with helmets and plates but that they suffered from his battle-axe. Thus he advanced, like another Hector, thinking to recover and conquer the field, from his own prowess, until he was met by three spears that were pointed at him. One struck him on the shoulder, another on the stomach, and the third entered his thigh. He could never disengage himself from these spears, but was borne to the ground, fighting desperately. From that time he never rose again. Some of his knights and squires had followed him, but not all; for, though the moon shone, it was rather dark. The three English lancers knew that they had struck down some person of considerable rank, but never thought it was Earl Douglas. Had they known it, they would have been so rejoiced that their courage would have been redoubled, and the fortune of the day had consequently been determined to their side. The Scots were ignorant also of their loss until the battle was over, otherwise they would certainly, from despair, have been discomfited.

I will relate what befell the earl afterwards. As soon as he fell, his head was cleaved by a battle-axe, the spear thrust through his thigh, and the main body of the English marched over him, without paying any attention, not supposing him to be their principal enemy. In another part of the field, the Earl of March and Dunbar combated valiantly; and the English gave the Scots full employment who had followed the Earl of Douglas, and had engaged with the two Percies. The Earl of Moray behaved so gallantly in pursuing the English that they knew not how to resist him. Of all the battles that have been described in this history, great and small, this of which I am now speaking was the best fought and the most severe; for there was not a man, knight, or squire who did not acquit himself gallantly, hand to hand with the enemy. It resembled something that of Cocherel, which was as long and as hardily disputed. The sons of the Earl of Northumberland, Sir Henry and Sir Ralph Percy, who were the leaders of this expedition, behaved themselves like good knights in the combat. Almost a similar accident befel Sir Ralph as that which happened to the Earl of Douglas; for, having advanced too far, he was surrounded by the enemy and severely wounded, and, being out of breath, surrendered himself to a Scots knight, called Sir John Maxwell, who was under the command and of the household of the Earl of Moray.

When made prisoner, the knight asked him who he was, for it was dark, and he knew him not. Sir Ralph was so weakened by loss of blood, which was flowing from his wound, that he could scarcely avow himself to be Sir Ralph Percy. "Well," replied the knight, "Sir Ralph, rescued or not, you are my prisoner; my name is Maxwell." "I agree to it," said Sir Ralph. "But pay some attention to me, for I am so desperately wounded that my drawers and greaves are full of blood." Upon this the Scots knight was very attentive to him; when suddenly hearing the cry of Moray hard by, and perceiving the earl's banner advancing to him, Sir John addressed himself to the Earl of Moray and said, "My lord, I present you with Sir Ralph Percy as a prisoner; but let good care be taken of him, for he is very badly wounded." The earl was much pleased at this, and replied, "Maxwell, thou hast well earned thy spurs this day." He then ordered his men to take every care of Sir Ralph, who bound up and staunched his wounds. The battle still continued to rage, and no one could say at that moment which side would be the conqueror, for there were very many captures and rescues that never came to my knowledge.

The young Earl of Douglas had this night performed wonders in arms. When he was struck down, there was a great crowd round him, and he could not raise himself; for the blow on his head was mortal. His men had followed him as closely as they were able, and there came to him his cousins, Sir James Lindsay, Sir John and Sir Walter Sinclair, with other knights and squires. They found by his side a gallant knight, that had constantly attended him, who was his chaplain, and had at this time exchanged his profession for that of a valiant man-at-arms. The whole night he had followed the earl, with his battle-axe in hand, and had by his exertions more than once repelled the English. This conduct gained the thanks of his countrymen and turned out to his advantage, for in the same year he was promoted to the archdeaconry and made canon of Aberdeen. His name was Sir William of North Berwick. To say the truth, he was well formed in all his limbs to shine in battle, and was severely wounded at this combat. When these knights came to the Earl of Douglas, they found him in a melancholy state, as well as one of his knights, Sir Robert Hart, who had fought by his side the whole of the night, and now lay beside him, covered with fifteen wounds from lances and other weapons.

Sir John Sinclair asked the earl, "Cousin, how fares it with you?" "But so so," replied he. "Thanks to God, there are but few of my ancestors who have died in chambers or in their beds. I bid you, therefore, revenge my death, for I have but little hope of living, as my heart becomes every minute more faint. Do you, Walter and Sir John Sinclair, raise up my banner, for certainly it is on the ground, from the death of David Campbell, that valiant squire who bore it, and who refused knighthood from my hands this day, though he was equal to the most eminent knights for courage and loyalty; and continue to shout 'Douglas!' but do not tell friend or foe whether I am in your company or not; for, should the enemy know the truth, they will be greatly rejoiced."

The two brothers Sinclair and Sir John Lindsay obeyed his orders. The banner was raised, and "Douglas!" shouted. Their men, who had remained behind, hearing the shouts of "Douglas!" so often repeated, ascended a small eminence and pushed their lances with such courage that the English were repulsed, and many killed or struck to the ground. The Scots, by thus valiantly driving the enemy beyond the spot where the Earl of Douglas lay dead—for he had expired on giving his last orders—arrived at his banner, which was borne by Sir John Sinclair. Numbers were continually increasing, from the repeated shouts of "Douglas!" and the greater part of the Scots knights and squires were now there. The Earls of Moray and March, with their banners and men, came thither also. When they were all thus collected, perceiving the English retreat, they renewed the battle with greater vigor than before.

To say the truth, the English had harder work than the Scots, for they had come by a forced march that evening from Newcastle-on-Tyne, which was eight English leagues distant, to meet the Scots, by which means the greater part were exceedingly fatigued before the combat began. The Scots, on the contrary, had reposed themselves, which was to them of the utmost advantage, as was apparent from the event of the battle. In this last attack, they so completely repulsed the English that the latter could never rally again, and the former drove them far beyond where the Earl of Douglas lay on the ground. Sir Henry Percy, during this attack, had the misfortune to fall into the hands of the Lord Montgomery, a very valiant knight of Scotland. They had long fought hand to hand with much valor and without hindrance from any one; for there was neither knight nor squire of either party who did not find there his equal to fight with, and all were fully engaged. In the end, Sir Henry was made prisoner by the Lord Montgomery.

CHAPTER XXXVIII

EDWARD THE BLACK PRINCE

"ICH DIEN"

The last hero of English chivalry with whom we have to do is Edward the Black Prince. And as the most characteristic part of the knighthood of this most knightly of English princes, we have selected the battles of Crecy and of Poitiers.

THE BATTLE OF CRECY

The English, who were drawn up in three divisions and seated on the ground, on seeing their enemies advance, rose undauntedly up, and fell into their ranks. That of the prince[11] was the first to do so, whose archers were formed in the matter of a portcullis or harrow, and the men-at-arms in the rear. The Earls of Northumberland and Arundel, who commanded the second division, had posted themselves in good order on his wing, to assist and succor the prince if necessary.

You must know that these kings, earls, barons, and lords of France did not advance in any regular order, but one after the other, or anyway most pleasing to themselves. As soon as the King of France came in sight of the English, his blood began to boil, and he cried out to his marshals, "Order the Genoese forward, and begin the battle, in the name of God and St. Denis." There were about fifteen thousand Genoese crossbowmen, but they were quite fatigued, having marched on foot that day six leagues, completely armed and with their crossbows. They told the constable they were not in a fit condition to do any great things that day in battle. The Earl of

354

EDWARD THE BLACK PRINCE

Alençon, hearing this, said, "This is what one gets by employing such scoundrels, who fall off when there is any need of them." During this time, a heavy rain fell, accompanied by thunder and a very terrible eclipse of the sun; and before this rain a great flight of crows hovered in the air over all those battalions, making a loud noise. Shortly afterwards it cleared up, and the sun shone very bright, but the Frenchmen had it in their faces, and the Englishmen in their backs. When the Genoese were somewhat in order, and approached the English, they set up a loud shout, in order to frighten them; but they remained quite still, and did not seem to attend to it. Then they set up a second shout and advanced a little forward, but the English never moved. They hooted a third time, advancing with their crossbows presented, and began to shoot. The English archers then advanced one step forward, and shot their arrows with such force and quickness that it seemed as if it snowed. When the Genoese felt these arrows, which pierced their arms, heads, and through their armor, some of them cut the strings of their crossbows, others flung them on the ground, and all turned about and retreated quite discomfited. The French had a large body of men-at-arms on horseback, richly dressed, to support the Genoese. The King of France, seeing them thus fall back, cried out, "Kill me those scoundrels, for they stop up our road without any reason." You would then have seen the above-mentioned men-at-arms lay about them, killing all they could of these runaways.

The English continued shooting as vigorously and quickly as before; some of their arrows fell among the horsemen who were sumptuously equipped, and, killing and wounding many, made them caper and fall among the Genoese, so that they were in such confusion that they could never rally again. The valiant King of Bohemia was slain there. He was called Charles of Luxembourg, for he was the son of the gallant king and emperor, Henry of Luxembourg. Having heard the order of battle, he inquired where his son, the Lord Charles, was. His attendants answered that they did not know, but believed he was fighting. The king said to them, "Gentlemen, you are all my people, my friends and brethren at arms this day; therefore, as I am blind, I request of you to lead me so far into the engagement that I may strike one stroke with my sword." The knights replied they would directly lead him forward; and in order that they might not lose him in the crowd, they fastened all the reins of their horses together, and put the king at their head, that he might gratify his wish, and advanced towards the enemy. The Lord Charles of Bohemia, who already signed his name as King of Germany, and bore the arms, had come in good order to the engagement; but when he perceived that it was likely to turn against the French, he departed, and I do not well know what road he took. The king, his father, had rode in among the enemy, and made good use of his sword, for he and his companions had fought most gallantly. They had advanced so far that they were all slain; and on the morrow they were found on the ground, with their horses all tied together.

The Earl of Alençon advanced in regular order upon the English to fight with them, as did the Earl of Flanders in another part. These two lords, with their detachments, coasting, as it were, the archers, came to the prince's battalion, where they fought valiantly for a length of time. The King of France was eager to march to the place where he saw their banners displayed, but there was a hedge of archers before him. He had that day made a present of a handsome black horse to Sir John of Hainault, who had mounted on it a knight of his that bore his banner, which horse ran off with him and forced his way through the English army, and, when about to return, stumbled and fell into a ditch and severely wounded him. He would have been dead if his page had not followed him round the battalions and found him unable to rise. He had not, however, any other hindrance than from his horse; for the English did not quit the ranks that day to make prisoners. The page alighted and raised him up; but he did not return the way he came, as he would have found it difficult from the crowd.

This battle, which was fought on a Saturday between la Broyes and Crecy, was very murderous and cruel; and many gallant deeds of arms were performed that were never known. Towards evening, many knights and squires of the French had lost their masters. They wandered up and down the plain, attacking the English in small parties. They were soon destroyed, for the English had determined that day to give no quarter, or hear of ransom from any one.

Early in the day, some French, Germans, and Savoyards had broken through the archers of the prince's battalion and had engaged with the men-at-arms; upon which the second battalion came to his aid, and it was time, for otherwise he would have been hard pressed. The first division, seeing the danger they were in, sent a knight in great haste to the King of England, who was posted upon an eminence near a wind-mill. On the knight's arrival, he said, "Sir, the Earl of Warwick, the Lord Stafford, the Lord Reginald Cobham, and the others who are about your son, are vigorously attacked by the French; and they entreat that you would come to their assistance with your battalion, for, if their numbers should increase, they fear he will have too much to do." The king replied, "Is my son dead, unhorsed, or so badly wounded that he cannot support himself?" "Nothing of the sort, thank God," rejoined the knight; "but he is in so hot an engagement that he has great need of your help." The king answered, "Now, Sir Thomas, return back to those that sent you, and tell them from me not to send again for me this day, or expect that I shall come, let what will happen, as long as my son has life; and say that I command them to let the boy win his spurs; for I am determined, if it please God, that all the glory and honor of this day shall be given to him and to those into whose care I have entrusted him." The knight returned to his lords and related the king's answer, which mightily encouraged them and made them repent they ever sent such a message.

Late after vespers, the King of France had not more about him than sixty men, every one included. Sir John of Hainault, who was of the number, had once remounted the king; for his horse had been killed under him by an arrow. He said to the king, "Sir, retreat whilst you have an opportunity, and do not expose yourself so simply; if you have lost this battle, another time you will be the conqueror." After he had said this, he took the bridle of the king's horse and led him off by force, for he had before entreated him to retire. The king rode on until he came to the castle of la Broyes, where he found the gates shut, for it was very dark. The king ordered the governor of it to be summoned. He came upon the battlements and asked who it was that called at such an hour. The king answered, "Open, open, governor; it is the fortune of France." The governor, hearing the king's voice, immediately descended, opened the gate, and let down the bridge. The king and his company entered the castle; but he had only with him five barons, Sir John of Hainault and four more. The king would not bury himself in such a place as that, but, having taken some refreshments, set out again with his attendants about midnight, and rode on, under the direction of guides who were well acquainted with the country, until, about daybreak, he came to Amiens, where he halted. This Saturday the English never quitted their ranks in pursuit of any one, but remained on the field, guarding their position and defending themselves against all who attacked them. The battle was ended at the hour of vespers.

When, on this Saturday night, the English heard no more hooting or shouting, nor any more crying out to particular lords or their banners, they looked upon the field as their own, and their enemies as beaten. They made great fires and lighted torches because of the obscurity of the night. King Edward then came down from his post, who all that day had not put on his helmet, and, with his whole battalion, advanced to the Prince of Wales, whom he embraced in his arms and kissed, and said, "Sweet son, God give you good perseverance; you are my son, for most loyally have you acquitted yourself this day; you are worthy to be a sovereign." The prince bowed down very low and humbled himself, giving all honor to the king, his father. The English during the night made frequent thanksgiving to the Lord for the happy issue of the day, and without rioting; for the king had forbidden all riot or noise.

At Crecy the Black Prince won his spurs, but the great achievement of his life was his victory at Poitiers —a battle fought by him alone with his army, when his father, Edward III, was absent from France in England. At the peace of Bretagne, agreed upon after the battle, several provinces were ceded by France to England, and these Edward added to his dominions in Guienne, and formed for himself a separate kingdom, which he ruled until his death. He never came to the throne of England; his son, Richard II, succeeded Edward III.

THE BATTLE OF POITIERS[12]

On Sunday morning, the King of France, who was very impatient to combat the English, ordered a solemn mass to be sung in his pavilion, and he and his four sons received the communion. Mass being over, there came to him many barons of France, as well as other great lords who held fiefs in the neighborhood, according to a summons they had received for a council. They were a considerable time debating; at last it was ordered that the whole army should advance into the plain, and that each lord should display his banner and push forward in the name of God and St. Denis. Upon this the trumpets of the army sounded, and every one got himself ready, mounted his horse, and made for that part of the plain where the king's banner was fluttering in the wind. There might be seen all the nobility of France, richly dressed out in brilliant armor, with banners and pennons gallantly displayed; for all the flower of the French nobility was there; no knight nor squire, for fear of dishonor, dared to remain at home. By the advice of the constable and the marshals, the army was divided into three battalions, each consisting of sixteen thousand men-at-arms, who had before shown themselves men of tried courage. The Duke of Orleans commanded the first battalion, where there were thirty-six banners and twice as many pennons. The second was under command of the Duke of Normandy, and his two brothers, the Lord Lewis and Lord John. The King of France commanded the third.

Whilst these battalions were forming, the king called to him the Lord Eustace de Ribeaumont, the Lord John de Landas, and the Lord Guiscard de Beaujeu, and

said to them, "Ride forward as near the English army as
you can, and observe their countenance, taking notice
of their numbers, and examine which will be the most
advantageous manner to combat them, whether on horseback or on foot." The three knights left the king to
obey his commands. The king was mounted on a white
palfrey, and, riding to the head of his army, said aloud,
"You men of Paris, Chartres, Rouen, and Orleans have
been used to threaten what you would do to the English if you could find them, and wished much to meet
them in arms; now that wish shall be granted. I will lead
you to them, and let us see how you will revenge yourselves for all the mischief and damage they have done
you. Be assured we will not part without fighting." Those
who heard him replied, "Sir, through God's assistance
we will most cheerfully meet them."

At this instant, the three knights returned, and pushing through the crowd, came to the king, who asked
what news they had brought. Sir Eustace de Ribeaumont,
whom his companions had requested to be their spokes-
man, answered, "Sir, we have observed accurately the
English; they may amount, according to our estimate,
to about two thousand men-at-arms, four thousand archers, and fifteen hundred footmen. They are in a very
strong position; but we do not imagine they can make
more than one battalion; nevertheless, they have posted
themselves with great judgment, have fortified all the
road along the hedge side, and lined the hedges with
part of their archers; for, as that is the only road for an
attack, one must pass through the midst of them. This
lane has no other entry; for it is so narrow that scarcely
can four men ride abreast in it. At the end of this
lane, amidst vines and thorns, where it is impossible to
ride or march in any regular order, are posted the
men-at-arms on foot; and they have drawn up before
them their archers in the manner of a harrow, so that it
will be no easy matter to defeat them." The king asked
in what manner they would advise him to attack them.
"Sir," replied Sir Eustace, "on foot; except three hundred of the most expert, to break, if possible, this body
of archers; and then your battalions must advance quickly
on foot, attack the men-at-arms hand to hand, and com-

bat them valiantly. This is the best advice that I can give you, and if any one know a better, let him say it." The king replied, "Thus shall it be, then." And, in company with his two marshals, he rode from battalion to battalion and selected, in conformity to their opinions, three hundred knights and squires of the greatest repute in his army, each well armed and mounted on the best of horses. Soon after, the battalion of the Germans was formed, who were to remain on horseback, to assist the marshals; they were commanded by the Earls of Salzburg, Neydo, and Nassau. King John was armed in royal armor, and nineteen others like him.

When the battalions of the King of France were drawn up, and each lord posted under his proper banner, and informed how they were to act, it was ordered that all those who were armed with lances should shorten them to the length of five feet, that they might be the more manageable and that every one should take off his spurs. As the French were on the point of marching to their enemies, the Cardinal of Perigord, who had left Poitiers that morning early, came full gallop to the king, making him a low reverence, and entreated him that he might be allowed to go to the Prince of Wales, to endeavor to make peace between him and the King of France. The king answered, "It is very agreeable to us; but make haste back again."

So then the cardinal set off and went in all speed to the prince; but though he spent all this Sunday in riding from one army to another, he could not make terms which were thought honorable alike by the king and by the Prince of Wales. That same day, the French kept in their quarters, where they lived at their ease, having plenty of provisions; whilst the English, on the other hand, were but badly off, nor did they know whither to go for forage, as they were so straitly kept by the French they could not move without danger. This Sunday they made many mounds and ditches round where the archers were posted, the better to secure them.

On Monday morning, the prince and his army were soon in readiness, and as well arranged as on the former day. The French were also drawn out by sunrise. The cardinal, returning again that morning, imagined that by his exhortations he could pacify both parties; but the French told him to return when he pleased and not attempt bringing them any more treaties or pacifications, else worse might betide him. When the cardinal saw that he labored in vain, he took leave of the King of France and set out towards the Prince of Wales, to whom he said, "Fair son, exert yourself as much as possible, for there must be a battle; I cannot by any means pacify the King of France." The prince replied, "that such were the intentions of him and his army; and God defend the right." The cardinal then took leave of him and returned to Poitiers.

The arrangement of the prince's army, in respect to the battalions, was exactly the same as what the three knights before named had related to the King of France, except that at this time he had ordered some valiant and intelligent knights to remain on horseback, similar to the battalion of the French marshals, and had also commanded three hundred men-at-arms, and as many archers on horseback, to post themselves on the right, on a small hill, that was not too steep nor too high, and, by passing over its summit, to get round the wings of the Duke of Normandy's battalions, who was in person at the foot of it. These were all the alterations the prince had made in his order of battle; he himself was with the main body, in the midst of the vineyards, the whole completely armed, with their horses near, if there should be any occasion for them. They had fortified and inclosed the weaker parts with their wagons and baggage.

And when the Prince of Wales saw, from the departure of the cardinal without being able to obtain any honorable terms, that a battle was inevitable, and that the King of France held both him and his army in great contempt, he thus addressed himself to them: "Now, my gallant fellows, what though we be a small body when compared to the army of our enemies; do not let us be cast down on that account, for victory does not always follow numbers, but where the Almighty God pleases to bestow it. If, through good fortune, the day shall be ours, we will gain the greatest honor and glory in this world; if the contrary should happen, and we be slain, I have a father and beloved brethren alive, and you all have some relations or good friends, who will

be sure to revenge our deaths. I therefore entreat of
you to exert yourselves and combat manfully; for, if it
please God and St. George, you shall see me this day
act like a true knight." By such words and arguments as
these the prince harangued his men, as did the marshals,
by his orders, so that they were all in high spirits. Sir
John Chandos placed himself near the prince, to guard
and advise him; and never, during that day, would he
on any account quit his post.

The Lord James Audley remained also a considerable
time near him; but, when he saw that they must certainly engage, he said to the prince: "Sir, I have ever
served most loyally my lord your father and yourself,
and shall continue so to do as long as I have life. Dear
sir, I must now acquaint you that formerly I made a
vow, if ever I should be engaged in any battle where the
king, your father, or any of his sons were, that I would
be the foremost in the attack, and the best combatant on
his side, or die in the attempt. I beg, therefore, most
earnestly, as a reward for any services I may have done,
that you would grant me permission honorably to quit
you, that I may post myself in such wise to accomplish
my vow." The prince granted this request and, holding out his hand to him, said: "Sir James, God grant
that this day you may shine in valor above all other
knights." The knight then set off and posted himself at
the front of the battalion, with only four squires whom
he had detained with him to guard his person. The Lord
James was a prudent and valiant knight; and by his
advice the army had thus been drawn up in order of
battle. The Lord James began to advance, in order to
fight with the battalion of the marshals. Sir Eustace
d'Ambreticourt, being mounted, placed his lance in its
rest and, fixing his shield, struck spurs into his horse
and galloped up to this battalion. A German knight, perceiving Sir Eustace quit his army, left his battalion that
was under the command of Earl John of Nassau, and
made up to him. The shock of their meeting was so
violent that they both fell to the ground. The German was
wounded in the shoulder, so that he could not rise again
so nimbly as Sir Eustace, who, when upon his legs, after
he had taken breath, was hastening to the knight that
lay on the ground; but five German men-at-arms came

upon him, struck him down, and made him prisoner.
They led him to those that were attached to the Earl of
Nassau, who did not pay much attention to him, nor do
I know if they made him swear himself their prisoner;
but they tied him to a car with some of their harness.

The engagement now began on both sides, and the battalion of the marshals was advancing before those who
were intended to break the battalion of the archers, and
had entered the lane where the hedges on both sides
were lined by the archers, who, as soon as they saw
them fairly entered, began shooting with their bows in
such an excellent manner from each side of the hedge
that the horses, smarting under the pain of the wounds
made by their bearded arrows, would not advance, but
turned about, and, by their unruliness, threw their
masters, who could not manage them; nor could those
that had fallen get up again for the confusion, so that
this battalion of the marshals could never approach
that of the prince. However, there were some knights
and squires so well mounted that, by the strength of
their horses, they passed through and broke the
hedge, but, in spite of their efforts, could not get up
to the battalion of the prince. The Lord James Audley,
attended by his four squires, had placed himself, sword
in hand, in front of this battalion much before the rest,
and was performing wonders. He had advanced through
his eagerness so far that he engaged the Lord Arnold
d'Andreghen, marshal of France, under his banner when
they fought a considerable time, and the Lord Arnold
was roughly enough treated. The battalion of the marshals
was soon after put to the rout by the arrows of the
archers and the assistance of the men-at-arms, who
rushed among them as they were struck down and seized
and slew them at their pleasure. The Lord Arnold
d'Andreghen was there made prisoner, but by others
than the Lord James Audley or his four squires, for that
knight never stopped to make any one his prisoner that
day, but was the whole time employed in fighting and
following his enemies. In another part, the Lord John
Clermont fought under his banner as long as he was able,
but being struck down, he could neither get up again nor
procure his ransom; he was killed on the spot. In a
short time, this battalion of the marshals was totally dis-

comfited; for they fell back so much on each other that
the army could not advance, and those who were in the
rear, not being able to get forward, fell back upon the
battalion commanded by the Duke of Normandy, which
was broad and thick in the front, but it was soon thin
enough in the rear; for when they learnt that the marshals had been defeated, they mounted their horses and
set off. At this time, a body of English came down from
the hill, and, passing along the battalions on horseback,
accompanied by a large body of archers, fell upon one
of the wings of the Duke of Normandy's division. To
say the truth, the English archers were of infinite service to their army, for they shot so thickly and so well
that the French did not know what way to turn themselves to avoid their arrows. By this means they kept
advancing by little and little and gained ground. When
the English men-at-arms perceived that the first battalion
was beaten, and that the one under the Duke of Normandy was in disorder and beginning to open, they
hastened to mount their horses, which they had ready
prepared close at hand. As soon as they were all
mounted, they gave a shout of "St. George for Guienne!"
and Sir John Chandos said to the prince, "Sir, sir, now
push forward, for the day is ours. God will this day put
it in your hand. Let us make for our adversary, the King
of France; for where he is will lie the main stress of
the business. I well know that his valor will not let him
fly; and he will remain with us, if it please God and St.
George; but he must be well fought with, and you have
before said that you would show yourself this day a good
knight." The prince replied: "John, get forward; you
shall not see me turn my back this day, but I will always be among the foremost." He then said to Sir Walter
Woodland, his banner-bearer, "Banner, advance, in the
name of God and St. George." The knight obeyed the
commands of the prince; and the prince upon this
charged the division of the Duke of Athens, and very
sharp the encounter was, so that many were beaten
down. The French, who fought in large bodies, cried out,
"Montjoye St. Dennis!" and the English answered them
with "St. George for Guienne!" The prince next met the
battalion of Germans under command of the Earl of
Salzburg, the Earl of Nassau, and the Earl of Neydo;

but they were soon overthrown and put to flight. The English archers shot so well that none dared to come within reach of their arrows, and they put to death many who could not ransom themselves. Then the above-named earls were slain there, as well as many other knights and squires attached to them. In the confusion, Sir Eustace d'Ambreticourt was rescued by his own men, who remounted him. He afterwards performed many gallant deeds of arms and made good captures that day.

When the battalion of the Duke of Normandy saw the prince advancing so quick upon them, they bethought themselves how to escape. The sons of the king, the Duke of Normandy, the Earl of Poitiers, and the Earl of Touraine, who were very young, too easily believed what those under whose management they were placed said to them. However, the Lord Guiscard d'Angle and Sir John de Saintré, who were near the earl of Poitiers, would not fly, but rushed into the thickest of the combat. The three sons of the king, according to the advice given them, galloped away, with upwards of eighty lances who had never been near the enemy, and took the road to Chavigny.

Now the king's battalion advanced in good order to meet the English; many hard blows were given with swords, battle-axes, and other warlike weapons. The King of France, with the Lord Philip, his youngest son, attacked the division of the marshals, the Earls of Warwick and Suffolk, and in this combat were engaged many very noble lords on both sides.

The Lord James Audley, with the assistance of his four squires, was always engaged in the heat of the battle. He was severely wounded in the body, head, and face; and, as long as his breath permitted him, he maintained the fight and advanced forward. He continued to do so until he was covered with blood. Then, towards the close of the engagement, his four squires, who were his body guard, took him, and led him out of the engagement, very weak and wounded, towards a hedge, that he might cool and take breath. They disarmed him as gently as they could, in order to examine his wounds, dress them, and sew up the most serious.

It often happens that fortune in war and love turns out more favorable and wonderful than could have been hoped for or expected. To say the truth, this battle, which was fought near Poitiers, in the plains of Beauvoir and Maupertuis, was very bloody and perilous. Many gallant deeds of arms were performed that were never known, and the combatants on either side suffered much. King John himself did wonders. He was armed with a battle-axe, with which he fought and defended himself; and if a fourth of his people had behaved as well, the day would have been his own. The Earl of Tancarville, in endeavoring to break through the crowd, was made prisoner close to him, as were also Sir James de Bourbon, Earl of Ponthieu, and the Lord John d'Artois, Earl of Eu. The pursuit continued even to the gates of Poitiers, where there was much slaughter and overthrow of men and horses; for the inhabitants of Poitiers had shut their gates and would suffer none to enter; upon which account there was great butchery on the causeway before the gate, where such numbers were killed or wounded that several surrendered themselves the moment they spied an Englishman; and there were many English archers who had four, five, or six prisoners.

There was much pressing at this time through eagerness to take the king; and those who were nearest to him and knew him, cried out, "Surrender yourself, surrender yourself, or you are a dead man." In that part of the field was a young knight from St. Omer, who was engaged by a salary in the service of the King of England. His name was Denys de Morbeque, who for five years had attached himself to the English on account of having been banished in his younger days from France for a murder committee in an affray at St. Omer. It fortunately happened for this knight that he was at the time near to the King of France when he was so much pulled about. He, by dint of force, for he was very strong and robust, pushed through the crowd and said to the king in very good French, "Sire, sire, surrender yourself." The king, who found himself very disagreeably situated, turning to him, asked, "To whom shall I surrender myself; to whom? Where is my cousin, the Prince of Wales? If I could see him, I would speak to him." "Sire," replied Sir Denys, "he is not here; but surrender yourself to me, and I will lead you to him." "Who are you?" said the king. "Sire, I am Denys de Morbeque, a knight from Artois, but I serve the King of England because I cannot belong to France, having forfeited all I possess there." The king then gave him his right-hand glove and said, "I surrender myself to you." There was much crowding and pushing about, for every one was eager to cry out, "I have taken him." Neither the king nor his youngest son Philip were able to get forward and free themselves from the throng.

The Prince of Wales, who was as courageous as a lion, took great delight that day to combat his enemies. Sir John Chandos, who was near his person and had never quitted it during the whole of the day, nor stopped to take any prisoners, said to him toward the end of the battle, "Sir, it will be proper for you to halt here and plant your banner on the top of this bush, which will serve to rally your forces that seem very much scattered; for I do not see any banners or pennons of the French, nor any considerable bodies able to rally against us; and you must refresh yourself a little, as I perceive you are very much heated." Upon this, the banner of the prince was placed on a high bush; the minstrels began to play, and trumpets and clarions to do their duty. The prince took off his helmet, and the knights attendant on his person and belonging to his chamber were soon ready, and pitched a small pavilion of crimson color, which the prince entered. Liquor was then brought to him and the other knights who were with him. They increased every moment; for they were returning from the pursuit, and stopped there, surrounded by their prisoners.

As soon as the two marshals were come back, the prince asked them if they knew anything of the King of France. They replied, "No, sir, not for a certainty; but we believe he must be either killed or taken prisoner, since he has never quitted his battalion." The prince then, addressing the Earl of Warwick and Lord Cobham, said, "I beg of you to mount your horses and ride over the field, so that on your return you may bring me some certain intelligence of him." The two barons, immediately mounting their horses, left the prince and made for a small hillock, that they might look about them. From their stand they perceived a crowd of men-at-arms on foot, who were advancing very slowly. The King of France was in the midst of them, and in great danger; for the

French and Gascons had taken him from Sir Denys de Morbeque and were disputing who should have him, the stoutest bawling out, "It is I who have got him." "No, no," replied the others, "we have him." The king, to escape this peril, said, "Gentlemen, gentlemen, I pray you conduct me and my son in a courteous manner to my cousin the prince; and do not make such a riot over my capture, for I am so great a lord that I can make all sufficiently rich." These words, and others which fell from the king, appeased them a little, but the disputes were always beginning again, and they did not move a step without rioting. When the two barons saw this troop of people, they descended from the hillock and, sticking spurs into their horses, made up to them. On their arrival, they asked what was the matter. They were answered that it was the King of France, who had been made prisoner, and that upwards of ten knights and squires challenged him at the same time as belonging to each of them. The two barons then pushed through the crowd by main force and ordered all to draw aside. They commanded, in the name of the prince and under pain of instant death, that every one should keep his distance and not approach unless ordered or desired so to do. They all retreated behind the king; and the two barons, dismounting, advanced to the king with profound reverence and conducted him in a peaceable manner to the Prince of Wales.

Soon after the Earl of Warwick and the Lord Reginald Cobham had left the prince, as has been above related, he inquired from those knights around him of Lord James Audley, and asked if any one knew what was become of him. "Yes, sir," replied some of the company, "he is very badly wounded, and is lying in a litter hard by." "By my troth," replied the prince, "I am sore vexed that he is so wounded. See, I beg of you, if he be able to bear being carried hither; otherwise I will come and visit him." Two knights directly left the prince, and, coming to Lord James, told him how desirous the prince was of seeing him. "A thousand thanks to the prince," answered Lord James, "for condescending to remember so poor a knight as myself." He then called eight of his servants and had himself borne in his litter to where the prince was. When he was come into his presence, the prince bent down over him and embraced him, saying, "My lord James, I am bound to honor you very much, for by your valor this day you have acquired glory and renown above us all, and your prowess has proved you the bravest knight." Lord James replied, "My lord, you have a right to say whatever you please, but I wish it were as you have said. If I have this day been forward to serve you, it has been to accomplish a vow that I had made, and ought not to be so much thought of." "Sir James," answered the prince, "I and all the rest of us deem you the bravest knight on our side in this battle; and to increase your renown and furnish you withal to pursue your career of glory in war, I retain you henceforward forever as my knight, with five hundred marcs of yearly revenue, which I will secure to you from my estates in England." "Sir," said Lord James, "God make me deserving of the good fortune you bestow upon me." At these words, he took leave of the prince, as he was very weak, and his servants carried him back to his tent. He could not have been at a great distance when the Earl of Warwick and Lord Reginald Cobham entered the pavilion of the prince and presented the King of France to him. The prince made a very low obeisance to the king and gave him as much comfort as he was able, which he well knew how to administer. He ordered wine and spices to be brought, which he presented to the king himself, as a mark of great affection.

Thus was this battle won, as you have heard related, in the plains of Maupertuis, two leagues from the city of Poitiers, on the 19th day of September, 1356. It commenced about nine o'clock, and was ended by noon; but the English were not all returned from the pursuit, and it was to recall his people that the prince had placed his banner upon a high bush. They did not return till late after vespers from pursuing the enemy. It was reported that all the flower of French knighthood was slain, and that, with the king and his son the Lord Philip, seventeen earls, without counting barons, knights, or squires, were made prisoners, and from five to six thousand of all sorts left dead in the field. When they were all collected, they found they had twice as many prisoners as themselves. They therefore consulted, if, considering the risk they might run, it would not be more advisable to ransom them on the spot. This was done; and the prisoners found the English and Gascons very civil; for there were many set at liberty that day on their promise of coming to Bordeaux before Christmas to pay their ransom.

When all were returned to their banners, they retired to their camp, which was adjoining to the field of battle. Some disarmed themselves and did the same to their prisoners, to whom they showed every kindness; for whoever made any prisoners, they were solely at his disposal to ransom or not, as he pleased. It may be easily supposed that all those who accompanied the prince were very rich in glory and wealth, as well by the ransoms of his prisoners as by the quantities of gold and silver plate, rich jewels, and trunks stuffed full of belts that were weighty from their gold and silver ornaments and furred mantles. They set no value on armor, tents, or other things; for the French had come there as magnificently and richly dressed as if they had been sure of gaining the victory.

When the Lord James Audley was brought back to his tent after having most respectfully thanked the prince for his gift, he did not remain long before he sent for his brother, Sir Peter Audley, and some more. They were all of his relations. He then sent for his four squires that had attended upon him that day, and, addressing himself to the knights, said: "Gentlemen, it has pleased my lord the prince to give me five hundred marcs as a yearly inheritance, for which gift I have done him very trifling bodily service. You see here these four squires who have always served me most loyally, and especially in this day's engagement. What glory I may have gained has been through their means and by their valor, on which account I wish to reward them. I therefore give and resign into their hands the gift of five hundred marcs which my lord the prince has been pleased to bestow on me, in the same form and manner that it has been presented to me. I disinherit myself of it and give it to them simply and without a possibility of revoking it." The knights looked on each other and said, "It is becoming the noble mind of Lord James to make such a gift;" and then unanimously added: "May the Lord God remember you for it! We will bear witness of this gift to them wheresoever and whensoever they may call upon us." They then took leave of him, when some went to the Prince of Wales, who that night was to give a supper to the King of France from his own provisions; for the French had brought vast quantities with them, which were now fallen into the hands of the English, many of whom had not tasted bread for the last three days.

When evening was come, the Prince of Wales gave a supper in his pavilion to the King of France and to the greater part of the princes and barons who were prisoners. The prince seated the King of France and his son the Lord Philip at an elevated and well-covered table; and with them were some other French lords of high rank. The other knights and squires were placed at different tables. The prince himself served the king's table, as well as the others, with every mark of humility, and would not sit down at it, in spite of all his entreaties for him to do so, saying that he was not worthy of such an honor, nor did it appertain to him to seat himself at the table of so great a king or of so valiant a man as he had shown himself by his actions that day. He added also, with a noble air: "Dear sir, do not make a poor meal because the Almighty God has not gratified your wishes in the event of this day; for be assured that my lord and father will show you every honor and friendship in his power and will arrange for your ransom so reasonably that you will henceforward always remain friends. In my opinion, you have cause to be glad that the success of this battle did not turn out as you desired; for you have this day acquired such high renown for prowess that you have surpassed all the best knights on your side. I do not, dear sir, say this to flatter you, for all those of our side who have seen and observed the actions of each party have unanimously allowed this to be your due, and decree you the prize and garland for it." At the end of this speech, there were murmurs of praise heard from every one; and the French said the prince had spoken truly and nobly, and that he would be one of the most gallant princes in Christendom if God should grant him life to pursue his career of glory.

NOTES

1. From the revised edition of *The Age of Chivalry,* by Edward Everett Hale, published in 1884.

2. Richard I (Lion-Heart) of England (1157–1199).

3. The preceding narrative is taken from the chronicle of Richard of Devizes; what follows is from the chronicle of Geoffrey of Vinsauf. The latter is the English chronicler of the Third Crusade, history and itinerary of King Richard I (1189–92), which followed the capture of Jerusalem (1187) by Saladin. This Crusade ended with a truce between Richard and Saladin. The English chronicler is usually called Geoffrey de Winesalf. But see *The Romance of Richard the Lion-Hearted,* tr. and ed. by Bradford B. Broughton, Dutton (New York, 1966), pp. 147–229.

4. The term *Saracens* in the Middle Ages applied commonly to Moslems (Arabs, Moors, Seljuk Turks). They won the Crusades, of course. *Bedouin* is Arabic for "desert dwellers." The Bedouins Richard met were a Semitic, nomadic people of Arabia, converted to Islam.

5. The Knights Hospitalers and Knights Templar were the principal Crusading Orders who fought for the Latin Kingdom of Jerusalem and for the Christian rulers and pilgrims who sought to own Jerusalem, control it, and defend it against Islam.

6. There were five Kings of Jerusalem named Baldwin. They defended their Latin Kingdom from 1100 to 1186. The next year Saladin (1137–*c.*1193) conquered the Crusader kingdom. He was the Sultan of Egypt, and by far the more chivalrous warrior.

7. It is customary to give a catalogue of heroes to whom the author's favorite (in this case, King Richard I) can be compared, as here: Hercules (vs. Antaeus), Achilles, Hector, Alexander the Great, Charlemagne's Roland, Judas Maccabeus, and Richard.

8. The verses came from the English poet Michael Drayton (1563–1631), who was famous for historical, lyric, and pastoral poetry.

9. Thomas Percy (1729–1811) is the English scholar and clergyman who collected *Reliques of Ancient English Poetry* (3 vols., 1765): 175 English and Scottish ballads thus saved for posterity.

10. Sir Henry Percy (1364–1403) is the character named Hotspur in William Shakespeare's play *Henry IV.* Hotspur died in battle against the king.

11. King Edward III (1312–1377) of England and son, the Black Prince (1330–1376), on August 26, 1346, defeated King Philippe VI of France (1293–1350), and the flower of French chivalry, at Crécy-en-Ponthieu, Somme, northern France.

12. At Poitiers, the ancient capital of Poitou in western France, in 1356, Edward the Black Prince defeated French and Burgundian chivalry. But it was Joan of Arc who defeated England, saved France (1429), and won the Hundred Years War.

LEGENDS OF CHARLEMAGNE

OR

ROMANCE OF THE MIDDLE AGES

How Agrican with all his northern powers
Besieged Albracca, as romances tell;
The city of Galaphron, from thence to win
The fairest of her sex, Angelica,
His daughter, loved of many prowest knights,
Both paynim, and the peers of Charlemain.

Paradise Lost

PREFACE

Besides the education which schools and colleges impart, there is still another kind necessary to completeness. It is that which has for its object a knowledge of polite literature. In the intercourse of polished society, a young person will more frequently need an acquaintance with the creations of fancy than with the discoveries of science or the speculations of philosophy.

In an age when intellectual darkness enveloped Western Europe, a constellation of brilliant writers arose in Italy. Of these, Pulci (born in 1431), Boiardo (1434), and Ariosto (1474) took for their subjects the romantic fables which had for many ages been transmitted in the lays of bards and the legends of monkish chroniclers. These fables they arranged in order, adorned with the embellishments of fancy, amplified from their own invention, and stamped with immortality. It may safely be asserted that, as long as civilization shall endure, these productions will retain their place among the most cherished creations of human genius.

In two previous works, *The Age of Fable* and *The Age of Chivalry,* the author of this volume has endeavored to supply to the modern reader such knowledge of the fables of classical and mediæval literature as is needed to render intelligible the allusions which occur in reading and conversation. This volume is intended to carry out the same design. Like its predecessors, it aspires to a higher character than that of a work of mere amusement. It claims to be useful, in acquainting its readers with the subjects of the works of the great poets of Italy. Some knowledge of these is expected of every well-educated young person.

In reading these romances, we cannot fail to observe how the primitive inventions have been used, again and

377

again, by successive generations of fabulists. The Siren of Ulysses is the prototype of the Siren of Orlando, and the character of Circe reappears in Alcina. The fountains of Love and Hatred may be traced to the story of Cupid and Psyche; and similar effects produced by a magic draught appear in the tale of Tristram and Isoude, and, substituting a flower for the draught, in Shakespeare's "Midsummer Night's Dream." There are many other instances of the same kind which the reader will recognize without our assistance.

The sources whence we derive these stories are, first, the Italian poets named above; next, the "Romans de Chevalerie" of the Comte de Tressan; lastly, certain German collections of popular tales. Some chapters have been borrowed from Leigh Hunt's Translations from the Italian Poets. It seemed unnecessary to do over again what he had already done so well; yet, on the other hand, those stories could not be omitted from the series without leaving it incomplete.

T. B.

INTRODUCTION

Now finally we are in full romance. The hero Orlando will go mad, not from combat fatigue, but from the pains of love. And here we are, in pseudo-history, among recognizable personages like King Arthur and Charlemagne, and having a real topography, with landmarks that we also recognize, in countries near and/or very distant. We have our heroical hero Orlando, who was Charlemagne's warrior Roland—mad or sane. And we have always succumbed to the allure of an Oriental Princess like Angelica.

Our primary, poetical author is Ludovico Ariosto (1474–1533), an Italian. He was a contemporary of other renowned achievers of the Renaissance: Christopher Columbus and Amerigo Vespucci, and other Italians like Raphael, Leonardo da Vinci, and Michelangelo. Ariosto's own great achievement was a poem in which the hero Orlando goes mad for love. The poem was written in *ottava rima,* eight verses to a stanza, rhymed AB AB AB CC. The poetic form, and this scenario, were borrowed from earlier Italian poets named Boiardo (1441–1494) and Luigi Pulci (1432–1484). The latter sets a stage for us: We are as of now in Charlemagne's Palace Court around the year 800, *ottava-rima* style, Lord Byron translating Pulci:

VIII.
Twelve paladins had Charles in court, of whom
    The wisest and most famous was Orlando;
Him the traitor Gan conducted to the tomb
    In Roncesvalles, as the villain plann'd too,
While the horn rang so loud and knell'd the doom
    Of their sad rout, though he did all knight can do;
And Dante in his comedy has given
    To him a happy seat with Charles in heaven.

The great Byron struggles here, as we see. *Whom-tomb-doom* are not bad. *Orlando-too-do* are less good. *Given-heaven,* passable. However, Sir John Harrington has been since 1591 the prime translator of Ariosto's *Orlando Furioso,* a task he performed at the request of Her Majesty, Queen Elizabeth I. Royalty then much admired both romantic subject and poetic form. Lancelot, like Orlando, had earlier been driven mad, more probably by combat fatigue, however, or by his failure to be crowned King of the Grail Castle.

The three Italian poets wrote voluminously—some forty thousand verses about a lovesick Orlando, who in Lancelot's style went furiously insane. Both Boiardo and Ariosto served the tastes of high nobility as the Arthurian poets from France had served under the patronage of King Henry II of England and his noble French queen, Eleanor. They served the ducal House of Este in Ferrara, which had already ruled that city and dukedom for some three hundred years.

Their prime subject was Orlando in love—so much in love that he really did go mad. The ladies in Ferrara probably felt very gratified to have this power over a great hero-warrior-courtier.

Love is the internal story, however. Externally, the subject is war. Politically, Charlemagne and his deputy Roland (Orlando in Italian) are fighting Saracens. Now, you might say: "Yes, but Charlemagne fought 'Saracens' at 'Roncesvalles' in the Pyrenees Mountains between France and Spain some years before 800. Are we with Charlemagne (c.800) or now in the sixteenth century with the Este family?" So saying, you will have put your finger on the problem here. The answer is both.

One should really never mention in one sentence these two areas of thought, history and romance. Yes, Charlemagne was crowned emperor by the pope in the year 800; he fought Moors in Spain; they were Moslems. Ariosto stretches a point when he writes, in apparent disregard of history, that Charlemagne fought "Saracens" in Africa. In Ariosto's romance, then, Charlemagne, the Saracens, and Orlando/Roland are all legendary.

War is one of our two prime subjects. The real war that underlies Ariosto's poem is the fall of Constantinople to Islamic warriors in 1453, which catastrophe also plunged Europe into panic. The failure of the Crusades—in no small measure the fault of the Lion-Hearted Richard I—had opened the gates of western Europe to conquest by Islam. The real war is East vs. West, Christian vs. Moslem.

The real Charlemagne, Patrician of Rome, was King of the Franks (768–814), and Emperor of the West (800–814). He was the grandson of Charles Martel (*c.*688–741), who had won what everybody in the West has always considered one of the decisive victories of history: the Battle of Tours (France) in 732. At that royal city of towers, Martel turned back the Moorish invasion of France. Charlemagne had also done his share by defeating "Saracens" at the gates of Spain before 800.

The hero Roland, whom Charlemagne left in command of his rear guard, died there in the Pyrenees and was interred in the celebrated Romanesque cathedral of Saint Sernin at Toulouse. If so, he also was historical. Charlemagne's chronicler Einhard (or Eginhard) called the hero not Roland but "Hruodlandus." Einhard (*c.*770–840) was a Frankish scholar at Charlemagne's famous Palace School at Aachen (Aix-la-Chapelle in French). His Roland is the hero of one of the world's most gorgeous epics, *The Song of Roland* (translated in *Medieval Myths* by Norma Lorre Goodrich, Meridian, 1994). In the epic Roland is affianced to a lady named Aude. He is not madly or otherwise particularly attached to her. He never cries her name at the hour of his very oratorical death, but loudly the name of his dear friend-in-arms, Olivier. It is Aude who loves Roland madly. She demands her fiancé be returned to wed her. She refuses to accept Charlemagne's excuse. "Produce him," she shrieks. Finally, but sooner than later, she drops dead from unrequited love. This drama has besmirched Charlemagne's name. Now everybody wants to know how, and why, and wherefore Charlemagne "lost" Roland and the rear guard down in those passes of the gruesome Pyrenees—very impressive, very dark, volcanic mountains. We never know why Roland died there.

Not content to leave it at that, Ariosto takes us another giant step back in time to *c.*400–500, the Dark Ages

of King Arthur. Thus, the writers of romances in the
Renaissance come to join novelists in the twentieth century, both purposely disorienting the reader by utilizing
the techniques of an upset chronology: *"une chronologie
bouleversée."* Ariosto moves from Charlemagne back to
the early Dark Ages when King Arthur fought invasions
into Britain while his contemporary across the Channel
was King Clovis I (481–511), who founded the Frankish
monarchy. It was Clovis, ancestor of Charlemagne, who
defeated Romans and expelled them from Gaul, which
he re-baptized as "France." In a chronic war King Clovis
defeated Romans, Germans, Burgundians, and Visigoths
to found a kingdom that endured for four hundred years.
In 496 Clovis was baptized Christian at the request of
his devout queen, Clotilda, who then retired to a convent
for the rest of her life. Their four sons followed him on
the throne of France. These invasion years, which Ariosto keeps constantly in his readers' minds, are appropri-
ately called "The Age of Clovis" in France and "The
Age of Arthur" in Britain.

Neither period was an age of courtly love—far from
it—despite Sir Thomas Malory's attempts to modernize
Arthurian Britain. Nor were the members of the court
of King Clovis or the palace court of Charlemagne, to
which that Emperor summoned serious historians and
theologians from western cathedral schools, under any
compulsion to go mad for love. Even Lancelot, a fellow
pupil of Arthur's Queen Guinevere, was obliged to do
her military service, much as the feudal order of Charlemagne's time required his vassals to perform for him.
Unable to stomach the barbarity of the Dark Ages, great
ladies like Saint Bridget and Saint Clotilda chose the
convent. In Ariosto's scenario they go gallivanting mer-
rily through "pretty" forests that have been cleansed of
brigands and rapists.

In Ariosto's *Orlando Furioso* we have three, recurring,
principal themes that are intricately interwoven. Despite
a skewed geography of fairly familiar names, we are in-
volved really and seriously in a long war that could be
called "The Defense of Europe from Asia." (The Hellespont, with the ruins of the City Troy upon its palisade,
has divided us again.) Or it could be called "Christianity

vs. Islam." Therefore, Ariosto is justified in setting up for us the great confrontations of history as he chooses to address them, romantically:

1. *King Arthur vs. Anglo-Saxon invasions of Great Britain.* Result: Arthur died and the Saxons kept coming.

2. *Charlemagne vs. the Moors in Spain.* Result: Charlemagne died, and the Moors remained in Spain for some seven hundred years.

3. *The Crusaders vs. Saladin and other Asian and African Moslems.* Result: the Crusaders died, and Islam held Jerusalem. Despite the victory of Godefroy de Bouillon, King Baldwin I, and Tancred of Sicily in the First Crusade (1095–99), the Holy Sepulcher and tomb of Christ passed out of Christian control.

The masked, underlying theme of *Orlando Furioso* is the series of disasters following the fall of Jerusalem. Having failed to defeat Charles Martel and then his descendant Charlemagne at the Straits of Gibraltar, which is the western entrance from Asia (via Africa) into Europe, the warriors of Islam returned to the eastern gate. Crossing the Hellespont, they took Constantinople by storm in 1453, and changed its name to Istanbul.

Constantinople had reigned as capital of the Byzantine Empire, a second Rome, from the victories of Constantine the Great (A.D. 324) until its conquest by the Turks in 1453. Chroniclers in far-distant France only heard the terrible news on Christmas Eve, 1453, while the French king was hosting a masquerade party. The horror and grief experienced at that instant by the courtiers and their sovereigns can hardly be imagined, much less expressed now.

This disaster was followed by the advance into central Europe of Islamic warriors: Hungary (1521), Germany (1532), until a naval victory by Italians and allies won the battle of Lepanto (October 7, 1571). There the Turkish navy was clearly defeated.

Even while Ariosto was writing *Orlando Furioso,* early in the sixteenth century, the French army under their King Charles VIII was invading Italy. Nor did they retreat until the following year. Understandably, then, war is the prime preoccupation of Ariosto. Our question follows logically: Why all this preoccupation with Orlando going insane because of his love for the lovely Angelica, just because she does not return his affection?

Ariosto has countered our objections (in Sir John Harrington's translation):

> Yet when a man is bent to speak his worst
> That in despite he can of women say,
> He calls them but incontinent and cursed;
> No greater fault he to their charge can lay.[1]

Both Hesiod and the Bible have explained why all women were accursed forever, but the charge of incontinence on their parts seems strange. When Orlando goes mad for unrequited love, how can Ariosto charge to women an inability to restrain their passions, and especially their sexual appetites?

Harrington's editor, Rudolf Gottfried, has a most satisfactory answer. The poet had completed his stanza by accusing men: they rob and despoil, break into and burst open houses; they betray cities, countries, and towns; they commit murder and practice usury. Women, says Harrington, are free of such sins. Such crimes, he said, are "proper to men."

Gottfried explains in his Introduction (p. 16ff.) that irony underlies Ariosto's poem, and that this irony, which we too find ridiculous, was so intended. The Italian poet speaks tongue in cheek. His irony is at times comic, as here, but also commonly pathetic and/or violent. When Ariosto needles contemporary woman-haters, he laughs secretly to himself, thinking that if the coats fits, they can put it on. When they act like fools, they are pathetic. When they love killing, shedding blood, piling high hordes of corpses, then that exaggerated violence turns the readers' admiration sour. Even the hero Ruggiero (or Rogero) looks plain silly, flying around on his monstrous and uncontrollable "griffith horse" (p. 133). And the wise priestess Melissa ("Her gown ungirt, her hair about her head," p. 71) is inappropriately dressed to be quoting Merlin and the Lady of the Lake, and viewing their sacred tombs. And Harrington makes matters worse by having Merlin's "dead carcass" reside there beside his "living soul," and then prophesy.

Poor Harrington labored for eleven years to translate thirty-three thousand verses of Ariosto, leaving the English short by six thousand. Perhaps he was consoled by his own irony for an unsuccessful career and the punishment of unrewarded and unappreciated work. Perhaps he took comfort in Ariosto's attacks, comical, pathetic, and/or violent, against court life in Italy, which doubtless much resembled Harrington's perception of court life in Elizabethan England. For all her virtues, Queen Elizabeth I, godmother of our Harrington, was a murderous queen. Court life there as abroad thrived upon malice, jealousy, and evil. Thus, Ariosto made use, as Gottfried saw it, of an otherwise chaotic and often senseless world.

Ariosto amply illustrates the chaos created by young lovers and their foolishness in the two major love stories that come and go across the complicated web of this fiction. One brilliantly colored thread tells the triumphs and defeats of a love that should have led to the altar, a happy ending, orange blossoms, and white lace for Angelica, as a bride for her suitor, Orlando. The poet here seems to have envisioned this glamorous and desirable heroine as a Chinese beauty. Centuries before, the Sultans of Persia had sought to marry such lovely girls. The Persian Rustam also wedded one such and remained by her side until she was properly pregnant. She bore and raised by herself the hero Sohrab. Despite her Latin name, Angelica is also identified by Ariosto as "Circassian," which makes her Islamic and a Turk; but then later as born in (Marco Polo's) Cathay, which would make her Chinese. Romance simply forgives a skewed geography. The romancer does not feel obliged to be consistent.

The second love story is even more peculiar than the first. The Moorish hero Ruggiero here does not go mad; he converts to Christianity. His beloved is the warrior maid Bradamante—a girl possessed of such virtues as tolerance, determination, martial spirit, and superior athletic prowess. Hers is an ancient name, we learn; for she will bear the House of Este. She, and not unangelic Angelica, is the true special heroine of the romance.

The pleasures of love enjoyed by Ruggiero and the sorceress Alcina on her island (which sounds like Japan) consist of "all joys" (Canto VII, stanza 31) in that "fair abode." Life in romance?

> Two or three times a day they change their dress,
> For many different purposes designed.
> Always they hold themselves in readiness
> For banquets, jousts, and feasts of every kind.
> By shady hills, or where the fountain plays,
> They read of lovers in the olden days.[2]

Ariosto first reveals Bradamante in combat (I, 69–70), as if she were drawn from Joan of Arc, Maid of Orléans (d. 1431). Canto II (stanza 31) makes her importance clear:

> I mean the celebrated Maid; she is
> The one who felled the monarch with her lance:
> Daughter of Aymon and of Beatrice,
> A sister whom Rinaldo proudly flaunts,
> Who for her courage, might and expertise
> By Charlemagne and all the Peers of France
> Is held in no less honour than her brother,
> For they are known to equal the other.[3]

Bradamante had gone to Merlin's tomb to hear him prophesy, and he had told her that by her union "mankind will see renewed the age of gold" (III, 18). In our two love stories we have opposites: a philandering maiden in one story, a philandering hero in the other. Which philanderer do you suppose will be pardoned, the hero or the heroine? The world of romance guarantees freedom to the poet and a disregard for history, fact, truth geographical or chronological. What he gains in these areas, he loses in psychology, which must seem true in personal relations, at least once in a while. Sex, beauty, youth, love, fun, and high adventure primary-color the romance.

The best adventures in *Orlando Furioso* may be its voyages. An admirable American historian who wrote a superb history of the ancient world (Vol. I: *The Orient and Greece,* 1926) was Michael Ivanovich Rostovtzeff (born in Russia in 1870). He noted that human beings can be understood by the historians as characterized by their overwhelming love of travel. Ariosto delights us with his travel episodes, such as Angelica surviving shipwreck on the red volcanic Hebrides, off the stormy west coast of Scotland, although chained naked in that wild sea. Unbelievably she survives that ordeal! Ruggiero's first journey from the south of France westward across the Atlantic, West Indies, Pacific Ocean to Alcina's island would have been envied by the real, intrepid navigators like Vasco da Gama, Christopher Columbus, Amerigo Vespucci, Ferdinand Magellan, Sir Francis Drake, and Sir Walter Raleigh. Orlando's sea cruise to Zealand via Brittany, Antwerp, and the Orkney Islands must have been very enjoyable, particularly its entry into Roskilde Fjord at Copenhagen itself. The true hero Ruggiero bested Orlando, however, with his three-thousand-mile journey on a winged quadruped. It was Orlando, however, who found the Lady of the Lake asleep, a scene Bulfinch also truly enjoyed. He must have understood Orlando's despair that he rescued the staked-out, naked Angelica, only to have her prove both ungenerous and unfaithful.

Wandering with maids and heroes from one familiar place of romance to another, the Celtic necropolis on its island in the Rhône River to Shakespeare's Forest of Arden, to Queen Guinevere's Fountain of the Pine, we meet all over again Tristan, Isolde, and Owain (Yvain).

NOTES

1. *Ariosto's Orlando Furioso,* tr. by Sir John Harrington, ed. by Rudolf Gottfried, Indiana University Press (Bloomington, 1963). See Canto XXVIII, p. 214.

2. *Orlando Furioso,* 2 vols., tr. and Introduction by Barbara Reynolds, Penguin (Harmondsworth, 1975), p. 249.

3. Aymon is the father of Renaud (Ariosto's Rinaldo) in the French epic *Les quatre fils Aymon.* French poets knew Bradamante as the "Virginal Knight." She wore white armor and a white plume on her helmet. Her spear magically unhorsed any opponent. Joan of Arc bore the arms of the royal House of Orléans: blue fleur-de-lys on a silver field.

THE PEERS, OR PALADINS

The twelve most illustrious knights of Charlemagne were called peers, for the equality that reigned among them; while the name of paladins, also conferred on them, implies that they were inmates of the palace and companions of the king. Their names are not always given alike by the romancers, yet we may enumerate the most distinguished of them as follows: Orlando or Roland (the former the Italian, the latter the French form of the name), favorite nephew of Charlemagne; Rinaldo of Montalban, cousin of Orlando; Namo, Duke of Bavaria; Salomon, King of Brittany; Turpin, the Archbishop; Astolpho, of England; Ogier, the Dane; Malagigi, the Enchanter; and Florismart, the friend of Orlando. There were others who are sometimes named as paladins, and the number cannot be strictly limited to twelve. Charlemagne himself must be counted one, and Ganelon, or Gano, of Mayence, the treacherous enemy of all the rest, was rated high on the list by his deluded sovereign, who was completely the victim of his arts.

We shall introduce more particularly to our readers a few of the principal peers, leaving the others to make their own introduction, as they appear in the course of our narrative. We begin with Orlando.

ORLANDO

Milon, or Milone, a knight of great family and distantly related to Charlemagne, having secretly married

Bertha, the Emperor's sister, was banished from France and excommunicated by the Pope. After a long and miserable wandering on foot as mendicants, Milon and his wife arrived at Sutri, in Italy, where they took refuge in a cave, and in that cave Orlando was born. There his mother continued, deriving a scanty support from the compassion of the neighboring peasants, while Milon, in quest of honor and fortune, went into foreign lands. Orlando grew up among the children of the peasantry, surpassing them all in strength and manly graces. Among his companions in age, though in station far more elevated, was Oliver, son of the governor of the town. Between the two boys a feud arose that led to a fight, in which Orlando thrashed his rival; but this did not prevent a friendship springing up between the two which lasted through life.

Orlando was so poor that he was sometimes half naked. As he was a favorite of the boys, one day four of them brought some cloth to make him clothes. Two brought white and two red; and from this circumstance Orlando took his coat-of-arms, or *quarterings*.

When Charlemagne was on his way to Rome to receive the imperial crown, he dined in public in Sutri. Orlando and his mother that day had nothing to eat, and Orlando, coming suddenly upon the royal party and seeing abundance of provisions, seized from the attendants as much as he could carry off and made good his retreat in spite of their resistance. The Emperor, being told of this incident, was reminded of an intimation he had received in a dream, and ordered the boy to be followed. This was done by three of the knights, whom Orlando would have encountered with a cudgel on their entering the grotto had not his mother restrained him. When they heard from her who she was, they threw themselves at her feet and promised to obtain her pardon from the Emperor. This was easily effected. Orlando was received into favor by the Emperor, returned with him to France, and so distinguished himself that he became the most powerful support of the throne and of Christianity.*

* It is plain that Shakespeare borrowed from this source the similar incident in his "As you Like it." The names of characters in the play, Orlando, Oliver, Rowland, indicate the same thing.

ROLAND AND FERRAGUS

Orlando, or Roland, particularly distinguished himself by his combat with Ferragus. Ferragus was a giant, and moreover his skin was of such impenetrable stuff that no sword could make any impression upon it. The giant's mode of fighting was to seize his adversary in his arms and carry him off, in spite of all the struggles he could make. Roland's utmost skill only availed to keep him out of the giant's clutches, but all his efforts to wound him with the sword were useless. After long fighting, Ferragus was so weary that he proposed a truce, and when it was agreed upon, he lay down and immediately fell asleep. He slept in perfect security, for it was against all the laws of chivalry to take advantage of an adversary under such circumstances. But Ferragus lay so uncomfortably for the want of a pillow that Orlando took pity upon him, and brought a smooth stone, and placed it under his head. When the giant woke up, after a refreshing nap, and perceived what Orlando had done, he seemed quite grateful, became sociable, and talked freely in the usual boastful style of such characters. Among other things, he told Orlando that he need not attempt to kill him with a sword, for that every part of his body was invulnerable, except this; and as he spoke, he put his hand to the vital part, just in the middle of his breast. Aided by this information, Orlando succeeded, when the fight was renewed, in piercing the giant in the very spot he had pointed out and giving him a death-wound. Great was the rejoicing in the Christian camp, and many the praises showered upon the victorious paladin by the Emperor and all his host.

On another occasion, Orlando encountered a puissant Saracen warrior and took from him, as the prize of victory, the sword Durindana. This famous weapon had once belonged to the illustrious Prince Hector of Troy. It was of the finest workmanship and of such strength and temper that no armor in the world could stand against it.

A ROLAND FOR AN OLIVER

Guerin de Montglave held the lordship of Vienne, subject to Charlemagne. He had quarrelled with his sovereign, and Charles laid siege to his city, having ravaged the neighboring country. Guerin was an aged warrior, but relied for his defence upon his four sons and two grandsons, who were among the bravest knights of the age. After the siege had continued two months, Charlemagne received tidings that Marsilius, king of Spain, had invaded France, and, finding himself unopposed, was advancing rapidly in the southern provinces. At this intelligence, Charles listened to the counsel of his peers and consented to put the quarrel with Guerin to the decision of Heaven, by single combat between two knights, one of each party, selected by lot. The proposal was acceptable to Guerin and his sons. The names of the four, together with Guerin's own, who would not be excused, and of the two grandsons, who claimed their lot, being put into a helmet, Oliver's was drawn forth, and to him, the youngest of the grandsons, was assigned the honor and the peril of the combat. He accepted the award with delight, exulting in being thought worthy to maintain the cause of his family. On Charlemagne's side Roland was the designated champion, and neither he nor Oliver knew who his antagonist was to be.

They met on an island in the Rhône, and the warriors of both camps were ranged on either shore, spectators of the battle. At the first encounter, both lances were shivered, but both riders kept their seats, immovable. They dismounted and drew their swords. Then ensued a combat which seemed so equal that the spectators could not form an opinion as to the probable issue. Two hours and more the knights continued to strike and parry, to thrust and ward, neither showing any sign of weariness, nor ever being taken at unawares. At length Orlando struck furiously upon Oliver's shield, burying Durindana in its edge so deeply that he could not draw it back, and Oliver, almost at the same moment, thrust so vigorously upon Orlando's breastplate that his sword snapped off at the handle. Thus were the two warriors left weaponless. Scarcely pausing a moment, they rushed upon one another, each striving to throw his adversary to the ground, and failing in that, each snatched at the other's helmet to tear it away. Both succeeded, and at the same moment they stood bareheaded face to face, and Roland recognized Oliver, and Oliver Roland. For a moment they stood still; and the next, with open arms, rushed into one another's embrace. "I am conquered," said Orlando. "I yield me," said Oliver.

The people on the shore knew not what to make of all this. Presently they saw the two late antagonists standing hand in hand, and it was evident the battle was at an end. The knights crowded round them and with one voice hailed them as equals in glory. If there were any who felt disposed to murmur that the battle was left undecided, they were silenced by the voice of Ogier the Dane, who proclaimed aloud that all had been done that honor required and declared that he would maintain that award against all gainsayers.

The quarrel with Guerin and his sons being left undecided, a truce was made for four days, and in that time, by the efforts of Duke Namo on the one side and of Oliver on the other, a reconciliation was effected. Charlemagne, accompanied by Guerin and his valiant family, marched to meet Marsilius, who hastened to retreat across the frontier.

RINALDO

Rinaldo was one of the four sons of Aymon, who married Aya, the sister of Charlemagne. Thus Rinaldo was nephew to Charlemagne and cousin of Orlando.

When Rinaldo had grown old enough to assume arms, Orlando had won for himself an illustrious name by his exploits against the Saracens, whom Charlemagne and his brave knights had driven out of France. Orlando's fame excited a noble emulation in Rinaldo. Eager to go in pursuit of glory, he wandered in the country near Paris, and one day saw at the foot of a tree a superb horse, fully equipped and loaded with a complete suit of armor. Rinaldo clothed himself in the armor and mounted the horse, but took not the sword. On the day when, with his brothers, he had received the honor of knighthood from the Emperor, he had sworn never to bind a sword to his side till he had wrested one from some famous knight.

Rinaldo took his way to the forest of Arden, celebrated for so many adventures. Hardly had he entered it when he met an old man, bending under the weight of years, and learned from him that the forest was infested with a wild horse, untamable, that broke and overturned everything that opposed his career. To attack him, he said, or even to meet him, was certain death. Rinaldo, far from being alarmed, showed the most eager desire to combat the animal. This was the horse Bayard, afterwards so famous. He had formerly belonged to Amadis of Gaul. After the death of that hero, he had been held under enchantment by the power of a magician, who predicted that, when the time came to break the spell, he should be subdued by a knight of the lineage of Amadis, and not less brave than he.

To win this wonderful horse, it was necessary to conquer him by force or skill; for from the moment when he should be thrown down, he would become docile and manageable. His habitual resort was a cave on the borders of the forest; but, woe be to any one who should approach him, unless gifted with strength and courage more than mortal. Having told this, the old man departed. He was not, in fact, an old man, but Malagigi, the enchanter, cousin of Rinaldo, who, to favor the enterprises of the young knight, had procured for him the horse and armor which he so opportunely found, and now put him in the way to acquire a horse unequalled in the world.

Rinaldo plunged into the forest and spent many days in seeking Bayard, but found no traces of him. One day he encountered a Saracen knight, with whom he made acquaintance, as often happened to knights, by first meeting him in combat. This knight, whose name was Isolier, was also in quest of Bayard. Rinaldo succeeded in the encounter, and so severe was the shock that Isolier was a long time insensible. When he revived, and was about to resume the contest, a peasant who passed by (it was Malagigi) interrupted them with the news that the

terrible horse was near at hand, advising them to unite
their powers to subdue him, for it would require all their
ability.

Rinaldo and Isolier, now become friends, proceeded
together to the attack of the horse. They found Bayard
and stood a long time, concealed by the wood, admiring his strength and beauty.

A bright bay in color (whence he was called Bayard),
with a silver star in his forehead, and his hind feet white,
his body slender, his head delicate, his ample chest filled
out with swelling muscles, his shoulders broad and full,
his legs straight and sinewy, his thick mane falling over
his arching neck—he came rushing through the forest,
regardless of rocks, bushes, or trees, rending everything
that opposed his way and neighing defiance.

He first descried Isolier and rushed upon him. The
knight received him with lance in rest, but the fierce
animal broke the spear, and his course was not delayed
by it for an instant. The Spaniard adroitly stepped aside
and gave way to the rushing tempest. Bayard checked
his career and turned again upon the knight, who had already drawn his sword. He drew his sword, for he had no
hope of taming the horse; that, he was satisfied, was impossible.

Bayard rushed upon him, fiercely rearing, now on this
side, now on that. The knight struck him with his sword,
where the white star adorned his forehead, but struck in
vain and felt ashamed, thinking that he had struck feebly,
for he did not know that the skin of that horse was so
tough that the keenest sword could make no impression
upon it.

Whistling fell the sword once more, and struck with
greater force, and the fierce horse felt it and drooped his
head under the blow, but the next moment turned upon his
foe with such a buffet that the pagan fell, stunned and
lifeless, to the earth.

Rinaldo, who saw Isolier fall and thought that his life
was reft, darted towards the horse and, with his fist, gave
him such a blow on the jaws that the blood tinged his
mouth with vermilion. Quicker than an arrow leaves the
bow, the horse turned upon him and tried to seize his arm
with his teeth.

The knight stepped back, and then, repeating his blow, struck him on the forehead. Bayard turned and kicked with both his feet with a force that would have shattered a mountain. Rinaldo was on his guard and evaded his attacks, whether made with head or heels. He kept at his side, avoiding both; but, making a false step, he at last received a terrible blow from the horse's foot, and at the shock almost fainted away. A second such blow would have killed him, but the horse kicked at random, and a second blow did not reach Rinaldo, who in a moment recovered himself. Thus the contest continued until by chance Bayard's foot got caught between the branches of an oak. Rinaldo seized it and, putting forth all his strength and address, threw him on the ground.

No sooner had Bayard touched the ground than all his rage subsided. No longer an object of terror, he became gentle and quiet, yet with dignity in his mildness.

The paladin patted his neck, stroked his breast, and smoothed his mane, while the animal neighed and showed delight to be caressed by his master. Rinaldo, seeing him now completely subdued, took the saddle and trappings from the other horse and adorned Bayard with the spoils.

Rinaldo became one of the most illustrious knights of Charlemagne's court—indeed, the most illustrious, if we except Orlando. Yet he was not always so obedient to the Emperor's commands as he should have been, and every fault he committed was sure to be aggravated by the malice of Gan, Duke of Maganza, the treacherous enemy of Rinaldo and all his house.

At one time Rinaldo had incurred the severe displeasure of Charlemagne and been banished from court. Seeing no chance of being ever restored to favor, he went to Spain and entered into the service of the Saracen king, Ivo. His brothers, Alardo, Ricardo, and Ricciardetto, accompanied him, and all four served the king so faithfully that they rose to high favor with him. The king gave them land in the mountains on the frontiers of France and Spain, and subjected all the country round to Rinaldo's authority. There was plenty of marble in the mountains, the king furnished workmen, and they built a castle for Rinaldo, surrounded with high walls, so as to be almost impregnable. Built of white stone and placed on the brow of a marble promontory, the castle shone like a star, and Rinaldo gave it the name of Montalban. Here he assembled his friends, many of whom were banished men like himself, and the country people furnished them with provisions in return for the protection the castle afforded. Yet some of Rinaldo's men were lawless, and sometimes the supplies were not furnished in sufficient abundance, so that Rinaldo and his garrison got a bad name for taking by force what they could not obtain by gift; and we sometimes find Montalban spoken of as a nest of free-booters, and its defenders called a beggarly garrison.

Charlemagne's displeasure did not last long, and at the time our history commences, Rinaldo and his brothers were completely restored to the favor of the Emperor; and none of his cavaliers served him with greater zeal and fidelity than they, throughout all his wars with the Saracens and pagans.

THE TOURNAMENT

It was the month of May, and the feast of Pentecost. Charlemagne had ordered magnificent festivities and summoned to them, besides his paladins and vassals of the crown, all strangers, Christian or Saracen, then sojourning at Paris. Among the guests were King Grandonio, from Spain; and Ferrau, the Saracen, with eyes like an eagle; Orlando and Rinaldo, the Emperor's nephews; Duke Namo; Astolpho, of England, the handsomest man living; Malagigi, the Enchanter; and Gano, of Maganza, that wily traitor, who had the art to make the Emperor think he loved him, while he plotted against him.

High sat Charlemagne at the head of his vassals and his paladins, rejoicing in the thought of their number and their might, while all were sitting and hearing music and feasting, when suddenly there came into the hall four enormous giants, having between them a lady of incomparable beauty, attended by a single knight. There were many ladies present who had seemed beautiful till she made her appearance, but after that they all seemed nothing. Every Christian knight turned his eyes to her, and every pagan crowded round her, while she, with a sweetness that might have touched a heart of stone, thus addressed the Emperor:

"High-minded lord, the renown of your worthiness and of the valor of these your knights, which echoes from sea to sea, encourages me to hope that two pilgrims, who have come from the ends of the world to behold you, will not have encountered their fatigue in vain. And, before I show the motive which has brought us hither, learn that this knight is my brother Uberto and that I am his sister Angelica. Fame has told us of the jousting this day appointed, and so the prince my brother has come to prove his valor and to say that, if any of the knights here assembled choose to meet him in the joust, he will encounter them, one by one, at the stair of Merlin, by the Fountain of the Pine. And his conditions are these: No knight who chances to be thrown shall be allowed to renew the combat, but shall remain prisoner to my brother, but if my brother be overthrown, he shall depart out of the country, leaving me as the prize of the conqueror."

Now it must be stated that this Angelica and her brother, who called himself Uberto, but whose real name was Argalia, were the children of Galafron, king of Cathay, who had sent them to be the destruction of the Christian host; for Argalia was armed with an enchanted lance which unfailingly overthrew everything it touched, and he was mounted on a horse, a creature of magic, whose swiftness outstripped the wind. Angelica possessed also a ring which was a defence against all enchantments and, when put into the mouth, rendered the bearer invisible. Thus Argalia was expected to subdue and take prisoners whatever knights should dare to encounter him; and the charms of Angelica were relied on to entice the paladins to make the fatal venture, while her ring would afford her easy means of escape.

When Angelica ceased speaking, she knelt before the king and awaited his answer, and everybody gazed on her with admiration. Orlando especially felt irresistibly drawn towards her, so that he trembled and changed countenance. Every knight in the hall was infected with the same feeling, not excepting old white-headed Duke Namo and Charlemagne himself.

All stood for a while in silence, lost in the delight of looking at her. The fiery youth Ferrau could hardly restrain himself from seizing her from the giants and carrying her away; Rinaldo turned as red as fire; while Malagigi, who had discovered by his art that the stranger was not speaking truth, muttered softly, as he looked at her, "Exquisite false creature! I will play thee such a trick for this as will leave thee no cause to boast of thy visit."

Charlemagne, to detain her as long as possible before him, delayed his assent till he had asked her a number of questions, all which she answered discreetly, and then the challenge was accepted.

As soon as she was gone, Malagigi consulted his book and found out the whole plot of the vile, infidel king Galafron, as we have explained it, so he determined to seek the damsel and frustrate her designs. He hastened to the appointed spot and there found the prince and his sister in a beautiful pavilion, where they lay asleep, while the four giants kept watch. Malagigi took his book and cast a spell out of it, and immediately the four giants fell into a deep sleep. Drawing his sword (for he was a belted knight), he softly approached the young lady, intending to despatch her at once; but, seeing her look so lovely, he paused for a moment, thinking there was no need of hurry, as he believed his spell was upon her and she could not wake. But the ring which she wore secured her from the effect of the spell, and some slight noise, or whatever else it was, caused her at that moment to awake. She uttered a great cry, and flew to her brother, and waked him. By the help of her knowledge of enchantment, they took and bound fast the magician, and seizing his book, turned his arts against himself. Then they summoned a crowd of demons and bade them seize their prisoner and bear him to king Galafron, at his great city of Albracca, which they did, and, on his arrival, he was locked up in a rock under the sea.

While these things were going on, all was uproar at Paris, since Orlando insisted upon being the first to try the adventure at the stair of Merlin. This was resented

by the other pretenders to Angelica, and all contested
his right to the precedence. The tumult was stilled by
the usual expedient of drawing lots, and the first prize
was drawn by Astolpho. Ferrau, the Saracen, had the
second, and Grandonio the third. Next came Berlinghieri,
and Otho; then Charles himself, and, as his ill fortune
would have it, after thirty more, the indignant Orlando.

Astolpho, who drew the first lot, was handsome, brave,
and rich. But, whether from heedlessness or want of skill,
he was an unlucky jouster and very apt to be thrown,
an accident which he bore with perfect good humor, always ready to mount again and try to mend his fortune,
generally with no better success.

Astolpho went forth upon his adventure with great
gaiety of dress and manner, encountered Argalia, and
was immediately tilted out of the saddle. He railed at
fortune, to whom he laid all the fault; but his painful
feelings were somewhat relieved by the kindness of Angelica, who, touched by his youth and good looks, granted
him the liberty of the pavilion and caused him to be
treated with all kindness and respect.

The violent Ferrau had the next chance in the encounter, and was thrown no less speedily than Astolpho;
but he did not so easily put up with his mischance.
Crying out, "What are the emperor's engagements to
me?" he rushed with his sword against Argalia, who,
being forced to defend himself, dismounted and drew his
sword, but got so much the worse of the fight that he
made a signal of surrender and, after some words, listened to a proposal of marriage from Ferrau to his sister.
The beauty, however, feeling no inclination to match
with such a rough and savage-looking person, was so
dismayed at the offer that, hastily bidding her brother
to meet her in the forest of Arden, she vanished from
the sight of both by means of the enchanted ring.
Argalia, seeing this, took to his horse of swiftness and
dashed away in the same direction. Ferrau pursued him,
and Astolpho, thus left to himself, took possession of
the enchanted lance in place of his own, which was
broken, not knowing the treasure he possessed in it,
and returned to the tournament. Charlemagne, finding
the lady and her brother gone, ordered the jousting to

proceed as at first intended, in which Astolpho, by aid of the enchanted lance, unhorsed all comers against him, equally to their astonishment and his own.

The paladin Rinaldo, on learning the issue of the combat of Ferrau and the stranger, galloped after the fair fugitive in an agony of love and impatience. Orlando, perceiving his disappearance, pushed forth in like manner; and, at length, all three are in the forest of Arden, hunting about for her who is invisible.

Now, in this forest, there were two fountains, the one constructed by the sage Merlin, who designed it for Tristram and the fair Isoude *; for such was the virtue of this fountain that a draught of its waters produced an oblivion of the love which the drinker might feel, and even produced aversion for the object formerly beloved. The other fountain was endowed with exactly opposite qualities, and a draught of it inspired love for the first living object that was seen after tasting it. Rinaldo happened to come to the first-mentioned fountain, and, being flushed with heat, dismounted, and quenched in one draught both his thirst and his passion. So, far from loving Angelica as before, he hated her from the bottom of his heart, became disgusted with the search he was upon, and, feeling fatigued with his ride, finding a sheltered and flowery nook, laid himself down and fell asleep.

Shortly after came Angelica, but, approaching in a different direction, she espied the other fountain, and there quenched her thirst. Then, resuming her way, she came upon the sleeping Rinaldo. Love instantly seized her, and she stood rooted to the spot.

The meadow round was all full of lilies of the valley and wild roses. Angelica, not knowing what to do, at length plucked a handful of these and dropped them, one by one, on the face of the sleeper. He woke up, and, seeing who it was, received her salutations with averted countenance, remounted his horse, and galloped away. In vain the beautiful creature followed and called after him, in vain asked him what she had done to be so despised. Rinaldo disappeared, leaving her in despair, and

* See their story in *The Age of Chivalry.*

she returned in tears to the spot where she had found him sleeping. There, in her turn, she herself lay down, pressing the spot of earth on which he had lain, and, out of fatigue and sorrow, fell asleep.

As Angelica thus lay, fortune conducted Orlando to the same place. The attitude in which she was sleeping was so lovely that it is not to be conceived, much less expressed. Orlando stood gazing like a man who had been transported to another sphere. "Am I on earth," he exclaimed, "or am I in Paradise? Surely it is I that sleep, and this is my dream."

But his dream was proved to be none in a manner which he little desired. Ferrau, who had slain Argalia, came up, raging with jealousy, and a combat ensued which awoke the sleeper.

Terrified at what she beheld, she rushed to her palfrey and, while the fighters were occupied with one another, fled away through the forest. The champions continued their fight till they were interrupted by a messenger, who brought word to Ferrau that king Marsilius, his sovereign, was in pressing need of his assistance, and conjured him to return to Spain. Ferrau, upon this, proposed to suspend the combat, to which Orlando, eager to pursue Angelica, agreed. Ferrau, on the other hand, departed with the messenger to Spain.

Orlando's quest for the fair fugitive was all in vain. Aided by the powers of magic, she made a speedy return to her own country.

But the thought of Rinaldo could not be banished from her mind, and she determined to set Malagigi at liberty and to employ him to win Rinaldo, if possible, to make her a return of affection. She accordingly freed him from his dungeon, unlocking his fetters with her own hands, and restored him his book, promising him ample honors and rewards, on condition of his bringing Rinaldo to her feet.

Malagigi, accordingly, with the aid of his book, called up a demon, mounted him, and departed. Arrived at his destination, he inveigled Rinaldo into an enchanted bark, which conveyed him, without any visible pilot, to an island where stood an edifice called Joyous Castle. The whole island was a garden. On the western side, close to the sea, was the palace, built of marble, so clear and polished that it reflected the landscape about it. Rinaldo leapt ashore and soon met a lady, who invited him to enter. The house was as beautiful within as without, full of rooms adorned with azure and gold and with noble paintings. The lady led the knight into an apartment painted with stories and, opening to the garden, through pillars of crystal, with golden capitals. Here he found a bevy of ladies, three of whom were singing in concert, while another played on an instrument of exquisite accord and the rest danced round about them. When the ladies beheld him coming, they turned the dance into a circuit round him, and then one of them, in the sweetest manner, said, "Sir knight, the tables are set, and the hour for the banquet is come"; and, with these words, still dancing, they drew him across the lawn in front of the apartment to a table that was spread with cloth of gold and fine linen, under a bower of damask roses by the side of a fountain.

Four ladies were already seated there, who rose and placed Rinaldo at their head, in a chair set with pearls. And truly, indeed, was he astonished. A repast ensued, consisting of viands the most delicate and wines, as fragrant as they were fine, drunk out of jewelled cups; and, when it drew towards its conclusion, harps and lutes were heard in the distance, and one of the ladies said in the knight's ear: "This house and all that you see in it are yours; for you alone was it built, and the builder is a queen. Happy indeed must you think yourself, for she loves you, and she is the greatest beauty in the world. Her name is Angelica."

The moment Rinaldo heard the name he so detested he started up, with a changed countenance, and, in spite of all that the lady could say, broke off across the garden and never ceased hastening till he reached the place where he landed. The bark was still on the shore. He sprang into it and pushed off, though he saw nobody in it but himself. It was in vain for him to try to control its movements, for it dashed on as if in fury, till it reached a distant shore covered with a gloomy forest. Here Rinaldo, surrounded by enchantments of a very different sort from those which he had lately resisted, was entrapped into a pit.

The pit belonged to a castle called Altaripa, which was hung with human heads and painted red with blood. As the paladin was viewing the scene with amazement, a hideous old woman made her appearance at the edge of the pit and told him that he was destined to be thrown to a monster, who was only kept from devastating the whole country by being supplied with living human flesh. Rinaldo said, "Be it so; let me but remain armed as I am, and I fear nothing." The old woman laughed in derision. Rinaldo remained in the pit all night, and the next morning was taken to the place where the monster had his den. It was a court surrounded by a high wall. Rinaldo was shut in with the beast, and a terrible combat ensued. Rinaldo was unable to make any impression on the scales of the monster, while he, on the contrary, with his dreadful claws, tore away plate and mail from the paladin. Rinaldo began to think his last hour was come and cast his eyes around and above to see if there was any means of escape. He perceived a beam projecting from the wall at the height of some ten feet, and, taking a leap almost miraculous, he succeeded in reaching it and in flinging himself up across it. Here he sat for hours, the hideous brute continually trying to reach him. All at once he heard the sound of something coming through the air like a bird, and suddenly Angelica herself alighted on the end of the beam. She held something in her hand towards him and spoke to him in a loving voice. But the moment Rinaldo saw her, he commanded her to go away, refused all her offers of assistance, and at length declared that, if she did not leave him, he would cast himself down to the monster and meet his fate.

Angelica, saying she would lose her life rather than displease him, departed; but first she threw to the monster a cake of wax she had prepared and spread around him a rope knotted with nooses. The beast took the bait, and, finding his teeth glued together by the wax, vented his fury in bounds and leaps, and, soon getting entangled in the nooses, drew them tight by his struggles, so that he could scarcely move a limb.

Rinaldo, watching his chance, leapt down upon his back, seized him round the neck, and throttled him, not relaxing his grip till the beast fell dead.

Another difficulty remained to be overcome. The walls were of immense height, and the only opening in them was a grated window of such strength that he could not break the bars. In his distress, Rinaldo found a file which Angelica had left on the ground and, with the help of this, effected his deliverance.

What further adventures he met with will be told in another chapter.

THE SIEGE OF ALBRACCA

At the very time when Charlemagne was holding his plenary court and his great tournament, his kingdom was invaded by a mighty monarch, who was moreover so valiant and strong in battle that no one could stand against him. He was named Gradasso, and his kingdom was called Sericane. Now, as it often happens to the greatest and the richest to long for what they cannot have, and thus to lose what they already possess, this king could not rest content without Durindana, the sword of Orlando, and Bayard, the horse of Rinaldo. To obtain these he determined to war upon France, and for this purpose put in array a mighty army.

He took his way through Spain, and, after defeating Marsilius, the king of that country, in several battles, was rapidly advancing on France. Charlemagne, though Marsilius was a Saracen, and had been his enemy, yet felt it needful to succor him in this extremity from a consideration of common danger, and, with the consent of his peers, despatched Rinaldo with a strong body of soldiers against Gradasso.

There was much fighting, with doubtful results, and Gradasso was steadily advancing into France. But, impatient to achieve his objects, he challenged Rinaldo to single combat, to be fought on foot, and upon these conditions: If Rinaldo conquered, Gradasso agreed to give up all his prisoners and return to his own country; but if Gradasso won the day, he was to have Bayard.

The challenge was accepted, and would have been fought had it not been for the arts of Malagigi, who just then returned from Angelica's kingdom with set purpose to win Rinaldo to look with favor upon the fair princess who was dying for love of him. Malagigi drew Rinaldo away from the army by putting on the semblance of Gradasso and, after a short contest, pretending to fly before him, by which means Rinaldo was induced to follow him into a boat, in which he was borne away and entangled in various adventures, as we have already related.

The army, left under the command of Ricciardetto, Rinaldo's brother, was soon joined by Charlemagne and all his peerage, but experienced a disastrous rout, and the Emperor and many of his paladins were taken prisoners. Gradasso, however, did not abuse his victory; he took Charles by the hand, seated him by his side, and told him he warred only for honor. He renounced all conquests, on condition that the Emperor should deliver to him Bayard and Durindana, both of them the property of his vassals, the former of which, as he maintained, was already forfeited to him by Rinaldo's failure to meet him as agreed. To these terms Charlemagne readily acceded.

Bayard, after the departure of his master, had been taken in charge by Ricciardetto and sent back to Paris, where Astolpho was in command, in the absence of Charlemagne. Astolpho received with great indignation the message despatched for Bayard and replied by a herald that "he would not surrender the horse of his kinsman Rinaldo, without a contest. If Gradasso wanted the steed, he might come and take him, and that he, Astolpho, was ready to meet him in the field."

Gradasso was only amused at this answer, for Astolpho's fame as a successful warrior was not high, and Gradasso willingly renewed with him the bargain which he had made with Rinaldo. On these conditions the battle was fought. The enchanted lance, in the hands of Astolpho, performed a new wonder, and Gradasso, the terrible Gradasso, was unhorsed.

He kept his word, set free his prisoners, and put his
army on the march to return to his own country, renewing his oath, however, not to rest till he had taken
from Rinaldo his horse and from Orlando his sword, or
lost his life in the attempt.

Charlemagne, full of gratitude to Astolpho, would
have kept him near his person and loaded him with
honors, but Astolpho preferred to seek Rinaldo, with
the view of restoring to him his horse, and departed from
Paris with that design.

Our story now returns to Orlando, whom we left fascinated with the sight of the sleeping beauty, who, however, escaped him while engaged in the combat with
Ferrau. Having long sought her in vain through the recesses of the wood, he resolved to follow her to her father's court. Leaving, therefore, the camp of Charlemagne, he travelled long in the direction of the East,
making inquiry everywhere, if, perchance, he might get
tidings of the fugitive. After many adventures, he arrived one day at a place where many roads crossed, and,
meeting there a courier, he asked him for news. The
courier replied that he had been despatched by Angelica
to solicit the aid of Sacripant, king of Circassia, in favor
of her father Galafron, who was besieged in his city, Albracca, by Agrican, king of Tartary. This Agrican had
been an unsuccessful suitor to the damsel, whom he now
pursued with arms. Orlando thus learned that he was
within a day's journey of Albracca; and feeling now secure of Angelica, he proceeded with all speed to her city.

Thus journeying, he arrived at a bridge, under which
flowed a foaming river. Here a damsel met him with a
goblet and informed him that it was the usage of this
bridge to present the traveller with a cup. Orlando accepted the offered cup and drank its contents. He had no
sooner done so than his brain reeled, and he became
unconscious of the object of his journey and of everything else. Under the influence of this fascination, he followed the damsel into a magnificent and marvellous
palace. Here he found himself in company with many
knights, unknown to him and to each other, though if it
had not been for the Cup of Oblivion of which they all

had partaken, they would have found themselves brothers in arms.

Astolpho, proceeding on his way to seek Rinaldo, splendidly dressed and equipped, as was his wont, arrived in Circassia and found there a great army encamped under the command of Sacripant, the king of that country, who was leading it to the defence of Galafron, the father of Angelica. Sacripant, much struck by the appearance of Astolpho and his horse, accosted him courteously and tried to enlist him in his service; but Astolpho, proud of his late victories, scornfully declined his offers and pursued his way. King Sacripant was too much attracted by his appearance to part with him so easily and, having laid aside his kingly ornaments, set out in pursuit of him.

Astolpho next day encountered on his way a stranger knight, named Sir Florismart, Lord of the Sylvan Tower, one of the bravest and best of knights, having as his guide a damsel, young, fair, and virtuous, to whom he was tenderly attached, whose name was Flordelis. Astolpho, as he approached, defied the knight, bidding him yield the lady, or prepare to maintain his right by arms. Florismart accepted the contest, and the knights encountered. Florismart was unhorsed and his steed fell dead, while Bayard sustained no injury by the shock.

Florismart was so overwhelmed with despair at his own disgrace and the sight of the damsel's distress that he drew his sword, and was about to plunge it into his own bosom. But Astolpho held his hand, told him that he contended only for glory, and was contented to leave him the lady.

While Florismart and Flordelis were vowing eternal gratitude, King Sacripant arrived and, coveting the damsel of the one champion as much as the horse and arms of the other, defied them to the joust. Astolpho met the challenger, whom he instantly overthrew, and presented his courser to Florismart, leaving the king to return to his army on foot.

The friends pursued their route, and ere long Flordelis discovered, by signs which were known to her, that they were approaching the waters of Oblivion, and advised them to turn back, or to change their course. This the knights would not hear of, and, continuing their march, they soon arrived at the bridge where Orlando had been taken prisoner.

The damsel of the bridge appeared as before with the enchanted cup, but Astolpho, forewarned, rejected it with scorn. She dashed it to the ground, and a fire blazed up which rendered the bridge unapproachable. At the same moment the two knights were assailed by sundry warriors, known and unknown, who, having no recollection of anything, joined blindly in defence of their prison-house. Among these was Orlando, at sight of whom Astolpho, with all his confidence not daring to encounter him, turned and fled, owing his escape to the strength and fleetness of Bayard.

Florismart, meanwhile, overlaid by fearful odds, was compelled to yield to necessity and comply with the usage of the fairy. He drank of the cup and remained prisoner with the rest. Flordelis, deprived of her two friends, retired from the scene and devoted herself to untiring efforts to effect her lover's deliverance. Astolpho pursued his way to Albracca, which Agrican was about to besiege. He was kindly welcomed by Angelica, and enrolled among her defenders. Impatient to distinguish himself, he one night sallied forth alone, arrived in Agrican's camp, and unhorsed his warriors right and left by means of the enchanted lance. But he was soon surrounded and overmatched and made prisoner to Agrican.

Relief was, however, at hand; for as the citizens and soldiers were one day leaning over their walls, they descried a cloud of dust, from which horsemen were seen to prick forth, as it rolled on towards the camp of the besiegers. This turned out to be the army of Sacripant, which immediately attacked that of Agrican, with the view of cutting a passage through his camp to the besieged city. But Agrican, mounted upon Bayard, taken from Astolpho, but not armed with the lance of gold, the virtues of which were unknown to him, performed wonders and rallied his scattered troops, which had given way to the sudden and unexpected assault. Sacripant, on the other hand, encouraged his men by the most desperate acts of valor, having as an additional incentive to his courage the sight of Angelica, who showed herself upon the city walls.

There she witnessed a single combat between the two leaders, Agrican and Sacripant. In this, at length, her defender appeared to be overmatched, when the Circassians broke the ring and separated the combatants, who were borne asunder in the rush. Sacripant, severely wounded, profited by the confusion and escaped into Albracca, where he was kindly received and carefully tended by Angelica.

The battle continuing, the Circassians were at last put to flight, and, being intercepted between the enemy's lines and the town, sought for refuge under the walls. Angelica ordered the drawbridge to be let down and the gates thrown open to the fugitives. With these Agrican, not distinguished in the crowd, entered the place, driving both Circassians and Cathayans before him, and the portcullis being dropped, he was shut in.

For a time the terror which he inspired put to flight all opposers, but when at last it came to be known that few or none of his followers had effected an entrance with him, the fugitives rallied and surrounded him on all sides. While he was thus apparently reduced to the last extremities, he was saved by the very circumstance which threatened him with destruction. The soldiers of Angelica, closing upon him from all sides, deserted their defences, and his own besieging army entered the city in a part where the wall was broken down.

In this way was Agrican rescued, the city taken, and the inhabitants put to the sword. Angelica, however, with some of the knights who were her defenders, among whom was Sacripant, saved herself in the citadel, which was planted upon a rock.

The fortress was impregnable, but it was scantily victualled and ill provided with other necessaries. Under these circumstances, Angelica announced to those blockaded with her in the citadel her intention to go in quest of assistance, and, having plighted her promise of a speedy return, she set out, with the enchanted ring upon her finger. Mounted upon her palfrey, the damsel passed through the enemy's lines and by sunrise, was many miles clear of their encampment.

It so happened that her road led her near the fatal bridge of Oblivion, and, as she approached it, she met a damsel weeping bitterly. It was Flordelis, whose lover, Florismart, as we have related, had met the fate of Orlando and many more and fallen a victim to the enchantress of the cup. She related her adventures to Angelica and conjured her to lend what aid she might to rescue her lord and his companions. Angelica, accordingly, watching her opportunity and aided by her ring, slipped into the castle unseen, when the door was opened to admit a new victim. Here she speedily disenchanted Orlando and the rest by a touch of her talisman. But Florismart was not there. He had been given up to Falerina, a more powerful enchantress, and was still in durance. Angelica conjured the rescued captives to assist her in the recovery of her kingdom, and all departed together for Albracca.

The arrival of Orlando, with his companions, nine in all, and among the bravest knights of France, changed at once the fortunes of the war. Wherever the great paladin came, pennon and standard fell before him. Agrican in vain attempted to rally his troops. Orlando kept constantly in his front, forcing him to attend to nobody else. The Tartar king at length bethought him of a stratagem. He turned his horse, and made a show of flying in despair. Orlando dashed after him as he desired, and Agrican fled till he reached a green place in a wood, where there was a fountain.

The place was beautiful, and the Tartar dismounted to refresh himself at the fountain, but without taking off his helmet or laying aside any of his armor. Orlando was quickly at his back, crying out, "So bold, and yet a fugitive! How could you fly from a single arm and think to escape?"

The Tartar king had leaped on his saddle the moment he saw his enemy, and when the paladin had done speaking, he said, in a mild voice, "Without doubt you are the best knight I ever encountered, and fain would I leave you untouched for your own sake, if you would cease to hinder me from rallying my people. I pretended to fly, in order to bring you out of the field. If you insist upon fighting, I must needs fight and slay you, but I call the sun in the heavens to witness I would rather not. I should be very sorry for your death."

The Count Orlando felt pity for so much gallantry, and he said, "The nobler you show yourself, the more it grieves me to think that, in dying without a knowledge of the true faith, you will be lost in the other world. Let me advise you to save body and soul at once. Receive baptism, and go your way in peace."

Agrican replied: "I suspect you to be the paladin Orlando. If you are, I would not lose this opportunity of fighting with you to be King of Paradise. Talk to me no more about your things of another world, for you will preach in vain. Each of us for himself, and let the sword be umpire."

The Saracen drew his sword, boldly advancing upon Orlando, and a combat began, so obstinate and so long, each warrior being a miracle of prowess, that the story says it lasted from noon till night. Orlando then, seeing the stars come out, was the first to propose a respite.

"What are we to do," said he, "now that daylight has left us?"

Agrican answered readily enough, "Let us repose in this meadow and renew the combat at dawn."

The repose was taken accordingly. Each tied up his horse and reclined himself on the grass, not far from the other, just as if they had been friends, Orlando by the fountain, Agrican beneath a pine. It was a beautiful clear night, and, as they talked together before addressing themselves to sleep, the champion of Christendom, looking up at the firmament, said, "That is a fine piece of workmanship, that starry spectacle; God made it all, that moon of silver, and those stars of gold, and the light of day, and the sun—all for the sake of humankind."

"You wish, I see, to talk of matters of faith," said the Tartar. "Now I may as well tell you at once that I have no sort of skill in such matters, nor learning of any kind. I never could learn any thing when I was a boy. I hated it so that I broke the man's head who was commissioned to teach me; and it produced such an effect on others that nobody ever afterwards dared so much as show me a book. My boyhood was therefore passed, as it should be, in horsemanship and hunting and learning to fight. What is the good of a gentleman's poring all day over a book? Prowess to the knight and preaching to the clergyman; that is my motto."

"I acknowledge," returned Orlando, "that arms are the first consideration of a gentleman; but not at all that he does himself dishonor by knowledge. On the contrary, knowledge is as great an embellishment of the rest of his attainments as the flowers are to the meadow before us; and as to the knowledge of his Maker, the man that is without it is no better than a stock or a stone or a brute beast. Neither without study can he reach anything of a due sense of the depth and divineness of the contemplation."

"Learned or not learned," said Agrican, "you might show yourself better bred than by endeavoring to make me talk on a subject on which you have me at a disadvantage. If you choose to sleep, I wish you good night; but if you prefer talking, I recommend you to talk of fighting or of fair ladies. And, by the way, pray tell me, are you not that Orlando who makes such a noise in the world? And what is it, pray, that brings you into these parts? Were you ever in love? I suppose you must have been; for to be a knight, and never to have been in love, would be like being a man without a heart in his breast."

The count replied: "Orlando I am, and in love I am. Love has made me abandon everything, and brought me into these distant regions, and, to tell you all in one word, my heart is in the hands of the daughter of King Galafron. You have come against him with fire and sword to get possession of his castles and his dominions; and I have come to help him, for no object in the world but to please his daughter and win her beautiful hand. I care for nothing else in existence."

Now when the Tartar king, Agrican, heard his antagonist speak in this manner, and knew him to be indeed Orlando and to be in love with Angelica, his face changed color for grief and jealousy, though it could not be seen for the darkness. His heart began beating with such violence that he felt as if he should have died.

"Well," said he to Orlando, "we are to fight when it is daylight, and one or other is to be left here, dead on the ground. I have a proposal to make to you—nay, an entreaty. My love is so excessive for the same lady that I beg you to leave her to me. I will owe you my thanks, and give up the siege, and put an end to the war. I cannot bear that any one should love her and that I should live to see it. Why, therefore, should either of us perish? Give her up. Not a soul shall know it."

"I never yet," answered Orlando, "made a promise which I did not keep, and nevertheless I own to you that, were I to make a promise like that, and even swear to keep it, I should not. You might as well ask me to tear away the limbs from my body and the eyes out of my head. I could as well live without breath itself as cease loving Angelica."

Agrican had hardly patience to let him finish speaking ere he leapt furiously on horseback, though it was midnight. "Quit her," said he, "or die!"

Orlando, seeing the infidel getting up and not being sure that he would not add treachery to fierceness, had been hardly less quick in mounting for the combat. "Never," exclaimed he; "I never could have quitted her if I would, and now I would not if I could. You must seek her by other means than these."

Fiercely dashed their horses together, in the night-time, on the green mead. Despiteful and terrible were the blows they gave and took by the moonlight. Agrican fought in a rage; Orlando was cooler. And now the struggle had lasted more than five hours, and day began to dawn, when the Tartar king, furious to find so much trouble given him, dealt his enemy a blow sharp and violent beyond conception. It cut the shield in two as if it had been made of wood, and, though blood could not be drawn from Orlando, because he was fated, it shook and bruised him as if it had started every joint in his body.

His *body* only, however, not a particle of his soul. So dreadful was the blow which the paladin gave in return, that not only shield, but every bit of mail on the body of Agrican was broken in pieces, and three of his ribs cut asunder.

The Tartar, roaring like a lion, raised his sword with still greater vehemence than before and dealt a blow on the paladin's helmet, such as he had never yet received from mortal man. For a moment it took away his senses. His sight failed, his ears tinkled, his frightened horse turned about to fly; and he was falling from the saddle when the very action of falling threw his head upwards and thus recalled his recollection.

"What a shame is this!" thought he; "how shall I ever again dare to face Angelica! I have been fighting, hour after hour, with this man, and he is but one, and I call myself Orlando! If the combat last any longer, I will bury myself in a monastery and never look on sword again."

Orlando muttered with his lips closed and his teeth ground together; and you might have thought that fire instead of breath came out of his nose and mouth. He raised his sword Durindana with both his hands and sent it down so tremendously on Agrican's shoulder that it cut through breastplate down to the very haunch, nay, crushed the saddle-bow, though it was made of bone and iron, and felled man and horse to the earth. Agrican turned as white as ashes and felt death upon him. He called Orlando to come close to him, with a gentle voice, and said, as well as he could: "I believe on Him who died on the cross. Baptize me, I pray thee, with the fountain, before my senses are gone. I have lived an evil life, but need not to be rebellious to God in death also. May He who came to save all the rest of the world save me!" And he shed tears, that great king, though he had been so lofty and fierce.

Orlando dismounted quickly, with his own face in tears. He gathered the king tenderly in his arms and took and laid him by the fountain, on a marble rim that it had, and then he wept in concert with him heartily, and asked his pardon, and so baptized him in the water of the fountain, and knelt and prayed to God for him with joined hands.

He then paused and looked at him, and when he perceived his countenance changed and that his whole person was cold, he left him there on the marble rim of the fountain, all armed as he was, with the sword by his side and the crown upon his head.

We left Rinaldo when, having overcome the monster, he quitted the castle of Altaripa and pursued his way on foot. He soon met with a weeping damsel, who, being questioned as to the cause of her sorrow, told him she was in search of one to do battle to rescue her lover, who had been made prisoner by a vile enchantress, together with Orlando and many more. The damsel was Flordelis, the lady-love of Florismart, and Rinaldo promised his assistance, trusting to accomplish the adventure either by valor or skill. Flordelis insisted upon Rinaldo's taking her horse, which he consented to do, on condition of her mounting behind him.

As they rode on through a wood, they heard strange noises, and Rinaldo, reassuring the damsel, pressed forward towards the quarter from which they proceeded. He soon perceived a giant standing under a vaulted cavern, with a huge club in his hand and of an appearance to strike the boldest spirit with dread. By the side of the cavern was chained a griffin, which, together with the giant, was stationed there to guard a wonderful horse, the same which was once Argalia's. This horse was a creature of enchantment, matchless in vigor, speed, and form, which disdained to share the diet of his fellow-steeds—corn or grass—and fed only on air. His name was Rabican.

This marvellous horse, after his master Argalia had been slain by Ferrau, finding himself at liberty, returned to his native cavern, and was here stabled under the protection of the giant and the griffin. As Rinaldo approached, the giant assailed him with his club. Rinaldo defended himself from the giant's blows and gave him one in return, which, if his skin had not been of the toughest, would have finished the combat. But the giant, though wounded, escaped and let loose the griffin. This monstrous bird towered in air and thence pounced down upon Rinaldo, who, watching his opportunity, dealt her a desperate wound. She had, however, strength for another fight, and kept repeating her attacks, which Rinaldo parried as he could, while the damsel stood trembling by, witnessing the contest.

The battle continued, rendered more terrible by the approach of night, when Rinaldo determined upon a desperate expedient to bring it to a conclusion. He fell, as if fainting from his wounds, and, on the close approach of the griffin, dealt her a blow which sheared away one of her wings. The beast, though sinking, griped him fast with her talons, digging through plate and mail; but Rinaldo plied his sword in utter desperation and at last accomplished her destruction.

Rinaldo then entered the cavern and found there the wonderful horse, all caparisoned. He was coal-black, except for a star of white on his forehead, and one white foot behind. For speed he was unrivalled, though in strength he yielded to Bayard. Rinaldo mounted upon Rabican and issued from the cavern.

As he pursued his way, he met a fugitive from Agrican's army, who gave such an account of the prowess of a champion who fought on the side of Angelica that Rinaldo was persuaded this must be Orlando, though at a loss to imagine how he could have been freed from captivity. He determined to repair to the scene of the contest to satisfy his curiosity, and Flordelis, hoping to find Florismart with Orlando, consented to accompany him.

While these things were doing, all was rout and dismay in the Tartarian army, from the death of Agrican. King Galafron, arriving at this juncture with an army for the relief of his capital, Albracca, assaulted the enemy's camp and carried all before him. Rinaldo had now reached the scene of action, and was looking on as an unconcerned spectator, when he was espied by Galafron. The king instantly recognized the horse Rabican, which he had given to Argalia when he sent him forth on his ill-omened mission to Paris. Possessed with the idea that the rider of the horse was the murderer of Argalia, Galafron rode at Rinaldo and smote him with all his force. Rinaldo was not slow to avenge the blow, and it would have gone hard with the king had not his followers instantly closed round him and separated the combatants.

Rinaldo thus found himself, almost without his own choice, enlisted on the side of the enemies of Angelica, which gave him no concern, so completely had his draught from the fountain of hate steeled his mind against her.

For several successive days the struggle continued, without any important results, Rinaldo meeting the bravest knights of Angelica's party and defeating them one after the other. At length he encountered Orlando, and the two knights bitterly reproached one another for the cause they had each adopted, and engaged in a furious combat. Orlando was mounted upon Bayard, Rinaldo's horse, which Agrican had by chance become possessed of, and Orlando had taken from him as the prize of victory. Bayard would not fight against his master, and Orlando was getting the worse of the encounter, when suddenly Rinaldo, seeing Astolpho, who for love of him had arrayed himself on his side, hard beset by numbers, left Orlando to rush to the defence of his friend. Night prevented the combat from being renewed, but a challenge was given and accepted for their next meeting.

But Angelica, sighing in her heart for Rinaldo, was not willing that he should be again exposed to so terrible a venture. She begged a boon of Orlando, promising she would be his, if he would do her bidding. On receiving his promise, she enjoined him to set out without delay to destroy the garden of the enchantress Falerina, in which many valiant knights had been entrapped and were imprisoned.

Orlando departed, on his horse Brigliadoro, leaving Bayard in disgrace for his bad deportment the day before. Angelica, to conciliate Rinaldo, sent Bayard to him, but Rinaldo remained unmoved by this, as by all her former acts of kindness.

When Rinaldo learned of Orlando's departure, he yielded to the entreaties of the lady of Florismart, and prepared to fulfil his promise and rescue her lover from the power of the enchantress. Thus both Rinaldo and Orlando were bound upon the same adventure, but unknown to one another.

The castle of Falerina was protected by a river, which

was crossed by a bridge, kept by a ruffian who challenged all comers to the combat; and such was his strength that he had thus far prevailed in every encounter, as appeared by the arms of various knights which he had taken from them and piled up as a trophy on the shore. Rinaldo attacked him, but with as bad success as the rest, for the bridge-ward struck him so violent a blow with an iron mace that he fell to the ground. But when the villain approached to strip him of his armor, Rinaldo seized him, and the bridge-ward, being unable to free himself, leapt with Rinaldo into the lake, where they both disappeared.

Orlando, meanwhile, in discharge of his promise to Angelica, pursued his way in quest of the same adventure. In passing through a wood, he saw a cavalier, armed at all points and mounted, keeping guard over a lady who was bound to a tree, weeping bitterly. Orlando hastened to her relief, but was exhorted by the knight not to interfere, for she had deserved her fate by her wickedness. In proof of which he made certain charges against her. The lady denied them all, and Orlando believed her, defied the knight, overthrew him, and, releasing the lady, departed with her seated on his horse's croup.

While they rode, another damsel approached on a white palfrey, who warned Orlando of impending danger and informed him that he was near the garden of the enchantress. Orlando was delighted with the intelligence and entreated her to inform him how he was to gain admittance. She replied that the garden could only be entered at sunrise and gave him such instructions as would enable him to gain admittance. She gave him also a book in which was painted the garden and all that it contained, together with the palace of the false enchantress, where she had secluded herself for the purpose of executing a magic work in which she was engaged. This was the manufacture of a sword capable of cutting even through enchanted substances. The object of this labor, the damsel told him, was the destruction of a knight of the west, by name Orlando, who, she had read in the book of Fate, was coming to demolish her garden. Having thus instructed him, the damsel departed.

Orlando, finding he must delay his enterprise till the next morning, now lay down and was soon asleep. Seeing this, the base woman whom he had rescued, and who was intent on making her escape to rejoin her paramour, mounted Brigliadoro and rode off, carrying away Durindana.

When Orlando awoke, his indignation, as may be supposed, was great on the discovery of the theft; but, like a good knight and true, he was not to be diverted from his enterprise. He tore off a huge branch of an elm to supply the place of his sword; and, as the sun rose, took his way towards the gate of the garden, where a dragon was on his watch. This he slew by repeated blows, and entered the garden, the gate of which closed behind him, barring retreat. Looking round him, he saw a fair fountain, which overflowed into a river, and in the centre of the fountain a figure, on whose forehead was written—

> The stream which waters violet and rose,
> From hence to the enchanted palace goes.

Following the banks of this flowing stream and rapt in the delights of the charming garden, Orlando arrived at the palace and, entering it, found the mistress, clad in white, with a crown of gold upon her head, in the act of viewing herself in the surface of the magic sword. Orlando surprised her before she could escape, deprived her of the weapon, and holding her fast by her long hair, which floated behind, threatened her with immediate death if she did not yield up her prisoners and afford him the means of egress. She, however, was firm of purpose, making no reply, and Orlando, unable to move her either by threats or entreaties, was under the necessity of binding her to a beech and pursuing his quest as he best might.

He then bethought him of his book, and consulting it, found that there was an outlet to the south, but that to reach it, a lake was to be passed, inhabited by a siren, whose song was so entrancing as to be quite irresistible to whoever heard it; but his book instructed him how to protect himself against this danger. According to its directions, while pursuing his path, he gathered abundance of flowers, which sprung all around, and filled his helmet and his ears with them; then listened if he heard the birds sing. Finding that, though he saw the gaping beak, the swelling throat, and ruffled plumes, he could not catch a note, he felt satisfied with his defence and advanced toward the lake. It was small but deep, and so clear and tranquil that the eye could penetrate to the bottom.

He had no sooner arrived upon the banks than the waters were seen to gurgle, and the siren, rising midway out of the pool, sung so sweetly that birds and beasts came trooping to the waterside to listen. Of this Orlando heard nothing, but, feigning to yield to the charm, sank down upon the bank. The siren issued from the water with the intent to accomplish his destruction. Orlando seized her by the hair, and while she sang yet louder (song being her only defence) cut off her head. Then, following the directions of his book, he stained himself all over with her blood.

Guarded by this talisman, he met successively all the monsters set for defence of the enchantress and her garden, and at length found himself again at the spot where he had made captive the enchantress, who still continued fastened to the beech. But the scene was changed. The garden had disappeared, and Falerina, before so haughty, now begged for mercy assuring him that many lives depended upon the preservation of hers. Orlando promised her life upon her pledging herself for the deliverance of her captives.

This, however, was no easy task. They were not in her possession, but in that of a much more powerful enchantress, Morgana, the Lady of the Lake, the very idea of opposing whom made Falerina turn pale with fear. Representing to him the hazards of the enterprise, she led him towards the dwelling of Morgana. To approach it he had to encounter the same uncourteous bridgeward who had already defeated and made captive so many knights, and last of all, Rinaldo. He was a churl of the most ferocious character, named Arridano. Morgana had provided him with impenetrable armor and endowed him in such a manner that his strength always

increased in proportion to that of the adversary with
whom he was matched. No one had ever yet escaped
from the contest, since, such was his power of endurance,
he could breathe freely under water. Hence, having grappled with a knight and sunk with him to the bottom of
the lake, he returned, bearing his enemy's arms in
triumph to the surface.

While Falerina was repeating her cautions and her
counsels, Orlando saw Rinaldo's arms erected in form
of a trophy among other spoils made by the villain, and,
forgetting their late quarrel, determined upon revenging
his friend. Arriving at the pass, the churl presuming to
bar the way, a desperate contest ensued, during which
Falerina escaped. The churl, finding himself overmatched at a contest of arms, resorted to his peculiar
art, grappled his antagonist, and plunged with him into
the lake. When he reached the bottom, Orlando found
himself in another world, upon a dry meadow, with the
lake overhead, through which shone the beams of our
sun, while the water stood on all sides like a crystal
wall. Here the battle was renewed, and Orlando had in
his magic sword an advantage which none had hitherto
possessed. It had been tempered by Falerina so that no
spells could avail against it. Thus armed, and counter-
vailing the strength of his adversary by his superior skill
and activity, it was not long before he laid him dead
upon the field.

Orlando then made all haste to return to the upper
air, and, passing through the water, which opened a way
before him (such was the power of the magic sword),
he soon regained the shore and found himself in a field,
as thickly covered with precious stones as the sky is
with stars.

Orlando crossed the field, not tempted to delay his
enterprise by gathering any of the brilliant gems spread
all around him. He next passed into a flowery meadow,
planted with trees, covered with fruit and flowers and
full of all imaginable delights.

In the middle of this meadow was a fountain, and
fast by it lay Morgana, asleep; a lady of a lovely aspect,
dressed in white and vermilion garments, her forehead well
furnished with hair, while she had scarcely any behind.

While Orlando stood in silence contemplating her beauty, he heard a voice exclaim, "Seize the fairy by the forelock, if thou hopest fair success." But his attention was arrested by another object, and he heeded not the warning. He saw on a sudden an array of towers, pinnacles and columns, palaces, with balconies and windows, extended alleys with trees—in short, a scene of architectural magnificence surpassing all he had ever beheld. While he stood gazing in silent astonishment, the scene slowly melted away and disappeared.*

When he had recovered from his amazement, he looked again toward the fountain. The fairy had awaked and risen, and was dancing round its border with the lightness of a leaf, timing her footsteps to this song:

Who in this world would wealth and treasure share,
Honor, delight, and state, and what is best,
Quick let him catch me by the lock of hair
Which flutters from my forehead; and be blest.

But let him not the proffered good forbear,
Nor till he seize the fleeting blessing rest;
For present loss is sought in vain to-morrow,
And the deluded wretch is left in sorrow.

The fairy, having sung thus, bounded off and fled from the flowery meadow over a high and inaccessible mountain. Orlando pursued her through thorns and rocks, while the sky gradually became overcast, and at last he was assailed by tempest, lightning, and hail.

While he thus pursued, a pale and meagre woman issued from a cave, armed with a whip, and, treading close upon his steps, scourged him with vigorous strokes. Her name was Repentance, and she told him it was her office to punish those who neglected to obey the voice of Prudence and seize the fairy Fortune when he might.

Orlando, furious at this chastisement, turned upon his tormentor, but might as well have stricken the wind. Finding it useless to resist, he resumed his chase of the fairy, gained upon her, and made frequent snatches at her white

* This is a poetical description of a phenomenon which is said to be really exhibited in the strait of Messina, between Sicily and Calabria. It is called Fata Morgana, or Mirage.

and vermilion garments, which still eluded his grasp.
At last, on her turning her head for an instant, he
profited by the chance and seized her by the forelock.
In an instant, the tempest ceased, the sky became serene,
and Repentance retreated to her cave.

Orlando now demanded of Morgana the keys of her
prison, and the fairy, feigning a complacent aspect, delivered up a key of silver, bidding him to be cautious
in the use of it, since to break the lock would be to
involve himself and all in inevitable destruction, a caution which gave the count room for long meditation and
led him to consider

> How few amid the suitors who importune
> The dame, know how to turn the keys of Fortune.

Keeping the fairy still fast by the forelock, Orlando
proceeded toward the prison, turned the key, without
occasioning the mischiefs apprehended, and delivered the
prisoners.

Among these were Florismart, Rinaldo, and many
others of the bravest knights of France. Morgana had
disappeared, and the knights, under the guidance of
Orlando, retraced the path by which he had come. They
soon reached the field of treasure. Rinaldo, finding himself amidst this mass of wealth, remembered his needy
garrison of Montalban and could not resist the tempta-
tion of seizing part of the booty. In particular a golden
chain studded with diamonds was too much for his self-
denial, and he took it, and was bearing it off, notwithstanding the remonstrances of Orlando, when a violent
wind caught him and whirled him back as he approached
the gate. This happened a second and a third time, and
Rinaldo at length yielded to necessity, rather than to the
entreaties of his friends, and cast away his prize.

They soon reached the bridge and passed over without hindrance to the other side, where they found the
trophy decorated with their arms. Here each knight resumed his own, and all, except the paladins and their
friends, separated as their inclinations or duty prompted.
Dudon the Dane, one of the rescued knights, informed
the cousins that he had been made prisoner by Mor-

gana while in the discharge of an embassy to them from
Charlemagne, who called upon them to return to the
defence of Christendom. Orlando was too much fascinated
by Angelica to obey this summons, and, followed by the
faithful Florismart, who would not leave him, returned
towards Albracca. Rinaldo, Dudon, Iroldo, Prasildo, and
the others took their way towards the west.

THE INVASION OF FRANCE

Agramant, King of Africa, convoked the kings, his
vassals, to deliberate in council. He reminded them of
the injuries he had sustained from France, that his father
had fallen in battle with Charlemagne, and that his early
years had hitherto not allowed him to wipe out the stain
of former defeats. He now proposed to them to carry
war into France.

Sobrino, his wisest councillor, opposed the project,
representing the rashness of it; but Rodomont, the young
and fiery king of Algiers, denounced Sobrino's counsel
as base and cowardly, declaring himself impatient for
the enterprise. The king of the Garamantes, venerable for
his age and renowned for his prophetic lore, interposed,
and assured the king that such an attempt would be sure
to fail, unless he could first get on his side a youth
marked out by destiny as the fitting compeer of the most
puissant knights of France, the young Rogero, descended
in direct line from Hector of Troy. This prince was
now a dweller upon the mountain Carena, where Atlantes,
his foster-father, a powerful magician, kept him in retirement, having discovered by his art that his pupil
would be lost to him if allowed to mingle with the world.
To break the spells of Atlantes and draw Rogero from
his retirement, only one means was to be found. It was
a ring possessed by Angelica, Princess of Cathay, which
was a talisman against all enchantments. If this ring could
be procured, all would go well; without it, the enterprise
was desperate.

Rodomont treated this declaration of the old prophet with scorn, and it would probably have been held of little weight by the council, had not the aged king, oppressed by the weight of years, expired in the very act of reaffirming his prediction. This made so deep an impression on the council that it was unanimously resolved to postpone the war until an effort should be made to win Rogero to the camp.

King Agramant thereupon proclaimed that the sovereignty of a kingdom should be the reward of whoever should succeed in obtaining the ring of Angelica. Brunello, the dwarf, the subtlest thief in all Africa, undertook to procure it.

In prosecution of this design, he made the best of his way to Angelica's kingdom and arrived beneath the walls of Albracca while the besieging army was encamped before the fortress. While the attention of the garrison was absorbed by the battle that raged below, he scaled the walls, approached the princess unnoticed, slipped the ring from her finger, and escaped unobserved. He hastened to the seaside, and, finding a vessel ready to sail, embarked, and arrived at Biserta, in Africa. Here he found Agramant, impatient for the talisman which was to foil the enchantments of Atlantes and to put Rogero into his hands. The dwarf, kneeling before the king, presented him with the ring, and Agramant, delighted at the success of his mission, crowned him in recompense King of Tingitana.

All were now anxious to go in quest of Rogero. The cavalcade accordingly departed and in due time arrived at the mountain of Carena.

At the bottom of this was a fruitful and well-wooded plain, watered by a large river, and from this plain was descried a beautiful garden on the mountain-top, which contained the mansion of Atlantes; but the ring, which discovered what was before invisible, could not, though it revealed this paradise, enable Agramant or his followers to enter it. So steep and smooth was the rock by nature that even Brunello failed in every attempt to scale it. He did not, for this, despair of accomplishing the object; but, having obtained Agramant's consent, caused the assembled courtiers and knights to celebrate a tournament upon the plain below. This was done with the view of seducing Rogero from his fastness, and the stratagem was attended with success.

Rogero joined the tourney, and was presented by Agramant with a splendid horse, Frontino, and a magnificent sword. Having learned from Agramant of his intended invasion of France, he gladly consented to join the expedition.

Rodomont, meanwhile, was too impatient to wait for Agramant's arrangements, and embarked with all the forces he could raise, made good his landing on the coast of France, and routed the Christians in several encounters. Previously to this, however, Gano, or Ganelon (as he is sometimes called), the traitor, enemy of Orlando and the other nephews of Charlemagne, had entered into a traitorous correspondence with Marsilius, the Saracen King of Spain, whom he invited into France. Marsilius, thus encouraged, led an army across the frontiers and joined Rodomont. This was the situation of things when Rinaldo and the other knights who had obeyed the summons of Dudon set forward on their return to France.

When they arrived at Buda, in Hungary, they found the king of that country about despatching his son, Ottachiero, with an army to the succor of Charlemagne. Delighted with the arrival of Rinaldo, he placed his son and troops under his command. In due time, the army arrived on the frontiers of France and, united with the troops of Desiderius, King of Lombardy, poured down into Provence. The confederate armies had not marched many days through this gay tract before they heard a crash of drums and trumpets behind the hills, which spoke the conflict between the paynims, led by Rodomont, and the Christian forces. Rinaldo, witnessing from a mountain the prowess of Rodomont, left his troops in charge of his friends and galloped towards him with his lance in rest. The impulse was irresistible, and Rodomont was unhorsed. But Rinaldo, unwilling to avail himself of his advantage, galloped back to the hill and, having secured Bayard among the baggage, returned to finish the combat on foot.

During this interval the battle had become general, the Hungarians were routed, and Rinaldo, on his return, had the mortification to find that Ottachiero was wounded and Dudon taken prisoner. While he sought Rodomont in order to renew the combat, a new sound of drums and trumpets was heard, and Charlemagne, with the main body of his army, was descried advancing in battle array.

Rodomont, seeing this, mounted the horse of Dudon, left Rinaldo, who was on foot, and galloped off to encounter this new enemy.

Agramant, accompanied by Rogero, had by this time made good his landing, and joined Rodomont with all his forces. Rogero eagerly embraced this first opportunity of distinguishing himself and spread terror wherever he went, encountering in turn and overthrowing many of the bravest knights of France. At length he found himself opposite to Rinaldo, who, being interrupted, as we have said, in his combat with Rodomont, and unable to follow him, being on foot, was shouting to his late foe to return and finish their combat. Rogero also was on foot, and seeing the Christian knight so eager for a contest, proffered himself to supply the place of his late antagonist. Rinaldo saw at a glance that the Moorish prince was a champion worthy of his arm and gladly accepted the defiance. The combat was stoutly maintained for a time; but now fortune declared decisively in favor of the infidel army, and Charlemagne's forces gave way at all points in irreparable confusion. The two combatants were separated by the crowd of fugitives and pursuers, and Rinaldo hastened to recover possession of his horse. But Bayard, in the confusion, had got loose, and Rinaldo followed him into a thick wood, thus becoming effectually separated from Rogero.

Rogero, also seeking his horse in the medley, came where two warriors were engaged in mortal combat. Though he knew not who they were, he could distinguish that one was a paynim and the other a Christian; and, moved by the spirit of courtesy, he approached them and exclaimed, "Let him of the two who worships Christ pause and hear what I have to say. The army of Charles is routed and in flight, so that if he wishes to follow his leader he has no time for delay." The Christian knight, who was none other than Bradamante, a female war-

rior, in prowess equal to the best of knights, was thunder-
struck with the tidings, and would gladly leave the contest undecided and retire from the field; but Rodomont,
her antagonist, would by no means consent. Rogero, indignant at his discourtesy, insisted upon her departure,
while he took up her quarrel with Rodomont.

The combat, obstinately maintained on both sides, was
interrupted by the return of Bradamante. Finding herself
unable to overtake the fugitives and reluctant to leave
to another the burden and risk of a contest which belonged to herself, she had returned to reclaim the combat.
She arrived, however, when her champion had dealt his
enemy such a blow as obliged him to drop both his
sword and bridle. Rogero, disdaining to profit by his
adversary's defenceless situation, sat apart, upon his
horse, while that of Rodomont bore his rider, stunned
and stupefied, about the field.

Bradamante approached Rogero, conceiving a yet
higher opinion of his valor on beholding such an instance
of forbearance. She addressed him, excusing herself for
leaving him exposed to an enemy from his interference
in her cause, pleading her duty to her sovereign as the
motive. While she spoke, Rodomont, recovered from his
confusion, rode up to them. His bearing was, however,
changed, and he disclaimed all thoughts of further contest with one who, he said, "had already conquered him
by his courtesy." So saying, he quitted his antagonist,
picked up his sword, and spurred out of sight.

Bradamante was now again desirous of retiring from
the field, and Rogero insisted on accompanying her,
though yet unaware of her sex.

As they pursued their way, she inquired the name
and quality of her new associate; and Rogero informed
her of his nation and family. He told her that Astyanax,
the son of Hector of Troy, established the kingdom of
Messina in Sicily. From him were derived two branches,
which gave origin to two families of renown. From one
sprang the royal race of Pepin and Charlemagne, and
from the other that of Reggio, in Italy. "From that of
Reggio am I derived," he continued. "My mother, driven
from her home by the chance of war, died in giving me
life, and I was taken in charge by a sage enchanter,

who trained me to feats of arms amidst the dangers of the desert and the chase."

Having thus ended his tale, Rogero entreated a similar return of courtesy from his companion, who replied, without disguise, that she was of the race of Clermont, and sister to Rinaldo, whose fame was perhaps known to him. Rogero, much moved by this intelligence, entreated her to take off her helmet, and, at the discovery of her face, remained transported with delight.

While absorbed in this contemplation, an unexpected danger assailed them. A party which was placed in a wood, in order to intercept the retreating Christians, broke from its ambush upon the pair, and Bradamante, who was uncasqued, was wounded in the head. Rogero was in fury at this attack, and Brandamante, replacing her helmet, joined him in taking speedy vengeance on their enemies. They cleared the field of them, but became separated in the pursuit; and Rogero, quitting the chase, wandered by hill and vale in search of her whom he had no sooner found than lost.

While pursuing this quest, he fell in with two knights, whom he joined, and engaged them to assist him in the search of his companion, describing her arms, but concealing, from a certain feeling of jealousy, her quality and sex.

It was evening when they joined company, and having ridden together through the night, the morning was beginning to break, when one of the strangers, fixing his eyes upon Rogero's shield, demanded of him by what right he bore the Trojan arms. Rogero declared his origin and race, and then, in his turn, interrogated the inquirer as to his pretensions to the cognizance of Hector, which he bore. The stranger replied, "My name is Mandricardo, son of Agrican, the Tartar king, whom Orlando treacherously slew. I say *treacherously*, for in fair fight he could not have done it. It is in search of him that I have come to France, to take vengeance for my father, and to wrest from him Durindana, that famous sword, which belongs to me and not to him." When the knights demanded to know by what right he claimed Durindana, Mandricardo thus related his history:

"I had been, before the death of my father, a wild

and reckless youth. That event awakened my energies
and drove me forth to seek for vengeance. Determined
to owe success to nothing but my own exertions, I departed without attendants or horse or arms. Travelling
thus alone and on foot, I espied one day a pavilion,
pitched near a fountain, and entered it, intent on adventure. I found therein a damsel of gracious aspect,
who replied to my inquiries that the fountain was the
work of a fairy whose castle stood beyond a neighboring hill, where she kept watch over a treasure which
many knights had tried to win, but fruitlessly, having
lost their life or liberty in the attempt. This treasure was
the armor of Hector, prince of Troy, whom Achilles
treacherously slew. Nothing was wanting but his sword
Durindana, and this had fallen into the possession of a
queen named Penthesilea, from whom it passed through
her descendants to Almontes, whom Orlando slew, and
thus became possessed of the sword. The rest of Hector's
arms were saved and carried off by Æneas, from whom
this fairy received them in recompense of service rendered. "If you have the courage to attempt their acquisition," said the damsel, "I will be your guide."

Mandricardo went on to say that he eagerly embraced
the proposal, and being provided with horse and armor
by the damsel, set forth on his enterprise, the lady accompanying him.

As they rode, she explained the dangers of the quest.
The armor was defended by a champion, one of the
numerous unsuccessful adventurers for the prize, all of
whom had been made prisoners by the fairy and compelled to take their turn, day by day, in defending the
arms against all comers. Thus speaking, they arrived at
the castle, which was of alabaster overlaid with gold.
Before it, on a lawn, sat an armed knight on horseback,
who was none other than Gradasso, King of Sericane,
who, in his return home from his unsuccessful inroad
into France had fallen into the power of the fairy, and
was held to do her bidding. Mandricardo, upon seeing
him, dropt his visor and laid his lance in rest. The champion of the castle was equally ready, and each spurred
towards his opponent. They met one another with equal
force, splintered their spears, and, returning to the charge,

encountered with their swords. The contest was long and doubtful, when Mandricardo, determined to bring it to an end, threw his arms about Gradasso, grappled with him, and both fell to the ground. Mandricardo, however, fell uppermost and, preserving his advantage, compelled Gradasso to yield himself conquered. The damsel now interfered, congratulating the victor and consoling the vanquished as well as she might.

Mandricardo and the damsel proceeded to the gate of the castle, which they found undefended. As they entered, they beheld a shield suspended from a pilaster of gold. The device was a white eagle on an azure field, in memory of the bird of Jove, which bore away Ganymede, the flower of the Phrygian race. Beneath was engraved the following couplet:

> Let none with hand profane my buckler wrong
> Unless he be himself as Hector strong.

The damsel, alighting from her palfrey, made obeisance to the arms, bending herself to the ground. The Tartar king bowed his head with equal reverence; then advancing towards the shield, touched it with his sword. Thereupon an earthquake shook the ground, and the way by which he had entered closed. Another and an opposite gate opened and displayed a field bristling with stalks and grain of gold. The damsel, upon this, told him that he had no means of retreat but by cutting down the harvest which was before him and by uprooting a tree which grew in the middle of the field. Mandricardo, without replying, began to mow the harvest with his sword, but had scarce smitten thrice when he perceived that every stalk that fell was instantly transformed into some poisonous or ravenous animal, which prepared to assail him. Instructed by the damsel, he snatched up a stone and cast it among the pack. A strange wonder followed; for no sooner had the stone fallen among the beasts than they turned their rage against one another and rent each other to pieces. Mandricardo did not stop to marvel at the miracle, but proceeded to fulfil his task and uproot the tree. He clasped it round the trunk and made vigorous efforts to tear it up by the roots. At each effort fell a shower of leaves, that were instantly changed into birds of prey, which attacked the knight, flapping their wings in his face, with horrid screeching. But undismayed by this new annoyance, he continued to tug at the trunk till it yielded to his efforts. A burst of wind and thunder followed, and the hawks and vultures flew screaming away.

But these only gave place to a new foe, for from the hole made by tearing up the tree issued a furious serpent, and, darting at Mandricardo, wound herself about his limbs with a strain that almost crushed him. Fortune, however, again stood his friend, for, writhing under the folds of the monster, he fell backwards into the hole, and his enemy was crushed beneath his weight.

Mandricardo, when he was somewhat recovered, and assured himself of the destruction of the serpent, began to contemplate the place into which he had fallen, and saw that he was in a vault incrusted with costly metals and illuminated by a live coal. In the middle was a sort of ivory bier, and upon this was extended what appeared to be a knight in armor, but was in truth an empty trophy, composed of the rich and precious arms once Hector's, to which nothing was wanting but the sword. While Mandricardo stood contemplating the prize, a door opened behind him, and a bevy of fair damsels entered, dancing, who, taking up the armor, piece by piece, led him away to the place where the shield was suspended; where he found the fairy of the castle seated in state. By her he was invested with the arms he had won, first pledging his solemn oath to wear no other blade but Durindana, which he was to wrest from Orlando, and thus complete the conquest of Hector's arms.

THE INVASION OF FRANCE

CONTINUED

Mandricardo, having completed his story, now turned to Rogero and proposed that arms should decide which of the two was most worthy to bear the symbol of the Trojan knight.

Rogero felt no other objection to this proposal than the scruple which arose on observing that his antagonist was without a sword. Mandricardo insisted that this need be no impediment, since his oath prevented him from using a sword until he should have achieved the conquest of Durindana.

This was no sooner said than a new antagonist started up in Gradasso, who now accompanied Mandricardo. Gradasso vindicated his prior right to Durindana, to obtain which he had embarked (as was related in the beginning) in that bold inroad upon France. A quarrel was thus kindled between the kings of Tartary and Sericane. While the dispute was raging, a knight arrived upon the ground, accompanied by a damsel, to whom Rogero related the cause of the strife. The knight was Florismart, and his companion Flordelis. Florismart succeeded in bringing the two champions to accord, by informing them that he could bring them to the presence of Orlando, the master of Durindana.

Gradasso and Mandricardo readily made truce in order to accompany Florismart, nor would Rogero be left behind.

As they proceeded on their quest, they were met by a dwarf, who entreated their assistance in behalf of his lady, who had been carried off by an enchanter, mounted on a winged horse. However unwilling to leave the question of the sword undecided, it was not possible for the knights to resist this appeal. Two of their number, Gradasso and Rogero, therefore accompanied the dwarf, Mandricardo persisted in his search for Orlando, and Florismart, with Flordelis, pursued their way to the camp of Charlemagne.

Atlantes, the enchanter, who had brought up Rogero and cherished for him the warmest affection, knew by his art that his pupil was destined to be severed from him and converted to the Christian faith through the influence of Bradamante, that royal maiden with whom chance had brought him acquainted. Thinking to thwart the will of Heaven in this respect, he now put forth all his arts to entrap Rogero into his power. By the aid of his subservient demons, he reared a castle on an inaccessible height in the Pyrenean mountains, and, to make it a pleasant abode to his pupil, contrived to entrap and convey thither knights and damsels many a one, whom chance had brought into the vicinity of his castle. Here, in a sort of sensual paradise, they were but too willing to forget glory and duty and to pass their time in indolent enjoyment.

It was by the enchanter that the dwarf had now been sent to tempt the knights into his power.

But we must now return to Rinaldo, whom we left interrupted in his combat with Rodomont. In search of his late antagonist, and intent on bringing their combat to a decision, he entered the forest of Arden, whither he suspected Rodomont had gone. While engaged on this quest, he was surprised by the vision of a beautiful child dancing naked, with three damsels as beautiful as himself. While he was lost in admiration at the sight, the child approached him and, throwing at him handfuls of roses and lilies, struck him from his horse. He was no sooner down than he was seized by the dancers, by whom he was dragged about and scourged with flowers till he fell into a swoon. When he began to revive, one of the group approached him and told him that his punishment was the consequence of his rebellion against that power before whom all things bend; that there was but one remedy to heal the wounds that had been inflicted, and that was to drink of the waters of Love. Then they left him.

Rinaldo, sore and faint, dragged himself towards a fountain which flowed near by, and, being parched with thirst, drank greedily and almost unconsciously of the water, which was sweet to the taste, but bitter at the heart. After repeated draughts, he recovered his strength and recollection and found himself in the same place where Angelica had formerly awakened him with a rain of flowers, and whence he had fled in contempt of her courtesy.

This remembrance of the scene was followed by the recognition of his crime; and, repenting bitterly his ingratitude, he leaped upon Bayard, with the intention of hastening to Angelica's country and soliciting his pardon at her feet.

Let us now retrace our steps and revert to the time when the paladins, having learned from Dudon the summons of Charlemagne to return to France to repel the invaders, had all obeyed the command, with the exception of Orlando, whose passion for Angelica still held him in attendance on her. Orlando, arriving before Albracca, found it closely beleaguered. He, however, made his way into the citadel and related his adventures to Angelica, from the time of his departure up to his separation from Rinaldo and the rest, when they departed to the assistance of Charlemagne. Angelica, in return, described the distresses of the garrison and the force of the besiegers; and in conclusion prayed Orlando to favor her escape from the pressing danger and escort her into France. Orlando, who did not suspect that love for Rinaldo was her secret motive, joyfully agreed to the proposal, and the sally was resolved upon.

Leaving lights burning in the fortress, they departed at nightfall and passed in safety through the enemy's camp. After encountering numerous adventures, they reached the seaside and embarked on board a pinnace for France. The vessel arrived safely, and the travellers, disembarking in Provence, pursued their way by land. One day, heated and weary, they sought shelter from the sun in the forest of Arden, and chance directed Angelica to the fountain of Disdain, of whose waters she eagerly drank.

Issuing thence, the count and damsel encountered a stranger-knight. It was no other than Rinaldo, who was just on the point of setting off on a pilgrimage in search of Angelica, to implore her pardon for his insensibility and urge his new-found passion. Surprise and delight at first deprived him of utterance, but soon recovering himself, he joyfully saluted her, claiming her as his and exhorting her to put herself under his protection. His presumption was repelled by Angelica with disdain, and Orlando, enraged at the invasion of his rights, challenged him to decide their claims by arms.

Terrified at the combat which ensued, Angelica fled amain through the forest and came out upon a plain covered with tents. This was the camp of Charlemagne, who led the army of reserve destined to support the troops which had advanced to oppose Marsilius. Charles, having heard the damsel's tale, with difficulty separated the two cousins and then consigned Angelica, as the cause of quarrel, to the care of Namo, Duke of Bavaria, promising that she should be his who should best deserve her in the impending battle.

But these plans and hopes were frustrated. The Christian army, beaten, at all points, fled from the Saracens; and Angelica, indifferent to both her lovers, mounted a swift palfrey and plunged into the forest, rejoicing, in spite of her terror, at having regained her liberty. She stopped at last in a tufted grove, where a gentle zephyr blew and whose young trees were watered by two clear runnels, which came and mingled their waters, making a pleasing murmur. Believing herself far from Rinaldo and overcome by fatigue and the summer heat, she saw with delight a bank covered with flowers so thick that they almost hid the green turf, inviting her to alight and rest. She dismounted from her palfrey and turned him loose, to recruit his strength with the tender grass which bordered the streamlets. Then, in a sheltered nook tapestried with moss and fenced in with roses and hawthorn-flowers, she yielded herself to grateful repose.

She had not slept long when she was awakened by the noise made by the approach of a horse. Starting up, she saw an armed knight who had arrived at the bank of the stream. Not knowing whether he was to be feared or not, her heart beat with anxiety. She pressed aside the leaves to allow her to see who it was, but scarce dared to breathe for fear of betraying herself. Soon the knight threw himself on the flowery bank and, leaning his head on his hand, fell into a profound reverie. Then arousing himself from his silence, he began to pour forth complaints, mingled with deep sighs. Rivers of tears flowed down his cheeks, and his breast seemed to labor with a hidden flame. "Ah, vain regrets!" he exclaimed; "cruel fortune! Others triumph, while I endure hopeless misery! Better a thousand times to lose life than wear a chain so disgraceful and so oppressive!"

Angelica, by this time, had recognized the stranger, and perceived that it was Sacripant, King of Circassia, one of the worthiest of her suitors. This prince had fol-

lowed Angelica from his country, at the very gates of
the day, to France, where he heard with dismay that
she was under the guardianship of the paladin Orlando,
and that the Emperor had announced his decree to
award her as the prize of valor to that one of his nephews who should best deserve her.

As Sacripant continued to lament, Angelica, who had
always opposed the hardness of marble to his sighs,
thought with herself that nothing forbade her employing
his good offices in this unhappy crisis. Though firmly
resolved never to accept him as a spouse, she yet felt
the necessity of giving him a gleam of hope in reward
for the service she required of him. All at once, like
Diana, she stepped forth from the arbor. "May the gods
preserve thee," she said, "and put far from thee all hard
thoughts of me!" Then she told him all that had befallen
her since she parted with him at her father's court, and
how she had availed herself of Orlando's protection to
escape from the beleaguered city. At that moment the
noise of horse and armor was heard as of one approaching, and Sacripant, furious at the interruption, resumed
his helmet, mounted his horse, and placed his lance in
rest. He saw a knight advancing, with scarf and plume
of snowy whiteness. Sacripant regarded him with angry
eyes, and, while he was yet some distance off, defied him
to the combat. The other, not moved by his angry tone
to make reply, put himself on his defence. Their horses,
struck at the same moment with the spur, rushed upon
one another with the impetuosity of a tempest. Their
shields were pierced each with the other's lance, and
only the temper of their breastplates saved their lives.
Both the horses recoiled with the violence of the shock,
but the unknown knight's recovered itself at the touch
of the spur; the Saracen king's fell dead, and bore down
his master with him. The white knight, seeing his enemy
in this condition, cared not to renew the combat, but,
thinking he had done enough for glory, pursued his way
through the forest, and was a mile off before Sacripant
had got free from his horse.

As a ploughman, stunned by a thunder-clap which
has stricken dead the oxen at his plough, stands motionless, sadly contemplating his loss, so Sacripant stood,

confounded and overwhelmed with mortification at having Angelica a witness of his defeat. He groaned, he sighed, less from the pain of his bruises than for the shame of being reduced to such a state before her. The princess took pity on him and consoled him as well as she could. "Banish your regrets, my lord," she said, "this accident has happened solely in consequence of the feebleness of your horse, which had more need of rest and food than of such an encounter as this. Nor can your adversary gain any credit by it, since he has hurried away, not venturing a second trial." While she thus consoled Sacripant, they perceived a person approach, who seemed a courier, with bag and horn. As soon as he came up, he accosted Sacripant and inquired if he had seen a knight pass that way, bearing a white shield and with a white plume to his helmet. "I have, indeed, seen too much of him," said Sacripant; "it is he who has brought me to the ground; but at least I hope to learn from you who that knight is." "That I can easily inform you," said the man; "know then that, if you have been overthrown, you owe your fate to the high prowess of a lady as beautiful as she is brave. It is the fair and illustrious Bradamante who has won from you the honors of victory."

At these words, the courier rode on his way, leaving Sacripant more confounded and mortified than ever. In silence he mounted the horse of Angelica, taking the lady behind him on the croup, and rode away in search of a more secure asylum. Hardly had they ridden two miles when a new sound was heard in the forest, and they perceived a gallant and powerful horse, which, leaping the ravines and dashing aside the branches that opposed his passage, appeared before them, accoutred with a rich harness adorned with gold.

"If I may believe my eyes, which penetrate with difficulty the underwood," said Angelica, "that horse that dashes so stoutly through the bushes is Bayard, and I marvel how he seems to know the need we have of him, mounted as we are both on one feeble animal." Sacripant, dismounting from the palfrey, approached the fiery courser and attempted to seize his bridle, but the disdainful animal, turning from him, launched at him a volley of kicks enough to have shattered a wall of marble. Bayard then approached Angelica with an air as gentle and loving as a faithful dog could his master after a long separation. For he remembered how she had caressed him and even fed him in Albracca. She took his bridle in her left hand, while with her right she patted his neck. The beautiful animal, gifted with wonderful intelligence, seemed to submit entirely. Sacripant, seizing the moment to vault upon him, controlled his curvetings, and Angelica, quitting the croup of the palfrey, regained her seat.

But, turning his eyes toward a place where was heard a noise of arms, Sacripant beheld Rinaldo. That hero now loves Angelica more than his life, and she flies him as the timid crane the falcon.

The fountain of which Angelica had drunk produced such an effect on the beautiful queen that, with distressed countenance and trembling voice, she conjured Sacripant not to wait the approach of Rinaldo, but to join her in flight.

"Am I, then," said Sacripant, "of so little esteem with you that you doubt my power to defend you? Do you forget the battle of Albracca, and how, in your defence, I fought single-handed against Agrican and all his knights?"

Angelica made no reply, uncertain what to do; but already Rinaldo was too near to be escaped. He advanced menacingly to the Circassian king, for he recognized his horse.

"Vile thief," he cried, "dismount from that horse, and prevent the punishment that is your due for daring to rob me of my property. Leave, also, the princess in my hands, for it would indeed be a sin to suffer so charming a lady and so gallant a charger to remain in such keeping."

The King of Circassia, furious at being thus insulted, cried out, "Thou liest, villain, in giving me the name of thief, which better belongs to thyself than to me. It is true, the beauty of this lady and the perfection of this horse are unequalled; come on, then, and let us try which of us is most worthy to possess them."

At these words the King of Circassia and Rinaldo at-

tacked one another with all their force, one fighting on
foot, the other on horseback. You need not, however,
suppose that the Saracen king found any advantage in
this; for a young page, unused to horsemanship, could
not have failed more completely to manage Bayard than
did this accomplished knight. The faithful animal loved
his master too well to injure him, and refused his aid as
well as his obedience to the hand of Sacripant, who could
strike but ineffectual blows, the horse backing when he
wished him to go forward, and dropping his head and
arching his back, throwing out with his legs, so as almost
to shake the knight out of the saddle. Sacripant, seeing
that he could not manage him, watched his opportunity,
rose on his saddle, and leapt lightly to the earth; then,
relieved from the embarrassment of the horse, renewed
the combat on more equal terms. Their skill to thrust
and parry were equal; one rises, the other stoops; with
one foot set firm, they turn and wind, to lay on strokes
or to dodge them. At last Rinaldo, throwing himself on
the Circassian, dealt him a blow so terrible that Fus-
berta, his good sword, cut in two the buckler of Sacripant, although it was made of bone, and covered with a
thick plate of steel well tempered. The arm of the Saracen was deprived of its defence, and almost palsied with
the stroke. Angelica, perceiving how victory was likely
to incline and shuddering at the thought of becoming the
prize of Rinaldo, hesitated no longer. Turning her horse's
head, she fled with the utmost speed; and, in spite of the
round pebbles which covered a steep descent, she
plunged into a deep valley, trembling with the fear that
Rinaldo was in pursuit. At the bottom of this valley she
encountered an aged hermit, whose white beard flowed
to his middle and whose venerable appearance seemed
to assure his piety.

This hermit, who appeared shrunk by age and fasting,
travelled slowly, mounted upon a wretched ass. The
princess, overcome with fear, conjured him to save her
life and to conduct her to some port of the sea, whence
she might embark and quit France, never more to hear
the odious name of Rinaldo.

The old hermit was something of a wizzard. He comforted Angelica and promised to protect her from all

peril. Then he opened his scrip and took from thence a book, and had read but a single page when a goblin, obedient to his incantations, appeared, under the form of a laboring man, and demanded his orders. He received them, transported himself to the place where the knights still maintained their conflict, and boldly stepped between the two.

"Tell me, I pray you," he said, "what benefit will accrue to him who shall get the better in this contest? The object you are contending for is already disposed of, for the Paladin Orlando, without effort and without opposition, is now carrying away the Princess Angelica to Paris. You had better pursue them promptly, for if they reach Paris, you will never see her again."

At these words you might have seen those rival warriors confounded, stupefied, silently agreeing that they were affording their rival a fair opportunity to triumph over them. Rinaldo, approaching Bayard, breathes a sigh of shame and rage and swears a terrible oath that, if he overtakes Orlando, he will tear his heart out. Then mounting Bayard and pressing his flanks with his spurs, he leaves the King of Circassia on foot in the forest.

Let it not appear strange that Rinaldo found Bayard obedient at last, after having so long prevented any one from even touching his bridle; for that fine animal had an intelligence almost human; he had fled from his master only to draw him on the track of Angelica and enable him to recover her. He saw when the princess fled from the battle, and Rinaldo being then engaged in a fight on foot, Bayard found himself free to follow the traces of Angelica. Thus he had drawn his master after him, not permitting him to approach, and had brought him to the sight of the princess. But Bayard now, deceived like his master with the false intelligence of the goblin, submits to be mounted and to serve his master as usual, and Rinaldo, animated with rage, makes him fly toward Paris, more slowly than his wishes, though the speed of Bayard outstripped the winds. Full of impatience to encounter Orlando, he gave but a few hours that night to sleep. Early the next day he saw before him the great city, under the walls of which the Emperor Charles had collected the scattered remains of his army. Foreseeing that he would soon be attacked on all sides, the Emperor had caused the ancient fortifications to be repaired and new ones to be built, surrounded by wide and deep ditches. The desire to hold the field against the enemy made him seize every means of procuring new allies. He hoped to receive from England aid sufficient to enable him to form a new camp, and as soon as Rinaldo rejoined him, he selected him to go as his ambassador into England, to plead for auxiliaries. Rinaldo was far from pleased with this commission, but he obeyed the Emperor's commands, without giving himself time to devote a single day to the object nearest his heart. He hastened to Calais and lost not a moment in embarking for England, ardently desiring a hasty despatch of his commission and a speedy return to France.

BRADAMANTE AND ROGERO

Bradamante, the knight of the white plume and shield, whose sudden appearance and encounter with Sacripant we have already told, was in quest of Rogero, from whom chance had separated her, almost at the beginning of their acquaintance. After her encounter with Sacripant, Bradamante pursued her way through the forest, in hopes of rejoining Rogero, and arrived at last on the brink of a fair fountain.

This fountain flowed through a broad meadow. Ancient trees overshadowed it, and travellers, attracted by the sweet murmur of its waters, stopped there to cool themselves. Bradamante, casting her eyes on all sides to enjoy the beauties of the spot, perceived, under the shade of a tree, a knight reclining, who seemed to be oppressed with the deepest grief.

Bradamante accosted him and asked to be informed of the cause of his distress. "Alas! my lord," said he, "I lament a young and charming friend, my affianced wife, who has been torn from me by a villain—let me rather call him a demon—who, on a winged horse, descended from the air, seized her, and bore her screaming to his den. I have pursued them over rocks and through ravines till my horse is no longer able to bear me, and I now wait only for death." He added that already a vain attempt on his behalf had been made by two knights whom chance had brought to the spot. Their names were Gradasso, King of Sericane, and Rogero, the Moor. Both had been overcome by the wiles of the enchanter, and were added to the number of the captives, whom he held in an impregnable castle, situated on the height of the mountain. At the mention of Rogero's name, Bradamante started with delight, which was soon changed to an opposite sentiment when she heard that her lover was a prisoner in the toils of the enchanter. "Sir Knight," she said, "do not surrender yourself to despair; this day may be more happy for you than you think, if you will only lead me to the castle which enfolds her whom you deplore."

The knight responded, "After having lost all that made life dear to me, I have no motive to avoid the dangers of the enterprise, and I will do as you request; but I forewarn you of the perils you will have to encounter. If you fall, impute it not to me."

Having thus spoken, they took their way to the castle, but were overtaken by a messenger from the camp, who had been sent in quest of Bradamante to summon her back to the army, where her presence was needed to reassure her disheartened forces and withstand the advance of the Moors.

The mournful knight, whose name was Pinabel, thus became aware that Bradamante was a scion of the house of Clermont, between which and his own of Mayence there existed an ancient feud. From this moment the traitor sought only how he might be rid of the company of Bradamante, from whom he feared no good would come to him, but rather mortal injury, if his name and lineage became known to her. For he judged her by his own base model, and, knowing his ill deserts, he feared to receive his due.

Bradamante, in spite of the summons to return to the army, could not resolve to leave her lover in captivity and determined first to finish the adventure on which she was engaged. Pinabel leading the way, they at length arrived at a wood in the centre of which rose a steep, rocky mountain. Pinabel, who now thought of nothing else but how he might escape from Bradamante, proposed to ascend the mountain to extend his view, in order to discover a shelter for the night, if any there might be within sight. Under this pretence he left Bradamante and advanced up the side of the mountain till he came to a cleft in the rock, down which he looked and perceived that it widened below into a spacious cavern. Meanwhile, Bradamante, fearful of losing her guide, had followed close on his footsteps, and rejoined him at the mouth of the cavern. Then the traitor, seeing the impossibility of escaping her, conceived another design. He told her that before her approach he had seen in the cavern a young and beautiful damsel, whose rich dress announced her high birth, who with tears and lamentations implored assistance; that before he could descend to relieve her, a ruffian had seized her and hurried her away into the recesses of the cavern.

Bradamante, full of truth and courage, readily believed this lie of the Mayencian traitor. Eager to succor the damsel, she looked round for the means of facilitating the descent, and seeing a large elm with spreading branches, she lopped off with her sword one of the largest and thrust it into the opening. She told Pinabel to hold fast to the larger end, while, grasping the branches with her hands, she let herself down into the cavern.

The traitor smiled at seeing her thus suspended, and, asking her in mockery, "Are you a good leaper?" he let go the branch with perfidious glee and saw Bradamante precipitated to the bottom of the cave. "I wish your whole race were there with you," he muttered, "that you might all perish together."

But Pinabel's atrocious design was not accomplished. The twigs and foliage of the branch broke its descent, and Bradamante, not seriously injured, though stunned with her fall, was reserved for other adventures.

As soon as she recovered from the shock, Bradamante cast her eyes around and perceived a door, through which she passed into a second cavern, larger and loftier than the first. It had the appearance of a subterranean temple. Columns of the purest alabaster adorned it and supported the roof; a simple altar rose in the middle; a lamp, whose radiance was reflected by the alabaster walls, cast a mild light around.

Bradamante, inspired by a sense of religious awe, approached the altar, and, falling on her knees, poured forth her prayers and thanks to the Preserver of her life, invoking the protection of his power. At that moment, a small door opened and a female issued from it, with naked feet and flowing robe and hair, who called her by her name and thus addressed her: "Brave and generous Bradamante, know that it is a power from above that has brought you hither. The spirit of Merlin, whose last earthly abode was in this place, has warned me of your arrival and of the fate that awaits you. This famous grotto," she continued, "was the work of the enchanter Merlin; here his ashes repose. You have no doubt heard how this sage and virtuous enchanter ceased to be. Victim of the artful fairy of the lake, Merlin, by a fatal compliance with her request, laid himself down living in his tomb, without power to resist the spell laid upon him by that ingrate, who retained him there as long as he lived. His spirit hovers about this spot, and will not leave it until the last trumpet shall summon the dead to judgment. He answers the questions of those who approach his tomb, where perhaps you may be privileged to hear his voice."

Bradamante, astonished at these words and the objects which met her view, knew not whether she was awake or asleep. Confused, but modest, she cast down her eyes, and a blush overspread her face. "Ah, what am I," said she, "that so great a prophet should deign to speak to me!" Still, with a secret satisfaction, she followed the priestess, who led her to the tomb of Merlin. This tomb was constructed of a species of stone hard and resplendent like fire. The rays which beamed from the stone sufficed to light up that terrible place, where the sun's rays never penetrated; but I know not whether that light was the effect of a certain phosphorescence of the stone itself, or of the many talismans and charms with which it was wrought over.

Bradamante had hardly passed the threshold of this

sacred place when the spirit of the enchanter saluted her with a voice firm and distinct. "May thy designs be prosperous, oh, chaste and noble maiden, the future mother of heroes, the glory of Italy, and destined to fill the whole world with their fame. Great captains, renowned knights, shall be numbered among your descendants, who shall defend the Church and restore their country to its ancient splendor. Princes, wise as Augustus and the sage Numa shall bring back the age of gold.* To accomplish these grand destinies it is ordained that you shall wed the illustrious Rogero. Fly then to his deliverance, and lay prostrate in the dust the traitor who has snatched him from you and now holds him in chains!"

Merlin ceased with these words and left to Melissa, the priestess, the charge of more fully instructing the maiden in her future course. "To-morrow," said she, "I will conduct you to the castle on the rock where Rogero is held captive. I will not leave you till I have guided you through this wild wood, and I will direct you on your way so that you shall be in no danger of mistaking it."

The next morning Melissa conducted Bradamante, between rocks and precipices, crossing rapid torrents, and traversing intricate passes, employing the time in imparting to her such information as was necessary to enable her to bring her design to a successful issue.

"Not only would the castle, impenetrable by force, and that winged horse of his baffle your efforts, but know that he possesses also a buckler whence flashes a light so brilliant that the eyes of all who look upon it are blinded. Think not to avoid it by shutting your eyes, for how then will you be able to avoid his blows and make him feel your own? But I will teach you the proper course to pursue.

"Agramant, the Moorish prince, possesses a ring stolen from a queen of India, which has power to render of no avail all enchantments. Agramant, knowing that Rogero is of more importance to him than any one of his

---

* This prophecy is introduced by Ariosto in this place to compliment the noble house of Este, the princes of his native state, the dukedom of Ferrara.

warriors, is desirous of rescuing him from the power of the enchanter, and has sent for that purpose Brunello, the most crafty and sagacious of his servants, provided with his wonderful ring, and he is even now at hand, bent on this enterprise. But, beautiful Bradamante, as I desire that no one but yourself shall have the glory of delivering from thraldom your future spouse, listen while I disclose the means of success. Following this path which leads by the seashore, you will come ere long to a hostelry, where the Saracen Brunello will arrive shortly after you. You will readily know him by his stature, under four feet, his great disproportioned head, his squint eyes, his livid hue, his thick eyebrows joining his tufted beard. His dress, moreover, that of a courier, will point him out to you.

"It will be easy for you to enter into conversation with him, announcing yourself as a knight seeking combat with the enchanter, but let not the knave suspect that you know anything about the ring. I doubt not that he will offer to be your guide to the castle of the enchanter. Accept his offer, but take care to keep behind him till you come in sight of the brilliant dome of the castle. Then hesitate not to strike him dead, for the wretch deserves no pity, and take from him the ring. But let him not suspect your intention, for by putting the ring into his mouth he will instantly become invisible and disappear from your eyes."

Saying thus, the sage Melissa and the fair Bradamante arrived near the city of Bordeaux, where the rich and wide River Garonne pours the tribute of its waves into the sea. They parted with tender embraces. Bradamante, intent wholly on her purpose, hastened to arrive at the hostelry, where Brunello had preceded her a few moments only. The young heroine knew him without difficulty. She accosted him and put to him some slight questions, to which he replied with adroit falsehoods. Bradamante, on her part, concealed from him her sex, her religion, her country, and the blood from whence she sprung. While they talk together, sudden cries are heard from all parts of the hostelry. "O queen of heaven!" exclaimed Bradamante, "what can be the cause of this sudden alarm?" She soon learned the cause. Host, chil-

dren, domestics, all, with upturned eyes, as if they saw a
comet or a great eclipse, were gazing on a prodigy which
seemed to pass the bounds of possibility. She beheld
distinctly a winged horse, mounted with a cavalier in
rich armor, cleaving the air with rapid flight. The wings
of this strange courser were wide extended and covered
with feathers of various colors. The polished armor of
the knight made them shine with rainbow tints. In a
short time, the horse and rider disappeared behind the
summits of the mountains.

"It is an enchanter," said the host, "a magician who
often is seen traversing the air in that way. Sometimes
he flies aloft as if among the stars, and at others, skims
along the land. He possesses a wonderful castle on the
top of the Pyrenees. Many knights have shown their
courage by going to attack him, but none have ever returned, from which it is to be feared they have lost either
their life or their liberty."

Bradamante, addressing the host, said, "Could you
furnish me a guide to conduct me to the castle of this
enchanter?" "By my faith," said Brunello, interrupting,
"that you shall not seek in vain; I have it all in writing,
and I will myself conduct you." Bradamante, with
thanks, accepted him for her guide.

The host had a tolerable horse to dispose of, which
Bradamante bargained for, and the next day, at the first
dawn of morning, she took her route by a narrow valley,
taking care to have the Saracen Brunello lead the way.

They reached the summit of the Pyrenees, whence one
may look down on France, Spain, and the two seas.
From this height they descended again by a fatiguing
road into a deep valley. From the middle of this valley
an isolated mountain rose, composed of rough and per-
pendicular rock, on whose summit was the castle, surrounded with a wall of brass. Brunello said, "Yonder is
the stronghold where the enchanter keeps his prisoners;
one must have wings to mount thither; it is easy to see
that the aid of a flying horse must be necessary for the
master of this castle, which he uses for his prison and
for his abode."

Bradamante, sufficiently instructed, saw that the time
had now come to possess herself of the ring; but she

could not resolve to slay a defenseless man. She seized Brunello before he was aware, bound him to a tree, and took from him the ring which he wore on one of his fingers. The cries and entreaties of the perfidious Saracen moved her not. She advanced to the foot of the rock whereon the castle stood and, to draw the magician to the combat, sounded her horn, adding to it cries of defiance.

The enchanter delayed not to present himself, mounted on his winged horse. Bradamante was struck with surprise mixed with joy when she saw that this person, described as so formidable, bore no lance nor club, nor any other deadly weapon. He had only on his arm a buckler, covered with a cloth, and in his hand an open book. As to the winged horse, there was no enchantment about him. He was a natural animal, of a species which exists in the Riphæan mountains. Like a griffin, he had the head of an eagle, claws armed with talons, and wings covered with feathers, the rest of his body being that of a horse. This strange animal is called a Hippogriff.

The heroine attacked the enchanter on his approach, striking on this side and on that, with all the energy of a violent combat, but wounding only the wind; and, after this pretended attack had lasted some time, dismounted from her horse, as if hoping to do battle more effectually on foot. The enchanter now prepares to employ his sole weapon, by uncovering the magic buckler which never failed to subdue an enemy by depriving him of his senses. Bradamante, confiding in her ring, observed all the motions of her adversary, and, at the unveiling of the shield, cast herself on the ground, pretending that the splendor of the shield had overcome her, but in reality to induce the enchanter to dismount and approach her.

It happened according to her wish. When the enchanter saw her prostrate, he made his horse alight on the ground and, dismounting, fixed the shield on the pommel of his saddle and approached in order to secure the fallen warrior. Bradamante, who watched him intently, as soon as she saw him near at hand, sprang up, seized him vigorously, threw him down, and, with the same chain which the enchanter had prepared for herself, bound him fast, without his being able to make any effectual resistance.

The enchanter, with the accents of despair, exclaimed, "Take my life, young man!" but Bradamante was far from complying with such a wish. Desirous of knowing the name of the enchanter and for what purpose he had formed with so much art this impregnable fortress, she commanded him to inform her.

"Alas!" replied the magician, while tears flowed down his cheeks, "it is not to conceal booty, nor for any culpable design, that I have built this castle; it was only to guard the life of a young knight, the object of my tenderest affection, my art having taught me that he is destined to become a Christian, and to perish, shortly after, by the blackest of treasons.

"This youth, named Rogero, is the most beautiful and most accomplished of knights. It is I, the unhappy Atlantes, who have reared him from his childhood. The call of honor and the desire of glory led him from me to follow Agramant, his prince, in his invasion of France, and I, more devoted to Rogero than the tenderest of parents, have sought the means of bringing him back to this abode, in the hope of saving him from the cruel fate that menaces him.

"For this purpose I have got him in my possession by the same means as I attempted to employ against you, and by which I have succeeded in collecting a great many knights and ladies in my castle. My purpose was to render my beloved pupil's captivity light, by affording him society to amuse him and keep his thoughts from running on subjects of war and glory. Alas! my cares have been in vain! Yet, take, I beseech you, whatever else I have, but spare me my beloved pupil. Take this shield, take this winged courser, deliver such of your friends as you may find among my prisoners, deliver them all if you will, but leave me my beloved Rogero; or, if you will snatch him too from me, take also my life, which will cease then to be to me worth preserving."

Bradamante replied: "Old man, hope not to move me by your vain entrea*   . It was precisely the liberty of Rogero that I require. You would keep him here in bondage and in slothful pleasure to save him from a fate which you forsee. Vain old man! how can you forsee his fate when you could not foresee your own? You desire me to take your life. No, my arm and my soul refuse the request." This said, she required the magician to go before and guide her to the castle. The prisoners were set at liberty, though some, in their secret hearts, regretted the voluptuous life which was thus brought to an end. Bradamante and Rogero met one another with transports of joy.

They descended from the mountain to the spot where the encounter had taken place. There they found the Hippogriff, with the magic buckler in its wrapper, hanging to his saddle-bow. Bradamante advanced to seize the bridle; the Hippogriff seemed to wait her approach, but before she reached him, he spread his wings and flew away to a neighboring hill, and in the same manner, a second time, eluded her efforts. Rogero and the other liberated knights dispersed over the plain and hill-tops to secure him, and at last the animal allowed Rogero to seize his rein. The fearless Rogero hesitated not to vault upon his back, and let him feel his spurs, which so roused his mettle that, after galloping a short distance, he suddenly spread his wings and soared into the air. Bradamante had the grief to see her lover snatched away from her at the very moment of reunion. Rogero, who knew not the art of directing the horse, was unable to control his flight. He found himself carried over the tops of the mountains, so far above them that he could hardly distinguish what was land and what water. The Hippogriff directed his flight to the west and cleaved the air as swiftly as a new-rigged vessel cuts the waves, impelled by the freshest and most favorable gales.

ASTOLPHO AND THE ENCHANTRESS

In the long flight which Rogero took on the back of the Hippogriff, he was carried over land and sea, unknowing whither. As soon as he had gained some control over the animal, he made him alight on the nearest land. When he came near enough to earth, Rogero leapt lightly from his back and tied the animal to a myrtle-tree. Near the spot flowed the pure waters of a fountain, surrounded by cedars and palm-trees. Rogero laid aside his shield, and, removing his helmet, breathed with delight the fresh air, and cooled his lips with the waters of the fountain. For we cannot wonder that he was excessively fatigued, considering the ride he had taken. He was preparing to taste the sweets of repose when he perceived that the Hippogriff, which he had tied by the bridle to a myrtle-tree, frightened at something, was making violent efforts to disengage himself. His struggles shook the myrtle-tree so that many of its beautiful leaves were torn off, and strewed the ground.

A sound like that which issues from burning wood seemed to come from the myrtle-tree, at first faint and indistinct, but growing stronger by degrees, and at length was audible as a voice which spoke in this manner: "Oh, knight, if the tenderness of your heart corresponds to the beauty of your person, relieve me, I pray you, from this tormenting animal. I suffer enough inwardly without having outward evils added to my lot."

Rogero, at the first accents of this voice, turned his eyes promptly on the myrtle, hastened to it, and stood fixed in astonishment when he perceived that the voice issued from the tree itself. He immediately untied his horse and, flushed with surprise and regret, exclaimed, "Whoever thou art, whether mortal or the goddess of these woods, forgive me, I beseech you, my involuntary fault. Had I imagined that this hard bark covered a being possessed of feeling, could I have exposed such a beautiful myrtle to the insults of this steed? May the sweet influences of the sky and air speedily repair the injury I have done! For my part, I promise by the sovereign lady of my heart to do everything you wish in order to merit your forgiveness."

At these words the myrtle seemed to tremble from root to stem, and Rogero remarked that a moisture as of tears trickled down its bark, like that which exudes from a log placed on the fire. It then spoke: "The kindness which inspires your words compels me to disclose to you who I once was and by what fatility I have been changed into this shape. My name was Astolpho, cousin of Orlando and Rinaldo, whose fame has filled the earth. I was myself reckoned among the bravest paladins of France and was by birth entitled to reign over England, after Otho, my father. Returning from the distant east, with Rinaldo and many other brave knights, called home to aid with our arms the great Emperor of France, we reached a spot where the powerful enchantress Alcina possessed a castle on the borders of the sea. She had gone to the waterside to amuse herself with fishing, and we paused to see how, by her art, without hook or line, she drew from the water whatever she would.

"Not far from the shore an enormous whale showed a back so broad and motionless that it looked like an island. Alcina had fixed her eyes on me and planned to get me into her power. Addressing us, she said: 'This is the hour when the prettiest mermaid in the sea comes regularly every day to the shore of yonder island. She sings so sweetly that the very waves flow smoother at the sound. If you wish to hear her, come with me to her resort.' So saying, Alcina pointed to the fish, which we all supposed to be an island. I, who was rash, did not hesitate to follow her, but swam my horse over, and mounted on the back of the fish. In vain Rinaldo and Dudon made signs to me to beware; Alcina, smiling, took me in charge, and led the way. No sooner were we mounted upon him than the whale moved off, spreading his great fins, and cleft rapidly the waters. I then saw my folly, but it was too late to repent. Alcina soothed my anger and professed that what she had done was for love of me. Ere long we arrived at this island, where at first everything was done to reconcile me to my lot and to make my days pass happily away. But soon Alcina, sated with her conquest, grew indifferent, then weary of me, and at last, to get rid of me, changed me into this form, as she had done to many lovers before me, making some of them olives, some palms, some cedars, changing others into fountains, rocks, or even into wild beasts. And thou, courteous knight, whom accident has brought to this enchanted isle, beware that she get not the power over thee, or thou shalt haply be made like us, a tree, a fountain, or a rock."

Rogero expressed his astonishment at this recital. Astolpho added that the island was in great part subject to the sway of Alcina. By the aid of her sister Morgana, she had succeeded in dispossessing a third sister, Logestilla, of nearly the whole of her patrimony, for the whole isle was hers originally by her father's bequest. But Logestilla was temperate and sage, while the other sisters were false and voluptuous. Her empire was divided from theirs by a gulf and chain of mountains, which alone had thus far prevented her sister from usurping it.

Astolpho here ended his tale, and Rogero, who knew that he was the cousin of Bradamante, would gladly have devised some way for his relief; but, as that was out of his power, he consoled him as well as he could, and then begged to be told the way to the palace of Logestilla and how to avoid that of Alcina. Astolpho directed him to take the road to the left, though rough and full of rocks. He warned him that this road would present serious obstacles; that troops of monsters would oppose his passage, employed by the art of Alcina to prevent her subjects from escaping from her dominion. Rogero thanked the myrtle and prepared to set out on his way.

He at first thought he would mount the winged horse, and scale the mountain on his back; but he was too uncertain of his power to control him to wish to encounter the hazard of another flight through the air, besides that he was almost famished for the want of food. So he led the horse after him and took the road on foot, which for some distance led equally to the dominions of both the sisters.

He had not advanced more than two miles when he saw before him the superb city of Alcina. It was surrounded with a wall of gold, which seemed to reach the skies. I know that some think that this wall was not of real gold, but only the work of alchemy; it matters not; I prefer to think it gold, for it certainly shone like gold.

A broad and level road led to the gates of the city, and from this another branched off, narrow and rough, which led to the mountain region. Rogero took without hesitation the narrow road, but he had no sooner entered upon it than he was assailed by a numerous troop which opposed his passage.

You never have seen anything so ridiculous, so extraordinary, as this host of hobgoblins were. Some of them bore the human form from the neck to the feet, but had the head of a monkey or a cat; others had the legs and the ears of a horse; old men and women, bald and hideous, ran hither and thither as if out of their senses, half clad in the shaggy skins of beasts; one rode full speed on a horse without a bridle, another jogged along mounted on an ass or a cow; others, full of agility, skipped about and clung to the tails and manes of the animals which their companions rode. Some blew horns, others brandished drinking-cups; some were armed with spits, and some with pitchforks. One, who appeared to be the captain, had an enormous belly and a gross fat head; he was mounted on a tortoise that waddled, now this way, now that, without keeping any one direction.

One of these monsters, who had something approaching the human form, though he had the neck, ears, and muzzle of a dog, set himself to bark furiously at Rogero, to make him turn off to the right and reënter upon the road to the gay city; but the brave chevalier exclaimed, "That will I not, so long as I can use this sword," and he thrust the point directly at his face. The monster tried to strike him with a lance, but Rogero was too quick for him and thrust his sword through his body, so that it appeared a hand's breadth behind his back. The paladin, now giving full vent to his rage, laid about him vigorously among the rabble, cleaving one to the teeth, another to the girdle; but the troop was so numerous, and in spite of his blows pressed around him so close, that, to clear his way, he must have had as many arms as Briareus.

If Rogero had uncovered the shield of the enchanter which hung at his saddle-bow, he might easily have vanquished this monstrous rout; but perhaps he did not think of it, and perhaps he preferred to seek his defence nowhere but in his good sword. At that moment, when his perplexity was at its height, he saw issue from the city gate two young beauties, whose air and dress proclaimed their rank and gentle nurture. Each of them was mounted on a unicorn, whose whiteness surpassed that of ermine. They advanced to the meadow where Rogero was contending so valiantly against the hobgoblins, who all retired at their approach. They drew near, they extended their hands to the young warrior, whose cheeks glowed with the flush of exercise and modesty. Grateful for their assistance, he expressed his thanks and, having no heart to refuse them, followed their guidance to the gate of the city.

This grand and beautiful entrance was adorned by a portico of four vast columns, all of diamond. Whether they were real diamond or artificial, I cannot say. What matter is it, so long as they appeared to the eye like diamond, and nothing could be more gay and splendid.

On the threshold and between the columns was seen a bevy of charming young women, who played and frolicked together. They all ran to receive Rogero and conducted him into the palace, which appeared like a paradise.

We might well call by that name this abode, where the hours flew by, without account, in ever-new delights. The bare idea of satiety, want, and, above all, of age, never entered the minds of the inhabitants. They experienced no sensations except those of luxury and gaiety; the cup of happiness seemed for them ever-flowing and exhaustless. The two young damsels to whom Rogero owed his deliverance from the hobgoblins conducted him to the apartment of their mistress. The beautiful Alcina advanced and greeted him with an air at once dignified and courteous. All her court surrounded the paladin and rendered him the most flattering attentions. The castle was less admirable for its magnificence than for the charms of those who inhabited it. They were of either sex, well matched in beauty, youth, and grace; but among this charming group the brilliant Alcina shone, as the sun outshines the stars. The young warrior was fascinated. All that he had heard from the myrtle-tree appeared to him but a vile calumny. How could he suspect that falsehood and treason veiled themselves under smiles and the ingenuous air of truth? He doubted not that Astolpho had deserved his fate, and perhaps a punish-

ment more severe; he regarded all his stories as dictated
by a disappointed spirit and a thirst for revenge. But
we must not condemn Rogero too harshly, for he was
the victim of magic power.

They seated themselves at table, and immediately harmonious lyres and harps waked the air with the most
ravishing notes. The charms of poetry were added, in
entertaining recitals; the magnificence of the feast would
have done credit to a royal board. The traitress forgot
nothing which might charm the paladin and attach him
to the spot, meaning, when she should grow tired of him,
to metamorphose him as she had done others. In the
same manner passed each succeeding day. Games of
pleasant exercise, the chase, the dance, or rural sports
made the hours pass quickly, while they gave zest to the
refreshment of the bath, or sleep.

Thus Rogero led a life of ease and luxury, while
Charlemagne and Agramant were struggling for empire.
But I cannot linger with him, while the amiable and
courageous Bradamante is night and day directing her
uncertain steps to every spot where the slightest chance
invites her, in the hope of recovering Rogero.

I will therefore say that, having sought him in vain
in fields and in cities, she knew not whither next to
direct her steps. She did not apprehend the death of
Rogero. The fall of such a hero would have reëchoed
from the Hydaspes to the farthest river of the west; but,
not knowing whether he was on the earth or in the air,
she concluded, as a last resource, to return to the cavern which contained the tomb of Merlin, to ask of him
some sure direction to the object of her search.

While this thought occupied her mind, Melissa, the
sage enchantress, suddenly appeared before her. This
virtuous and beneficent magician had discovered by her
spells that Rogero was passing his time in pleasure and
idleness, forgetful of his honor and his sovereign. Not
able to endure the thought that one who was born to be
a hero should waste his years in base repose and leave
a sullied reputation in the memory of survivors, she saw
that vigorous measures must be employed to draw him
forth into the paths of virtue. Melissa was not blinded
by her affection for the amiable paladin, like Atlantes,

who, intent only on preserving Rogero's life, cared nothing for his fame. It was that old enchanter whose arts had guided the Hippogriff to the isle of the too charming Alcina, where he hoped his favorite would learn to forget honor and lose the love of glory.

At the sight of Melissa, joy lighted up the countenance of Bradamante and hope animated her breast. Melissa concealed nothing from her, but told her how Rogero was in the toils of Alcina. Bradamante was plunged in grief and terror; but the kind enchantress calmed her, dispelled her fears, and promised that before many days she would lead back the paladin to her feet.

"My daughter," she said, "give me the ring which you wear and which possesses the power to overcome enchantments. By means of it, I doubt not but that I may enter the stronghold where the false Alcina holds Rogero in durance, and may succeed in vanquishing her and liberating him." Bradamante unhesitatingly delivered her the ring, recommending Rogero to her best efforts. Melissa then summoned by her art a huge palfrey, black as jet, excepting one foot, which was bay. Mounted upon this animal, she rode with such speed that by the next morning she had reached the abode of Alcina.

She here transformed herself into the perfect resemblance of the old magician Atlantes, adding a palmbreadth to her height and enlarging her whole figure. Her chin she covered with a long beard, and seamed her whole visage well with wrinkles. She assumed also his voice and manner and watched her chance to find Rogero alone. At last she found him, dressed in a rich tunic of silk and gold, a collar of precious stones about his neck, and his arms, once so rough with exercise, decorated with bracelets. His air and his every motion indicated effeminacy, and he seemed to retain nothing of Rogero but the name; such power had the enchantress obtained over him.

Melissa, under the form of his old instructor, presented herself before him, wearing a stern and serious visage. "Is this, then," she said, "the fruit of all my labors? Is it for this that I fed you on the marrow of bears and lions, that I taught you to subdue dragons and, like Hercules, strangle serpents in your youthful

grasp, only to make you, by all my cares, a feeble
Adonis? My nightly watchings of the stars, of the yet
warm fibres of animals, the lots I have cast, the points
of nativity that I have calculated, have they all falsely
indicated that you were born for greatness? Who could
have believed that you would become the slave of a base
enchantress? Oh, Rogero, learn to know this Alcina,
learn to understand her arts and to countervail them.
Take this ring, place it on your finger, return to her
presence, and see for yourself what are her real charms."

At these words, Rogero, confused, abashed, cast his
eyes upon the ground and knew not what to answer.
Melissa seized the moment, slipped the ring on his finger, and the paladin was himself again. What a thunder-
clap to him! Overcome by shame, he dared not to encounter the looks of his instructor. When at last he
raised his' eyes, he beheld not that venerable form, but
the priestess Melissa, who in virtue of the ring now
appeared in her true person. She told him of the motives
which had led her to come to his rescue, of the griefs
and regrets of Bradamante, and of her unwearied search
for him. "That charming Amazon," she said, "sends you
this ring, which is a sovereign antidote to all enchantments. She would have sent you her heart in my hands,
if it would have had greater power to serve you."

It was needless for Melissa to say more. Rogero's love
for Alcina, being but the work of enchantment, vanished
as soon as the enchantment was withdrawn, and he now
hated her with an equal intensity, seeing no longer anything in her but her vices, and feeling only resentment
for the shame that she had put upon him.

His surprise when he again beheld Alcina was no less
than his indignation. Fortified by his ring from her enchantments, he saw her as she was, a monster of ugliness. All her charms were artificial and, truly viewed,
were rather deformities. She was, in fact, older than
Hecuba or the Sibyl of Cumæ; but an art, which it is
to be regretted our times have lost, enabled her to appear charming and to clothe herself in all the attractions
of youth. Rogero now saw all this, but, governed by the
counsels of Melissa, he concealed his surprise, assumed
under some pretext his armor, long neglected, and bound

to his side Belisarda, his trusty sword, taking also the
buckler of Atlantes, covered with its veil.

He then selected a horse from the stables of Alcina,
without exciting her suspicions; but he left the Hippogriff by the advice of Melissa, who promised to take
him in charge and train him to a more manageable state.
The horse he took was Rabican, which belonged to
Astolpho. He restored the ring to Melissa.

Rogero had not ridden far when he met one of the
huntsmen of Alcina, bearing a falcon on his wrist, and
followed by a dog. The huntsman was mounted on a
powerful horse and came boldly up to the paladin, demanding, in a somewhat imperious manner, whither he
was going so rapidly. Rogero disdained to stop or to
reply, whereupon the huntsman, not doubting that he was
about making his escape, said, "What if I, with my falcon, stop your ride?" So saying, he threw off the bird,
which even Rabican could not equal in speed. The huntsman then leapt from his horse, and the animal, open-
mouthed, darted after Rogero with the swiftness of an
arrow. The huntsman also ran as if the wind or fire bore
him, and the dog was equal to Rabican in swiftness.
Rogero, finding flight impossible, stopped and faced his
pursuers; but his sword was useless against such foes.
The insolent huntsman assailed him with words and
struck him with his whip, the only weapon he had; the
dog bit his feet, and the horse drove at him with his
hoofs. At the same time, the falcon flew over his head
and over Rabican's and attacked them with claws and
wings, so that the horse in his fright began to be un-
manageable. At that moment the sound of trumpets and
cymbals was heard in the valley, and it was evident
that Alcina had ordered out all her array to go in pursuit. Rogero felt that there was no time to be lost and
luckily remembered the shield of Atlantes, which he bore
suspended from his neck. He unveiled it, and the charm
worked wonderfully. The huntsman, the dog, the horse,
fell flat; the trembling wings of the falcon could no
longer sustain her, and she fell senseless to the ground.
Rogero, rid of their annoyances, left them in their trance
and rode away.

Meanwhile, Alcina, with all the force she could muster, sallied forth from her palace in pursuit. Melissa, left behind, took advantage of the opportunity to ransack all the rooms, protected by the ring. She undid one by one all the talismans and spells which she found, broke the seals, burned the images, and untied the hagknots. Thence, hurrying through the fields, she disenchanted the victims changed into trees, fountains, stones, or brutes, all of whom recovered their liberty, and vowed eternal gratitude to their deliverer. They made their escape, with all possible despatch, to the realms of the good Logestilla, whence they departed to their several homes.

Astolpho was the first whom Melissa liberated, for Rogero had particularly recommended him to her care. She aided him to recover his arms, and particularly that precious golden-headed lance which once was Argalia's. The enchantress mounted with him upon the winged horse and in a short time arrived through the air at the castle of Logestilla, where Rogero joined them soon after.

In this abode the friends passed a short period of delightful and improving intercourse with the sage Logestilla and her virtuous court; and then each departed, Rogero with the Hippogriff, ring, and bucklet, Astolpho with his golden lance and mounted on Rabican, the fleetest of steeds. To Rogero Logestilla gave a bit and bridle suited to govern the Hippogriff; and to Astolpho a horn of marvellous powers, to be sounded only when all other weapons were unavailing.

THE ORC

We left the charming Angelica at the moment when, in her flight from her contending lovers, Sacripant and Rinaldo, she met an aged hermit. We have seen that her request to the hermit was to furnish her the means of gaining the sea-coast, eager to avoid Rinaldo, whom she hated, by leaving France and Europe itself. The pretended hermit, who was no other than a vile magician,

knowing well that it would not be agreeable to his false
gods to aid Angelica in this undertaking, feigned to comply with her desire. He supplied her a horse, into which
he had by his arts caused a subtle devil to enter, and,
having mounted Angelica on the animal, directed her
what course to take to reach the sea.

Angelica rode on her way without suspicion, but when
arrived at the shore, the demon urged the animal headlong into the water. Angelica in vain attempted to turn
him back to the land; he continued his course till, as
night approached, he landed with his burden on a sandy
headland.

Angelica, finding herself alone, abandoned in this
frightful solitude, remained without movement, as if stupefied, with hands joined and eyes turned towards heav-
en, till at last, pouring forth a torrent of tears, she
exclaimed: "Cruel fortune, have you not yet exhausted
your rage against me! To what new miseries do you
doom me? Alas! then, finish your work! Deliver me a
prey to some ferocious beast, or by whatever fate you
choose bring me to an end. I will be thankful to
you for terminating my life and my misery." At last,
exhausted by her sorrows, she fell asleep and sunk prostrate on the sand.

Before recounting what next befell, we must declare
what place it was upon which the unhappy lady was
now thrown. In the sea that washes the coast of Ireland
there is an island called Ebuda, whose inhabitants, once
numerous, had been wasted by the anger of Proteus till
there were now but few left. This deity was incensed
by some neglect of the usual honors which he had in
old times received from the inhabitants of the land, and,
to execute his vengeance, had sent a horrid sea-monster,
called an Orc, to devour them. Such were the terrors
of his ravages that the whole people of the isle had
shut themselves up in the principal town and relied on
their walls alone to protect them. In this distress they
applied to the oracle for advice, and were directed to
appease the wrath of the sea-monster by offering to
him the fairest virgin that the country could produce.

Now it so happened that the very day when this dreadful oracle was announced, and when the fatal mandate

had gone forth to seek among the fairest maidens of the land one to be offered to the monster, some sailors, landing on the beach where Angelica was, beheld that beauty as she lay asleep.

Oh, blind Chance! whose power in human affairs is but too great, canst thou then abandon to the teeth of a horrible monster those charms which different sovereigns took arms against one another to possess? Alas! the lovely Angelica is destined to be the victim of those cruel islanders.

Still asleep, she was bound by the Ebudians, and it was not until she was carried on board the vessel that she came to a knowledge of her situation. The wind filled the sails and wafted the ship swiftly to the port, where all that beheld her agreed that she was unquestionably the victim selected by Proteus himself to be his prey. Who can tell the screams, the mortal anguish of this unhappy maiden, the reproaches she addressed even to the heavens themselves, when the dreadful information of her cruel fate was made known to her? I cannot; let me rather turn to a happier part of my story.

Rogero left the palace of Logestilla, careering on his flying courser far above the tops of the mountains, and borne westward by the Hippogriff, which he guided with ease, by means of the bridle that Melissa had given him. Anxious as he was to recover Bradamante, he could not fail to be delighted at the view his rapid flight presented of so many vast regions and populous countries as he passed over in his career. At last he approached the shores of England, and perceived an immense army in all the splendor of military pomp, as if about to go forth flushed with hopes of victory. He caused the Hippogriff to alight not far from the scene and found himself immediately surrounded by admiring spectators, knights, and soldiers, who could not enough indulge their curiosity and wonder. Rogero learned, in reply to his questions, that the fine array of troops before him was the army destined to go to the aid of the French Emperor, in compliance with the request presented by the illustrious Rinaldo, as ambassador of King Charles, his uncle.

By this time the curiosity of the English chevaliers was partly gratified in beholding the Hippogriff at rest,

and Rogero, to renew their surprise and delight, remounted the animal, and, clapping spurs to his sides, made
him launch into the air with the rapidity of a meteor,
and directed his flight still westwardly, till he came within sight of the coasts of Ireland. Here he descried what
seemed to be a fair damsel, alone, fast chained to a
rock which projected into the sea. What was his astonishment when, drawing nigh, he beheld the beautiful
Princess Angelica. That day she had been led forth and
bound to the rock, there to wait till the sea-monster
should come to devour her. Rogero exclaimed as he
came near, "What cruel hands, what barbarous soul,
what fatal chance can have loaded thee with those
chains?" Angelica replied by a torrent of tears, at first
her only response; then, in a trembling voice, she disclosed to him the horrible destiny for which she was
there exposed. While she spoke, a terrible roaring was
heard far off on the sea. The huge monster soon came in
sight, part of his body appearing above the waves, and
part concealed. Angelica, half dead with fear, abandoned
herself to despair.

Rogero, lance in rest, spurred his Hippogriff towards
the Orc and gave him a thrust. The horrible monster
was like nothing that nature produces. It was but one
mass of tossing and twisting body, with nothing of the
animal but head, eyes, and mouth, the last furnished
with tusks like those of the wild boar. Rogero's lance
had struck him between the eyes; but rock and iron are
not more impenetrable than were his scales. The knight,
seeing the fruitlessness of the first blow, prepared to give
a second. The animal, beholding upon the water the
shadow of the great wings of the Hippogriff, abandoned
his prey and turned to seize what seemed nearer. Rogero took the opportunity and dealt him furious blows on
various parts of his body, taking care to keep clear of
his murderous teeth; but the scales resisted every attack.
The Orc beat the water with his tail till he raised a foam
which enveloped Rogero and his steed, so that the knight
hardly knew whether he was in the water or the air. He
began to fear that the wings of the Hippogriff would be
so drenched with water that they would cease to sustain him. At that moment Rogero bethought him of the

magic shield which hung at his saddle-bow; but the fear
that Angelica would also be blinded by its glare discouraged him from employing it. Then he remembered the
ring which Melissa had given him, the power of which
he had so lately proved. He hastened to Angelica and
placed it on her finger. Then, uncovering the buckler, he,
turned its bright disk full in the face of the detestable
Orc. The effect was instantaneous. The monster, deprived
of sense and motion, rolled over on the sea and lay
floating on his back. Rogero would fain have tried the
effect of his lance on the now exposed parts, but Angelica implored him to lose no time in delivering her from
her chains, before the monster should revive. Rogero,
moved with her entreaties, hastened to do so and, having unbound her, made her mount behind him on the
Hippogriff. The animal, spurning the earth, shot up into
the air and rapidly sped his way through it. Rogero, to
give time to the princess to rest after her cruel agita-
tions, soon sought the earth again, alighting on the shore
of Brittany. Near the shore a thick wood presented itself, which resounded with the songs of birds. In the
midst, a fountain of transparent water bathed the turf of
a little meadow. A gentle hill rose near by. Rogero, making the Hippogriff alight in the meadow, dismounted and
took Angelica from the horse.

When the first tumults of emotion had subsided, Angelica, casting her eyes downward, beheld the precious
ring upon her finger, whose virtues she was well acquainted with, for it was the very ring which the Saracen
Brunello had robbed her of. She drew it from her finger
and placed it in her mouth, and, quicker than we can tell
it, disappeared from the sight of the paladin.

Rogero looked around him on all sides, like one frantic, but soon remembered the ring which he had so lately
placed on her finger. Struck with the ingratitude which
could thus recompense his services, he exclaimed:
"Thankless beauty, is this then the reward you make me?
Do you prefer to rob me of my ring rather than receive
it as a gift? Willingly would I have given it to you, had
you but asked it." Thus he said, searching on all sides,
with arms extended, like a blind man, hoping to recover

by the touch what was lost to sight; but he sought in vain. The cruel beauty was already far away.

Though sensible of her obligations to her deliverer, her first necessity was for clothing, food, and repose. She soon reached a shepherd's hut, where, entering unseen, she found what sufficed for her present relief. An old herdsman inhabited the hut, whose charge consisted of a drove of mares. When recruited by repose, Angelica selected one of the mares from the flock and, mounting the animal, felt the desire revive in her mind of returning to her home in the east, and for that purpose would gladly have accepted the protection of Orlando or of Sacripant across those wide regions which divided her from her own country. In hopes of meeting with one or the other of them, she pursued her way.

Meanwhile, Rogero, despairing of seeing Angelica again, returned to the tree where he had left his winged horse, but had the mortification to find that the animal had broken his bridle and escaped. This loss, added to his previous disappointment, overwhelmed him with vexation. Sadly he gathered up his arms, threw his buckler over his shoulders, and, taking the first path that offered, soon found himself within the verge of a dense and wide-spread forest.

He had proceeded for some distance when he heard a noise on his right and, listening attentively, distinguished the clash of arms. He made his way toward the place whence the sound proceeded, and found two warriors engaged in mortal combat. One of them was a knight of a noble and manly bearing, the other a fierce giant. The knight appeared to exert consummate address in defending himself against the massive club of the giant, evading his strokes or parrying them with sword or shield. Rogero stood spectator of the combat, for he did not allow himself to interfere in it, though a secret sentiment inclined him strongly to take part with the knight. At length he saw with grief the massive club fall directly on the head of the knight, who yielded to the blow and fell prostrate. The giant sprang forward to despatch him and, for that purpose, unlaced his helmet, when Rogero, with dismay, recognized the face of Bradamante. He cried aloud, "Hold, miscreant!" and sprang forward with drawn sword. Whereupon the giant, as if he cared not to enter upon another combat, lifted Bradamante on his shoulders and ran with her into the forest.

Rogero plunged after him, but the long legs of the giant carried him forward so fast that the paladin could hardly keep him in sight. At length they issued from the wood, and Rogero perceived before him a rich palace, built of marble and adorned with sculptures executed by a master hand. Into this edifice, through a golden door, the giant passed, and Rogero followed; but, on looking round, saw nowhere either the giant or Bradamante. He ran from room to room, calling aloud on his cowardly foe to turn and meet him, but got no response, nor caught another glimpse of the giant or his prey. In his vain pursuit he met, without knowing them, Ferrau, Florismart, King Gradasso, Orlando, and many others, all of whom had been entrapped like himself into this enchanted castle. It was a new stratagem of the magician Atlantes to draw Rogero into his power and to secure also those who might by any chance endanger his safety. What Rogero had taken for Bradamante was a mere phantom. That charming lady was far away, full of anxiety for her Rogero, whose coming she had long expected.

The Emperor had committed to her charge the city and garrison of Marseilles, and she held the post against the infidels with valor and discretion. One day Melissa suddenly presented herself before her. Anticipating her questions, she said, "Fear not for Rogero; he lives, and is as ever true to you; but he has lost his liberty. The fell enchanter has again succeeded in making him a prisoner. If you would deliver him, mount your horse and follow me." She told her in what manner Atlantes had deceived Rogero, in deluding his eyes with the phantom of herself in peril. "Such," she continued, "will be his arts in your own case, if you penetrate the forest and approach that castle. You will think you behold Rogero, when, in fact, you see only the enchanter himself. Be not deceived, plunge your sword into his body, and trust me when I tell you that, in slaying him, you will restore not only Rogero, but with him many of the bravest knights of France, whom the wizard's arts have withdrawn from the camp of their sovereign."

Bradamante promptly armed herself and mounted her horse. Melissa led her by forced journeys, by field and forest, beguiling the way with conversation on the theme which interested her hearer most. When at last they reached the forest, she repeated once more her instructions and then took her leave, for fear the enchanter might espy her and be put on his guard.

Bradamante rode on about two miles when suddenly she beheld Rogero, as it appeared to her, hard pressed by two fierce giants. While she hesitated, she heard his voice calling on her for help. At once the cautions of Melissa lost their weight. A sudden doubt of the faith and truth of her kind monitress flashed across her mind. "Shall I not believe my own eyes and ears?" she said and rushed forward to his defence. Rogero fled, pursued by the giants, and Bradamante followed, passing with them through the castle gate. When there, Bradamante was undeceived, for neither giant nor knight was to be seen. She found herself a prisoner, but had not the consolation of knowing that she shared the imprisonment of her beloved. She saw various forms of men and women, but could recognize none of them; and their lot was the same with respect to her. Each viewed the others under some illusion of the fancy, wearing the semblance of giants, dwarfs, or even four-footed animals, so that there was no companionship or communication between them.

ASTOLPHO'S ADVENTURES CONTINUED, AND ISABELLA'S BEGUN

When Astolpho escaped from the cruel Alcina, after a short abode in the realm of the virtuous Logestilla, he desired to return to his native country. Logestilla lent him the best vessel of her fleet to convey him to the mainland. She gave him at parting a wonderful book, which taught the secret of overcoming all manner of enchantments, and begged him to carry it always with him, out of regard for her. She also gave him another gift, which surpassed everything of the kind that mortal workmanship can frame; yet it was nothing in appearance but a simple horn.

Astolpho, protected by these gifts, thanked the good fairy, took leave of her, and set out on his return to France. His voyage was prosperous, and, on reaching the desired port, he took leave of the faithful mariners and continued his journey by land. As he proceeded over mountains and through valleys, he often met with bands of robbers, wild beasts, and venomous serpents, but he had only to sound his horn to put them all to flight.

Having landed in France, and traversed many provinces on his way to the army, he one day, in crossing a forest, arrived beside a fountain and alighted to drink. While he stooped at the fountain, a young rustic sprang from the copse, mounted Rabican, and rode away. It was a new trick of the enchanter Atlantes. Astolpho, hearing the noise, turned his head just in time to see his loss; and, starting up, pursued the thief, who, on his part, did not press the horse to his full speed, but just kept in sight of his pursuer till they both issued from the forest; and then Rabican and his rider took shelter in a castle which stood near. Astolpho followed and penetrated without difficulty within the court-yard of the castle, where he looked around for the rider and his horse, but could see no trace of either, nor any person of whom he could make inquiry. Suspecting that enchantment was employed to embarrass him, he bethought him of his book and, on consulting it, discovered that his suspicions were well founded. He also learned what course to pursue. He was directed to raise the stone which served as a threshold, under which a spirit lay pent, who would willingly escape and leave the castle free of access. Astolpho applied his strength to lift aside the stone. Thereupon the magician put his arts in force. The castle was full of prisoners, and the magician caused that to all of them Astolpho should appear in some false guise—to some a wild beast, to others a giant, to others a bird of prey. Thus all assailed him, and would quickly have made an end of him, if he had not bethought him of his horn. No sooner had he blown a blast than, at the horrid larum, fled the cavaliers and the necromancer with them, like a flock of pigeons at the sound of the fowler's gun. Astolpho then renewed his efforts on the stone and turned it over. The under face was all inscribed with magical characters, which the knight defaced, as directed by his book; and no sooner had he done so than the castle, with its walls and turrets, vanished into smoke.

The knights and ladies set at liberty were, besides Rogero and Bradamante, Orlando, Gradasso, Florismart, and many more. At the sound of the horn they fled, one and all, men and steeds, except Rabican, which Astolpho secured, in spite of his terror. As soon as the sound had ceased, Rogero recognized Bradamante, whom he had daily met during their imprisonment, but had been prevented from knowing by the enchanter's arts. No words can tell the delight with which they recognized each other and recounted mutually all that had happened to each since they were parted. Rogero took advantage of the opportunity to press his suit and found Bradamante as propitious as he could wish, were it not for a single obstacle, the difference of their faiths. "If he would obtain her in marriage," she said, "he must in due form demand her of her father, Duke Aymon, and must abandon his false prophet and become a Christian." The latter step was one which Rogero had for some time intended taking, for reasons of his own. He therefore gladly accepted the terms and proposed that they should at once repair to the abbey of Vallombrosa, whose towers were visible at no great distance. Thither they turned their horses' heads, and we will leave them to find their way without our company.

I know not if my readers recollect that, at the moment when Rogero had just delivered Angelica from the voracious Orc, that scornful beauty placed her ring in her mouth and vanished out of sight. At the same time the Hippogriff shook off his bridle, soared away, and flew to rejoin his former master, very naturally returning to his accustomed stable. Here Astolpho found him, to his very great delight. He knew the animal's powers, having seen Rogero ride him, and he longed to fly abroad over all the earth and see various nations and peoples from his airy course. He had heard Logestilla's directions how to guide the animal, and saw her fit a bridle to his head. He therefore was able, out of all the bridles he found in the stable, to select one suitable, and, placing Rabican's saddle on the Hippogriff's back, nothing seemed to prevent his immediate departure. Yet before he went, he bethought him of placing Rabican in hands where he would be safe and whence he might recover him in time of need. While he stood deliberating where he should find a messenger, he saw Bradamante approach. That fair warrior had been parted from Rogero on their way to the abbey of Vallombrosa by an inopportune adventure which had called the knight away. She was now returning to Montalban, having arranged with Rogero to join her there. To Bradamante, therefore, his fair cousin, Astolpho committed Rabican, and also the lance of gold, which would only be an encumbrance in his aerial excursion. Bradamante took charge of both; and Astolpho, bidding her farewell, soared in air.

Among those delivered by Astolpho from the magician's castle was Orlando. Following the guide of chance, the paladin found himself at the close of day in a forest, and stopped at the foot of a mountain. Surprised to discern a light which came from a cleft in the rock, he approached, guided by the ray, and discovered a narrow passage in the mountainside, which led into a deep grotto.

Orlando fastened his horse, and then, putting aside the bushes that resisted his passage, stepped down from rock to rock till he reached a sort of cavern. Entering it, he perceived a lady, young and handsome, as well as he could discover through the signs of distress which agitated her countenance. Her only companion was an old woman, who seemed to be regarded by her young partner with terror and indignation. The courteous paladin saluted the women respectfully and begged to know by whose barbarity they had been subjected to such imprisonment.

The younger lady replied, in a voice often broken with sobs:

"Though I know well that my recital will subject me to worse treatment by the barbarous man who keeps me here, to whom this woman will not fail to report it, yet I will not hide from you the facts. Ah! why should I fear his rage? If he should take my life, I know not what better boon than death I can ask.

"My name is Isabella. I am the daughter of the King of Galicia, or rather I should say misfortune and grief are my parents. Young, rich, modest, and of tranquil temper, all things appeared to combine to render my lot happy. Alas! I see myself to-day poor, humbled, miserable, and destined perhaps to yet further afflictions. It is a year since, my father having given notice that he would open the lists for a tournament at Bayonne, a great number of chevaliers from all quarters came together at our court. Among these, Zerbino, son of the King of Scotland, victorious in all combats, eclipsed by his beauty and his valor all the rest. Before departing from the court of Galicia, he testified the wish to espouse me, and I consented that he should demand my hand of the king, my father. But I was a Mahometan, and Zerbino a Christian, and my father refused his consent. The prince, called home by his father to take command of the forces destined to the assistance of the French Emperor, prevailed on me to be married to him secretly and to follow him to Scotland. He caused a galley to be prepared to receive me and placed in command of it the chevalier Oderic, a Biscayan famous for his exploits both by land and sea. On the day appointed, Oderic brought his vessel to a seaside resort of my father's, where I embarked. Some of my domestics accompanied me, and thus I departed from my native land.

"Sailing with a fair wind, after some hours we were assailed by a violent tempest. It was to no purpose that we took in all sail; we were driven before the wind directly upon the rocky shore. Seeing no other hopes of safety, Oderic placed me in a boat, followed himself with a few of his men, and made for land. We reached it through infinite peril, and I no sooner felt the firm land beneath my feet than I knelt down and poured out heartfelt thanks to the Providence that had preserved me.

"The shore where we landed appeared to be uninhabited. We saw no dwelling to shelter us, no road to lead us to a more hospitable spot. A high mountain rose before us, whose base stretched into the sea. It was here the infamous Oderic, in spite of my tears and entreaties, sold me to a band of pirates, who fancied I might be an acceptable present to their prince, the Sultan of Morocco. This cavern is their den, and here they keep me under the guard of this woman, until it shall suit their convenience to carry me away."

Isabella had hardly finished her recital when a troop of armed men began to enter the cavern. Seeing the Prince Orlando, one said to the rest, "What bird is this we have caught, without even setting a snare for him?" Then addressing Orlando, "It was truly civil in you, friend, to come hither with the handsome coat of armor and vest, the very things I want." "You shall pay for them, then," said Orlando, and, seizing a half-burnt brand from the fire, he hurled it at him, striking his head and stretching him lifeless on the floor.

There was a massy table in the middle of the cavern, used for the pirates' repasts. Orlando lifted it and hurled it at the robbers as they stood clustered in a group toward the entrance. Half the gang were laid prostrate, with broken heads and limbs; the rest got away as nimbly as they could.

Leaving the den and its inmates to their fate, Orlando, taking Isabella under his protection, pursued his way, for some days, without meeting with any adventure.

One day, they saw a band of men advancing, who seemed to be guarding a prisoner, bound hand and foot, as if being carried to execution. The prisoner was a youthful cavalier, of a noble and ingenuous appearance. The band bore the ensigns of Count Anselm, head of the treacherous house of Maganza. Orlando desired Isabella to wait, while he rode forward to inquire the meaning of this array. Approaching, he demanded of the leader who his prisoner was and of what crime he had been guilty. The man replied that the prisoner was a murderer, by whose hand Pinabel, the son of Count Anselm, had been treacherously slain. At these words, the prisoner exclaimed, "I am no murderer, nor have I been in any way the cause of the young man's death." Orlando, knowing the cruel and ferocious character of the chiefs of the house of Maganza, needed no more to satisfy him that the youth was the victim of injustice. He commanded the leader of the troop to release his victim and, receiving an insolent reply, dashed him to the earth with a stroke of his lance; then, by a few vigorous blows, dispersed the band, leaving deadly marks on those who were slowest to quit the field.

Orlando then hastened to unbind the prisoner and to assist him to reclothe himself in his armor, which the false Magencian had dared to assume. He then led him to Isabella, who now approached the scene of action. How can we picture the joy, the astonishment, with which Isabella recognized in him Zerbino, her husband, and the prince discovered her whom he had believed overwhelmed in the waves! They embraced one another and wept for joy. Orlando, sharing in their happiness, congratulated himself in having been the instrument of it. The princess recounted to Zerbino what the illustrious paladin had done for her, and the prince threw himself at Orlando's feet and thanked him as having twice preserved his life.

While these exchanges of congratulation and thankfulness were going on, a sound in the underwood attracted their attention, and caused the two knights to brace their helmets and stand on their guard. What the cause of the interruption was, we shall record in another chapter.

MEDORO

France was at this time the theatre of dreadful events. The Saracens and the Christians, in numerous encounters, slew one another. On one occasion Rinaldo led an attack on the infidel columns, broke and scattered them, till he found himself opposite to a knight whose armor (whether by accident or choice, it matters not) bore the blazon of Orlando. It was Dardinel, the young and brave prince of Zumara, and Rinaldo remarked him by the slaughter he spread all around. "Ah," said he to himself, "let us pluck up this dangerous plant before it has grown to its full height."

As Rinaldo advanced, the crowd opened before him, the Christians to let his sword have free course, the pagans to escape its sweep. Dardinel and he stood face to face. Rinaldo exclaimed, fiercely, "Young man, whoever gave you that noble buckler to bear made you a dangerous gift; I should like to see how you are able to defend those quarterings, red and white. If you cannot defend them against me, how pray will you do so when Orlando challenges them?" Dardinel replied: "Thou shalt learn that I can defend the arms I bear and shed new glory upon them. No one shall rend them from me but with life." Saying these words, Dardinel rushed upon Rinaldo with sword uplifted.

The chill of mortal terror filled the souls of the Saracens when they beheld Rinaldo advance to attack the prince, like a lion against a young bull. The first blow came from the hand of Dardinel, and the weapon rebounded from Mambrino's helmet without effect. Rinaldo smiled and said, "I will now show you if my strokes are more effectual." At these words, he thrust the unfortunate Dardinel in the middle of his breast. The blow was so violent that the cruel weapon pierced the body and came out a palm-breadth behind his back. Through this wound the life of Dardinel issued with his blood, and his body fell helpless to the ground.

As a flower which the passing plough has uprooted languishes and droops its head, so Dardinel, his visage covered with the paleness of death, expires, and the hopes of an illustrious race perish with him.

Like waters kept back by a dike, which, when the dike is broken, spread abroad through all the country, so the Moors, no longer kept in column by the example of Dardinel, fled in all directions. Rinaldo despised too much such easy victories to pursue them; he wished for no combats but with brave men. At the same time, the other paladins made terrible slaughter of the Moors. Charles himself, Oliver, Guido, and Ogier the Dane carried death into their ranks on all sides.

The infidels seemed doomed to perish to a man on that dreadful day; but the wise king, Marsilius, at last put some slight degree of method into the general rout. He collected the remnant of the troops, formed them into a battalion, and retreated in tolerable order to his camp. That camp was well fortified by intrenchments and a broad ditch. Thither the fugitives hastened, and by degrees all that remained of the Moorish army was brought together there.

The Emperor might perhaps that night have crushed his enemy entirely; but not thinking it prudent to expose his troops, fatigued as they were, to an attack upon a camp so well fortified, he contended himself with encompassing the enemy with his troops, prepared to make a regular siege. During the night, the Moors had time to see the extent of their loss. Their tents resounded with lamentations. This warrior had to mourn a brother, that a friend; many suffered with grievous wounds, all trembled at the fate in store for them.

There were two young Moors, both of humble rank, who gave proof at that time of attachment and fidelity rare in the history of man. Cloridan and Medoro had followed their prince, Dardinel, to the wars of France. Cloridan, a bold huntsman, combined strength with activity. Medoro was a mere youth, his cheeks yet fair and blooming. Of all the Saracens, no one united so much grace and beauty. His light hair was set off by his black and sparkling eyes. The two friends were together on guard at the rampart. About midnight they gazed on the scene in deep dejection. Medoro, with tears in his eyes, spoke of the good prince Dardinel and could not endure the thought that his body should be cast out on the plain, deprived of funeral honors. "Oh, my friend," said he, "must then the body of our prince be the prey of wolves and ravens? Alas! when I remember how he loved me, I feel that, if I should sacrifice my life to do him honor, I should not do more than my duty. I wish, dear friend, to seek out his body on the battlefield and give it burial, and I hope to be able to pass through King Charles's camp without discovery, as they are probably all asleep. You, Cloridan, will be able to say for me, if I should die in the adventure, that gratitude and fidelity to my prince were my inducements."

Cloridan was both surprised and touched with this proof of the young man's devotion. He loved him tenderly and tried for a long time every effort to dissuade him from his design, but he found Medoro determined to accomplish his object or die in the endeavor.

Cloridan, unable to change his purpose, said, "I will go with you, Medoro, and help you in this generous enterprise. I value not life compared with honor, and if I did, do you suppose, dear friend, that I could live without you? I would rather fall by the arms of our enemies than die of grief for the loss of you."

When the two friends were relieved from their guard duty, they went without any followers into the camp of the Christians. All there was still; the fires were dying out; there was no fear of any attempt on the part of the Saracens, and the soldiers, overcome by fatigue or wine, slept secure, lying upon the ground in the midst of their arms and equipage. Cloridan stopped, and said, "Medoro, I am not going to quit this camp without taking vengeance for the death of our prince. Keep watch, be on your guard that no one shall surprise us; I mean to mark a road with my sword through the ranks of our enemies." So saying, he entered the tent where Alpheus slept, who a year before had joined the camp of Charles, and pretended to be a great physician and astrologer. But his science had deceived him, if it gave him hope of dying peacefully in his bed at a good old age; his lot was to die with little warning. Cloridan ran his sword through his heart. A Greek and a German followed, who had been playing late at dice: fortunate if they had continued their game a little longer; but they never reckoned a throw like this among their chances. Cloridan next came to the unlucky Grillon, whose head lay softly on his pillow. He dreamed probably of the feast from which he had but just retired; for when Cloridan cut off his head, wine flowed forth with the blood.

The two young Moors might have penetrated even to the tent of Charlemagne, but knowing that the paladins encamped around him kept watch by turns, and judging that it was impossible they should all be asleep, they were

afraid to go too near. They might also have obtained
rich booty, but intent only on their object, they crossed
the camp and arrived at length at the bloody field, where
bucklers, lances, and swords lay scattered in the midst
of corpses of poor and rich, common soldier and prince,
horses and pools of blood. This terrible scene of carnage
would have destroyed all hope of finding what they were
in search of until dawn of day, were it not that the
moon lent the aid of her uncertain rays.

Medoro raised his eyes to the planet and exclaimed,
"O holy goddess, whom our fathers have adored under
three different forms—thou who displayest thy power
in heaven, on earth, and in the underworld—thou who
art seen foremost among the nymphs chasing the beasts
of the forest—cause me to see, I implore thee, the spot
where my dear master lies, and make me all my life
long follow the example which thou dost exhibit of works
of charity and love."

Either by accident, or that the moon was sensible of
the prayer of Medoro, the cloud broke away, and the
moonlight burst forth as bright as day. The rays seemed
especially to gild the spot where lay the body of Prince
Dardinel, and Medoro, bathed in tears and with bleeding
heart, recognized him by the quarterings of red and white
on his shield.

With groans stifled by his tears, and lamentations in
accents suppressed, not from any fear for himself, for
he cared not for life, but lest any one should be roused
to interrupt their pious duty while yet incomplete, he
proposed to his companion that they should together bear
Dardinel on their shoulders, sharing the burden of the
beloved remains.

Marching with rapid strides under their precious load,
they perceived that the stars began to grow pale and
that the shades of night would soon be dispersed by the
dawn. Just then Zerbino, whose extreme valor had urged
him far from the camp in pursuit of the fugitives, returning, entered the wood in which they were. Some knights
in his train perceived at a distance the two brothers-in-
arms. Cloridan saw the troop and, observing that they
dispersed themselves over the plain as if in search of
booty, told Medoro to lay down the body, and let each

save himself by flight. He dropped his part, thinking that
Medoro would do the same; but the good youth loved
his prince too well to abandon him, and continued to
carry his load singly as well as he might, while Cloridan made his escape. Near by there was a part of the
wood tufted as if nothing but wild animals had ever penetrated it. The unfortunate youth, loaded with the weight
of his dead master, plunged into its recesses.

Cloridan, when he perceived that he had evaded his
foes, discovered that Medoro was not with him. "Ah!"
exclaimed he, "how could I, dear Medoro, so forget myself as to consult my own safety without heeding yours?"
So saying, he retraced the tangled passes of the wood toward the place from whence he had fled. As he approached, he heard the noise of horses and the menacing
voices of armed men. Soon he perceived Medoro, on
foot, with the cavaliers surrounding him. Zerbino, their
commander, bade them seize him. The unhappy Medoro
turned now this way, now that, trying to conceal himself
behind an oak or a rock, still bearing the body, which he
would by no means leave. Cloridan, not knowing how to
help him, but resolved to perish with him, if he must perish, takes an arrow, fits it to his bow, discharges it, and
pierces the breast of a Christian knight, who falls helpless
from his horse. The others look this way and that, to discover whence the fatal bolt was sped. One, while demanding of his comrades in what direction the arrow
came, received a second in his throat, which stopped his
words and soon closed his eyes to the scene.

Zerbino, furious at the death of his two comrades,
ran upon Medoro, seized his golden hair, and dragged
him forward to slay him. But the sight of so much youth
and beauty commanded pity. He stayed his arm. The
young man spoke in suppliant tones. "Ah! signor," said
he, "I conjure you by the God whom you serve, deprive
me not of life until I shall have buried the body of the
prince, my master. Fear not that I will ask you any
other favor; life is not dear to me; I desire death as
soon as I shall have performed this sacred duty. Do
with me then as you please. Give my limbs a prey to
the birds and beasts, only let me first bury my prince."
Medoro pronounced these words with an air so sweet

and tender that a heart of stone would have been moved
by them. Zerbino was so to the bottom of his soul. He
was on the point of uttering words of mercy, when a
cruel subaltern, forgetting all respect to his commander,
plunged his lance into the breast of the young Moor.
Zerbino, enraged at this brutality, turned upon the wretch
to take vengeance, but he saved himself by a precipitate
flight.

Cloridan, who saw Medoro fall, could contain himself
no longer. He rushed from his concealment, threw down
his bow, and, sword in hand, seemed only desirous of
vengeance for Medoro, and to die with him. In a moment, pierced through and through with many wounds,
he exerts the last remnant of his strength in dragging
himself to Medoro, to die embracing him. The cavaliers
left them thus, to rejoin Zerbino, whose rage against the
murderer of Medoro had drawn him away from the spot.

Cloridan died; and Medoro, bleeding copiously, was
drawing near his end when help arrived.

A young maiden approached the fallen knights at this
critical moment. Her dress was that of a peasant-girl,
but her air was noble and her beauty celestial; sweetness and goodness reigned in her lovely countenance.
It was no other than Angelica, the Princess of Cathay.

When she had recovered that precious ring, as we
have before related, Angelica, knowing its value, felt
proud in the power it conferred, travelled alone without fear, not without a secret shame that she had ever
been obliged to seek protection in her wanderings of
the Count Orlando and of Sacripant. She reproached herself, too, as with a weakness, that she had ever thought
of marrying Rinaldo; in fine, her pride grew so high as
to persuade her that no man living was worthy to as-
pire to her hand.

Moved with pity at the sight of the young man
wounded, and melted to tears at hearing the cause, she
quickly recalled to remembrance the knowledge she had
acquired in India, where the virtues of plants and the
art of healing formed part of the education even of
princesses. The beautiful queen ran into the adjoining
meadow to gather plants of virtue to stanch the flow of
blood. Meeting on her way a countryman on horseback

seeking a strayed heifer, she begged him to come to her assistance and endeavor to remove the wounded man to a more secure asylum.

Angelica, having prepared the plants by bruising them between two stones, laid them with her fair hand on Medoro's wound. The remedy soon restored in some degree the strength of the wounded man, who, before he would quit the spot, made them cover with earth and turf the bodies of his friend and of the prince. Then surrendering himself to the pity of his deliverers, he allowed them to place him on the horse of the shepherd and conduct him to his cottage. It was a pleasant farmhouse on the borders of the wood, bearing marks of comfort and competency. There the shepherd lived with his wife and children. There Angelica tended Medoro, and there, by the devoted care of the beautiful queen, his sad wound closed over, and he recovered his perfect health.

Oh, Count Rinaldo, Oh, King Sacripant! what availed it you to possess so many virtues and such fame? What advantage have you derived from all your high deserts? Oh, hapless king, great Agrican! if you could return to life, how would you endure to see yourself rejected by one who will bow to the yoke of Hymen in favor of a young soldier of humble birth? And thou, Ferrau, and ye numerous others who a hundred times have put your lives at hazard for this cruel beauty, how bitter will it be to you to see her sacrifice you all to the claims of the humble Medoro!

There, under the low roof of a shepherd, the flame of Hymen was lighted for this haughty queen. She takes the shepherd's wife to serve in place of mother, the shepherd and his children for witnesses, and marries the happy Medoro.

Angelica, after her marriage, wishing to endow Medoro with the sovereignty of the countries which yet remained to her, took with him the road to the east. She had preserved through all her adventures a bracelet of gold enriched with precious stones, the present of the Count Orlando. Having nothing else wherewith to reward the good shepherd and his wife, who had served her with so much care and fidelity, she took the bracelet from her arm and gave it to them, and then the newly married couple directed their steps towards those mountains which separate France and Spain, intending to wait at Barcelona a vessel which should take them on their way to the east.

ORLANDO MAD

Orlando, on the loss of Angelica, laid aside his crest and arms and arrayed himself in a suit of black armor, expressive of his despair. In this guise, he carried such slaughter among the ranks of the infidels that both armies were astonished at the achievements of the stranger knight. Mandricardo, who had been absent from the battle, heard the report of these achievements and determined to test for himself the valor of the knight so extolled. He it was who broke in upon the conference of Zerbino and Isabella and their benefactor, Orlando, as they stood, occupied in mutual felicitations, after the happy reunion of the lovers by the prowess of the paladin.

Mandricardo, after contemplating the group for a moment, addressed himself to Orlando in these words: "Thou must be the man I seek. For ten days and more I have been on thy track. The fame of thy exploits has brought me hither, that I may measure my strength with thine. Thy crest and shield prove thee the same who spread such slaughter among our troops. But these marks are superfluous, and if I saw thee among a hundred, I should know thee by thy martial bearing to be the man I seek."

"I respect thy courage," said Orlando; "such a design could not have sprung up in any but a brave and generous soul. If the desire to see me has brought thee hither, I would, if it were possible, show thee my inmost soul. I will remove my visor that you may satisfy your curiosity; but when you have done so, I hope that you will also try and see if my valor corresponds to my appearance."

"Come on," said the Saracen, "my first wish was to see and know thee; I will now gratify my second."

Orlando, observing Mandricardo, was surprised to see no sword at his side, nor mace at his saddle-bow. "And what weapon hast thou," said he, "if thy lance fail thee?"

"Do not concern yourself about that," said Mandricardo; "I have made many good knights give ground with no other weapon than you see. Know that I have sworn an oath never to bear a sword until I win back that famous Durindana that Orlando, the paladin, carries. That sword belongs to the suit of armor which I wear; that only is wanting. Without doubt it was stolen, but how it got into the hands of Orlando I know not. But I will make him pay dearly for it when I find him. I seek him the more anxiously that I may avenge with his blood the death of King Agrican, my father, whom he treacherously slew. I am sure he must have done it by treachery, for it was not in his power to subdue in fair fight such a warrior as my father."

"Thou liest," cried Orlando, "and all who say so lie. I am Orlando, whom you seek; yes, I am he who slew your father honorably. Hold, here is the sword: you shall have it if your courage avails to merit it. Though it belongs to me by right, I will not use it in this dispute. See, I hang it on this tree: you shall be master of it, if you bereave me of life; not else."

At these words, Orlando drew Durindana and hung it on one of the branches of a tree near by.

Both knights, boiling with equal ardor, rode off in a semicircle, then rushed together with reins thrown loose and struck one another with their lances. Both kept their seats, immovable. The splinters of their lances flew into the air, and no weapon remained for either but the fragment which he held in his hand. Then those two knights, covered with iron mail, were reduced to the necessity of fighting with staves, in the manner of two rustics who dispute the boundary of a meadow, or the possession of a spring.

These clubs could not long keep whole in the hands of such sturdy smiters, who were soon reduced to fight with naked fists. Such warfare was more painful to him that gave than to him that received the blows. They next clasped and strained each his adversary, as Hercules did Antæus. Mandricardo, more enraged than Orlando, made violent efforts to unseat the paladin and dropped the rein of his horse. Orlando, more calm, perceived it. With one hand he resisted Mandricardo, with the other he twitched the horse's bridle over the ears of the animal. The Saracen dragged Orlando with all his might, but Orlando's thighs held the saddle like a vise. At last the efforts of the Saracen broke the girths of Orlando's horse; the saddle slipped; the knight, firm in his stirrups, slipped with it and came to the ground hardly conscious of his fall. The noise of his armor in falling startled Mandricardo's horse, now without a bridle. He started off in full career, heeding neither trees nor rocks nor broken ground. Urged by fright, he ran with furious speed, carrying his master, who, almost distracted with rage, shouted and beat the animal with his fists, and thereby impelled his flight. After running thus three miles or more, a deep ditch opposed their progress. The horse and rider fell headlong into it and did not find the bottom covered with feather-beds or roses. They got sadly bruised, but were lucky enough to escape without any broken limbs.

Mandricardo, as soon as he gained his feet, seized the horse by his mane with fury, but, having no bridle, could not hold him. He looked round in hopes of finding something that would do for a rein. Just then fortune, who seemed willing to help him at last, brought that way a peasant with a bridle in his hand, who was in search of his farm horse that had strayed away.

Orlando, having speedily repaired his horse's girths, remounted and waited a good hour for the Saracen to return. Not seeing him, he concluded to go in search of him. He took an affectionate leave of Zerbino and Isabella, who would willingly have followed him; but this the brave paladin would by no means permit. He held it unknightly to go in search of an enemy accompanied by a friend, who might act as a defender. Therefore, desiring them to say to Mandricardo, if they should meet him, that his purpose was to tarry in the neighborhood three days and then repair to the camp of Charlemagne, he took down Durindana from the tree and proceeded in

the direction which the Saracen's horse had taken. But
the animal, having no guide but its terror, had so
doubled and confused its traces that Orlando, after two
days spent in the search, gave up the attempt.

It was about the middle of the third day when the
paladin arrived on the pleasant bank of a stream which
wound through a meadow enamelled with flowers. High
trees, whose tops met and formed an arbor, overshadowed the fountain, and the breeze which blew through
their foliage tempered the heat. Hither the shepherds
used to resort to quench their thirst and to enjoy the
shelter from the midday sun. The air, perfumed with
the flowers, seemed to breathe fresh strength into their
veins. Orlando felt the influence, though covered with
his armor. He stopped in this delicious arbor, where everything seemed to invite to repose. But he could not have
chosen a more fatal asylum. He there spent the most
miserable moments of his life.

He looked around and noted with pleasure all the
charms of the spot. He saw that some of the trees were
carved with inscriptions—he drew near and read them,
and what was his surprise to find that they composed
the name of Angelica. Farther on, he found the name
of Medoro mixed with hers. The paladin thought he
dreamed. He stood like one amazed—like a bird that,
rising to fly, finds its feet caught in a net.

Orlando followed the course of the stream and came
to one of its turns, where the rocks of the mountain
bent in such a way as to form a sort of grotto. The
twisted stems of ivy and the wild vine draped the entrance of this recess, scooped by the hand of nature.

The unhappy paladin, on entering the grotto, saw letters which appeared to have been lately carved. They
were verses which Medoro had written in honor of his
happy nuptials with the beautiful queen. Orlando tried
to persuade himself it must be some other Angelica whom
those verses celebrated, and as for Medoro, he had never
heard his name. The sun was now declining, and Orlando remounted his horse and went on his way. He
soon saw the roof of a cottage whence the smoke ascended; he heard the barking of dogs and the lowing of
cattle, and arrived at a humble dwelling which seemed

to offer an asylum for the night. The inmates, as soon as they saw him, hastened to render him service. One took his horse, another his shield and cuirass, another his golden spurs. This cottage was the very same where Medoro had been carried, deeply wounded—where Angelica had tended him and afterwards married him. The shepherd who lived in it loved to tell everybody the story of this marriage, and soon related it, with all its details, to the miserable Orlando.

Having finished it, he went away and returned with the precious bracelet which Angelica, grateful for his services, had given him as a memorial. It was the one which Orlando had himself given her.

This last touch was the finishing stroke to the excited paladin. Frantic, exasperated, he exclaimed against the ungrateful and cruel princess who had disdained him, the most renowned, the most indomitable of all the paladins of France—him, who had rescued her from the most alarming perils—him, who had fought the most terrible battles for her sake—she to prefer to him a young Saracen! The pride of the noble count was deeply wounded. Indignant, frantic, a victim to ungovernable rage, he rushed into the forest, uttering the most frightful shrieks.

"No, no!" cried he, "I am not the man they take me for! Orlando is dead! I am only the wandering ghost of that unhappy count, who is now suffering the torments of hell!"

Orlando wandered all night, as chance directed, through the wood, and at sunrise his destiny led him to the fountain where Medoro had engraved the fatal inscription. The frantic paladin saw it a second time with fury, drew his sword, and hacked it from the rock.

Unlucky grotto! You shall no more attract by your shade and coolness, you shall no more shelter with your arch either shepherd or flock. And you, fresh and pure fountain, you may not escape the rage of the furious Orlando! He cast into the fountain branches, trunks of trees which he tore up, pieces of rocks which he broke off, plants uprooted, with the earth adhering, and turf and bushes, so as to choke the fountain and destroy the purity of its waters. At length, exhausted by his violent exertions, bathed in sweat, breathless, Orlando sunk panting upon the earth, and lay there insensible three days and three nights.

The fourth day he started up and seized his arms. His helmet, his buckler, he cast far from him; his hauberk and his clothes he rent asunder; the fragments were scattered through the wood. In fine, he became a furious madman. His insanity was such that he cared not to retain even his sword. But he had no need of Durindana, nor of other arms, to do wonderful things. His prodigious strength sufficed. At the first wrench of his mighty arm, he tore up a pine-tree by the roots. Oaks, beeches, maples, whatever he met in his path, yielded in like manner. The ancient forest soon became as bare as the borders of a morass, where the fowler has cleared away the bushes to spread his nets. The shepherds, hearing the horrible crashing in the forest, abandoned their flocks to run and see the cause of this unwonted uproar. By their evil star, or for their sins, they were led thither. When they saw the furious state the count was in, and his incredible force, they would fain have fled out of his reach, but in their fears lost their presence of mind. The madman pursued them, seized one, and rent him limb from limb, as easily as one would pull ripe apples from a tree. He took another by the feet and used him as a club to knock down a third. The shepherds fled; but it would have been hard for any to escape, if he had not at that moment left them to throw himself with the same fury upon their flocks. The peasants, abandoning their ploughs and harrows, mounted on the roofs of buildings and pinnacles of the rocks, afraid to trust themselves even to the oaks and pines. From such heights they looked on, trembling at the raging fury of the unhappy Orlando. His fists, his teeth, his nails, his feet, seize, break, and tear cattle, sheep, and swine, the most swift in flight alone being able to escape him.

When at last terror had scattered everything before him, he entered a cottage which was abandoned by its inhabitants and there found that which served for food. His long fast had caused him to feel the most ravenous hunger. Seizing whatever he found that was eatable, whether roots, acorns, or bread, raw meat or cooked, he gorged it indiscriminately.

Issuing thence again, the frantic Orlando gave chase to whatever living thing he saw, whether men or animals. Sometimes he pursued the deer and hind, sometimes he attacked bears and wolves, and with his naked hands killed and tore them and devoured their flesh.

Thus he wandered, from place to place, through France, imperilling his life a thousand ways, yet always preserved by some mysterious providence from a fatal result. But here we leave Orlando for a time, that we may record what befell Zerbino and Isabella after their parting with him.

The prince and his fair bride waited, by Orlando's request, near the scene of the battle for three days, that, if Mandricardo should return, they might inform him where Orlando would give him another meeting. At the end of that time, their anxiety to know the issue led them to follow Orlando's traces, which led them at last to the wood where the trees were inscribed with the names of Angelica and Medoro. They remarked how all these inscriptions were defaced, and how the grotto was disordered, and the fountain clogged with rubbish. But that which surprised them and distressed them most of all was to find on the grass the cuirass of Orlando, and not far from it his helmet, the same which the renowned Almontes once wore.

Hearing a horse neigh in the forest, Zerbino turned his eyes in that direction and saw Brigliadoro, with the bridle yet hanging at the saddle-bow. He looked round for Durindana and found that famous sword, without the scabbard, lying on the grass. He saw also the fragments of Orlando's other arms and clothing scattered on all sides over the plain.

Zerbino and Isabella stood in astonishment and grief, not knowing what to think, but little imagining the true cause. If they had found any marks of blood on the arms or on the fragments of the clothing, they would have supposed him slain, but there were none. While they were in this painful uncertainty, they saw a young peasant approach. He, not yet recovered from the terror of the scene which he had witnessed from the top of a rock, told them the whole of the sad events.

Zerbino, with his eyes full of tears, carefully collected all the scattered arms. Isabella also dismounted to aid him in the sad duty. When they had collected all the pieces of that rich armor, they hung them like a trophy on a pine; and to prevent their being violated by any passers-by, Zerbino inscribed on the bark this caution: "These are the arms of the paladin Orlando."

Having finished this pious work, he remounted his horse, and just then a knight rode up and requested Zerbino to tell him the meaning of the trophy. The prince related the facts as they had happened; and Mandricardo, for it was that Saracen knight, full of joy, rushed forward and seized the sword, saying, "No one can censure me for what I do; this sword is mine; I can take my own wherever I find it. It is plain that Orlando, not daring to defend it against me, has counterfeited madness to excuse him in surrendering it."

Zerbino vehemently exclaimed, "Touch not that sword. Think not to possess it without a contest. If it be true that the arms you wear are those of Hector, you must have got them by theft and not by prowess."

Immediately they attacked one another with the utmost fury. The air resounded with thick-falling blows. Zerbino, skilful and alert, evaded for a time with good success the strokes of Durindana, but at length a terrible blow struck him on the neck. He fell from his horse, and the Tartar king, possessed of the spoils of his victory, rode away.

ZERBINO AND ISABELLA

Zerbino's pain at seeing the Tartar prince go off with the sword surpassed the anguish of his wound; but now the loss of blood so reduced his strength that he could not move from where he fell. Isabella, not knowing whither to resort for help, could only bemoan him and chide her cruel fate. Zerbino said, "If I could but leave thee, my best beloved, in some secure abode, it would not distress me to die; but to abandon thee so, without protection, is sad indeed." She replied, "Think not to leave me, dear-

est; our souls shall not be parted; this sword will give me
the means to follow thee." Zerbino's last words implored
her to banish such a thought, but live and be true to his
memory. Isabella promised, with many tears, to be faithful to him so long as life should last.

When he ceased to breathe, Isabella's cries resounded
through the forest and reached the ears of a reverend
hermit, who hastened to the spot. He soothed and calmed
her, urging those consolations which the word of God
supplies, and at last brought her to wish for nothing else
but to devote herself for the rest of life wholly to religion.
As she could not bear the thoughts of leaving her dead
lord abandoned, the body was, by the good hermit's aid,
placed upon the horse and taken to the nearest inhabited
place, where a chest was made for it, suitable to be carried with them on their way. The hermit's plan was to
escort his charge to a monastery, not many days' journey
distant, where Isabella resolved to spend the remainder
of her days. Thus they travelled day after day, choosing
the most retired ways, for the country was full of armed
men. One day a cavalier met them and barred their way.
It was no other than Rodomont, King of Algiers, who had
just left the camp of Agramant, full of indignation at the
treatment he had received from Doralice. At sight of the
lovely lady and her reverend attendant, with their horse
laden with a burden draped with black, he asked the
meaning of their journey. Isabella told him her affliction
and her resolution to renounce the world and devote herself to religion and to the memory of the friend she had
lost. Rodomont laughed scornfully at this and told her
that her project was absurd, that charms like hers were
meant to be enjoyed, not buried, and that he himself
would more than make amends for her dead lover. The
monk, who promptly interposed to rebuke this impious
talk, was commanded to hold his peace; and still persist-
ing, was seized by the knight and hurled over the edge of
the cliff, where he fell into the sea, and was drowned.

Rodomont, when he had got rid of the hermit, again
applied to the sad lady, heartless with affright, and, in the
language used by lovers, said, "she was his very heart,
his life, his light." Having laid aside all violence, he
humbly sued that she would accompany him to his re-

treat, near by. It was a ruined chapel from which the monks had been driven by the disorders of the time, and which Rodomont had taken possession of. Isabella, who had no choice but to obey, followed him, meditating as she went what resource she could find to escape out of his power and keep her vow to her dead husband, to be faithful to his memory as long as life should last. At length she said, "If, my lord, you will let me go and fulfil my vow, and my intention, as I have already declared it, I will bestow upon you what will be to you of more value than a hundred women's hearts. I know an herb, and I have seen it on our way, which, rightly prepared, affords a juice of such power, that the flesh, if laved with it, becomes impenetrable to sword or fire. This liquor I can make, and will, to-day, if you will accept my offer; and when you have seen its virtue, you will value it more than if all Europe were made your own."

Rodomont, at hearing this, readily promised all that was asked, so eager was he to learn a secret that would make him as Achilles was of yore. Isabella, having collected such herbs as she thought proper, and boiled them, with certain mysterious signs and words, at length declared her labor done, and, as a test, offered to try its virtue on herself. She bathed her neck and bosom with the liquor, and then called on Rodomont to smite with all his force and see whether his sword had power to harm. The pagan, who during the preparations had taken frequent draughts of wine, and scarce knew what he did, drew his sword at the word and struck across her neck with all his might, and the fair head leapt sundered from the snowy neck and breast.

Rude and unfeeling as he was, the pagan knight lamented bitterly this sad result. To honor her memory, he resolved to do a work as unparalleled as her devotion. From all parts round he caused laborers to be brought, and had a tower built to enclose the chapel, within which the remains of Zerbino and Isabella were entombed. Across the stream which flowed near by he built a bridge, scarce two yards wide, and added neither parapet nor rail. On the top of the tower a sentry was placed, who, when any traveller approached the bridge, gave notice to his master. Rodomont thereupon sallied out and defied the approaching knight to fight him upon the bridge, where any chance step a little aside would plunge the rider headlong in the stream. This bridge he vowed to keep until a thousand suits of armor should be won from conquered knights, wherewith to build a trophy to his victim and her lord.

Within ten days the bridge was built, and the tower was in progress. In a short time many knights, either seeking the shortest route or tempted by a desire of adventure, had made the attempt to pass the bridge. All, without exception, had lost either arms or life, or both, some falling before Rodomont's lance, others precipitated into the river. One day, as Rodomont stood urging his workmen, it chanced that Orlando in his furious mood came thither and approached the bridge. Rodomont halloed to him, "Halt, churl; presume not to set foot upon that bridge; it was not made for such as you!" Orlando took no notice, but pressed on. Just then a gentle damsel rode up. It was Flordelis, who was seeking her Florismart. She saw Orlando and, in spite of his strange appearance, recognized him. Rodomont, not used to have his commands disobeyed, laid hands on the madman, and would have thrown him into the river, but to his astonishment found himself in the grip of one not so easily disposed of. "How can a fool have such strength?" he growled between his teeth. Flordelis stopped to see the issue, where each of these two puissant warriors strove to throw the other from the bridge. Orlando at last had strength enough to lift his foe with all his armor and fling him over the side, but had not wit to clear himself from him, so both fell together. High flashed the wave as they together smote its surface. Here Orlando had the advantage; he was naked, and could swim like a fish. He soon reached the bank and, careless of praise or blame, stopped not to see what came of the adventure. Rodomont, entangled with his armor, escaped with difficulty to the bank. Meantime, Flordelis passed the bridge unchallenged.

After long wandering without success, she returned to Paris and there found the object of her search; for Florismart, after the fall of Albracca, had repaired thither. The joy of meeting was clouded to Florismart by the news which Flordelis brought of Orlando's wretched plight. The last she had seen of him was when he fell with Rodomont into the stream. Florismart, who loved Orlando like a brother, resolved to set out immediately, under guidance of the lady, to find him and bring him where he might receive the treatment suited to his case. A few days brought them to the place where they found the Tartar king still guarding the bridge. The usual challenge and defiance was made, and the knights rode to encounter one another on the bridge. At the first encounter both horses were overthrown, and, having no space to regain their footing, fell with their riders into the water. Rodomont, who knew the soundings of the stream, soon recovered the land, but Florismart was carried downward by the current, and landed at last on a bank of mud where his horse could hardly find footing. Flordelis, who watched the battle from the bridge, seeing her lover in this piteous case, exclaimed aloud, "Ah! Rodomont, for love of her whom dead you honor, have pity on me, who love this knight, and slay him not. Let it suffice he yields his armor to the pile, and none more glorious will it bear than his." Her prayer, so well directed, touched the pagan's heart, though hard to move, and he lent his aid to help the knight to land. He kept him a prisoner, however, and added his armor to the pile. Flordelis, with a heavy heart, went her way.

We must now return to Rogero, who, when we parted with him, was engaged in an adventure which arrested his progress to the monastery whither he was bound with the intention of receiving baptism, and thus qualifying himself to demand Bradamante as his bride. On his way, he met with Mandricardo, and the quarrel was revived respecting the right to wear the badge of Hector. After a warm discussion, both parties agreed to submit the question to King Agramant, and for that purpose took their way to the Saracen camp. Here they met Gradasso, who had his controversy also with Mandricardo. This warrior claimed the sword of Orlando, denying the right of Mandricardo to possess it in virtue of his having found it abandoned by its owner. King Agramant strove in vain to reconcile these quarrels, and was forced at last to consent that the points in dispute should be settled by one combat, in which Mandricardo should meet one of the other champions, to whom should be committed the cause of both. Rogero was chosen by lot to maintain Gradasso's cause and his own. Great preparations were made for this signal contest. On the appointed day it was fought in the presence of Agramant and of the whole army. Rogero won it; and Mandricardo, the conqueror of Hector's arms, the challenger of Orlando, and the slayer of Zerbino, lost his life. Gradasso received Durindana as his prize, which lost half its value in his eyes, since it was won by another's prowess, not his own.

Rogero, though victorious, was severely wounded, and lay helpless many weeks in the camp of Agramant, while Bradamante, ignorant of the cause of his delay, expected him at Montalban. Thither he had promised to repair in fifteen days, or twenty at furthest, hoping to have obtained by that time an honorable discharge from his obligations to the Saracen commander. The twenty days were passed, and a month more, and still Rogero came not, nor did any tidings reach Bradamante accounting for his absence. At the end of that time, a wandering knight brought news of the famous combat and of Rogero's wound. He added, what alarmed Bradamante still more, that Marphisa, a female warrior, young and fair, was in attendance on the wounded knight. He added that the whole army expected that, as soon as Rogero's wounds were healed, the pair would be united in marriage.

Bradamante, distressed by this news, though she believed it but in part, resolved to go immediately and see for herself. She mounted Rabican, the horse of Astolpho, which he had committed to her care, and took with her the lance of gold, though unaware of its wonderful powers. Thus accoutred, she left the castle and took the road toward Paris and the camp of the Saracens.

Marphisa, whose devotion to Rogero in his illness had so excited the jealousy of Bradamante, was the twin sister of Rogero. She, with him, had been taken in charge when an infant by Atlantes, the magician, but while yet a child she had been stolen away by an Arab tribe. Adopted by their chief, she had early learned horsemanship and skill in arms, and at this time had come to the camp of Agramant with no other view than to see and test for herself the prowess of the warriors of either camp, whose fame rang through the world. Arriving at the very moment of the late encounter, the name of Rogero, and some few facts of his story which she learned, were enough to suggest the idea that it was her brother whom she saw victorious in the single combat. Inquiry satisfied the two of their near kindred, and from that moment Marphisa devoted herself to the care of her new-found and much-loved brother.

In those moments of seclusion Rogero informed his sister of what he had learned of their parentage from old Atlantes. Rogero, their father, a Christian knight, had won the heart of Galaciella, daughter of the Sultan of Africa, and sister of King Agramant, converted her to the Christian faith, and secretly married her. The sultan, enraged at his daughter's marriage, drove her husband into exile and caused her, with her infant children, Rogero and Marphisa, to be placed in a boat and committed to the winds and waves, to perish, from which fate they were saved by Atlantes. On hearing this, Marphisa exclaimed, "How can you, brother, leave our parents unavenged so long, and even submit to serve the son of the tyrant who so wronged them?" Rogero replied that it was but lately he had learned the full truth; that when he learned it, he was already embarked with Agramant, from whom he had received knighthood, and that he only waited for a suitable opportunity when he might with honor desert his standard and at the same time return to the faith of his fathers. Marphisa hailed this resolution with joy and declared her intention to join with him in embracing the Christian faith.

We left Bradamante when, mounted on Rabican and armed with Astolpho's lance, she rode forth, determined to learn the cause of Rogero's long absence. One day, as she rode, she met a damsel, of visage and of manners fair, but overcome with grief. It was Flordelis, who was seeking far and near a champion capable of liberating and avenging her lord. Flordelis marked the approaching warrior and, judging from appearances, thought she had found the champion she sought. "Are you, Sir Knight," she said, "so daring and so kind as to take up my cause against a fierce and cruel warrior who has made prisoner of my lord, and forced me thus to be a wanderer and a suppliant?" Then she related the events which had happened at the bridge. Bradamante, to whom noble enterprises were always welcome, readily embraced this, and the rather as in her gloomy forebodings she felt as if Rogero was forever lost to her.

Next day the two arrived at the bridge. The sentry descried them approaching and gave notice to his lord, who thereupon donned his armor and went forth to meet them. Here, as usual, he called on the advancing warrior to yield his horse and arms an oblation to the tomb. Bradamante replied, asking by what right he called on the innocent to do penance for his crime. "Your life and your armor," she added, "are the fittest offering to her tomb, and I, a woman, the fittest champion to take them." With that she couched her spear, spurred her horse, and ran to the encounter. King Rodomont came on with speed. The trampling sounded on the bridge like thunder. It took but a moment to decide the contest. The golden lance did its office, and that fierce Moor, so renowned in tourney, lay extended on the bridge. "Who is the loser now?" said Bradamante, but Rodomont, amazed that a woman's hand should have laid him low, could not or would not answer. Silent and sad, he raised himself, unbound his helm and mail, and flung them against the tomb; then, sullen and on foot, left the ground, but first gave orders to one of his squires to release all his prisoners. They had been sent off to Africa. Besides Florismart, there were Sansonnet and Oliver, who had ridden that way in quest of Orlando and had both in turn been overthrown in the encounter.

Bradamante, after her victory, resumed her route and in due time reached the Christian camp, where she readily learned an explanation of the mystery which had caused her so much anxiety. Rogero and his fair and brave sister, Marphisa, were too illustrious by their station and exploits not to be the frequent topic of discourse even among their adversaries, and all that Bradamante was anxious to know reached her ear, almost without inquiry.

We now return to Gradasso, who, by Rogero's victory

had been made possessor of Durindana. There now only remained to him to seek the horse of Rinaldo; and the challenge, given and accepted, was yet to be fought with that warrior, for it had been interrupted by the arts of Malagigi. Gradasso now sought another meeting with Rinaldo and met with no reluctance on his part. As the combat was for the possession of Bayard, the knights dismounted and fought on foot. Long time the battle lasted. Rinaldo, knowing well the deadly stroke of Durindana, used all his art to parry or avoid its blow. Gradasso struck with might and main, but well nigh all his strokes were spent in air, or if they smote, they fell obliquely and did little harm.

Thus had they fought long, glancing at one another's eyes and seeing naught else, when their attention was arrested perforce by a strange noise. They turned and beheld the good Bayard attacked by a monstrous bird. Perhaps it was a bird, for such it seemed; but when or where such a bird was ever seen I have nowhere read, except in Turpin; and I am inclined to believe that it was not a bird, but a fiend, evoked from underground by Malagigi and thither sent on purpose to interrupt the fight. Whether a fiend or a fowl, the monster flew right at Bayard and clapped his wings in his face. Thereat the steed broke loose and ran madly across the plain, pursued by the bird, till Bayard plunged into the wood, and was lost to sight.

Rinaldo and Gradasso, seeing Bayard's escape, agreed to suspend their battle till they could recover the horse, the object of contention. Gradasso mounted his steed and followed the foot-marks of Bayard into the forest. Rinaldo, never more vexed in spirit, remained at the spot, Gradasso having promised to return thither with the horse, if he found him. He did find him, after long search, for he had the good fortune to hear him neigh. Thus he became possessed of both the objects for which he had led an army from his own country and invaded France. He did not forget his promise to bring Bayard back to the place where he had left Rinaldo; but, only muttering, "Now I have got him, he little knows me who expects me to give him up; if Rinaldo wants the horse, let him seek him in India, as I have sought him in France,"—he made the best of his way to Arles, where his vessels lay; and in possession of the two objects of his ambition, the horse and the sword, sailed away to his own country.

ASTOLPHO IN ABYSSINIA

When we last parted with the adventurous paladin Astolpho, he was just commencing that flight over the countries of the world from which he promised himself so much gratification. Our readers are aware that the eagle and the falcon have not so swift a flight as the Hippogriff on which Astolpho rode. It was not long, therefore, before the paladin, directing his course toward the southeast, arrived over that part of Africa where the great River Nile has its source. Here he alighted and found himself in the neighborhood of the capital of Abyssinia, ruled by Senapus, whose riches and power were immense. His palace was of surpassing splendor; the bars of the gates, the hinges and locks, were all of pure gold; in fact, this metal, in that country, is put to all those uses for which we employ iron. It is so common that they prefer for ornamental purposes rock crystal, of which all the columns were made. Precious stones of different kinds, rubies, emeralds, sapphires, and topazes, were set in ornamental designs, and the walls and ceilings were adorned with pearls.

It is in this country those famous balms grow of which there are some few plants in that part of Judæa called Gilead. Musk, ambergris, and numerous gums, so precious in Europe, are here in their native climate. It is said the Sultan of Egypt pays a vast tribute to the monarch of this country to hire him not to cut off the source of the Nile, which he might easily do, and cause the river to flow in some other direction, thus depriving Egypt of the source of its fertility.

At the time of Astolpho's arrival in his dominions, this monarch was in great affliction. In spite of his riches and the precious productions of his country, he was in danger

of dying of hunger. He was a prey to a flock of obscene
birds called harpies, which attacked him whenever he sat
at meat and with their claws snatched, tore, and scattered everything, overturning the vessels, devouring the
food, and infecting what they left with their filthy touch.
It was said this punishment was inflicted upon the king because, when young, and filled with pride and presumption,
he had attempted to invade with an army the terrestrial
paradise, which is situated on the top of a mountain
whence the Nile draws its source. Nor was this his only
punishment. He was struck blind.

Astolpho, on arriving in the dominions of this monarch,
hastened to pay him his respects. King Senapus received
him graciously and ordered a splendid repast to be prepared in honor of his arrival. While the guests were
seated at table, Astolpho filling the place of dignity at
the king's right hand, the horrid scream of the harpies
was heard in the air, and soon they approached, hovering
over the tables, seizing the food from the dishes, and
overturning everything with the flapping of their broad
wings. In vain the guests struck at them with knives and
any weapons which they had, and Astolpho drew his
sword and gave them repeated blows, which seemed to
have no more effect upon them than if their bodies had
been made of tow.

At last Astolpho thought of his horn. He first gave
warning to the king and his guests to stop their ears; then
blew a blast. The harpies, terrified at the sound, flew
away as fast as their wings could carry them. The paladin
mounted his Hippogriff and pursued them, blowing his
horn as often as he came near them. They stretched their
flight towards the great mountain, at the foot of which
there is a cavern, which is thought to be the mouth of the
infernal abodes. Hither those horrid birds flew, as if to
their home. Having seen them all disappear in the recess,
Astolpho cared not to pursue them farther, but, alighting, rolled huge stones into the mouth of the cave and
piled branches of trees therein, so that he effectually
barred their passage out, and we have no evidence of
their ever having been seen since in the outer air.

After this labor, Astolpho refreshed himself by bath-
ing in a fountain whose pure waters bubbled from a cleft

of the rock. Having rested awhile, an earnest desire seized him of ascending the mountain which towered above him. The Hippogriff bore him swiftly upwards and landed him on the top of the mountain, which he found to be an extensive plain.

A splendid palace rose in the middle of this plain, whose walls shone with such brilliancy that mortal eyes could hardly bear the sight. Astolpho guided the winged horse towards this edifice and made him poise himself in the air while he took a leisurely survey of this favored spot and its environs. It seemed as if nature and art had striven with one another to see which could do the most for its embellishment.

Astolpho, on approaching the edifice, saw a venerable man advance to meet him. This personage was clothed in a long vesture as white as snow, while a mantle of purple covered his shoulders and hung down to the ground. A white beard descended to his middle, and his hair, of the same color, overshadowed his shoulders. His eyes were so brilliant that Astolpho felt persuaded that he was a blessed inhabitant of the heavenly mansions.

The sage, smiling benignantly upon the paladin, who from respect had dismounted from his horse, said to him: "Noble chevalier, know that it is by the Divine will you have been brought to the terrestrial paradise. Your mortal nature could not have borne to scale these heights and reach these seats of bliss if it were not the will of Heaven that you should be instructed in the means to succor Charles and to sustain the glory of our holy faith. I am prepared to impart the needed counsels; but before I begin, let me welcome you to our sojourn. I doubt not your long fast and distant journey have given you a good appetite."

The aspect of the venerable man filled the prince with admiration; but his surprise ceased when he learned from him that he was that one of the Apostles of our Lord to whom he said, "I will that thou tarry till I come."

St. John, conducting Astolpho, rejoined his companions. These were the patriarch Enoch and the prophet Elijah, neither of whom had yet seen his dying day, but, taken from our lower world, were dwelling in a region of peace and joy, in a climate of eternal spring, till the last trumpet shall sound.

The three holy inhabitants of the terrestrial paradise received Astolpho with the greatest kindness, carried him to a pleasant apartment, and took great care of the Hippogriff, to whom they gave such food as suited him, while to the prince they presented fruits so delicious that he felt inclined to excuse our first parents for their sin in eating them without permission.

Astolpho, having recruited his strength, not only by these excellent fruits, but also by sweet sleep, roused himself at the first blush of dawn and, as soon as he left his chamber, met the beloved Apostle coming to seek him. St. John took him by the hand and told him many things relating to the past and the future. Among others, he said, "Son, let me tell you what is now going on in France. Orlando, the illustrious prince who received at his birth the endowment of strength and courage more than mortal, raised up as was Samson of old to be the champion of the true faith, has been guilty of the basest ingratitude in leaving the Christian camp when it most needed the support of his arm, to run after a Saracen princess, whom he would fain marry, though she scorns him. To punish him, his reason has been taken away, so that he runs naked through the land, over mountains and through valleys, without a ray of intelligence. The duration of his punishment has been fixed at three months, and that time having nearly expired, you have been brought hither to learn from us the means by which the reason of Orlando may be restored. True, you will be obliged to make a journey with me, and we must even leave the earth and ascend to the moon, for it is in that planet we are to seek the remedy for the madness of the paladin. I propose to make our journey this evening, as soon as the moon appears over our head."

As soon as the sun sunk beneath the seas, and the moon presented its luminous disk, the holy man had the chariot brought out in which he was accustomed to make excursions among the stars, the same which was employed long ago to convey Elijah up from earth. The saint made Astolpho seat himself beside him, took the reins, and giving the word to the coursers, they bore them upward with astonishing celerity.

At length, they reached the great continent of the

moon. Its surface appeared to be of polished steel, with here and there a spot which, like rust, obscured its brightness. The paladin was astonished to see that the earth, with all its seas and rivers, seemed but an insignificant spot in the distance.

The prince discovered in this region so new to him rivers, lakes, plains, hills, and valleys. Many beautiful cities and castles enriched the landscape. He saw also vast forests and heard in them the sound of horns and the barking of dogs, which led him to conclude that the nymphs were following the chase.

The knight, filled with wonder at all he saw, was conducted by the saint to a valley, where he stood amazed at the riches strewed all around him. Well he might be so, for that valley was the receptacle of things lost on earth, either by men's fault, or by the effect of time and chance. Let no one suppose we speak here of kingdoms or of treasures; they are the toys of Fortune, which she dispenses in turning her wheel; we speak of things which she can neither give nor take away. Such are reputations, which appear at one time so brilliant and a short time after are heard of no more. Here, also, are countless vows and prayers for unattainable objects, lovers' sighs and tears, time spent in gaming, dressing, and doing nothing, the leisure of the dull and the intentions of the lazy, baseless projects, intrigues, and plots; these and such like things fill all the valley.

Astolpho had a great desire to understand all that he saw, and which appeared to him so extraordinary. Among the rest, he observed a great mountain of blown bladders, from which issued indistinct noises. The saint told him these were the dynasties of Assyrian and Persian kings, once the wonder of the earth, of which now scarce the name remains.

Astolpho could not help laughing when the saint said to him, "All these hooks of silver and gold that you see are the gifts of courtiers to princes, made in the hope of getting something better in return." He also showed him garlands of flowers in which snares were concealed; these were flatteries and adulations, meant to deceive. But nothing was so comical as the sight of numerous grasshoppers which had burst their lungs with chirping. These, he told him, were sonnets, odès, and dedications addressed by venal poets to great people.

The paladin beheld with wonder what seemed a lake of spilled milk. "It is," said the saint, "the charity done by frightened misers on their death-beds." It would take too long to tell all that the valley contained: meannesses, affectations, pretended virtues, and concealed vices were there in abundance.

Among the rest, Astolpho perceived many days of his own lost, and many imprudent sallies which he had made, and would have been glad not to have been reminded of. But he also saw among so many lost things a great abundance of one thing which men are apt to think they all possess and do not think it necessary to pray for— good sense. This commodity appeared under the form of a liquor, most light and apt to evaporate. It was therefore kept in vials, firmly sealed. One of these was labelled, "The sense of the paladin Orlando."

All the bottles were ticketed, and the sage placed one in Astolpho's hand, which he found was his own. It was more than half full. He was surprised to find there many other vials which contained almost the whole of the wits of many persons who passed among men for wise. Ah, how easy it is to lose one's reason! Some lose theirs by yielding to the sway of the passions; some, in braving tempests and shoals in search of wealth; some, by trusting too much to the promises of the great; some, by setting their hearts on trifles. As might have been expected, the bottles which held the wits of astrologers, inventors, metaphysicians, and above all, of poets, were in general the best filled of all.

Astolpho took his bottle, put it to his nose, and inhaled it all; and Turpin assures us that he was for a long time afterwards as sage as one could wish; but the Archbishop adds that there was reason to fear that some of the precious fluid afterwards found its way back into the bottle. The paladin took also the bottle which belonged to Orlando. It was a large one, and quite full.

Before quitting the planetary region, Astolpho was conducted to an edifice on the borders of a river. He was shown an immense hall full of bundles of silk, linen, cotton, and wool. A thousand different colors, brilliant or dull, some quite black, were among these skeins. In one part of the hall an old woman was busy winding off yarns from all these different bundles. When she had finished a skein, another ancient dame took it and placed it with others; a third selected from the fleeces spun and mingled them in due proportions. The paladin inquired what all this might be. "These old women," said the saint, "are the Fates, who spin, measure, and terminate the lives of mortals. As long as the thread stretches in one of those skeins, so long does the mortal enjoy the light of day; but nature and death are on the alert to shut the eyes of those whose thread it spun."

Each one of the skeins had a label of gold, silver, or iron, bearing the name of the individual to whom it belonged. An old man, who, in spite of the burden of years, seemed brisk and active, ran without ceasing to fill his apron with these labels, and carried them away to throw them into the river, whose name was Lethe. When he reached the shore of the river, the old man shook out his apron, and the labels sunk to the bottom. A small number only floated for a time, hardly one in a thousand. Numberless birds, hawks, crows, and vultures hovered over the stream, with clamorous cries, and strove to snatch from the water some of these names; but they were too heavy for them, and after a while the birds were forced to let them drop into the river of oblivion. But two beautiful swans, of snowy whiteness, gathered some few of the names and returned with them to the shore, where a lovely nymph received them from their beaks, and carried them to a temple placed upon a hill, and suspended them for all time upon a sacred column, on which stood the statue of Immortality.

Astolpho was amazed at all this and asked his guide to explain it. He replied, "The old man is Time. All the names upon the tickets would be immortal if the old man did not plunge them into the river of oblivion. Those clamorous birds which make vain efforts to save certain of the names are flatterers, pensioners, venal rhymesters, who do their best to rescue from oblivion the unworthy names of their patrons; but all in vain; they may keep them from their fate a little while, but ere long the river of oblivion must swallow them all.

"The swans, that with harmonious strains carry certain names to the temple of Eternal Memory, are the great poets, who save from oblivion worse than death the names of those they judge worthy of immortality. Swans of this kind are rare. Let monarchs know the true breed, and fail not to nourish with care such as may chance to appear in their time."

THE WAR IN AFRICA

When Astolpho had descended to the earth with the precious phial, St. John showed him a plant of marvellous virtues, with which he told him he had only to touch the eyes of the King of Abyssinia to restore him to sight. "That important service," said the saint, "added to your having delivered him from the harpies, will induce him to give you an army wherewith to attack the Africans in their rear and force them to return from France to defend their own country." The saint also instructed him how to lead his troops in safety across the great deserts, where caravans are often overwhelmed with moving columns of sand. Astolpho, fortified with ample instructions, remounted the Hippogriff, thanked the saint, received his blessing, and took his flight down to the level country.

Keeping the course of the River Nile, he soon arrived at the capital of Abyssinia and rejoined Senapus. The joy of the king was great when he heard again the voice of the hero who had delivered him from the harpies. Astolpho touched his eyes with the plant which he had brought from the terrestrial paradise, and restored their sight. The king's gratitude was unbounded. He begged him to name a reward, promising to grant it, whatever it might be. Astolpho asked an army to go to the assistance of Charlemagne, and the king not only granted him a hundred thousand men, but offered to lead them himself.

The night before the day appointed for the departure

of the troops, Astolpho mounted his winged horse and directed his flight towards a mountain, whence the fierce South-wind issues, whose blast raises the sands of the Nubian Desert and whirls them onward in overwhelming clouds. The paladin, by the advice of St. John, had prepared himself with a leather bag, which he placed adroitly, with its mouth open, over the vent whence issues this terrible wind. At the first dawn of morning, the wind rushed from its cavern to resume its daily course, and was caught in the bag and securely tied up. Astolpho, delighted with his prize, returned to his army, placed himself at their head, and commenced his march. The Abyssinians traversed without danger or difficulty those vast fields of sand which separate their country from the kingdoms of Northern Africa, for the terrible South-wind, taken completely captive, had not force enough left to blow out a candle.

Senapus was distressed that he could not furnish any cavalry, for his country, rich in camels and elephants, was destitute of horses. This difficulty the saint had foreseen and had taught Astolpho the means of remedying. He now put those means in operation. Having reached a place whence he beheld a vast plain and the sea, he chose from his troops those who appeared to be the best made and the most intelligent. These he caused to be arranged in squadrons at the foot of a lofty mountain which bordered the plain, and he himself mounted to the summit to carry into effect his great design. Here he found vast quantities of fragments of rock and pebbles. These he set rolling down the mountain's side, and, wonderful to relate, as they rolled they grew in size, made themselves bodies, legs, necks, and long faces. Next they began to neigh, to curvet, to scamper on all sides over the plain. Some were bay, some roan, some dapple, some chestnut. The troops at the foot of the mountain exerted themselves to catch these new-created horses, which they easily did, for the miracle had been so considerate as to provide all the horses with bridles and saddles. Astolpho thus suddenly found himself supplied with an excellent corps of cavalry, not fewer (as Archbishop Turpin asserts) than eighty thousand strong. With these troops Astolpho reduced all the country to subjection, and at last arrived before the walls of Agramant's capital city, Biserta, to which he laid siege.

We must now return to the camp of the Christians, which lay before Arles, to which city the Saracens had retired after being defeated in a night attack led on by Rinaldo. Agramant here received the tidings of the invasion of his country by a fresh enemy, the Abyssinians, and learned that Biserta was in danger of falling into their hands. He took counsel of his officers and decided to send an embassy to Charles, proposing that the whole quarrel should be submitted to the combat of two warriors, one from each side, according to the issue of which it should be decided which party should pay tribute to the other, and the war should cease. Charlemagne, who had not heard of the favorable turn which affairs had taken in Africa, readily agreed to this proposal, and Rinaldo was selected on the part of the Christians to sustain the combat.

The Saracens selected Rogero for their champion. Rogero was still in the Saracen camp, kept there by honor alone, for his mind had been opened to the truth of the Christian faith by the arguments of Bradamante, and he had resolved to leave the party of the infidels on the first favorable opportunity and to join the Christian side. But his honor forbade him to do this while his former friends were in distress; and thus he waited for what time might bring forth, when he was startled by the announcement that he had been selected to uphold the cause of the Saracens against the Christians, and that his foe was to be Rinaldo, the brother of Bradamante.

While Rogero was overwhelmed with this intelligence, Bradamante on her side felt the deepest distress at hearing of the proposed combat. If Rogero should fall, she felt that no other man living was worthy of her love; and if, on the other hand, Heaven should resolve to punish France by the death of her chosen champion, Bradamante would have to deplore her brother, so dear to her, and be no less completely severed from the object of her affections.

While the fair lady gave herself up to these sad thoughts, the sage enchantress, Melissa, suddenly appeared before her. "Fear not, my daughter," said she, "I shall find a way to interrupt this combat which so distresses you."

Meanwhile, Rinaldo and Rogero prepared their weapons for the conflict. Rinaldo had the choice, and decided that it should be on foot and with no weapons but the battle-axe and poniard. The place assigned was a plain between the camp of Charlemagne and the walls of Arles.

Hardly had the dawn announced the day appointed for this memorable combat when heralds proceeded from both sides to mark the lists. Ere long the African troops were seen to advance from the city, Agramant at their head, his brilliant arms adorned in the Moorish fashion, his horse a bay with a white star on his forehead. Rogero marched at his side, and some of the greatest warriors of the Saracen camp attended him, bearing the various parts of his armor and weapons. Charlemagne, on his part, proceeded from his intrenchments, ranged his troops in semi-circle, and stood surrounded by his peers and paladins. Some of them bore portions of the armor of Rinaldo, the celebrated Ogier the Dane bearing the helmet which Rinaldo took from Mambrino. Duke Namo of Bavaria and Salomon of Bretagne bore two axes, of equal weight, prepared for the occasion.

The terms of the combat were then sworn to with the utmost solemnity by all parties. It was agreed that, if from either part any attempt was made to interrupt the battle, both combatants should turn their arms against the party which should be guilty of the interruption; and both monarchs assented to the condition that, in such case, the champion of the offending party should be discharged from his allegiance and at liberty to transfer his arms to the other side.

When all the preparations were concluded, the monarchs and their attendants retired each to his own side, and the champions were left alone. The two warriors advanced with measured steps towards each other and met in the middle of the space. They attacked one another at the same moment, and the air resounded with the blows they gave. Sparks flew from their battle-axes, while the velocity with which they managed their weapons astonished the beholders. Rogero, always remembering that his antagonist was the brother of his betrothed, could not aim a deadly wound; he strove only to ward off those levelled against himself. Rinaldo, on the other hand, much as he esteemed Rogero, spared not his blows, for he eagerly desired victory for his own sake and for the sake of his country and his faith.

The Saracens soon perceived that their champion fought feebly and gave not to Rinaldo such blows as he received from him. His disadvantage was so marked that anxiety and shame were manifest on the countenance of Agramant. Melissa, one of the most acute enchantresses that ever lived, seized this moment to disguise herself under the form of Rodomont, that rude and impetuous warrior, who had now for some time been absent from the Saracen camp. Approaching Agramant, she said, "How could you, my lord, have the imprudence of selecting a young man without experience to oppose the most redoubtable warrior of France? Surely you must have been regardless of the honor of your arms and of the fate of your empire! But it is not too late. Break without delay the agreement which is sure to result in your ruin." So saying, she addressed the troops who stood near. "Friends," said she, "follow me; under my guidance every one of you will be a match for a score of those feeble Christians." Agramant, delighted at seeing Rodomont once more at his side, gave his consent, and the Saracens, at the instant, couched their lances, set spurs to their steeds, and swept down upon the French. Melissa, when she saw her work successful, disappeared.

Rinaldo and Rogero, seeing the truce broken, and the two armies engaged in general conflict, stopped their battle; their martial fury ceased at once, they joined hands and resolved to act no more on either side until it should be clearly ascertained which party had failed to observe its oath. Both renewed their promise to abandon forever the party which had been thus false and perjured.

Meanwhile, the Christians, after the first moment of surprise, met the Saracens with courage redoubled by rage at the treachery of their foes. Guido the Wild, brother and rival of Rinaldo, Griffon and Aquilant, sons of Oliver, and numerous others whose names have already been celebrated in our recitals beat back the assailants and, at last, after prodigious slaughter, forced them to take shelter within the walls of Arles.

We will now return to Orlando, whom we last heard of as furiously mad and doing a thousand acts of violence in his senseless rage. One day, he came to the borders of a stream which intercepted his course. He swam across it, for he could swim like an otter, and on the other side saw a peasant watering his horse. He seized the animal, in spite of the resistance of the peasant, and rode it with furious speed till he arrived at the sea-coast, where Spain is divided from Africa by only a narrow strait. At the moment of his arrival, a vessel had just put off to cross the strait. She was full of people who, with glass in hand, seemed to be taking a merry farewell of the land, wafted by a favorable breeze.

The frantic Orlando cried out to them to stop and take him in; but they, having no desire to admit a madman to their company, paid him no attention. The paladin thought this behavior very uncivil and, by force of blows, made his horse carry him into the water in pursuit of the ship. The wretched animal soon had only his head above water, but as Orlando urged him forward, nothing was left for the poor beast but either to die or swim over to Africa.

Already Orlando had lost sight of the bark; distance and the swell of the sea completely hid it from his sight. He continued to press his horse forward, till at last it could struggle no more and sunk beneath him. Orlando, nowise concerned, stretched out his nervous arms, puffing the salt water from before his mouth, and carried his head above the waves. Fortunately, they were not rough; scarce a breath of wind agitated the surface; otherwise, the invincible Orlando would then have met his death. But fortune, which it is said favors fools, delivered him from this danger and landed him safe on the shore of Ceuta. Here he rambled along the shore till he came to where the black army of Astolpho held its camp.

Now it happened, just before this time, that a vessel filled with prisoners which Rodomont had taken at the bridge had arrived, and, not knowing of the presence of the Abyssinian army, had sailed right into port, where of course the prisoners and their captors changed places, the former being set at liberty and received with all joy, the latter sent to serve in the galleys. Astolpho thus found himself surrounded with Christian knights, and he and his friends were exchanging greetings and felicitations when a noise was heard in the camp, and seemed to increase every moment.

Astolpho and his friends seized their weapons, mounted their horses, and rode to the quarter whence the noise proceeded. Imagine their astonishment when they saw that the tumult was caused by a single man, perfectly naked, and browned with dirt and exposure, but of a force and fury so terrible that he overturned all that offered to lay hands on him.

Astolpho, Dudon, Oliver, and Florismart gazed at him with amazement. It was with difficulty they knew him. Astolpho, who had been warned of his condition by his holy monitor, was the first to recognize him. As the paladins closed round Orlando, the madman dealt one and another a blow of his fist, which, if they had not been in armor, or he had had any weapon, would probably have despatched them; as it was, Dudon and Astolpho measured their length on the sand. But Florismart seized him from behind, Sansonnet and another grasped his legs, and at last they succeeded in securing him with ropes. They took him to the waterside and washed him well, and then Astolpho, having first bandaged his mouth so that he could not breathe except through his nose, brought the precious phial, uncorked it, and placed it adroitly under his nostrils, when the good Orlando took it all up in one breath. Oh, marvellous prodigy! The paladin recovered in an instant all his intelligence. He felt like one who had awaked from a painful dream, in which he had believed that monsters were about to tear him to pieces. He seemed prostrated, silent, and abashed. Florismart, Oliver, and Astolpho stood gazing upon him, while he turned his eyes around and on himself. He seemed surprised to find himself naked, bound, and stretched on the seashore. After a few moments he recognized his friends and spoke to them in a tone so tender that they hastened to unbind him and to supply him with garments. Then they exerted themselves to console him, to diminish the weight with which his spirits were oppressed, and to make him forget the wretched condition into which he had been sunk.

Orlando, in recovering his reason, found himself also delivered from his insane attachment to the Queen of Cathay. His heart felt now no further influenced by the recollection of her than to be moved with an ardent desire to retrieve his fame by some distinguished exploit. Astolpho would gladly have yielded to him the chief command of the army, but Orlando would not take from the friend to whom he owed so much the glory of the campaign; but in everything the two paladins acted in concert and united their counsels. They proposed to make a general assault on the city of Biserta, and were only waiting a favorable moment when their plan was interrupted by new events.

Agramant, after the bloody battle which followed the infraction of the truce, found himself so weak that he saw it was in vain to attempt to remain in France. So, in concert with Sobrino, the bravest and most trusted of his chiefs, he embarked to return to his own country, having previously sent off his few remaining troops in the same direction. The vessel which carried Agramant and Sobrino approached the shore where the army of Astolpho lay encamped before Biserta, and, having discovered this fact before it was too late, the king commanded the pilot to steer eastward, with a view to seek protection of the King of Egypt. But the weather becoming rough, he consented to the advice of his companions and sought harbor in an island which lies between Sicily and Africa. There he found Gradasso, the warlike King of Sericane, who had come to France to possess himself of the horse Bayard and the sword Durindana, and, having procured both these prizes, was returning to his own country.

The two kings, who had been companions in arms under the walls of Paris, embraced one another affectionately. Gradasso learned with regret the reverses of Agramant and offered him his troops and his person. He strongly deprecated resorting to Egypt for aid. "Remember the great Pompey," said he, "and shun that fatal shore. My plan," he continued, "is this: I mean to

challenge Orlando to single combat. Possessed of such a
sword and steed as mine, if he were made of steel or
bronze, he could not escape me. He being removed, there
will be no difficulty in driving back the Abyssinians. We will rouse against them the Moslem nations
from the other side of the Nile, the Arabians, Persians,
and Chaldeans, who will soon make Senapus recall his
army to defend his own territories."

Agramant approved this advice except in one particular. "It is for me," said he, "to combat Orlando; I cannot
with honor devolve that duty on another."

"Let us adopt a third course," said the aged warrior
Sobrino. "I would not willingly remain a simple spectator of such a contest. Let us send three squires to the
shore of Africa to challenge Orlando and any two of his
companions in arms to meet us three in this island of
Lampedusa."

This counsel was adopted; the three squires sped on
their way, and now presented themselves and rehearsed
their message to the Christian knights.

Orlando was delighted, and rewarded the squires with
rich gifts. He had already resolved to seek Gradasso and
compel him to restore Durindana, which he had learned
was in his possession. For his two companions, the count
chose his faithful friend Florismart and his cousin Oliver.

The three warriors embarked, and sailing with a favorable wind, the second morning showed them, on their
right, the island where this important battle was to be
fought. Orlando and his two companions, having landed,
pitched their tent. Agramant had placed his opposite.

Next morning, as soon as Aurora brightened the edges
of the horizon, the warriors of both parties armed themselves and mounted their horses. They took their positions, face to face, lowered their lances, placed them in
rest, clapped spurs to their horses, and flew to the
charge. Orlando met the charge of Gradasso. The paladin
was unmoved, but his horse could not sustain the terrible
shock of Bayard. He recoiled, staggered, and fell some
paces behind. Orlando tried to raise him, but, finding his
efforts unavailing, seized his shield and drew his famous
Balisardo. Meanwhile, Agramant and the brave Oliver

gained no advantage, one or the other; but Florismart unhorsed the King Sobrino. Having brought his foe to the ground, he would not pursue his victory, but hastened to attack Gradasso, who had overthrown Orlando. Seeing him thus engaged, Orlando would not interfere, but ran with sword upraised upon Sobrino and, with one blow, deprived him of sense and motion. Believing him dead, he next turned to aid his beloved Florismart. That brave paladin, neither in horse nor arms equal to his antagonist, could but parry and evade the blows of the terrible Durindana. Orlando, eager to succor him, was delayed for a moment in securing and mounting the horse of the King Sobrino. It was but an instant, and with sword upraised he rushed upon Gradasso, who, noways disconcerted at the onset of this second foe, shouted his defiance and thrust at him with his sword, but, having miscalculated the distance, scarcely reached him and failed to pierce his mail. Orlando, in return, dealt him a blow with Balisardo, which wounded, as it fell, face, breast, and thigh, and, if he had been a little nearer, would have cleft him in twain. Sobrino, by this time recovered from his swoon, though severely wounded, raised himself on his legs and looked to see how he might aid his friends. Observing Agramant hard pressed by Oliver, he thrust his sword into the bowels of the latter's horse, which fell and bore down his master, entangling his leg as he fell, so that Oliver could not extricate himself. Florismart saw the danger of his friend and ran upon Sobrino with his horse, overthrew him, and then turned to defend himself from Agramant. They were not unequally matched, for though Agramant, mounted on Brigliadoro, had an advantage over Florismart, whose horse was but indifferent, yet Agramant had received a serious wound in his encounter with Oliver.

Nothing could exceed the fury of the encounter between Orlando and Gradasso. Durindana, in the hands of Gradasso, clove asunder whatever it struck; but such was the skill of Orlando, who perfectly knew the danger to which he was exposed from a stroke of that weapon, it had not yet struck him in such a way as to inflict a wound. Meanwhile, Gradasso was bleeding from many wounds, and his rage and incaution increased

every moment. In his desperation, he lifted Durindana
with both hands and struck so terrible a blow full on the
helmet of Orlando that, for a moment, it stunned the
paladin. He dropped the reins, and his frightened
horse scoured with him over the plain. Gradasso turned
to pursue him, but at that moment saw Florismart in the
very act of striking a fatal blow at Agramant, whom he
had unhorsed. While Florismart was wholly intent upon
completing his victory, Gradasso plunged his sword into
his side. Florismart fell from his horse and bathed the
plain with his blood.

Orlando recovered himself just in time to see the
deed. Whether rage or grief predominated in his breast,
I cannot tell; but, seizing Balisardo with fury, his first
blow fell upon Agramant, who was nearest to him, and
smote his head from his shoulders. At this sight, Gradasso,
for the first time, felt his courage sink and a dark presentiment of death come over him. He hardly stood on his
defence when Orlando cast himself upon him and gave
him a fatal thrust. The sword penetrated his ribs and
came out a palm's breadth on the other side of his body.

Thus fell beneath the sword of the most illustrious
paladin of France the bravest warrior of the Saracen host.
Orlando then, as if despising his victory, leaped lightly
to the ground and ran to his dear friend Florismart,
embraced him, and bathed him with his tears. Florismart
still breathed. He could even command his voice to utter
a few parting words: "Dear friend, do not forget me—
give me your prayers—and oh! be a brother to Flordelis."
He died in uttering her name.

After a few moments given to grief, Orlando turned to
look for his other companion and his late foes. Oliver
lay oppressed with the weight of his horse, from which he
had in vain struggled to liberate himself. Orlando extri-
cated him with difficulty; he then raised Sobrino from
the earth and committed him to his squire, treating
him as gently as if he had been his own brother. For this
terrible warrior was the most generous of men to a fallen
foe. He took Bayard and Brigliadoro, with the arms of
the conquered knights; their bodies and their other spoils
he remitted to their attendants.

But who can tell the grief of Flordelis when she saw

the warriors return and found not Florismart, as usual
after absence, hasten to her side. She knew by the aspect
of the others that her lord was slain. At the thought,
and before the question could pass her lips, she fell senseless upon the ground. When life returned, and she learned
the truth of her worst fears, she bitterly upbraided herself
that she had let him depart without her. "I might have
saved him by a single cry when his enemy dealt him that
treacherous blow, or I might have thrown myself between and given my worthless life for his. Or, if no more,
I might have heard his last words, I might have given
him a last kiss." So she lamented, and could not be comforted.

ROGERO AND BRADAMANTE

After the interruption of the combat with Rinaldo, as
we have related, Rogero was perplexed with doubts what
course to take. The terms of the treaty required him to
abandon Agramant, who had broken it, and to transfer his
allegiance to Charlemagne; and his love for Bradamante
called him in the same direction; but unwillingness to
desert his prince and leader in the hour of distress
forbade this course. Embarking, therefore, for Africa,
he took his way to rejoin the Saracen army, but was arrested midway by a storm which drove the vessel on a
rock. The crew took to their boat, but that was quickly
swamped in the waves, and Rogero with the rest were
compelled to swim for their lives. Then, while buffeting
the waves, Rogero bethought him of his sin in so long
delaying his Christian profession and vowed in his heart
that, if he should live to reach the land, he would no
longer delay to be baptized. His vows were heard and answered; he succeeded in reaching the shore, and was aided
and relieved on landing by a pious hermit, whose cell
overlooked the sea. From him he received baptism, having first passed some days with him, partaking his hum-

ble fare and receiving instruction in the doctrines of the Christian faith.

While these things were going on, Rinaldo, who had set out on his way to seek Gradasso and recover Bayard from him, hearing on his way of the great things which were doing in Africa, repaired thither to bear his part in them. He arrived too late to do more than join his friends in lamenting the loss of Florismart and to rejoice with them in their victory over the pagan knights. On the death of their king, the Africans gave up the contest, Biserta submitted, and the Christian knights had only to dismiss their forces and return home. Astolpho took leave of his Abyssinian army and sent them back, laden with spoil, to their own country, not forgetting to intrust to them the bag which held the winds, by means of which they were enabled to cross the sandy desert again without danger, and did not untie it till they reached their own country.

Orlando now, with Oliver, who much needed the surgeon's care, and Sobrino, to whom equal attention was shown, sailed in a swift vessel to Sicily, bearing with him the body of Florismart, to be laid in Christian earth. Rinaldo accompanied them, as did Sansonnet and the other Christian leaders. Arrived at Sicily, the funeral was solemnized with all the rites of religion, and with the profound grief of those who had known Florismart or had heard of his fame. Then they resumed their course, steering for Marseilles. But Oliver's wound grew worse instead of better, and his sufferings so distressed his friends that they conferred together, not knowing what to do. Then said the pilot, "We are not far from an isle where a holy hermit dwells alone in the midst of the sea. It is said none seek his counsel or his aid in vain. He hath wrought marvellous cures, and if you resort to that holy man, without doubt he can heal the knight." Orlando bade him steer thither, and soon the bark was laid safely beside the lonely rock; the wounded man was lowered into their boat and carried by the crew to the hermit's cell. It was the same hermit with whom Rogero had taken refuge after his shipwreck, by whom he had been baptized, and with whom he was now staying, absorbed in sacred studies and meditations.

The holy man received Orlando and the rest with
kindness and inquired their errand; and being told that
they had come for help for one who, warring for the
Christian faith, was brought to perilous pass by a sad
wound, he straightway undertook the cure. His applica-
tions were simple, but they were seconded by his prayers.
The paladin was soon relieved from pain, and in a few
days his foot was perfectly restored to soundness. Sobrino, as soon as he perceived the holy monk perform
that wonder, cast aside his false prophet, and, with con-
trite heart, owned the true God, and demanded baptism
at his hands. The hermit granted his request, and also by
his prayers restored him to health, while all the Christian knights rejoiced in his conversion almost as much as
at the restoration of Oliver. More than all, Rogero felt
joy and gratitude and daily grew in grace and faith.

Rogero was known by fame to all the Christian
knights, but not even Rinaldo knew him by sight, though
he had proved his prowess in combat. Sobrino made
him known to them, and great was the joy of all when
they found one whose valor and courtesy were renowned
through the world no longer an enemy and unbeliever,
but a convert and champion of the true faith. All press
about the knight; one grasps his hand, another locks
him fast in his embrace; but more than all the rest, Rinaldo cherished him, for he more than any knew his
worth.

It was not long before Rogero confided to his friend
the hopes he entertained of a union with his sister, and
Rinaldo frankly gave his sanction to the proposal. But
causes unknown to the paladin were at that very time
interposing obstacles to its success.

The fame of the beauty and worth of Bradamante
had reached the ears of the Grecian Emperor Constantine, and he had sent Charlemagne to demand the hand
of his niece for Leo, his son and the heir to his dominions. Duke Aymon, her father, had only reserved his
consent until he should first have spoken with his son
Rinaldo, now absent.

The warriors now prepared to resume their voyage.
Rogero took a tender farewell of the good hermit who
had taught him the true faith. Orlando restored to him

the horse and arms which were rightly his, not even asserting his claim to Balisardo, that sword which he himself had won from the enchantress.

The hermit gave his blessing to the band, and they reembarked. The passage was speedy, and very soon they arrived in the harbor of Marseilles.

Astolpho, when he had dismissed his troops, mounted the Hippogriff and, at one flight, shot over to Sardinia, thence to Corsica, thence, turning slightly to the left, hovered over Provence, and alighted in the neighborhood of Marseilles. There he did what he had been commanded to do by the holy saint; he unbridled the Hippogriff and turned him loose to seek his own retreats, never more to be galled with saddle or bit. The horn had lost its marvellous power ever since the visit to the moon.

Astolpho reached Marseilles the very day when Orlando, Rinaldo, Oliver, Sobrino, and Rogero arrived there. Charles had already heard the news of the defeat of the Saracen kings and all the accompanying events. On learning of the approach of the gallant knights, he sent forward some of his most illustrious nobles to receive them, and himself, with the rest of his court, kings, dukes, and peers, the queen, and a fair and gorgeous band of ladies, set forward from Arles to meet them.

No sooner were the mutual greetings interchanged than Orlando and his friends led forward Rogero and presented him to the Emperor. They vouch him son of Rogero, Duke of Risa, one of the most renowned of Christian warriors, by adverse fortune stolen in his infancy and brought up by Saracens in the false faith, now by a kind Providence converted and restored to fill the place his father once held among the foremost champions of the throne and Church.

Rogero had alighted from his horse and stood respectfully before the Emperor. Charlemagne bade him remount and ride beside him, and omitted nothing which might do him honor in sight of his martial train. With pomp triumphal and with festive cheer, the troop returned to the city; the streets were decorated with garlands, the houses hung with rich tapestry, and flowers fell like rain upon the conquering host from the hands of fair dames and damsels, from every balcony and window. So welcomed, the mighty Emperor passed on till he reached the royal palace, where many days he feasted, high in hall, with his lords, amid tourney, revel, dance, and song.

When Rinaldo told his father, Duke Aymon, how he had promised his sister to Rogero, his father heard him with indignation, having set his heart on seeing her united to the Grecian emperor's son. The Lady Beatrice, her mother, also appealed to Bradamante herself to reject a knight who had neither title nor lands and give the preference to one who would make her Empress of the wide Levant. But Bradamante, though respect forbade her to refuse her mother's entreaty, would not promise to do what her heart repelled, and answered only with a sigh, until she was alone, and then gave a loose to tears.

Meanwhile Rogero, indignant that a stranger should presume to rob him of his bride, determined to seek the Prince of Greece and defy him to mortal combat. With this design he donned his armor, but exchanged his crest and emblazonment and bore instead a white unicorn upon a crimson field. He chose a trusty squire and, commanding him not to address him as Rogero, rode on his quest. Having crossed the Rhine and the Austrian countries into Hungary, he followed the course of the Danube till he reached Belgrade. There he saw the imperial ensigns spread, and white pavilions, thronged with troops, before the town. For the Emperor Constantine was laying siege to the city to recover it from the Bulgarians, who had taken it from him not long before.

A river flowed between the camp of the emperor and the Bulgarians, and at the moment when Rogero approached, a skirmish had begun between the parties from either camp, who had approached the stream for the purpose of watering. The Greeks in that affray were four to one and drove back the Bulgarians in precipitate rout. Rogero, seeing this, and animated only by his hatred of the Grecian prince, dashed into the middle of the flying mass, calling aloud on the fugitives to turn. He encountered first a leader of the Grecian host in splendid armor, a nephew of the Emperor, as dear to him as a son. Rogero's lance pierced shield and armor and stretched the warrior breathless on the plain. Another and another fell before him, and astonishment and terror arrested the advance of the Greeks, while the Bulgarians, catching courage from the cavalier, rally, change front, and chase the Grecian troops, who fly in their turn. Leo, the prince, was at a distance when this sudden skirmish rose, but not so far but that he could see distinctly, from an elevated position which he held, how the changed battle was all the work of one man, and could not choose but admire the bravery and prowess with which it was done. He knew by the blazonry displayed that the champion was not of the Bulgarian army, though he furnished aid to them. Although he suffered by his valor, the prince could not wish him ill, for his admiration surpassed his resentment. By this time the Greeks had regained the river, and, crossing it by fording or swimming, some made their escape, leaving many more prisoners in the hands of the Bulgarians. Rogero, learning from some of the captives that Leo was at a point some distance down the river, rode thither with a view to meet him, but arrived not before the Greek prince had retired beyond the stream, and broken up the bridge. Day was spent, and Rogero, wearied, looked round for a shelter for the night. He found it in a cottage, where he soon yielded himself to repose. It so happened, a knight who had narrowly escaped Rogero's sword in the late battle also found shelter in the same cottage, and, recognizing the armor of the unknown knight, easily found means of securing him as he slept, and next morning carried him in chains and delivered him to the Emperor. By him he was in turn delivered to his sister Theodora, mother of the young knight, the first victim of Rogero's spear. By her he was cast into a dungeon, till her ingenuity could devise a death sufficiently painful to satiate her revenge.

Bradamante, meanwhile, to escape her father's and mother's importunity, had begged a boon of Charlemagne, which the monarch pledged his royal word to grant; it was that she should not be compelled to marry any one unless he should first vanquish her in single combat. The Emperor, therefore, proclaimed a tournament in these words: "He that would wed Duke Aymon's daughter must contend with the sword against that dame, from the sun's rise to his setting; and if, in that time, he is not overcome, the lady shall be his."

Duke Aymon and the Lady Beatrice, though much incensed at the course things had taken, brought their daughter to court to await the day appointed for the tournament. Bradamante, not finding there him whom her heart required, distressed herself with doubts what could be the cause of his absence. Of all fancies, the most painful one was that he had gone away to learn to forget her, knowing her father's and her mother's opposition to their union, and despairing to contend against them. But oh, how much worse would be the maiden's woe, if it were known to her what her betrothed was then enduring!

He was plunged in a dungeon where no ray of daylight ever penetrated, loaded with chains and scantily supplied with the coarsest food. No wonder despair took possession of his heart, and he longed for death as a relief, when one night (or one day, for both were equally dark to him) he was roused with the glare of a torch, and saw two men enter his cell. It was the Prince Leo, with an attendant, who had come as soon as he had learned the wretched fate of the brave knight whose valor he had seen and admired on the field of battle. "Cavalier," said he, "I am one whom thy valor hath so bound to thee that I willingly peril my own safety to lend thee aid." "Infinite thanks I owe you," replied Rogero, "and the life you give me I promise faithfully to render back upon your call, and promptly to stake it at all times for your service." The prince then told Rogero his name and rank, at hearing which a tide of contending emotions almost overwhelmed Rogero. He was set at liberty and had his horse and arms restored to him.

Meanwhile, tidings arrived of King Charles's decree that whoever aspired to the hand of Bradamante must first encounter her with sword and lance. This news made the Grecian prince turn pale, for he knew he was no match for her in fight. Communing with himself, he sees how he may make his wit supply the place of valor and employ the French knight, whose name was still unknown to him, to fight the battle for him. Rogero heard the proposal with extreme distress; yet it seemed worse than death to deny the first request of one to whom he owed his life. Hastily he gave his assent "to do in all things that which Leo should command." Afterward, bitter repentance came over him; yet, rather than confess his change of mind, death itself would be welcome. Death seems his only remedy; but how to die? Sometimes he thinks to make none but a feigned resistance, and allow her sword a ready access, for never can death come more happily than if her hand guide the weapon. Yet this will not avail, for, unless he wins the maid for the Greek prince, his debt remains unpaid. He had promised to maintain a real, not a feigned encounter. He will then keep his word and banish every thought from his bosom except that which moved him to maintain his truth.

The young prince, richly attended, set out, and with him Rogero. They arrived at Paris, but Leo preferred not to enter the city and pitched his tents without the walls, making known his arrival to Charlemagne by an embassy. The monarch was pleased, and testified his courtesy by visits and gifts. The prince set forth the purpose of his coming and prayed the Emperor to dispatch his suit—"to send forth the damsel who refused ever to take in wedlock any lord inferior to herself in fight; for she should be his bride, or he would perish beneath her sword."

Rogero passed the night before the day assigned for the battle like that which the felon spends, condemned to pay the forfeit of his life on the ensuing day. He chose to fight with sword only, and on foot, for he would not let her see Frontino, knowing that she would recognize the steed. Nor would he use Balisardo, for against that enchanted blade all armor would be of no avail, and the sword that he did take he hammered well upon the edge to abate its sharpness. He wore the surcoat of Prince Leo and his shield, emblazoned with a golden, double-headed eagle. The prince took care to let himself be seen by none.

Bradamante, meanwhile, prepared herself for the combat far differently. Instead of blunting the edge of her falchion, she whets the steel, and would fain infuse into it her own acerbity. As the moment approached, she seemed to have fire within her veins, and waited impatiently for the trumpet's sound. At the signal, she drew her sword and fell with fury upon her Rogero. But as a well-built wall or aged rock stands unmoved the fury of the storm, so Rogero, clad in those arms which Trojan Hector once wore, withstood the strokes which stormed about his head and breast and flank. Sparks flew from his shield, his helm, his cuirass; from direct and back strokes, aimed now high, now low, falling thick and fast, like hailstones on a cottage roof; but Rogero, with skilful ward, turns them aside, or receives them where his armor is a sure protection, careful only to protect himself, and with no thought of striking in return. Thus the hours passed away, and, as the sun approached the west, the damsel began to despair. But so much the more her anger increases, and she redoubles her efforts, like the craftsman who sees his work unfinished while the day is well nigh spent. Oh, miserable damsel! didst thou know whom thou wouldst kill—if, in that cavalier matched against thee thou didst but know Rogero, on whom thy very life-threads hang, rather than kill him thou wouldst kill thyself, for he is dearer to thee than life.

King Charles and the peers, who thought the cavalier to be the Grecian prince, viewing such force and skill exhibited, and how without assaulting her the knight defended himself, were filled with admiration, and declared the champions well matched and worthy of each other.

When the sun was set, Charlemagne gave the signal for terminating the contest, and Bradamante was awarded to Prince Leo as a bride. Rogero, in deep distress, returned to his tent. There Leo unlaced his helmet and kissed him on both cheeks. "Henceforth," said he, "do with me as you please, for you cannot exhaust my gratitude." Rogero replied little, laid aside the ensigns he had worn, and resumed the unicorn, then hasted to withdraw himself from all eyes. When it was midnight he rose, saddled Frontino, and sallied from his tent, taking that direction which pleased his steed. All night he rode, absorbed in bitter woe, and called on Death as alone capable of relieving his sufferings. At last he entered a forest and penetrated into its deepest recesses. There he unharnessed Frontino and suffered him to wander where he would. Then he threw himself down on the ground and poured forth such bitter wailings that the birds and beasts, for none else heard him, were moved to pity with his cries.

Not less was the distress of the lady Bradamante, who, rather than wed any one but Rogero, resolved to break her word and defy kindred, court, and Charlemagne himself; and, if nothing else would do, to die. But relief came from an unexpected quarter. Marphisa, sister of Rogero, was a heroine of warlike prowess equal to Bradamante. She had been the confidante of their loves, and felt hardly less distress than themselves at seeing the perils which threatened their union. "They are already united by mutual vows," she said, "and in the sight of Heaven what more is necessary?" Full of this thought, she presented herself before Charlemagne and declared that she herself was witness that the maiden had spoken to Rogero those words which they who marry swear, and that the compact was so sealed between the pair that they were no longer free, nor could forsake, the one the other, to take another spouse. This her assertion she offered to prove, in single combat, against Prince Leo or any one else.

Charlemagne, sadly perplexed at this, commanded Bradamante to be called, and told her what the bold Marphisa had declared. Bradamante neither denied nor confirmed the statement, but hung her head and kept silence. Duke Aymon was enraged, and would fain have set aside the pretended contract on the ground that, if made at all, it must have been made before Rogero was baptized, and therefore void. But not so thought Rinaldo, nor the good Orlando, and Charlemagne knew not which way to decide, when Marphisa spoke thus:

"Since no one else can marry the maiden while my brother lives, let the prince meet Rogero in mortal combat, and let him who survives take her for his bride."

This saying pleased the Emperor, and was accepted by the prince, for he thought that, by the aid of his unknown champion, he should surely triumph in the fight. Proclamation was therefore made for Rogero to appear and defend his suit; and Leo, on his part, caused search to be made on all sides for the knight of the unicorn.

Meanwhile Rogero, overwhelmed with despair, lay stretched on the ground in the forest night and day without food, courting death. Here he was discovered by one of Leo's people, who, finding him resist all attempts to remove him, hastened to his master, who was not far off, and brought him to the spot. As he approached, he heard words which convinced him that love was the cause of the knight's despair; but no clew was given to guide him to the object of that love. Stooping down, the prince embraced the weeping warrior and, in the tenderest accents, said: "Spare not, I entreat you, to disclose the cause of your distress, for few such desperate evils betide mankind as are wholly past cure. It grieves me much that you would hide your grief from me, for I am bound to you by ties that nothing can undo. Tell me, then, your grief, and leave me to try if wealth, art, cunning, force, or persuasion cannot relieve you. If not, it will be time enough, after all has been tried in vain, to die."

He spoke in such moving accents that Rogero could not choose but yield. It was some time before he could command utterance; at last he said, "My lord, when you shall know me for what I am, I doubt not you, like myself, will be content that I should die. Know, then, I am that Rogero whom you have so much cause to hate, and who so hated you that, intent on putting you to death, he went to seek you at your father's court. This I did because I could not submit to see my promised bride borne off by you. But, as man purposes and God disposes, your great courtesy, well tried in time of sore need, so moved my fixed resolve that I not only laid aside the hate I bore, but purposed to be your friend forever. You then asked of me to win for you the lady Bradamante, which was all one as to demand of me my heart and soul. You know whether I served you faithfully or not. Yours is the lady; possess her in peace; but ask me not to live to see it. Be content rather that I die, for vows have passed between myself and her which forbid that while I live she can lawfully wive with another."

So filled was gentle Leo with astonishment at these words that for a while he stood silent, with lips unmoved and steadfast gaze, like a statue. And the discovery that

the stranger was Rogero not only abated not the good
will he bore him, but increased it, so that his distress
for what Rogero suffered seemed equal to his own. For
this, and because he would appear deservedly an emper-
or's son, and, though in other things outdone, would not
be surpassed in courtesy, he says: "Rogero, had I known,
that day when your matchless valor routed my troops,
that you were Rogero, your virtue would have made me
your own, as then it made me while I knew not my foe,
and I should have no less gladly rescued you from Theodora's dungeon. And if I would willingly have done so
then, how much more gladly will I now restore the gift of
which you would rob yourself to confer it upon me. The
damsel is more due to you than to me, and though I
know her worth, I would forego not only her, but life itself, rather than distress a knight like you."

This and much more he said to the same intent, till at
last Rogero replied, "I yield and am content to live, and
thus a second time owe my life to you."

But several days elapsed before Rogero was so far restored as to return to the royal residence, where an embassy had arrived from the Bulgarian princes to seek the
knight of the unicorn and tender to him the crown of
that country, in place of their king, fallen in battle.

Thus were things situated when Prince Leo, leading
by the hand Rogero, clad in the battered armor in which
he had sustained the conflict with Bradamante, presented
himself before the king. "Behold," he said, "the champion who maintained from dawn to setting sun the ardu-
ous contest; he comes to claim the guerdon of the fight."
King Charlemagne, with all his peerage, stood amazed,
for all believed that the Grecian prince himself had fought
with Bradamante. Then stepped forth Marphisa and said,
"Since Rogero is not here to assert his rights, I, his sister,
undertake his cause, and will maintain it against whoever shall dare dispute his claim." She said this with so
much anger and disdain that the prince deemed it no
longer wise to feign, and withdrew Rogero's helmet from
his brow, saying, "Behold him here!" Who can describe
the astonishment and joy of Marphisa! She ran and threw
her arms about her brother's neck, nor would give way
to let Charlemagne and Rinaldo, Orlando, Dudon, and

the rest who crowded round, embrace him and press friendly kisses on his brow. The joyful tidings flew fast by many a messenger to Bradamante, who in her secret chamber lay lamenting. The blood that stagnated about her heart flowed at that notice so fast that she had well nigh died for joy. Duke Aymon and the Lady Beatrice no longer withheld their consent, and pledged their daughter to the brave Rogero before all that gallant company.

Now came the Bulgarian ambassadors and, kneeling at the feet of Rogero, besought him to return with them to their country, where, in Adrianople, the crown and sceptre were awaiting his acceptance. Prince Leo united his persuasions to theirs and promised, in his royal father's name, that peace should be restored on their part. Rogero gave his consent, and it was surmised that none of the virtues which shone so conspicuously in him so availed to recommend Rogero to the Lady Beatrice as the hearing her future son-in-law saluted as a sovereign prince.

THE BATTLE OF RONCESVALLES

After the explusion of the Saracens from France, Charlemagne led his army into Spain, to punish Marsilius, the king of that country, for having sided with the African Saracens in the late war. Charlemagne succeeded in all his attempts and compelled Marsilius to submit and pay tribute to France. Our readers will remember Gano, otherwise called Gan, or Ganelon, whom we mentioned in one of our early chapters as an old courtier of Charlemagne, and a deadly enemy of Orlando, Rinaldo, and all their friends. He had great influence over Charles, from equality of age and long intimacy; and he was not without good qualities: he was brave and sagacious, but envious, false, and treacherous. Gan prevailed on Charles to send him as ambassador to Marsilius, to arrange the tribute. He embraced Orlando over and over again at taking leave, using such pains to seem loving and sincere that his hypocrisy was manifest to every one but the old monarch. He fastened with equal tenderness on Oliver, who smiled contemptuously in his face and thought to himself, "You may make as many fair speeches as you choose, but you lie." All the other paladins who were present thought the same, and they said as much to the Emperor, adding that Gan should on no account be sent ambassador to the Spaniards. But Charles was infatuated.

Gan was received with great honor by Marsilius. The king, attended by his lords, came fifteen miles out of Saragossa to meet him, and then conducted him into the city with acclamations. There was nothing for several days but balls, games, and exhibitions of chivalry, the ladies throwing flowers on the heads of the French knights, and the people shouting, "France! Mountjoy and St. Denis!"

After the ceremonies of the first reception, the king and the ambassador began to understand one another. One day they sat together in a garden on the border of a fountain. The water was so clear and smooth it reflected every object around, and the spot was encircled with fruit-trees which quivered with the fresh air. As they sat and talked, as if without restraint, Gan, without looking the king in the face, was enabled to see the expression of his countenance in the water, and governed his speech accordingly. Marsilius was equally adroit, and watched the face of Gan while he addressed him. Marsilius began by lamenting, not as to the ambassador, but as to the friend, the injuries which Charles had done him by invading his dominions, charging him with wishing to take his kingdom from him and give it to Orlando; till at length he plainly uttered his belief that, if that ambitious paladin were but dead, good men would get their rights.

Gan heaved a sigh, as if he was unwillingly compelled to allow the force of what the king said; but, unable to contain himself long, he lifted up his face, radiant with triumphant wickedness, and exclaimed: "Every word you utter is truth; die he must, and die also must Oliver, who struck me that foul blow at court. Is it treachery to punish affronts like these? I have planned everything—I have settled everything already with their besotted master. Orlando will come to your borders—to Roncesvalles

—for the purpose of receiving the tribute. Charles will await him at the foot of the mountains. Orlando will bring but a small band with him: you, when you meet him, will have secretly your whole army at your back. You surround him, and who receives tribute then?"

The new Judas had scarcely uttered these words when his exultation was interrupted by a change in the face of nature. The sky was suddenly overcast, there was thunder and lightning, a laurel was split in two from head to foot, and the Carob-tree under which Gan was sitting, which is said to be the species of tree on which Judas Iscariot hung himself, dropped one of its pods on his head.

Marsilius, as well as Gan, was appalled at this omen, but on assembling his soothsayers they came to the conclusion that the laurel-tree turned the omen against the Emperor, the successor of the Caesars, though one of them renewed the consternation of Gan by saying that he did not understand the meaning of the tree of Judas, and intimating that perhaps the ambassador could explain it. Gan relieved his vexation by anger; the habit of wickedness prevailed over all other considerations; and the king prepared to march to Roncesvalles at the head of all his forces.

Gan wrote to Charlemagne to say how humbly and submissively Marsilius was coming to pay the tribute into the hands of Orlando, and how handsome it would be of the Emperor to meet him half-way, and so be ready to receive him after the payment at his camp. He added a brilliant account of the tribute and the accompanying presents. The good Emperor wrote in turn to say how pleased he was with the ambassador's diligence, and that matters were arranged precisely as he wished. His court, however, had its suspicions still, though they little thought Gan's object in bringing Charles into the neighborhood of Roncesvalles was to deliver him into the hands of Marsilius, after Orlando should have been destroyed by him.

Orlando, however, did as his lord and sovereign desired. He went to Roncesvalles, accompanied by a moderate train of warriors, not dreaming of the atrocity that awaited him. Gan, meanwhile, had hastened back to

France, in order to show himself free and easy in the
presence of Charles, and secure the success of his plot;
while Marsilius, to make assurance doubly sure, brought
into the passes of Roncesvalles no less than three armies,
which were successively to fall on the paladin in case of
the worst, and so extinguish him with numbers. He had
also, by Gan's advice, brought heaps of wine and good
cheer to be set before his victims in the first instance;
"for that," said the traitor, "will render the onset the
more effective, the feasters being unarmed. One thing,
however, I must not forget," added he; "my son Baldwin
is sure to be with Orlando; you must take care of his
life for my sake."

"I give him this vesture off my own body," said the
king; "let him wear it in the battle, and have no fear.
My soldiers shall be directed not to touch him."

Gan went away rejoicing to France. He embraced the
sovereign and the court all round with the air of a man
who had brought them nothing but blessings, and the old
king wept for very tenderness and delight.

"Something is going on wrong, and looks very black,"
thought Malagigi, the good wizard; "Rinaldo is not here,
and it is indispensably necessary that he should be. I
must find out where he is, and Ricciardetto, too, and
send for them with all speed."

Malagigi called up by his art a wise, terrible, and
cruel spirit, named Ashtaroth. "Tell me, and tell me
truly, of Rinaldo," said Malagigi to the spirit. The
demon looked hard at the paladin and said nothing. His
aspect was clouded and violent.

The enchanter, with an aspect still cloudier, bade
Ashtaroth lay down that look, and made signs as if he
would resort to angrier compulsion; and the devil,
alarmed, loosened his tongue, and said, "You have not
told me what you desire to know of Rinaldo."

"I desire to know what he has been doing and where he
is."

"He has been conquering and baptizing the world, east
and west," said the demon, "and is now in Egypt with
Ricciardetto."

"And what has Gan been plotting with Marsilius?" inquired Malagigi; "and what is to come of it?"

"I know not," said the devil. "I was not attending to Gan at the time, and we fallen spirits know not the future. All I discern is that by the signs and comets in the heavens, something dreadful is about to happen—something very strange, treacherous, and bloody—and that Gan has a seat ready prepared for him in hell."

"Within three days," cried the enchanter loudly, "bring Rinaldo and Ricciardetto into the pass of Roncesvalles. Do it, and I hereby undertake to summen thee no more."

"Suppose they will not trust themselves with me?" said the spirit.

"Enter Rinaldo's horse, and bring him, whether he trust thee or not."

"It shall be done," returned the demon.

There was an earthquake, and Ashtaroth disappeared.

Marsilius now made his first movement towards the destruction of Orlando by sending before him his vassal, King Blanchardin, with his presents of wines and other luxuries. The temperate but courteous hero took them in good part and distributed them as the traitor wished; and then Blanchardin, on pretence of going forward to salute Charlemagne, returned and put himself at the head of the second army, which was the post assigned him by his liege-lord. King Falseron, whose son Orlando had slain in battle, headed the first army, and King Balugante the third. Marsilius made a speech to them in which he let them into his design, and concluded by recommending to their good will the son of his friend Gan, whom they would know by the vest he had sent him, and who was the only soul amongst the Christians they were to spare.

This son of Gan, meanwhile, and several of the paladins, who distrusted the misbelievers and were anxious at all events to be with Orlando, had joined the hero in the fated valley; so that the little Christian host, considering the tremendous valor of their lord and his friends, were not to be sold for nothing. Rinaldo, alas! the second thunderbolt of Christendom, was destined not to be there in time to meet the issue. The paladins in vain begged Orlando to be on his guard against treachery and send for a more numerous body of men. The great heart of

the Champion of the Faith was unwilling to harbor suspicion as long as he could help it. He refused to summon aid which might be superfluous; neither would he
do anything but what his liege-lord had directed. And yet
he could not wholly repress a misgiving. A shadow had
fallen on his heart, great and cheerful as it was. The
anticipations of his friends disturbed him, in spite of the
face with which he met them. Perhaps by a certain fore-
sight he felt his death approaching; but he felt bound not
to encourage the impression. Besides, time pressed; the
moment of the looked-for tribute was at hand, and little combinations of circumstances determine often the
greatest events.

King Marsilius was to arrive early next day with the
tribute, and Oliver, with the morning sun, rode forth to
reconnoitre and see if he could discover the peaceful
pomp of the Spanish court in the distance. He rode up the
nearest height, and from the top of it beheld the first
army of Marsilius already forming in the passes. "Oh,
devil Gan," he exclaimed, "this then is the consummation
of thy labors!" Oliver put spurs to his horse and galloped back down the mountain to Orlando.

"Well," cried the hero, "what news?"

"Bad news," said his cousin, "such as you would
not hear of yesterday. Marsilius is here in arms, and all
the world is with him."

The paladins pressed round Orlando and entreated
him to sound his horn, in token that he needed help.
His only answer was to mount his horse and ride up
the mountain with Sansonetto.

As soon, however, as he cast forth his eyes and beheld what was round about him, he turned in sorrow,
and looked down into Roncesvalles, and said, "Oh, miserable valley! the blood shed in thee this day will color
thy name forever."

Orlando's little camp were furious against the Saracens. They armed themselves with the greatest impatience. There was nothing but lacing of helmets and
mounting of horses, while good Archbishop Turpin went
from rank to rank exhorting and encouraging the warriors of Christ. Orlando and his captains withdrew for
a moment to consultation. He fairly groaned for sorrow,

and at first had not a word to say, so wretched he felt at having brought his people to die in Roncesvalles. Then he said: "If it had entered into my heart to conceive the King of Spain to be such a villain, never would you have seen this day. He has exchanged with me a thousand courtesies and good words; and I thought that the worse enemies we had been before, the better friends we had become now. I fancied every human being capable of this kind of virtue on a good opportunity, saving, indeed, such base-hearted wretches as can never forgive their very forgivers; and of these I did not suppose him to be one. Let us die, if die we must, like honest and gallant men, so that it shall be said of us, it was only our bodies that died. The reason why I did not sound the horn was partly because I thought it did not become us, and partly because our liege-lord could hardly save us, even if he heard it." And with these words Orlando sprang to his horse, crying, "Away, against the Saracens!" But he had no sooner turned his face than he wept bitterly and said, "O Holy Virgin, think not of me, the sinner Orlando, but have pity on these thy servants!"

And now, with a mighty dust and an infinite sound of horns and tambours which came filling the valley, the first army of the infidels made its appearance, horses neighing, and a thousand pennons flying in the air. King Falseron led them on, saying to his officers: "Let nobody dare to lay a finger on Orlando. He belongs to myself. The revenge of my son's death is mine. I will cut the man down that comes between us."

"Now friends," said Orlando, "every man for himself, and St. Michael for us all! There is not one here that is not a perfect knight." And he might well say it, for the flower of all France was there, except Rinaldo and Ricciardetto—every man a picked man, all friends and constant companions of Orlando.

So the captains of the little troop and of the great army sat looking at one another and singling one another out as the latter came on, and then the knights put spear in rest and ran for a while two and two in succession, one against the other.

Astolpho was the first to move. He ran against Arlotto of Soria, and thrust his antagonist's body out of the saddle and his soul into the other world. Oliver encountered Malprimo and, though he received a thrust which hurt him, sent his lance right through the heart of Malprimo.

Falseron was daunted at this blow. "Truly," thought he, "this is a marvel." Oliver did not press on among the Saracens—his wound was too painful—but Orlando now put himself and his whole band in motion, and you may guess what an uproar ensued. The sound of the rattling of blows and helmets was as if the forge of Vulcan had been thrown open. Falseron beheld Orlando coming so furiously that he thought him a Lucifer who had burst his chain, and was quite of another mind than when he purposed to have him all to himself. On the contrary, he recommended himself to his gods and turned away, meaning to wait for a more auspicious season of revenge. But Orlando hailed him, with a terrible voice, saying, "Oh, thou traitor! was this the end to which old quarrels were made up?" Then he dashed at Falseron with a fury so swift and, at the same time, with a mastery of his lance so marvellous that, though he plunged it in the man's body so as instantly to kill him, and then withdrew it, the body did not move in the saddle. The hero himself, as he rushed onwards, was fain to see the end of a stroke so perfect, and turning his horse back, touched the carcass with his sword, and it fell on the instant!

When the infidels beheld their leader dead, such fear fell upon them that they were for leaving the field to the paladins, but they were unable. Marsilius had drawn the rest of his forces round the valley like a net, so that their shoulders were turned in vain. Orlando rode into the thick of them, and wherever he went thunderbolts fell upon helmets. Oliver was again in the fray, with Walter and Baldwin, Avino and Avolio, while Archbishop Turpin had changed his crosier for a lance and chased a new flock before him to the mountains.

Yet what could be done against foes without number? Marsilius constantly pours them in. The paladins are as units to thousands. Why tarry the horses of Rinaldo and Ricciardetto?

The horses did not tarry, but fate had been quicker than enchantment. Ashtaroth had presented himself to

Rinaldo in Egypt, and, after telling his errand, he and Foul-mouth, his servant, entered the horses of Rinaldo and Ricciardetto, which began to neigh, and snort, and leap with the fiends within them, till off they flew through the air over the pyramids and across the desert, and reached Spain and the scene of action just as Marsilius brought up his third army. The two paladins on their horses dropped right into the midst of the Saracens and began making such havoc among them that Marsilius, who overlooked the fight from a mountain, thought his soldiers had turned against one another. Orlando beheld it, and guessed it could be no other but his cousins, and pressed to meet them. Oliver coming up at the same moment, the rapture of the whole party is not to be expressed. After a few hasty words of explanation, they were forced to turn again upon the enemy, whose numbers seemed perfectly without limit.

Orlando, making a bloody passage towards Marsilius, struck a youth on the head, whose helmet was so strong as to resist the blow, but at the same time flew off. Orlando prepared to strike a second blow when the youth exclaimed, "Hold! You loved my father; I am Bujaforte!" The paladin had never seen Bujaforte, but he saw the likeness to the good old man, his father, and he dropped his sword. "Oh, Bujaforte," said he, "I loved him indeed; but what does his son do here fighting against his friends?"

Bujaforte could not at once speak for weeping. At length he said: "I am forced to be here by my lord and master, Marsilius; and I have made a show of fighting, but have not hurt a single Christian. Treachery is on every side of you. Baldwin himself has a vest given him by Marsilius, that everybody may know the son of his friend Gan and do him no harm."

"Put your helmet on again," said Orlando, "and behave just as you have done. Never will your father's friend be an enemy to the son."

The hero then turned in fury to look for Baldwin, who was hastening towards him, at that moment, with friendliness in his looks.

" 'T is strange," said Baldwin, "I have done my duty as well as I could, yet nobody will come against me.

I have slain right and left, and cannot comprehend what it is that makes the stoutest infidels avoid me."

"Take off your vest," said Orlando contemptuously, "and you will soon discover the secret, if you wish to know it. Your father has sold us to Marsilius, all but his honorable son."

"If my father," said Baldwin, impetuously tearing off the vest, "has been such a villain, and I escape dying, I will plunge this sword through his heart. But I am no traitor, Orlando, and you do me wrong to say it. Think not I can live with dishonor."

Baldwin spurred off into the fight, not waiting to hear another word from Orlando, who was very sorry for what he had said, for he perceived that the youth was in despair.

And now the fight raged beyond all it had done before; twenty pagans went down for one paladin, but still the paladins fell. Sansonetto was beaten to earth by the club of Grandonio, Walter d'Amulion had his shoulder broken, Berlinghieri and Ottone were slain, and at last Astolpho fell, in revenge of whose death Orlando turned the spot where he died into a lake of Saracen blood. The luckless Bujaforte met Rinaldo, and, before he could explain how he seemed to be fighting on the Saracen side, received such a blow upon the head that he fell, unable to utter a word. Orlando, cutting his way to a spot where there was a great struggle and uproar, found the poor youth Baldwin, the son of Gan, with two spears in his breast. "I am no traitor now," said Baldwin, and those were the last words he said. Orlando was bitterly sorry to have been the cause of his death, and tears streamed from his eyes. At length down went Oliver himself. He had become blinded with his own blood, and smitten Orlando without knowing him. "How now, cousin," cried Orlando, "have you too gone over to the enemy?" "Oh, my lord and master," cried the other, "I ask your pardon. I can see nothing; I am dying. Some traitor has stabbed me in the back. If you love me, lead my horse into the thick of them, so that I may not die unavenged."

"I shall die myself before long," said Orlando, "out of very toil and grief; so we will go together."

Orlando led his cousin's horse where the press was thickest, and dreadful was the strength of the dying man and his tired companion. They made a street through which they passed out of the battle, and Orlando led his cousin away to his tent, and said, "Wait a little till I return, for I will go and sound the horn on the hill yonder."

" 'T is of no use," said Oliver, "my spirit is fast going, and desires to be with its Lord and Saviour."

He would have said more, but his words came from him imperfectly, like those of a man in a dream, and so he expired.

When Orlando saw him dead, he felt as if he was alone on the earth, and he was quite willing to leave it; only he wished that King Charles, at the foot of the mountains, should know how the case stood before he went. So he took up the horn and blew it three times, with such force that the blood burst out of his nose and mouth. Turpin says that at the third blast the horn broke in two.

In spite of all the noise of the battle, the sound of the horn broke over it like a voice out of the other world. They say that birds fell dead at it, and that the whole Saracen army drew back in terror. Charlemagne was sitting in the midst of his court when the sound reached him; and Gan was there. The Emperor was the first to hear it.

"Do you hear that?" said he to his nobles. "Did you hear the horn as I heard it?"

Upon this they all listened, and Gan felt his heart misgive him. The horn sounded a second time.

"What is the meaning of this?" said Charles.

"Orlando is hunting," observed Gan, "and the stag is killed."

But when the horn sounded yet a third time, and the blast was one of so dreadful a vehemence, everybody looked at the other, and then they all looked at Gan in fury. Charles rose from his seat.

"This is no hunting of the stag," said he. "The sound goes to my very heart. Oh, Gan! Oh, Gan! Not for thee do I blush, but for myself. Oh, foul and monstrous villain! Take him, gentlemen, and keep him in close prison. Would to God I had not lived to see this day!"

But it was no time for words. They put the traitor in
prison, and then Charles with all his court took his way
to Roncesvalles, grieving and praying.

It was afternoon when the horn sounded, and half an
hour after it when the Emperor set out; and meantime
Orlando had returned to the fight that he might do his
duty, however hopeless, as long as he could sit his horse.
At length he found his end approaching, for toil and
fever, and rode all alone to a fountain where he had before quenched his thirst. His horse was wearier than he,
and no sooner had his master alighted than the beast,
kneeling down as if to take leave and to say, "I have
brought you to a place of rest," fell dead at his feet.
Orlando cast water on him from the fountain, not wishing to believe him dead; but when he found it to no purpose, he grieved for him as if he had been a human
being, and addressed him by name with tears, and asked
forgiveness if he had ever done him wrong. They say
that the horse, at these words, opened his eyes a little, and looked kindly at his master, and then stirred
never more. They say also that Orlando, then, summon-
ing all his strength, smote a rock near him with his
beautiful sword Durindana, thinking to shiver the steel
in pieces and so prevent its falling into the hands of the
enemy; but though the rock split like a slate and a great
cleft remained ever after to astonish the eyes of pilgrims, the sword remained uninjured.

And now Rinaldo and Ricciardetto came up, with Turpin, having driven back the Saracens, and told Orlando that the battle was won. Then Orlando knelt
before Turpin and begged remission of his sins, and Turpin gave him absolution. Orlando fixed his eyes on the
hilt of his sword, as on a crucifix, and embraced it,
and he raised his eyes and appeared like a creature
seraphical and transfigured, and, bowing his head, he
breathed out his pure soul.

And now King Charles and his nobles came up. The
Emperor, at sight of the dead Orlando, threw himself, as
if he had been a reckless youth, from his horse, and embraced and kissed the body, and said: "I bless thee, Orlando; I bless thy whole life, and all that thou wast, and
all that thou ever didst, and the father that begat thee;

and I ask pardon of thee for believing those who brought thee to thine end. They shall have their reward, oh, thou beloved one! But indeed it is thou that livest, and I who am worse than dead."

Horrible to the Emperor's eyes was the sight of the field of Roncesvalles. The Saracens indeed had fled, conquered; but all his paladins but two were left on it dead, and the whole valley looked like a great slaughterhouse, trampled into blood and dirt and reeking to the heat. Charles trembled to his heart's core for wonder and agony. After gazing dumbly on the place, he cursed it with a solemn curse and wished that never grass might grow in it again, nor seed of any kind, neither within it nor on any of its mountains around, but the anger of Heaven abide over it forever.

Charles and his warriors went after the Saracens into Spain. They took and fired Saragossa, and Marsilius was hung to the carob-tree under which he had planned his villainy with Gan; and Gan was hung and drawn and quartered in Roncesvalles, amidst the execrations of the country.

RINALDO AND BAYARD

Charlemagne was overwhelmed with grief at the loss of so many of his bravest warriors at the disaster of Roncesvalles, and bitterly reproached himself for his credulity in resigning himself so completely to the counsels of the treacherous Count Gan. Yet he soon fell into a similar snare when he suffered his unworthy son Charlot to acquire such an influence over him that he constantly led him into acts of cruelty and injustice that in his right mind he would have scorned to commit. Rinaldo and his brothers, for some slight offence to the imperious young prince, were forced to fly from Paris and to take shelter in their castle of Montalban; for Charles had publicly said, if he could take them, he would hang them all. He sent numbers of his bravest knights to arrest them, but all without success. Either Rinaldo foiled their efforts and sent them back, stripped of their armor and of their glory, or, after meeting and conferring with him, they came back and told the king they could not be his instruments for such a work.

At last Charles himself raised a great army and went in person to compel the paladin to submit. He ravaged all the country round about Montalban, so that supplies of food should be cut off, and he threatened death to any who should attempt to issue forth, hoping to compel the garrison to submit for want of food.

Rinaldo's resources had been brought so low that it seemed useless to contend any longer. His brothers had been taken prisoners in a skirmish, and his only hope of saving their lives was in making terms with the king.

So he sent a messenger, offering to yield himself and his castle if the king would spare his and his brothers' lives. While the messenger was gone, Rinaldo, impatient to learn what tidings he might bring, rode out to meet him. When he had ridden as far as he thought prudent he stopped in a wood and, alighting, tied Bayard to a tree. Then he sat down, and, as he waited, he fell asleep. Bayard meanwhile got loose and strayed away where the grass tempted him. Just then came along some country people, who said to one another, "Look, is not that the great horse Bayard that Rinaldo rides? Let us take him, and carry him to King Charles, who will pay us well for our trouble." They did so, and the king was delighted with his prize, and gave them a present that made them rich to their dying day.

When Rinaldo woke he looked round for his horse, and, finding him not, he groaned, and said, "Oh, unlucky hour that I was born! How fortune persecutes me!" So desperate was he that he took off his armor and his spurs, saying, "What need have I of these, since Bayard is lost?" While he stood thus lamenting, a man came from the thicket, seemingly bent with age. He had a long beard hanging over his breast and eyebrows that almost covered his eyes. He bade Rinaldo good day. Rinaldo thanked him and said, "A good day I have hardly had since I was born." Then said the old man, "Signor Rinaldo, you must not despair, for God will make all

things turn to the best." Rinaldo answered, "My trouble
is too heavy for me to hope relief. The king has taken
my brothers and means to put them to death. I thought
to rescue them by means of my horse Bayard, but while
I slept some thief has stolen him." The old man replied,
"I will remember you and your brothers in my prayers. I
am a poor man; have you not something to give me?"
Rinaldo said, "I have nothing to give," but then he recollected his spurs. He gave them to the beggar and said,
"Here, take my spurs. They are the first present my
mother gave me when my father, Count Aymon, dubbed
me knight. They ought to bring you ten pounds."

The old man took the spurs, and put them into his
sack, and said, "Noble sir, have you nothing else you can
give me?" Rinaldo replied, "Are you making sport of
me? I tell you truly if it were not for shame to beat one
so helpless, I would teach you better manners." The old
man said, "Of a truth, sir, if you did so, you would do a
great sin. If all had beaten me of whom I have begged,
I should have been killed long ago, for I ask alms in
churches and convents, and wherever I can." "You say
true," replied Rinaldo, "if you did not ask, none would
relieve you." The old man said, "True, noble sir, therefore I pray if you have anything more to spare, give it
me." Rinaldo gave him his mantle and said, "Take it,
pilgrim. I give it you for the love of Christ, that God
would save my brothers from a shameful death and
help me to escape out of King Charles's power."

The pilgrim took the mantle, folded it up, and put it
into his bag. Then a third time he said to Rinaldo, "Sir,
have you nothing left to give me that I may remember
you in my prayers?" "Wretch!" exclaimed Rinaldo, "do
you make me your sport?" and he drew his sword and
struck at him; but the old man warded off the blow with
his staff and said, "Rinaldo, would you slay your cousin
Malagigi?" When Rinaldo heard that, he stayed his hand
and gazed doubtingly on the old man, who now threw
aside his disguise and appeared to be indeed Malagigi.
"Dear cousin," said Rinaldo, "pray forgive me. I did not
know you. Next to God, my trust is in you. Help my
brothers to escape out of prison, I entreat you. I have
lost my horse and therefore cannot render them any as-

sistance." Malagigi answered, "Cousin Rinaldo, I will enable you to recover your horse. Meanwhile, you must do as I say."

Then Malagigi took from his sack a gown, and gave it to Rinaldo to put on over his armor, and a hat that was full of holes, and an old pair of shoes to put on. They looked like two pilgrims, very old and poor. Then they went forth from the wood and, after a little while, saw four monks riding along the road. Malagigi said to Rinaldo, "I will go meet the monks and see what news I can learn."

Malagigi learned from the monks that on the approaching festival there would be a great crowd of people at court, for the prince was going to show the ladies the famous horse Bayard that used to belong to Rinaldo. "What!" said the pilgrim; "is Bayard there?" "Yes," answered the monks; "the king has given him to Charlot, and, after the prince has ridden him, the king means to pass sentence on the brothers of Rinaldo and have them hanged." Then Malagigi asked alms of the monks, but they would give him none, till he threw aside his pilgrim garb and let them see his armor, when, partly for charity and partly for terror, they gave him a golden cup adorned with precious stones that sparkled in the sunshine.

Malagigi then hastened back to Rinaldo and told him what he had learned.

The morning of the feast-day, Rinaldo and Malagigi came to the place where the sports were to be held. Malagigi gave Rinaldo his spurs back again and said, "Cousin, put on your spurs, for you will need them." "How shall I need them," said Rinaldo, "since I have lost my horse?" Yet he did as Malagigi directed him.

When the two had taken their stand on the border of the field among the crowd, the princes and ladies of the court began to assemble. When they were all assembled, the king came also, and Charlot with him, near whom the horse Bayard was led, in the charge of grooms, who were expressly enjoined to guard him safely. The king, looking round on the circle of spectators, saw Malagigi and Rinaldo, and observed the splendid cup that they had, and said to Charlot, "See, my son, what a brilliant cup those two pilgrims have got. It seems to be worth a hundred ducats." "That is true," said Charlot; "let us go and ask where they got it." So they rode to the place where the pilgrims stood, and Charlot stopped Bayard close to them. The horse snuffed at the pilgrims, knew Rinaldo, and caressed his master. The king said to Malagigi, "Friend, where did you get that beautiful cup?" Malagigi replied, "Honorable sir, I paid for it all the money I have saved from eleven years' begging in churches and convents. The Pope himself has blessed it and given it the power that whosoever eats or drinks out of it shall be pardoned of all his sins." Then said the king to Charlot, "My son, these are right holy men; see how the dumb beast worships them."

Then the king said to Malagigi, "Give me a morsel from your cup, that I may be cleared of my sins." Malagigi answered, "Illustrious lord, I dare not do it, unless you will forgive all who have at any time offended you. You know that Christ forgave all those who had betrayed and crucified him." The king replied, "Friend, that is true; but Rinaldo has so grievously offended me that I cannot forgive him, nor that other man, Malagigi, the magician. These two shall never live in my kingdom again. If I catch them, I will certainly have them hanged. But tell me, pilgrim, who is that man who stands beside you?" "He is deaf, dumb, and blind," said Malagigi. Then the king said again, "Give me to drink of your cup, to take away my sins." Malagigi answered, "My lord king, here is my poor brother, who for fifty days has not heard, spoken, nor seen. This misfortune befell him in a house where we found shelter, and the day before yesterday we met with a wise woman, who told him the only hope of a cure for him was to come to some place where Bayard was to be ridden, and to mount and ride him; that would do him more good than anything else." Then said the king, "Friend, you have come to the right place, for Bayard is to be ridden here to-day. Give me a draught from your cup, and your companion shall ride upon Bayard." Malagigi, hearing these words, said, "Be it so." Then the king, with great devotion, took a spoon and dipped a portion from the pilgrim's cup, believing that his sins should be thereby forgiven.

When this was done, the king said to Charlot, "Son, I

request that you will let this sick pilgrim sit on your horse, and ride if he can, for by so doing he will be healed of all his infirmities." Charlot replied, "That will I gladly do." So saying, he dismounted, and the servants took the pilgrim in their arms and helped him on the horse.

When Rinaldo was mounted, he put his feet in the stirrups and said, "I would like to ride a little." Malagigi, hearing him speak, seemed delighted and asked him whether he could see and hear also. "Yes," said Rinaldo, "I am healed of all my infirmities." When the king heard it, he said to Bishop Turpin, "My lord bishop, we must celebrate this with a procession, with crosses and banners, for it is a great miracle."

When Rinaldo remarked that he was not carefully watched, he spoke to the horse and touched him with the spurs. Bayard knew that his master was upon him, and he started off upon a rapid pace, and in a few moments was a good way off. Malagigi pretended to be in great alarm. "Oh, noble king and master," he cried, "my poor companion is run away with; he will fall and break his neck." The king ordered his knights to ride after the pilgrim and bring him back, or help him if need were. They did so, but it was in vain. Rinaldo left them all behind him and kept on his way till he reached Montalban. Malagigi was suffered to depart, unsuspected, and he went his way, making sad lamentation for the fate of his comrade, who he pretended to think must surely be dashed to pieces.

Malagigi did not go far, but, having changed his disguise, returned to where the king was and employed his best art in getting the brothers of Rinaldo out of prison. He succeeded; and all three got safely to Montalban, where Rinaldo's joy at the rescue of his brothers and the recovery of Bayard was more than tongue can tell.

DEATH OF RINALDO

The distress in Rinaldo's castle for want of food grew more severe every day, under the pressure of the siege. The garrison were forced to kill their horses, both to save the provision they would consume and to make food of their flesh. At last, all the horses were killed except Bayard, and Rinaldo said to his brothers, "Bayard must die, for we have nothing else to eat." So they went to the stable and brought out Bayard to kill him. But Alardo said, "Brother, let Bayard live a little longer; who knows what God may do for us?"

Bayard heard these words, and understood them as if he was a man, and fell on his knees, as if he would beg for mercy. When Rinaldo saw the distress of his horse, his heart failed him, and he let him live.

Just at this time, Aya, Rinaldo's mother, who was the sister of the Emperor, came to the camp, attended by knights and ladies, to intercede for her sons. She fell on her knees before the king and besought him that he would pardon Rinaldo and his brothers; and all the peers and knights took her side and entreated the king to grant her prayer. Then said the king, "Dear sister, you act the part of a good mother, and I respect your tender heart and yield to your entreaties. I will spare your sons their lives, if they submit implicitly to my will."

When Charlot heard this, he approached the king and whispered in his ear. And the king turned to his sister and said, "Charlot must have Bayard, because I have given the horse to him. Now go, my sister, and tell Rinaldo what I have said."

When the Lady Aya heard these words, she was delighted, thanked God in her heart, and said, "Worthy king and brother, I will do as you bid me." So she went into the castle, where her sons received her most joyfully and affectionately, and she told them the king's offer. Then Alardo said, "Brother, I would rather have the king's enmity than give Bayard to Charlot, for I believe he will kill him." Likewise said all the brothers. When Rinaldo heard them, he said, "Dear brothers, if we may win our forgiveness by giving up the horse, so be it. Let us make our peace, for we cannot stand against the king's power." Then he went to his mother, and told her they would give the horse to Charlot, and more, too, if the king would pardon them and forgive all that they had done against his crown and dignity. The lady returned to Charles and told him the answer of her sons.

When the peace was thus made between the king and the sons of Aymon, the brothers came forth from the castle, bringing Bayard with them, and, falling at the king's feet, begged his forgiveness. The king bade them rise and received them into favor in the sight of all his noble knights and counsellors, to the great joy of all, especially of the Lady Aya, their mother. Then Rinaldo took the horse Bayard, gave him to Charlot, and said, "My lord and prince, this horse I give to you; do with him as to you seems good." Charlot took him, as had been agreed on. Then he made the servants take him to the bridge and throw him into the water. Bayard sank to the bottom, but soon came to the surface again and swam, saw Rinaldo looking at him, came to land, ran to his old master, and stood by him as proudly as if he had understanding, and would say, "Why did you treat me so?" When the prince saw that, he said, "Rinaldo, give me the horse again, for he must die." Rinaldo replied, "My lord and prince, he is yours without dispute," and gave him to him. The prince then had a millstone tied to each foot, and two to his neck, and made them throw him again into the water. Bayard struggled in the water, looked up to his master, threw off the stones, and came back to Rinaldo.

When Alardo saw that, he said, "Now must thou be disgraced forever, brother, if thou give up the horse again." But Rinaldo answered, "Brother, be still. Shall I for the horse's life provoke the anger of the king again?" Then Alardo said, "Ah, Bayard! what a return do we make for all thy true love and service!" Rinaldo gave the horse to the prince again and said, "My lord, if the horse comes out again, I cannot return him to you any more, for it wrings my heart too much." Then Charlot had Bayard loaded with the stones as before and thrown into the water, and commanded Rinaldo that he should not stand where the horse would see him. When Bayard rose to the surface, he stretched his neck out of the water and looked round for his master, but saw him not. Then he sunk to the bottom.

Rinaldo was so distressed for the loss of Bayard that he made a vow to ride no horse again all his life long, nor to bind a sword to his side, but to become a hermit.

He resolved to betake himself to some wild wood, but first to return to his castle, to see his children and to appoint to each his share of his estate.

So he took leave of the king and of his brothers and returned to Montalban, and his brothers remained with the king. Rinaldo called his children to him, and he made his eldest born, Aymeric, a knight, and made him lord of his castle and of his land. He gave to the rest what other goods he had, and kissed and embraced them all, commended them to God, and then departed from them with a heavy heart.

He had not travelled far when he entered a wood, and there met with a hermit, who had long been retired from the world. Rinaldo greeted him, and the hermit replied courteously and asked him who he was and what was his purpose. Rinaldo replied, "Sir, I have led a sinful life; many deeds of violence have I done, and many men have I slain, not always in a good cause, but often under the impulse of my own headstrong passions. I have also been the cause of the death of many of my friends, who took my part, not because they thought me in the right, but only for love of me. And now I come to make confession of all my sins and to do penance for the rest of my life, if perhaps the mercy of God will forgive me." The hermit said, "Friend, I perceive you have fallen into great sins and have broken the commandments of God, but his mercy is greater than your sins; and if you repent from your heart and lead a new life, there is yet hope for you that he will forgive you what is past." So Rinaldo was comforted, and said, "Master, I will stay with you, and what you bid me I will do." The hermit replied, "Roots and vegetables will be your food; shirt or shoes you may not wear; your lot must be poverty and want, if you stay with me." Rinaldo replied, "I will cheerfully bear all this and more." So he remained three whole years with the hermit, and after that his strength failed, and it seemed as if he was like to die.

One night the hermit had a dream, and heard a voice from heaven which commanded him to say to his companion that he must without delay go to the Holy Land and fight against the heathen. The hermit, when he heard that voice, was glad, and, calling Rinaldo, he said,

"Friend, God's angel has commanded me to say to you that you must without delay go to Jerusalem and help our fellow-Christians in their struggle with the infidels." Then said Rinaldo, "Ah! master, how can I do that? It is over three years since I made a vow no more to ride a horse, nor take a sword or spear in my hand." The hermit answered, "Dear friend, obey God, and do what the angel commanded." "I will do so," said Rinaldo, "and pray for me, my master, that God may guide me right." Then he departed, and went to the seaside, and took ship and came to Tripoli in Syria.

And as he went on his way, his strength returned to him, till it was equal to what it was in his best days. And though he never mounted a horse, nor took a sword in his hand, yet with his pilgrim's staff he did good service in the armies of the Christians; and it pleased God that he escaped unhurt, though he was present in many battles, and his courage inspired the men with the same. At last a truce was made with the Saracens, and Rinaldo, now old and infirm, wishing to see his native land again before he died, took ship and sailed for France. When he arrived, he shunned to go to the resorts of the great and preferred to live among the humble folk, where he was unknown. He did country work and lived on milk and bread, drank water, and was therewith content. While he so lived, he heard that the city of Cologne was the holiest and best of cities, on account of the relics and bodies of saints who had there poured out their blood for the faith. This induced him to betake himself thither. When the pious hero arrived at Cologne, he went to the monastery of St. Peter and lived a holy life, occupied night and day in devotion. It so happened that at that time, in the next town to Cologne, there raged a dreadful pestilence. Many people came to Rinaldo, to beg him to pray for them, that the plague might be stayed. The holy man prayed fervently, and besought the Lord to take away the plague from the people, and his prayer was heard. The stroke of the pestilence was arrested, and all the people thanked the holy man and praised God.

Now there was at this time at Cologne a bishop, called Agilolphus, who was a wise and understanding man, who led a pure and secluded life and set a good example to

others. This bishop undertook to build the Church of St.
Peter, and gave notice to all stone-masons and other
workmen round about to come to Cologne, where they
should find work and wages. Among others came Rinaldo; and he worked among the laborers and did more
than four or five common workmen. When they went to
dinner, he brought stone and mortar so that they had
enough for the whole day. When the others went to bed,
he stretched himself out on the stones. He ate bread
only, and drank nothing but water, and had for his wages
but a penny a day. The head-workman asked him his
name and where he belonged. He would not tell, but said
nothing and pursued his work. They called him St. Peter's
workman, because he was so devoted to his work.

When the overseer saw the diligence of this holy
man, he chid the laziness of the other workmen and
said, "You receive more pay than this good man, but
do not do half as much work." For this reason the other
workmen hated Rinaldo and made a secret agreement
to kill him. They knew that he made it a practice to go
every night to a certain church to pray and give alms. So
they agreed to lay wait for him with the purpose to kill
him. When he came to the spot, they seized him and beat
him over the head till he was dead. Then they put his
body into a sack, and stones with it, and cast it into the
Rhine, in the hope the sack would sink to the bottom
and be there concealed. But God willed not that it should
be so, but caused the sack to float on the surface and be
thrown upon the bank. And the soul of the holy martyr
was carried by angels, with songs of praise, up to the
heavens.

Now at that time the people of Dortmund had become
converted to the Christian faith; and they sent to the
Bishop of Cologne and desired him to give them some of
the holy relics that are in such abundance in that city. So
the bishop called together his clergy to deliberate what
answer they should give to this request. And it was determined to give to the people of Dortmund the body of
the holy man who had just suffered martyrdom.

When now the body with the coffin was put on the
cart, the cart began to move toward Dortmund without
horses or help of men, and stopped not till it reached

the place where the church of St. Rinaldo now stands. The bishop and his clergy followed the holy man to do him honor, with singing of hymns, for a space of three miles. And St. Rinaldo has ever since been the patron of that place, and many wonderful works has God done through him, as may be seen in the legends.

HUON OF BORDEAUX

When Charlemagne grew old, he felt the burden of government become heavier year by year, till at last he called together his high barons and peers to propose to abdicate the empire and the throne of France in favor of his sons, Charlot and Lewis.

The Emperor was unreasonably partial to his eldest son; he would have been glad to have had the barons and peers demand Charlot for their only sovereign; but that prince was so infamous, for his falsehood and cruelty, that the council strenuously opposed the Emperor's proposal of abdicating and implored him to continue to hold a sceptre which he wielded with so much glory.

Amaury of Hauteville, cousin of Ganelon and now head of the wicked branch of the house of Maganza, was the secret partisan of Charlot, whom he resembled in his loose morals and bad dispositions. Amaury nourished the most bitter resentment against the house of Guienne, of which the former duke, Sevinus, had often rebuked his misdeeds. He took advantage of this occasion to do an injury to the two young children whom the Duke Sevinus had left under the charge of the Duchess Alice, their mother; and, at the same time, to advance his interest with Charlot by increasing his wealth and power. With this view, he suggested to the prince a new idea.

He pretended to agree with the opinion of the barons; he said that it would be best to try Charlot's capacity for government by giving him some rich provinces before placing him upon the throne; and that the Emperor, without depriving himself of any part of his realm, might give Charlot the investiture of Guienne. For although seven years had passed since the death of Sevinus, the young duke, his son, had not yet repaired to the court of Charlemagne to render the homage due to his lawful sovereign.

We have often had occasion to admire the justice and wisdom of the advice which on all occasions the Duke Namo of Bavaria gave to Charlemagne, and he now discountenanced, with indignation, the selfish advice of Amaury. He represented to the Emperor the early age of the children of Sevinus and the useful and glorious services of their late father, and proposed to Charlemagne to send two knights to the duchess, at Bordeaux, to summon her two sons to the court of the Emperor, to pay their respects and render homage.

Charlemagne approved this advice and sent two chevaliers to demand the two young princes of their mother. No sooner had the duchess learned the approach of the two knights than she sent distinguished persons to receive them; and as soon as they entered the palace, she presented herself before them, with her elder and younger sons, Huon and Girard.

The deputies, delighted with the honors and caresses they received, accompanied with rich presents, left Bordeaux with regret and, on their return, represented to Charlemagne that the young Duke Huon seemed born to tread in the footsteps of his brave father, informing him that in three months the young princes of Guienne would present themselves at his court.

The duchess employed the short interval in giving her sons her last instructions. Huon received them in his heart, and Girard gave as much heed to them as could be expected from one so young.

The preparations for their departure having been made, the duchess embraced them tenderly, commending them to the care of Heaven, and charged them to call, on their way, at the celebrated monastery of Cluny, to visit the abbot, the brother of their father. This abbot, worthy of his high dignity, had never lost an opportunity of doing good, setting an example of every excellence and making virtue attractive by his example.

He received his nephews with the greatest magnificence; and, aware how useful his presence might be to them with Charlemagne, whose valued counsellor he was, he took with them the road to Paris.

When Amaury learned what reception the two deputies of Charlemagne had received at Bordeaux, and the arrangements made for the visit of the young princes to the Emperor's court, he suggested to Charlot to give him a troop of his guards, with which he proposed to lay wait for the young men in the wood of Montlery, put them to death, and thereby give the Prince Charlot possession of the duchy of Guienne.

A plan of treachery and violence agreed but too well with Charlot's disposition. He not only adopted the suggestion of Amaury, but insisted upon taking a part in it. They went out secretly, by night, followed by a great number of attendants, all armed in black, to lie in ambuscade in the wood where the brothers were to pass.

Girard, the younger of the two, having amused himself as he rode by flying his hawk at such game as presented itself, had ridden in advance of his brother and the Abbot of Cluny. Charlot, who saw him coming, alone and unarmed, went forth to meet him, sought a quarrel with him, and threw him from his horse with a stroke of his lance. Girard uttered a cry as he fell; Huon heard it and flew to his defence with no other weapon than his sword. He came up with him and saw the blood flowing from his wound. "What has this child done to you, wretch?" he exclaimed to Charlot. "How cowardly to attack him when unprepared to defend himself!" "By my faith," said Charlot, "I mean to do the same by you. Know that I am the son of Duke Thierry of Ardennes, from whom your father, Sevinus, took three castles; I have sworn to avenge him, and I defy you." "Coward," answered Huon, "I know well the baseness that dwells in your race; worthy son of Thierry, use the advantage that your armor gives you; but know that I fear you not." At these words, Charlot had the wickedness to put his lance in rest and to run upon Huon, who had barely time to wrap his arm in his mantle. With this feeble buckler he received the thrust of the lance. It penetrated the mantle, but missed his body. Then, rising upon his stirrups, Sir Huon struck Charlot so terrible a blow with his sword that the helmet was cleft asunder, and his head, too. The dastardly prince fell dead upon the ground.

Huon now perceived that the wood was full of armed men. He called the men of his suite, and they hastily put themselves in order, but nobody issued from the wood to attack him. Amaury, who saw Charlot's fall, had no desire to compromit himself; and, feeling sure that Charlemagne would avenge the death of his son, he saw no occasion for his doing anything more at present. He left Huon and the Abbot of Cluny to bind up the wound of Girard, and, having seen them depart and resume their way to Paris, he took up the body of Charlot, and, placing it across a horse, had it carried to Paris, where he arrived four hours after Huon.

The Abbot of Cluny presented his nephew to Charlemagne, but Huon refrained from paying his obeisance, complaining grievously of the ambush which had been set for him, which he said could not have been without the Emperor's permission. Charlemagne, surprised at a charge which his magnanimous soul was incapable of meriting, asked eagerly of the abbot what were the grounds of the complaints of his nephew. The abbot told him faithfully all that had happened, informing him that a coward knight, who called himself the son of Thierry of Ardennes, had wounded Girard, and run upon Huon, who was unarmed; but by his force and valor he had overcome the traitor and left him dead upon the plain.

Charlemagne indignantly disavowed any connection with the action of the infamous Thierry, congratulated the young Duke upon his victory, himself conducted the two brothers to a rich apartment, stayed to see the first dressing applied to the wound of Girard, and left the brothers in charge of Duke Namo of Bavaria, who, having been a companion in arms of the Duke Sevinus, regarded the young men almost as if they were his own sons.

Charlemagne had hardly quitted them when, returning to his chamber, he heard cries and saw through the window a party of armed men just arrived. He recognized Amaury, who bore a dead knight stretched across a horse; and the name of Charlot was heard among the exclamations of the people assembled in the court-yard.

Charles's partiality for this unworthy son was one of

his weaknesses. He descended in trepidation to the court-yard, ran to Amaury, and uttered a cry of grief on recognizing Charlot. "It is Huon of Bordeaux," said the traitor Amaury, "who has massacred your son before it was in my power to defend him." Charlemagne, furious at these words, seized a sword and flew to the apartment of the two brothers to plunge it into the heart of the muderer of his son. Duke Namo stopped his hand for an instant, while Charles told him the crime of which Huon was accused. "He is a peer of the realm," said Namo, "and if he is guilty, is he not here in your power, and are not we peers the proper judges to condemn him to death? Let not your hand be stained with his blood." The Emperor, calmed by the wisdom of Duke Namo, summoned Amaury to his presence. The peers assembled to hear his testimony, and the traitor accused Huon of Bordeaux of having struck the fatal blow, without allowing Charlot an opportunity to defend himself, and though he knew that his opponent was the Emperor's eldest son.

The Abbot of Cluny, indignant at the false accusation of Amaury, advanced and said, "By Saint Benedict, sire, the traitor lies in his throat. If my nephew has slain Charlot, it was in his own defence, and after having seen his brother wounded by him, and also in ignorance that his adversary was the prince. Though I am a son of the Church," added the good abbot, "I forget not that I am a knight by birth. I offer to prove with my body the lie upon Amaury, if he dares sustain it, and I shall feel that I am doing a better work to punish a disloyal traitor, than to sing lauds and matins."

Huon to this time had kept silent, amazed at the black calumny of Amaury; but now he stepped forth and, addressing Amaury, said: "Traitor! darest thou maintain in arms the lie thou hast uttered?" Amaury, a knight of great prowess, despising the youth and slight figure of Huon, hesitated not to offer his glove, which Huon seized; then, turning again to the peers, he said: "I pray you let the combat be allowed me, for never was there a more legitimate cause." The Duke Namo and the rest, deciding that the question should be remitted to the judgment of Heaven, the combat was ordained, to which Charlemagne unwillingly consented. The young Duke was restored to the charge of Duke Namo, who the next morning invested him with the honors of knighthood and gave him armor of proof, with a white shield. The Abbot of Cluny, delighted to find in his nephew sentiments worthy of his birth, embraced him, gave him his blessing, and hastened to the church of St. Germains to pray for him, while the officers of the king prepared the lists for the combat.

The battle was long and obstinate. The address and agility of Huon enabled him to avoid the terrible blows which the ferocious Amaury aimed at him. But Huon had more than once drawn blood from his antagonist. The effect began to be perceived in the failing strength of the traitor; at last he threw himself from his horse and, kneeling, begged for mercy. "Spare me," he said, "and I will confess all. Aid me to rise and lead me to Charlemagne." The brave and loyal Huon, at these words, put his sword under his left arm and stretched out his right to raise the prostrate man, who seized the opportunity to give him a thrust in the side. The hauberk of Huon resisted the blow, and he was wounded but slightly. Transported with rage at this act of baseness, he forgot how necessary for his complete acquittal the confession of Amaury was, and without delay dealt him the fatal blow.

Duke Namo and the other peers approached, had the body of Amaury dragged forth from the lists, and conducted Huon to Charlemagne. The Emperor, however, listening to nothing but his resentment and grief for the death of his son, refused to be satisfied; and under the plea that Huon had not succeeded in making his accuser retract his charge, seemed resolved to confiscate his estates and to banish him forever from France. It was not till after long entreaties on the part of Duke Namo and the rest that he consented to grant Huon his pardon, under conditions which he should impose.

Huon approached, and knelt before the Emperor, rendered him homage, and cried him mercy for the involuntary killing of his son. Charlemagne would not receive the hands of Huon in his own, but touched him with his sceptre, saying, "I receive thy homage, and pardon thee the death of my son, but only on one condition. You shall go immediately to the court of the Sultan Gaudisso; you shall present yourself before him as he sits at meat; you shall cut off the head of the most illustrious guest whom you shall find sitting nearest to him; you shall kiss three times on the mouth the fair princess his daughter, and you shall demand of the sultan, as token of tribute to me, a handful of the white hair of his beard and four grinders from his mouth."

These conditions caused a murmur from all the assembly. "What!" said the Abbot of Cluny; "slaughter a Saracen prince without first offering him baptism?" "The second condition is not so hard," said the young peers, "but the demand that Huon is bound to make of the old Sultan is very uncivil, and will be hard to obtain."

The Emperor's obstinacy when he had once resolved upon a thing is well known. To the courage of Huon nothing seemed impossible. "I accept the conditions," said he, silencing the intercessions of the old Duke of Bavaria; "my liege, I accept my pardon at this price. I go to execute your commands, as your vassal and a peer of France."

The Duke Namo and the Abbot of Cluny, being unable to obtain any relaxation of the sentence passed by Charlemagne, led forth the young duke, who determined to set out at once on his expedition. All that the good abbot could obtain of him was that he should prepare for this perilous undertaking by going first to Rome, to pay his homage to the Pope, who was the brother of the Duchess Alice, Huon's mother, and from him demand absolution and his blessing. Huon promised it and forthwith set out on his way to Rome.

HUON OF BORDEAUX

CONTINUED

Huon, having traversed the Apennines and Italy, arrived at the environs of Rome, where, laying aside his armor, he assumed the dress of a pilgrim. In this attire he presented himself before the Pope, and not till after he had made a full confession of his sins did he announce himself as his nephew. "Ah! my dear nephew," exclaimed the Holy Father, "what harder penance could I impose than the Emperor has already done? Go in peace, my son," he added, absolving him, "I go to intercede for you with the Most High." Then he led his nephew into his palace and introduced him to all the cardinals and princes of Rome as the Duke of Guienne, son of the Duchess Alice, his sister.

Huon, at setting out, had made a vow not to stop more than three days in a place. The Holy Father took advantage of this time to inspire him with zeal for the glory of Christianity, and with confidence in the protection of the Most High. He advised him to embark for Palestine, to visit the Holy Sepulchre, and to depart thence for the interior of Asia.

Loaded with the blessings of the Holy Father, Huon, obeying his counsels, embarked for Palestine, arrived, and visited with the greatest reverence the holy places. He then departed and took his way towards the east. But, ignorant of the country and of the language, he lost himself in a forest and remained three days without seeing a human creature, living on honey and wild fruits which he found on the trees. The third day, seeking a passage through a rocky defile, he beheld a man in tattered clothing, whose beard and hair covered his breast and shoulders. This man stopped on seeing him, observed him, and recognized the arms and bearing of a French knight. He immediately approached and exclaimed, in the language of the South of France, "God be praised! Do I indeed behold a chevalier of my own country, after fifteen years passed in this desert without seeing the face of a fellow-countryman?"

Huon, to gratify him still more, unlaced his helmet and came towards him with a smiling countenance. The other regarded him with more surprise than at first. "Good Heaven!" he exclaimed, "was there ever such a resemblance! Ah, noble sir," he added, "tell me, I beseech you, of what country and race you come?" "I require," replied Huon, "before telling you mine, that you first reveal your own; let it suffice you at present to know that I am a Christian, and that in Guienne I was born." "Ah! Heaven grant that my eyes and my heart do not deceive me," exclaimed the unknown; "my name is Sherasmin; I am brother to Guire, the Mayor of Bordeaux. I was taken prisoner in the battle where my dear and illustrious master, Sevinus, lost his life. For three years I endured the miseries of slavery; at length I broke my chains and escaped to this desert, where I have sustained myself in solitude ever since. Your features recall to me my beloved sovereign, in whose service I was from my infancy till his death." Huon made no reply but by embracing the old man, with tears in his eyes. Then Sherasmin learned that his arms enfolded the son of the Duke Sevinus. He led him to his cabin and spread before him the dry fruits and honey which formed his only aliment.

Huon recounted his adventures to Sherasmin, who was moved to tears at the recital. He then consulted him on the means of conducting his enterprise. Sherasmin hesitated not to confess that success seemed impossible; nevertheless, he swore a solemn oath never to abandon him. The Saracen language, which he was master of, would be serviceable to them when they should leave the desert and mingle with men.

They took the route of the Red Sea and entered Arabia. Their way lay through a region which Sherasmin described as full of terrors. It was inhabited by Oberon, King of the Fairies, who made captive such knights as were rash enough to penetrate into it, and transformed them into Hobgoblins. It was possible to avoid this district at the expense of somewhat lengthening their route; but no dangers could deter Huon of Bordeaux; and the brave Sherasmin, who had now resumed the armor of a knight, reluctantly consented to share with him the dangers of the shorter route.

They entered a wood and arrived at a spot whence alleys branched off in various directions. One of them seemed to be terminated by a superb palace, whose gilded roofs were adorned with brilliant weathercocks covered with diamonds. A superb chariot issued from the gate of the palace and drove towards Huon and his companion, as if to meet them half-way. The prince saw no one in the chariot but a child apparently about five years old, very beautiful, and clad in a robe which glittered with precious stones. At the sight of him, Sherasmin's terror was extreme. He seized the reins of Huon's horse and turned him about, hurrying the prince away and assuring him that they were lost if they stopped to parley with the mischievous dwarf, who, though he appeared a child, was full of years and of treachery. Huon was sorry to lose sight of the beautiful dwarf, whose aspect had nothing in it to alarm; yet he followed his friend, who urged on his horse with all possible speed. Presently a storm began to roar through the forest, the daylight grew dim, and they found their way with difficulty. From time to time they seemed to hear an infantine voice, which said, "Stop, Duke Huon; listen to me: it is in vain you fly me!"

Sherasmin only fled the faster, and stopped not until he had reached the gate of a monastery of monks and nuns, the two communities of which were assembled at that time in a religious procession. Sherasmin, feeling safe from the malice of the dwarf in the presence of so many holy persons and the sacred banners, stopped to ask an asylum, and made Huon dismount also. But at that moment they were joined by the dwarf, who blew a blast upon an ivory horn which hung from his neck. Immediately the good Sherasmin, in spite of himself, began to dance like a young collegian, and seizing the hand of an aged nun, who felt as if it would be her death, they footed it briskly over the grass, and were imitated by all the other monks and nuns, mingled together, forming the strangest dancing-party ever beheld. Huon alone felt no disposition to dance, but he came near dying of laughter at seeing the ridiculous postures and leaps of the others.

The dwarf, approaching Huon, said, in a sweet voice and in Huon's own language, "Duke of Guienne, why do you shun me? I conjure you, in Heaven's name, speak to me." Huon, hearing himself addressed in this serious manner and knowing that no evil spirit would dare to use the holy name in aid of his schemes, replied, "Sir, whoever you are, I am ready to hear and answer you." "Huon, my friend," continued the dwarf, "I always loved your race, and you have been dear to me ever since your birth. The gracious state of conscience in which you were when you entered my wood has protected you from all enchantments, even if I had intended to practise any upon you. If these monks, these nuns, and even your friend Sherasmin had had a conscience as pure as yours, my horn would not have set them dancing; but where is the monk or the nun who can always be deaf to the voice of the tempter, and Sherasmin in the desert has often doubted the power of Providence."

At these words Huon saw the dancers overcome with exertion. He begged mercy for them, the dwarf granted it, and the effect of the horn ceased at once; the nuns got rid of their partners, smoothed their dresses, and hastened to resume their places in the procession. Sherasmin, overcome with heat, panting, and unable to stand on his legs, threw himself upon the grass and began, "Did not I tell you—" He was going on in an angry tone, but the dwarf, approaching, said, "Sherasmin, why have you murmured against Providence? Why have you thought evil of me? You deserved this light punishment; but I know you to be good and loyal; I mean to show myself your friend, as you shall soon see." At these words, he presented him a rich goblet. "Make the sign of the cross on this cup," said he, "and then believe that I hold my power from the God you adore, whose faithful servant I am, as well as you. Sherasmin obeyed, and on the instant the cup was filled with delicious wine, a draught of which restored vigor to his limbs and made him feel young again. Overcome with gratitude, he threw himself on his knees, but the dwarf raised him, and bade him sit beside him, and thus commenced his history:

"Julius Cæsar, going by sea to join his army, was driven by a storm to take shelter in the island of Celea, where dwelt the fairy Glorianda. From this renowned pair I draw my birth. I am the inheritor of that which was most admirable in each of my parents: my father's heroic qualities and my mother's beauty and magic art. But a malicious sister of my mother's, in revenge for some slight offence, touched me with her wand when I was only five years old and forbade me to grow any bigger; and my mother, with all her power, was unable to annul the sentence. I have thus continued in-

fantile in appearance, though full of years and experience.
The power which I derive from my mother I use sometimes for my own diversion, but always to promote justice and to reward virtue. I am able and willing to assist
you, Duke of Guienne, for I know the errand on which
you come hither. I presage for you, if you follow my
counsels, complete success, and the beautiful Clarimunda for a wife."

When he had thus spoken, he presented to Huon the
precious and useful cup, which had the faculty of filling
itself when a good man took it in his hand. He gave him
also his beautiful horn of ivory, saying to him, "Huon,
when you sound this gently, you will make the hearers
dance, as you have seen; but if you sound it forcibly,
fear not that I shall hear it, though at a hundred leagues'
distance, and will fly to your relief; but be careful not to
sound it in that way, unless upon the most urgent occasion."

Oberon directed Huon what course he should take to
reach the country of the Sultan Gaudisso. "You will encounter great perils," said he, "before arriving there, and
I fear me," he added, with tears in his eyes, "that you
will not in everything obey my directions, and in that
case you will suffer much calamity." Then he embraced
Huon and Sherasmin and left them.

Huon and his follower travelled many days through
the desert before they reached any inhabited place, and
all this while the wonderful cup sustained them, furnish-
ing them not only wine, but food also. At last they came
to a great city. As day was declining, they entered its
suburbs, and Sherasmin, who spoke the Saracen language perfectly, inquired for an inn where they could
pass the night. A person who appeared to be one of the
principal inhabitants, seeing two strangers of respectable
appearance making this inquiry, stepped forward and
begged them to accept the shelter of his mansion. They
entered, and their host did the honors of his abode with a
politeness which they were astonished to see in a Saracen.
He had them served with coffee and sherbet, and all was
conducted with great decorum, till one of the servants
awkwardly overturned a cup of hot coffee on the host's
legs, when he started up, exclaiming in very good Gascon,

"Blood and thunder! you blockhead, you deserve to be thrown over the mosque!"

Huon could not help laughing to see the vivacity and the language of his country thus break out unawares. The host, who had no idea that his guests understood his words, was astonished when Huon addressed him in the dialect of his country. Immediately confidence was established between them; especially when the domestics had retired. The host, seeing that he was discovered and that the two pretended Saracens were from the borders of the Garonne, embraced them and disclosed that he was a Christian. Huon, who had learned prudence from the advice of Oberon, to test his host's sincerity, drew from his robe the cup which the Fairy-king had given him and presented it empty to the host. "A fair cup," said he, "but I should like it better if it was full." Immediately it was so. The host, astonished, dared not put it to his lips. "Drink boldly, my dear fellow-countryman," said Huon; "your truth is proved by this cup, which only fills itself in the hands of an honest man." The host did not hesitate longer; the cup passed freely from hand to hand; their mutual cordiality increased as it passed, and each recounted his adventures. Those of Huon redoubled his host's respect, for he recognized in him his legitimate sovereign: while the host's narrative was in these words:

"My name is Floriac; this great and strong city, you will hear with surprise and grief, is governed by a brother of Duke Sevinus, and your uncle. You have no doubt heard that a young brother of the Duke of Guienne was stolen away from the seashore, with his companions, by some corsairs. I was then his page, and we were carried by those corsairs to Barbary, where we were sold for slaves. The Barbary prince sent us as part of the tribute which he yearly paid to his sovereign, the Sultan Gaudisso. Your uncle, who had been somewhat puffed up by the flattery of his attendants, thought to increase his importance with his new master by telling him his rank. The sultan, who, like a true Mussulman, detested all Christian princes, exerted himself from that moment to bring him over to the Saracen faith. He succeeded but too well. Your uncle, seduced by the arts of the santons and by the pleasures and indulgences which the sultan allowed him, committed the horrid crime of apostasy; he renounced his baptism and embraced Mahometanism. Gaudisso then loaded him with honors, made him espouse one of his nieces, and sent him to reign over this city and adjoining country. Your uncle preserved for me the same friendship which he had had when a boy; but all his caresses and efforts could not make me renounce my faith. Perhaps he respected me in his heart for my resistance to his persuasians, perhaps he had hopes of inducing me in time to imitate him. He made me accompany him to this city, of which he was master, he gave me his confidence, and permits me to keep in my service some Christians, whom I protect for the sake of their faith."

"Ah!" exclaimed Huon, "take me to this guilty uncle. A prince of the house of Guienne, must he not blush at the cowardly abandonment of the faith of his fathers?"

"Alas!" replied Floriac, "I fear he will neither be sensible of shame at your reproaches, nor of pleasure at the sight of a nephew so worthy of his lineage. Brutified by sensuality, jealous of his power, which he often exercises with cruelty, he will more probably restrain you by force or put you to death."

"Be it so," said the brave and fervent Huon, "I could not die in a better cause; and I demand of you to conduct me to him to-morrow, after having told him of my arrival and my birth." Floriac still objected, but Huon would take no denial, and he promised obedience.

Next morning Floriac waited upon the governor and told him of the arrival of his nephew, Huon of Bordeaux, and of the intention of the prince to present himself at his court that very day. The governor, surprised, did not immediately answer, though he at once made up his mind what to do. He knew that Floriac loved Christians and the princes of his native land too well to aid in any treason to one of them; he therefore feigned great pleasure at hearing of the arrival of the eldest born of his family at his court. He immediately sent Floriac to find him; he caused his palace to be put in festal array, his divan to be assembled, and, after giving some secret orders, went himself to meet his nephew, whom he introduced under his proper name and title to all the great officers of his court.

Huon burned with indignation at seeing his uncle with forehead encircled with a rich turban, surmounted with a crescent of precious stones. His natural candor made him receive with pain the embraces which the treacherous governor lavished upon him. Meanwhile, the hope of finding a suitable moment to reproach him for his apostasy made him submit to those honors which his uncle caused to be rendered to him. The governor evaded with address the chance of being alone with Huon, and spent all the morning in taking him through his gardens and palace. At last, when the hour of dinner approached, and the governor took him by the hand to lead him into the dining-hall, Huon seized the opportunity and said to him in a low voice, "Oh, my uncle! Oh, Prince, brother of the Duke Sevinus! in what condition have I the grief and shame of seeing you!" The governor pretended to be moved, pressed his hand, and whispered in his ear, "Silence! my dear nephew; to-morrow morning I will hear you fully."

Huon, comforted a little by these words, took his seat at the table by the side of the governor. The mufti, some cadis, agas, and santons, filled the other places. Sherasmin sat down with them; but Floriac, who would not lose sight of his guests, remained standing and passed in and out to observe what was going on within the palace. He soon perceived a number of armed men gliding through the passages and antechambers connected with the dining-hall. He was about to enter to give his guests notice of what he had seen when he heard a violent noise and commotion in the hall. The cause was this.

Huon and Sherasmin were well enough suited with the first course, and ate with good appetite; but the people of their country not being accustomed to drink only water at their meals, Huon and Sherasmin looked at one another, not very well pleased at such a regimen. Huon laughed outright at the impatience of Sherasmin, but soon, experiencing the same want himself, he drew forth Oberon's cup and made the sign of the cross. The cup filled, and he drank it off, and handed it to Sherasmin, who followed his example. The governor and his officers, seeing this abhorred sign, contracted their brows and sat in silent consternation. Huon pretended not to observe it, and having filled the cup again, handed it to his uncle, saying, "Pray join us, dear uncle; it is excellent Bordeaux wine, the drink that will be to you like mother's milk." The governor, who often drank in secret with his favorite sultanas the wines of Greece and Shiraz, never in public drank anything but water. He had not for a long time tasted the excellent wines of his native land; he was sorely tempted to drink what was now handed to him, it looked so bright in the cup, outshining the gold itself. He stretched forth his hand, took the brimming goblet and raised it to his lips, when immediately it dried up and disappeared. Huon and Sherasmin, like Gascons as they were, laughed at his astonishment. "Christian dogs!" he exclaimed, "do you dare to insult me at my own table? But I will soon be revenged." At these words he threw the cup at the head of his nephew, who caught it with his left hand while, with the other, he snatched the turban, with its crescent, from the governor's head and threw it on the floor. All the Saracens started up from table, with loud outcries, and prepared to avenge the insult. Huon and Sherasmin put themselves on their defence and met with their swords the scimitars directed against them. At this moment, the doors of the hall opened and a crowd of soldiers and armed eunuchs rushed in, who joined in the attack upon Huon and Sherasmin. The prince and his followers took refuge on a broad shelf or sideboard, where they kept at bay the crowd of assailants, making the most forward of them smart for their audacity. But more troops came pressing in, and the brave Huon, inspired by the wine of Bordeaux and not angry enough to lose his relish for a joke, blew a gentle note on his horn, and no sooner was it heard than it quelled the rage of the combatants and set them to dancing. Huon and Sherasmin, no longer attacked, looked down from their elevated position on a scene the most singular and amusing. Very soon the sultanas, hearing the sound of the dance, and finding their guards withdrawn, came into the hall and mixed with the dancers. The favorite sultana seized upon a young santon, who performed jumps two feet high; but soon the long dresses of this couple got intermingled and threw them down. The santon's beard was caught in the sultana's necklace, and they could not disentangle them. The governor by no means approved this familiarity, and took two steps forward to get at the santon, but he stumbled over a prostrate dervise and measured his length on the floor. The dancing continued till the strength of the performers was exhausted, and they fell, one after the other, and lay helpless. The governor at length made signs to Huon that he would yield everything, if he would but allow him to rest. The bargain was ratified; the governor allowed Huon and Sherasmin to depart on their way, and even gave them a ring which would procure them safe passage through his country and access to the Sultan Gaudisso. The two friends hastened to avail themselves of this favorable turn, and, taking leave of Floriac, pursued their journey.

HUON OF BORDEAUX

CONTINUED

Huon had seen many beauties at his mother's court, but his heart had never been touched with love. Honor had been his mistress, and in pursuit of that he had never found time to give a thought to softer cares. Strange that a heart so insensible should first be touched by something so unsubstantial as a dream; but so it was.

The day after the adventure with his uncle, night overtook the travellers as they passed through a forest. A grotto offered them shelter from the night dews. The magic cup supplied their evening meal, for such was its virtue that it afforded not only wine, but more solid fare when desired. Fatigue soon threw them into profound repose. Lulled by the murmur of the foliage and breathing the fragrance of the flowers, Huon dreamed that a lady more beautiful than he had ever before seen hung over him and imprinted a kiss upon his lips. As he stretched out his arms to embrace her, a sudden gust of wind swept her away.

Huon awoke in an agony of regret. A few moments

sufficed to afford some consolation in showing him that
what had passed was but a dream; but his perplexity and
sadness could not escape the notice of Sherasmin.
Huon hesitated not to inform his faithful follower of
the reason of his pensiveness, and got nothing in return
but his rallyings for allowing himself to be disturbed by
such a cause. He recommended a draught from the fairy
goblet, and Huon tried it with good effect.

At early dawn, they resumed their way. They travelled
till high noon, but said little to one another. Huon was
musing on his dream, and Sherasmin's thoughts flew back
to his early days on the banks of the flowery Garonne.

On a sudden they were startled by the cry of distress, and, turning an angle of the wood, came where a
knight hard pressed was fighting with a furious lion. The
knight's horse lay dead, and it seemed as if another moment would end the combat, for terror and fatigue
had quite disabled the knight for further resistance. He
fell, and the lion's paw was raised over him, when a blow
from Huon's sword turned the monster's rage upon a new
enemy. His roar shook the forest, and he crouched in
act to spring, when, with the rapidity of lightning,
Huon plunged his sword into his side. He rolled over on the
plain in the agonies of death.

They raised the knight from the ground, and Sherasmin
hastened to offer him a draught from the fairy cup. The
wine sparkled to the brim, and the warrior put forth his
lips to quaff it, but it shrunk away and did not even wet
his lips. He dashed the goblet angrily on the ground, with
an exclamation of resentment. This incident did not tend
to make either party more acceptable to the other,
and what followed was worse. For when Huon said, "Sir
knight, thank God for your deliverance"—"Thank Mahomet, rather, yourself," said he, "for he has led you this
day to render service to no less a personage than the
Prince of Hyrcania."

At the sound of this blasphemy, Huon drew his sword
and turned upon the miscreant, who, little disposed to
encounter the prowess of which he had so lately seen
proof, betook himself to flight. He ran to Huon's horse,
and, lightly vaulting on his back, clapped spurs to his
side, and galloped out of sight.

The adventure was vexatious, yet there was no remedy. The prince and Sherasmin continued their journey with the aid of the remaining horse as they best might. At length, as evening set in, they descried the pinnacles and towers of a great city full before them, which they knew to be the famous city of Bagdad.

They were well nigh exhausted with fatigue when they arrived at its precincts, and in the darkness, not knowing what course to take, were glad to meet an aged woman, who, in reply to their inquiries, offered them such accommodations as her cottage could supply. They thankfully accepted the offer and entered the low door. The good dame busily prepared the best fare her stores supplied—milk, figs, and peaches—deeply regretting that the bleak winds had nipped her almond-trees.

Sir Huon thought he had never in his life tasted any fare so good. The old lady talked while her guests ate. She doubted not, she said, they had come to be present at the great feast in honor of the marriage of the sultan's daughter, which was to take place on the morrow. They asked who the bridegroom was to be, and the old lady answered, "The Prince of Hyrcania," but added, "Our princess hates him, and would rather wed a dragon than him." "How know you that?" asked Huon, and the dame informed him that she had it from the princess herself, who was her foster-child. Huon inquired the reason of the princess's aversion, and the woman, pleased to find her chat excite so much interest, replied that it was all in consequence of a dream. "A dream!" exclaimed Huon. "Yes! a dream. She dreamed that she was a hind, and that the prince, as a hunter, was pursuing her, and had almost overtaken her when a beautiful dwarf appeared in view, drawn in a golden car, having by his side a young man of yellow hair and fair complexion, like one from a foreign land. She dreamed that the car stopped where she stood, and that, having resumed her own form, she was about to ascend it when suddenly it faded from her view, and with it the dwarf and the fair-haired youth. But from her heart that vision did not fade, and from that time her affianced bridegroom, the Hyrcanian prince, had become odious to her sight. Yet the sultan, her father, by no means regarding such a cause as suffi-

cient to prevent the marriage, had named the morrow as
the time when it should be solemnized, in presence of his
court and many princes of the neighboring countries,
whom the fame of the princess's beauty and the bridegroom's splendor had brought to the scene."

We may suppose this conversation woke a tumult of
thoughts in the breast of Huon. Was it not clear that Providence led him on and cleared the way for his happy success? Sleep did not early visit the eyes of Huon that
night; but, with the sanguine temper of youth, he in-
dulged his fancy in imagining the sequel of his strange
experience.

The next day, which he could not but regard as the
decisive day of his fate, he prepared to deliver the message of Charlemagne. Clad in his armor, fortified with his
ivory horn and his ring, he reached the palace of Gaudisso when the guests were assembled at the banquet.
As he approached the gate, a voice called on all true be-
lievers to enter; and Huon, the brave and faithful
Huon, in his impatience passed in under that false pretension. He had no sooner passed the barrier than he
felt ashamed of his baseness, and was overwhelmed
with regret. To make amends for his fault, he ran forward
to the second gate and cried to the porter, "Dog of a
misbeliever, I command you, in the name of Him who
died on the cross, open to me!" The points of a hundred
weapons immediately opposed his passage. Huon then
remembered for the first time the ring he had received
from his uncle, the governor. He produced it and demanded to be led to the sultan's presence. The officer
of the guard recognized the ring, made a respectful obeisance, and allowed him free entrance. In the same way,
he passed the other doors to the rich saloon where the
great sultan was at dinner with his tributary princes. At
sight of the ring, the chief attendant led Huon to the
head of the hall and introduced him to the sultan
and his princes as the ambassador of Charlemagne. A
seat was provided for him near the royal party.

The Prince of Hyrcania, the same whom Huon had rescued from the lion, and who was the destined bridegroom of the beautiful Clarimunda, sat on the sultan's
right hand, and the princess herself on his left. It chanced

that Huon found himself near the seat of the princess, and hardly were the ceremonies of reception over before he made haste to fulfil the commands of Charlemagne by imprinting a kiss upon her rosy lips, and after that a second, not by command, but by good will. The Prince of Hyrcania cried out, "Audacious infidel! take the reward of thy insolence!" and aimed a blow at Huon, which, if it had reached him, would have brought his embassy to a speedy termination. But the ingrate failed of his aim, and Huon punished his blasphemy and ingratitude at once by a blow which severed his head from his body.

So suddenly had all this happened that no hand had been raised to arrest it; but now Gaudisso cried out, "Seize the murderer!" Huon was hemmed in on all sides, but his redoubtable sword kept the crowd of courtiers at bay. But he saw new combatants enter and could not hope to maintain his ground against so many. He recollected his horn and, raising it to his lips, blew a blast almost as loud as that of Roland at Roncesvalles. It was in vain. Oberon heard it, but the sin of which Huon had been guilty in bearing, though but for a moment, the character of a believer in the false prophet, had put it out of Oberon's power to help him. Huon, finding himself deserted, and conscious of the cause, lost his strength and energy, was seized, loaded with chains, and plunged into a dungeon.

His life was spared for the time, merely that he might be reserved for a more painful death. The sultan meant that, after being made to feel all the torments of hunger and despair, he should be flayed alive.

But an enchanter more ancient and more powerful than Oberon himself interested himself for the brave Huon. That enchanter was Love. The Princess Clarimunda learned with horror the fate to which the young prince was destined. By the aid of her governante, she gained over the keeper of the prison and went herself to lighten the chains of her beloved. It was her hand that removed his fetters, from her he received supplies of food to sustain a life which he devoted from thenceforth wholly to her. After the most tender explanations the princess departed, promising to repeat her visit on the morrow.

The next day she came, according to promise, and again brought supplies of food. These visits were continued during a whole month. Huon was too good a son of the Church to forget that the amiable princess was a Saracen, and he availed himself of these interviews to instruct her in the true faith. How easy it is to believe the truth when uttered by the lips of those we love! Clarimunda ere long professed her entire belief in the Christian doctrines and desired to be baptized.

Meanwhile, the sultan had repeatedly inquired of the jailer how his prisoner bore the pains of famine, and learned to his surprise that he was not yet much reduced thereby. On his repeating the inquiry, after a short interval, the keeper replied that the prisoner had died suddenly, and had been buried in the cavern. The sultan could only regret that he had not sooner ordered the execution of the sentence.

While these things were going on, the faithful Sherasmin, who had not accompanied Huon in his last adventure, but had learned by common rumor the result of it, came to the court in hopes of doing something for the rescue of his master. He presented himself to the sultan as Solario, his nephew. Guadisso received him with kindness, and all the courtiers loaded him with attentions. He soon found means to inform himself how the princess regarded the brave but unfortunate Huon, and, having made himself known to her, confidence was soon established between them. Clarimunda readily consented to assist in the escape of Huon and to quit with him her father's court to repair to that of Charlemagne. Their united efforts had nearly perfected their arrangement, a vessel was secretly prepared, and all things in forwardness for the flight, when an unlooked-for obstacle presented itself. Huon himself positively refused to go, leaving the orders of Charlemagne unexecuted.

Sherasmin was in despair. Bitterly he complained of the fickleness and cruelty of Oberon in withdrawing his aid at the very crisis when it was most necessary. Earnestly he urged every argument to satisfy the prince that he had done enough for honor and could not be held bound to achieve impossibilities. But all was of no avail, and he

knew not which way to turn, when one of those events occurred which are so frequent under Turkish despotisms.
A courier arrived at the court of the sultan, bearing the
ring of his sovereign, the mighty Agrapard, Caliph of
Arabia, and bringing the bow-string for the neck of Gaudisso. No reason was assigned; none but the pleasure of
the caliph is ever required in such cases; but it was
suspected that the bearer of the bow-string had persuaded the caliph that Gaudisso, whose rapacity was
well known, had accumulated immense treasures which
he had not duly shared with his sovereign, and thus had
obtained an order to supersede him in his emirship.

The body of Gaudisso would have been cast out a prey
to dogs and vultures had not Sherasmin, under the character of nephew of the deceased, been permitted to receive it and give it decent burial, which he did, but not till
he had taken possession of the beard and grinders,
agreeably to the orders of Charlemagne.

No obstacle now stood in the way of the lovers and
their faithful follower in returning to France. They sailed,
taking Rome in their way, where the Holy Father himself
blessed the union of his nephew, Duke Huon of Bordeaux,
with the Princess Clarimunda.

Soon afterwards they arrived in France, where Huon
laid his trophies at the feet of Charlemagne, and, being
restored to the favor of the Emperor, hastened to present himself and his bride to the duchess, his mother,
and to the faithful liegemen of his province of Guienne
and his city of Bordeaux, where the pair were received
with transports of joy.

OGIER THE DANE

Ogier the Dane was the son of Geoffroy, who wrested
Denmark from the pagans and reigned the first Christia
king of that country. When Ogier was born, and before
he was baptized, six ladies of ravishing beauty appeared
all at once in the chamber of the infant. They encircled
him, and she who appeared the eldest took him in her

arms, kissed him, and laid her hand upon his heart. "I give you," said she, "to be the bravest warrior of your times." She delivered the infant to her sister, who said, "I give you abundant opportunities to display your valor." "Sister," said the third lady, "you have given him a dangerous boon; I give him that he shall never be vanquished." The fourth sister added, as she laid her hand upon his eyes and his mouth, "I give you the gift of pleasing." The fifth said, "Lest all these gifts serve only to betray, I give you sensibility to return the love you inspire." Then spoke Morgana, the youngest and handsomest of the group, "Charming creature, I claim you for my own; and I give you not to die till you shall have come to pay me a visit in my isle of Avalon." Then she kissed the child and departed with her sisters.

After this, the king had the child carried to the font and baptized with the name of Ogier.

In his education, nothing was neglected to elevate him to the standard of a perfect knight and render him accomplished in all the arts necessary to make him a hero.

He had hardly reached the age of sixteen years when Charlemagne, whose power was established over all the sovereigns of his time, recollected that Geoffroy, Ogier's father, had omitted to render the homage due to him as Emperor and sovereign lord of Denmark, one of the grand fiefs of the empire. He accordingly sent an embassy to demand of the King of Denmark this homage, and on receiving a refusal couched in haughty terms, sent an army to enforce the demand. Geoffroy, after an unsuccessful resistance, was forced to comply, and as a pledge of his sincerity delivered Ogier, his eldest son, a hostage to Charles, to be brought up at his court. He was placed in charge of the Duke Namo of Bavaria, the friend of his father, who treated him like his own son.

Ogier grew up more and more handsome and amiable every day. He surpassed in form, strength, and address all the noble youths his companions; he failed not to be present at all tourneys; he was attentive to the elder knights and burned with impatience to imitate them. Yet his heart rose sometimes in secret against his condition as a hostage and as one apparently forgotten by his father.

The King of Denmark, in fact, was at this time occupied with new loves. Ogier's mother having died, he had married a second wife, and had a son named Guyon. The new queen had absolute power over her husband, and fearing that, if he should see Ogier again, he would give him the preference over Guyon, she had adroitly persuaded him to delay rendering his homage to Charlemagne, till now four years had passed away since the last renewal of that ceremony. Charlemagne, irritated at this delinquency, drew closer the bonds of Ogier's captivity until he should receive a response from the King of Denmark to a fresh summons which he caused to be sent to him.

The answer of Geoffroy was insulting and defiant, and the rage of Charlemagne was roused in the highest degree. He was at first disposed to wreak his vengeance upon Ogier, his hostage; but at the entreaties of Duke Namo, who felt towards his pupil like a father, consented to spare his life, if Ogier would swear fidelity to him as his liege-lord and promise not to quit his court without his permission. Ogier accepted these terms, and was allowed to retain all the freedom he had before enjoyed.

The Emperor would have immediately taken arms to reduce his disobedient vassal, if he had not been called off in another direction by a message from Pope Leo, imploring his assistance. The Saracens had landed in the neighborhood of Rome, occupied Mount Janiculum, and prepared to pass the Tiber and carry fire and sword to the capital of the Christian world. Charlemagne hesitated not to yield to the entreaties of the Pope. He speedily assembled an army, crossed the Alps, traversed Italy, and arrived at Spoleto, a strong place to which the Pope had retired. Leo, at the head of his cardinals, advanced to meet him and rendered him homage, as to the son of Pepin, the illustrious protector of the Holy See, coming, as his father had done, to defend it in the hour of need.

Charlemagne stopped but two days at Spoleto and, learning that the infidels, having rendered themselves masters of Rome, were besieging the Capitol, which could not long hold out against them, marched promptly to attack them.

The advanced posts of the army were commanded by Duke Namo, on whom Ogier waited as his squire. He did not yet bear arms, not having received the order of knighthood. The Oriflamme, the royal standard, was borne by a knight named Alory, who showed himself unworthy of the honor.

Duke Namo, seeing a strong body of the infidels advancing to attack him, gave the word to charge them. Ogier remained in the rear, with the other youths, grieving much that he was not permitted to fight. Very soon he saw Alory lower the Oriflamme and turn his horse in flight. Ogier pointed him out to the young men and, seizing a club, rushed upon Alory and struck him from his horse. Then, with his companions, he disarmed him, clothed himself in his armor, raised the Oriflamme, and, mounting the horse of the unworthy knight, flew to the front rank, where he joined Duke Namo, drove back the infidels, and carried the Oriflamme quite through their broken ranks. The duke, thinking it was Alory, whom he had not held in high esteem, was astonished at his strength and valor. Ogier's young companions imitated him, supplying themselves with armor from the bodies of the slain; they followed Ogier and carried death into the ranks of the Saracens, who fell back in confusion upon their main body.

Duke Namo now ordered a retreat, and Ogier obeyed with reluctance, when they perceived Charlemagne advancing to their assistance. The combat now became general, and was more terrible than ever. Charlemagne had overthrown Corsuble, the commander of the Saracens, and had drawn his famous sword, Joyeuse, to cut off his head, when two Saracen knights set upon him at once, one of whom slew his horse, and the other overthrew the Emperor on the sand. Perceiving by the eagle on his casque who he was, they dismounted in haste to give him his death-blow. Never was the life of the Emperor in such peril. But Ogier, who saw him fall, flew to his rescue. Though embarrassed with the Oriflamme, he pushed his horse against one of the Saracens and knocked him down, and, with his sword, dealt the other so vigorous a blow that he fell stunned to the earth. Then helping the Emperor to rise, he remounted him on the horse of one of the fallen knights. "Brave and generous Alory!" Charles exclaimed, "I owe to you my honor and my life!" Ogier made no answer; but, leaving Charlemagne surrounded by a great many of the knights who had flown to his succor, he plunged into the thickest ranks of the enemy and carried the Oriflamme, followed by a gallant train of youthful warriors, till the standard of Mahomet turned in retreat and the infidels sought safety in their intrenchments.

Then the good Archbishop Turpin laid aside his helmet and his bloody sword (for he always felt that he was clearly in the line of his duty while slaying infidels), took his mitre and his crosier, and intoned Te Deum.

At this moment, Ogier, covered with blood and dust, came to lay the Oriflamme at the feet of the Emperor. He was followed by a train of warriors of short stature, who walked ill at ease loaded with armor too heavy for them. Ogier knelt at the feet of Charlemagne, who embraced him, calling him Alory, while Turpin, from the height of the altar, blessed him with all his might. Then young Orlando, son of the Count Milone and nephew of Charlemagne, no longer able to endure this misapprehension, threw down his helmet and ran to unlace Ogier's, while the other young men laid aside theirs. Our author says he cannot express the surprise, the admiration, and the tenderness of the Emperor and his peers. Charles folded Ogier in his arms, and the happy fathers of those brave youths embraced them with tears of joy. The good Duke Namo stepped forward, and Charlemagne yielded Ogier to his embrace. "How much do I owe you," he said, "good and wise friend, for having restrained my anger! My dear Ogier! I owe you my life! My sword leaps to touch your shoulder, yours, and those of your brave young friends." At these words he drew that famous sword, Joyeuse, and, while Ogier and the rest knelt before him, gave them the accolade conferring on them the order of knighthood. The young Orlando and his cousin Oliver could not refrain, even in the presence of the Emperor, from falling upon Ogier's neck and pledging with him that brotherhood in arms, so dear and so sacred to the knights of old times; but Charlot, the Emperor's son, at the sight of the glory with which Ogier had covered himself, conceived the blackest jealousy and hate.

The rest of the day and the next were spent in the rejoicings of the army. Turpin, in a solemn service, implored the favor of Heaven upon the youthful knights and blessed the white armor which was prepared for them. Duke Namo presented them with golden spurs, Charles himself girded on their swords. But what was his astonishment when he examined that intended for Ogier! The loving fairy, Morgana, had had the art to change it and to substitute one of her own procuring, and when Charles drew it out of the scabbard, these words appeared written on the steel: "My name is Cortana, of the same steel and temper as Joyeuse and Durindana." Charles saw that a superior power watched over the destinies of Ogier; he vowed to love him as a father would, and Ogier promised him the devotion of a son. Happy had it been for both if they had always continued mindful of their promises.

The Saracen army had hardly recovered from its dismay when Carahue, King of Mauritania, who was one of the knights overthrown by Ogier at the time of the rescue of Charlemagne, determined to challenge him to single combat. With that view, he assumed the dress of a herald, resolved to carry his own message. The French knights admired his air and said to one another that he seemed more fit to be a knight than a bearer of messages.

Carahue began by passing the warmest eulogium upon the knight who bore the Oriflamme on the day of the battle, and concluded by saying that Carahue, King of Mauritania, respected that knight so much that he challenged him to the combat.

Ogier had risen to reply, when he was interrupted by Charlot, who said that the gage of the King of Mauritania could not fitly be received by a vassal, living in captivity; by which he meant Ogier, who was at that time serving as hostage for his father. Fire flashed from the eyes of Ogier, but the presence of the Emperor restrained his speech, and he was calmed by the kind looks of Charlemagne, who said, with an angry voice, "Silence, Charlot! By the life of Bertha, my queen, he who has saved my life is as dear to me as yourself. Ogier," he continued, "you are no longer a hostage. Herald! report my answer to your master, that never does knight of my court refuse a challenge on equal terms. Ogier the Dane accepts of his, and I myself am his security."

Carahue, profoundly bowing, replied, "My lord, I was sure that the sentiments of so great a sovereign as yourself would be worthy of your high and brilliant fame; I shall report your answer to my master, who I know admires you and unwillingly takes arms against you." Then, turning to Charlot, whom he did not know as the son of the Emperor, he continued, "As for you, Sir Knight, if the desire of battle inflames you, I have it in charge from Sadon, cousin of the King of Maritania, to give the like defiance to any French knights who will grant him the honor of the combat."

Charlot, inflamed with rage and vexation at the public reproof which he had just received, hesitated not to deliver his gage. Carahue received it with Ogier's, and it was agreed that the combat should be on the next day, in a meadow environed by woods and equally distant from both armies.

The perfidious Charlot meditated the blackest treason. During the night, he collected some knights unworthy of the name and like himself in their ferocious manners; he made them swear to avenge his injuries, armed them in black armor, and sent them to lie in ambush in the wood, with orders to make a pretended attack upon the whole party, but in fact to lay heavy hands upon Ogier and the two Saracens.

At the dawn of day, Sadon and Carahue, attended only by two pages to carry their spears, took their way to the appointed meadow; and Charlot and Ogier repaired thither also, but by different paths. Ogier advanced with a calm air, saluted courteously the two Saracen knights, and joined them in arranging the terms of combat.

While this was going on, the perfidious Charlot remained behind and gave his men the signal to advance. That cowardly troop issued from the wood and encompassed the three knights. All three were equally surprised at the attack, but neither of them suspected the other to have any hand in the treason. Seeing the attack made equally upon them all, they united their efforts to

resist it and made the most forward of the assilants bite
the dust. Cortana fell on no one without inflicting a mortal
wound, but the sword of Carahue was not of equal temper
and broke in his hands. At the same instant, his horse
was slain, and Carahue fell, without a weapon and entangled with his prostrate horse. Ogier, who saw it, ran
to his defence, and, leaping to the ground, covered the
prince with his shield, supplied him with the sword of
one of the fallen ruffians, and would have had him mount
his own horse. At that moment, Charlot, inflamed with
rage, pushed his horse upon Ogier, knocked him down,
and would have run him through with his lance if Sadon,
who saw the treason, had not sprung upon him and thrust
him back. Carahue leapt lightly upon the horse which
Ogier presented him and had time only to exclaim,
"Brave Ogier, I am no longer your enemy, I pledge to
you an eternal friendship," when numerous Saracen
knights were seen approaching, having discovered the
treachery, and Charlot with his followers took refuge in
the wood.

The troop which advanced was commanded by
Dannemont, the exiled King of Denmark, whom Geoffroy,
Ogier's father, had driven from his throne and compelled
to take refuge with the Saracens. Learning who Ogier
was, he instantly declared him his prisoner, in spite of
the urgent remonstrances and even threats of Carahue
and Sadon, and carried him, under a strong guard, to the
Saracen camp. Here he was at first subjected to the most
rigorous captivity, but Carahue and Sadon insisted so
vehemently on his release, threatening to turn their arms
against their own party if it was not granted, while Dannemont as eagerly opposed the measure, that Corsuble, the
Saracen commander, consented to a middle course and
allowed Ogier the freedom of his camp, upon his promise
not to leave it without permission.

Carahue was not satisfied with this partial concession.
He left the city next morning, proceeded to the camp of
Charlemagne, and demanded to be led to the Emperor.
When he reached his presence, he dismounted from his
horse, took off his helmet, drew his sword, and, holding
it by the blade, presented it to Charlemagne as he knelt
before him.

"Illustrious prince," he said, "behold before you the herald who brought the challenge to your knights from the King of Mauritania. The cowardly old King Dannemont has made the brave Ogier prisoner, and has prevailed on our general to refuse to give him up. I come to make amends for this ungenerous conduct by yielding myself, Carahue, King of Mauritania, your prisoner."

Charlemagne, with all his peers, admired the magnanimity of Carahue; he raised him, embraced him, and restored to him his sword. "Prince," said he, "your presence and the bright example you afford my knights consoles me for the loss of Ogier. Would to God you might receive our holy faith and be wholly united with us." All the lords of the court, led by Duke Namo, paid their respects to the King of Mauritania. Charlot only failed to appear, fearing to be recognized as a traitor; but the heart of Carahue was too noble to pierce that of Charlemagne by telling him the treachery of his son.

Meanwhile the Saracen army was rent by discord. The troops of Carahue clamored against the commander-in-chief because their king was left in captivity. They even threatened to desert the cause and turn their arms against their allies. Charlemagne pressed the siege vigorously, till at length the Saracen leaders found themselves compelled to abandon the city and betake themselves to their ships. A truce was made; Ogier was exchanged for Carahue, and the two friends embraced one another with vows of perpetual brotherhood. The Pope was reestablished in his dominions, and Italy being tranquil, Charlemagne returned, with his peers and their followers, to France.

OGIER THE DANE

CONTINUED

Charlemagne had not forgotten the offence of Geoffroy, the King of Denmark, in withholding homage, and now prepared to enforce submission. But at this crisis he was waited upon by an embassy from Geoffroy, acknowledging his fault and craving assistance against an army of invaders who had attacked his states with a force which he was unable to repel. The soul of Charlemagne was too great to be implacable, and he took this opportunity to test that of Ogier, who had felt acutely the unkindness of his father in leaving him, without regard or notice, fifteen years in captivity. Charles asked Ogier whether, in spite of his father's neglect, he was disposed to lead an army to his assistance. He replied, "A son can never be excused from helping his father by any cause short of death." Charlemagne placed an army of a thousand knights under the command of Ogier, and great numbers more volunteered to march under so distinguished a leader. He flew to the succor of his father, repelled the invaders, and drove them in confusion to their vessels. Ogier then hastened to the capital, but as he drew near the city, he heard all the bells sounding a knell. He soon learned the cause; it was the obsequies of Geoffroy, the King. Ogier felt keenly the grief of not having been permitted to embrace his father once more and to learn his latest commands; but he found that his father had declared him heir to his throne. He hastened to the church where the body lay; he knelt and bathed the lifeless form with his tears. At that moment a celestial light beamed all around, and a voice as of an angel said, "Ogier, leave thy crown to Guyon, thy brother, and bear no other title than that of 'The Dane.' Thy destiny is glorious, and other kingdoms are reserved for thee." Ogier obeyed the divine behest. He saluted his stepmother respectfully, and, embracing his brother, told him that he was content with his lot in being reckoned among the paladins of Charlemagne, and resigned all claims to the crown of Denmark.

Ogier returned covered with glory to the court of Charlemagne, and the Emperor, touched with this proof of his attachment, loaded him with caresses and treated him almost as an equal.

We pass in silence the adventures of Ogier for several ensuing years, in which the fairy-gifts of his infancy showed their force in making him successful in all enterprises, both of love and war. He married the charming

Belicene and became the father of young Baldwin, a youth who seemed to inherit in full measure the strength and courage of his father and the beauty of his mother. When the lad was old enough to be separated from his mother, Ogier took him to court and presented him to Charlemagne, who embraced him and took him into his service. It seemed to Duke Namo and all the elder knights as if they saw in him Ogier himself, as he was when a youth; and this resemblance won for the lad their kind regards. Even Charlot at first seemed to be fond of him, though after a while the resemblance to Ogier which he noticed had the effect to excite his hatred.

Baldwin was attentive to Charlot and lost no occasion to be serviceable. The prince loved to play chess, and Baldwin, who played well, often made a party with him.

One day Charlot was nettled at losing two pieces in succession; he thought he could, by taking a piece from Baldwin, get some amends for his loss; but Baldwin, seeing him fall into a trap which he had set for him, could not help a slight laugh, as he said, "Check-mate." Charlot rose in a fury, seized the rich and heavy chess-board, and dashed it with all his strength on the head of Baldwin, who fell, and died where he fell.

Frightened at his own crime, and fearing the vengeance of the terrible Ogier, Charlot concealed himself in the interior of the palace. A young companion of Baldwin hastened and informed Ogier of the event. He ran to the chamber and beheld the body of his child bathed in blood, and it could not be concealed from him that Charlot gave the blow. Transported with rage, Ogier sought Charlot through the palace, and Charlot, feeling safe nowhere else, took refuge in the hall of Charlemagne, where he seated himself at table with Duke Namo and Salomon, Duke of Brittany. Ogier, with sword drawn, followed him to the very table of the Emperor. When a cupbearer attempted to bar his way, he struck the cup from his hand and dashed the contents in the Emperor's face. Charles rose in a passion, seized a knife, and would have plunged it into his breast, had not Salomon and another baron thrown themselves between, while Namo, who retained his ancient influence over Ogier, drew him out of the room. Foreseeing the consequences of this violence, pitying Ogier and, in his heart, excusing him, Namo hurried him away before the guards of the palace could arrest him, made him mount his horse, and leave Paris.

Charlemagne called together his peers and made them take an oath to do all in their power to arrest Ogier and bring him to condign punishment. Ogier on his part sent messages to the Emperor, offering to give himself up on condition that Charlot should be punished for his atrocious crime. The Emperor would listen to no conditions, and went in pursuit of Ogier at the head of a large body of soldiers. Ogier, on the other hand, was warmly supported by many knights, who pledged themselves in his defence. The contest raged long, with no decisive results. Ogier more than once had the Emperor in his power, but declined to avail himself of his advantage and released him without conditions. He even implored pardon for himself, but demanded at the same time the punishment of Charlot. But Charlemagne was too blindly fond of his unworthy son to subject him to punishment for the sake of conciliating one who had been so deeply injured.

At length, distressed at the blood which his friends had lost in his cause, Ogier dismissed his little army and, slipping away from those who wished to attend him, took his course to rejoin the Duke Guyon, his brother. On his way, having reached the forest of Ardennes, weary with long travel, the freshness of a retired valley tempted him to lie down to take some repose. He unsaddled Beiffror, relieved himself of his helmet, lay down on the turf, rested his head on his shield, and slept.

It so happened that Turpin, who occasionally recalled to mind that he was Archbishop of Rheims, was at that time in the vicinity, making a pastoral visit to the churches under his jurisdiction. But his dignity of peer of France, and his martial spirit, which caused him to be reckoned among the "preux chevaliers" of his time, forbade him to travel without as large a rctinue of knights as he had of clergymen. One of these was thirsty, and knowing the fountain on the borders of which Ogier was reposing, he rode to it, and was struck by the sight of a knight stretched on the ground. He hastened back and let the Archbishop know, who approached the fountain and recognized Ogier.

The first impulse of the good and generous Turpin was to save his friend, for whom he felt the warmest attachment; but his archdeacons and knights, who also recognized Ogier, reminded the archbishop of the oath which the Emperor had exacted of them all. Turpin could not be false to his oath; but it was not without a groan that he permitted his followers to bind the sleeping knight. The archbishop's attendants secured the horse and arms of Ogier and conducted their prisoner to the Emperor at Soissons.

The Emperor had become so much imbittered by Ogier's obstinate resistance, added to his original fault, that he was disposed to order him to instant death. But Turpin, seconded by the good Dukes Namo and Salomon, prayed so hard for him that Charlemagne consented to remit a violent death, but sentenced him to close imprisonment, under the charge of the archbishop, strictly limiting his food to one quarter of a loaf of bread per day, with one piece of meat and a quarter of a cup of wine. In this way he hoped to quickly put an end to his life without bringing on himself the hostility of the King of Denmark and other powerful friends of Ogier. He exacted a new oath of Turpin to obey his orders strictly.

The good archbishop loved Ogier too well not to cast about for some means of saving his life, which he foresaw he would soon lose if subjected to such scanty fare, for Ogier was seven feet tall and had an appetite in proportion. Turpin remembered, moreover, that Ogier was a true son of the Church, always zealous to propagate the faith and subdue unbelievers; so he felt justified in practising on this occasion what in later times has been entitled "mental reservation," without swerving from the letter of the oath which he had taken. This is the method he hit upon.

Every morning he had his prisoner supplied with a quarter of a loaf of bread, made of two bushels of flour; to this he added a quarter of a sheep or a fat calf, and he had a cup made which held forty pints of wine, and allowed Ogier a quarter of it daily.

Ogier's imprisonment lasted long; Charlemagne was astonished to hear, from time to time, that he still held out; and when he inquired more particularly of Turpin, the good archibishop, relying on his own understanding of the words, did not hesitate to affirm positively that he allowed his prisoner no more than the permitted ration.

We forgot to say that, when Ogier was led prisoner to Soissons, the Abbot of Saint Faron, observing the fine horse Beiffror, and not having at the time any other favor to ask of Charlemagne, begged the Emperor to give him the horse, and had him taken to his abbey. He was impatient to try his new acquisition, and, when he had arrived in his litter at the foot of the mountain where the horse had been brought to meet him, mounted him and rode onward. The horse, accustomed to bear the enormous weight of Ogier in his armor, when he perceived nothing on his back but the light weight of the abbot, whose long robes fluttered against his sides, ran away, making prodigious leaps over the steep acclivities of the mountain, till he reached the convent of Jouaire, where, in sight of the abbess and her nuns, he threw the abbot, already half dead with fright, to the ground. The abbot, bruised and mortified, revenged himself on poor Beiffror, whom he condemned, in his wrath, to be given to the workmen to drag stones for a chapel that he was building near the abbey. Thus, ill fed, hard-worked, and often beaten, the noble horse Beiffror passed the time while his master's imprisonment lasted.

That imprisonment would have been as long as his life if it had not been for some important events which forced the Emperor to set Ogier at liberty.

The Emperor learned at the same time that Carahue, King of Mauritania, was assembling an army to come and demand the liberation of Ogier; that Guyon, King of Denmark, was prepared to second the enterprise with all his forces; and, worse than all, that the Saracens, under Bruhier, Sultan of Arabia, had landed in Gascony, taken Bordeaux, and were marching with all speed for Paris.

Charlemagne now felt how necessary the aid of Ogier was to him. But, in spite of the representations of Turpin, Namo, and Salomon, he could not bring himself to consent to surrender Charlot to such punishment as Ogier should see fit to impose. Besides, he believed that Ogier was without strength and vigor, weakened by imprisonment and long abstinence.

At this crisis he received a message from Bruhier, proposing to put the issue upon the result of a combat between himself and the Emperor or his champion, promising, if defeated, to withdraw his army. Charlemagne would willingly have accepted the challenge, but his counsellors all opposed it. The herald was therefore told that the Emperor would take time to consider his proposition, and give his answer the next day.

It was during this interval that the three dukes succeeded in prevailing upon Charlemagne to pardon Ogier and to send for him to combat the puissant enemy who now defied him; but it was no easy task to persuade Ogier. The idea of his long imprisonment and the recollection of his son, bleeding and dying in his arms by the blow of the ferocious Charlot, made him long resist the urgency of his friends. Though glory called him to encounter Bruhier, and the safety of Christendom demanded the destruction of this proud enemy of the faith, Ogier only yielded at last on condition that Charlot should be delivered into his hands to be dealt with as he should see fit.

The terms were hard, but the danger was pressing, and Charlemagne, with a returning sense of justice and a strong confidence in the generous though passionate soul of Ogier, at last consented to them.

Ogier was led into the presence of Charlemagne by the three peers. The Emperor, faithful to his word, had caused Charlot to be brought into the hall where the high barons were assembled, his hands tied and his head uncovered. When the Emperor saw Ogier approach, he took Charlot by the arm, led him towards Ogier, and said these words: "I surrender the criminal; do with him as you think fit." Ogier, without replying, seized Charlot by the hair, forced him on his knees, and lifted with the other hand his irresistible sword. Charlemagne, who expected to see the head of his son rolling at his feet, shut his eyes and uttered a cry of horror.

Ogier had done enough. The next moment he raised Charlot, cut his bonds, kissed him on the mouth, and hastened to throw himself at the feet of the Emperor.

Nothing can exceed the surprise and joy of Charlemagne at seeing his son unharmed and Ogier kneeling at his feet. He folded him in his arms, bathed him with tears, and exclaimed to his barons, "I feel at this moment that Ogier is greater than I." As for Charlot, his base soul felt nothing but the joy of having escaped death; he remained such as he had been, and it was not till some years afterwards he received the punishment he deserved, from the hands of Huon of Bordeaux, as we have seen in a former chapter.

OGIER THE DANE

CONTINUED

When Charlemagne had somewhat recovered his composure, he was surprised to observe that Ogier appeared in good case and had a healthy color in his cheeks. He turned to the archbishop, who could not help blushing as he met his eye. "By the head of Bertha, my queen," said Charlemagne, "Ogier has had good quarters in your castle, my Lord Archbishop; but so much the more am I indebted to you." All the barons laughed and jested with Turpin, who only said, "Laugh as much as you please, my lords; but for my part I am not sorry to see the arm in full vigor that is to avenge us on the proud Saracen."

Charlemagne immediately despatched his herald, accepting the challenge and appointing the next day but one for the encounter. The proud and crafty Bruhier laughed scornfully when he heard the reply accepting his challenge, for he had a reliance on certain resources besides his natural strength and skill. However, he swore by Mahomet to observe the conditions as proposed and agreed upon.

Ogier now demanded his armor, and it was brought to him in excellent condition, for the good Turpin had kept it faithfully; but it was not easy to provide a horse for the occasion. Charlemagne had the best horses of his stables brought out, except Blanchard, his own charger; but all in vain; the weight of Ogier bent their backs to the ground. In this embarrassment the archbishop remembered that the Emperor had given Beiffror to the Abbot of St. Faron, and sent off a courier in haste to re-demand him.

Monks are hard masters, and the one who directed the laborers at the abbey had but too faithfully obeyed the orders of the abbot. Poor Beiffror was brought back lean, spiritless, and chafed with the harness of the vile cart that he had had to draw so long. He carried his head down and trod heavily before Charlemagne; but when he heard the voice of Ogier he raised his head, he neighed, his eyes flashed, his former ardor showed itself by the force with which he pawed the ground. Ogier caressed him, and the good steed seemed to return his caresses; Ogier mounted him, and Beiffror, proud of carrying his master again, leapt and curvetted with all his youthful vigor.

Nothing being now wanted, Charlemagne, at the head of his army, marched forth from the city of Paris and occupied the hill of Montmartre, whence the view extended over the plain of St. Denis, where the battle was to be fought.

When the appointed day came, the Dukes Namo and Salomon, as seconds of Ogier, accompanied him to the place marked out for the lists, and Bruhier, with two distinguished emirs, presented himself on the other side.

Bruhier was in high spirits and jested with his friends, as he advanced, upon the appearance of Beiffror. "Is that the horse they presume to match with Marchevallée, the best steed that ever fed in the vales of Mount Atlas?" But now the combatants, having met and saluted each other, ride apart, to come together in full career. Beiffror flew over the plain and met the adversary more than half-way. The lances of the two combatants were shivered at the shock, and Bruhier was astonished to see almost at the same instant the sword of Ogier gleaming above his head. He parried it with his buckler and gave Ogier a blow on his helmet, who returned it with another, better aimed or better seconded by the temper of his blade, for it cut away part of Bruhier's helmet, and with it his ear and part of his cheek. Ogier, seeing the blood, did not immediately repeat his blow, and Bruhier seized the moment to gallop off on one side. As he rode, he took a vase of gold which hung at his saddle-bow and bathed with its contents the wounded part. The blood instantly ceased to flow, the ear and the flesh were restored quite whole, and the Dane was astonished to see his antagonist return to the ground as sound as ever.

Bruhier laughed at his amazement. "Know," said he, "that I possess the precious balm that Joseph of Arimathea used upon the body of the crucified one, whom you worship. If I should lose an arm, I could restore it with a few drops of this. It is useless for you to contend with me. Yield yourself, and, as you appear to be a strong fellow, I will make you first oarsman in one of my galleys."

Ogier, though boiling with rage, forgot not to implore the assistance of Heaven. "O Lord," he exclaimed, "suffer not the enemy of thy name to profit by the powerful help of that which owes all its virtue to thy divine blood." At these words, he attacked Bruhier again with more vigor than ever; both struck terrible blows, and made grievous wounds; but the blood flowed from those of Ogier, while Bruhier stanched his by the application of his balm. Ogier, desperate at the unequal contest, grasped Cortana with both hands and struck his enemy such a blow that it cleft his buckler and cut off his arm with it; but Bruhier at the same time launched one at Ogier, which, missing him, struck the head of Beiffror, and the good horse fell and drew down his master in his fall.

Bruhier had time to leap to the ground, to pick up his arm, and apply his balsam; then, before Ogier had recovered his footing, he rushed forward with sword uplifted to complete his destruction.

Charlemagne, from the height of Montmartre, seeing the brave Ogier in this situation, groaned, and was ready to murmur against Providence; but the good Turpin, raising his arms, with a faith like that of Moses, drew down upon the Christian warrior the favor of Heaven.

Ogier, promptly disengaging himself, pressed Bruhier with so much impetuosity that he drove him to a distance from his horse, to whose saddle-bow the precious balm was suspended; and very soon Charlemagne saw Ogier, now completely in the advantage, bring his enemy to his knees, tear off his helmet, and, with a sweep of his sword, strike his head from his body.

After the victory, Ogier seized Marchevallée, leaped upon his back, and became possessed of the precious flask, a few drops from which closed his wounds and restored his strength. The French knights who had been Bruhier's captives, now released, pressed round Ogier to thank him for their deliverance.

Charlemagne and his nobles, as soon as their attention was relieved from the single combat, perceived from their elevated position an unusual agitation in the enemy's camp. They attributed it at first to the death of their general, but soon the noise of arms, the cries of combatants, and new standards which advanced disclosed to them the fact that Bruhier's army was attacked by a new enemy.

The Emperor was right; it was the brave Carahue of Mauritania, who, with an army, had arrived in France, resolved to attempt the liberation of Ogier, his brother in arms. Learning on his arrival the changed aspect of affairs, he hesitated not to render a signal service to the Emperor by attacking the army of Bruhier in the midst of the consternation occasioned by the loss of its commander.

Ogier recognized the standard of his friend and, leaping upon Marchevallée, flew to aid his attack. Charlemagne followed with his army; and the Saracen host, after an obstinate conflict, was forced to surrender unconditionally.

The interview of Ogier and Carahue was such as might be anticipated of two such attached friends and accomplished knights. Charlemagne went to meet them, embraced them, and putting the King of Mauritania on his right and Ogier on his left, returned with triumph to Paris. There the Empress Bertha and the ladies of her court crowned them with laurels, and the sage and gallant Eginhard, chamberlain and secretary of the Emperor, wrote all these great events in his history.

A few days after, Guyon, King of Denmark, arrived in France with a chosen band of knights, and sent an ambassador to Charlemagne to say that he came, not as an enemy, but to render homage to him as the best knight of the time and the head of the Christian world. Charlemagne gave the ambassador a cordial reception and, mounting his horse, rode forward to meet the King of Denmark.

These great princes, being assembled at the court of Charles, held council together, and the ancient and sage barons were called to join it.

It was decided that the united Danish and Mauritanian armies should cross the sea and carry the war to the country of the Saracens, and that a thousand French knights should range themselves under the banner of Ogier the Dane, who, though not a king, should have equal rank with the two others.

We have not space to record all the illustrious actions performed by Ogier and his allies in this war. Suffice it to say they subdued the Saracens of Ptolemais and Judæa, and, erecting those regions into a kingdom, placed the crown upon the head of Ogier. Guyon and Carahue then left him, to return to their respective dominions. Ogier adopted Walter, the son of Guyon of Denmark, to be his successor in his kingdom. He superintended his education and saw the young prince grow up worthy of his cares. But Ogier, in spite of all the honors of his rank, often regretted the court of Charlemagne, the Duke Namo, and Salomon of Brittany, for whom he had the respect and attachment of a son. At last, finding Walter old enough to sustain the weight of government, Ogier caused a vessel to be prepared secretly, and, attended only by one squire, left his palace by night and embarked to return to France.

The vessel, driven by a fair wind, cut the sea with the swiftness of a bird; but on a sudden it deviated from its course, no longer obeyed the helm, and sped fast towards a black promontory which stretched into the sea. This was a mountain of loadstone, and, its attractive power increasing as the distance diminished, the vessel at last flew with the swiftness of an arrow towards it, and was dashed to pieces on its rocky base. Ogier alone saved himself and reached the shore on a fragment of the wreck.

Ogier advanced into the country, looking for some marks of inhabitancy, but found none. On a sudden he encountered two monstrous animals, covered with glittering scales, accompanied by a horse breathing fire. Ogier drew his sword and prepared to defend himself; but the monsters, terrific as they appeared, made no attempt to assail him, and the horse, Papillon, knelt down and appeared to court Ogier to mount upon his back. Ogier hesitated not to see the adventure through; he mounted Papillon, who ran with speed, and soon cleared the rocks and precipices which hemmed in and concealed a beautiful landscape. He continued his course till he reached a magnificent palace, and, without allowing Ogier time to admire it, crossed a grand court-yard adorned with colonnades, and entered a garden, where, making his way through alleys of myrtle, he checked his course and knelt down on the enamelled turf of a fountain.

Ogier dismounted and took some steps along the margin of the stream, but was soon stopped by meeting a young beauty, such as they paint the Graces, and almost as lightly attired as they. At the same moment, to his amazement, his armor fell off of its own accord. The young beauty advanced with a tender air and placed upon his head a crown of flowers. At that instant the Danish hero lost his memory; his combats, his glory, Charlemagne and his court, all vanished from his mind; he saw only Morgana, he desired nothing but to sigh forever at her feet.

We abridge the narrative of all the delights which Ogier enjoyed for more than a hundred years. Time flew by, leaving no impression of its flight. Morgana's youthful charms did not decay, and Ogier had none of those warnings of increasing years which less-favored mortals never fail to receive. There is no knowing how long this blissful state might have lasted if it had not been for an accident, by which Morgana one day, in a sportive moment, snatched the crown from his head.

That moment Ogier regained his memory and lost his contentment. The recollection of Charlemagne, and of his own relatives and friends, saddened the hours which he passed with Morgana. The fairy saw with grief the changed looks of her lover. At last she drew from him the acknowledgment that he wished to go, at least for a time, to revisit Charles's court. She consented with reluctance, and with her own hands helped to reinvest him with his armor. Papillon was led forth, Ogier mounted him, and, taking a tender adieu of the tearful Morgana, crossed at rapid speed the rocky belt which separated Morgana's palace from the borders of the sea.

The sea-goblins which had received him at his coming awaited him on the shore. One of them took Ogier on his back, and the other placing himself under Papillon, they spread their broad fins and, in a short time, traversed the wide space that separates the isle of Avalon from France. They landed Ogier on the coast of Languedoc and then plunged into the sea and disappeared.

Ogier remounted on Papillon, who carried him across the kingdom almost as fast as he had passed the sea. He arrived under the walls of Paris, which he would scarcely have recognized if the high towers of St. Genevieve had not caught his eye. He went straight to the palace of Charlemagne, which seemed to him to have been entirely rebuilt. His surprise was extreme, and increased still more on finding that he understood with difficulty the language of the guards and attendants in replying to his questions; and seeing them smile as they tried to explain to one another the language in which he addressed them. Presently the attention of some of the barons who were going to court was attracted to the scene, and Ogier, who recognized the badges of their rank, addressed them, and inquired if the Dukes Namo and Salomon were still residing at the Emperor's court. At this question the barons looked at one another in amazement; and one of the eldest said to the rest, "How much this knight resembles the portrait of my grand-uncle, Ogier the Dane." "Ah! my dear nephew, I am Ogier the Dane," said he; and he remembered that Morgana had told him that he was little aware of the flight of time during his abode with her.

The barons, more astonished than ever, concluded to conduct him to the monarch who then reigned, the great Hugh Capet.

The brave Ogier entered the palace without hesitation; but when, on reaching the royal hall, the barons directed him to make his obeisance to the King of France, he was astonished to see a man of short stature and large head, whose air, nevertheless was noble and martial, seated upon the throne on which he had so often seen Charlemagne, the tallest and handsomest sovereign of his time.

Ogier recounted his adventures with simplicity and unaffectedness. Hugh Capet was slow to believe him, but Ogier recalled so many proofs and circumstances, that at last he was forced to recognize the aged warrior to be the famous Ogier the Dane.

The king informed Ogier of the events which had taken place during his long absence; that the line of Charlemagne was extinct; that a new dynasty had commenced; that the old enemies of the kingdom, the Saracens, were still troublesome; and that at that very time an army of those miscreants was besieging the city of Chartres, to which he was about to repair in a few days to its relief. Ogier, always inflamed with the love of glory, offered the service of his arm, which the illustrious monarch accepted graciously, and conducted him to the queen. The astonishment of Ogier was redoubled when he saw the new ornaments and head-dresses of the ladies; still, the beautiful hair which they built up on their foreheads, and the feathers interwoven, which waved with so much grace, gave them a noble air that delighted him. His admiration increased when, instead of the old Empress Bertha, he saw a young queen who combined a majestic mien with the graces of her time of life, and manners candid and charming, suited to attach all hearts. Ogier saluted the youthful queen with a respect so profound that many of the courtiers took him for a foreigner, or at least for some nobleman brought up at a distance from Paris, who retained the manners of what they called the *old court.*

When the queen was informed by her husband that it was the celebrated Ogier the Dane whom he presented to

her, whose memorable exploits she had often read in the
chronicles of antiquity, her surprise was extreme, which
was increased when she remarked the dignity of his address, the animation and even the youthfulness of his
countenance. This queen had too much intelligence to believe hastily; proof alone could compel her assent; and
she asked him many questions about the old court of
Charlemagne, and received such instructive and appropriate answers as removed every doubt. It is to the
corrections which Ogier was at that time enabled to make
to the popular narratives of his exploits that we are indebted for the perfect accuracy and trustworthiness of
all the details of our own history.

King Hugh Capet, having received that same evening
couriers from the inhabitants of Chartres, informing him
that they were hard pressed by the besiegers, resolved
to hasten with Ogier to their relief.

Ogier terminated this affair as expeditiously as he had
so often done others. The Saracens having dared to offer
battle, he bore the Oriflamme through the thickest of
their ranks; Papillon, breathing fire from his nostrils,
threw them into disorder, and Cortana, wielded by his
invincible arm, soon finished their overthrow.

The king, victorious over the Saracens, led back the
Danish hero to Paris, where the deliverer of France received the honors due to his valor. Ogier continued some
time at the court, detained by the favor of the king and
queen; but ere long he had the pain to witness the death
of the king. Then it was that, impressed with all the per-
fections which he had discerned in the queen, he could
not withhold the tender homage of the offer of his hand.
The queen would perhaps have accepted it, she had even
called a meeting of her great barons to deliberate on
the proposition, when, the day before the meeting was to
be held, at the moment when Ogier was kneeling at her
feet, she perceived a crown of gold which an invisible
hand had placed on his brow, and in an instant a cloud
enveloped Ogier, and he disappeared forever from her
sight. It was Morgana, the fairy, whose jealousy was
awakened at what she beheld, who now resumed her
power and took him away to dwell with her in the
island of Avalon. There, in company with the great King

Arthur of Britain, he still lives, and when his illustrious friend shall return to resume his ancient reign, he will doubtless return with him and share his triumph.

INDEX

Abdalrahman, 380-81
Aber Alaw, 259
Aber Menei, 256
Aberfraw, 253
Abyssinia, 499-508
Accolade: defined, 42; by Charlemagne, 578
Achelous, Battle of, 54
Acre, 299-301
Æneas, 53, 431
Agilolphus, Bishop, 550-52
Agramant, King, 425-28, 447-48, 494-96, 508-10, 513-16
Agrapard, 574
Agrican, King, 407, 409-15, 417, 430
Agrivain, 78, 88, 109; and Launcelot, 178
Alardo, 396, 547-48
Albanact, 55
Albania, see Scotland
Albion, 53, 55, 63
Albracca, siege of, 407-15, 417, 426, 436
Alcina, 454-62
Alcuin, 386
Alençon, Earl of, 354-56
Alice, Duchess, 552-53, 558
Allobroges, King of the, 60
Almesbury, 190, 192
Almontes, 431
Alory, 577
Alpheus, 478
Altaripa, 404-5
Alyduke, Sir, 104
Amadis of Gaul, 394
Amaury of Hauteville, 552-57
Ambreticourt, Sir Eustace d', 363-64, 366
Ambreu, 220
Ambrosius, see Uther
Amhar, 220
Amren, 274
Anbessa, 380
Andegavia, 80
Andreghen, Lord Arnold d', 364
Andret, Sir, 128
Aneurin, 197-98
Angelica: and Orlando, 398-402, 413-15, 418, 425, 436; and Rinaldo, 399, 401-5, 416-19, 435-36, 440-43; at siege, 407-11; ring of,

425-26, 447-50, 459-61, 466, 481; and Sacripant, 437-42; and the Orc, 462-67; marries Medoro, 481-83, 486-87
Angle, Lord Guiscard d', 366
Anselm, Count, 474
Antenor, 55
Aquilant, 510
Aquitaine, 380-81
Arden, forest of, 394, 400, 435, 436
Arelivri, 220
Argalia (Uberto), 398-400, 402, 416
Argius, King of Ireland, 123-27
Ariosto, Lodovico, 67, 129, 377, 384-85, 447n.
Arles, 508-11, 520
Arlotto of Soria, 535-36
Armor, 44-45
Armorica, see Brittany
Arridano, 421-22
Arryfuerys, 220
Arthgallo (Artegal), 60-61
Arthur, King, 99, 108, 125-26, 138, 140, 143-44, 198-99, 200, 205, 219-21, 229-34, 260n.; chronicles of, 47; historical evidence of, 68-70; election and coronation of, 72-73, 80-82; his swords, 72-74, 85-87, 88, 188-89; 274; and Graal, 66, 146-47, 158-59; battles of, 68, 73-76, 78-79, 82-83, 180-87; and Kay, 79n.; slays giant, 84-85; and marriage of Gawain, 88-91; tournaments of, 114-17, 134-36, 160-61; enchanted by Lady of the Lake, 132-34; Perceval and, 153-57; wars with Launcelot, 179-84; seeks Owain, 212-15; and Kilwich, 272-76, 283-84, 286-87; and half-man, 275n.; supposed death of, 69-70, 184-90, 597-98; see also Guenever, Queen
Arundel, Earl of, 354
Arviragus, 62
Arvon, 256
Ascanius, 53
Ashtaroth, 532-33, 536-37
Assaracus, 54
Astolpho, 389, 397, 400-1, 406-7, 418, 518; enchanted, 453-55,

MERIDIAN

HEROES, GODS AND LEGENDS

☐ **BULFINCH'S MYTHOLOGY: THE AGE OF CHIVALRY and LEGENDS OF CHARLEMAGNE,** *Or Romance in the Middle Ages.* **With a New Foreword and Notes by Norma Lorre Goodrich.** Epics, sagas, and folklore of the fabulous Middle Ages, tales of great Christian kings, legends of King Arthur and the Round Table, the love story of Tristram and Isolde, the ancient Welsh myths and Frankish epics that are buried in Europe's history—all come to life in Thomas Bulfinch's enduring classic. (011531—$14.95)

☐ **BULFINCH'S MYTHOLOGY: THE AGE OF FABLE by Thomas Bulfinch. With a New Foreword and Notes by Norma Lorre Goodrich.** This is a brilliant reconstruction of the traditional myths that form the backbone of Western culture. It contains Bulfinch's complete, original text of the legends of Greece, Rome, and Scandinavia, as well as offering invaluable insights into the rich cultures and mythologies of ancient Egypt, Persia, and India. (011523—$12.95)

☐ **MYTHS OF THE GREEKS AND ROMANS by Michael Grant.** In this insightful and absorbing book, a distinguished historian and classical scholar demonstrates the dynamic effect that ancient mythology has had on the creative efforts of succeeding centuries. The author summarizes all the myths as well as the legends of the lesser gods and heroes, and traces their origins in historical fact or religious myth. He then shows how myths have continued to evolve throughout the ages. (011620—$14.95)

Prices slightly higher in Canada.